I0739543

Honor's Banner

Also by Charlsie Russell

The Devil's Bastard

Wolf Dawson

Epico Bayou

River's Bend

Camellia Creek

Honor's Banner

A Novel

Charlsie Russell

Loblolly Writer's House
Gulfport, Mississippi

Loblolly Writer's House
P.O. Box 7438
Gulfport, MS 39506-7438
Visit our website at www.loblollywritershouse.com

First Edition: October 2015

Library of Congress Control Number: 2015916475
Russell, Charlsie.
    Honor's banner: a novel

ISBN 978-0-9894302-2-7
1. Historical – Fiction

Book design by Lucretia Gibson
Copy editor, Nancy McDowell
Cover design by Lucretia Gibson: The "Bonnie Blue Flag." The emblem of sovereign states and their rights and a poignant reminder of a lost federal republic: truly Honor's Banner.

Printed and bound in the United States of America.

Author's Note

"Honor's Banner" is a sequel to my historical novel "Camellia Creek." Though this book can stand alone, I believe the reader will derive a greater degree of satisfaction by reading it in sequence with the earlier novel.

Charlsie Russell

Guide to Characters

Seth Parker - Maj., United States Marine Corps, assigned to the United States Army
  Hampton & Reeves Parker - Seth Parker's father and brother, respectively
    Hugh Henry James - Seth Parker's maternal grandfather from Fulton County, Kentucky
Rebecca Mackey - Daughter of Holland Calhoon and Isabel Hays; Eli Calhoon's half sister
  James Mackey - Rebecca Mackey's deceased husband, killed in the war
    Emily Mackey - Rebecca's sister-in-law, killed in a Union raid on Hickory Grove
      Eliza Mackey & Pearl - Rebecca Mackey's niece and ward, both orphans
Isabel Hays - Owner of The Pink Lady in Rodney, Rebecca Mackey's mother
  Marguerite Fortier, "Aunt Maggie" - Isabel's aunt in Rodney
Eli Calhoon - ex-Lt. Col., Confederate States Army, owner of Camellia Creek Plantation
  Alice Shelton Calhoon - Eli Calhoon's bride; a Northerner
    Holland & Rosalind Calhoon - Eli Calhoon's parents, both deceased
      Andrew Calhoon - Eli Calhoon's older brother, died in the war
        Hannah Calhoon - Eli Calhoon's younger sister, died during the war
Laura Calhoon Blackledge - Eli Calhoon's deceased sister-in-law and ex-lover
  Albert Blackledge - Laura's second husband; deceased owner of the Meridian Southern RR
Naomi Polk - Rosalind Calhoon's sister, Eli Calhoon's aunt, shot Eli; Seth Parker killed her
Peter Franklin - Alice Calhoon's uncle, ex-Union soldier, speculator
  Betty Franklin - Peter's wife, Alice Shelton's aunt, Jacob Shelton's sister
    Cassie Franklin - Peter and Betty's daughter, Alice Shelton's cousin
      Jonathan Franklin - Peter Franklin's nephew; recently murdered
        Eustacia "Stacy" Franklin - Jon Franklin's mother
Poynter Cummings - Editor of *The Port Gibson Chronicle*; shares work spaces with Seth Parker
Tobias Holbein - Eli Calhoon & Isabel Hays' lawyer and friend in Rodney, Mississippi
Sam Caruthers - Secessionist turned Republican Scalawag in Warren County
  Alma Caruthers - Sam Caruthers' wife
    Cole Terry & Wilson Caruthers - Sam Caruthers' sons
Lawrence Pendleton - Judge and anti-secessionist Whig from Warren County
William Haskers - Vice President of the U.S. National Bank in New Orleans
Jocelyn LeBlanc - Mulatto beauty, murdered twenty-five years earlier; Isabel Hays' niece
William Rothenham - Member of British economic delegation to Brazil; Isabel Hays' friend

Federal Officials & Northerners

Malcolm Byrnes - Col., United States Army, Seth Parker's immediate senior
Greg Dustin - Col., United States Army, Intelligence, War Department in Washington, D.C.
  Dan Fairchild - Special agent working fraud at Treasury, Dustin's brother-in-law
Edgar Chase - Maj., United States Army, Freedmen's Bureau, Madison County
  Amy Chase - His wife; works at the Bureau's Negro orphanage in Madison County
Don Hemple - Maj., United States Army, and Provost Marshal for Claiborne County
William Thatcher - Maj., United States Army, and Provost Marshal of Madison County
  Eleanor Thatcher - William Thatcher's wife, with Freedmen's Bureau in Madison County
Alan Guthrie - Treasury operative murdered in October 1865 in Hinds County
  Jacob Harding - Guthrie's brother-in-law, deceased, worked in Treasury Department
Jim Hurd - Deceased senior employee, who worked in Treasury Department's bank
Walter Miller - Treasury operative from Washington sent to work the Guthrie murder
  Felix Roscoe & Clem White - Hirelings of Walter Miller
Cecil Bowler - Treasury officer assigned to Warren County Clerk's office in Vicksburg
Douglas Ralston - Col., United States Army, Malcolm Byrnes' predecessor during hostilities

James Petersen - Lt. Col., United States Army, intelligence operative, disappeared in 1863
Jerry Phillips - Col., United States Army, District Provost Marshal at Vicksburg
Martin Trueblood - ex-Maj., United States Army, speculator, stationed in area during war
Thomas McKee - Capt., United States Army Engineer, with Eli Calhoon before he was shot
Faith Lawrence - Wife of U.S. Army officer; stopped Rebecca Mackey's questioning in 1863
Josiah Spate - Northern Methodist who has come to Madison County, Mississippi
   Ursula Spate - Josiah Spate's wife

State and local officials

Ephraim Lester - Doctor and coroner, Claiborne County, Mississippi
Tom Potts - Sheriff of Claiborne County
Tim Abrams - Superior Clerk for the Mississippi State Archives
Lyle Ferguson - County Clerk of Warren County

Domestic Negroes

Elvira Hinny - Auntie Elvie, freedwoman and midwife, nursemaid to Eli Calhoon
Brim Solomon - Freedman and childhood companion of Eli Calhoon, killed in *Camellia Creek*
Buck Pike - Freedman in the employ of Eli Calhoon
Jessie - "Uncle Jessie," freedman and caretaker at Muscatine Plantation
   Lettie - Jessie's daughter at Muscatine
Mattie - Freedwoman in employ of Rebecca Mackey, Mammy to Eliza Mackey and Pearl
Hector - Freedman in employ of Rebecca Mackey at Hickory Grove Plantation
Polly - Freedwoman in employ of Rebecca Mackey at Hickory Grove Plantation

Miscellaneous neighbors, friends, associates, many unseen in **Honor's Banner**

Wayne Hale - Killed in *Camellia Creek*
Robert Davis - Captain, Confederate States Army, in charge of a roving battery during war
Dr. Yancy - Sgt. Frank Zachary's deceased master
Helen Morgan - Dear friend of Becky's deceased sister-in-law, Emily Mackey

Seth Parker's Troops, from the Mississippi Native Guard, except as noted

Capt. Jubal Summers - ex-United States Colored Troops, New York

Sgt. Frank Zachary	*Pvt. Lawson*
Sgt. Richard Kushing - Zachary's relief, regular army	*Pvt. Hand*
Cpl. Peters	*Pvt. Ball*
Cpl. Daws	*Pvt. Spain*
Pvt. Price	

Employees and clientele at The Pink Lady in Rodney, Mississippi

Savannah Sutton - Isabel Hays' immediate subordinate in running the business
Mark Dicks - ex-Maj., United States Army, a regular patron of Isabel Hays' establishment
Mary Margaret - Working girl and favorite of Mark Dicks
David Wills - Col., United States Army, stationed in Baton Rouge, patron of The Pink Lady
Cheri - Working girl at The Pink Lady
Dinah & Thomas - Domestics working for Isabel at The Pink Lady

Prologue

Alan Guthrie left Fifteenth Avenue and made his way along the rear of the building that housed the State Department, before identifying himself to a sentry and slipping into the northern end of the Treasury Building's newly completed west wing. The hour approached midnight, and when he entered the well-lit hall, his measured pace became easier. Halfway down the corridor, he took the stairs to the second floor, then another flight to the third. He hadn't seen a soul, but he had heard the thumps and clanks of cleaning crews shaping up the hallowed halls of this gargantuan testimony to fiscal hegemony over a nation.

Alan opened Jacob Harding's office door to find his brother-in-law hunkered over his desk. Alan thought he might be sleeping, but when he stepped in, Jacob sat up. Alan closed the door, and Jacob swiveled away, averting his face.

"You hit her again," Alan said. He stopped in front of the desk. "She said you were drunk, but I already figured that when I saw her face. Where were the kids when you did that?"

Jacob pulled himself closer to the kneehole. "Asleep. I was late."

"Adelaide said you told her to pack."

"I want her to take the kids and go to your parents. I have to get away."

Alan narrowed his eyes, then looked around the office. The gas lamp overhead cast a soft glow over the room, which was a good fourteen foot square. A nice office, and Jacob's alone.

Certainly nicer than the slightly larger space one floor below that Alan shared with three other men. Jacob's salary was nicer, too. During Fessenden's brief tenure as Secretary, Jacob had been promoted to "clerk of clerks," as Alan called him. As far as Alan knew, nothing had happened to change that.

"Apparently you forgot to tell her you planned on leaving, too, just left her with the impression she was to get out."

"I never left her with that impression. She said that to win your sympathy."

"And she has it."

Jacob's face bore the resentment of a dog mistreated by its master. "Shit," Alan said, "you're not leaving. You're running." When Jacob didn't respond, Alan asked, "What have you done?"

"You don't know?" But he asked the question as if sure Alan did know.

"No."

Jacob straightened in his chair and reached for the top drawer on the right pedestal of his desk.

Alan said, "Don't," and Jacob hesitated.

"I'll be over the top of this desk and beating the hell out of you before you can pull it out, and I'll enjoy every minute of it. Now tell me what you're doing here this time of night, drunk, and why you hit my baby sister after I warned you I'd beat you within an inch of your life if you ever did it again."

"Why did you happen to come to the house tonight?" Jacob asked.

"Adelaide sent Edith for me after you left."

Jacob watched Alan warily, then said, "I hit your sister because she argued with me, and I don't have time to argue."

"Explain, perhaps?"

"Dammit, Alan, she's my wife. I don't have to explain to her or—"

"Explain it to me, then. Right now! What are you involved in?"

"Ah, so we're to pretend you don't know? All right, I'm trying to figure out how to cover up my misdeeds long enough to reach the Indian nations and, I hope, anonymity." He sat back. "I'm not as drunk as I thought if I could come up with 'anonymity.'"

"Why do you need to hide?"

Jacob's visage darkened. "Quit playing the innocent. I know you're behind this. You've been rank with jealousy ever since my promotion, so you brought your little team together to put me in my place."

"What's that supposed to mean?"

Again, Jacob reached for the desk drawer, but before touching it, he found Alan's eye. "May I?"

"Be careful."

Jacob opened the drawer. The revolver was there, as was a pint of whiskey, which is what he reached for. He pulled the cork and raised the half-empty bottle. "To a job well done, Alan.' He took a swig. "You've destroyed me along with your sister's livelihood." Jacob eyed the gun.

"Close the drawer," Alan said. When he did, Alan found a chair and sat. "What is this about?"

Jacob sat forward and brought the bottle down on the desk with a thud. He picked up a piece of paper lying in front of him, and taking a corner between his thumb and index finger, he flipped it and slid it toward Alan. "That, my dear brother, is the file copy of the letter of credit I took down to the bank this morning."

Alan picked it up, sat back in his chair, and started to read. "Damn," he said after a moment, "is this legitimate?"

"As per my instructions, the letter of credit is good. So is the bill of exchange that accompanied it to disbursing." Jacob repeated "disbursing" under his breath, and Alan's spine pricked.

"Chase signed the authorization over a year ago," Jacob continued. He slid a second piece of paper across the desk. "The thirtieth of June 1864, his last day at Treasury."

Alan looked at that document too. "And this hasn't been paid before now?"

Jacob glowered at him. "I know Chase's signature is a forgery, Alan. I'm not as big a fool as you think."

"You think that I'm behind an authorization bearing Chase's forged signature?"

"I think you and your friends are behind the entire mess."

"Why the devil would we forge Chase's signature? Why not McCulloch's?"

Jacob widened his eyes. "To implicate the man, one would suspect, and deflect attention from the real culprits. I'm sure that forgery didn't make it into the files anytime recently. It's been there, I would guess, since the summer of 1864."

Alan leaned back and regarded him coolly. "Why would you think that?"

"An educated guess. Your henchman brought me that authorization to justify my issuing the letter of credit."

"He knew this was in the file?"

"He knew it was there, because you and him put it there."

"I don't understand why you're trying to implicate me in this."

"Because you're jealous of me and you hate my guts. You two were in Arkansas together"—Jacob leaned forward and nodded at the authorization letter in Alan's hand—"and Mississippi. You were involved with those people out there. Even though Chase's signature is a forgery, the payout was approved. I checked the congressional record."

Alan drew in a calming breath. "How do you know Chase's signature is fraudulent?"

Jacob glared at him, and Alan laughed. "You don't know for sure, do you?"

"Why would he sign such a thing for those people?"

"Blackmail, murder, treason? Or something else. There are all sorts of reasons one could come up with."

"It would have been easier for you to find a good forger among all your victims than to put pressure on Chase."

"How deeply involved in this are you, Jacob?"

"I've signed the paperwork and sent it out."

"Why would you draft a letter of credit based on an authorization you suspect is a forgery?"

"I had little choice, and you know it."

Alan contemplated that, then he grinned. "So someone found out about your embezzling. I warned you."

"I borrowed the money. I always repaid it."

"I'd hazard a guess the kitty would turn up short right now, or you wouldn't have a problem. Who's blackmailing you, Jake? I really do want to know."

Jacob's face smoothed, and he sat back. "I'm not telling you just in case you really don't know."

Alan flexed his jaw. "Someone who befriended you, maybe? An associate of mine who's approached you within the past six months?" Alan's eyes narrowed. "Hmm, let's see, six months ago... That was about the same time you fractured Adelaide's cheek, wasn't it?"

"You son of a bitch, I knew you were involved. There was no other way he could have known so much."

"Other than he's smart, and you're stupid? He bluffed you is what he did, based on information I"—Alan smiled—"innocently provided him."

"You told him about my borrowing money."

"Misappropriation is what it is, Jake. Euphemistic for theft, and I didn't tell him, I didn't have to. It's obvious to anyone looking close enough that you've been living beyond your means."

Jacob covered his face with his hands. "Corinne's medicine—"

"You make enough. You were spending that money on liquor and whores."

The man looked up. "Yes, good whores, too. Adelaide was tired of being pregnant."

"Did he find those whores for you?"

Jacob blinked stupidly at him, and Alan sighed. "Of course he did. One of 'em got you drunk or drugged and seduced the information out of you. You were easy prey for him. Do you have any idea the kinds of things the man did during the war?"

"And you! How you operated during the war." Jacob leaned closer. "You compromised me."

"If you're still thinking I was part of this, think again. I care too much for my nieces and nephews, which brings up another question. If you're not getting part of this, did he offer you any money to draft that letter of credit?"

"He paid me a nominal sum."

"How much?"

"A thousand dollars."

"And you took it?"

Jacob nodded.

"Who else is involved?" Sensing Jacob's unease, Alan pressed. "Someone in disbursing, right?"

"Hurd," Jacob said.

For a long moment, Alan Guthrie just stared at his sister's husband. Then he said, "Poor ole Jim Hurd. I understand now why you find the territories so appealing. Was he part of this conspiracy?"

"No."

"But he signed the bill of exchange?"

"I took it down to him myself, watched him sign it. Then he started having second thoughts. He was uncomfortable with the sum and wanted to know why it had been held so long. I told him it was because of the war, but he said he wanted to discuss it with Spinner."

"And you told—"

"Yes," Jacob hissed. "I told the bastard we had a problem. I wanted out. I hoped with Hurd's questions, we would just pull the request before Hurd talked to Spinner."

"Jacob, Jacob, Jacob. There was no 'out' at that point. What were you going to do, tell Hurd it was all a mistake? What do you think he'd have done then?"

"You sound like your partner, and you wonder why I think you're part of this?"

"What happened with the bill of exchange?" Alan demanded.

"I went back to Hurd's office during lunch. I knew he walked home every day to eat with his wife. I found the bill in his top drawer. I retrieved it, drafted the forwarding letter, and sent it to the mail room." He shrugged. "Wells Fargo has it now. It's on its way to New Orleans. Every aspect of the transaction is legitimate including the identity of the executor." Jacob pushed a third letter across the desk.

Without looking up, Alan reached for it. This letter, as it turned out, provided the recipient authority to act as agent for the newly established account in New Orleans.

Alan looked at the name, then at Jacob, who wore a triumphant grin. Alan frowned. "You find some victory in this, Jake?"

"You're damn right I do. The addressee of that letter is not who you and your partner wanted me to send it to. You see, I did some research on this thing." He nodded at the letter Alan was still holding. "The person whose name you see there is the person whose name appeared on all the documentation for years and years. That's who it was supposed to go to, and that's where I sent it." He sneered and leaned back in his chair. "How are your plans looking now, you son of a bitch?"

Chapter One

Major Seth Parker, United States Marine Corps, on assignment with the United States Army, swung the door to Captain Jubal Summers' room wide.

"Did you find her?" he asked his immediate subordinate.

"She's in her room," Jubal said, "dressed. She says she's going back with you."

"You told her about Calhoon, I take it?"

"She guessed something more had happened."

"I'm ready."

Ah, he reflected as he spun on one heel, the melodious voice of the beautiful Isabel Leigh Hays sounded strained. That would be a first in his experience. She stood just inside the room, and if a heavy wool coat and a flop hat were all that was required for this journey, she was indeed ready. Had he managed to break the woman's cool exterior during fruitless probing into the murder of Alan Guthrie, would this horrific night have happened? Or were the events of the past eight hours related to the dead Treasury operative at all?

"The lake and creek have flooded," he said. "I can't get you to the house."

"How do you intend to get yourself to the house, Major?"

"Swim the horses."

She held her hands out palms up. "I have no doubt my horse can swim."

"Have you had occasion to swim that lake on horseback?"

9

"That's the only way you'd ever catch me swimming that lake, and then only under dire circumstances"—her voice broke—"such as Eli Calhoon's fighting for his life."

Seth knew there was a bond, and he'd wondered how strong it was. Now he guessed he knew, if still ignorant of the "why" of it.

As for himself, he was cold and wet, and his shoulder ached. He didn't want to go back out in that miserable weather to a place more miserable still. He'd killed an old woman tonight. A mean, murderous old woman, but an old woman nonetheless. He knew what he'd left out there earlier. God only knew what he'd walk back into. He wanted to find a dark room, by himself, and throw up. But even if there'd been no Isabel pressing him to hurry, he had to return to Camellia Creek tonight.

"You've been told Jon Franklin is dead?" he said to Isabel.

"Shot shortly after I left him, if I understand what Captain Summers told me. I assume that leaves me your primary suspect?"

"Of sorts. We need to talk about that, but it can wait."

He turned to Jubal. "Have you sent any men out there?"

"Daws is ready with Price, but knowing they wouldn't know where to cross, I had them wait on you. How did the Franklins react when you told 'em?"

"His mother is hysterical. The death appears to be a big blow to Peter Franklin, too. The missus is more shaken by the shooting of Calhoon. Her main concern is her niece. I imagine she'll be out there with Alice as soon as she can manage, but her sister-in-law is gonna need support, too."

At the door, Isabel shifted on her feet. "I'll get my bag. The corporal said he'd bring my horse from the livery. I'll meet you downstairs."

Seth brushed water from his greatcoat. He cursed once under his breath, then turned back to Jubal. "We need to talk to the sheriff. Naomi Polk's attempted murder of the Calhoons is a civil case." At least Seth thought it should be.

"So is Franklin's."

"Right now the last person known to have seen Jon Franklin alive is one of my few links to Alan Guthrie. We know Franklin was up to something nefarious, and the manner in which both murders were carried out is eerily similar."

"Lone travelers gettin' shot on a road isn't that uncommon in this state at present."

"That might be true, but I'm not lettin' go of Franklin's murder yet. Get the sheriff out of bed and to Camellia Creek, and make sure the office is manned come sunup."

Jubal nodded, and Seth, steeling himself for another cold, wet ride, stepped out of the room and started down the deserted hall.

Chapter Two

<u>Hickory Grove Plantation, Madison County, Mississippi, 3 January 1866</u>

With the baby's cry, warmth filled the womb of Rebecca Calhoon Mackey, then her breast, and she fought waking. Strong arms held her against a hard body, safe and warm. "James," she whispered, and prayed for his sweet breath upon her ear.

A gust of wind rattled the glass panes. She opened her eyes and watched the familiar shadows of naked limbs dance across the shades drawn over the upper half of the window. Her eyes burned. She was lying on her side, and the arms that held her were her own, weak defense against a frigid cold that permeated her lonely bedroom.

The storm had ended, the sky cleared, and the silver glow of the near-full moon rained down on the glistening earth. Heart heavy, she reached behind her just to make certain this was not a magical night after all. The bed was empty but for her, cold but for where she lay. She turned the clock face to the glowing windows and made the time out to be near five in the morning.

Again a baby cried, and she sat up. That much had been real. Becky found her footing on the frigid floor, colder even than the air around her. The storm had brought winter back with a fury. A northern winter. Grabbing her robe, but foregoing a search for slippers, Becky hurried from the room and down the dark hall. At its end, Mattie had lit a lamp, and Pearl's wails had subsided to whimpers. Becky heard the soft hum of Mattie's voice willing the child to quiet, and when Becky reached them, Pearl gave her a smile.

"She wuz wet," Mattie said, pinning the diaper and pulling the last of the little girl's clothing back into place.

Becky reached to take her. "She hasn't wet the bed in two weeks."

"Eliza gib her too much milk at suppa. Cain't turn my back on dat chil' fo' a instant."

A bright-eyed Pearl in her arms, Becky turned to where Eliza Mackey, her niece by marriage and heiress to Hickory Grove Plantation, or what was left of it, slumbered. "And then the little wench sleeps through the consequences."

"Wouldn't hab if'n I hadn't moved Pearl befo' I went to bed. Pearl be scared by all dat thundah, an' Miz Eliza got 'er outta da crib, min' you, an' I found da both 'em in missy's bed soun' to sleep when I come in. Served 'er right to wake up col' in Pearlie's pee.

Becky smiled and started for the rocker. "Then you'd be cleaning two of them up."

"Hmmpf. Heah, Miz Becky. You lets me do dat now, an' get on back to bed. Done got so col'."

"I'm wide awake, and I want to rock a baby. You get back in bed."

Mattie sighed, then reached for the bedding in the crib. "Had yo'se'f a bad dream, didn't you?"

"More disturbing than bad. I dreamed James was next to me again."

"Maybe he wuz."

Becky's trembling smile triggered a tear, and she swiped at it as she turned to sit. "If such things could happen, Mattie, don't you think it would be easier for me to simply close my eyes and not wake up. Go to him on the other side?"

"Ain't da same ovah der. Wouldn't be like it were in life. Masta James always be a sweet, sweet boy. Ain't 'im who's unhappy. He only worries fo' you, 'cause he loved you so. He knows 'im be all right, an' he knows you don' know dat. He comes to you rememberin' what it was like between you two, but dat he does fo' you, not 'im. Ain't what he needs no mo'. Yo still gots to lib yo life, and 'im knows dat. When yo fin'ly 'appy again, yo' won't be feelin' 'im no mo'. Him'll go where 'im belongs knowin' you gonna be all right."

Becky's chest weighted her body so that she feared it would collapse into itself. She kissed Pearl's cheek, and rocked. "I don't know that I'll ever be happy again. I don't even have a picture of him, Mattie. Not one thing that belonged to him, but on nights such as this one, I can smell him next to me. I fear one day I'll forget what he even looked—"

Mattie started at the first blow against the door, as did Pearl, cuddled in Becky's arms. A second hard knock followed the first, and another, echoing furiously down the corridor leading to the front door. Becky pressed the baby to her, then breathed. A fist had struck the door, not the butt of a rifle. Still, it was only five in the morning.

"Miz Becky, it be Buck," the familiar voice cried, causing her heart to race anew. She stood and passed Pearl to a quiet Mattie, then hurried down the hall. A quick slip of the bolt and turn of the key and she threw the door wide.

"Get inside," she cried, "you'll catch your death out on a night like this." The cold misery on his face did nothing to cover the anguish, but he pulled the hat from a head wrapped further by a wool scarf and stepped inside. The hat and heavy coat were wet. He'd been out, headed here from Camellia Creek, since before the storm had stopped. Becky braced. "What's happened?"

"Yo' mama sent one a dem nigga sol'jahs to da qua'tah afta midnight. She say come an' fetch you home to Camellia Creek. Masta Eli done been shot."

A chill coursed through her body. "Is he dead?" she forced out, part of her already resolved.

"Dat nigga tol' me he weren't yet but he be hu't bad."

"Who—"

"Don't know, Miz Becky." Buck was wringing his hat in his hands now. "Don't know what happened. Dat sol'ja didn't know much eitha. Jus' tell me Miz Isabel say hurry, so I done hurried."

Union soldiers, in league with whom?

Body shaking with anger, frustration and, yes, terror, Becky pushed away from the wall. Sam Caruthers had better not have played a part in this. Hiding behind Yankee soldiers wouldn't save him from an assassin's bullet, not this time. She was running out of things worth living for.

Chapter Three

Seth stepped into the sickroom, rank with the stench of carbolic acid, blood, and sweat. The room was dark except for a low-burning lantern on the table beside the bed. There were a number of people holed up within, all still and quiet, but for Dr. Ephraim Lester, who appeared to be heading out.

"I need to talk to Alice," Seth said to him. He kept his voice low.

"Come ahead," Isabel said, her voice near normal. She stood at the foot of the bed silhouetted against the single light. The window shade glowed with the welcomed dawn. It had been a long night.

The doctor concurred with a nod. "No need to whisper. We'd be blessed to wake him." The man looked at Isabel, who had turned back to the patient on the bed. "I'm gonna take a break."

She moved then. "Elvie has breakfast, bless her. Get yourself something. You don't plan on leaving soon?"

"Not unless someone fetches me for some other poor soul who got himself shot last night."

"Jon Franklin's body is at the livery," Seth said. "Someone needs to 'bless' him dead."

"That would be me, I reckon. I'll go into town in a bit and file the report. Then I'll come back."

Despite his own conviction, the doctor had kept his voice low when he'd spoken, but maybe that had been fatigue. He'd been working on Eli Calhoon since nine o'clock last evening.

At the door he turned to Seth and asked, "Where's Zachary?"

"He's in the kitchen, too."

The doc waved his hand at the man on the bed. "Saved his life up to this point. Did a fine job. He needs to be told. Could you leave him here while I'm in town?"

"I will."

Last evening Sergeant Frank Zachary, 60th Mississippi Loyal Guards, United States Army Colored Troops, had assumed responsibility for the critically wounded Calhoon. He'd taken over the scene like he'd been senior man present. And when it came to the care of his patient, he'd remained in nominal charge until they got the doctor out here almost two hours later.

Dr. Lester disappeared out the door, and Seth sucked in a breath of the heavy air. Alice sat in a ladder-back chair, still as stone. She had one arm in a sling pressed against her breast, and near her right temple, blood matted her hair, despite Isabel's efforts to clean it up. Both injuries were the result of a vicious attack by Calhoon's aunt, Naomi Polk, a deranged murderess who had subsequently shot Eli Calhoon and whom Seth, in turn, had slain.

Seth reckoned Alice hadn't cried for several hours now, but she remained pale and glassy-eyed. He squatted in front of her. "Can you talk to me a minute?"

"I'll not leave him. We'll have to do it here."

"That's fine," he said softly. "Do you remember I told you Jon Franklin was dead?"

"Yes. You said someone shot him."

"And you told me he'd been here earlier in the afternoon, before the storm started."

"He attacked me. I drove him off with the poker. I didn't shoot him, Seth, and Eli didn't shoot him either."

"I know neither of you shot him. You told Isabel he said Naomi Polk put him up to coming here."

"Jon said Naomi told him Eli planned to kill both of us because he believed we were lovers, but Naomi told me she and Eli planned to kill me. I knew she was lying. *She* planned to kill me, yes, but Eli wasn't involved." Alice grimaced, as if in pain, then said, "I don't know why she needed Jon for that." She swallowed. "I think he meant to force me."

"To violate you?"

"Yes. His plan was to compromise my marriage and get my money."

Even if Alice had been willing, that would have gotten him only an adulteress, assuming he lived that long. Seth wasn't totally familiar with the laws of this state, but he knew enough about the terms of Alice's inheritance to know that the hefty fortune that came with Alice Shelton Calhoon was probably her husband's now and short of Calhoon's death, would remain his.

"Did Jon say anything else, anything to indicate why someone would have wanted to kill him?"

"I wanted to kill him."

He couldn't resist a smile. "Something less spontaneous. Did he indicate he feared for his life?"

"He said he was desperate for money." She shook her head. "But my leaving with him wouldn't get him my money. It was all a lie, Seth." She reached for the bedside table and grasped a book, then surprised him with a smile. "Could you open the shade now, so I can see? The sun is up." She looked at Eli Calhoon, propped on pillows and lying on his side. "My sweetheart has lived to see another bright, beautiful sunrise."

Yeah, well, if he woke up he'd see it. Seth didn't point that out to Alice.

"I'm going to read to him. If we're too quiet, he'll take it as a sign that we're all at peace, and he'll cross to the other side."

Seth squeezed her good shoulder, then caught Isabel's eye. "Could I talk to you outside?"

Chapter Four

Seth closed the door to Calhoon's study and motioned Isabel to a chair, but she didn't sit. The violent storm had precluded his talking to her at length on their ride out, and the situation presented on their arrival certainly had not been conducive to discussion.

"It was a large caliber bullet, through the heart. He died instantly."

"And I keep a Navy Colt under my carriage seat," she said. "Is that what you wish to point out? I will admit that at a range of six feet I am a damn good shot. Don't know if I could have got him through the heart, but I'd have been close. But, as I've already told you, he was driving his carriage and very much alive when we parted ways."

Seth wished she'd sit so he could. He was tired. He'd talked to Sheriff Tom Potts, who'd waded in, wet and gruff, about three this morning and had promised the man a written statement regarding the Naomi Polk shooting. They'd discussed the Franklin murder, but the sheriff seemed comfortable with Seth's pursuing it. Potts had left about an hour after he got here.

Seth turned to the bank of windows and looked down at Lake Elizabeth. Rather than swim the damn thing for a fourth time last night, he'd opted to stay with his handful of men here at Camellia Creek until the storm let up and the water receded. His attempt to sleep on Calhoon's settee in the parlor a little later had failed, his mind haunted by the evening before. The water was down now, the sodden land bridge visible.

"You turned on to the drive leading to Camellia Creek," he said. "My men found Franklin not too far west of that turnoff, so whoever killed him did so shortly after y'all went your separate ways."

"I assume so."

"You didn't hear the gunshot?"

"No, but from the sound of the thunder one would have thought the war had resumed. Between that and the rain pounding the top of my carriage, I'm not surprised. Did my 'escort' hear anything?"

Her escort had been a three-man detail he'd assigned to keep watch on her. "Peters didn't, but Daws and his men, who I'd sent in search of Jon Franklin, did. They passed up the main turnoff to Camellia Creek to check it out." Seth rubbed his shoulder. "You weren't expecting Franklin in Rodney last evening?"

"I was not. I told you the reason he was coming to me—he couldn't go home. He didn't want to have to explain why Alice had bloodied him."

"You didn't say anything to Lawson about coming to Camellia Creek."

"Because I hadn't planned to come to Camellia Creek, Major. Jon Franklin is aggressive with women. Nothing my girls hadn't been able to handle, but he hadn't met any resistance from them either. I knew Alice's response to his advances would have been different, and as she just told you, I was right. Jon told me someone had 'misled' him regarding Alice's regard for him, then he defamed Alice as a lunatic who'd reacted to his offer of safety by attacking him with a poker. I was certain all of that was an out-and-out lie, but despite the visible evidence she'd landed some successful blows on his person, I had no idea what he might have done to her and wanted to confirm she was all right."

"Can you add anything to what you heard her tell me?"

"Nothing. When I got here yesterday afternoon, Alice was not predisposed to dwell on the incident. She told me what Jon had said about Naomi, so I assume she was the person who 'misled' him regarding Alice. What Naomi did was plot with Jon to carry out this attack, which proved a dismal failure on his part. At the time I had no idea how dismal."

"Why were you coming to Port Gibson?" Seth asked.

The beautiful Isabel Hays narrowed her eyes. "I was on my way to visit my daughter Rebecca at Hickory Grove."

"We found you at the hotel in Port Gibson."

"I told Private Lawson before leaving Rodney that I would probably be staying the night at Port Gibson. He can confirm that."

He had confirmed that, that's why Seth had suspected she was at the hotel last night. He drew a long breath. "You told Alice you had business in Port Gibson, that's why you had to leave instead of riding out the storm here."

Isabel's eyes filled with tears. "Oh God, yes, and crossing that land bridge yesterday afternoon I was struck with an overwhelming sense of foreboding. I intended to turn around once I'd reached the other side and come back, wait with Alice until Eli got home, but I barely made it off the bridge when the torrent hit, and there was no coming back." She blinked back the tears. "The business to which I referred came up after I got here and learned Naomi was behind Jon's attack on Alice. I intended to have words with Naomi before leaving for Madison County. I went straight to her house, but as we all now know, she wasn't there. She was here trying to kill Alice. But just so you know, I believe someone other than her had been in the house before I arrived. I say that because there were boot tracks on the floor, large, definitely a man. The tracks led out the front door. I surmised, somewhat uncomfortably, that I'd frightened off whoever it was with my unexpected arrival."

Seth rubbed at the stubble on his chin. That was interesting. He nodded, then said, "If you weren't expecting Jon Franklin in Rodney last night, who knew he was on the Rodney Road?"

"I have no idea. Have you considered Jon's death might be nothing more than a robbery?"

"He had over seventy dollars in greenbacks in his wallet and a gold watch on his person. Who would have wanted him dead, Isabel?"

"Jon Franklin, to the best of my knowledge, was a conceited

ass, who thought much more of himself than others did. He was interested in getting wealthy under the conditions that today present themselves in Mississippi. There could have been a number of people who wouldn't have minded seeing him dead. The question you should be asking is who 'needed' him dead."

Seth let that sink in. "He came to you."

"That's true, Major, but I didn't need him dead and had no particular wish to see him dead—he still owed me money for one thing. Jon came to me because I know people. Enjoying my girls was a perquisite. He wanted to know who I knew."

"That's what I need, Mistress Hays, I need to know who you put him into contact with."

"I put him into contact with no one, and I advised him most strongly to continue to work with his uncle. Let me reiterate, Major Parker, that no one planning to kill Jon Franklin would have been aware he'd be on the road that evening. He hadn't planned to be himself."

"Someone could have followed him."

"That's true, but wouldn't I have passed them coming off the Camellia Creek cutoff?"

Seth furrowed his brow. "He entered the Rodney Road from the shortcut?"

"He did, I saw him pull out. That's what initially prompted my concern."

"Is that ingress to this farm well known?"

"To those of us familiar with the place, yes. It cuts almost two miles off the trek to Rodney, a trip that me and mine, and Holland Calhoon and his, made often. I concede it might be considered odd that Jon was aware of it. Are you thinking that someone followed him from here?"

"Could be."

"I'd have still had to pass that person." She raised her chin. "Or are you suggesting I'm protecting someone? Eli perhaps?"

He held her steady gaze for a long moment, then said, "You heard me tell Alice I know he didn't shoot Franklin. Calhoon was with Tom McKee at the same time you were with Alice. Franklin would have already been dead by that time, so no. I've ruled him out as Franklin's killer. What I find interesting, though, is Jon's familiarity with Camellia Creek. That could imply his killer is, too." He cocked his head. "Maybe he, or she, got off the road."

"He or she would have to know the lay of the land fairly well, because that drive was excavated along the bluff above the river's floodplain. It's a sheer drop on the west and a deep hollow on the east, you've seen it. It's barely wide enough for a carriage and hasn't been graded since before the war."

"There are woods."

"Bare woods. Not much cover this time of year."

"How heavy was the rain? I must assume you were focused on that narrow road."

She shrugged. "I concede a rider might have gotten down in the hollow and I missed him, but if you're insinuating a local killed him, I'm certain I will be of no further assistance to you. The men I am dealing with of late are either Northern or have Northern connections. They also have money and want more."

"Of late?"

"I've heard a lifetime of lucrative schemes hatched from local associations, not one of which I would share with an arrogant New York ass still wet behind the ears and attempting to find his footing in the slimy mud of Yankee corruption, so much easier for the likes of him here than at home, I'm certain. If Jon were involved with local thieves, he established those associations with no help from me."

"But him coming from where he came from, and them coming from where they came from, they might be quicker to kill him."

"Ah, sectional thievery, as quaint as it is ludicrous. You're savvy enough to know, Major, that the corruption embarked upon since the onset of Mr. Lincoln's war is limited in scope only by the greed and ruthlessness of the participants. If a local stalked and killed Jon Franklin it had nothing to do with his being a Northerner and everything to do with his, shall we say, ambitions, which very possibly threatened those of someone smarter and more ruthless than he."

"So we're not ruling out your Southern friends?"

She reached for the knob. "I've merely given you something to think about. If someone wanted Jon Franklin dead, I would not hazard a guess as to who or why."

He watched the door shut with a soft click, then he fell into his chair. She might not hazard a guess, but he'd bet his next paycheck against a full house that she could expound on someone "needing" him dead, or she'd have never brought it up.

Chapter Five

"Come on in," Cassie Franklin said, her voice soft.

The warmth inside the Franklin house felt good. This most recent early morning ride had left Seth near frozen, and his wool greatcoat was damp, despite his having worn a tarred-canvas poncho over it all night in the rain. Cassie closed the door behind him. A central hall stretched out before him, and from its far end, Betty Franklin rushed forward.

"How is Eli?" she asked, her voice hushed in deference to a subdued household. The drapes were drawn in the front rooms to either side of him, leaving them dark as well as quiet, and just down the hall from where the two women had gathered around him, what he presumed to be a foyer mirror was covered with a black cloth.

"He's alive," Seth said.

"Is he going to survive?"

"I don't know."

Cassie, her eyes anxious, had moved around him to stand by her mother. He hadn't seen the girl in the wee hours of this morning when he'd awakened Peter Franklin to tell him his nephew was dead.

"The doctor was still there when I left. Worked on him most of the night. He's unconscious."

"And Alice?"

"All I can tell you for certain is she won't leave his side."

"The Hinny woman's with her?"

"Most assuredly. Mrs. Franklin, all the servants are near the house, and there's an old family friend there, too, as well as two of my men."

The pretty Mrs. Franklin wrung her hands, then took his elbow, starting them down the hall. "Peter's in his study. I've got to get out there. If that young man dies on her, she'll take his gun and kill herself right there on the spot, I know it. She'll not be able to grieve for another man."

"Mama, she won't do that. I think she will simply lose her mind."

And not find it this time, Seth thought, recalling lunch with Alice only two months ago, during the course of which she'd shared her grief over the battlefield deaths of her father and brothers.

"Are you going back out there soon? Peter is so upset he doesn't know what to do next. I hate to ask him to take me. I thought I might return with you?"

"You're welcome to, but I'm heading into town after speaking to your husband. I probably won't be returning until near dinner-time."

She nodded. Quietly she tapped a door near the end of the hall, then opened it. "Major Parker is here, dear." She looked at Seth before moving out of his way. "I'll let you know before you leave, but I need to get out there before that, I fear."

Peter Franklin, a blanket over his shoulders, rose from his chair in front of a cheery fire, at odds with the atmosphere of this grieving house. Someone had opened his drapes and the south-facing room was relatively bright. The older man extended a cold hand, and Seth took it.

"How are Calhoon and Alice?"

"It's a critical situation out there, but he was still alive when I left."

"Have a seat," Franklin said, returning to his own chair. "I need to take Betty out there, and I think getting out will do me good."

"How's the other Mrs. Franklin holding up?"

"Not well."

"I don't want to bother her. Did you have a chance to ask her what I wanted?"

"Jon told her he had a meeting last evening in Port Gibson, but she overheard him ask Luther, my yard man, if the phaeton could manage the roads to Camellia Creek. Luther told him he thought it could. Eustacia then proceeded to question Jon about his 'business' at Camellia Creek. He responded that it did not concern her. It's unfortunate that he was too often disrespectful to his mama, but she could be difficult, and she never stopped treating him like a child."

Peter Franklin had been speaking to the hands he'd folded in his lap. Now he looked at Seth. "Eustacia has been questioning him of late regarding his activities, drinking and late nights. I imagine she snuck out after him, which is why she overheard his conversation with Luther. My cook tells me their subsequent discussion became quite vocal, but we had become accustomed to their arguing. Eustacia accused Jon of trying to make trouble for Alice and to keep away, and she insisted he leave the carriage here if he were determined to go because I might need it later. He told her, and she confirmed this to me, that he did have a meeting in Port Gibson last evening and since it looked like rain, and he didn't want to get wet, that he would take the carriage, which, of course, he did."

"Do you have any idea who he planned to meet in Port Gibson?"

"I do not, nor do I know if there really was such a meeting. He might have told Eustacia that to preclude further argument."

"Could his meeting have been with Naomi Polk?"

"Why do you ask that?"

"From what Jon told Alice during his visit yesterday, it appears Miss Polk was behind his going out there and confronting Alice with this supposed threat posed by Eli Calhoon."

Franklin looked away.

"Do you know anything about his relationship with Naomi Polk?"

"No." After a moment, the man leaned back in his chair. "Dear God," he said, "what do you think that woman was up to?"

Seth drew in a breath. "I think she meant to kill Calhoon and

Alice. What she had planned with or for your nephew I'm not sure. Have you seen his body?"

Franklin gave his head a little shake. "I planned to go to the livery in a bit."

"The doctor hasn't seen it yet, either, but in addition to the bullet hole in his chest, you'll find other injuries on him."

"What sort of injuries?"

"A noticeable bite on his mouth and bruises on his torso and limbs, blows from Alice's poker."

Peter Franklin gave him a blank stare, and Seth regretted adding to the man's anxiety.

"I had a pretty coherent talk with your niece this morning. Jon attacked her yesterday afternoon, and she fought him off."

The man's narrowed eyes closed tight. "When you said Alice was injured last night, I assumed the Polk woman."

"Her major injuries were done by Naomi Polk. Alice won the battle with your nephew, but I wanted you to know that Jon indicated he needed her money."

"I realize now that all he ever wanted was her money." Peter Franklin's eyes were open now. "Fool that I am, I was determined he should have it, but not to gamble away on risky ventures. I truly thought he'd establish himself and the two of them would be happy. Alice never had any interest in my nephew, Parker. I understand why, now, and for better or worse, she's in love with Calhoon."

"And what risky venture was your nephew involved in?"

"I'm merely guessing about that. My brother left his wife and son very comfortable, yet the money was gone within two years. I thought Eustacia had control of the assets. She bought his way out of military service, but there was a lot more money than required for that."

"So you don't know what plans he had for Alice's money?"

"Jon was supposed to be working with me. We were speculating in land."

The door opened, and Cassie entered with a tray. She looked at Seth and smiled. "Mama thought you two might like some coffee." She set the tray, with its porcelain pot, cups, and saucers, as well as silver spoons, on a table in front of them. "Luther found two of your men in the carriage house," she said to Seth. "We've put them in the kitchen where it's warmer."

Seth nodded—"Thank you"—and looked at Peter Franklin. "I want to check your carriage, if I could. Try to find the bullet that killed Jon. I figure it's lodged in the back of the seat unless it passed through completely."

"Of course." Peter looked back at his daughter. "Tell your mother to pack some things. I'll take her out to Camellia Creek in a little bit. We need to check on Alice."

"You want Mama to stay out there?"

"I think she should."

Cassie started to speak, but Peter said, "I'll be leaving in just a couple of days, honey, to take your aunt and cousin back to New York, so you'll not have to deal with your Aunt Stacey long."

Her hand on his shoulder, Cassie bent over and kissed the man's cheek. "I'll be fine, Papa, you know I grate on her nerves much more than she grates on mine."

He patted her hand. "I don't believe you let anything bother you, sweetheart. Now run along and tell your mama, and let the major and me get on with our talk."

Porcelain cups tinkled against their respective saucers as Franklin set them out. "Betty knows I hate these damn little cups. They don't hold but a swallow. She only drags them out for company." He handed Seth a filled cup of steaming brew, then raised his own in semblance of a toast. "Consider yourself honored."

Seth mimicked the salute and took a swallow. Hot, and a strong, bitter brew to boot. "A woman by the name of Isabel Hays passed your nephew on the Rodney Road last evening, not too long before he was shot. She and he were well acquainted."

When Franklin didn't respond, Seth said. "Do you know who she is?"

"I do, and I am aware that Jon visited her place."

"How long have you known?"

Franklin's brief rally with Cassie's interruption had passed. "A couple of months."

"Did you ever discuss his activities there?"

"I beg your pardon?"

"More goes on there than whoring, Mr. Franklin. I've been aware for some time that Jon had been interested in cultivating business contacts."

"Was the woman able to tell you anything?"

"She says she didn't introduce Jon to anyone who would require his services. She considered him empty air."

Franklin thrust a hand through his head of thick, white hair. "We were supposed to be partners. As it turns out, I must assume he was dealing with, or attempting to deal with, people of whom I am unaware."

"Was it his murder that made you realize this or did you know before?"

"I've suspected for several weeks. Look, Parker, I know you need names, but honestly I don't have any for you. Right now, I want to get Jon buried beside my brother in New York, then I'll return and direct my attention to helping you."

"Do you think his mother might know anything?"

"Good Lord, no. As I indicated earlier, he didn't even want her aware of what he and I were doing." He shook his head. "Obviously he regarded me in similar light. To tell you the truth, I'm crushed by not only my nephew's death, but his apparent perfidy. I would like the opportunity to clear this up, if possible."

Seth finished his coffee and stood. "Finding his killer might help."

Franklin stood, too, and extended a hand.

"When do you plan on leaving?" Seth asked.

"As soon as authorities give me the body. I am going into town later and see what I can learn regarding travel. I haven't tried to get anywhere in the northeast from here, and I have no idea how difficult it's going to be."

"Rail would be a nightmare, constantly switching from train to stage, at least through most of Virginia. Going up the river might not be bad. You could probably switch to rail at Wheeling, but for ease of travel you might think about the Pearl River to the Gulf on a small packet. Better yet, hire a flatboat at the ferry landing at Georgetown in Copiah County where the Gallatin-Westville Road crosses the Pearl. River's high, and I'm told small boats can manage the lower rapids this time of year. From there, go on to Mobile and catch a steamer to New York. It'll take longer, but you won't have to worry about moving the casket from one conveyance to another."

"I'll look at that," the man said, moving toward the door. "I've already decided against trying to get there overland."

"*It* was new," Cassie Franklin told Seth and shook her head. "Papa ordered it before we left Chicago. We'd never had anything like a phaeton before, but he said the family had gotten so big since the war ended, we needed it. It arrived Grand Gulf shortly before Christmas. I think he'll probably sell it now, and we've hardly used it."

Seth was on his knees in the cramped space between the carriage's two seats. Pocket knife held in fingers so numbed by cold they were near useless, he was doing his damnedest to recover the bullet that had killed Jon Franklin the afternoon before. It had passed through Franklin, then exploded out the back to the carriage's front seat to bury itself in the plush padding of the one behind it. Poor light in the carriage house hindered Seth's effort, and he was adding to the vehicle's damage.

"Got it," he said. He stood up and held the crushed projectile between thumb and index finger for Jubal Summers to see, before dropping it in the black man's palm.

"Large caliber, like we thought."

Seth jumped from the carriage, and Jubal stepped back. Cassie, bundled up in coat and bonnet, drew closer to them. Her father had left them minutes ago to retrieve mules and the wagon from the barn. Given the condition of the roads this morning, Seth had advised against taking the carriage to Camellia Creek.

"Let's check something," he said to Jubal and strode outside the carriage house and mounted Boone. Ducking his head beneath the wide double door he brought the horse alongside the carriage, the seat of which sat high.

"Given the angle of the bullet's path, I'd guess the shooter was on horseback."

"Yeah, but that two-wheeler of the Hays woman sits higher than this one, and she could have stood," Jubal said.

True, and an observation Seth wished Jubal hadn't made in front of Cassie Franklin, who now stepped outside the carriage house at the noisy approach of another vehicle.

Peter Franklin drove the farm wagon into their line of sight and set the brake before jumping down. "Did you find it?" he asked Seth.

"I did. Afraid I did more damage to the seat though."

Franklin scowled. "The least of my concerns at the moment. I should have never bought that thing. It's a city carriage."

"Papa, Major Parker thinks the killer might have been mounted, but Captain Summers is apparently suspicious of some woman named Hays."

Peter whipped his head toward Seth. "You think she killed him?"

Seth fought the urge to release a long sigh. "Not necessarily, but given the height of her carriage seat, I can't rule her out."

Chapter Six

Naomi Polk's clapboard house on Farmer's Street, like most structures in this little Southern hamlet, had been pretty once. The roof of the two-storied structure rose into the limbs of surrounding water oaks and pecan trees, and it boasted a front porch cordoned by posts and spindled colonnades, all in need of paint.

Seth, Jubal, and Private Hand found Isabel's horse and two-wheeler, with a mulish-looking army horse tethered to it, in the back, the home's primary ingress and egress. Corporal Daws stood at the top of the back porch steps, loaded with sheets and blankets. He'd been about to descend. Isabel Hays followed him onto the porch and pulled the door shut behind her.

"What's happening here?" Seth said, dismounting.

Isabel gave him a courtesy smile, then grabbed a rickety railing with her free hand. In the other, she carried a Bible.

"I came back when Dr. Lester did. We're out of clean sheets, what with Eli's injury, and Elvie can't get the bloody ones washed and dried fast enough. I decided to pilfer Naomi's place.

"Here, darling," she said to Daws. "Just stack them on top of these." She again looked at Seth. "Holland paid for everything here, anyway. This"—she held out the ancient tome for them to see and continued in an embittered voice—"he inherited from his paternal grandmother, there being no sisters or female cousins. It disappeared the night of the Federal raid on Camellia Creek. The witch said the raiders burned it. She lied, obviously, and I'm taking it back where it belongs. I also found a dress to bury her in."

Seth perused Daws, who had finished putting the items on the floor of the carriage. "And you?"

Isabel sashayed to the front of the conveyance. "He insisted on accompanying me. Apparently he thought you wanted him to."

"I did." Seth stepped over and gave her a hand into the seat, then turned to Daws. "What did she take?"

The young man appeared taken aback. "Jes' dem sheets, an' blankets, an' stuff, far as I know, suh."

Isabel looked down from her perch. "Pray tell, Major Parker, what do you suspect me of doing?"

"Removing evidence." He wanted to search Naomi Polk's home for anything that might shed some light on the woman's dealings with Jon Franklin, and he didn't want anyone else removing things from the house before he had that opportunity, most especially the last person known to see Franklin alive. He walked around and rummaged through the pile of bed sheets and blankets piled in the carriage. Nothing. When he looked at the Bible on the seat beside her, she picked it up and thrust it under his nose. He didn't take it.

"I'm looking for something that might clue me as to what Naomi Polk was up to."

"Something more complicated than revenge?"

"Maybe that's all it was, Miss Hayes, but that doesn't explain to my satisfaction why Jon Franklin was working with her."

"Stupidity, perhaps?"

"I'll let you and the rest of her family know when you're allowed back in here, if you don't mind."

"Of course, Major. I did not mean to offend, and for your edification, I told you this morning that I believe someone was in this house before me. I now have cause to believe that person came back after I left. I'm referring to the chair in the bedroom."

Seth opened his mouth to ask, but Isabel said, "You'll see for yourself." She picked up the reins.

"You're returning to Camellia Creek?"

"As soon as I have checked out of the hotel. I need to get my things." She glanced down on the wrinkled garb she'd worn to Camellia Creek in the storm last night. "I do so want to get out of my pioneer woman outfit."

He stepped back from the carriage. "I'm surprised you left with Calhoon's condition so perilous."

"As I said, we're going to need clean sheets for all our beds." She gestured to the rear of the carriage where the corporal stood. "Do I get to keep Daws?"

Seth found his man and said, "Stay with her."

*N*othing inside Naomi Polk's cold and dingy home would have alerted Seth to someone having recently searched it. Isabel said the damaged chair was upstairs, but down, the spartan rooms appeared neat and tidy, if one didn't take into account a fireplace in need of shoveling.

"I'll start with the secretary over here," he said to Jubal. "You take the upstairs and listen for what might be loose floorboards as you're walking around."

Twenty minutes later, his search of the secretary and every other nook and cranny Seth could find downstairs completed, he went up to help Jubal, who was in the only furnished bedroom of three. There was an attic access in the hall, but Jubal told him that was the first place he'd looked.

"This is the most interesting thing I've found," he told Seth and pointed. "Isabel Hays' chair."

Seth studied a ragged rent in the chair's upholstery. "Looks like a bayonet."

"Yeah," Jubal said, "but look here. These cut threads indicate it had been sewed up, then cut again. Could have been as recent as this morning."

"We need to talk to Daws."

Chapter Seven

Ephraim Lester weighed the remains of the shell in his hand. "Forty-four," the doctor said.

At Seth's side, Jubal Summers stirred, interested. Private Hand did nothing. "You're sure?" Seth asked.

"It's a guess, but I've made many a sound guess in my day and handled more than my share of spent bullets. This one's the worse for wear, but..." He reached for a scale behind him, placed it on the apothecary chest situated to one side of his desk, then from his pocket, drew another small mass of metal. He held it up between thumb and forefinger so they could see. "This is the bullet I dug out of Eli Calhoon's pelvic bone last night." He tossed it in the left dish, then the bullet Seth had given him into the right. The right lowered a fraction in relation to the left.

"Now we know Naomi Polk shot Eli with a standard-issue 1851 Navy Colt, which takes a .36 caliber bullet." He pointed to the right scale. "The bullet that killed Franklin is heavier. My educated guess says a .44."

"So an Army Colt."

"Something that fires a .44 is all I can tell you. I have something else. From the angle of the bullet's entry and exit, I'd say the killer was on a large horse and looking down on his victim."

"A carriage seat?"

"Wagon or stagecoach maybe. Not any of the private coaches we've ever seen in these parts. I think you need to stick with a man on horseback." He handed Seth a piece of folded note paper. "Found that in a pocket inside Franklin's coat."

Good linen stationery on which the words 'S. Caruthers' had been written in a distinct, flowing script.

Seth looked at Jubal. "I thought the men checked his pockets?"

"They—"

"Came from a pocket sewn into the lining. Some tailors put them in as a defense against pickpockets. They'd have had to strip him down to find it. That job was left for me."

Seth again looked at the note. "Isn't this fellow a well-known politician here in the state?"

"Yep, Sam Caruthers, north of us. He was a respected Whig politician, then a leader of the Union Party. Family's been around since before statehood, bulk of folks round here aren't holdin' this particular Caruthers in too high esteem of late."

"Guess you'll rule out the Hays woman, now," Jubal said, following Seth through the gate of Ephraim Lester's front walk. Private Hand pulled the gate shut behind them.

"I knew by the size of the hole in Franklin's back the little .22 she carries around in her reticule wasn't the weapon." He rubbed the stubble on his chin. "I did consider that Navy Colt under her carriage seat a possibility, especially with her having cleaned it recently, but it's good to rule her out completely, at least in the Franklin murder."

"You still suspect her in Guthrie's?"

"I suspect her of knowing more than she's telling. She admitted going to Naomi Polk's house to confront the woman about her intrigue with Jon Franklin. That tells me Miss Hays has at least an inkling of what they might have been up to."

"A little less comfort and a little more pressure might help our effort."

"Still think I'm coddling her, Jubal? Because if you're thinking I can make her talk, it's going to take a lot more pressure."

"She has her weak points."

Indeed she did. One lay in bed at Camellia Creek fighting for his life, the other was her daughter in Madison County. Jubal was aware of both.

"The trick is knowing when to press the advantage," Seth said, "otherwise the opportunity is lost." He lessened his stride, at the same time twisting his body to bring Hand into the conversation. "I'm gonna check at the newspaper and see if the courier from Vicksburg left me anything. Then I'm gonna ride back out to Camellia Creek. I want to talk to Daws about that damaged chair without the distracting presence of Isabel Hays. There's no reason for us all to be dead on our feet. You two get back to quarters and get some sleep."

Chapter Eight

The Port Gibson Chronicle's front office was warm when Seth stepped inside. Of course, out of that brutal north wind it would have been warm inside relative to out, even if somebody didn't already have the stoves going.

To his right, Private Ball rose to attention and greeted him with a smart salute. Seth returned the greeting, the oddity of saluting inside and uncovered having worn off long ago.

"You the only one here?"

"Cawpral Peters be in da office, suh." He nodded at the closed door. "But he ain't doin' nuthin'."

"You are just in the nick of time, Major," Poynter Cummings said from the threshold of his office. "I was fixin' to go ransom my horse from the livery and ride out to Camellia Creek. Rumors are things got real exciting after you left here yesterday afternoon."

Seth turned from where he hung his coat and kepi near the door. "The source, no doubt, is my troops."

"Them and the sheriff's wife, and word has spread like proverbial wildfire. I want first dibs."

"Because you're in stiff competition with which other papers here in town?"

"For your information, Major, I wake up most mornings not knowing which provocateurs from the *Chicago Tribune* are expounding on lies for their radical readership up north. I sure don't want them beating me on something legitimate."

Seth stepped behind the counter of *The Chronicle's* front room. Two months ago he'd commandeered space here from which to launch his investigation into the Alan Guthrie murder. The site was ideal. Not only was it in downtown Port Gibson, seat of

Claiborne County, where Guthrie had reportedly centered his work, but the newspaper's editor was front and foremost with reporting not only Guthrie's untimely demise, but also the theft of confiscated Federal cotton on which Seth's senior originally believed the Treasury agent's murder had been predicated.

Seth opened the door to his office and found Corporal Peters, deck of cards in hand, playing solitaire. The young man jumped to his feet.

"As you were. Seen the runner yet?"

"No, suh."

"I want to send a detailed report up to Colonel Byrnes about last night. If he comes in, don't let him leave."

"Yes, suh."

Seth left the door wide and turned to Cummings. "You got time to talk?"

"You are jesting, right?" He swept his arm wide, inviting Seth into his office.

"Word is you shot Naomi Polk," Cummings said, closing the door behind them.

"Word's right, but she didn't give me much choice."

"She shot Calhoon?" Cummings took a seat at his desk.

"Yep."

"How's he doin'?"

"Barely hanging on when I left."

"That doesn't sound promising."

"His bride is reading to him. He's unconscious, but Alice swears he can hear her." Seth sat and rubbed his palms along the worn, velvet arms of the balloon-back gentleman's chair. His mother had several like it throughout his Bluegrass Kentucky home, and he favored the style and comfort. He slouched in an effort to rest his aching shoulder against its padded back.

"Why do you think the Polk woman shot him?"

"You heard our conversation yesterday afternoon," he said, working his shoulder. "She was trying to convince me Calhoon meant to kill Alice, the very woman he stepped in front of Naomi Polk's bullet to save last evening."

"So, he was protecting his wife."

"And you know what else is really interesting?" Seth said, without confirming the obvious, "Jon Franklin, the man Naomi Polk said Calhoon believed was sleeping with his wife, is also dead."

"I heard. Did Calhoon kill him?"

"Nope. He was with an army engineer at the time Franklin was shot. But Franklin had been at Camellia Creek yesterday afternoon. In fact, he'd left the place right before he was killed. He'd made inappropriate overtures to the missus while her husband was out."

"Are you sure Calhoon didn't kill him?"

"Positive." Seth massaged his shoulder all the time eyeing Cummings. "So what do you think, Mr. Newspaper Editor?"

"Sounds like a nice fit with your Guthrie murder."

Seth had considered a connection, but not something he'd term a "nice fit."

"Why?" he asked. "The only thing tying Franklin to Guthrie is the speculative chance Eli Calhoon knew both men."

"There's the way they died. Shot down on a lonely road with a bullet through the heart."

"And I have the bullet that killed Franklin, but not the one that killed Guthrie. Look, the only official reason I'm involved with Franklin now is because my men found his body. Unless Franklin's being a Northerner turns out to be an issue, his murder will probably be turned over to the locals."

"I think there could be a connection."

A prospect Seth favored. "Could you elaborate?"

"Franklin used to come see me from time to time. He liked to discuss individuals, I assume, he wanted to get to know better, and he displayed interest in the cotton 'trade.' A little later into the fall, he expressed a particular interest in the Guthrie murder.'

And that was, indeed, worth knowing. "You tell such a good story. Could be he was just curious about that, too."

"Self-aggrandizing individuals don't possess curiosity about anything that doesn't benefit them. Something happened to pique

Jon's interest. Have Peter Franklin make an issue out of it, keep you involved."

Seth cocked his head and studied Cummings. Why would the man, correctly, assume he wanted to stay involved?

When Seth said nothing, Cummings picked up a pencil and started tapping its blunt end on the desktop. The man watched the tap, tap, tap, then stopped and looked across the desk's marred surface to Seth. "I could start my own investigation, you know."

"I thought you already had."

"Not on Jon Franklin."

He knew now Cummings was fishing.

"Might be we could work together," Cummings said.

Seth had always believed this man knew more than he let on. That, or he had a damn good instinct for Seth's needs. Seth sat forward, giving up his effort with the chair's padded back. His shoulder felt like somebody was driving a pike into it. "Might be we could."

He tilted his head to the left and stretched his left arm behind his head to his right shoulder. Cummings watched for a moment, then pulled open a desk drawer, removed a small brown bottle, and set it on the desk. He rose and poured a glass of water.

"Paregoric," the man said, inverting the bottle and placing two drops in the water. He set the glass in front of Seth. "Doc told me one drop. You're bigger. I'm surprised those surgeons didn't give you a supply of morphine for what ails you. War wound, I take it?"

Seth reached for the glass. "They offered, but I've seen what addiction to that stuff can do and given that my shoulder aches every time the weather turns cold, I'd have been a sure candidate for dependency."

Cummings nodded at the glass in Seth's hand and sat back down. "That could prove just as bad. It's not as effective on my headaches any longer."

"I don't make a habit of this stuff either, but my shoulder's unusually bad this morning. Thanks." He drank the mixture.

"And it's your body's demand for more dope that's causing the headaches, I'd guess."

"Doc says that, too."

"You told me last fall that you had a working relationship with Alan Guthrie regarding cotton thieving. I took that to mean cotton thieving is what he was working on. Shortly thereafter, I'm pointed in the direction of a man who was indeed stealing cotton, but now doesn't appear to have been in the area at the time Guthrie would have been ordered here to break up his alleged cotton-theft ring. In other words, from what I'm seeing, Guthrie's arrival predates the establishment of Calhoon's cotton-thieving business. So I'm thinking what brought Guthrie to Mississippi, and, allegedly, to Calhoon, must have been something other than cotton thieving. Do you understand what I'm saying?"

The newspaperman gave Seth a long, hard study. Finally, he sighed. "Guthrie approached me, but not to share what I knew about cotton thieving. He wanted to use the cotton story as his cover for being here."

"So, he wasn't here about cotton. Dammit, Cum—"

The editor raised a palm. "Not *specifically* about cotton. He came to me because he'd read one of my articles in the paper. He told me he was a Treasury operative and that he was in the area investigating potential threats to the central government, which included the theft of Federal property. Discretion, he said, was required. He wanted my support in perpetuating the ruse and in return he would help me gather whatever information he could to expose corrupt Federal officials."

"And you believed that?"

"I didn't trust him, if that's what you mean, but I figured if nothing else, he was providing me fodder by making me privy to his own activities."

"So you're saying his alleged interest in cotton thefts was only a cover story for something else?"

"Yes, but he was vague as to exactly what that something else was, and his tone was arrogant, which I didn't appreciate. But didn't place much store in it, since I hadn't done anything wrong.

Further, I consider threats to me and my own, from a Federal, as a personal challenge."

"He indicated that ex-Confederates were involved in whatever thefts he was trying to uncover?"

"Like I said, his quest was vague. In short, he demanded my support in abetting his recovery of United States Government property. I consider what does or does not belong to the United States relative."

"Did you tell him that?"

"I told him that I would be as cooperative with him as he proved to me. I emphasized to the man that my focus was bringing the glorious soldiers of rapine, now stealing from, 'nominally,' their own, to justice and that I would happily allow him to bask in my successes if he had such a requirement."

"How did he react?"

Cummings snorted. "As if he thought I actually believed there was such a thing as an honest Treasury agent. He intimated that I should tell him anything I knew of ancillary thefts of government property, regardless of the thieves' alignment, and further suggested I recruit individuals willing to inform on those participating in such crimes. I never found anyone for him to cultivate."

"Did you try?"

"I considered hashing it over with my brother-in-law, just to see if we could infiltrate whatever the man was trying to build here, but only a few days later, Guthrie was dead. At the time, I regarded his stated objective to investigate thefts against the government as a bone thrown my way merely to draw me in. Further, I considered his implied objective to infiltrate groups who planned to resist Federal tyranny even more suspect. Looking back, I, blinded by my own prejudice, could have misinterpreted his intent or his intelligence." Cummings hesitated a moment, then said, "Now I'd be willing to countenance either."

Seth was feeling the effect of the drug, and he toyed with the thought Cummings had given it to him on purpose. "I think if I were planning to covertly insert men into a hostile group in order to spy on it, I'd be real sure of whoever I broached my plan with."

Seth allowed a grin to spread across his face. "And it sure as hell wouldn't be you."

"My point exactly, which led me to conclude that wasn't his real intent or he was not an effective agent."

"So, a lone man on a single mission?"

"A man on an ad hoc mission," Cummings stated matter-of-factly.

"Why didn't you tell me that suspicion before now?"

"You've just now got around to asking for my suspicions."

"I'd have always welcomed your 'suspicions.'"

"Well, then, maybe I've just now gotten around to wanting to offer them."

"Me and my own?"

"I beg your pardon."

"You made a comment moments ago about protecting 'me and my own.' To what did you refer?"

"To myself and the people of the South."

"In opposition to the United States?"

"In opposition to an administration rife with tyranny."

"What you're spouting is sedition."

"My having just lost the war, your opinion is fact."

"Were you as candid with Guthrie?"

"I was more discreet."

"Why less so with me?"

"I like you, Parker. You exude an aura of justice. Plus, I believe you and I could develop a successful partnership."

Seth smirked. "You don't think I'll ask you to betray your own?"

"People who do that are as treacherous as the people they recruit."

They could philosophize on this for hours, and he didn't have time. "You're digressing."

Cummings said nothing, and Seth said, "Do you know a man named Sam Caruthers."

"I do."

"Did Guthrie ever ask you about him?"

Cummings laughed. "He did not. Good God, Parker, why did you ask that?"

"Has Isabel or Tobias Holbein mentioned the two men knowing each other?"

"Not in my presence, but I don't keep company with either, as a rule."

"In someone else's presence?"

"I'm not playing word games. I know of no connection between Alan Guthrie and Sam Caruthers, nor would I expect to. Caruthers isn't from around here."

"But you do know him?"

"I've dined with and interviewed him on occasion over the years—influential in politics and all that, you know."

Seth seized the arms of his chair, ready to pull himself to his feet.

"Caruthers is a resident of Warren County," Cummings said. The lilt in the man's voice was leading, and Seth narrowed his eyes.

"What point are you trying to make?"

"One might expect, if someone were investigating him, they'd do so a little closer to his stomping ground, wouldn't you think?"

Seth fell back into his chair and studied Cummings, who appeared to be waiting for a question. After a moment, Seth said, "Did Guthrie ask you about anyone from around here?"

"Holland Calhoon, Andrew Calhoon, Eli Calhoon, and the sister, Hannah Calhoon."

Inwardly, Seth cursed Poynter Cummings. Then he said, "You gave me the damn drug intending to tell me that."

Cummings frowned. "Why would I do that?"

"In hopes that my ensuing physical euphoria would keep me from killing you. What did he ask?"

"He wanted to know where he could find them."

"And what did you tell him?"

"Dead, dead, believed dead, and dead."

"And this was in the context of stolen government property and infiltrating seditious groups?"

Cummings locked his jaw. "In the same conversation, not the same context."

"Are you splitting hairs, here, Cummings? Why did he say he wanted to talk to them?"

"He never really stated he wanted to talk to them, just curious as to their whereabouts. He'd been out to Camellia Creek and talked to Naomi Polk. She told him the family was gone and wouldn't be back, never hinted she was a relation. He just assumed she'd moved in when they moved out. That's another reason he came to me. He figured I would know every resident in the county.

"He wanted to know the dates and locations of Holland's and Andrew's deaths, but seemed particularly concerned over the supposed disappearance of Eli. I assured him Eli's status would be best described as missing rather than a disappearance. He wanted to know if there were other relations. I told him where to find Andrew Calhoon's widow, Laura Blackledge, and I told him there was an illegitimate daughter."

"Laura and Naomi Polk are both dead now, Cummings. If you'd told me —"

"I didn't know they were going to die, and when you showed up here last fall, I sure wasn't going to help you railroad a man into a murder conviction."

"That wouldn't —"

"That's exactly what would have happened, and you know it. I didn't know why Guthrie was looking at the Calhoons, and I still don't, but I can guarantee you that's why Laura told you Calhoon might have known Guthrie, because Guthrie approached her looking for him, and she couldn't be sure he hadn't found him."

Laura Blackledge had been murdered by Naomi Polk a little over a month ago. At the time, Seth had seriously considered Eli Calhoon had killed her, the violent result of passion twisted by betrayal. Now the whys and wherefores of Laura's murder were murky, the only confirmed thing being that Naomi Polk was her killer.

"You can sugarcoat it anyway you want," Seth said. "You were being uncooperative."

Cummings leaned back. "Damn right, but I've warmed to you now."

"Who and where is the bastard daughter?"

"Rebecca Mackey. War widow. She's in Madison County last I heard, but I told Guthrie I didn't know where she was."

Seth gave himself a moment before he spoke. "Holland Calhoon is the father of Isabel Hays' daughter?"

"He is. You know her?"

"I saw her a little over a week ago at The Pink Lady, right after Christmas." Inwardly, Seth cursed. She'd been talking to her brother's bride. It all made sense now, and therein lay the tale. Isabel Hays had borne Holland Calhoon a daughter, out of wedlock, some twenty-odd years ago. Seth had suspected an intimate tie between Calhoon's father and Isabel, but he'd not factored in a child. That kinship could neutralize the suggestion of illegal conspiracy between Eli Calhoon and Isabel. Then again, complicity might be stronger than ever.

"Do you know if Guthrie found her?" Seth asked.

"I don't, but it's interesting he was returning from Madison County when he was shot, so one might assume he was looking."

"You're real quick to throw the illegitimate daughter out there, but not Calhoon."

Cummings laughed in obvious disbelief. "You're not implying she shot the man on the Trace are you?"

Lord God in heaven, he hoped not. "Do you find it as odd as I do that Guthrie came to you instead of the sheriff in his search for county residents?"

"Wasn't odd if he didn't want local law enforcement to know he was looking for them."

And it wouldn't have been farfetched for Guthrie to assume local law enforcement was hostile to him, not that it would have been a deterrent.

"Now tell me," Cummings said, "why you think Guthrie was looking for Caruthers?"

"I don't. Caruthers' name came up in passing. I take it the white populace isn't too fond of him?"

"I don't know how fond black Mississippians are of him either. The only folks around here who are 'fond' of him for sure aren't from here. He made his bed with you boys in blue before Grant ever crossed the river, and he's been betraying his friends and neighbors ever since, all to his own benefit. I find it absolutely stupefying that some hothead hasn't put a bullet in his brain. Now tell me truthfully, in what context did Caruthers' name come up?"

Seth smiled and pulled himself out of the chair. "I've got to check some things first, then I can probably tell you. I just don't want to see it in the paper. Have you told anyone else about Guthrie's looking for the Calhoons?"

"Nope."

"Let's keep it between us for right now."

"I thought you'd say that. That's why I finally decided to let you know. I can keep secrets, Parker, and I'm gonna hold you to Caruthers."

Chapter Nine

"Already to'h when we got to da room, suh," Daws told Seth when he asked his corporal about the rip in the chair at Naomi Polk's home. "We gots der at da same time 'cause Miz Isabel say dats where da Polk woman keeps her sheets an' quilts an' dats what we come fo'. She take a good long look at dat tear an' scrunched 'er mou'f up a bit. Reached inside like she thought she might fin' somethin', but she didn't say nuthin' to me 'bout it.

"She cussed dat ole woman good, though, when she opened da blanket box an' found dat ole Bible. Say it be da Calhoon Bible an' didn't belong der. She opened da cover an' lights into dat ole dead woman agin'. Say dat ole witch dun dezecrated it." He grinned. "'Dezecrated it', she said."

"And she didn't take anything else?"

"No, suh. Looked through all da draws upstairs an' in dat furniture by da fireplace downstairs, but she didn't take nuthin', not dat I saw, but she be wif me mosta da time loadin' me up wif blankets and pillows an' such."

"How many trips did you make down to the carriage?"

"Two."

"And she was with you then?"

"Yes, suh, she had 'er own load da fu'st time. Only dat las' time, when y'all rode up did she lag behin' me an' not too long den. Beggin' yo' pah'don, Majah, but do I needs to be doin' mo when watchin' 'er?"

"We've ruled her out as Jon Franklin's killer. Don't interfere with her, just watch what she does and report to me or the captain. Good report."

He followed Daws out of the spacious office that Alice told

him he could use while in her home. His corporal was headed for the kitchen. Aunt Elvie had been cooking earlier, and she showed more patience with them all now. Seth loitered in the hall, trying to decide what to do next. He was hungry and tried to remember when last he'd eaten. Lunch yesterday, he thought, but despite his pangs he didn't have an appetite.

The back door rattled, and he turned from where he stood in the empty central hall and peered through the dim dining room to see who'd entered from the mud porch. A woman, her back to him at the moment, closed the back door and shut off the cold draft on which rode the scent of lilac. It was her, of course, it had to be, and now he knew the reason for it. His stomach had begun to quake before Rebecca Mackey turned and started through the dim dining room.

Bundled in winter garb, she stepped into the light. She had him in her sights, too, and she stopped, as surprised to see him as he was to see her, if the look on her face meant anything, like their encounter only days ago in Rodney. Her cheeks were flush from the cold, her eyes bright. It was late morning, and he understood she made her home in Madison County. She must have started out before first light and traveled hard.

Her eyes filled with tears, and she said in a voice filled with anguish, "Did you shoot him?"

"No," he answered, and he took a step toward the broad foyer separating them. "Naomi—"

The door to the sickroom opened, and the lovely Mrs. Mackey jerked her head that way. She swiped at her cheek, then sobbed "Aunt Elvie?" as Elvira Hinny, withered and slightly hunkered, stepped from the room with a bowl filled with water and wet rags stained with blood.

Rebecca took a step toward the aged Negress, who looked at her with eyes that brightened perceptibly. The woman nodded in acknowledgement and probably would have spoken, but the door to the room opened again.

"I thought that was you I heard," Isabel Hays said, quietly pulling the door shut behind her.

51

Rebecca stepped around the black woman and closer to her mother. "He's alive?"

"At the moment," Isabel said.

"Lasted da night and pawt of dis day," Elvira said, looking first at Isabel, then back to Becky. "Him's gonna pull through dis, you all is gonna see. Each hour him keeps on, makes him's chances better." Her voice had broken with her final words, and Rebecca hugged the old Negress to her and laid her head on the kerchief covering Aunt Elvie's hair.

Seth watched the three of them, braced for a renewal of grief in a place twisted from years of loss. Isabel Hays stood a little apart from the other two, the old black woman still in the embrace of the young white one until Rebecca finally straightened and freed her. "Goin' to get mo' hot watah, now," the old woman said. "Dinnah's done, too." She ambled into the dining room and out the back door on her way to the cookhouse.

"What in God's name happened?" Rebecca asked her mother in a voice clogged with tears.

Isabel's eyes moved from her daughter, to him, then back to her daughter. Rebecca had followed her mother's gaze to him, and that's where her eyes lingered when Isabel said, "Naomi shot him. She was trying to kill Alice."

"Sweet heaven," Rebecca said, her attention back on Isabel, "is Alice all right?"

"She's in there reading Machiavelli to him."

Rebecca, who now reached for the bow securing her hat, frowned at her mother, and Isabel gave her a tear-filled laugh.

"He's unconscious, has been since it happened. Naomi wasn't the only one a bit mad here, I fear."

Seth stepped closer, his eyes on Becky. "Alice thinks if things are too quiet, he'll take it as an opportunity to cross over."

"And she's determined he will not leave her," Isabel added. "She was hurt, but not too seriously, relatively speaking." A smile creased Isabel's face. "She's going to have a baby, darling."

Rebecca choked on something between a laugh and a sob. "Oh, Mama, I do hope this first one is a boy."

Isabel swiped at a tear.

"How badly is she hurt?"

"Naomi hit her in the shoulder with a poker. Ephraim was able to immobilize the injured arm, but he fears her collarbone is broken."

"She also took a blow to the head," Seth said softly, "but she won't take anything for pain because she's afraid it will put her to sleep. She's sure she's the only one who can keep him this side of the Styx."

Tears welled in Rebecca's gray eyes, but she blinked them back, let out a little breath, and turned back to her mother. "Perhaps I can help."

"I've tried to relieve her. She absolutely refuses."

"You're simply a should-have-been stepmother, I'm his sister. I'll convince her he'll listen to me. I'll need to find something to read other than those boring *Discourses* though."

Isabel reached for Becky's coat when the younger woman slipped it off. "Buck returned with you?"

"Hector's with me. We came on horseback as soon as I could dress. I left Buck there to thaw out and rest. He's gonna bring Mattie and the girls later today on the stage. Hector will pick them up in Port Gibson." Becky looked at her mother. "I didn't know how long I'd be here, and I can't leave them at Hickory Grove."

"Of course not." Isabel turned to the closed door, the black coat still draped over one arm.

"I'll take it," Seth said, then reached for the hat Becky held. She looked at him as if not sure what he was about. "Your hat," he said, and she handed it to him.

"Where is Aunt Naomi?" she asked her mother, and Seth tensed.

Isabel took Rebecca's elbow and guided her toward the closed door. "She's in Andrew and Eli's room, quite dead."

"I killed her," he said and turned his back when the beauty looked at him. He went into the parlor and disposed of Rebecca Mackey's outerwear over the back of the worn settee.

"I don't believe he had time to give the action much thought," he heard Isabel say, "and thank goodness for it."

He heard the squeak of the door, and turned. Now that he'd had a chance to talk to Daws about the ripped chair, he was ready to talk to her. "Miss Hays," he said, throwing his voice across the room and hall, "I need to..."

A gentle click confirmed the closing of the sickroom door, and he sighed. That was all right. He was exhausted. His questions could wait till after dinnertime.

The subtle scents of fear and blood permeated the acrid scent of potent astringents. Not even the comforting smell of coal oil and wood smoke from the glowing stove had banished the gloom determined to have its way. In front of Becky sat Alice, her soft, but compelling voice a shield holding back the yet-to-be-defeated spectre of Death hovering in the dark corners of this room. Becky felt her hackles rise.

Her determined sister-in-law gave Becky heart, despite the gray figure that lay on his side in the bed. Cautious, she stepped forward, not wanting to disturb him, although Alice seemed to think the more he knew of life around him, the better. On Becky's left, another dark-headed woman stepped behind her, whispered something to her mother, then left the room.

Becky touched Alice's shoulder. Alice jerked, and Becky withdrew her hand. She'd forgotten Alice's injury. The auburn-haired beauty gave her a blank stare, and Becky squatted beside her. "I'm Becky, remember, Eli's sister?"

Alice's eyes widened with recognition, then teared, and she reached for Becky's hand. "Of course, I do." Not letting go of Becky's hand, she turned to Eli on the bed. "I'm distracted, that's all. I do apologize."

With her free hand, Becky squeezed the one covering hers, then rose and pulled a three-legged stool beside Alice. "I'm here now. You must rest. I'll read to him."

Alice shook her head. "I'll not leave him."

"You must take care of yourself if you're to care for him."

Alice reached out and touched him. "I will rest once he's decided he's going to stay."

"Don't you think he has—"

"No. His body is wounded. Where he is right now he's protected from the pain. He knows he'll suffer if he comes back. He hasn't decided he wants to."

"Where he is, he can rest for the long fight in front of him. He knows he wants to live or he'd already be gone."

"I'm not sure. We've never done anything but fight, and I'm fighting with him still to stay with me."

"I don't believe you've never done anything but fight."

Alice rose and kissed his lips. "We fought to find each other, and we did. I won't let him give up on us now. We're going to have a baby, and he's going to help me raise him." She sat back down, settled the open book in her lap, and turned the page.

Becky looked to her mother, who stood at the foot of the bed watching them. "His injuries?"

"The bullet broke a rib, which deflected it down and through the liver. It lodged in his right pelvic bone. Ephraim got the bullet. The pelvic bone fractured, but will heal given time. The rib punctured his right lung. It's deflated, that's why he's on his side. The doctor got the bleeding stopped in the liver, but he told me no matter what, livers have a strong tendency to heal. Right now, Ephraim is worried about the blood loss and possible infection."

"It was Seth Parker's Sergeant Zachary," Alice said, "who curbed the bleeding until the doctor got here. Dr. Lester says he saved his life."

"I must thank him."

Alice nodded and returned to the book.

"Our daddy used to take Livy and compare it to the chapters Machiavelli referenced. Drawing parallels between the fate of the Roman Republic and our own interested him."

Alice stopped reading. "Livy?"

Isabel moved toward them. "Marcus Livius, *The History of Rome*, Machiavelli's inspiration for *The Discourses*."

Alice twisted to better see Isabel. "I don't recall Eli reading about the history of Rome. I don't remember seeing any such work in the library."

"The library was gutted the night the Federals came," Becky said. "What they didn't rip apart or burn, they took with them, but the Calhoon collection of books was quite impressive once." Becky nodded at the one Alice held. "The reason that one survived is because Daddy was reading it that night beside Hannah's bed. She was very ill."

Alice nodded. "Eli told me the soldiers were afraid to enter the room. Do you think he would enjoy Livy?"

"I can't believe he's enjoying Machiavelli. I think his interest must stem from a desire to understand what Daddy found so intriguing."

Alice wrinkled her nose at the book she held. "Honestly, I think it was because there was nothing else to read."

Isabel laughed gently. "You *must* be enjoying it immensely, Alice," Isabel said.

"I think something more entertaining would help me stay awake. But the important thing is that Eli be interested."

It would be the voice that interested him, Becky thought, not the content.

And Alice was the one to read to him, after all.

<h1 style="text-align:center">Chapter Ten</h1>

"The Carutherses are old landowners in Warren County," said Isabel. "They have holdings in Hinds County also. Pray do tell, Major, why did you ask me to write his name?"

Seth was studying the *S. Caruthers* she'd written, at his request, on a separate piece of notepaper.

"Do you do business with him?"

"If you are referring to my primary business, no. Not him, his forefathers, nor his progeny have ever crossed the threshold of The Pink Lady as it is now. However, when Sam was a young man, years before my original benefactor, Isaac Baker, died, he visited the house relatively often. Dinner, cards, and business, and by that, I speak of legitimate endeavors. Sam, as well as Holland, Toby Holbein, and others, were in Isaac's circle of friends. Those friendships are the connection, not business."

"So you know him pretty well?"

She pursed her lips. "Tell me your interest."

He let her rendition of the man's name float to the surface of the desk. "Dr. Lester found a piece of paper with that name written on it in one of Jon Franklin's pockets."

Isabel glanced to the desk at what she'd written. "And you were trying to confirm I hadn't given it to him? Or that I had?"

"That was my intent, yes."

"Which one, darling?"

"Take your pick. I didn't have a preference, though your having done it would solve that mystery."

"And now you're still looking for who put Jon into contact with Sam Caruthers. Despite your lack of 'preference', darling, I'm certain you're disappointed it wasn't me."

He folded his arms over his chest. "A little."

"Well, for your information, I've been acquainted with Sam Caruthers all my adult life, and I entered adult life at a relatively tender age." She waved her hand, then began to pace. "Sam was a moderate Unionist, who finally succumbed to secessionist fever. It was 'politic' at the time. But once hostilities commenced, he expressed nothing but criticism as to how Davis executed the war. In 1862 he removed both his military-aged sons to England, out of harm's way. There were other unpatriotic actions he took in the years following. He survived the war solvent. I wouldn't say better off than when the war started. The Confederacy, if nothing else, managed to wreak havoc on his cotton fields, especially those in Louisiana, but certainly he's better off than most. I could spell out for you how he managed that, but you're not stupid, so I imagine you can figure it out on your own."

"Was it his, shall we say, waning loyalty to the Confederacy that resulted in his falling out with Holland Calhoon?"

She stopped her pacing. "I never said anything about a falling out with Holland."

"You implied it with the inflection of your voice."

"To quote Holland, 'by Samuel Caruthers' own standards he committed treason against one country, then turned around and betrayed another, the second compounded by the betrayal of everything he should have held dear, his state, his neighbors, his friends.' He lacks both honor and conviction. Those, too, were Holland's words, but I concur."

"'Honor and conviction?' That sounds strange coming from you."

"Au contraire, Major Parker. Lack of honor, perhaps, but I am not a man, so I do not have to live up to that ill-conceived masculine abstraction. And when it comes to conviction, no one who really knows me doubts whose side I was on. As for everyone else, I do not care what they think."

"So, was there a specific act that brought Caruthers' lack of honor and conviction to the fore for Holland Calhoon?"

"In the summer of 1863, Samuel Caruthers declared himself a

loyal citizen and, with the encouragement of the occupying forces, took Muscatine, which Becky had, technically speaking, abandoned when she went to Madison County to help her widowed sister-in-law, Emily, with their ailing father-in-law. Holland's dismay regarding Sam's action was aggravated by a distant kinship between the two. Holland felt betrayed."

Her voice had been clipped, and he met her eyes, assuring her he'd noted it.

"Why did Caruthers want Muscatine?" he asked.

"It's improved farmland. It really is quite a nice little farm."

"So now this Sam Caruthers is assessing the present political climate?"

"He assessed both the political and military climate three years ago, which has left him in a position to 'exploit' the present political climate. That is what he's doing now. Might I see what Ephraim found on Jon's person?"

Seth hesitated, then reached inside his blouse, removed the annotated piece of stationery, and handed it to her. She studied first the name, then the paper itself, even turning it over to peruse the back of it. After a moment, she smirked.

"All right," she said, "there is something more. Back in the early thirties, Sam offered Holland's uncle top dollar for five hundred acres making up most of what is now Muscatine. When Seamus refused the offer, Sam tried to bring the Calhoons in on a railroad charter scheduled to be brought before the legislature. The proposed right-of-way, as you've probably guessed, crossed those same acres Sam had tried to purchase. I do believe Seamus showed some interest, but the depression of '37 ended the initiative. Perhaps Sam is still dreaming of railroads."

"And do you think Jon Franklin might have been interested in a railroad?"

"Given his ambition, I think it's possible."

"Is the proposal legitimate?"

"If there even is such a proposal, I would assume so. It was way back then, but as you're probably aware, wheeling and dealing for land can be ruthless."

"And you know for certain—"

"I do not know if that's the reason Jon had Sam's name on his person, but I do know that I didn't give him the name, and now, given the comparison"—she nodded at her handwriting sample on the desk—"you also know that."

He moved back to the desk. "The railroad wouldn't have terminated in the hinterland of Warren County. Do you know the proposed terminus?"

"Natchez for the near term." She opened her arms wide. "Tomorrow, who knows? The Pacific perhaps? But alas, such dreams are dead to us now, or do you suppose Congress will use Southern tax dollars to subsidize their cronies' building a transcontinental railroad along a southern route in the near future?" She tightened her jaw. "Or ever?"

Seth held her gaze. "Miss Hays, is it fair to assume the right-of-way continued across Camellia Creek?"

"Decades ago, stops were suggested for Port Gibson, then Fayette. But Grand Gulf to Rodney was an alternative proposal. Depending on the final decision, Camellia Creek may have been involved."

"Captain Summers and I found the damaged chair in Naomi Polk's home. Corporal Daws confirmed the damage was already done when y'all arrived. He said you showed interest in it. Why?"

She raised her chin, then cocked her head to one side. "I told you I was in that house yesterday afternoon in search of Naomi. When I went up to her bedroom, I noted that damaged chair and the fine workmanship she had put into its repair. I touched the area and felt what I concluded was interfacing to aid in the stitching. I now conclude whatever I'd felt was paper, because this morning, the rip was open and whatever I'd felt the day before was gone."

"How do I know you didn't remove whatever it was yesterday afternoon?"

She sighed. "You don't, but I didn't."

He rubbed his eyes and moved in the direction of the chair he longed to sit in. "Did this Sam Caruthers know Alan Guthrie?"

"I've been wondering when you'd get back to your original investigation. And that, sir, is a question Mr. Caruthers could, no doubt, answer for you. I assume you'll be speaking with him soon?"

She assumed correctly, and Seth wondered if something had spurred her to send him that direction. "It would be nice to know the truth when I ask him."

"You won't get it from me. Alan Guthrie did not mention Sam Caruthers to me, nor have I discussed Guthrie on the few occasions I've seen Sam lately."

"What did—"

"My daughter's property, Muscatine."

"Speaking of meetings, Jon Franklin's mother says he planned to meet someone in Port Gibson the day he was killed. Did he happen to mention such a meeting to you?"

"As a matter of fact he did."

Seth stifled a quick intake of breath. "Why didn't you tell me that before now?"

"Because I didn't want you to know." She sauntered his way, still holding the original scrap of fine linen stationery with *S. Caruthers* inscribed on it. "Now it doesn't matter. Jon's meeting was with Sam Caruthers, and as you know, Jon didn't make it. He asked me to convey his regrets."

"You were protecting this Caruthers for some odd reason?"

"Hardly. Besides, Sam didn't make it to Port Gibson either. I spoke briefly to his younger son, Wilson. He did not elaborate on why he was meeting with Jon."

"You're helpful all of a sudden, Miss Hays. Why?"

"My motives are selfish, I assure you. For her entire life, Rebecca's father provided for her, and I was happy to let him. He gave her a stable home, an education, and arranged a good marriage for her with a fine young man—no small feat considering who her mother is. Unfortunately the newlyweds began wedded bliss on the eve of a nightmare. Though she fancied herself deeply in love with him, she and James Mackey really never had the chance to get to know each other. However, I have no doubt he would have kept her safe and secure. With the loss of her father and husband, that responsibility now falls on Eli, who, as you know, may not survive the next hour. In a word, I'm worried for Becky and her brother, hence my cooperation today."

"Is Caruthers a threat?"

"He does have Muscatine." She passed him the annotated paper, and before he could respond, she said, "The stationery belonged to Rebecca and Eli's sister, Hannah. You can probably find more of it in the drawers to her secretary, which is now in the bedroom shared by Eli and Alice." She pursed her lips, then pivoted and started for the study door. Upon reaching it, she stopped and turned. "Take your investigation north to Sam, with my blessing. Ask him about the terminus of his proposed railroad. You might even tell him I told you to. I'd like that." She nodded at the paper he still held in his hand. "And now we know who put the ill-fated Jonathan Franklin in touch with whom."

Seth was still pondering that subtle suggestion she'd offered regarding the railroad terminus. Now, he bridled, looked at the note, then back to her. "Who?"

"That distinctive flowing 'S' belonged to none other than the recently departed Naomi Polk. It is a pity you had to kill her before we had a chance to talk to her." She laughed. "Perhaps Sam will shed some light on the matter for you. Sam approached her about investing in his railroad way back then, you know? She had a little money from her father. Holland advised her against it."

Chapter Eleven

Becky glanced at the tray of dirty dishes Betty Franklin deposited on the cookhouse table. "She ate good," Becky said.

"I ate most of it. I don't see how she has enough energy left to chew. I try to make her feel guilty because of the baby, but she says she'll only throw it up. She wants coffee. Is there any?"

Becky started for the stove. "Yes, but she should drink Aunt Elvie's tea. That helps her nausea."

"She's trying to stay awake."

"You empty the tray, and we'll get her a cup. Just pile the dishes on the table, I'll wash them later."

This woman, Becky now knew, was Alice's aunt. There was a daughter, too, Alice's cousin Cassie, who, Becky'd been told remained in Port Gibson helping her father and the murdered Jon Franklin's mother prepare for the funeral trip to New York. Soon enough Cassie would join the group standing vigil over Alice and Eli here at Camellia Creek.

The back door to the kitchen opened, bringing in a gust of cold air, and Becky watched Elvira Hinny slip inside. All these interlopers, and Becky included herself, had invaded the kitchen which Aunt Elvie surely regarded as her exclusive territory, now that Naomi Polk was dead. Becky knew the old woman wasn't pleased about that, but she'd played a good martyr so far. Elvie put a kitten on the floor, and Becky met her eyes. "We'll be out of your way in a minute, Auntie."

"I fear if we lose him," Betty said, drawing Becky's attention. "she will shrivel up and die. That or she'll take her own life. I spent many a sleepless night fearing she'd do that after we learned of Michael."

Becky set the filled cup of steaming brew on the tray. "He was the last brother?"

"Yes."

Becky almost said she was sorry, but couldn't bring herself to do it. It had been them, after all, who'd chosen war. "Such a waste," was all she said, and a stupid platitude it was for an unforgivable act of aggression.

"Indeed."

Becky wondered if the woman would be so agreeable if she knew her thoughts. She pushed the topless sugar bowl toward Betty Franklin, that and a pitcher of cream—Eli had a cow. "I know she likes cream and sugar, but I don't know how much. I'll let you fix it."

"I jus' fed you, now git!"

Becky scooped up the calico kitten dodging Elvie's feet. "Where did she come from?"

"Eli give it to Miz Alice at Chris'mas time," Elvie said. "She puts a lot a sto' in dat cat. Naomi tried to drown it. Dat's why Eli run 'er off da farm."

Nothing about Naomi Polk shocked Becky any longer.

"Alice named her Mercy," Betty Franklin said, then returned to the clumps of brown sugar. "Her daddy had given her a calico when she was little, and there was a mouse in this kitchen."

Becky set the cat in the crook of her folded arm. The kitten purred, and Betty Franklin placed a piece of raw sugar in Alice's cup. Becky found the presence of this sometime domineering Northerner in her father's house irritating, but was thankful for it. Goodness knows she didn't know how she'd have dealt with stubborn little Alice, who was the source of more worry than actual trouble. Even now Alice was awake, reading that God-awful tome to Eli, sure she was keeping him alive. Becky considered being forced to lie there and listen to Machiavelli would drive her to *seek* oblivion.

At the stove behind her, Aunt Elvie snorted. "Ain't seen no mouse. I'm thinkin' it be da ghos' of Jocelyn LeBlanc 'erse'f keepin' Alice safe from Naomi Po'k's poison."

Betty Franklin turned quickly and looked at Auntie. "So you do think she was poisoned that time?"

"Nevah once say she weren't poisoned dat night. Jus' say I didn't do it."

"Y'all think Aunt Naomi tried to kill Alice before the other night?"

"I thought—"

"Easy to see sech, lookin' back now what's happened cone happened. You thought Eli done it."

Becky stared at the Franklin woman, who huffed, then caught Becky's eye before returning to Alice's coffee. "I took into account all he had to gain should she die, that's all. And considering the...." Betty stirred the brew, then placed the spoon aside.

"Considering what?" Becky prodded.

"Nothing," Betty said and glared over her shoulder at Elvie.

"Hmmpf!" the old Negress said and turned away. "You needs to be talkin' to Miz Alice 'bout dat, young missy. She be da one tell you 'bout dem's joinin' in marriage if'n 'er wants you to know."

"Suffice it to say their courtship was unorthodox."

Betty Franklin said nothing more, but she'd noticeably relaxed with auntie's words. Becky couldn't be quite so dismissive, though she tried not to let it show. The simple fact the woman had, for even a moment, considered Eli capable of plotting murder against Alice was hateful.

"Alice asked me about books by Livy," Betty Franklin said to her. "I think she'd like me to find her one."

"He was a Roman historian," Becky said. "I believe you can blame me for her interest."

"Is there such a book here?"

"Not any longer that I know of, but there is an edition of *Wealth of Nations* in the middle drawer of the desk. At least there was the last time I was here. I'll try to find it. Tell her I'll bring it. Eli likes that one, too."

Becky placed the kitten on a straight-back kitchen chair, and turned to Elvie. "I don't believe there's been a cat in this kitchen since Duchess died."

The old woman placed a cast-iron lid on the pot of peas she'd been stirring. "Yo' Aunt Naomi wouldn't have it."

"Duchess?" Betty Franklin asked.

Becky gave the kitten a last scratch between her ears and started for the door. "Supposedly she was Hannah's cat. She was very old when she died."

"Oldah dan Hannah," Elvie said, checking the cornbread in the oven.

Becky stopped at the door. For a moment her eyes burned, and she said wistfully, "Duchess died in the late fall. Hannah and I were at school. Daddy didn't tell us till we came home for Christmas. Remember how Hannah cried, Auntie?"

"Po ole cat were de'f and near blind. 'Magin' she were happy to go."

"And you didn't cry?" Betty Franklin asked Becky.

Becky gave her head a little shake and opened the breezeway door. She'd wept like a baby, she recalled, standing in front of the fresh mound of dirt where Andy had buried sweet Duchess beside generations of other family pets. "I'll try and find that book."

*B*ecky saw notated paper on Eli's desk when she entered the study, broad flowing strokes, but not in Eli's hand. The handsome, towheaded marine officer, Seth Parker, had commandeered this desk, and after the noon meal, he'd asked her mother in here to talk. Becky scanned his notes where they lay. *Jon Franklin, Naomi.* Becky's heart beat faster. *Sam Caruthers*, and — with trembling fingers, she reached for the paper — *Guthrie*.

A footfall alerted her, and she looked up to find Seth Parker in the doorway, watching. She laid the paper back on the desk.

"My notes on the Franklin murder."

Becky swallowed. "I wondered who did it."

He came on in the room. "I don't know yet, but I'd be appreciative of any help I can get."

"I'm sorry I have none to offer." Anxious now to retrieve the book she sought and beat a quick retreat, she stooped in front of the desk's right pedestal, only to straighten when he approached. Dreading the subject she feared he would broach, she said, "I thank you for the other night. It's my understanding, but for your timely arrival both Eli and Alice would be dead."

"Thanks isn't necessary, but you are welcome."

"Are you all right?"

He opened his mouth to speak, but she knew she might have misled him and said, "I'm referring to your shooting Aunt Naomi."

"I hesitated a moment too long, I'm afraid."

She squatted in front of the desk. "That is understandable, considering she was a woman."

He said nothing. The darn drawer was stuck. She wanted out of here. "I'm sorry you had to do it."

"Me, too."

She struggled with the drawer, concentrating more on the awkward silence than the cubby's refusal to open.

"I went to Muscatine when I arrived in November," he said.

There, he was going to the place she didn't want to go.

"The farm was pretty much abandoned. There was a Negro girl there, about fourteen, who was reluctant to talk to me."

"Lettie, Uncle Jessie's daughter. I left him as caretaker only a couple of months after your people retrieved you. Her reluctance stemmed from your blue uniform, I imagine."

"I wondered how you were, but your Lettie was stingy with information. She did tell me you were well, to ease my mind, I guess. Said you'd gone to your husband's people in Madison County. You being a married woman, I figured it best to pursue no more. Seeing you at The Pink Lady, in widow's weeds, was a shock."

She looked up. He had moved closer and now stood looking down on her over the corner of the desk. What was she to make of this handsome man who had blundered into her life...twice?

"No doubt desperate times led you to believe I was seeking employment."

He smiled at that. "I couldn't think at all, actually. I simply wanted to talk to you, find out how you were."

She dropped her gaze from his and reached for the bottom drawer. It opened, but was empty. She returned to the stubborn middle drawer. The one above it was missing. Eli had been putting this desk back together since he returned home. "I'm fine," she answered, looking across the kneehole to the adjacent pedestal. Only gaping holes where drawers once glided easily. She yanked on the stuck drawer.

"Could I help?" he asked and stepped around to where she was. She stepped back when he bent to grasp the handle, and he yanked the drawer open. Adam Smith's *Wealth of Nations* bumped against the front of the drawer. He picked it up, read the title, then looked at her with a frown. "Is this what you're looking for?"

"Yes," she said, reaching for it.

He placed it in her hands. "Heavy reading."

"For heavy times," she said and attempted to close the drawer with a crepe-covered knee. Parker slammed it shut with his foot.

"This desk is the worse for wear," he said.

"This desk is the worse for abuse." She regretted her snip. "The book is for Alice, she wishes to read it to Eli."

"Ah."

"I do believe she's had more of Machiavelli than most can endure."

Parker was standing in front of her, too close, and effectively blocking her route to the door. She considered turning to go around the desk, but retreat would be obvious then, and any attempt on his part to block her exit would be awkward.

"From what I gathered," he said, "you went to the Mackey plantation."

"Hickory Grove. My father-in-law had suffered a stroke. My sister-in-law was there alone with her little girl. We'd just learned of our husbands' deaths." She did turn then to circle around the desk no matter the consequences. "They were together, the same unit. They and their manservants all perished together. Artillery shell, we were informed. There was a number of dead, all from their unit. Neighbors. It was a terrible time for the community."

She was on the other side of the desk heading to the door and rambling on about something she was certain held no interest to him. He made no move to stop her.

Seth watched her retreat. She wanted to get out of this room and away from him.

"I just wanted to thank you. Offer my services if you're in need, Becky."

She stopped short at his use of her given name and turned. He met her stare. "My life is yours," he said. "I remember you asking me my name, then calling me by it. Given the circumstances, then as well as now, reciprocity did not seem inappropriate."

"I don't want your life, sir, or your familiarity. I need nothing from you at all, and please be advised your thanks is not necessary, either. I can assure you that had I the opportunity, I would have surrendered you to Confederate forces and you would have either been traded or sat the war out in a prison camp."

Seth's stomach clenched. She hadn't simply rejected his offer of friendship, she'd cast it back in his face. More hurt than angry, he stepped from behind the desk and closer to where she stood at the threshold. "'He will not survive, Robert, if you move him from this bed. Leave him here until he's regained some strength. You cannot care for a wounded prisoner.'

"'We would not care for a wounded prisoner' responded Robert, who I assume was Captain Robert Davis, commander of the roving battery I'd been sent to reconnoiter, 'But, Becky dearest,' the man had continued, 'what will you do with him if he does survive?'"

Her nostrils flared as he recited that brief encounter from almost three years earlier.

"'I doubt he'll survive, given his wounds. I just pray that if such a thing happens to James some other woman somewhere will try to make his last hours comfortable, as I am doing for this man.'"

Tears filled her eyes. "Obviously I overestimated the grievous nature of your injuries, Major Parker."

"What you did is underestimate how much your words meant to a wounded man. I would have died in your home but for the timely appearance of that Federal patrol that so fortuitously landed me in the hands of a capable surgeon. He told me that you'd controlled the bleeding, not to mention that I know you stood between me and Robert's designs."

"Who was more than kind himself for allowing me to keep you. He could have taken you by force. I couldn't have stopped him."

"He would have taken me then and there, but for your entreaty."

Her eyes still glistened, and now a sneer marred her pretty face. "Yes, well, the war was still young then, and as you know, Major, 'humane' is not how one wins a war. I would not be so now."

His heart beating faster, he said, "Well, it's too late, now, Mrs. Mackey, you've lost."

She glanced over him, head to foot, then reached for the knob.

He stepped after her. "I'm sorry for your loss, Rebecca, but I didn't lob the artillery shell that killed your husband. Letting me die would have made no difference."

He heard the strangled sob she managed to keep lodged in her throat, but he saw the tear before she turned, saw her hand swipe it away. She turned back to him. "I apologize for my behavior just now, and I thank you for your condolence."

She opened the door and walked toward the sickroom. He watched her, numbed as much by her unexpected animosity as he was by her heartfelt regret for speaking as she had. He'd been right though, and he was all the more pleased with himself for recognizing her attack for what it was, self-recrimination for offering kindness and hope to an enemy where fate had offered nothing in return.

For their surviving when James Mackey had perished.

Chapter Twelve

"Martin hired a flatboat in Jackson. He's going to meet us at Georgetown over in Copiah County day after tomorrow."

The man talking to Betty Franklin looked up when Becky stepped from the breezeway into the kitchen. Now he rose. The kitchen was the warmest room at Camellia Creek, and despite its boarded windows, battered table, and eclectic collection of chairs and stools, the most comfortable and lived-in, detached from the house though it was.

"Peter, dear," Betty said, "this is Eli's half sister, Rebecca Mackey."

Becky hurried forward and extended a hand. "Mr. Franklin."

"The pleasure is mine, Mrs. Mackey."

Becky hesitated. "Alice and Mama wanted coffee, but I can—"

"You're fine dear," Betty said dismissively. "Peter's just telling me his travel plans. He's leaving in the morning."

"I am sorry for your loss, sir, and please retake your seat. I'll get the coffee."

"You've decided to go up the east coast, then?" Mrs. Franklin continued to her spouse.

"We'll take a packet to Mobile. The Pearl is less a guess than the railroads, apparently. From Mobile we'll catch a steamboat to New York, but we'll probably come back by the Mississippi."

"Eustacia?"

"As of right now, she's planning on returning with me."

"She'd be better off to stay in New York," Betty Franklin said. "She does, at least, have friends there."

"She doesn't have friends there."

"Her sister's in Massachusetts."

The mister raised his hands, palms up. "Betty, please...."

Mrs. Franklin made a sibilant sound, then leaned forward to hug him. "What of Martin?"

Becky walked to the rear stoop and pulled the bottle of cream from the top step. She transferred a bit to a pitcher and returned the cream to the outdoor cold.

"I'll try and persuade him to come back with me for a visit, but he might want to return to Vicksburg, then come down for a longer stay."

"Either way he decides will be wonderful. His presence will offset that of Eustacia."

"If she does come back, I believe her being with us will be temporary."

"Of course, darling." Betty Franklin's voice was calm, even pleasant, but completely lacking in conviction, and the haggard Mr. Franklin blew out an exasperated breath.

"I don't know what else to do."

"You've enough on your mind. We'll deal with this later. Is she packed?"

"Cassie helped her."

"Cassie did it, you mean."

"Cassie informed me, Elizabeth, that you told her to pack everything the woman owned, so quit..."

The man glanced at Becky when his wife held up a hand to quiet him. "My love to Martin," she said, leaning forward to kiss his cheek. "Do persuade him to visit. What time do you leave?"

Peter Franklin rose when his wife did. "Early. I'm told with all this rain the Port Gibson-Gallatin road is boggy in places, and I have no idea what the road is like east of Gallatin. That's why I'm giving myself two days. Is Major Parker still here?"

Betty looked around at Becky.

"He left around two," Becky said. "I assume he returned to Port Gibson. Some of his men are here. Would you like me to try and find them?"

"No, no," he said, bending over to kiss his wife. "I'll check his office either this afternoon or in the morning before we leave. I thought perhaps he's learned something more about that name he found in Jon's pocket. I believe he was going to talk to that Hays woman."

Betty Franklin's eyes widened. "Isabel Hays is Rebecca's mother, dear."

"Oh," he said and twisted to see Becky. "I didn't realize.'

The man's red face would have been from what he meant to say next, not what he'd said. That or what the man had been thinking. "I know he talked to my mother this morning, Mr. Franklin. I've not been made privy to their conversation."

"The major will tell me anything pertinent, I'm sure."

Becky raised the tray. "I'll go so you can give your wife a proper farewell. I hope your trip is a safe one."

Chapter Thirteen

The black sergeant was in the room with Alice, when Becky entered during midmorning of the second full day. Alice had relinquished her rocker next to the bed and taken a seat in the straight-back chair she'd occupied yesterday. Isabel had found the rocker in the parlor where Alice had apparently moved it after marrying Eli. Several generations of infant ancestors had been soothed to sleep in that chair. Holland Calhoon had been using it by Hannah's bedside the night he died, thus the century-old relic, hewn from hickory growing along North Carolina's French Broad, had survived the terror the night the marauders came. Marauders too scared to cross Hannah's threshold once they learned she had yellow fever.

The sergeant was talking to Alice, who murmured something in response. The young woman looked to be bordering on madness, her eyes were so bright, but her movements and coherence appeared balanced, and when the Negro turned back to Eli, Alice looked anxiously at him, too, deathly still on the bed.

"Gotta say, Colonel, I'da nevah thought da likes a you would get yo'se'f shot dis a way. Sho', I know'd you was tryin' to save yo woman an' all, an' dat clouded yo' thinkin' steppin' in front a dat gun, but dat ain't no excuse now fo' yo' sleepin' da days away." He chuckled and patted the bed where Eli's arm was hidden beneath the covers. "Yo got yo'se'f some wo'k to live dis down. Shot by some ole crazy woman, I swear to goodness! Den you was saved by a damn Yankee. You come on now and get yo' Rebel ass back heah an' take care a dis little lady gonna have yo' baby. She be tar'd now, lookin' a mite peaked."

The man was quiet a moment, his head bowed in a silent

prayer. He rose then, forage cap in hand. "Here, Miz Alice," he said and held out a hand to pull her from her seat. "You sits yo'se'f back 'ere by 'im. He do know you heah. Hurd what I tol' 'im, too. Him'll be back soon nuff, you'll see. Gatherin' him's strength's all."

Alice held to the man's hand as she took her seat. "Thank you for coming to see him."

"You welcome, Miz Alice, you sho' welcome."

He turned then and saw Becky by the door. She'd seen him before, but now, realizing he was the one, Becky took her first good look at him. He nodded and would have bypassed her and quietly left the room, but she reached out and touched his arm. "You're Sergeant Zachary?"

"Yes'm."

"I want to thank you for what you did."

"Yo' welcome, but ain't no need. It were da Christian thing to do. 'Sides, I kinda like 'im."

Becky studied his face. "I would guess he likes you, too." She felt tears welling in her eyes, but she blinked them back. "I hope he heard your reprimand."

Zachary chuckled softly. "Oh, he heah me all right. Ain't near 'bout far away as we be thinkin'. Thought I saw an eyelid flit justa hair. I bes' go check on Daws. Probably tryin' to talk ole auntie outa mo' a my chicken."

The door closed silently at her back, and she took the chair Alice had vacated. Alice reached for the foot of the bed and Smith's heavy tome that she'd laid aside during Zachary's visit. She looked to be a good hundred pages into it. "Mama said she thinks your nausea's passed this morning. Your aunt is making you a plate."

"Rice and peas, I told her. I do feel better."

"You look exhausted, Alice."

"Aunt Betty told me that if Eli opens his eyes, I'll frighten him back to wherever he's been."

Becky laughed. "You're not that bad, but do try to eat. For the baby if nothing else."

Alice nodded, then said, "I heard your little girls this morning. Your mother told me Eliza is your niece by marriage."

"Yes, she and our little orphan Pearl and Mattie got here last evening."

"Does Eli know them?"

"He does. Eliza remembers him well. Pearl is only two. He's seen them both since he returned. Have they disturbed you?"

"Not at all. The weather is cold?"

"Not as bad as yesterday, but still pretty nippy." She wanted to add that fresh air would do Alice good, but knew better than to try.

Alice rose suddenly and stooped over Eli, an action that caused Becky's heart to lurch. Alice placed her hand on his chest, then, book in hand, retook her seat. Becky released a breath she hadn't realized she'd been holding. "His breathing is so shallow," Alice said, "he frightens me."

Becky glanced at her brother. He frightened her, too, but not as much as Alice did sometimes.

Chapter Fourteen

Seth left Jubal Summers in charge of the office in Port Gibson along with two of his men. Zachary and Daws were safely ensconced at Camellia Creek, and he'd offered up Privates Spain and Ball to help Peter Franklin move his nephew's remains east to the ferry landing on the Pearl River at Georgetown. Corporal Peters and Private Hand he took with him. Peters was literate and Hand was a damn fine shot in case they needed backing up along sometimes dangerous roads. He talked to Don Hemple, Claiborne County's provost, and let him know he'd be gone for several days. There'd been no problems with his troops from any quarter, but he did worry when he was out of contact. He could trust Don to intervene with the locals should any incidents arise between his black troops and the white populace.

They took the Port Gibson-Vicksburg road Friday morning to track down Samuel Caruthers, whose home was in Warren County, about ten miles south and a bit east of Vicksburg. A wealthy cotton farmer, Caruthers also raised corn and cane, and still dabbled in timber, a legacy of his grandfather who'd long ago found dual solvency in the practice of law and harvesting the forests along the county's verdant creeks and river banks. A Whig, Sam Caruthers had never held political office, but twice he'd made a credible performance against Democratic opponents, and he had put money toward successful state candidates during the past thirty years. Over the decades he'd had many friends sit the federal and local courts. He'd successfully argued against secession in 1850, then succumbed to the fever that inundated the South in 1860 and 1861. He was influential in choosing the Warren County candidate at the State Secession Convention that voted for Mississippi's leaving the Union. In the summer of 1863, and many of his neighbors say it was well before Grant crossed the Mississippi at Bruinsburg, he'd pragmatically conceded to the might of military arms and cooperated with (his now less-than-friendly neighbors say "worked for") the occupying forces for the "good of the people of the state."

No matter how one embellished the reasons for Samuel Caruthers' double treachery, there was no getting around the fact that Seth felt a personal dislike for the man before even meeting him. He didn't attribute that to the man's apparent feet of clay—Seth figured the man's feet were made of anything but. Sam Caruthers suffered from overweening ambition. When sectional strife threatened that ambition he'd switched sides. When military might swamped that choice, he'd switched sides again, not taking him back to where he'd been in the beginning—those old enemies were now all but obliterated. New players were in town, ready to begin a new game, and he'd kept himself in a position to ante up.

But where Seth could admire a principled man who might take advantage of situations to achieve a desired end, his take on Caruthers was that the man had no principles. His gut told him that upon reaching the apex of his coveted designs, Caruthers would not even espouse the delusion that his power furthered some public good. The only good Sam Caruthers cared about perpetuating was that which furthered him and his.

Seth found Caruthers' house easily enough, the result of having reviewed a map in Don Hemple's office that showed every road and hamlet known in the southwest portion of Mississippi, but once there, Sam Caruthers' wife, a pretty and charming woman, told him that Caruthers and their younger son were in Washington County and wouldn't be home for a fortnight. Monday week she advised, when pressed, but he should wait for even later in the week to return, just to make sure.

Seth could put the delay to good use. Earlier he'd debated with himself on the value of going to Jackson and searching the legislative journals on that thirties-era railroad before meeting

Caruthers. Further, he wanted to pass on what he'd learned from Poynter Cummings about Alan Guthrie to the Madison and Hinds county provosts and the respective county sheriffs.

Major Thatcher, the Madison County provost, wasn't at work that late Saturday morning. Thatcher's clerk gave him directions to the man's house, and Seth and his troops got there at the same time the family was sitting down to dinner. They put Seth in the main dining room and shuttled his troops off to the detached kitchen. Seth hadn't planned on joining the family for its noon meal, but imposition had stopped concerning him years ago. They were a happy bunch of Yankees, Thatcher in his prime with a no-nonsense and handsome wife, and three children, all old enough to join the adults at the table. Besides, there was something a woman enjoyed in providing a home-cooked meal to a displaced male. Why deny Eleanor Thatcher one of life's simple pleasures?

In his reports on Guthrie's murder, Thatcher had commented on Guthrie's evasiveness as to what exactly he was doing in the area. Though Madison County had not had jurisdiction over the murder—Guthrie having been killed in Hinds County— Thatcher's input was more valuable in that he'd actually talked to the man who'd been working in Madison County the day of his death. His murder on the Natchez Trace in Hinds County had been inadvertent as far as anyone could tell—assuming his murder was even related to why he was in the area. On the day they'd actually spoken, Guthrie had told Thatcher he was working cotton thefts and was in the area searching for an abandoned church, which he'd found. He'd required nothing but directions to the Trace, which Thatcher had provided. Guthrie's stated purpose would have been readily accepted, but for Guthrie's lack of interest in a stolen bale of cotton the provost was working and his refusal to tell Thatcher the significance of the church.

"I have a source now telling me Guthrie's alleged interest in cotton thieving was only a cover story," Seth had clarified to Thatcher in his parlor after the meal.

"A cover for what?"

And therein lay the crux of the matter. Seth knew Guthrie

had been searching for the Calhoons, but he had no idea why, and that's what he told Bill Thatcher. He also reiterated, in confidence, what Cummings told him regarding Guthrie's possible effort to recruit operatives to infiltrate traitorous groups.

Later that day, Seth repeated the same story to the Madison County sheriff and the provost and sheriff in Hinds County. He omitted the part about "infiltrating traitorous groups" when briefing the two sheriffs, but he did follow up with the Madison County sheriff on the unidentified church Guthrie claimed to have found. The sheriff had no new information as to which one it was.

Chapter Fifteen

Alice Calhoon woke with a start. Her head throbbed, so did her heart. The tome she'd been reading aloud had slid from her lap and thudded against the floor. The room was bright, and sunlight shined on her husband's peaceful face. She closed her eyes, angry and frustrated with herself. She'd fallen asleep during the night. How long...? No, she'd extinguished the coal oil lamp herself, and not so long ago. She needed to stand, walk around, wash Eli's face. Her own, too. She should bathe. How many days had it been now? The chamber pot reeked of last night's stale urine, and she wondered how badly *she* smelled. She sat forward and leaned down, reaching for the heavy book. The rocker creaked loudly when she did, then popped when her pose became more awkward.

"Did you tell me we were gonna have a baby?"

Eli's voice was weak, but his question was clear and directed at her. She caught the rocker's arm to keep from toppling from the chair and, with her eyes closed tight, whispered a prayer of thanks to a God, whom she believed, not so very long ago, had forsaken her. She raised her head to find Eli's eyes open, watching her, and she started to cry. "Ten," she said, moving to sit beside him on the bed. She stayed his attempt to roll over, pushed his jet hair back from his face, and kissed him. "We're going to have ten babies."

His attempt to smile contorted into a grimace, and he asked, "Alice, what is wrong with me?"

Juggling a porcelain pitcher and clean towels, Becky pushed open the door to the sickroom, then turned to stone when she saw

Alice draped over Eli, the woman's soft weeping interspersed with whispered words and desperate shakes of her head. Guilt-charged grief slammed into Becky, lightheaded now and befuddled. She'd checked them only minutes ago, as she had off and on during the night. Alice had been dozing, then, and Becky hadn't the heart to wake her.

Now she had to get the grieving Alice up, make some attempt to comfort her, though she wasn't sure she had the strength herself. It was not yet half past seven and dawn still broke late so early in January, but she heard movement upstairs and thought Betty Franklin would surely be up and about. She should get her. Betty was the best person to help Alice now.

Quietly, Becky set the pitcher and towels on the chest near the door, then startled at the sound of her brother's voice. Tears stung her eyes, and she covered her mouth to stifle a cry of relief. She stood there a moment, composing herself from the dual shocks, then stepped around the foot of the bed until she could see Eli. He saw her before she could acknowledge her presence. Alice followed his eyes and turned a smiling, tear-streaked face to Becky.

"Oh, Becky, he's come back to me."

Chapter Sixteen

Becky stepped into the foyer from the dining room and collided with Dr. Lester. "Where's Aunt Elvie?" he asked, grasping her elbow, steadying himself as much as her. He turned her
back the way she'd come.

"In the kitchen. What's wrong?"

He shook his head—"Nothing"—then guided her through the
back door, across the porch and breezeway and back into the
kitchen. "Ah, Isabel, I was looking for you, too. That chicken
broth you're working on, Auntie?"

The Negress nodded her cloth-covered head. "Can 'im eats?"

"Yes, but only liquids," he said and took a seat. "Nothing
solid, the broth is exactly what we need. We're a long way from
out of the woods with him. I've expected fever for the past three
days, given the operation, and he's very weak. Pneumonia could
be a threat, and infection aside, probably the biggest one. He'll
have trouble fighting off either one, so the more weapons we can
get in him, the better." He eyed Elvie. "I've given Alice laudanum
and instructions for the pain, but I don't have anything better
than your witch's brew for fever and infection. Do you need anything from me?"

Elvie shook her head. "I'll make da tea soon as I done heah."

"And that little gal he's married to is gonna fall flat on her face
if she doesn't get some rest. She's already suffered a bout of pneumonia, from which I reckon she'd just fully recovered when this
happened. The pregnancy saps her strength even more."

"I'll set up a cot for her in his room," Becky said and pushed
a cup of coffee in front of the doctor. Elvie gave him a plate of bis-
cuit and rabbit fricassee. "She refuses to leave him."

Dr. Lester started to say something, but Isabel said, "She's not going to rest, Ephraim, unless she's with him."

A welcome interruption to their quietude, Becky thought, as she watched Tobias Holbein make his way from the dining room into the foyer. Isabel, who sat reading to Becky's two wards from one of Hannah's old nursery books, had yet to see him. Mattie sat at the window removing the hems from Eliza's summer dresses. They'd gotten Alice bathed and even got her to lie down after she'd eaten a plate of Buck's rabbits Aunt Elvie had cooked up this morning. Eli slept, by all indications comfortably. They'd gotten broth and laudanum in him.

Becky rose when Mr. Holbein entered, and she extended her hand.

"How is he?" he asked.

"He woke up this morning." She couldn't suppress a smile. "We've fed him. He's better."

"I expected you yesterday," Isabel said joining them. On the settee, Eliza had the book and was now reading to Pearl.

"I was in Grand Gulf when your message arrived in Rodney. I didn't get it till I got back, which was this morning. I flagged down the next paddle wheeler headed north."

"Business in Grand Gulf?"

"I had a meeting, yes."

Becky sensed the undercurrent in her mother's voice with the word "business." She sensed it again in Holbein's reply.

"Do you have any idea what that mad woman was thinking?" Holbein asked Isabel.

"I think I do. Let's you and I talk in Holland's office."

Becky's jaw clenched at being purposefully left out of the conversation. Mr. Holbein glanced at her and, in what appeared an afterthought, looked around the parlor with its scarred walls and boarded windows. "I haven't been in this house since we buried Holland and Hannah."

"We've cleaned it up a bit since then," Isabel said, heading out of the room.

Holbein shook his head. "It was such a beautiful home. They sure made a mess of things."

Becky walked over and sat beside the two girls. Down the hall she heard the door to her father's office click shut, but nary a squeak accompanied its closing. Eliza handed her the book. Becky handed it back. "You two stay right here."

She looked at Mattie, who acknowledged that she'd heard.

𝒩ot a whisper from the turning knob, or the slight opening of the door.

"When does he expect him?" Isabel asked.

Becky's intent had been to enter and demand inclusion. Given the unanticipated boon of forthright discussion due to their not knowing she was in the hall, listening, she opted to remain where she was for as long as she could.

"I suspect there'll be more than one, and their arrival will depend on travel," Holbein answered, "but Sam's expecting him within the week. He says it was the unexplained shortage of gold in New Orleans that forced the issue."

"I would have thought the missing authorization letter would have been the catalyst, especially when Guthrie showed up."

"Remember that you and I are not sure who is hiding what from whom back there. Whoever's involved has to be careful."

"Do you think they'll force Parker out?" Isabel asked.

"I have no idea what his role will be. There's push and pull at different levels between War and Treasury."

"One will prove as ruthless as the other."

"Which could serve us well if we can keep them at odds."

"You'll tell Sam it was Naomi, not me. That will buy a little time."

"He'd already figured out the part about Naomi and Franklin, my sweet. Convincing Sam she got her hands on my authorization letter is a different matter. Could Guthrie have spelled it out for her?"

Becky heard the groaning of the chair followed by the swish of her mother's skirts. "No one had to spell it out for her, Toby.

She lived in this house. She made a point of knowing everything that went on, most of which was none of her concern."

"I meant that to mislead Sam."

"Oh, yes, that might work. I cannot believe she passed that to Jon. Sam must have been apoplectic."

"You've got to give Naomi credit. She had both of them under her thumb, and if you're right, she intended Franklin to take that knowledge to the grave."

"I can't help but wonder what Sam would have eventually done about her. She'd become reckless."

"You've no business accusing anyone of being reckless, Isabel. What did you learn in New Orleans?"

Isabel's laughter filled the air. "Willie says that all continues to go well and we have nothing to worry about."

"You and I have plenty to worry about. At least, I do, thanks to you."

"You should have confided in me sooner."

"I never intended to confide in you at all. My plan was to let it expire."

For a moment silence prevailed, and Becky tensed with the thought she'd been found out. Then her mother said, "Holland's the reason, darling, that even if you had told me everything, I'd have still gone behind your back and did what I did."

"Did you really believe I had betrayed Holland?"

In the hall, Becky closed her eyes tight.

"The day I violated your trust and looked at what you'd stowed in my safe I certainly did."

"Shame on you."

"I feel no shame. You should have never been working with him behind Holland's back."

"Until now, I haven't been involved since I wrote that request for review."

"Which set everything in motion."

"I didn't want to believe that," Mr. Holbein said, "but now I fear you're right."

"Have you confronted Sam?"

"I'm waiting for the right time." Again a pause. "Do you know if Becky has said anything to Eli regarding her suspicions?"

"I've warned her not to. She certainly won't right now, not with him so weak."

"Did you broach the reason for her bolting after Christmas when you told her Parker wanted to talk to her?"

"Toby, I haven't had a chance! I was on my way to Hickory Grove, when all this happened."

Becky, heart pounding in her chest and her body stiff from the effort of keeping still, listened to slippered feet in tandem with the sway of skirt against petticoats inside the room upon which she was eavesdropping. Her mother had started pacing.

"I think you might be worried over nothing. If Guthrie had spoken to her, don't you think she would have said something to you after he turned up murdered?"

"Not if she were involved in his death."

Becky furrowed her brow. Good God!

"You actually believe Becky followed and shot that man on the Trace?"

"Of course not, but she could know about someone else having done it, which would be just as bad."

"You mean Eli?"

"If Guthrie needed shooting, Eli would have been the more likely of the two of them to have done it."

"Eli's not a cold-blooded killer."

"It's been a long, hard war, Toby, and who said it was in cold blood?"

"He wasn't even here."

"We don't know *where* he was."

Behind her, Becky heard the dining room's back door open. Whoever was coming, couldn't miss her listening at the door. Not wanting to arouse suspicions, particularly those of Seth Parker, she slipped quickly into the room.

Tobias Holbein sat on the settee facing the desk. Her mother stood at the windows looking down at the lake. Both had their backs to her.

Isabel turned and saw her at the same moment Becky closed the door with a resounding click. Mr. Holbein turned in his chair, and dismay washed over his face.

"I want to know what's going on," Becky said.

Both their surprised faces had suddenly gone blank. They would think, she realized with some satisfaction, that she'd just opened the door. They had no idea how much she'd overheard.

Tobias Holbein turned from her to Isabel. "It's past time to tell her something."

Her mother raised her chin. "Come in," she said.

Relieved, Becky took a seat on the settee by Mr. Holbein.

"We're discussing Naomi's motivation, darling. It's no secret she considered herself mistress of Camellia Creek, and if Eli was not going to let her be so, and his marriage to Alice substantiated that, she decided to get rid of both of them."

"I understand what was driving Aunt Naomi, Mama. What I'm curious about is what she offered Jon Franklin to go along with her."

"She told him about Sam's railroad."

"And his attack on Alice?"

"The attack was the result of his frustrated seduction, which Naomi had convinced him Alice would agree to. He'd been counting on her money for his railroad investment."

Becky swallowed her frustration. She didn't want to give herself away, at least not yet. "That doesn't work for me, Mama, anymore than it works for anybody else. He couldn't possibly have believed Alice would leave with him."

"I'm not so sure, not if you take into account what Naomi probably told him about Eli and Alice's relationship."

"And his believing Northerners could get away with murder down here isn't farfetched," Mr. Holbein added.

Becky's gaze moved from one to the other. Her mother and lawyer were trying to convince her of something they didn't believe themselves. "I know there's more you're not telling me."

"Darling," Isabel said, sitting beside her on the settee, "Toby and I don't know the answer."

"You say Aunt Naomi passed the information on Caruthers' railroad to Franklin. Did she also tell him that Sam Caruthers orchestrated the raid that took my father's life? Is that what Franklin was threatening Caruthers with?"

Isabel narrowed her eyes on Becky, as Holbein gave Isabel a wary glance. "You don't know that for sure." he said.

"I do know it, and you know it, too. Both of you do. What I can't do is prove it. Can you?"

Isabel shot back to her feet. Mr. Holbein, with apparent concern, followed her pacing before returning his attention to Becky. "Even if someone finds proof, honey, it wouldn't be a threat to Sam. He'd have laughed in Franklin's face."

"Even if it could be proved Sam was behind it," Isabel said, "the powers that be wouldn't care."

"Obviously he's done something that someone cares about or he wouldn't have been kowtowing to Aunt Naomi. What was that?"

Again, Isabel narrowed her eyes on Becky, but Holbein deflected Becky's question with, "You need to be careful what you say to Eli."

"I don't intend to involve him. When he got back, all he cared about was continuing the fight, but now he has Alice and a baby on the way. He has reasons to live."

"Implying you don't!" her mother cried. "What have you been up to, Rebecca?"

"Finding out what I can about Sam Caruthers' doings."

"How?" Isabel snapped, and Becky stiffened.

"By listening at doors you've shut in my face. You have details I want."

"How long were you out there?"

Calm, Tobias Holbein reached over and took Becky's hand. "I know you've visited the county clerk's office in Vicksburg. Since everyone, including Sam Caruthers, knows you want Muscatine back, that hasn't alarmed anyone yet. Muscatine we can handle through legal channels."

"And justice for my father?"

"There are better ways for getting even," her mother said.

"You are not helping matters, Isabel," Holbein said, his voice still calm.

Isabel huffed at that, then retook her place on Becky's other side. "Listen to me. You are to do nothing more. *Nothing.* You know nothing, and you are doing nothing, and that's the best possible approach for you right now. Sam Caruthers is dangerous, and he's made associations with ruthless individuals. These are men who are stealing from their own government, and they are killing one another for the spoils." Gently, Isabel touched her arm. "As long as you remain ignorant, they have no reason to hurt you."

"Ignorance does not keep one safe from these people, Mama."

"It could protect others," Mr. Holbein said gently.

"And I do not want Sam to know you suspect him of playing a part in the raid on Camellia Creek," Isabel said.

Becky turned on Holbein. "You're working with Caruthers. He trusts you."

"Toby is with us," Isabel said sharply. "And yes, Sam does trust him, and we want to keep it that way."

"And what about that Guthrie fellow, the dead Treasury agent? What is it that Mr. Holbein thought Guthrie spelled out for Aunt Naomi and that you, Mother, think she already knew?"

"You followed us to the door." Again, Isabel stood. "You've been out there all along."

Becky ignored that and asked, "Who's coming that will make things more dangerous?"

Holbein looked furtively at Isabel, who said, "A Treasury agent is coming."

"Because of Guthrie?" Becky asked.

"Yes. Has Eli ever mentioned Alan Guthrie to you?"

Becky was feeling, not so much calmer, but more resolved. They were patronizing her, using her perceived duty to Eli to keep her in check. But she wasn't a child. She was a full-grown woman, who'd lost a loving husband and their baby. She wasn't stupid, either. Yes, she would like to reap vengeance, but not at the price of injustice for those she loved. She understood where her priorities lay and wouldn't be browbeaten into subjection, and she wouldn't be made to feel guilty for the actions she took. She was no longer sure her objectives meshed with those of her mother and Tobias Holbein. And she couldn't know, because they shut her out.

"He has not," she answered.

When Becky didn't elaborate further, her mother squared her shoulders. "Is Parker's investigation of the Guthrie murder the reason you left Rodney so suddenly after Christmas?"

The murder of a Treasury agent had been the last thing on her mind, at least until her mother told her Eli was a suspect. The arrival of Seth Parker, in fact, had obliterated every thought in her head, even the thrill of meeting Eli's bride. "And why would that have been?"

"Had Guthrie contacted you, Rebecca?" her mother snapped.

"You know why he was here, don't you?"

"Quit answering my questions with questions. Had he contacted you?"

Becky rose from her seat. "Tell me what he had to do with Eli and Aunt Naomi and Sam Caruthers, and even Jon Franklin."

"Rebecca," her mother said. "Answer me, please."

"Did this Guthrie happen to have red hair?"

Isabel closed her eyes. "Damn."

Chapter Seventeen

Seth, with Peters sitting beside him, spent a good part of the next week in Jackson researching that thirties-era railroad charter. Private Hand he loaned to the county provost, who kept him busy performing odd jobs and making local courier runs. The provost could always use an extra man.

Seth had expected some difficulty finding the old legislative journals. They were all intact, that much he knew, but he figured it wasn't going to be easy putting his hands on the archives he needed. Prior to Grant's arrival in Jackson in 1863, the capital had moved east to the relative safety of Macon, then Columbus in Noxubee and Lowndes Counties respectively. The archives had gone with the capital, but though everything had returned to Jackson, much was still in disarray. A civil employee told Seth the 1836 journal was still crated, but a taciturn clerk spent more time finding Seth a place to work than pinpointing the location of the journal. Seth was about to ask him how he'd found the thing so fast, when another man, this one more wizened, plopped the 1837 journal in front of him, grunted, and asked him his interest, because, he said, "A while back there was another officer from your headquarters over in Vicksburg interested in those same books." With that, the man stuck out his hand. "I'm Tim Abrams, Superior Clerk for the State Archives."

"He was researching the charter of a railroad back in 1836?" Seth asked and rose from his straight-back chair to take Abrams' outstretched hand. "Seth Parker."

"Yes, sir," the older man said. At the same time he waved his younger assistant away, then made a point of studying Seth's uniform. "Marine?"

"I am. Assigned to the Army, however. When was the person you're referring to here?"

"Last summer. At the time, it took me a while to find the journals. We hadn't been back in Jackson long. I took the opportunity, since I'd gone to the trouble to unpack them, to file them properly. Ralph would still be looking if I hadn't heard him complaining that they were missing from the crates. I am curious about the interest in an old railroad charter that never came to fruition."

"I don't know what the other man's interest was," Seth said — though he wanted to know — "but I'm investigating a murder."

Abrams flexed his jaw. He was a frail looking fella of average height. Seth figured him to be pushing seventy if he were a day, but who knows how the war had treated him.

"Murder old or new?"

"The murder was about a week ago now. We're not sure of the motivation, but surmising it had something to do with greed."

"Well, that narrows it down. A United States marine is investigating a murder that somehow ties to an obsolete railroad charter? Sounds far-fetched to my old ears, but there's not much I can do to dissuade you. You people have proven the lengths you'll go to mess in other folks' affairs. I can tell you the fella was a major in the Union Army. He wasn't very forthcoming regarding his interest. He did tell me he was stationed in Vicksburg and implied his work was official."

"Do you recall his name?"

"I do not, but I have it in last year's receipts. He asked me to get him a copy of the map marking the right-of-way for the railroad in Warren, Claiborne, Jefferson, and Adams counties." Mr. Abrams pulled a folder from the back of one journal and opened it. "You see here?" He handed Seth the annotated map. "This is the one he wanted. I had the copy made at the *Clarion*. He picked it up the following week, and he paid me for costs. I gave him a receipt. That's where the name's recorded."

"Could you get me that name? And" — he handed Abrams the original map — "I'd like a copy, too."

The man took the map, but the old codger was scrutinizing Seth so thoroughly he thought he might have to pull out the authorizing order Malcolm had given him back in November. Abrams turned abruptly. "Take your time with those journals, Major. They make for dull reading. I'll find you the name. I don't know what you're looking for that might solve your murder, but I can tell you that this fella was more interested in the physical layout of the railroad than its corporate structure or financing."

That was information worth knowing and supported Seth's belief as to why Caruthers wanted Muscatine. Subsequent identification of last summer's researcher, however, didn't prove particularly enlightening, but only because Seth had never heard of "M. Trueblood". He didn't believe he'd have ever figured out the name, either, if Abrams hadn't deciphered enough of the scribbling to recall "Trueblood." Trueblood might not have anything to do with the events Seth was investigating, but he couldn't quite bring himself to believe that additional interest in Caruthers' old railroad venture was mere coincidence.

*H*e and Corporal Peters spent long hours over a number of days reviewing the legislative journals for 1836 and 1837 and taking notes on pieces of mismatched notepaper, stationery, and foolscap that the provost's office scrounged up for them—a favor in return for Private Hand. Paper was not in great supply at the moment, a fact Seth hadn't considered when he started this endeavor. Fortunately, the notes weren't copious because that railroad had taken up only so much of the agenda those years.

The charter wasn't revoked until the fall of 1837, when economic conditions nationwide deemed cost of the north-south railroad fiscally imprudent—not just for the state, but, as it turned out, for investors who opted to hold on to their money. Improved times found lackluster interest among the Democratic-controlled legislature and Caruthers' initiative fizzled, another Whig venture the Democrats said Mississippians couldn't afford. Wading through the journals had proven time-consuming, but between committee discussions, fiscal assessments, and two topographical studies, Seth left Jackson feeling he'd exhausted what the state legislature had to offer on the subject.

And then there was the Meridian Southern.

Two months ago, Laura Calhoon Blackledge, one-time bride of Andrew Calhoon, Eli's older brother, had been murdered by Naomi Polk allegedly because she posed a threat to Eli. At the time of her death, Laura had been the widow of Albert Blackledge who had made his way from New York to St. Louis, and finally Natchez, while still a young man. There he'd practiced law and invested in shipping. With Andrew Jackson's election, and the subsequent opening of the Choctaw cessions, Blackledge had acquired large land holdings. Railroad speculation was the result of his success, not a means to it. He'd built The Meridian Southern, his primary asset, in the early fifties. Unlike the east-west Southern Railroad connecting Meridian to Jackson and finally to Vicksburg via the older Vicksburg-Clinton Railroad, Blackledge's Meridian Southern traveled southwest, linking Meridian directly with Mississippi's cultural and financial center at Natchez. Now, considering all he'd learned in the past week, Seth couldn't help but wonder if Naomi Polk hadn't had another reason for killing Blackledge's widow.

Chapter Eighteen

"Was hopin' dat yarrow would draw out da poison," Becky heard Frank Zachary tell Alice.

Dr. Lester was near Eli's bed, but not as close as Zachary, who had just removed the poultice he'd placed on the weeping wound in Eli's abdomen two hours earlier. "My ole missus used it reg'lar on 'er menfolk and 'er people. Swo' by it, she did." The sergeant looked at Dr. Lester. "Doc Yancy used it, too. He b'lieved in da ole folks' ways an' dem we learnt from da Injuns."

"Many a doctor swears by yarrow, Alice," Dr. Lester said. "I am praying..." With gentle fingers he pushed down on the reddened skin around Eli's wound. It oozed and the doctor made a sibilant sound. "It's not working, Frank, because the infection is deep inside. He's weak. I didn't want to open this thing and clean it out, but looks like I'm gonna have to."

Alice drew in a stuttered breath, and Becky sighed inwardly. The young woman was wrought with worry once again. During the wee hours of this morning, Becky'd been awake in the old rocking chair, unable to sleep. Her stimulant had been Sam Caruthers and whatever her mother and lawyer were keeping from her. Alice had been asleep, but Eli was visibly agitated and, Becky soon realized, too miserable with fever to sleep.

She hadn't wanted to wake Alice, who was really sleeping for the first time in ten days. But his fever had come on fast, and a quick check of his wound found it festering. Eli had cringed in disgust. Shortly after, he'd slipped into semi-consciousness, and Becky had left an anxious Alice in charge and gone upstairs for Elvie and Betty Franklin. In the kitchen, she found Zachary and Daws sleeping on the floor. She hadn't seen hide nor hair of

Parker or the rest of his troop in days. Zachary had jumped up immediately and, after a quick perusal of the patient, sent Laws to fetch the doctor in Port Gibson.

A worn and weary Dr. Ephraim Lester had arrived about sunup. He told Becky he'd removed the appendix of a forty-four-year-old Confederate during the night, but the man had died anyway. He'd been called too late to get the diseased organ out before it burst.

*B*ecky remained at the foot of the bed where she couldn't see much, given all the people hovering over Eli. She couldn't escape the vile stench of the infection, though, and God it was awful. Her discreet location for smelling and not seeing, and puking if she must, also left her in position to open and close the door for Elvie, who kept up the supply of hot water from the kitchen.

Betty Franklin had moved Alice aside early on. She was too tired, the older woman warned, and risked doing Eli more harm than good. So Alice sat on the other side of the bed, holding Eli's hand during the whole gruesome process, despite his passing out early on. It had been Sergeant Zachary, not Betty Franklin, who had done the most to assist the doctor.

"His breathing and heartbeat are strong," the doctor said, securing the dressing.

"Looks like you got all da pus, doc."

The doctor nodded. "It's in the good Lord's hands now."

At the foot of the bed, Becky said a silent prayer. The doctor turned and looked at Elvie, who started his way with a bowl of clean water. He washed and dried his hands, then rolled down his sleeves. "He's passed out, but he should wake soon. Aunt Elvie, have that chokeberry tea ready for him." He looked at Becky, and she moved closer. "Continue the laudanum. He's gonna need it. Elvie, you can give him some of that yarrow tea, too, if his stomach can handle more. I'm not sure it will stave off more infection, didn't help a whole lot last time, but it's better than not." He found Frank Zachary. "I can trust you to keep an eye on these dressings till I get back?"

"If'n da cap'n don' sen' me off somewheres."

"And remember to wash with soap and hot water before you touch him."

"I will, suh. Doc Yancy b'lieve dat, too, but I didn't have time dat fus' night."

"I'm not faultin' you, Frank. He'd have died that night had you not controlled the bleeding as quick as you did. I'm just remindin' you." The doctor looked at the women surrounding him. "The main thing is to get any sustenance in him you can coax him to take. Broth and lots of water. When it comes down to it, the human body can fight infection on its own, if it's strong enough. Let's give him all the help we can."

The doctor turned to the bed. "He's stable for the moment, Alice. If the infection hasn't spread to somewhere we don't know about, his temperature should drop. He's not where he was before. He's sleeping, do you understand?"

"I do understand, Doctor, thank you."

"He appears determined to survive this."

"We're going to have ten children," she said softly, more to Eli than the doctor.

Ephraim Lester found Betty Franklin. "Alice needs to get out of this room for a bit. She needs a good, filling meal, and she needs to rest."

"I'll see to it," Betty said.

Frank Zachary snuck from the room, and Dr. Lester reached for his coat draped over the extra chair. When Alice got up and sat in the rocker, Betty Franklin put her hands on her niece's shoulders as if to pull her up.

"I'll come," Alice said, "as soon as you have a plate for me."

Her aunt relented. "We'll eat in the dining room so you can hear him when he wakes."

Becky took the straight-back chair. "I'll be right here while you're gone."

Alice looked at her. "I'll wash and change, too, so I won't look so wicked when he wakes." She rocked back in the chair. "I'd like a clean dress."

Cassie Franklin had slipped into the room when her mother opened the door. She rushed to Alice, and with a flourish and a teasing smile, she squatted in front of her cousin's chair and wrinkled her nose. "The rest of us would like that, too. I'll get everything ready. You can bathe before dinner if you like."

Chapter Nineteen

"I met with the man once, Major," Sam Caruthers said when Seth broached the subject of Jon Franklin. "That was the week between Christmas and New Years. He was interested in investing in a project I've been looking at for some time."

"What project, sir?"

Samuel Caruthers smiled. Not a gracious smile, but one denoting irritation. He was a handsome man, silver-haired. Seth figured him to be in his sixties. In addition to his wife, who'd greeted Seth warmly again this morning, Sam Caruthers had two sons, the younger of whom, Wilson, joined them in the well-appointed parlor of Caruthers' rambling bayou plantation home. It didn't look as if anything in this room had been damaged by the recent conflict. In fact, it was a bit on the crowded side, and Seth wondered how much of his neighbors' personal property Sam Caruthers had confiscated in addition to their land.

"I trust to your discretion, Major. A railroad project."

"Your plans are confidential?"

"At the present, there is a great deal of land speculation occurring. My project has elicited some interest, which led to the unfortunate Mr. Franklin's inquiries."

"And did you welcome Mr. Franklin's interest in your proposed railroad?"

"Had he capital to invest I might have. As it turned out, he was wasting my time. Franklin approached a friend of mine, Tobias Holbein of Rodney, on the advice of another individual, whom Franklin declined to identify. Given Franklin's name, I felt compelled to meet with him."

Seth opened his mouth to ask, but Caruthers anticipated him.

"There are, or were, two Franklins. The elder has purchased some land required for my proposed right-of-way. I was already suspicious that word had leaked out regarding my speculative rail before Toby Holbein approached me with Jon Franklin's request that we meet."

"Can you guess who that mutual acquaintance was?" Because Seth sure could, but confirmation would be best from Caruthers' own lips.

"I know lots of people, a number of whom know I'm interested in building a railroad. I am perturbed, to say the least, but I am not yet in a position to accuse any of my associates of trying to get ahead of me on this matter."

"Do you plan for the railroad to follow the same route that was approved by the legislature back in 1836?"

In the chair next to Seth, Wilson Caruthers moved his foot. Seth looked at him, but saw only what amounted to a bored listener. The younger man sat back in his wing chair, and Seth returned his attention to the senior Caruthers, who said, "You've been doing some research."

"I have. Vicksburg to Natchez with stops in Port Gibson and Fayette."

"Correct. A little to the west of Jackson, Albert Blackledge's Meridian Southern pushed south to Natchez, providing that city a much desired route east. His successful venture was funded with private money in the fifties and usurped my older initiative to link Natchez to Vicksburg, then east to Jackson and Meridian. With Blackledge's rail now out of commission, it appears an excellent opportunity to resurrect my old rail."

Seth gave passing thought to Caruthers' having given unsolicited recommendations to General Sherman.

"And who, if I might ask, informed you of my interest in a railroad?"

"Isabel Hays," Seth said without hesitation. "She sends her regards."

Sam Caruthers responded with a tight smile. There appeared to be no surprise there.

"Did Jon Franklin offer to sell you the land he and his uncle had acquired?"

"Undercutting his uncle, you mean? No. The younger man's interest was investment in the railroad itself."

Seth had begun to suspect that. "Tobias Holbein is your lawyer?" he asked.

"My lawyer is Zebulon Hatters in Jackson. Mr. Holbein had occasion to serve my father on a matter here and there over the years. Toby and I have been friends since we were young men, so I assume that's why Franklin approached him."

"You and Mr. Holbein were mutual acquaintances of Isaac Baker, I believe."

"Ah," Sam Caruthers said, "you've done a great deal of talking with Isabel."

At Seth's side, Wilson Caruthers said, "Does that surprise you, Dad?"

Seth looked at the younger man, leaning forward now with a big grin on his face. Seth ignored the innuendo and turned back to the father. "She is the last person known to have seen Jon Franklin alive. He told her he had a meeting with you in Port Gibson the night he was killed and asked her to convey his apologies for not attending."

"I requested the meeting, but given the weather that evening, I sent Wilson in my stead. It was he to whom Isabel passed the apology."

"And the reason you wanted to meet with him?"

"We had determined that Mr. Franklin would not fit into our organization."

"Was Naomi Polk aware of this new railroad venture?"

A hint of agitated surprise lit the man's face, then disappeared. "Why do you ask that?"

"There was a piece of paper in Jon Franklin's pocket with your name on it. The handwriting has been identified as belonging to Naomi Polk, and it's my understanding she was a potential investor in that original railroad."

"That you would have learned from Isabel, and yes, the Polk

woman was a potential investor way back then. Her brother-in-law advised against it, and his word was sacrosanct with her. And no, I had not approached her about investing this time. Now, given her note in Franklin's pocket, we could assume Miss Polk was the person who pointed the younger Franklin in the direction of Tobias Holbein, and hence to me."

Seth found it odd that Naomi Polk sent Jon Franklin to a man not Caruthers' lawyer to inquire about the railroad. What had she known about Caruthers and Holbein?

"Did you have a reason for wanting Jon Franklin dead, Mr. Caruthers?"

"I did not."

"Have you ever heard of a man named Trueblood?"

Sam Caruthers frowned at him in genuine surprise. "I knew a Martin Trueblood. He worked for Colonel Ralston over at your headquarters during the war. I had occasion to work with the man in regards to my capacity as steward"—he smiled—"shall we say, of certain confiscated properties. How, if I might ask, did you come up with his name?"

"Evidence indicates he'd shown interest in your old right-of-way last summer."

"That is interesting."

Both interesting and disconcerting if Caruthers' grimace meant anything.

"Is it safe to assume he was aware of your new proposal?"

"It is, but as far as I know he's returned to northern climes."

Seth rose. "One more thing, Mr. Caruthers, now that I have a clearer understanding of your workings with Colonel Ralston's department. Did you ever have occasion to meet a Treasury agent by the name of Alan Guthrie?"

"The operative killed over in Hinds County last fall?"

"The same."

"I never met the man."

Chapter Twenty

"That's good, Buck, thank you," Isabel told Eli's hand. She folded together four fifty-cent greenbacks and held it out to him. He refused it.

"Take it," Isabel said, "you're working for a wage, now."

"Wo'ked fo' wage off 'n on my whole life, Miz Iz'bel. Masta Eli ain't missed my pay yet."

Becky watched her mother take the black man's hand and stuff the bills into it. The move reminded Becky she should speak to Alice about paying Eli's two servants. She doubted her sister-in-law had given any thought to it. "Aunt Elvie has collards and peas in the kitchen," Becky told Buck. "Best you hurry before Daws and Spain eat it all."

A grin spread across the man's dark face, glistening with sweat in the yellow glow of the lamps lighting the dark room. "Now, dat be fine pay fo' dis day's wo'k, Miz Becky." He gave Isabel a two-fingered salute and left, brushing by Becky, clean sheets in hand, at the door.

Becky eyed Aunt Naomi's unmade bed, which Buck, with some voluntary help from Corporal Daws and Private Spain, had completed reassembling in Andrew and Eli's old room. Actually "voluntary" was being gracious. Becky figured her mother had slipped them a fair number of greenbacks, too.

"Do you think you could ever bring yourself to sleep in her bed?" she asked her mother.

Isabel took the sheets from Becky and plopped them at the foot of the tick mattress. "Holland paid for this bed," she said, "and we had to do something. With you and your entourage and the Franklin women here, finding comfortable places for everyone to sleep is proving a challenge. Besides, they're sleeping in it. You and I will stay in your room. We'll move the two daybeds from upstairs."

Becky took a corner of the sheet her mother shook out. "Mama, when you were talking to Mr. Holbein, I overheard him mention a trip to New Orleans. What—"

"You overheard too much." Isabel snatched the sheet hard enough that she pulled it from Becky's fingers. Becky breathed out and regained hold of her side of the sheet, and her mother straightened. "But in answer to your question, it was a quick trip. An old acquaintance was there on business."

Encouraged, Becky asked, "Would that be Willie?"

"Yes."

"Does he have a last name?"

"No."

Becky drew a calming breath. "And what has he to do with whatever it is you and Mr. Holbein do not have to concern yourselves over?"

Her mother shot her a jaundiced look. "He's an investor. A German, but I believe he's in the employ of the Bank of England. He thought he could bring me a nice sum in return for an investment in a joint British-Brazilian firm. Toby isn't comfortable with the expenditure."

"You have money to invest in Brazil?"

"The war resulted in a change in clientele, darling, not a dearth. Yes I have money for investments, and I choose not to deal with the North."

"I'm glad you're not dealing with the North."

"I'm not dealing with the North in this, darling, but life must go on. We are chained to them, now."

"And their tariffs."

"Oh, they're going to industrialize you, dear."

"And make us as filthy as they are."

"Literally and figuratively if they have their way." The bottom sheet was on, and Isabel was reaching for a top one. Becky turned to the boarded windows. In this room, those faced south

"Hannah used to complain that Andrew and Eli got the best room in the house," she said. "From where I'm standing, you could look out and watch the path to the mill disappear into the woods. The japonica bloomed from Christmas until the azaleas took over in the spring. The boys didn't appreciate them."

"Here," Isabel said and held out the sheet. "The camellias are out there, blooming as we stand here, and come next Christmas through the spring they'll bloom again. Help me finish this bed."

"We can't see them."

"Eli will have the windows fixed by Christmas." Isabel shook out the sheet, and it floated down to the mattress.

Across from her, Becky grabbed a corner and smoothed it into place. "I should get over to Aunt Naomi's and see what else we need to move out of there."

"I don't think we need to tell the Franklin women we stowed her away in this room for days before we got her in the ground."

"I wish we could have returned her to Tennessee."

"We didn't have time for that, darling, and you were generous to bury her on Camellia Creek. I don't think Eli would have."

"He can move her into town when he's able"—Becky tucked the sheet—"but I think we should leave her. She thought she belonged here at Camellia Creek, and she did die in this house. If we move her, she'll probably haunt this place."

"And she'd be a terrible haint, even a dangerous one."

"Where did she get this mattress, I wonder?"

"This one's filled with cotton. She had a fine feather mattress, another expense Holland made to ease his guilt for moving her out of this place. Yankee troops ripped it open and pulled the feathers out."

"Boys at play," Becky said, and her stomach quivered. "But they did worse things."

On the other side of the bed, her mother stilled, then said, "Darling, where are her quilts?"

Becky nodded to the stack on the floor behind the door.

"Pick one of them," Isabel said, "and let's get this done, all right?"

There were only two quilts, and Becky didn't debate her choice, simply grabbed the top one.

Once they had it on the bed, Isabel studied the squares, taking time to finger the stitches. "She pieced both these quilts herself. Looks like they came from other quilts. She probably salvaged scraps from the carnage the soldiers had made of those they didn't take with them. Cotton cloth was hard to come by. Her work is beautiful."

"Cotton cloth is still hard to come by. It's a pity she never found a man with whom to make a home and family."

"As far as she was concerned, she had."

"Daddy, you mean?"

"Most assuredly."

"From what Alice has told me about Jocelyn, I understand why you never married Daddy. You never explained it to me."

Isabel sat on the bed. "You never asked."

"I didn't think it was any of my business." Becky sat on the other side of the bed across from her.

"Perhaps it wasn't."

"You know, I spent most of my life in this house, and Jocelyn never contacted me, but Alice moves in and—"

Her mother's laugh sang out. "Alice *believes* Jocelyn contacted her." Isabel stretched her hand across the bed and took Becky's. "You must remember that growing up you were happy. You had your mother and father and brothers and sister. Eli had the same question—why did Jocelyn choose Alice? But Alice claims it was because she listened to Jocelyn, and the rest of us did not.

"Now, if I understand the things Betty Franklin has told me about Alice, when Eli brought her here, she was grieving terribly over her father and brothers. We might go so far as to presume grief had touched her sanity."

"Mrs. Franklin said that she feared Alice was going to kill herself."

"As we all thought Jocelyn had done. That grief, that longing for death made Alice, I guess one could say, more susceptible to contact from the other side."

"Mattie says similar things about me and James, but she says it's because he worries for me."

"You're talking to James?"

Becky blinked, then shook herself. "No, Mama, not like that. I dream of him, feel his presence."

"Memories, darling, that's what they are. James is at rest. He's not looking for you to avenge his 'murder.'"

"And Daddy?"

"Are you talking to your father, too?"

"No, Mother, I am not."

Isabel gave her head a shake and rose. "Let's make an agreement. Until your father contacts you with instructions to destroy Sam Caruthers, you let things lie."

Becky stood, too. "You're taking this too lightly. Shall I let Muscatine lie, too?"

"I'm not taking anything lightly. I'm trying to keep you out of harm's way."

"I've been in harm's way since the spring of 1863. We all have been. I'm not a child."

"How about I avenge your father?"

Becky picked up one of two pillows she'd placed on top of the bureau. "I don't intend to stop trying to get my property back, Mama, and if I come across anything implicating that person in my father's death, I will act on it."

"By bringing it to me."

"If the situation warrants."

"Toby is working with Sam. He'll take the issue of Muscatine to court if necessary. Sam thinks you'll stay at Hickory Grove and he can wait you out."

"Oh, bull. He couldn't possibly believe such. Hickory Grove belongs to Eliza, and once the church has its business in order and sends another preacher, there won't be a place—"

"I know all that, dear."

"If Caruthers pays the taxes, what sort of claim will that give him to Muscatine?"

"The taxes will be deferred."

"For how long?"

"Until the Radicals have full control of Congress and the Presidency."

"Do you think the Democrats in the North will let—"

"Darling," Isabel said, "I'm not sure they can do anything to stop it. Party hatred was one of the primary reasons for the war, and northern Democrats were part and parcel to it. They fomented sectional strife for no other reason than to create division within the Whig party until they destroyed it and left us with the monster in power today."

"A concise assessment, Mother?"

"The men who visit my pleasure palace do more than enjoy my girls, darling. They discuss politics, constantly. Of course, there's very little grace and political theory discussed today, given the boorish brutes now seeking power." Becky tossed her mother a pillow, and she caught it. "But for the fact it was the South that paid the price I'd find great pleasure seeing the northern Democrats get their just deserts."

"I want to raise Eliza at Muscatine. It's home and so much closer to Camellia Creek than I am now. I just need to hold on to her property until she reaches her majority."

"Since you are so adamant about spurning my financial help, have you considered you might have to sell Hickory Grove in order to provide for her?"

"I won't do that, not willingly, but providing for her makes having Muscatine more important, but that has nothing to do with justice for Daddy."

"Justice for your father is a different matter. Be satisfied right now that getting Muscatine back will thwart Sam."

"I'd wanted Eli to go to Washington with me and request a pardon, but he said he wouldn't grovel to those usurpers and he wouldn't let me either. He planned to move back into the house, and see what Caruthers would do about that. Now I fear he's had all the showdowns he can handle."

"Certainly Alice has, and the showdown would have been with the sheriff at best and Federal troops at worst. I swear young men are pathetically stupid, and you, too, if you gave credence to such idiocy." Isabel reached for the pillowcase Becky tossed across the bed. "Let me resolve this."

"What's Caruthers really up to, Mother?"

Isabel situated the pillow at the head of the bed. "Personal gain, nothing more sinister than that."

"You are being facetious."

"I'm telling the truth."

"You're stating the obvious and adding nothing of value. You imply he killed my father to get his hands on Camellia Creek in order to advance his railroad, so I don't understand why you're trying to convince me he's simply going to hand Muscatine back to me."

Isabel reached over, silently requesting the pillow Becky still held.

"Is that why Aunt Naomi planned her carnage here? Was she working for Sam Caruthers?"

"Naomi Polk was working for herself. Eli had angered her, and she was blind to anything short of destroying him."

"Oh, Mama, tell me the truth."

"Trust me in this, please." Isabel situated the second pillow on the bed. "Put the extra quilt down at the foot in case it turns real cold again."

Chapter Twenty-one

The Warren County Courthouse had survived the siege and bombardments that had gone hand in hand with Grant's taking Vicksburg in 1863. Not unscathed, but certainly it had weathered well, relatively speaking. Most importantly the county's records were intact.

Seth stood at a worn counter looking at the land record book, pulled for him by a county clerk, who was overseen by a bored-looking Federal minion. Hanging on the wall just behind and to one side of him was the section map of the county. He'd known generally where Muscatine was, taking up disparate parts of sections 14, 7, 8, and 3 located within range 2 and spreading south to north over township 13. Looking at the map, its parcels colored and annotated to distinguish ownership, he was pretty sure he could pinpoint the spot where he and his fellow reconnoiterers had come ashore that fateful day in April 1863—a small western portion of a large tract, colored yellow, touched the Mississippi. They'd come ashore at that landing, he was certain of it. The name "Mackey," printed boldly across the section, had been lined through. The name "Caruthers" had been written beneath it, and though he didn't have the Claiborne County record book available to him, he suspected part of James and Rebecca Mackey's holdings fell in northwestern Claiborne County, ending on the north bank of the Big Black, which separated the northwest section of the county from the county proper.

Six hundred fifty acres had been deeded to James Thomas Mackey and Rebecca Calhoon Mackey on the 7th of June 1860. He figured her for eighteen or nineteen when she'd wed young James.

Seth conjured the scent of lilac, overpowering that of blood and antiseptic, the feel of a cool hand against his fevered brow, the soft feminine murmurs of encouragement and comfort to drown out the unrelenting pain that succumbed only to intermittent bouts of unconsciousness. He wondered how she remembered that day and night, assuming she dwelled on it at all, and he knew her memories would not mirror his. Her tender recollections, she reserved for a ghost.

He turned from the map to the record book. The settling-in of James and Rebecca Mackey had not been, as he already knew, the beginning of Muscatine. He read a moment, then motioned to the graying clerk, who was busy recording information in newer books.

"Can I see this earlier deed," he asked and pointed to a line in the record. It took the man only a moment to recover the deed book. He had, without question, the order and relative content of each volume etched in his memory. More than likely, he had worked in this office for decades, the bound volumes of land deeds, wills, and death certificates precious wards bequeathed him by the trusting folk of Warren County. This time the clerk noted the page from the index with a soft "Ah," and turned to the requested deed. He slid the book back around for Seth to see.

The deed was filed in 1802 by Seamus McGowan Calhoon, validating, a note in the upper right hand corner said, an earlier deed on record in Adams County. A checkmark and a poorly crafted word he made out to be 'Trueblue' was written in pencil beneath it, and he squinted to confirm the name he was reading. Seth looked up and found the eyes of the clerk, who must have misinterpreted the unspoken question on his face.

"Probably Spanish," he said before Seth could speak. "But could be an old English grant the Spanish honored. You need to go to Natchez and see what they got in their records."

"Do you know what this annotation beneath it is for?"

The man turned the book so he could see. "Clerk verified he'd checked the deed is all. That particular fella worked for Colonel Ralston confiscating property and farmin' it back out to the loyal citizens." He'd said the last two words with unveiled contempt, then adjusted the book back to Seth's line of sight and started to return to his business.

"Trueblood was the man's name?"

"That's him," the man answered. "Federal officer. Got to the point Trueblood was here so often he knew my books 'bout well as me."

"Did he show interest in other counties' records?"

"How should I know?" he snapped. "I'm responsible for Warren County. You'll have to go to the clerks of other counties to find that out."

"Have you seen him lately?"

"Ain't seen 'im in months."

If he'd even been born as of 1802, Holland Calhoon would have been a baby. Seamus was the uncle Isabel had referenced, the one Caruthers had tried to purchase the land from. He squinted up at the annotated map. "I need to know the holdings of Samuel Caruthers here in Warren County."

The man Seth took to be a Federal overseer rose. "Caruthers is one of our loyal citizens, Major."

And why should the man assume he would care? Or was it that this man had an interest in those who had questions about the formidable Mr. Caruthers?

"Cecil Bowler," he said and extended a hand. Seth took it. "Seems every day a local walks in, pardon in hand, and wants his land back. That's why I'm here, to validate and coordinate the return of property. President Johnson's been real quick to return the land to those who claim to be the rightful owners and all too quick to push our loyal citizens and the freedmen aside."

Bowler was trim of build and sported a neat mustache and spectacles. His suit was black and brushed, his shoes shined — which he'd have had done this morning, because Vicksburg's streets were not conducive to groomed footwear at the moment. Seth judged the man to be in his forties.

"You're Treasury?"

"I am."

Seth glanced at the clerk, then returned his gaze to Bowler. "I'm interested in the property Mr. Caruthers is the undisputed owner of here in Warren County."

Bowler frowned, and Seth turned to the clerk. "He did own land in this county before the war, am I correct?"

"A significant amount of land, and some of what he's now claimin'"—the clerk turned and glared at Bowler—"as a loyal member of the Union, butts up against what he already owned. Some of that would be the property you were just lookin' at."

Seth's interest lay with that old right-of-way.

The clerk made a point of taking in Seth's uniform, as if he were trying to catch a whiff of something unpleasant. Apparently deciding Seth might not be particularly foul, after all, he walked around the counter to the map Seth had been studying earlier. With his index finger, he traced an imaginary line from just above Muscatine's north quarter, up through one whole township, east across what appeared nearly a full range, then diagonally down to the Big Black and west to Muscatine's easternmost property line. This parcel was colored blue and on closer inspection, Seth could see the name "Caruthers" printed across what was in fact a long, narrow swath.

Behind the counter, Cecil Bowler looked on with interest. "Mr. Ferguson here has been working that Mackey dispute for the past few months."

Months?

"The interest in this property goes back a long, long ways," Ferguson said. "Don't know the whole of it, but there was an issue with a railroad charter back in the thirties. Ain't seen much interest until three years ago, when Sam Caruthers declared himself a loyal citizen and squatted on it."

"Mackey's widow is a Calhoon from Claiborne County south of us," the clerk continued. "This land has been in her family for generations. She's been in here off an' on since last spring. She's one of the few fighting Caruthers. Rest of the folks he's stole from is gone or dead, I reckon. She wanted me to draw up a copy of the deed. Says hers was lost in a fire over in Madison County."

Seth frowned, ready to ask about the fire, then imagined the old coot's response to an event that took place in Madison County.

"I know about Sam Caruthers and his doings. And I know the likes of who he's dealin' with these days. A flea on a mangy dog."

Cecil Bowler cleared his throat and drew Seth's attention. "Mr. Caruthers, as a loyal Union man, has invoked the ire of many of his fellow—"

"Loyal Union man, my ass," Ferguson ground out. "He was a die-hard secessionist till Grant set up camp, not that treachery such as that would matter to a generation of Northerners that spat on the Constitution. His loyalty depends on whichever army is present. Whig he was back when there were such things. Greedy bastard will fit right in with the likes of the rest of you Republicans. You deserve the likes of 'im."

Seth came from a mix of old National Republican and Whig stock, but his father and paternal grandfather had voted for Breckenridge the year of Lincoln's election. They had opposed secession. Disillusioned with Lincoln and the Republicans, as well as the North in general, they'd not voted in the '64 election. His maternal grandfather, from cotton-growing Fulton County, was another story, and it wasn't a Whig one.

"You gave Mrs. Mackey her deed?" Seth asked.

"I did." The old man leaned over the counter. "Flagged that I weren't supposed to do nothin' for 'er, but I did it anyways."

The man turned and glared at Bowler, who calmly said, "Her husband was a large landowner in Madison County. Her father and brother, from whose estate the contested property derives, are also Thirteenthers. There is merely a question as to whether or not Mrs. Mackey requires a presidential pardon."

Seth wondered if she'd inherited any right to the property in Madison County. He studied Bowler a moment longer. Administrative, he thought, merely following instructions. Whoever had decided Muscatine was not to be returned to its rightful owner, at least for the short term, was not this man. What Seth found particularly interesting was Bowler's being so well versed on James Mackey's status as well as that of Eli Calhoon.

Chapter Twenty-two

The army corporal stepped from the rear hallway back into the room. "Those records are gone, sir, but the captain knew him. Says for you to come on back."

Seth followed the man out of the front room of a large frame building that had been seized back in July of 1863 to serve as the administrative center for Union forces comprising the Department of Mississippi, Southwest. This wasn't his first time in the building or his first meeting with Captain Jacob Schuler, United States Army. Seth had checked into this headquarters back in November, and he and Jubal Summers had officially received his eight Negro troops in this very building. He had not, however, been in Schuler's office.

"Sorry, Major," the graying officer said, motioning Seth into a straight-back chair, "but we've been clearing out old records in preparation for the next phase of occupation. Martin Trueblood's documents went back to Indiana with him."

"Nice office," Seth said, looking around. Relatively speaking, it was. Small in contrast to the rest of this building, it was larger than many offices Seth had seen.

"Colonel Ralston's old space. The broom closet I occupied until last September is down the hall."

Seth grinned. "Nice coup."

"Administration was not one of Ralston's many hats. I simply got lucky. When he left, his hats were either divvied up or deleted. As you well know, your Colonel Byrnes wears one of them. I'm stuck accounting for records, primarily personnel."

"Ah."

"Major Trueblood left for home last July. He was a captain

with the 161st Indiana when he was wounded during the siege. Then he came down with pneumonia. His regiment moved on without him, the adjutant's intent to muster him out. Unlike many soldiers, he didn't want to go and juggled for a transfer to the occupying staff. I worked his reassignment, which is why I remember him. He had a good record and was an accountant in real life. We were swamped with a logistical nightmare given the freedmen, refugees, and confiscated Confederate property. Accounting for such was sorely undermanned, so we managed to transfer Trueblood to staff and kept him. He got his promotion to major here."

"He was a bookkeeper?" Seth asked, because he wanted him to be more. Schuler smiled.

"Not of the money kind, if that's what you're thinking. Wasn't long before he'd moved from recording property acquisitions to assisting Colonel Ralston in running the department, hence the promotion. This past June when the 161st wanted the man back so it could muster him out, the colonel started to fight it." Schuler shrugged. "Then the Army shipped the colonel off to California and the fight ended. We sent Trueblood home."

"Trueblood had occasion to work with confiscated cotton?"

"Ralston's department was responsible for confiscated anything."

"Did Trueblood work with Treasury?"

"Intimately, and they were all tangled up with military intelligence, too."

"Have you seen him recently or heard of him being back in Mississippi?"

"I have not, which makes me curious about your questions."

"He showed some interest in land associated with a proposed railroad right-of-way here in Mississippi. The tie is purely speculative, but another man also believed to be interested in that railroad was murdered not long ago in Claiborne County. Trueblood isn't suspect. I merely want to talk to him to see if I can glean information as to who the murdered man might have been dealing with here in the area."

Schuler looked thoughtful, then said, "Trueblood's been gone for months."

"Given his interest, he might return. I'd appreciate your letting Colonel Byrnes over in special operations know if you see him."

He started to get up, but Schuler said, "You know, there was a woman in here asking about Trueblood. Wasn't too long after he left. July or August I'd guess. She wanted to talk to him."

"Do you recall her name?"

He shook his head. "Nope, but she was pretty, blond. That's why I remember her."

"Mature?"

"Young, dressed in widow's weeds."

Rebecca. He'd have bet on Isabel, but Becky made sense. "Were you able to help her?"

"I didn't tell her anything. Given what Ralston was involved in, I wasn't about to confirm or deny anything to people who are looking for his folks. Who knows what they're after."

"How did she react to your response?"

"Stoically."

Chapter Twenty-three

"How soon before he arrives?" Seth asked.

Malcolm Byrnes removed a pipe stem from between his lips. "Any day now. I imagine he plans on recruiting locally."

"But I'm already involved."

"Yes, but is he gonna want to keep you involved?" Malcolm rose. Seth started up, too, but Malcolm waved him down. "Keep your seat. My leg's bothering me. I need to stretch." He looked out the window behind him. "The war for which a man like me waits a lifetime has been over nine months."

"There's the west."

"The west is out. I can no longer sit a horse for any length of time. Besides, if guerrilla war develops here in the South, this is where I want to be."

"Then you're thinking Guthrie's death does have something to do with covert operations?"

"It has less to do with what I'm thinking than what they're thinking in Washington. Who knows what they have planned, or who they have it planned against. I was sent here to do a particular kind of job." Malcolm returned to his desk. "The murder of a Treasury agent on a discreet assignment fits under my charter. Its resolution requires knowledge of matters to which I have not been made privy, and that angers me. What it's boiling down to is a power struggle in Washington, which, if I were realistic, I'd admit Treasury has already won. The military assets that conducted intelligence gathering during the war are being consolidated in Treasury, and the civilian War Department is part and parcel of it. Those in control of the government want those intelligence assets to survive the war, but they want them directly under civilian control, not Army. And the threat of insurrection is real."

"Because they're fomenting it."

"They look at it as continued Southern resistance to what the founders intended."

Seth blew out a breath. "That's not how they see it, that's how they intend to 'sell' it."

Malcolm studied him. "Your lack of discretion is gonna get you in trouble, if you're not careful."

"I'm talking to you and we're saying the same thing, even if we see the consequences differently."

Malcolm stared a moment longer, then smirked. "And your Kentucky hide is always safe with me."

They were more than senior and subordinate. Four years ago, Seth had saved Malcolm Byrnes' life during a demonstration to a joint Army-Navy staff of the firing of one of Admiral Porter's proposed mortars. The mortar misfired, blowing up the gun mount and killing six men and injuring nine others, which included some of the observers sitting to the rear of the mount. Malcolm Byrnes had been among those observers.

Seth and some fellow sailors and marines had been watching from amidships their gunboat, moored outside the firing area. They hadn't been part of the demonstration, just curious and a bit bored. Malcolm and two others had been blown into the water. Grievously wounded from the force of the explosion, Malcolm had been unconscious. Seth had jumped in and saved him, and though several members of his crew had also participated in the rescue attempt, the other two bodies had not been recovered for hours.

Malcolm Byrnes had not forgotten. When his intelligence staff, as part of a joint Army-Navy operation on the Mississippi, needed an immediate replacement officer, he'd requested Seth — whom he'd gotten to know well and who was nominally part of the flagship crew — fill it, and Seth had spent a stressful nine months torn between a marine colonel at the flotilla level and an army colonel, then Malcolm's immediate senior, at the joint staff level.

In late April 1863, it had been Lieutenant Colonel Malcolm Byrnes who'd sent a patrol to recover the missing member of a small detachment that had come under fire while reconnoitering a Confederate battery north of the Big Black. Out of boredom, Seth, then a first lieutenant, had finagled duty with the reconnoiterers, and he was the only man wounded when they'd found the damn battery, or it had found them. That particular foray hadn't been Seth's first time ashore, but earlier incursions had occurred under cover of darkness, and though he'd gathered information, he'd done so without the misfortune of making contact with the enemy.

With the aid of Confederate forces eager to be rid of the injured man, the Federal patrol had recovered him at the home of Rebecca Mackey. The Federals left her minus a patient and a buckboard, but otherwise unharmed and unhindered. For Seth, his reconnoitering days were done, if he didn't count the present.

Malcolm sat back and drew on his pipe. "None of us regulars like the way things are going. Now, 'rumor's' telling me Treasury is going to take this case. This thing has had a foul odor since it landed on my desk. The implication to find a Southerner to blame screamed that someone was hiding something.

"I asked for you not only because I knew you liked this kind of work, but because I knew you wouldn't look at the investigation through the eyes of a crazed zealot drunk on a preconceived concept of patriotism. The Radicals might be gearing up to take control, but McCulloch is no radical, so you can bet on Treasury's plans for its own little fiefdom. The fall elections will tell the tale, but I fear what we're seeing now is just the beginning. Murders, like that of Guthrie and this Franklin fella from the North, will be excuses for whatever, whoever, has planned at any given time. Two months ago you offered them the perfect suspect in Calhoon, now you've snatched him back."

"Guthrie was looking for the entire family, Malcolm."

"Which secret service operatives will translate to mean an entire family of seditionists."

"The Franklin murder?"

"You and I both know you're not even sure it fits. Look, what I suspect that you've done with Calhoon is foul up something Treasury has working here in Mississippi, else they wouldn't be sending an operative out here to take this away from us. General Wood agrees that something is going on which Army should be privy to." Malcolm shrugged. "Your investigation is a mixed blessing. It looks like you've forced them to act when they preferred to lay low. But with Treasury's intervention, we could lose our upper hand before we find out what they're up to."

"You think we're out, then?"

"I think we will be unless we can come up with an inventive way to stay in before this fella gets here."

When Malcolm made no further comment, Seth asked, "What do you know of my Negroes?"

"Not that it looks like it's gonna matter, but the 60th will be mustered out next month. Six of your men were drawn from it, including Sergeant Zachary."

Peters, Hand, Spain, Lawson, and Ball were the other five. "Is there any way to re —"

"I've tried, but I barely get my mouth open before the chief of staff cuts me off. The Negro has served his purpose being turned against his own, now he's gonna be cut free."

Seth looked at him. "Your lack of discretion is gonna get you in trouble one day."

Malcolm chuckled, and Seth sighed. "The others?"

"March probably. I might can hold on to Jubal Summers for you if he'd be willing to accept reassignment to his old New York regiment. It'd be a paper transfer. He'd remain here with you, but to tell you the truth, I don't know how much longer that unit will be active either."

"Why not here on staff?" Seth asked, his voice carrying more than a hint of anger.

"A couple of the officers know Summers, or of him. He's got a surly arrogance about him, and they don't like him."

"He'd be with me."

"There is no support and less cooperation."

Seth blew out a breath. "Frank Zachary has expressed a desire to remain in the army."

"He could try for reassignment to another unit that doesn't have a date yet for deactivation, but to tell you the truth, everyone knows it's coming. Units are not accepting additional personnel." Malcolm picked up his pipe. "Good man, Zachary?"

"A damned good NCO and one of the best excuses for a human being you can find on this planet. Better than a lot of your white sergeants I've had the misfortune to come across, both as NCOs and human beings I might add."

Malcolm grinned. "Coming from a marine, I don't know that you're paying the man a great compliment. Look Seth, there's rumors that the Army might try some experiment out west, using Negro units against the Indians, but there's nothing firm with that. Pass that along to him and any of the others who might be interested. If I recall, I made sure you got the best of the lot with that group I rounded up for you."

Seth nodded. "Damn good for their being army." Seth leaned forward in his chair. "Segregated units?"

"That's one thing I'm sure of. My guess is that the officers will be white."

Seth smirked.

"What?"

"Funny that full integration worked with the Confederacy."

"Yeah, well all their officers were white, too. And if I might be allowed to remind you, Major, in the end nothing worked for the Confederacy, so I don't believe that's a standard we wish to aspire to."

Seth watched Malcolm knock the refuse from his pipe bowl into his palm. "Marlene's in Memphis or I'd ask you home for dinner. How about joining me at the officers' mess? Then we'll return to my place and get drunk. I can quote Webster and you can quote Clay, and we'll console ourselves with how damn pleased they'd be over what has happened."

The results perhaps, but not necessarily the costs. Seth rose. "'Go home, Mr. Mendenhall, and attend to your own business, and I will endeavor to see to mine.' There, I've exhausted my Clay quotes. The floor's clear for you and Webster."

"Now that I think about it, I'm not sure I know any Webster quotes, not verbatim anyway."

"Look, Malcolm, getting drunk sounds particularly appealing, but I wanna catch a southbound packet and try to catch Holbein before he closes up shop for the night. We're running out of time."

Chapter Twenty-four

ecky found her mother at the dining room table, pen in hand, leaning over the first recto page of the old Calhoon Bible.

"What are you doing?"

"Repairing the damage Naomi Polk did to this record. I swear at this moment I hope there is a hell and that witch is in it."

Becky pulled out the side chair and sat next to her. "What did she do?"

"Marked through your name. Holland put you in here himself."

She felt her stomach drop. "How bad is the damage?"

"She used India ink to obliterate it completely. I've rewritten the entry"

But it would no longer be in her father's hand.

Isabel blew on the wet ink. "Is your brother comfortable?"

"He's sleeping, but he sat up while Caw Pruitt was here. I'm glad you brought the extra pillows. When we situate them right, it helps alleviate his pain. I didn't tell him where they came from. Alice is back to sleep, too. We're hoping she sleeps through the night. I'll relieve you about two, if you'll relieve Betty at ten."

Isabel closed the cover and looked at her. "Of course, darling. Have you eaten?"

"Yes, and you should too." Becky bit her bottom lip. "Mama, I haven't seen Major Parker in days. Do you think he's been 'forced out'?"

Her mother raised an eyebrow, but made no reference to her eavesdropping days ago. "Zachary and Daws are still here, so he's around somewhere."

"Do you know who he works for?"

Isabel turned slightly in her seat and studied Becky, who now regretted having asked. Instead of a prying question, her mother said, "He's working for the Army, but as you know, we've heard Treasury operatives might take over the investigation. Hence, my remark to Toby about Parker's being 'forced out.'"

"And who told Mr. Holbein about the operatives?"

"He has sources to which I am not privy."

"Are you privy to this one?"

"Your attempts to browbeat me are becoming bothersome. I am your mother, so stop it. Yes, I am, and I'm not telling you who it is."

"Fine, I have another question. I never got an answer regarding what Mr. Holbein implied Guthrie had spelled out for Aunt Naomi, and you countered she already knew. What did she already know?"

"Let me clarify what I just said. Don't ask me another thing about that conversation. You know I deplore eavesdropping. You get that from your Aunt Naomi."

"I'm not even related to her. It's you I'm related to."

A smile had formed on Isabel's lips, so Becky donned one, too. After a moment, she traced a finger over the gold-inlaid printing on the Bible's cover. "Did she take anything other than this?"

"I have no doubt. Any bit of knowledge she might use for her own benefit, she'd have taken for future use, and anything she never wanted seen again she burned."

"My birth certificate, Mama?"

"It's in the upstairs safe at The Pink Lady. And the official record is at the courthouse in Fayette." Isabel pushed out from the table and stood.

"Did she strike through the record of my marriage?"

"'Obliterated' would be a better way of putting it, and yes, I fixed that, too."

"I don't believe the mourning will ever pass."

Her mother stooped and hugged her. "The poignancy of loss will always be with you. It's part of you. If it weren't, you'd be someone less than who you are. But trust me, darling. You will be happy again. Now I'd like to get something to eat and lie down for a couple of hours before ten. Since Eli is doing better, I want to get to Rodney for a couple of days. I'm giving the missing Major Parker one more day, then I'm leaving."

"What difference does he make?"

"I want to take Daws with me, and I don't know if the sergeant will send him."

"Why—"

"Security, sweetheart. The roads are dangerous."

"Take Buck or Hector."

"They're needed here." Her mother started for the door and Becky pushed back from the table and stood. She picked up the Bible.

"You can leave it. I'll put it away later."

"I'll put it in the parlor."

"Put it in our room. I don't want to risk the girls getting ahold of it. The pages have become quite brittle."

"Mama, how much does Parker know?"

Isabel, her hand on the doorknob leading to the rear porch, cocked her head. "Not as much as he could potentially know after the Treasury operative gets here."

"Is it better or worse for us if they force him out, do you think?"

"There are some particularly unsavory characters making up the ranks of the Treasury service, but the same can be said for those who worked in military intelligence during the war. I can't answer your question. There are some very dark shades of blue out there, darling, and I'm not sure of the handsome major's color. But no matter the shade, it does not favor us."

Chapter Twenty-five

stout Negress drew the door wide, took one look at Seth, and said to Tobias Holbein, "You be eatin' in da dinin' room tonight, suh?"

"Yes, Irene," he told her. He removed his coat, then reached for Seth's greatcoat. Both he passed to the servant. "I've told Fancy. You'll find me and Major Parker in the study when supper's ready. Is the back bedroom suitable for guests?"

She laughed and shut the door with a clatter. "You know we always be ready in dis house, Mr. Toby."

"And I thank you heartily."

Holbein led him through what Seth judged to be a sleeping porch at the back of the house and into a central hall, flanked by rooms the doors to which were closed, save the one Seth followed Holbein into at the end of the hall. They'd entered a spacious, well-lit room, warmed by a fire in an undistinguished fireplace. This, no doubt, was the room where Tobias Holbein spent most of his time when home.

It was a nice house, unimpressive by local standards, or what until recently had been the standard, on the western edge of that district of Jefferson County known as Westside. Less than three years ago, the area had boasted numerous plantation homes, most now burned or abandoned, all certainly plundered and ravaged, their families and slaves dead or gone, and the surrounding fields fallow.

Holbein had bought the house more than thirty years ago, he'd told Seth on their short ride out. Over the years there'd been a wife and four daughters, two of whom died in childhood. The other two were married, and he also had, 'as a matter of fact', four grandchildren, three of whom were boys. One daughter was a war widow. All his progeny lived in New Orleans.

"I'm trying to persuade Angela to bring her two boys home and live with me here," he said, pouring them each three fingers of whiskey. "It's been lonely since the girls left."

"How long has your wife been gone?"

"Twenty-two years." He handed Seth his glass, then waved him toward one of two wing-back chairs in front of the fireplace. "I'm not a comely man, I know that. Was a wee bit better in my youth, but I had no desire to wed again. I'd found and loved a woman who loved me in return. I didn't want to replace her."

Seth sat, and Holbein took the other chair, leaned against its back, and, from all appearances, relaxed.

A graying darkie of around sixty had taken their horses when they'd dismounted outside the barn, and an affable cook Holbein called Fancy had greeted them in a warm kitchen, fragrant with the scent of supper. "Your slaves stayed with you."

"No slaves," Holbein said. He sipped his whiskey and closed his eyes. "Haven't been any here since I've owned it. There were at one time though. It was a working farm with over three hundred acres. I bought the house and six. Most of that six has grown up now, except what the servants use for gardening. Irene has been with me the past twenty-seven years, Fancy for nine, and old Po for thirty-one. I don't care for slavery, primarily because I don't trust people held in bondage." He caught Seth's eye. "Especially the ones living under my roof and cooking my food."

"Your employees, then, appear to think a lot of you."

"I'm pretty easy to work for. Penelope was a little more demanding of Irene and our cook. I just let Irene manage the house and everyone seems happy. I do get lonesome, especially now that most of my friends and neighbors have died, been killed, or packed up and left."

Seth figured it was loneliness that had compelled the lawyer to offer him supper and a place to sleep tonight. The only other place in Rodney was Isabel's Pink Lady, and hunkering down there would be neither wise nor discreet, given his doubts regarding Isabel and Alan Guthrie. Not that he was less doubtful about Tobias Holbein.

He'd gotten to Holbein's office at dusk, the evening air heavy with the threat of a cold rain. Seth figured he'd missed him for sure, but the lawyer was locking up. Faced with the prospect of a miserable night ride to his quarters in Port Gibson, he opted for damnation over being forced to return to Rodney the next day, especially when he had his objective standing right there in front of him. When Holbein realized Seth was determined to talk while he was equally desirous of going home, the older man had given up and invited Seth to his house.

"What's so important it couldn't wait till morning, Major?"

"Not so much the importance as the time lost. Have you heard from Isabel Hays in the past couple of weeks?"

"I saw Isabel, oh, just about ten...twelve days ago."

That surprised him. "Did she say anything about Calhoon?"

"He's regained consciousness. I saw him, too."

"You've been to Camellia Creek?"

"Got up there as soon as I heard about Eli."

Well, damn, this was an incestuous group. "Isabel told you about Sam Caruthers' name in Jon Franklin's pocket?"

"Written in Naomi Polk's hand."

"I've talked to Caruthers. He says Jon Franklin approached you for an introduction to him, but that Franklin wouldn't tell you who gave him your name."

"That is correct. Given Franklin's uncle was buying up the right-of-way, Sam agreed to talk to the nephew."

"And what did you make of Naomi Polk's involvement with Jon Franklin?"

"I think it's fair to assume her ultimate goal was to hurt Eli."

"Any idea how they met, who approached whom first?"

"Let me ask you this. If you were a young investor wishing to talk to a businessman up in Warren County, would you approach an impoverished spinster living in a dilapidated town house on the outskirts of Port Gibson?"

"Depends on what I heard she knew."

"He'd have heard nothing of Naomi Polk. She was not his kind of people. And when it comes to anyone hearing anything, that again would have been Naomi. She made a point of listening. Jon Franklin did not. I'm confident Naomi approached him."

Seth pondered that a minute. "You were Albert Blackledge's lawyer and subsequently Laura's?"

"I was."

"How much do you know about the Meridian Southern Railroad?"

"That rail was the primary east-west line between Natchez and Meridian, then points east, less than a decade old when the war started. Albert invested his own money in that railroad, ultimately every cent he had. There was a brief period in the late fifties when we thought he'd have to sell or lose it, but things bounced back in the nick of time. He rented it out, in a manner of speaking, to the Confederate Army, and between that promise of worthless script and Sherman's bummers, he lost everything."

"Laura?"

"Albert married Andrew Calhoon's twenty-one-year-old widow in the fall of '62. He was sixty-eight. He'd never wed, but he'd always been a ladies' man. Not handsome, mind you, but rugged. Still, by sixty-eight he'd grown old. Laura wanted the money, or security. They apparently always understood that. But though he never confessed it to me, I believe he hoped she'd give him an heir, preferably male. He suffered a heart attack in '64. His railroad was gone, and Laura had not conceived. He never recovered. He died last fall, a broken man."

Seth knew Blackledge had died shortly before he'd arrived in the area.

"He left his wife nothing?"

"He had nothing left. As far as the railroad goes, both engines had been damaged. They were moved north to Memphis and dismantled for spare parts. Most of the rolling stock was similarly dismantled or systematically destroyed. Miles of rail were ripped up, the ties stacked and burned. Laura might have put in a claim had she lived. That's what I would have advised, if she'd asked, but at the time of her death, she hadn't."

"They'd had a fine home just south of the Claiborne line on the river. It burned in the spring of '63. We never knew how or why. Albert abandoned the land and bought a place in Port Gibson, her home, which was subsequently plundered by Union forces. At the time of Laura's death, she was about to lose it. I received a letter from the mortgage holder just last week that the bank intended to take possession in March for lack of payments. Laura was desperate. I believe her survival plan was to marry Eli Calhoon."

"What was the relationship between the Meridian Southern and Sam Caruthers' railroad proposal of 1836? "

Holbein disappeared into the shadow of his armchair. "There was no 'relationship' as you put it. The Meridian Southern basically usurped the purpose of Sam's railroad of almost twenty years prior, that being access from the east to Natchez and did so more directly, therefore more efficiently, than Sam's proposed route. But Sam had long before resolved his railroad would not be built. He'd turned his interest to shipping on the Big Black and the Mississippi, and, of course, to cotton. Though I perceived a hint of jealousy on Sam's part when Blackledge's rail came to the fore, I don't think others did. Blackledge built that thing with his own money. Whig that he was, Sam had tried to tap into state funds."

"And his new initiative to replace the Meridian Southern?"

Holbein leaned forward, again making himself visible. He appeared to contemplate Seth, who said, "He confirmed to me he has plans for a railroad."

"Well then, I believe he intends to replicate his 1836 charter, not rebuild the Meridian Southern."

"Why? You said yourself the Meridian Southern right-of-way is more efficient for the stated purpose."

"Sam argues that it'll be years before that mess is untangled in the federal courts. He doesn't want to wait."

Seth wasn't sure he believed that, especially considering the "friends" Sam Caruthers supposedly had among the Federals and the complete lack of any known opposition from The Meridian Southern side, all those with any possible claim now dead. He narrowed his eyes on Holbein. "Isabel told you that Naomi Polk admitted to killing Laura?"

"She did."

"Could the removal of entanglements have been a reason for Naomi's killing her?"

Holbein frowned. "It was my understanding that Laura was attempting to blame the murder of one of their neighbors on Eli and Naomi killed her to shut her up. Are you instead implying Naomi was actually working in concert with Sam when she killed Laura in order to remove impediments against the Meridian Southern?"

"Unless she was working with someone else trying to expedite the 'untangling' of The Meridian Southern's ownership."

"And who would that be?"

"Have you ever heard of a man named Martin Trueblood?"

"I have not," Holbein answered. "Why?"

"I came across his name in my research. As of last summer, he was showing an interest in that old '36 railroad right-of-way. He was an army officer. Worked confiscated property in Vicksburg during the war. Mr. Caruthers knew him and, in my opinion, was disturbed by the man's interest in his new initiative."

"Hmmm...do you have anything to indicate this Trueblood is interested in the Meridian Southern right-of-way?"

"No."

"So why would you think Naomi's murdering Laura was about the railroad?"

"I think it's more that I'm not comfortable with the reason I *do* have for the murder." Seth filled him in on Naomi Polk's visit to his office that stormy afternoon before she'd shot Calhoon. At the time, she'd tried to implicate her nephew for the murder of not only Wayne Hale, the neighbor who'd killed Calhoon's ex-slave and his young family, but also Laura. Further, she said he intended to kill Alice and Jon Franklin, whom he believed were lovers conspiring against him. Her conscience, Naomi said, had gotten the better of her. Having apparently noted skepticism on the part of him and Jubal Summers, Naomi had finally confessed what she claimed was the real truth, that Eli killed both Wayne Hale and Laura because they knew he'd played a part in the Guthrie murder.

Holbein hadn't interrupted him, but listened intently. "For sure, she knew she hadn't sold me on Calhoon's killing Laura, and I figured he might get a medal for killing Hale. At the time, and I'm still thinking, she threw in the Guthrie murder to keep me on Calhoon's trail. What's nagging me is that Naomi said specifically Laura Blackledge was blackmailing Calhoon with what she knew of Alan Guthrie's murder. More, though—it was Laura herself who told me she believed Calhoon knew Guthrie."

"Did she tell you why she believed that?"

"No, which led me ultimately to believe she'd been lying. But now I'm thinking, if she were lying, why not go for the whole caboodle, tell me straight out that she knew for a fact Calhoon knew Guthrie?"

"Maybe she feared getting caught up in an out-and-out lie."

"Or maybe she thought they might have met."

"And why would she think that?"

Seth leaned forward, hands on his thighs, and looked Holbein straight in the eye. "I have a source that tells me Alan Guthrie was in the area looking for the Calhoons."

Tobias Holbein said nothing, but he didn't drop his gaze.

"This same source sent Guthrie to Laura."

"And Laura sent Guthrie back here to Rodney and Isabel."

Seth sat upright. "Why the hell didn't you tell me that at the beginning?"

"Because I don't know if Guthrie ever found Eli. Neither does Isabel and quite frankly, neither of us wanted to give you anything to fuel your fire. Isabel was about ready to strangle Laura herself."

"Has anyone, other than me, asked Calhoon if he actually met the man?"

"We didn't. If he wasn't already aware of Guthrie's interest, we didn't want him to know about it."

"Don't you think he'd be better off knowing if a murdered man had been looking for him?"

Holbein took another sip of his whiskey and turned back to the fire.

Seth leaned back in his own chair. "You didn't want Calhoon asking questions. That's the only thing I can think of."

"Think all you want, Major, but Eli's innocent curiosity about the man would have drawn attention he was better off without."

"Did Guthrie ask about Rebecca Mackey?"

Holbein laid his head back and finished off his whiskey. "I believe Laura told him about Becky, unless it was your source."

Seth hoped Becky wasn't aware of Guthrie's search, because he didn't want her involved. "Did he contact her?"

"As far as I know he did not."

"What did he want with the family?"

"According to Guthrie, the family had perpetrated a great fraud against the government of the United States. He told me I was part of it and unless I cooperated he would expose that fraud as aiding and abetting sedition." Toby suddenly plopped his empty tumbler down on top of the little Queen Anne table beside him and leaned over the arm rest, closer to Seth. "There aren't many things I despise so much as an arrogant ass telling me what I am or am not a part of. I told him I had never been part of any fraud perpetrated against the United States Government, nor to the best of my knowledge had the Calhoons. I demanded proof of his accusations, and when he didn't produce any, I told him to get out of my office."

"And he left?"

"He'd have been back, I'm sure, but his unwanted presence in our midst was thankfully short-lived, and no, it was not me that made that so."

"You come across as protective of the Calhoons. Do they need protecting?"

"Under the present conditions, yes, but not because they're

guilty. They need protection because of a perception of guilt and an absence of justice."

"Calhoon more so than his sister?"

"Not if someone were to make a case for their having conspired together to kill the man."

Seth's stomach tensed. "Could you give me a motive for their having done such a thing?"

With a deep breath, Tobias Holbein rose from his chair and refilled his tumbler. "Why, I assume that would be the bastard's exposing whatever fraud we supposedly perpetrated against the United States Government."

"And you don't know what that was supposed to have been?"

"We participated in no fraud, Parker. I would venture to say that the only malfeasance conducted against the United States Government was perpetrated by its own members in league with the same."

The Negress Irene stuck her head in the door. "Me and Fancy done got suppa on da table, Mr. Toby. Y'all bes' come on befo' it gits col'. Didn't know'd you'd be bringin' home comp'ny. We ain't got da heat goin'."

Seth tipped his tumbler to his lips. The whiskey burned, warming him. "Just so you know, Treasury agents are en route from Washington to assume the Guthrie investigation."

Toby rose. "You've been my only surprise over the last two months, Major. I've expected Treasury from the start. Do you think you'll manage to keep yourself involved?"

$\mathcal{S}$eth mulled it all over as he lay beneath the clean sheets in Tobias Holbein's dark back bedroom and listened to a steady rain on the cedar shingles overhead. This piece and that, laying it all out in his head, forcing it to fit, tearing it apart and starting over. Naomi Polk's murder of Laura and her subsequent recruitment of Jon Franklin to help her eliminate the Calhoons. Franklin's murder, Sam Caruthers' reaction to the name Trueblood, and that 1836 right-of-way that proved Sam Caruthers needed not only Muscatine but also Camellia Creek if he was going to resurrect his old railroad, already superseded by a more efficient, albeit defunct, route. Caruthers' line simply didn't work from a good business standpoint, but did work if the objective was to surreptitiously drive Eli Calhoon off Camellia Creek. Then there was Holbein's knowing all along that Guthrie had been looking for the Calhoons. How did the fraud, which Guthrie referenced, fit with that old charter or was the railroad even related at all? And most importantly, how much did Rebecca Mackey know of Alan Guthrie's reason for being here and his subsequent death?

Chapter Twenty-six

"Colonel thinks Treasury is going to take the Guthrie case," Seth told Jubal Summers in finishing his summation of his trips to Madison, Hinds, Warren, and even down to Jefferson County.

Seth had left Holbein's home before sunrise and ridden back to Port Gibson under a gray sky. It was a little after nine now. The sun was trying to break through, and the temperature was dropping with the clearing of the skies.

Jubal was in the office when he got here, but he'd had little to report. Calhoon appeared to be getting stronger, despite the cleaning out of an abscess over a week ago, and Jubal had given Isabel Hays permission to move the bedroom furniture from Naomi Polk's house to Camellia Creek. Spain and Daws had helped. Jubal had been present at the Port Gibson end throughout the loading.

"What's gonna happen to us if Treasury does take it?" Jubal asked.

"We've still got the Franklin murder to deal with."

"That's nothin'."

"I don't know why you would say that. Franklin was to meet a well-known state politician friendly to the national government the evening he was killed."

"According to you, there's no tie between Guthrie and that Mr. Caruthers, and there's no tie between Franklin and Guthrie."

"None that we can see. That's why we investigate."

"The only thing we've accomplished with all this investigating is to lose our jobs."

"And where, Captain, do you think we'd be right now if we'd arrested Calhoon a month ago on Laura Blackledge's word?"

"A man would be waitin' trial instead of laid up with a gun-shot in his belly, and we wouldn't be regarded as incompetent."

Seth's gut knotted. "Is that what you think? Calhoon would already be tried and in prison or hanged, and someone would have probably gotten away with God-only-knows what."

"What does it matter as long as we got the killer? We're not supposed to be worryin' about what somebody else is gettin' away with. The government wanted a murderer caught, not for us to be speculatin' on a bunch of reasons why we shouldn't catch him."

"Such as not having enough evidence to arrest him, much less put him on trial?"

"The evidence we had went against him," Jubal said, louder than necessary. "There wasn't anything else. I don't know how you figure things the way you do, like you think somebody back in Washington is plotting to hang a Southern traitor for no reason."

"That Southern traitor could be a convenience."

"Guthrie was lookin' for him. Guthrie found him. He killed Guthrie."

It wasn't just what Jubal was saying, but the way he was saying it. Seth wasn't sure what to make of the man's hostility. Maybe he did feel Seth had let them all down. "Colonel Byrnes was hoping for a catalyst to provoke Treasury to show its hand. Coming up with a scapegoat to fit Treasury's need would have been playing into their hands. Why," Seth asked, "was Guthrie looking for Calhoon? And what would have compelled Calhoon to kill him?"

"The way I'm seein' it, the whys don't matter. Lookin' more and more like Army's wantin' Calhoon to walk free just to oppose the Federal government."

Seth had planned on sharing Malcolm's thoughts on the ongoing push-pull between Treasury and the military for control of intelligence assets, but he was fast coming to the conclusion that might do more harm than good. He and Jubal were working toward different goals, and Seth realized, Jubal not only didn't see the big picture, he wasn't interested in seeing it...or hell, maybe he did, and the picture he saw was opposite the one Seth was looking at. "Daws and Zachary still out at Camellia Creek?" he asked.

"Yes. Spain's here and the provost has put the others to work. Seems like we should at least be findin' more cotton thieves."

"That's the provost's job. Ours is to find Guthrie's killer."

"Instead we're investigatin' railroads and protectin' Southern slave owners."

"Not relevant, Captain. What does Hemple have my men doing?"

"Peters is servin' as a clerk. The rest are being used as runners or doin' whatever comes up."

He'd realized early on Malcolm had given him too many men, but he knew better than to give them back. Once that happened they'd have been gone for good. There wasn't much in the way of sympathy among seniors for a mid-level officer stupid enough to voluntarily give up assets. But he well knew that Don Hemple was short of men, so his were being gainfully employed and kept out of trouble, so to hell with their not having made an ill-advised arrest.

"I need to talk to Cummings, and so you know, the 60th will be gone by the end of next month, as will six of our men. We need to get the troops together in the next couple of days and let them know. The two remaining won't be far behind. This thing about Treasury is between you and me for right now."

"And we're done with the Guthrie murder?"

"I'm not done with either Guthrie or Franklin until the United States Army tells me we are to stand down."

And he might not be done then.

"Naomi Polk?" Poynter Cummings repeated, then smiled.

"Yep, Isabel Hays says it was her handwriting, and Caruthers confirmed to me that he'd met with Jon Franklin. Holbein didn't seem surprised either that she would have been the one to approach Jon Franklin and drop Caruthers' name."

"Holbein thinks the Polk woman approached Jon Franklin with information regarding Caruthers' railroad?"

"He doesn't think it would have happened the other way around," Seth clarified. "As far as he's concerned, Naomi Polk initiated the plot."

"How well did Holbein know Franklin?"

"I would assume not very. He drew his assessment from that one time Franklin approached him wanting an introduction to Caruthers." Seth blew out a quick breath. "Unless Isabel Hays was involved in that, too."

"So your question is?"

"How did Naomi Polk know to approach Franklin? She had to have known he was interested in contacting Sam Caruthers."

Cummings nodded in apparent agreement. "Or that he was interested in contacting somebody who could help him realize his ambitions. That was Franklin's goal when he got here last summer." He held up an index finger. "I think Laura and Jon Franklin may have known each other."

"Why do you say that?"

"The day after Laura asked me where to find you, Jon Franklin visited. Like I told you a couple of weeks ago, he and I shared information periodically. His amounted to little more than gossip he picked up, normally through his associations over in Rodney. In return, I would bring him up to date on my cotton-thieving investigation. It was my opinion at the time he was considering getting in, and I warned him the market was already cornered by men who would not welcome his presence. But Franklin was one of those young fellas who knows more than everybody else, if you understand my meaning. Anyway, in the spirit of cooperation, I told him about the find over at the Ferris place, which I was getting ready to put in print anyway, and I told him about Laura Blackledge coming to see me the day before. The implication was, of course, that he'd try and confirm she had been your source."

"Did he?"

"He didn't come to see me after that. Now that I think about that, maybe I'd become unnecessary, and he no longer required my services."

"But Jon Franklin's interest in Guthrie predated that, correct?"

"A little bit, yes." Cummings eyed Seth beneath veiled lids. "Laura was your source, wasn't she?"

"Yeah, and Naomi Polk killed her."

Cummings quickly sat forward in his seat. "And that's a bone I'd like to pick with you, Parker. I found out that little tidbit from the sheriff. Seems you forgot to mention that the morning after the rampage at Camellia Creek."

Seth stretched his legs in front of him before bending his knees and rising. "Must have slipped my mind with everything else going on.

"But think on this, Cummings, since you're such a good thinker anyway. Try to come up with a reason, other than Naomi Polk's claim that she was protecting Eli Calhoon from Laura, as to why she would have wanted the woman dead?"

Chapter Twenty-seven

"Caruthers admitted having met with Jon Franklin," Seth told Isabel. They were standing near Calhoon's desk in the study at Camellia Creek. She hadn't sat, so he didn't either. "Tobias Holbein was the intermediary. Jon wouldn't tell him who had given him the name. We now know, of course, it was Naomi Polk."

"You've talked to Toby?"

"Yes, he confirmed everything and didn't seem surprised that Naomi had been the person to send Jon to him."

"No, he wouldn't have been, certainly not in retrospect. Toby and Holland were close friends, and Holland had told him plenty about Naomi over the years. She was quite extraordinary in her behavior, and I do not mean to imply that in a good way." Isabel raised one shoulder. "Though she certainly wasn't all bad."

Seth frowned.

"She was an exceptional cook, homemaker. She mastered every form of needlecraft and sewing one could imagine. She managed the making of scented soaps. Two of Camellia Creek's slaves helped her and they sold them in the market, and she provided them a generous percentage. She had quite a little factory going back in the early fifties." Isabel smiled. "Dora and Ophie kept it going after Naomi went to live in town."

"Did she continue to take a percentage?"

"Not as far as I know, and neither did Holland. They were his slaves. Got to the point they could cover the overhead, and they kept the profit." She sauntered to the vicinity of the settee he'd moved in front of the desk this morning. "Did you mention me to Sam?" she asked.

"I think I got across to him whatever subtle message you intended."

She smiled. "I do appreciate that. Did you ask him if he knew Guthrie?"

"Said he'd never met the man. Caruthers did confirm he was interested in building that railroad he proposed back in '36. According to him, the railroad was the reason Franklin contacted him."

"And your impression of what he thought of Franklin's interest?"

The sound of children's voices distracted him, then he said, "I can tell you, without a doubt in my mind, that he didn't think much of it. According to Caruthers, Jon wanted a place on the board."

Isabel chuckled, and looked around him, out the window. "That does so sound like dear, foolish Jon."

He turned to the bank of windows that looked out on the dark surface of ancient Lake Elizabeth, well in front of the house. Two children were advancing down the gentle slope toward the water, one perhaps five or six, the other a toddler. The older was white, the baby he wasn't sure. Both were bundled against the cold and followed closely by a Negress, dressed in black.

"My daughter's niece, Eliza, and the baby of Eliza's mammy."

"The woman with them?"

"Mattie, Eliza's mother's mammy. The baby's Pearl. Her mother was Bea. She died of fever when Pearl was two weeks old. Eliza will not let Pearl out of her sight."

Indeed, Eliza, head down, held to the stumbling Pearl's hand and appeared to be talking to the baby incessantly. Then Eliza stopped short and watched Jubal Summers and Corporal Peters cross the bridge at the north end of the lake. Peters waved to them, and Eliza waved back. Seth had told Jubal to gather up Peters and bring him to Camellia Creek as soon as Don Hemple could let him go. Seth meant to replace him with Daws. Both men could stand relief from present duties.

The older child dropped the baby's hand and turned to

Mattie, who bent to listen. After a moment, the old woman shook her head and straightened, and the older girl again reached for the baby.

"The niece," he said, "does she have an aversion to Negro troops?"

"Aversion?"

He turned and looked at Isabel watching him now from the settee, where she'd finally sat while his back was turned.

"Does she have some reason to be afraid of them?"

"Blue uniforms, most definitely, but not Negro troops per se. To the best of my knowledge there were none there that day."

"What day?"

"The day a troop of Union soldiers made a not-so-polite visit to the home of Thomas Mackey, who reputedly had a stockpile of baled cotton in his barn, at least a dozen good horses, and two sons in Confederate service." Isabel smiled. "Johnston had already relieved Thomas of his horses and the cotton had been removed to safer climes, and both his sons were dead. Indeed, Thomas himself had succumbed to sickness and grief a fortnight before their visit. But both his daughters-in-law were there as were Eliza and the slaves. Some of those noble soldiers decided to avail themselves of Bea, who was young and pretty and of mixed blood. She'd been collecting eggs when they arrived unannounced. Three of them dragged her into the barn. Emily, Becky's sister-in-law, would have none of that and decided to put a stop to it. She used rather poor judgment in grabbing Thomas' scatter gun before leaving the big house." Isabel gave him a sad smile. "She was a fiery girl, Luke Mackey's Emily. Becky went with her. They left by the back door as the lieutenant in charge of the group entered the front, back from his fruitless search for horses and cotton.

"I don't know the full details of what happened in the barn, but I do know that Emily fired both barrels, killing one and wounding another of the rapists before being shot herself. Becky was pregnant"—Seth felt the color drain from his cheeks—"she was roughly handled. She doesn't talk about it."

"Becky was going to have a baby?"

Isabel narrowed her eyes on him. "Yes, six months along. One of the more humane members of the troop retrieved her from the fray. The lieutenant managed to regain order. Given Emily's use of armed offense, in defense of Bea, the lieutenant burned the main house and outbuildings. Emily was grievously wounded and left in the care of her servants. Becky was arrested and taken to Vicksburg. Emily died later that same day. It was eight days before I was able to retrieve Rebecca from where they ultimately confined her." Isabel held his gaze. "She was no longer pregnant when she was brought to me. She'd gone into labor. The baby was stillborn, a boy. He'd have carried the Mackey name. She wasn't even allowed to recover his tiny body."

Seth, mute and numb, remained standing.

Isabel cleared her throat. "If we've exhausted the subject of my daughter and her wards, might we return to the reason you asked me in here?"

He opened his mouth to speak, then frowned. Isabel said, "Jon's desire to be a member of Sam's board of directors."

"Ah, yes. You say he was foolish, Isabel, but no one could be so foolish as to think Sam Caruthers would place an investor on his board who had nothing to invest."

"Not even Jon, I'm sure. But if you're asking me if I know what he offered Sam, I cannot tell you."

Still reeling from what he'd learned about Rebecca, Seth walked back to the desk and pulled out the swivel chair. "Have you ever heard the name Martin Trueblood?"

"I have not. Who is he?"

"He worked at headquarters during the war, in contraband and confiscated property. I found evidence in Jackson that he also had an interest in Sam Caruthers' old railroad. Caruthers knew him and seemed perturbed when I informed him Trueblood had been researching that old right-of-way."

"That's understandable. Did you ask Toby about him?"

"He says he never heard of him either."

Seth thought of Captain Shuler's mention of the young

widow who'd been looking for Trueblood. If Isabel were aware Rebecca had made inquiries about the man, she surely would have known Trueblood's name. He started to persist, then decided against it. Trueblood he'd save for Becky.

He rose, she didn't. "Speaking of Holbein, he mentioned he'd been up here. I assume you sent word to him."

"I informed him that Eli had been seriously wounded. He's a close friend of the Calhoons."

"So I've always understood. Still, I couldn't help but wonder if you didn't have an additional reason for wanting to talk to him, such as informing him of Naomi Polk's note in Jon Franklin's pocket."

She smiled. "I'm sure he mentioned we discussed it."

Seth smiled in return, but not as pleasantly. "Did the two of you agree beforehand on what you'd tell me?"

"Why, Major, you lead me to believe you think we are conspiring against you."

"Well, I'll tell you this, it is the belief of my immediate senior that Treasury intends to take the Guthrie murder case out of Army's hands. If that proves true, your situation might become more uncomfortable."

"Is that to imply the United States Army isn't cooperating with the government on this matter?"

His thoughts jumped to Jubal, but he immediately pushed the implication aside. "I believe you might find me the lesser of two evils," he said.

She rose. "But an evil nonetheless. Let's see what happens after the operative arrives."

It was the matter-of-fact way she said those words, cool and composed, not harried, or even doubtful. And the choice of the word "operative" gave her away. Like Holbein, she wasn't surprised by Treasury's action. Maybe they wanted Treasury on the case, maybe they had friends there. Seth leaned back on the desk.

"I hear Calhoon is doing better."

"Getting stronger every day. Dr. Lester thinks the danger of more infection has passed. Eli can move all his limbs. He pees in a pan, eats broth from a bowl...well, actually someone, usually Alice, spoon-feeds him. He's starting to complain about that, the broth I mean, not being spoon-fed."

"Ah yes, a growing disdain for broth is always a good sign. He's speaking and thinking coherently?"

"For short periods."

Seth furrowed his brow, and Isabel clarified, "He tires easily."

"Has he been out of bed?"

"No. He can move, but the rib and that fractured pelvis hurt him quite a bit. He's yet to put weight on his right leg. And he's still sleeping a lot, but part of that is the laudanum."

"I'd like to talk to him."

"You'll need to speak to his primary nurse and mother of his unborn child, but since you are now considered a hero around here, I doubt that will be a problem."

Chapter Twenty-eight

Seth found the newly arrived Jubal Summers and Peters out in back of the kitchen with Frank Zachary, and he took a seat beside Jubal on the kitchen stoop's next-to-bottom step. Peters sidled closer to Zachary, and Seth heard something about coffee.

"Go on round by the mud porch," Seth said. He didn't want to maneuver out of the way of men climbing up and down the steps. "And tell Daws to leave Aunt Elvie alone and get out here." His men were driving the poor woman crazy always asking for something special. They were worse than kids.

The corporal grinned at Zachary, then started toward the front of the cookhouse. Frank Zachary stepped closer to the two men sitting on the stoop. "I'm gonna try for some collards."

"You better find her some. She tells me y'all are eating the Calhoons out of house and home."

"These people can afford food," Jubal said.

"It's not the paying for it. It's the finding it."

"Their nigger workers think so much of them, they can scrounge some up."

Seth declined comment. "You think your patient can live without you now?" he asked Zachary, "'cause I got a job for you."

"Doc's thinkin' he's gonna pull through."

Someone started to open the kitchen door above and behind them, but a quick shout caused it to shut again. Moments later Seth heard his two corporals on the mud porch. A chill wind followed the two of them around the kitchen's west corner.

He had them all now, his captain and his senior enlisted

"I received word from Colonel Byrnes a couple of days ago that the 60th will be decommissioned by the end of next month."

He looked at Zachary. "That includes you and Peters. We need to be gatherin' information as to benefits and options for the men. I'd like to brief them in a couple of days."

"Freedmen's Bureau is the place to go," Jubal said.

"What if we want to stay in the army?" Peters asked.

"I asked about that. Right now that is not an option. All the Negro units will be disbanded by the end of the summer, but there's a proposal afoot to form Negro units to fight the Indians in the west."

Daws snorted. "Injuns still burn people alive?"

"Not s'posed to get yo'se'f captured," Peters said.

"An' how you s'posed to keep dat from happ'nin' if you out-numbered an' surrounded?"

"Die fightin'."

Cup of coffee in hand, Daws looked at Peters. "Ain't much of a choice if ya ask me."

"You just survived a war," Jubal said.

"Ain't no Reb boys sayin' dey was gonna burn me alive."

"Injuns ain't either," the sergeant said. "We'll get whatcha need, Majah, to gib' da men some thoughts on what to do nex'."

A child's voice drew their attention to the east corner of the cookhouse. A moment later, the little girl he'd seen by the lake, her tiny charge in tow, emerged around the building. The black mammy and—his heart thumped—Rebecca Mackey followed. The older girl, Eliza was her name, saw them. She stopped dead still, then dropping the baby's hand, she covered her mouth, as quickly uncovered it, and cried out. "I *knew* it was you. I just knew it!" And Rebecca's eyes widened as the little person rushed forward on a beeline for Jubal Summers. Before Jubal realized what was happening, little hands had grasped his. "Jim!" the girl said. Eyes brimming, she twisted her head and looked at Becky, rushing up to them. "It is Jim. He's come home."

"No, dearest, it's—"

"I knew," she said, her high-pitched voice filled with excite-ment, "when I saw him on the bridge it was Jim." She looked back at a dumbstruck Jubal, his own large hands still captured.

"No," Rebecca said, forcing Eliza's fingers from Jubal's thumbs.

"No, no, Aunt Becky," the girl cried, her voice just short of a wail. Again the small hands grasped Jubal's, and Seth knew the man was fighting the urge to shake the child off. "It's him, it's Jim"—her lips began to quiver and now a thread of doubt tinged her voice. She turned to Becky. "Look at him."

"Eliza, darling," Becky said, squatting beside the child. "You look at him. He's in a Yankee uniform. Your daddy's Jim would not be wearing a Yankee uniform."

The girl, her bright eyes blinking back tears now, turned back to Jubal Summers. She raised her palm and laid it against his jaw, and he lifted his head to escape her touch, then he stilled and let her touch him. With her free hand, she wiped a tear from her cheek. "The Yankees stole him, the ones that killed Daddy." She looked at Seth, accusation in her eyes and in her tone.

"Naw, young missy," Daws, who now stood with one booted foot on the porch step, said. "He be from New Yawk. Was me dem Yankees stole."

"Daws," Seth reprimanded quietly.

The little face looked from Daws to him, then back to Jubal and finally, chin puckering, she twisted back around to Becky.

"Jim is with your daddy in heaven, darling, now let this man be." Miss Rebecca's voice was becoming a bit strained with emotion, too, Seth noted. He hadn't taken his eyes off her.

The little girl stepped back.

"What do you say?"

"I'm sorry," the child, barely able to speak now, said to Jubal. She balled a fist and swiped away a tear.

Now, Seth watched Jubal Summers, despiser of all things he perceived Southern, swallow hard. "It's all right."

"It's time for Pearl's nap, sweetheart," Becky said, rubbing Eliza's back and rising to her feet. "Go help Mattie."

The girl, head down, nodded, turned, and ran behind Becky. She took the hand of quiet Mattie, who waited, eyes glistening.

"I do apologize for my niece, Captain. Jim was her father's

body servant. They'd been together since shirtwaist. They died together in Virginia."

Jubal nodded. "No harm done," he said, but Seth wasn't so sure. Talk about being able to push someone down with a feather. Jubal Summers would have fallen hard enough to shake the earth to its core.

Becky smiled quickly and dimples appeared on her cheeks. "You do look like him. Amazing she remembers him so well. She hasn't"—her voice broke, and she raised her hem of black crepe and turned from them—"she was so little when last she saw him."

Chapter Twenty-nine

Becky and Mattie got both girls down. Pearl was ready, and Eliza, who was almost seven and rarely napped anymore, lay down beside her. The child hadn't spoken a word since leaving the men on the stoop.

Eliza had been four when she'd last seen her mother and father, but she retained sweet memories and often spoke of them. She hadn't cried for them in a long time, implying she accepted she would never see them again. This appearance of a man she'd been so certain was Jim Washington, only to learn it wasn't him, had crushed her, saddened Mattie, and left Becky fraught with emotion. Overwrought, Becky had swiped at an errant tear of her own, then brushed a kiss against Eliza's temple before retiring to her room downstairs to make up for lost sleep.

She woke groggy from a two-hour nap and almost stepped on Cassie Franklin, squatting on the floor between the dining room table and the cherry sideboard Rosalind Polk had brought with her from Tennessee when she wed Holland Calhoon. The sideboard was open, and Cassie appeared to be searching it.

"I do apologize," Becky said as Cassie scrambled to her feet.

"No need." Cassie smiled. "I told Alice this is a terrible arrangement of furniture in here, what with the sideboard interfering with the path to the back door."

"It's been this way for as long as I can remember. Can I help you find something?"

Cassie turned back to the table. "Mama thought it would be nice if we ate a late dinner in here. Something more formal.'

"Oh," Becky said, following Cassie's eyes to the scarred table. A covered basket sat in the middle of it and Becky wondered...

"Mama baked them early this morning. When you spelled her at two, she couldn't get to sleep. She hoped she'd be in and out of the kitchen before Miss Elvie woke, but she wasn't. Miss Elvie was none too pleased to find her in there at dawn. Oh, she didn't say anything, mind you, but Mama could tell by the slamming of doors and banging of pots."

"I fear we have a bigger problem than Aunt Elvie, who we can probably just ignore until one of us gets caught in a slamming door or hit by a pot. I don't know that we've enough place settings here —"

"Oh, we do. Alice's things are here." Cassie waved a hand toward the open sideboard. "They belonged to my Aunt Jenny."

"Alice's mother?"

"Yes, but I apologize. Mama just told me to go set the table. Alice is so preoccupied with Eli, we thought it wouldn't matter to her one way or the other, but perhaps we should have consulted you or Miss Isabel first."

Becky thought for a moment Cassie might be putting forth a slight given Becky's earlier question, but Cassie conveyed only honest apology.

"Not at all. This is Alice's home now, and if your mother thinks we can put together a proper sit-down dinner, I'm certainly not opposed."

Cassie gave her a quick smile and shut the door to the sideboard, allowing Becky to slip past. "Do you think you could say something to soothe Miss Elvie?"

Becky nodded, for what that was worth, and stepped onto the mud porch. The chilly morning had given way to a relatively warm and blustery afternoon. She might have dismissed Cassie's hope-filled question regarding Betty Franklin and Aunt Elvie's intransigence regarding the woman's attempts to use Elvie's kitchen, and Becky had little interest in sitting down to a semi-formal meal in the dark dining room, but bringing some order to this place wasn't a bad idea, and getting to know Alice's female relations appealed.

The back door squeaked when she opened it. Betty Franklin,

on tiptoes, was looking out the partially boarded east window. "Zachary and that Negro captain are down by the lake with those two little girls," she said. "I wonder where the nanny is? I don't think it's a good idea for those children to be alone with them."

Becky moved up behind Mrs. Franklin, who turned and saw her. "Oh, I thought you were Cassie."

"What are they doing?" Becky said, straining to see out the upper half of the dirty window.

"Skipping rocks on the water, it appears to me."

"Yes," Becky said, spying them. "Sergeant Zachary appears to be adept at it." She let loose a little laugh as Eliza's attempt arched in a loop and plopped in the lake. Pearl, watching contentedly, stood at Eliza's side. Captain Summers then made an attempt, not a very successful one, and Eliza stepped toward him apparently offering guidance. As bad as Summers' throw had been, it was certainly better than Eliza's, and judging from his mannerisms, he appeared to be pointing that out.

Betty Franklin turned from the window. "Your girls were in here earlier when Major Parker's men were eating. Eliza has taken a shine to Captain Summers."

"How was he with her?"

"Affable enough, I guess. I do think the men left to escape her pestering, but she followed them out, dragging the little one behind her. I swear Eliza thinks he's some sort of folk hero."

Becky turned to the woman. Her words had been frankly spoken, but Becky heard the censure in them.

"I'm surprised you're not concerned," the woman finished.

"Captain Summers reminds Eliza of someone she loves, Mrs. Franklin. Someone who showed her how to hold a newborn kitten, how to suck honeysuckle, and how to pick ripe blackberries without stepping on a copperhead."

"Surely there were other men in her life."

"There were, but they didn't come back to her. Jim did, at least that's what she thought when she first laid eyes on Captain Summers. He's revived a precious memory, and she's clinging to it." Becky turned back to the window. Zachary had moved over to Summers and was now demonstrating his expert throwing technique. "She's a loving and friendly child. I'll have to drag her away from him or she'll wear his patience thin."

"I believe that's a good idea. Negro men are known to show undue interest in white women."

Surprised less by the comment than its unexpected source, Becky said, "I've heard that, but I've never experienced such interest, and I've spent a great deal of my life around Negro men. I think it's probably a rumor put forth by white men who lust after colored women."

"Oh?" Betty Franklin said, her eyes widening a fraction. "That's a unique perspective."

Becky didn't understand why anyone would consider that thought unique. Since the sexual exploits of the white master and his female slaves made up a titillating portion of abolitionist propaganda, she figured Betty Franklin must have found fault in Becky's conclusion that it was a "white man's rumor."

"Oh, Mama"—Becky and Betty Franklin turned as one—"men like women, and women like men. It's no more complicated than that. It's the very differences in the two races that appeals to some in the same way that it's the differences in the genders that attract." Cassie Franklin gave her mother a knowledgeable look and stepped through the door, but didn't close it. Someone was coming up behind her.

"That is absurd, Cassie," her mother snapped. "There is a big difference in the attraction between genders and that of races. Those are two completely different things. One is natural, the other is not, and you are wrong in assuming otherwise. And in this case we are talking about a child."

"Mama, one might be natural, the other is not even relevant."

Betty Franklin opened her mouth, then shut it as Seth Parker filled the open doorway. He acknowledged all three women with a nod, then settled his gaze on Becky. If he'd heard Cassie's candid remarks, he gave no indication.

"Mrs. Mackey," Parker said, "could I speak with you?"

As much as she detested Northern hypocrisy and reveled in

Yankee ignorance, she preferred Betty Franklin's thoughts on the Negro male's unrestrained libido to being "spoken to" by Seth Parker. What could he want? Besides, with Cassie's input, their discussion had been shaping up to be a lively one.

"Mattie's on the front porch, Mrs. Franklin," Becky said, at the same time averting her eyes from Parker's. "For Captain Summers' sake, I'll send her down to gather the girls. Eliza can be trying."

*S*eth watched Becky, a question on her pretty face, brush past him and onto the breezeway separating the house and kitchen. He closed the kitchen door and turned to her. "I'd like to talk to you about your Aunt Naomi."

"Aunt Naomi?"

"It's you or your brother, and Alice tells me he's still not up to lengthy discussions."

From what Seth had gathered, Becky was more or less raised in this house. Odds were good she knew as much or more than Calhoon himself regarding Naomi Polk's relationship with the family.

A gust of wind caused her dress to billow and whipped a strand of hair across her face. The scent of lilac filled his senses. She brushed the hair out of her eyes and hugged her free arm to her waist. It occurred to Seth she'd rather not talk to him, but that would have more to do with him than the subject. "It relates to your brother's shooting, and the murder of Jon Franklin." There were other things, too, he planned to discuss with her

She didn't say yes, and she didn't say no, but when he said, "Let's get someplace warmer," and started toward the back door, she followed. In the dining room, the table was set.

"Are you certain Aunt Naomi's shooting Eli wasn't an accident?" she asked.

"I was there, remember? I can assure you that the bullet that hit your brother was meant for Alice, but tell me this, what would your brother have done if the woman had shot Alice?"

When she didn't respond, he said, "My opinion is that if he

hadn't killed your aunt on the spot, he'd have seen her hanged, and surely she realized that. She had to be planning on killing him, too."

"But why?" she asked, then stopped in the foyer and turned on him. "Let me speak to Mattie. I'll meet you in 'your' office."

She didn't like that, he supposed, his taking the liberty of confiscating her father's, now brother's, study for his own use.

"I did request a working space from Alice, if you must know," he told her moments later when she followed him into the room.

"I have no doubt."

"Would you like to sit?" he asked, nodding to the settee in front of the plantation desk. "You look like you're about to drop."

"I just rose from a nap, but thank you."

He pulled out his chair and swore he was gonna sit whether she did or not. "Sit," he said, then added, "please, so I can."

She did.

"Your husband has been dead going on three years, why are you still in widow's weeds?"

"Because I'm still mourning."

"And you dyed all your dresses black, or is it your only one?"

"Is there some point to these questions?"

"From what I've seen of her, I believe your mother would pro—"

"My mother respects my wishes to bide my time and discourage anyone from assuming I am ready to return to society, or what's left of it."

He studied her a long moment, then sat himself. "Tell me about your Aunt Naomi."

"She was Eli's aunt, his mother's half sister. She assumed the running of the household when Eli's mother, Rosalind, died. She was very efficient, but also domineering and meddlesome. I spent a good part of my life here. Mama was here often, too. She, Mama, I mean, had a room next to Daddy's. My mother and Aunt Naomi tolerated each other, you could say, but I knew Aunt Naomi didn't approve of Daddy's relationship with my mother."

"Did she say so to you?"

"I only know of her saying anything once, when I was very small. Apparently it was meant to be offensive to me. I don't recall what she said, because I didn't understand it. She said it in the kitchen. Only her and us kids were there. Andrew, who was older, and did understand, told Daddy, who had a talk with her."

"How did she treat you?"

"No different than she treated Hannah. She was not a loving person. She rarely showed affection, but was quick to scold and spank. She didn't have a lot of patience, but she took care of our material needs." Seth caught the hint of a smile on Becky's face. "When one of us was sick, she'd go to the quarter and find Aunt Elvie and bring her back to the house. Supposedly, that was because Aunt Elvie knew all the old folk medicines, but I believe it was primarily because Aunt Naomi couldn't deal with the sick, especially a sick child.

"Aunt Naomi was partial to the men in this house, Daddy, Andrew, and Eli. I liken it to her regarding Daddy as the king and Andy and Eli the heirs apparent. I don't think that was particularly unusual, at least not in Southern homes, but she doted on Daddy to the point of fawning. I don't think he would have minded so much if he had liked her more. Thinking back, there were probably other things I wasn't aware of. She offered unsolicited advice on subjects that really were of no concern to her. She had to have her own way, if you understand what I mean, but she had a sneaky way of getting it, leaving her as the root of discord, but often hard to pinpoint why.

"Hannah was almost two years older than me. When she was fourteen, Daddy suggested Aunt Naomi teach her to help with the house. I know for certain Hannah put him up to it. Aunt Naomi had isolated all the house slaves against her. Even Aunt Elvie, who'd been Rosalind Calhoon's personal servant and had remained a mammy to us children for years after Rosalind died, asked to return to the fields.

"A point of contention was always the kitchen. Aunt Naomi constantly interfered there. There was no reason for it. Camellia Creek had a good cook."

"She planned the meals?"

"It was one thing to plan a meal and ensure all the proper ingredients were available to those required to make them, but Aunt Naomi paid less attention to stocking and more to the cooking—particularly when the cook couldn't find the necessary accoutrements to complete the meal. For that, she always blamed the cook. Of course, everyone knew who was at fault. She was petty and interfering. That's just how she was. Andy used to say the cook would end up poisoning her one day."

"Was she abusive to the slaves?" He only asked to validate what Isabel had implied regarding the soap makers.

"Not usually, Daddy wouldn't allow that. And I don't know that she would have been anyway. However, the incident that finally propelled him to move her out of this house was when Hannah and Dolly, the cook, conspired to bake a lemon cake for Daddy's birthday without Aunt Naomi's knowledge. Dolly used the last of the lemon extract, and when Aunt Naomi learned of it she threw a hissy fit. It takes weeks to make the stuff. She ended up hitting Dolly with a wooden spoon. It was no more temper than she at times had used on us kids, but in Dolly's case, Aunt Naomi brought blood—busted her lip. Aunt Naomi excused the strike by saying Dolly had back-talked her. All Dolly really said was that she'd done what Hannah told her to.

"It was the last straw. Aunt Naomi may have been partial to the princes, but Daddy doted on his princesses. I do believe Hannah, very much her mother's daughter according to Aunt Elvie, knew how unhappy Aunt Naomi's presence made Daddy and she'd decided to replace her." Becky looked away wistfully. "Hannah was her daddy's girl and Aunt Naomi's bane for as long as I can remember. Aunt Naomi had fallen right into Hannah's trap when she hit Dolly, and Hannah told Daddy there was room for only one woman running this house."

Seth considered Hannah might well have shared some disagreeable traits with her Aunt Naomi.

"That's when your father moved Naomi to the house in Port Gibson?"

"Ten or more years ago, yes, but she was still here often. She acted as if what had happened were the natural course of things, that Hannah's ascension would be short-lived, as indeed it was."

"She wed?"

"When she was sixteen she went to a girls' school in Noxubee County. She didn't wed until the summer of 1859. Two years before that, Andrew had married Laura Ménier—"

"Your brother Eli's first love."

He saw her bridle slightly and regretted interrupting her. "There was some suspicion," he said, "that your brother had murdered her. Did you not know that?"

"You thought Eli *strangled* Laura?" She was gaping at him, and her not having known did surprise him somewhat.

"As opposed to shooting or knifing her?"

"Well, yes. Strangulation is so..., well, personal."

"As one might assume their relationship had been."

"Eli would have never killed her in that way." She shook her head. "He'd have never killed her in any way. But strangulation is absurd. Why would you have ever—"

"Rebecca, it is my opinion, speaking as a man, strangulation is the perfect crime of passion in terminating an intimate relationship with a treacherous or even difficult woman."

She was staring at him. "You would condone such a thing?"

"Which is why I did not arrest your brother at the time."

Her mouth fell open, and he laughed.

"That isn't funny!"

"And it's a moot point. Your Aunt Naomi confessed to Alice that she killed Laura."

"Hardly moot if you are in agreement with such executions."

Perhaps that flippant remark about his not having arrested Eli 'at the time' had been in poor taste. He certainly regretted it now, because he hadn't planned on getting hung up on a silly indiscretion. He leaned forward and brought his head over the desk closer to her. "I was teasing you. I do not condone strangling a woman, no matter how much she may deserve it. Now can you think of why your aunt would have wanted Laura dead?"

"She told Alice that Laura had accused Eli of killing Wayne Hale."

"The afternoon your brother was shot, your aunt tried to convince me of the same thing, and she said he had killed Laura to silence her. When I didn't get too excited at the thought he would have feared retribution in the killing of Hale, she brought up Laura's knowing he'd been involved in the Alan Guthrie murder."

He watched her eyes when he said Guthrie's name.

"The man from Treasury?"

"Yes, so it appears she had not only changed her mind in regards to protecting your brother, but was now doing everything she could to get him out of the way."

"Eli had run her off Camellia Creek."

"Would you say she was obsessed with this place?"

"Once I would have said she was obsessed with Daddy. According to what Mama told me, and things Hannah said, I think she considered herself the rightful matriarch of this place after Rosalind Calhoon died, that Camellia Creek's men belonged to her. It sounds sick, doesn't it?" She narrowed her eyes on him. "Not unlike the passionate strangling of women."

"I didn't mean it that way, and you know it. Now, from what you've told me regarding Naomi's obsession with the male line of this family—I can't help but question her motives for betraying your brother."

"He rejected her totally."

"So did your father. That didn't prove a deterrent. You yourself just said she considered that particular exile would be short-lived."

Becky gave her head a small shake. "In Daddy's mind, she always remained family. When Eli threw her off Camellia Creek, he told her never to step foot on this place again."

"You think she believed he would never relent?"

"I think that's possible."

"I think she may have considered him an obstacle."

"She could have never gotten Camellia Creek."

"She might have considered you for elimination also."

"You don't understand. There was no provision for her. She had no rights to this property, no matter who she eliminated."

"And if she'd made an alliance elsewhere?"

"You mean among the powers that be?"

He shrugged.

"Who are you thinking?"

"You tell me."

She set her jaw. "You said this had something to do with the Franklin murder. Who do you think?"

If she were thinking the man who had Muscatine, she wasn't going to tell him so. "I'd hoped," he said, "a good perspective on Naomi Polk would shed some light on Franklin's role in her scheme. For what I'm thinking to hold water, she needed someone to help her. The fabricated love triangle between Franklin, Alice, and your brother is easy to see, and that would have removed both Calhoon and Alice, but with Alice dead, Franklin had nothing to gain, and he had to have known that. Even if your aunt planned on killing Franklin, and I believe she did, she would have had to, at least, offer him something at the start, even if she never intended to pay up. And my next question is how did she come to approach, of all people, him?"

"How did she meet him, you mean?"

"In a manner of speaking."

"I would guess through Laura since she and Jon Franklin were lovers."

"I beg your pardon?"

"That's what Jon told Alice when he attacked her. I'm surprised Alice didn't tell you."

He wasn't. Alice had answered his questions on the morning after the attack, but physically exhausted, in pain, and distracted by her wounded husband she'd responded to his prompts, not analyzed answers to questions of which she was unaware.

"I need to talk to her again."

"Mama's in the room with them now. I know both Alice and Eli are sleeping and you absolutely cannot wake her, but as soon as she's up...." Becky had started to rise.

"That's fine, but I still have some questions for you."

She sat back down and folded her hands in her lap.

"Tell me what you're doing about Muscatine."

Her manner became instantly guarded. "Doing?"

"Your efforts to reclaim it."

"I've been told by persons at the Warren County clerk's office that I require a presidential pardon to get the land back. My mother and brother insist that I do not. Mama believes that Sam Caruthers is behind that requirement, and she has Mr. Holbein working with Mr. Caruthers to return the property to me."

"And why do you think Caruthers wants that land?"

"Mama believes it's for a railroad right-of-way."

"That old 1836 charter requires land that presently makes up part of Camellia Creek, too."

He saw the movement of her throat when she swallowed. "Are you asking me or are you telling me?"

"I'm telling you information I know you already know, and I point this out only because you're not readily sharing it with me."

"Very well, it is my understanding that for him to realize completion of his thirty-year-old-railroad scheme, he needs a part of Camellia Creek."

"And what else?"

"Should I care what else?"

"I don't know if you should care or not, but I think you know that he needs other parcels in Warren, Claiborne, Jefferson, and Adams Counties. He has some already, some he bought outright, some he claims as a loyal citizen. Few such parcels remain in the hands of their original owners. A few of those owners, particularly in Claiborne and Jefferson Counties, have sold portions of their property along the right-of-way to Peter Franklin, your brother for one."

"And what has this to do with me?"

Damn, she was making this hard. "I've turned up another name interested in that old right-of-way. What do you know of a Martin Trueblood?"

She stood abruptly and turned to the door.

"Hold on!"

She did stop. All she would have had to say was the man signed off on her property transfer in the record. She hadn't done that. Now she spun and glared at him.

"I know," he said, "you went to the army personnel office in Vicksburg looking for him. Why?"

She heaved in a breath and stalked back toward him. He rose from behind the desk. "Why did you need him, Rebecca?"

"Do you work for Ralston?"

The vehemence in her voice caught him off guard, and he tensed. "Ralston left last summer."

"Are you Ralston, then?"

"His relief you mean?"

"Whatever the term."

"My immediate senior's name is Malcolm Byrnes. He, like Ralston, is a full colonel, a couple of pay grades above mine. Colonel Byrnes relieved Ralston of his special operations job."

"Special operations? Is that what they call it?"

"That's what it's called now, at least that part of the job that deals with the murder of Federal agents."

"And what do they call the part that deals with the murder of Southern civilians?"

He opened his mouth to speak, but she shoved a palm in his face. "Wait! You don't need to tell me, I can make an educated guess. They called it war didn't they? *War*." Her face twisted. "War would have been bad enough if it had been justified but this war saw fit to murder civilians whose deaths offered no military advantage. Let's think about that. What would be a good term for that? Oh," she said, "how about 'opportunity,' taking advantage of a bad situation—a cover," she growled—"for rapine by a government, who along with its thugs...and its unconstitutional *Union*, can go to hell."

He didn't try to calm her. She was telling him something, despite her story being somewhat confused.

She'd held back the tears for a good part of her diatribe, but now she swiped at her cheeks.

"I wanted to know," she spat out in a staccato cadence, "what this Trueblood knew of the raid made on Camellia Creek in September of 1863, but you've inadvertently answered my real question, and I thank you, sir. And there was something else I wanted from Trueblood, but my telling you is of no value to me, so I'll keep it to myself."

She whirled again and made a beeline for the door.

"I know Alan Guthrie was looking for you the day he was shot," he called after her.

She spun back to look at him.

"You knew that, didn't you?"

Eyes glittering, she stared at him.

"He was looking for your entire family, all of you, Becky, Why?"

"I don't know what he wanted. I don't know what any of you horrible people want, but I know what I want, Major Parker. I want my farm back, and most of all, I want justice for my daddy, for my sister-in-law, and for my baby boy."

Chapter Thirty

Seth didn't try to stop her leaving. She was too upset, he was too confused. He'd been working two murders, which might, just might, relate to one another. Now Rebecca Mackey had presented him a tangential line dotted with cryptic clues. She said he had answered her question regarding Trueblood, but what had he, in return, given her? And her agitation with Ralston? Sweet Jesus. Seth knew enough about counter operations during the war to leave his blood cold. He pondered her incarceration in Vicksburg and her lost baby, and he chilled with realization.

Head high, Becky walked briskly past the pleasantly set table and out the back door, praying she crossed paths with no one before she got away from the house. No matter how high her head, how proud her chin, her eyes would give her away.

She didn't even think about a coat, and in the yard a balmy breeze whipped her skirt and tore at her hair. When the kitchen was a good ten yards behind her, she began to run against the billowing breeze. The clouds hung low, the air damp and chilled with the promise of mist and rain, and she ran all the way to Jocelyn's tree, no longer ominous with specters long relegated to childhood frights. Jocelyn was at rest now, Alice swore so.

Becky sank beneath its verdant branches and smoothed away the tears on her cheeks. Parker had seen those tears, and she'd been too distressed to care. Good heavens, what all had she said during her fit? She'd all but told him she wanted vengeance for the raids on Camellia Creek and Hickory Grove, which wasn't what she'd meant, but that's how he'd interpret it, and she guessed that's what it was. And she'd brought Trueblood into it.

No, he had. He'd brought up Trueblood, but she'd allowed herself to fall into his trap, if trap it was.

She sucked in a sharp breath. He'd said 'Martin.' Martin Trueblood, then indicated a link between Caruthers' old right-of-way and the man, confirming what she'd suspected for so long.

Her fit had brought her something after all.

The realization consoled her, and later, when she told Alice Parker wanted to talk to her about Jon and Laura, she'd agreed to fetch him to the sickroom. The sooner she faced him the better. She wasn't going to try and avoid him. He showed up here too unexpectedly. She'd thrown a fit and she'd wept in front of him, and the sooner he knew those dismal performances would prove of no advantage to him, the more comfortable she would be.

She found him in the kitchen, and he actually looked relieved to see her. But the question conveyed in his eyes went unspoken, because three of his men were with him, and she'd been glad, at least, for the restraint their presence offered—in point of fact, there was only so much resolve she dared risk.

Parker said he'd be there shortly. From what she heard of the conversation she'd interrupted, he was sending his men back to Port Gibson, and she couldn't help but wonder if he'd made sense out of something she'd said and now he was sending one of his troops to Vicksburg with a report for Ralston's relief.

Seth took Eli Calhoon's extended hand.

"Pardon my not getting up," Calhoon said, his voice weak. "I owe you."

The shake was surprisingly strong, but Seth figured Calhoon made a point of a strong handshake, and he wondered what it had taken out of the man to manage it.

"Actually, it was you I was expecting to shoot once we got in. Took me a moment to size up what was happening. Sorry I was a bit slow."

"I'da thought you might have shot me anyway, just for good measure."

"I'm not nearly as bad a fella as you Rebels make me out to be." He made a point then of finding Rebecca's eyes.

She held his gaze, trying to read something into his look. He had told her he knew Guthrie was looking for her the day he'd been shot. Becky knew now, because Parker had told her so not two hours earlier, that Guthrie had actually been looking for all the Calhoons. That's why Parker had been focused on Eli all along.

Eli coughed, and Becky tore her eyes from Parker. Her brother was in no condition to be hosting visitors, but Alice had wanted Parker to see Eli and vice versa. Becky wasn't convinced either man really wanted to see the other, but more than two weeks ago, Parker had saved the day, so Becky didn't argue. She patted the back of the rocker Alice had vacated for their honored guest. "Please sit," she said to Parker "and it's Alice you came to talk to."

Parker stepped toward the rocker, but he didn't sit. Alice still stood and so did Becky, busying herself with the cup of medicinal tea she'd intercepted from Aunt Elvie in the hall. She placed the fine china cup and saucer on the table beside the bed and indicated the chair next to it. "Elvie says it's for your stomach," she said to Alice. "You've had it before."

Alice took the seat, sipped the tea, and thanked her. "He just woke," she said to Seth. "I was about to wash his face."

"I'll do it." Becky scooted past Parker on her way to the wash bowl. "Sit," she commanded, and at the same time, she nodded to Alice. "Have your talk with Alice and don't wear my brother out."

He sat.

Becky carefully positioned herself on the other side of the bed and raised the wet rag to Eli's face. He turned away.

"I want Alice to do it."

Alice moved, and Becky held up a staying palm. "Don't you dare get up," she ordered. "He's joking." She glared down at her brother. "Shut up or I will suffocate you with this rag."

Seth watched Becky minister to her brother. Despite his playful smirk, Calhoon probably would have preferred Alice's care to his sister's. Seth's lips twitched when Becky caught him watching her. Again, she nodded at Alice. He responded by turning his attention to Calhoon, who, propped up by pillows, was watching him and Becky gauge each other. There was a lot Seth needed to talk to this man about, and it occurred to him Becky might not want him talking to her brother for reasons that had nothing to do with Calhoon's precarious health.

"Seth?" said Alice.

He turned to her, a tired version of the beautiful young woman he'd decided to court nearly three months earlier. "Doc says he's doin' better than could be expected," he said.

She looked at Calhoon, her expression soft. "He is."

"Look, I've got to get back to Port Gibson tonight, but before I leave I want to ask you about Jon Franklin."

Alice sat forward. "I haven't told Eli what happened to Jon."

Calhoon twisted his head and looked at his wife.

"He was murdered after he left here that day," Seth said.

A prolonged silence followed, then Calhoon said, "I didn't do it."

"We know. You've a sound alibi. We ran into Tom McKee on our way here that night. He led the charge across the flooded lake, then fetched the doc for you."

Alice reached out and took Calhoon's hand. "I did tell him all the good things. You've made some useful friends among us Northerners, darling."

Calhoon snorted, and Seth said to Alice, "How much have you told him about Franklin's visit that afternoon?"

"I told him about Naomi's plot to frame Eli for my murder because of an affair I allegedly had with Jon."

Again Seth focused on Calhoon. "Jon Franklin came to your house while you were with McKee. He confronted Alice with some story concocted by your aunt that you intended to kill him and Alice who, having been made aware of the plot, would be willing to rid herself of you and marry him. Suffice it to say he wouldn't take Alice's denial for an answer. She ended up beating him with a poker and driving him off the place."

Calhoon looked at Alice. "Did Naomi kill him?"

"Your aunt was apparently here the entire time. Isabel met Franklin on the Port Gibson-Rodney Road. My question is his relationship with your aunt. Did—"

"That's not why you're in here," Becky said, but Seth was already raising his hand.

"I'm getting to that." He turned back to Calhoon. "Did Jon Franklin really believe what he claimed Naomi Polk told him or was he perpetuating her lie? I gotta be honest with you that his believing Alice would willingly leave with him rings hollow. He'd have to be a complete idiot."

"They meant to kill me and Alice," Calhoon answered.

"Do you know that for certain?"

"Was I privy to their plot, you mean? No, just makes sense."

Seth nodded. "I can't see it any other way, either."

"That would not have gotten him my fortune," Alice said, "and he said he needed my money. What would he have to gain?"

"That's my question," Seth answered, "and does the answer have anything to do with why he was killed?"

Calhoon closed his eyes.

"He needs to rest," Becky said, furrowing her brow and gesticulating toward Alice with her chin.

Alice started to rise, and Seth knew he'd about worn out his welcome, even with his one sure friend.

"One more thing," he said to Alice. "Becky said you told her Jon and Laura had been lovers."

Alice's eyes moved from him, to Becky, then widened, and she jerked back to face him. "Oh! I had thought it very important when Jon told me. Remember the night Laura was killed? You told me she'd been with a man?"

"I do recall."

"And there was some suspicion on your part that the man was Eli?" She looked at her husband, whose eyes were open now.

watching her. She held her head proudly. "But I knew it wasn't him."

"I do remember all that, Alice," Seth said.

"I didn't worry about it so much after Naomi told me she'd killed Laura. It no longer seemed to matter." Alice looked at Seth, who encouraged her with a look. "Jon told me that he and Laura had been with each other."

And now Seth recalled Naomi had intimated the same thing that last night when she'd come to him and tried to convince him Calhoon was a killer. In his own defense, in retrospect, he'd believed little of what the woman said that evening.

Alice frowned. "Do you think it's important?"

"It could explain how Jon Franklin got involved with Naomi Polk."

"The Franklins hired one of my darkies," Calhoon whispered.

"Yes," Alice said suddenly. "Rose Walton, and Naomi was the one who arranged it. Aunt Betty and Naomi worked out the hiring, and Naomi Polk came to the house more than once."

So there was possibly more interface between Jon Franklin and Naomi Polk than Seth had realized.

"Aunt Naomi might've set Laura up with Franklin sooner than anyone thinks," Calhoon said. "She didn't want me and Laura together, and that's the sorta thing she'd have done to stop it."

Seth stood as Alice rose and bent over her husband. "You know," he said to Calhoon, "I asked Laura to try and get you to confess to your knowing Guthrie."

"Why me?"

Seth glanced at Becky, focused on him now, her gray eyes filled with suspicion. Yes, he was goading her, but he felt both compelled as well as justified. He returned to Calhoon. "It wasn't random. Laura told me she believed you'd met the man, but she didn't tell me why. In fact, she was evasive. Do you wonder why she told me that?"

"I *wondered* why you wanted to pin Guthrie's murder on me. Now I guess I know the answer."

Becky rose from the bed, her fists clenched. No doubt she was going to demand he leave the room, but when she took a step his way, he patted the air in front of her, silently bidding her to settle down. He turned back to Calhoon. "I don't have it all worked out yet. I'll let you good folks know when I have."

"I didn't kill your Treasury man, Parker," Calhoon said. "I never knew him. Discovered my cotton target on my own. This house was too damn lonely. I couldn't sleep nights. Fools were crossin' Camellia Creek on their way to that old landing. No more to it than that. And I'll lie under oath that I ever told you I was stealin' cotton."

"Get some rest," Seth told him, then nodded to Alice, before letting his eyes linger on Becky. "Like I said, I'd appreciate any help I can get." He turned and left the room.

*B*ecky watched Parker's back, then the door as it shut after him. She turned to find Alice's and Eli's eyes on her. Eli frowned. "What's goin' on, Becky?"

"He doesn't like me, and I don't like him."

Chapter Thirty-one

The rain had started during Seth and Sergeant Zachary's ride back from Camellia Creek last evening. It continued this morning. He'd eaten with his men over at the mess hall, a large canvas tent the provost had erected behind the building he and his handful of men shared with those making up the Claiborne County's Freedmen's Bureau. Food was adequate even if the drafty enclosure was damp and cold this morning. They'd stayed fairly dry, though more than one pair of feet encased in muddy boots or brogans ended up wet and cold.

After the meal, Seth had the sergeant gather the men and march them over to their work space at the newspaper office. He and Jubal Summers followed.

"You a damn fool, Bo Hand," Private Lawson said. "You ain't no African an' you don't wanna go back der, neitha. Dey ain't yo frien's an' fam'ly. Yo frien's an' fam'ly be heah. An' dem people still makin' slaves outa folks ovah yondah. How you think you get heah to begin wif? You think some white man sauntered hisse'f in an' *stole* you? You got no se'f respect fo' yo' race atall? You was sol' by yo own kin."

"I ain't nevah been sol' by nobody. Live my whole life at Marshfiel' befo' da wah."

"You know what I'z talkin' 'bout, Bo."

Ball, his back to the door, took a step toward Privates Hand and Lawson. "I know I don' wanna evah hol' a hoe ag'in long as I live. My mama got a freebawn cousin out in da Arizona territory. His mama bought 'er freedom mo'n fawty year ago an foun' 'erse'f a po white fahmah. Had 'em a place up on da Big Black.

Three li'l chil'en. Made a good life, too, till a spring flood washed dey crop away. Nex' summa come a drought. Dat cousin be fifteen den. His ole daddy died dat fall an' 'im an' 'is mama an' sistahs lived way poorer dan a nigga slave. Ain't gonna gib me no fawty acres an' some tools an' tell me to make a livin' off it."

"You make it soun' lak bein' a slave be good," Lawson said.

"Nexta wo'kin' a fahm by myse'f, it is. Think I'm gonna go to Arizona an' fin' my kin," Ball said. "Raise stock. A man'll really be free der."

Hand shook his head. "Bureau's wantin' us to sign contract fo' wo'k —"

"Dat's to protect you from da landowners —"

"Fo' a yeah?" Hand cried. "A whole yeah!"

"Ain't no contracts out in Arizona," Ball said.

"Yeah, but der be lots a mean Injuns out in Arizona," Lawson said.

"The one-year contracts were to ensure the landowners they would still have help in the fall," Seth said, walking through the open door of his office where Zachary had gathered the bulk of his troops. "But contracts are now being negotiated on a month by month basis, if that concerns any of you."

Those that had found a place to sit in the room stood when he entered, and he had, admittedly, lingered in the outer room with Jubal Summers when he'd heard them expressing their concerns regarding their futures.

"But you're going to have to work one way or the other."

Corporal Peters stepped forward, but Hand almost knocked him sideways to get to the front first. Ball opened his mouth to speak, and Zachary bellowed, "Quiet!"

They immediately settled, and Seth nodded. "Find a place to sit, all of you. We'll answer all your questions as best we can, and do our best to get answers for those we can't."

And for most of the next hour he did, supported by Zachary and Peters, who detailed what they'd found out at the Claiborne County Freedmen's Bureau. The result was more unanswered questions, and Seth resolved to get with Major Stockman and set up a more detailed brief for his men, not only outlining their options, but giving them some idea of how to act on them.

"What you gonna do wif'out us, Majah?" Ball asked at the end.

He hesitated, not sure of the answer, then said, "This was a special detail from the start. I don't know if I'll get replacements or not, but in a greater sense, there is no replacing you. No doubt about it, I'm gonna be way worse off."

Despite the terrible weather, Becky asked Buck to hitch up the wagon. He had to come to Port Gibson anyway for feed and Eli had asked her to have him check the current prices of wood. Eli thought they were too high over at Grand Gulf. Becky wasn't sure where Eli thought the merchants in Port Gibson were getting their inventory, but one or two might have a closer source. Buck dropped her off in front of the newspaper office.

It was warm and bright inside, the air acrid with wood smoke and tobacco. Becky swept back her veil. Seth Parker stood in the door to what she assumed to be his office; Poynter Cummings stood across from him, in the door to his. They'd been talking, she assumed about nothing consequential, since Parker had been laughing. So was Private Spain, sitting at his desk near the front door's entry. The latter jumped to his feet when she entered. She figured he was about to ask how he might be of service when she looked at Parker and said, "Could I talk to you?"

He held her gaze, then started toward the gate at the end of the counter, separating the paper's front room from the two rear offices. "Come in."

She smiled at Private Spain and asked him how he was. He was always happy. Then she nodded at Cummings, who responded with, "Mrs. Mackey," before he turned back into his office. She slipped through the gate Parker held for her. Once they were inside his spaces, he shut the door. "Be advised these walls are thin."

He referred to her raised voice from the day before. Resolved there'd be no more displays of emotion, she ignored the comment.

"Why did you say those things to Eli yesterday? You have him and Alice worried now, and there—"

"Let me have your coat."

She hesitated.

"Give it to me. You're not going to walk into my office, raise the unholy dickens with me, then scurry out. We need to talk. Rationally."

He was being purposefully insulting. She swallowed and removed her gloves, then coat. He glanced at her hat. She untied the bow and removed it also. "Sit down," he said.

Two chairs sat in front of his desk. She chose the one on her right, and he walked around the desk to his. "In answer to your question, I did not say what I did to worry your brother or Alice. I said what I did to provoke you."

And it had worked. Here she was in his office, on his ground. "What do you want?"

"I want you to tell me about Guthrie."

"I didn't know Guthrie. I never met the man."

"You knew he was looking for you and your brother and all the—"

"No, I didn't know he was looking for all of us until you told me yesterday. I did know he'd been looking for me the day he was murdered, but I didn't figure that out until long after he was dead, and that was by chance. At the time of his death I didn't even know he existed.

"I learned at Christmastime you were trying to blame the man's death on Eli. Mama told me that day I saw you at The Pink Lady, because I asked her what you were doing there."

"She hadn't brought up that little tidbit with you before that?"

"No, she keeps things from me. She said she didn't want to ruin the holidays with unnecessary worry. I have no idea why parents believe it wise to keep young girls, even grown women, ignorant, but they do. But with my having asked, she did tell me about Eli, then told me you'd asked to speak to me. Looking back, she must have thought you wanted to talk to me about Guthrie, but I knew why you wanted to see me, and I didn't want to talk to you, so I left Rodney. I was supposed to stay through the New Year. For sure, that made Mama even more suspicious that I'd known the man, but I hadn't an inkling."

"That would mean she knew all along Guthrie was looking for all you Calhoons."

"Possibly."

"She may well know why."

Becky blinked at him. "I don't know what she knows, but doubtless she knows more than she tells me. You'll have to talk to her."

"Go ahead with your story."

"When she told me you suspected Eli, I was worried, so I checked and found that this agent Guthrie had been killed on the ninth of October, and I didn't think Eli got back till after that."

"Or he didn't make his presence known until after."

"I could have killed the man as easily as Eli. More so, perhaps, because he came to my home."

That shut him up.

"And you're forcing me to get ahead of myself," Becky said.

"I apologize. Continue."

"I keep a journal in which I make a point of recording everything which might prove ultimately significant. Last October I took Eliza, accompanied by Mattie and our Pearl, to the home of Helen Morgan, Emily Mackey's dear friend in Jackson. Helen has a son who was turning six. She, too, is a war widow, and she'd so loved Emily and wanted Eliza present at the party. A small affair, but we were invited for the week."

Seth pushed back from the kneehole and angled the chair so that he was looking straight at her, and she wondered if he were growing impatient. She licked her lips. "When we returned, Polly, whom I'd left in the house, said a man had visited that very afternoon looking for me. He had, I imagine, told her his name, but Polly pays little attention to such things. The man said he would return within the week. He never did. Shortly thereafter, Eli returned and I, quite frankly, ceased to worry about much of anything for a while."

"Was the man in uniform?"

"Polly said he was dressed in a suit, and when I asked her to describe him, his only feature that impressed her was his red hair. She hadn't recognized him, and he didn't sound familiar to me."

"What day did you return from Jackson?"

"I'd written the entry on the tenth, the day following our return. I caught up on the whole journey then. I'd been too tired the night before."

"That means the visitor came on the ninth."

"Yes."

"Guthrie told the Madison County provost he'd been looking for a church."

"And he'd found it."

"You're living in an abandoned church?"

"I'm living in the parson's cottage across the road from the Hickory Grove Methodist Church. It's abandoned, as Guthrie indicated. There hasn't been a meeting there since the summer of '63."

"Have you discussed Guthrie with your brother?"

"No. Until after Christmas, when I asked Mama your purpose for being in Rodney, I had no interest in this Guthrie person. I didn't see Eli during that time, much less discuss the man's shooting with him, and I certainly don't want him worried with it now. I want you to leave him alone."

"If he killed Guthrie, I can't leave him alone, and even if I did, someone coming along after me won't, and might be even quicker to charge him, whether he's guilty or not."

"You can at least give him time to heal before you start browbeating him."

"I hardly think what I said to him yesterday would be considered browbeating, and like I said, it was you I was trying to provoke. Now tell me why you think this fella Martin Trueblood was involved in the attack on Camellia Creek."

Her heartbeat quickened. "He validated the transfers of property to Sam Caruthers and you told me yesterday he'd shown interest in the old railroad."

"He got wind of Caruthers' railroad, probably by virtue of his position at headquarters."

"He and Caruthers had a falling out is what happened, and Trueblood started buying the land he'd been helping Caruthers acquire as a 'loyal citizen.'"

"Do you know this for a fact? I said Trueblood had shown an interest in the railroad, but I haven't seen his name on any deeds."

"No, but I can read between the lines."

"Becky, that's not a missing entry between the lines, that's a hole in the paper, unless you know something you're not telling me."

She had her suspicions, which she had no intention of sharing with him at this time. She started to get up, but he moved faster, and she'd scarcely turned from her chair before his hand seized her wrist and he twisted her bodily around and reseated her. He hadn't been rough, but he had been firm. Hand still on her wrist, he squatted on one knee beside her. "Listen to me —"

"Trueblood worked for Ralston," she said, using her other hand to try to pry his fingers from her wrist. "And they were both helping Sam Caruthers steal his neighbors' properties."

"You don't know that."

"Just because you don't know that, doesn't mean I don't. And you wouldn't see it the way I do even if you did. Sam Caruthers played a part in the decision to attack my daddy's farm, and my daddy died."

"Then why doesn't Sam Caruthers have Camellia Creek to-day? Your brother was gone. You told me yesterday Naomi Polk had no claim."

"She must have had something, then, don't you think?"

Seth's gut churned at the thought Rebecca Mackey was re-fusing to tell him something he needed to know, but he'd be damned before he tried to force it out of her.

He held her eyes, steel gray and thick lashed, both features he'd noted before. A splash of freckles kissed the bridge of her nose and her cheeks. She had a pretty mouth.

"What aren't you telling me, Becky?"

"Listen to what I am telling you, Major Parker. There's more to this than a railroad right-of-way, and you are better able to find out what it is than I am. My dilemma is that I don't trust you'll bother, and I will not surrender any advantage I have so that you can use it against me."

He rubbed the inside of her captive wrist with his thumb, and he heard her breath quicken. Resisting her efforts to pull her arm away, he said, "Do you really believe I'd do that?"

He stopped the caress, and she gave up the struggle for her wrist. "You might think you can seduce information out of me with kind words and gentle caresses, sir, but no matter how kind or how gentle you pretend to be, I know the type of people you are working with...or for, and I know the kind of government you and they support.' She'd kept her voice soft, mimicking his. Now she moved her face closer to his. "They are foul, and there is no way you can help but be tainted by them."

"I'm a man, not a zealot, and I'm trying to solve a murder."

"You're a man in the service of a corrupt government trying to solve the murder of a man that concerns that government. Don't try and tell me you're the only one involved with this. I'm not stupid."

He held her gaze until she finally dropped her eyes. "I said some things to you yesterday in a fit of temper, things I haven't confided to my mother. What are you going to do with them?"

Gently, he squeezed her wrist, then he released his hold and stood. "I'm not going to use what you told me against you if that's what you fear." He wanted to tell her he would never hurt her, but he wasn't sure that was true, especially considering arresting her brother would hurt her almost as badly as his arresting her.

"I would appreciate you're not bringing our discussion up with my mother."

"Doesn't she already know Guthrie was looking for you?"

"Of course, but she doesn't know about Trueblood."

He started to ask what else she knew about Trueblood, but someone knocked on the door. She stood. Purposefully, he didn't move away, leaving them almost touching. Lilac wafted over him like a warm blanket. With just a quick movement and a tug he would have her pressed against him, safe and warm. Dear God, he wanted her. He stepped back and called, "Enter."

Spain stuck his head it. "Runna from da provost done brung you a telegram from Vicksbu'g, suh."

Chapter Thirty-two

Becky walked through the back door of Camellia Creek's kitchen to find Cassie seated at the table with one arm around Eliza, holding her close, and Pearl in her lap. Both Eliza and Cassie were laughing. Mattie was on the other side of the table. She'd been laughing, too.

"What," Becky asked, untying the scarf securing her bonnet, "is going on here?"

"Aunt Becky," Eliza said, "Pearl can read better than Miss Cassie."

That sent Cassie into fits of laughter again. "I merely pointed to this atrocious creature on the page and called it a cat, and Pearl immediately contradicted me and said it was a coon."

"But you can see 'raccoon' written right under it," Eliza said.

"Which means," Becky said, "that you, Eliza, are the only one who can actually read."

That started Cassie giggling again, and she turned the book around and pushed it across the table to Mattie. "I was looking at that awful picture, not trying to read the words, and I've never in my life seen a raccoon. If my efforts are no more appreciated than that, I'm giving you both back to Mattie. You for laughing at me, Eliza"—who she kissed atop her head—"and you, you little scamp"—she turned Pearl to face her, and the baby smiled when Cassie kissed her cheek—"for showing me up."

Becky took Pearl, who hugged her neck, and for a moment, eyes tight, Becky hugged her back, then she rounded the end of the table and settled the baby in Mattie's lap. Eliza had already scrambled onto the bench on the other side and was turning the page for Mattie's benefit.

"I don't know how the drive was for you this morning," Cassie said over her shoulder, "but I nearly froze."

"It's still cold."

Cassie had returned to her parents' rented home yesterday afternoon and spent the night. Their hired servants were there, but Betty Franklin liked to check on things anyway, and it had been days since either she or Cassie had been to the house. Becky knew all this because she'd been wanting to talk to Cassie since Seth Parker had given her Trueblood's first name. Now she followed her across the breezeway and into the main house.

"I'm sure this is nothing like Chicago in late January."

"No, it's not, but we had closed carriages, at least that's how I traveled if I went out at all. Actually, we spent a good part of the winter inside, especially for the past several years while Daddy was gone."

"And now he's gone again."

"Yes, but we don't have to worry so much now. Mama received a letter from him, posted days and days ago. If things went as planned, they buried Jon yesterday. Mama and I hope Daddy'll be back within a fortnight. Mama's worried cousin Martin might wish to take care of some other business while in New York—he's a speculator like Daddy, but his contacts are farther afield than Daddy's and she's afraid he'll delay their departure for business. She's sure he must have something brewing in New York." Cassie rolled her eyes. "Mama's other great fear is that Aunt Stacy will return with them."

"She doesn't want your aunt living with you?"

"Goodness, no. She and Mama do not like each other, and in defense of Mama, that is Aunt Stacy's fault. She can be quite horrid, and she'll be even more demanding now that she's lost Jon. I don't wish her ill, but I do hope she doesn't come back. She was never happy with us, the only saving grace being that she was with her son. With him gone, her only amusement would be to make the rest of us miserable."

"Some people can't be happy unless they're making others unhappy," Becky said.

She and Cassie had stopped in the hall outside the sickroom door, Becky en route her bedroom. Cassie, she assumed, meant to check on Alice.

"By that I presume you're referring to your Aunt Naomi?" Cassie said, then suddenly her expression drooped. "Unless you are talking about Northerners."

"Oh, no, Cassie, it was just a comment. I meant nothing specific by it." Becky smiled. "I was being philosophical."

"Oh"—Cassie's face perked up as quickly as it had fallen—"good."

Cassie turned to grab the doorknob and Becky said, "Your cousin, Martin Franklin. I overheard your parents talking before your father left. Will he be coming for a visit, then?"

"Mama and I still aren't sure." She giggled. "We don't even know if Daddy knows. I guess we'll find out when he gets here. And he isn't a Franklin. His mother was Daddy's mother's sister."

Becky held her breath, frightened that Cassie would leave it at that, and it appeared she would. When Cassie started to push the door open, Becky asked, "What is his last name, Cassie?"

"Oh, Trueblood. Martin Trueblood, and he is such a dear. At least Mama has always thought so."

Chapter Thirty-three

"Treasury is taking this," Malcolm told Seth. "I was hoping you would get here sooner so I could brief you fully, but—"

Outside the office, they heard the opening of the exterior door followed by the sound of brogans clomping on wood. Murmurs followed, commiseration with Malcolm's clerk. "That's them, so I'll make this quick. Suffice it to say that for proprietary reasons I've factored you in. I'll explain it all later. There might be a fight. Answer their questions regarding the case, but don't volunteer anything not already in your reports. Let me handle the rest."

A knock. Malcolm looked around Seth to the direction of the door.

"Come in," he hollered.

"I am curious, Major"—Felix Roscoe waved Seth's most recent report to Malcolm Byrnes in front of him—"as to whose side you're on?"

Seth wanted to look at Malcolm, who sat at his desk watching the verbal intercourse between him and Roscoe, but Seth had received his guidance. Explanations would have to wait regarding the attitude of the horse's ass sitting in a matching straight-back chair next to him, so he kept his eyes on Roscoe. "I beg your pardon?"

Roscoe again raised the papers in front of him. "Your sympathies are obvious."

"There are no sympathies reflected there, Mr. Roscoe, merely a reiteration of the facts."

"But nothing exonerating this Colonel Calhoon of the murder of Alan Guthrie, just of Jon Franklin."

"More importantly, in none of my reports is there anything substantiating Colonel Calhoon as the murderer of Alan Guthrie."

Two men had walked through the door of Malcolm's office. Walter Miller, senior of the two, occupied the comfortable wing chair reserved for guests. The man had spent a good part of the war here in the tri-state area of Louisiana, Arkansas, and Mississippi, but had been reassigned to Washington in the winter of '64. The other man was the beady-eyed Felix Roscoe, a long-ago émigré from New York City, who'd settled in St. Louis two decades before the war. Roscoe was a local hire, so to speak, in that he was not an official operative of Treasury. He and Miller had worked together during the "rebellion," hence Miller's tapping him to augment this assignment.

The man's black eyes narrowed. "You have the statement of Laura Blackledge that Calhoon met the man. The Polk woman later substantiated it."

"Naomi Polk, I believe, was feeding off my suspicions. Mrs. Blackledge said he might have met the man. But she was reticent to tell me why. As best I can determine, she didn't even know where Calhoon was at the time of Guthrie's death."

"As best you can determine," Roscoe ground out, "she put them in touch."

"Maybe, but I believe she would have confirmed that. She was plenty angry at Calhoon. So was Naomi Polk."

"Calhoon denies having ever spoken to Guthrie?" Miller asked.

"For what that's worth. You two appear to believe they actually did meet, and I'd like to know why."

"You validated the Blackledge woman's report regarding the cotton, didn't you?" Miller asked, his tone even and genial.

"The cotton was where she said it was. He denies it was his."

"Of course he denied it," Roscoe blurted. "But it was there, so why do you think she's lying about the two men having met?"

"I never said anything about her lying. My point is she didn't know one way or the other, of that I have no doubt."

Roscoe held his hands out, palms up. "You're splitting hairs."

"No, I'm not. If you have something more to add to Mrs. Blackledge's self-serving speculation, I'd like to know what it is."

"Enough, Roscoe, I get the Major's point." Miller leaned back in his chair, then reached for the report in Roscoe's hand. "Very well, Parker, what do you have regarding Alan's murder."

"You knew him?"

"Pretty well, as a matter of fact."

"Then you knew what he was doing here?"

"And I still do."

Miller stood at average height, shorter than Roscoe and certainly Seth. His fair hair was neat despite its need for a cut, a distraction, perhaps, for the crooked nose punctuated by a waxed handlebar mustache over thin lips. He had good teeth and a narrow face. His ensuing smile did not include his eyes. Seth waited, but he said nothing more.

"Give 'em what you've got on the murder, Major," Malcolm said.

"He was shot through the heart with a large-caliber bullet, unrecovered. How much effort was made to find evidence at the site of the shooting, I can only guess. He'd been dead four weeks when I arrived here. The Hinds County sheriff and the provost marshal assure me they did a good job checking the areas around where the body was moved and where they found blood on the road. There was nothing to indicate who killed the man or how many people were involved."

"You've seen his clothing?"

"Gone," Malcolm answered. "The sheriff shipped his clothes back to Pennsylvania on his body."

"Who paid for that?" Miller asked.

"His family." Again, it was Malcolm who answered.

Miller turned back to Seth. "Did the authorities mention anything about his clothing?"

"No."

Miller shrugged. "Folks traveling in troubled times sometimes sew their valuables into the lining of their clothes. I wondered if anyone noticed anything unusual about Guthrie's. Continue."

"Guthrie had spoken to Madison County's provost marshal earlier the day he was killed, but their discussion was in passing and dealt with a freedman accused of stealing a bale of cotton from one John Dunlap of Madison. According to the provost, Guthrie was looking for a church and found it. At the time he crossed paths with the provost he was on his way back to Port Gibson. Guthrie had not seemed eager to elaborate on his doings, and the provost, admittedly uninterested, and having the case of the stolen bale of cotton well in hand, did not press him further. Something he regretted after Guthrie was found dead."

"Is that incident what led the reporter in Port Gibson...'" Miller started rummaging through the papers he held.

"Cummings," Seth said.

"Yes, Poynter Cummings." Miller looked up. "He's familiar to me. Is that what led Cummings to tie Guthrie's murder to cotton thieving?"

"I don't believe he ever did that."

"He just reported the facts and"—Roscoe sneered when Seth looked at him—"let you draw your own conclusions?"

Malcolm cleared his throat. "That analysis was suggested before Major Parker was ever assigned to the murder, Mr. Roscoe, by General Slocum, with my concurrence."

"And your focus has been on the potential consequences of an army member's having killed a Treasury agent," Miller said.

"It was a concern."

"All the more reason, I would think," Roscoe said, "to prove that a Southerner committed the deed."

Malcolm leaned back in his chair. "It's the proving that's a problem. Given the present conditions here, anyone could have killed him. He had no money or jewelry on his person, nothing of value. It may or may not have been a random robbery, but if a Southerner did it, he'd have probably taken his clothes and shoes. Those are valuable. It's as likely another Treasury agent killed Guthrie." He'd said the last tongue-in-cheek, as if he didn't really believe it—just tossed it out there to agitate the two agents. They had, after all, started it by defaming the military.

"Did you interview any?" Roscoe asked.

"There were none in the general area," Malcolm said. "Nathan Purvis had detached in August, without relief. Bridgers was still in Jackson at the time and was interviewed personally by me shortly after. He claims not to have known Guthrie was here. Guthrie had not reported to headquarters at the time of his arrival in Mississippi in late September. We'd naturally assumed he was Purvis' replacement, but to this day, that's not been confirmed."

Miller cleared his throat. "Bridgers was a local hire. Ralston hired him on my recommendation. I believe he was no longer in Treasury's employ at the time. Army's perhaps?"

Malcolm shrugged. "He wasn't working for me, if that's what you're asking, but he was working."

Roscoe snorted. "For himself, maybe."

"Colonel," Miller said, "I do not believe a fellow operative killed Alan, nor do I believe a random disgruntled Southerner killed him. And for your and General Wood's peace of mind, rest assured that I do not believe an army officer killed him over stolen cotton. For reasons I will not delve into, I believe Alan's murder was premeditated and was directly related to what he was doing here. I am taking his death seriously."

"And you don't believe we have been? Where the devil have you been for the past three and a half months?"

Miller held up a hand. "I did not mean to imply you or your people have shirked this. In fact, the major's investigation will prove quite valuable."

Malcolm's swivel chair squeaked when he sat forward. "What was Guthrie doing here, Mr. Miller?"

"Why don't we say, for your purposes, he was investigating the thefts of cotton. It sits well for Treasury proper, and it should sit well with you."

"I take that to mean he was working covertly."

"Discretion is called for, Colonel, and I'd prefer to say no more on the matter."

"I want Major Parker to continue to work with you."

"I don't need him," Miller said.

"When we reported Guthrie's demise to Treasury, we got some cock 'n' bull story about a rich Republican donor uncle and a recommendation we find a Southerner to blame. I take it that story is no longer valid."

"You can continue to believe it if you wish."

"Don't patronize me, Miller."

Miller didn't appear bothered.

"We've got a second murder now," Malcolm continued, "and reason to believe it ties into the Guthrie killing. I intend to keep my man on it until McCulloch cajoles Stanton out of that one, too, but by then I'll have stirred up so much of your shit that it'll stink to high heaven."

"There's still a war going on here," Miller said.

"Damn right, and Army is on the front line. I'm not going to sit back and watch while Treasury disrupts my intelligence efforts from a thousand miles away."

"You may be on the front lines, Colonel," Roscoe said ominously, "but we're behind them."

Malcolm's eyes widened in faux surprise. "Is that so?"

Roscoe opened his mouth to speak, but Miller snapped— "Enough"—and looked at Malcolm. "The other murder you make reference to, I assume, is that of Jon Franklin?"

"Yes."

"I gather from the major's reports you're trying to draw a connection between Franklin and Sam Caruthers?"

"A friend of yours, I believe?" Malcolm said.

"Our paths crossed several years ago. I don't know that we consider each other friends. He's a pretty ambitious fellow. That being the case, he proved useful."

Roscoe was on the edge of his seat, looking at Malcolm with contempt in his eye. "What do Franklin and Caruthers have to do with Guthrie?"

"Maybe nothing, Felix," Miller said congenially, "but the Colonel's concerns, like ours, go beyond what is happening in this theater. He feels he is being betrayed at the cabinet level and is going to create something out here whether there is anything or not."

Roscoe was studying his senior through narrowed eyes. Prudent, he said nothing more, and Miller turned to Seth. "Very well, Major, convince me that Franklin's death might tie in to that of Alan Guthrie's."

Seth responded, trying to remember what he'd put in his recent report regarding Franklin's relationship with Laura Blackledge and Naomi Polk and that railroad, all the while keeping it separate from his gut feeling, which anyone, including himself, might construe as wishful thinking. The other thing was the way Jon Franklin had been killed, as if done by the same person who'd shot Guthrie months earlier.

"The Polk woman is Eli Calhoon's aunt, is that correct?" Miller said at the end.

"Yes," Malcolm confirmed before Seth could answer.

Miller rubbed his chin. "All right, Colonel, he continues to work the Franklin murder, but he reports to me."

"He reports to me and briefs you. You brief him on Guthrie."

"I've already told you, I don't need—"

"Then he reports to me and tells you nothing...about anything he turns up, which hurts you when he turns up the connection."

"If he turns up a connection," Roscoe said.

"All right," Miller said, "understanding he is not privileged as to why Guthrie was here."

Malcolm leaned back and stuck his pipe stem in his mouth. "Fine," he said through clenched teeth.

They broke up shortly after, Seth and the agents agreeing to meet the next morning to plan a course of action. The meeting had ended on a positive note, Miller thrusting his hand at Seth and saying he believed they'd work well together. Roscoe offered his hand, too, but said nothing. Malcolm called Seth back when he'd been about to exit.

"Close the door. "

Seth did and returned, this time to the upholstered chair.

"Look," Malcolm said, "the men who just walked out that

door are dangerous. They're operatives for a newly formed clandestine service under William Wood at Treasury. I know about Miller, the leader. He's the man accountable. Roscoe served in the army as an intelligence operative during the war, primarily in Missouri. What it boils down to is he was an anti-guerrilla guerrilla. A nasty fella. Miller knows him from Arkansas, and you can rest assured every obnoxious word out of his mouth Miller put there prior to our meeting.

"Miller, himself, was a henchman for Ben Butler in New Orleans."

General Ben Butler, Seth mused, the notorious occupier of New Orleans who had been discreetly relieved by Lincoln himself for the overt abuses and insult he heaped upon the subjugated populace while he controlled that city.

"He may be planning on hiring others, assuming he hasn't already done so. You may never see their faces. These men spent the war moving back and forth behind Confederate lines. They performed the kind of reconnaissance missions you envisioned for yourself had you not gotten yourself so severely wounded when you did. But they care nothing for discretion and are not governed by your inbred Southern honor. In fact, I'd go so far as to suggest the local hirelings aren't governed by *any* sense of honor. As for the official operatives, many are ex-military. They'd cut the throat of a sentry without blinking twice and never think about it after. During hostilities, when they weren't cutting throats or sabotaging the enemy rear, they were beating prisoners senseless in a self-professed effort to obtain information, and during their time off they terrorized, incarcerated, and interrogated citizens, including Northern ones, whom they judged to be traitors against their own ideals of loyalty. The war is over, but those who utilized such assets are not done. There's a lot of ruthless bastards back there carving out a niche for themselves in a nation that, based on its charter, should no longer require such assets, and the kind of government that falls out of this mess will tell the tale, and we're probably gonna be living with it from here on out."

"Men like them have always existed, Malcolm."

"You think I don't realize that? But there comes a time to set them aside. What happens with the likes of such men will tell us a great deal about the direction this nation is headed, and for better or worse, Southern intransigence is abetting it."

"There's a reason for Southern intransigence."

"And you can rest assured those who perceive any sort of gain from it will do everything they can to fuel it. What they have working now in the hallowed halls of Congress means the end of federalism as we know it. The restraints imposed on the central government by the Constitution have been removed, and you can bet they'll keep them off. And it's not just the Radicals, it's all of them, even the Democrats and the unaligned and, most importantly, those in the shadows holding the reins. They're all carving out their fiefdoms, and the price someone else has to pay is of no consequence. Their tools will be distraction and excuses for excess power. The easiest source for both will be Southern Reconstruction. Degradation of the Southern people is designed to increase discontent on Southern soil. It will be resisted with Southern blood. The whoremothers know Southerners are not going to hesitate to shed the blood of those they consider traitors and outsiders in return. The longer the politicians in Washington can keep that fire stoked, the longer they have to consolidate power everywhere." He looked at Seth, who had grown a bit nauseated from unanticipated anger and helpless frustration. "We either play the game, son, or we go home."

Malcolm pulled out his pocket watch. "It's been a long day. Marlene's expecting you for dinner. If you've got other plans, you'll need to cancel."

He didn't have plans and had, up to a few minutes ago, been hoping for an invite. Now he didn't have much of an appetite.

"Dinner's unofficially official. Rumor's in town and I want you to meet him. We'll chat after we eat, then you'll have a clearer picture of where my fiefdom lies."

Chapter Thirty-four

Becky stepped from her bedroom into the hall and spied Poynter Cummings closing the sickroom door. Heat flooded her, but before she could reach the man to berate him, he had spied her and beckoned her to come his way, at the same time starting toward her.

"Could I talk to you?" he asked when he reached her.

"You've spoken to Eli?" She hoped she'd made it clear from her tone that she didn't like it.

"I came here on the pretense of visiting your brother, but it's you I wanted to talk to."

"Have you seen my mother?"

"No. My topic is what you and Parker talked about."

She calmed and considered the possibilities presenting themselves to her now, then hiked her skirt and moved around him. "Come into the office."

"I want to know who you believe was behind the raid that took your father's life."

"Major Parker said the walls were thin, but it can't be that simple, Mr. Cummings. Did he put you up to coming here?"

"He said nothing to me about your conversation yesterday."

"Then he talked to someone else, and that someone is talking to you?"

"No, I really can hear what goes on in that room. It's one of the reasons I didn't fight the Federals' taking my work spaces. What Major Parker, and Alan Guthrie before him, claim to be working on interests me. So do their nominally private conversations."

195

"I'm not willing to tell you any more than what you heard me tell him yesterday."

She was on the settee. Now the newspaper editor sat beside her. "I know you don't trust me, but if you think I'm working with these people, you're wrong."

"You said Alan Guthrie used the space next to your office downtown?"

"Not really. He wasn't around long enough, but he did approach me, looking for your family. At the time he didn't know your father and older brother were dead, and no one knew where Eli was. He didn't know Hannah had died and he didn't even realize you existed."

"You told him about me?"

"I'm sorry to say I did. I also told him about Laura in town. He'd been out to Camellia Creek and talked to your aunt, but she didn't tell him anything, including being kin."

"Did you tell him she was?"

"I did."

"You talk too much, Mr. Cummings."

"Quid pro quo, my dear. The price of doing business. One hopes for a payoff worth the cost."

"And what do you want from me, and what will you give me in return?"

He smiled. "I want to know who Martin Trueblood is and why you think he was part of the raid on your daddy's farm."

"I believe that because he is the officer who checked off the paperwork transferring my Warren County property to Sam Caruthers."

"Somebody had to do that."

"I do believe he is known personally by Mr. Caruthers."

"So you think Sam Caruthers is behind your father's death?"

She rose. "There, you've jumped to the same wild conclusion I did, and before you ask, no, you may not quote me."

"I assure you, madam," he said, rising to stand beside her, "I'm a long way from putting anything in print. I'm an investigative reporter with a cause, not a gossip columnist. Do you know why Major Parker was summoned back to headquarters so suddenly?"

"If you know what was discussed in that room, you know he didn't confide in me."

"He might have told you later."

"To ensure you weren't informed?"

"Oh, he told me, and since you've been so helpful, I'll tell you. Treasury operatives have arrived at Vicksburg. Their interest is, supposedly, the Guthrie murder."

"He'll be working with them, then?"

"I don't know if he'll be working it any longer at all. My point is, you may need support in this, and he may not be able, for whatever reason, to provide it."

"I never expected him to provide me support."

"Just between me and you, I believe him to be a just and honest man. I've opened up a bit to him lately, and he's being more forthright with me. There's more to why Guthrie was out here than meets the eye. His looking for your family and for you, in tandem with your revelation that you believe Sam Caruthers was behind the raid on your family's farm, intrigues me, as I believe it must you...and Major Parker."

"The raid on Camellia Creek was two and a half years ago, and as far as I know, there is no link between Mr. Caruthers and this Guthrie person."

"No *known* link. Let's hope Major Parker returns. If that's the case, he may have additional information for us, or me, or maybe just you."

She cocked her head.

"And this is my reason for visiting you today. Should you find yourself in need of support, consider that I am on your side."

"You mean, if by some remote chance, Major Parker confides in me I should consider sharing confidences with you?"

"And I will do likewise."

"And have you made a similar agreement with him in regards to me?"

"No."

"Why would you trust me not to betray you to him?"

"Two reasons. You and I are on the same side and I don't really think he'd trust you with anything he wouldn't want me *not* to know. However, he may not be quick to agree that I *need* to know it, if that makes sense to you. That, Mrs. Mackey, is where I perceive your value to lie."

"Quid pro quo?"

His ensuing smile showed his teeth. "We'll simply be comparing information, so to speak."

"I will consider your offer should I need support."

He held out his hand. "That's a start."

He turned to the door. "Mr. Cummings...?"

"Yes?"

She'd been about to ask him if he'd talked to her mother about comparing information, then realized she'd be telling him that her mother knew something that she wasn't sharing with her daughter. "Never mind," she said.

<h1 align="center">Chapter Thirty-five</h1>

Yankee pot roast with rice and black-eyed peas on the side, finished off with sweet bread and butter. The dark-haired, fair-skinned Marlene Byrnes had apologized for the peas, but the food supply still lagged from time to time and it *was* late winter. Her cook, she told them, swore they were wonderful food, and Seth had agreed that they were. Of course, he'd eaten them all his life.

"Rumor," it turned out, had a name, that being Greg Dustin, a full colonel at the War Department. He was a tad taller than Malcolm and more than a tad leaner. They had graduated West Point together a lifetime ago, so they were the same age, had the same salt and pepper hair, carried the same style pipes in their right hands, and wore the same uniform right down to rank and regalia. All right, the regalia did vary some, but the point was their accoutrements indicated similar career paths and successes. Dustin had seemed genuinely pleased to finally meet Seth, about whom he'd heard quite a bit from Malcolm and even Marlene.

Brandy poured, Seth's cigar snipped and lit, and the colonels' pipes filling Malcolm's study with the scent of sweet tobacco, his two seniors relaxed in matching Sleepy Hollow armchairs replete with mismatched ottomans. Seth stretched out on a tapestry-upholstered settee.

Malcolm removed his pipe from between his teeth. "Greg's here, Seth, because Walter Miller's here."

"Does Miller know?"

"No. I only know Miller by sight. To the best of my knowledge he knows even less about me. Malcolm could have added that I came out here at the insistence of a member of Stanton's

199

staff." He chuckled. "That would be me. Officially I'm on furlough."

Malcolm poked out his bottom lip. "I knew Greg had a contact in Treasury, so I contacted him in December to see if he could find out what the hell was going on with the Guthrie murder."

"At that time, I showed more interest in the incident than anyone in Treasury," Dustin said. "By happenstance, that changed in early January when my brother-in-law, Dan Fairchild, the contact in Treasury Malcolm mentioned, was called off a counterfeiting assignment to work a fraud case that had taken place inside Treasury itself. Dan's specialty is counterfeiting, forgery, and fraud. For the most part, he spent the war ferreting out counterfeiters.

"Anyway, the apparent perpetrator of this fraud committed suicide—back in September. He had a drinking problem. The investigation subsequently showed he'd been embezzling. On the surface, none of this is relevant to what you're working on, but Dan did pass me a tidbit that interested those of us at the War Department who question the wholesale confiscation of military intelligence assets by the people over at Treasury. Alan Guthrie was the brother-in-law to the individual, who killed himself. Aware of my interest in Guthrie's murder, Dan told me Guthrie had worked special operations, which has been consolidated into Treasury's Secret Service."

"So Guthrie could have been working a covert operation?" Seth said.

"That was my guess and I immediately informed Malcolm here of what I'd learned. I have to be careful when using information culled from Dan. When push comes to shove, he's going to align with Treasury. It's been providing for him and his family for a long time now.

"About ten days ago, I asked Dan how his big case was going, and he said this Walter Miller, who is the primary individual he's been talking to about Guthrie most recently, left for New Orleans to work Guthrie's murder." Dustin drew on his pipe, then set it in the ashtray on the table beside him. "That was a little surprising to me, since from what Malcolm had said, Army was working it. I telegraphed Malcolm that Miller was en route and we might should construe something out of that."

"Note the plural 'we'," Malcolm said.

"I admit to being curious," Dustin said. "I talked it over with my immediate senior, another colonel, career army. Hmm, we thought, a dead operative in Mississippi apparently hushed up over at Treasury. We started giving serious thought as to what they were up to, especially with them saying nothing to us at either the national level or in theater. So here I am, on furlough."

Seth was feeling pretty mellow at the moment, lost as much in the intrigue of Washington politics as he was in his own murder cases.

"Miller beat you out here?"

"By almost a week."

"He's busy doing something," Malcolm said, "and it isn't talking to me."

"We know he hired Felix Roscoe," Dustin said. "Who knows who else he's seen and talked to."

Malcolm jabbed his pipe stem Seth's direction. "This is what has us concerned, Seth. What kind of operation is Miller concocting and why not a courtesy briefing to the Army to at least let us know they're working in the area? Do you recall how I goaded him with the Franklin murder this afternoon? His gracious deferment to my concern over the potential loss of military intelligence assets? The concerns of a lowly colonel stuck out here in the wilderness won't change Washington policy for an instant, and he and I both know it. Nor does he care one way or the other."

"He didn't want us in a position to foul up whatever it is he's working on," Seth said.

"So he humored me, and that was a dead giveaway, because frankly, I was shocked stupid at his agreeing to keep you in the investigation. At least now you have a vantage point from where you can keep an eye on this Guthrie thing." Malcolm shrugged. "And who knows, maybe you'll even come up with something tying the two together. No matter what, the two organizations should be sharing enough information so that we're keeping out of each other's way. We didn't even know Guthrie was in the area until he was dead."

"From what I've learned from Dan," Dustin said, "Guthrie's seniors are letting it be known that he was out here working rumors of insurrectionist activities on the part of Southerners not ready to accept the new order of things."

Seth blew out a breath. "That fills in the gaps of what Miller told us."

Malcolm leaned over to pick up his brandy.

"But why would Guthrie have been looking for Rebecca Mackey?" Seth asked.

"As a conspirator," Dustin said. "Hell, we hanged a woman last summer for conspiracy in the Lincoln assassination, and we could have probably hanged a lot more over the past five years. The woman should prove a weak point that Miller and Roscoe will have no trouble exploiting."

Seth felt his entire body tingle. Malcolm, watching him, said, "They'll regard her as a weak chink in Calhoon's mail. They'll target her. If she knows anything, they'll get it out of her. "

Seth fought not to react. Becky would no doubt risk life and limb to protect her brother, but he couldn't see Calhoon knowingly putting her in danger. Seth frowned at his senior. "Her older brother has been dead since Shiloh, her father for three years."

"The raid on her father's farm may have had a purpose other than the obvious," Dustin said.

Becky had all but said that. His head was starting to hurt. His own damn cigar smoke no doubt. "Come on, Colonel, the war was still going on. The only way for that argument to hold water is if the fight was considered a conspiracy against the government." They were both looking at him like he had two heads. "It was a war for independence, gentlemen, not an attempt to overthrow the United States Government, and you know it."

Malcolm waved a hand. "Seth's right, Greg, the attack on the

Calhoon farm wouldn't have had anything to do with what Guthrie was working on last fall."

Greg Dustin leaned back. "Well, he was looking for the old man and the kids, and he had a reason. Just keep that in mind."

Malcolm took the pipe from his mouth. "Eli Calhoon was late getting back from the fighting, right? Went down to Mexico?"

"Started that way. Says he stopped at the Rio Grande."

"He planned on searching out Jubal Early. That's what your report stated," Dustin clarified.

"He said it wasn't the fight he wanted, Colonel, and he came home."

"That can be interpreted in ominous ways."

"Yes it can," Malcolm agreed, looking at Dustin. "Everything from sedition and armed conflict to simply getting his farm operational again to thwart the likes of Thaddeus Stevens."

"I'm not sure what reasons you two have for not wanting to believe this Calhoon person was involved with Guthrie's death, but remember that Miller and his associate have read your reports, too."

"I'm not trying to save Calhoon's neck if it's not deserving of being saved," Malcolm said to Dustin. "I just want to know what Treasury is up to."

"And stop them if you can." Greg Dustin smiled, then picked up his brandy snifter and raised it in a toast. "To sabotaging Treasury." He and Malcolm drank.

Seth drank, too, then said, "You'd think they'd be more concerned with catching this whole seditious group they envision rather than arresting Calhoon."

"My guess is that they're planning to get him to expose his co-conspirators under interrogation," Dustin said. "I'm told Miller has proven adept at that."

"And I'm told he never got much worth using," Malcolm said, his voice mellow.

"Who told you that?"

"Associates. I've been aware of Miller and his operations in theater since '63. He's ruthless, and he's greedy. Problem is when you put a man under too much duress, you can't count on what he eventually tells you."

"Unless you've told him in advance what you want him to say," Seth said.

Greg Dustin nodded. "If a confession is all you want, the job is certainly easier."

"But the tactic doesn't serve one well if quality information is needed," Malcolm said.

"Very true." With that, Colonel Dustin downed what was left of his brandy and rose. Seth started up, too, but the man waved him back. "Keep your seat. I'm tired, long trip. I will leave you two to figure out how you're gonna persuade the likes of Walter Miller that he wants more than a confession." He winked at Malcolm and left the room.

Malcolm rose and poured Seth another brandy, then made his way back to his own chair. Through the haze of blue smoke, his senior studied him. Seth's stomach tightened with the scrutiny.

After a moment Malcolm said softly, "I recall the name, you know. I wish I'd saved the note that Confederate sergeant handed me, but I remember the gist well enough. 'There's a wounded Federal officer at the home of Mrs. James Mackey and we'd all be much obliged if you'd come fetch him before we're forced to bury him in our sacred soil. We will honor your flag of truce for twenty-four hours.' The note came replete with a map to Rebecca Mackey's front door."

Seth shifted his weight.

Malcolm laid his pipe on his desk. "In your reports you never pointed out the correlation, so I never asked, but I saw the look on your face minutes ago when Greg indicated her possible role in all this."

"She saved my life, Malcolm."

"Damn right she did, and you saved mine. But when I speak of you to others, they don't see in my face what I see in yours when speaking of her. I can look at you now and know your ephemeral Florence Nightingale has become flesh and blood. Do I need to take you off this?"

"Only if you mean to see me court-martialed for disobeying a direct order."

"How much do you trust this woman you've fallen in love with?"

Seth sucked in a breath, ready to protest, but the breath waylaid in his throat now choked him, and if he opened his mouth to speak, he'd sound like a girl. He waited a moment, swallowed, then said, "I wouldn't necessarily say I trust Rebecca Mackey at all, primarily because she doesn't trust me."

"Is she hiding something?"

"She's not a killer."

"Is she *hiding* anything?"

Seth rose, he couldn't sit still. "Yes, but I'm not sure what."

"What about her brother?"

"That would be my best guess to account for any subterfuge on her part, him and her mother. I think she'd go to great lengths to protect them both, but they both feel the same way about her."

"And after learning what we've learned today, do you still think Calhoon is innocent?"

Seth had a gut feeling of having learned a lot. He just needed time to put it all together. "I have no doubt that Calhoon is capable of killing, but he's not a murderer. Having confronted him with Guthrie, he's either the sort of poker player you don't want to share a table with or he never met the man."

Malcolm knocked the contents of his pipe bowl into his palm, then dumped the spent tobacco in the ashtray. "Whether he ever met Guthrie or not, Calhoon's involved, and if Calhoon's involved, that girl's involved, and if that girl's involved, I've known for a little while now, you're involved. Miller and his henchmen, spouting their dubious ideas of patriotism, will see to it. The organization those men work for is the offspring of McCulloch and Stanton. Think Walsingham, Cromwell, and Robespierre, and you'll have a better picture. You need to ascertain fast if that gal knows anything regarding seditious activities or if she thinks her brother's involved in such. Until you've got her on your side, you'd best tread real carefully between either group. And one thing you absolutely do not want to do is let those bastards know you care for her. If it turns out you are on different sides, they will use it against you. That would prove equally dangerous for her, too."

Seth watched Malcolm finish stuffing tobacco into his pipe bowl.

"And Colonel Dustin?"

"Like I said, an old friend. He courted my sister one summer while we were still at West Point. Their romance didn't prosper, but he and I have kept in touch over the years. We corresponded often during the war on operational matters. He's an old intelligence collector like me. Like I told you this afternoon, he says the civilian hierarchy at the War Department isn't going to stand in Treasury's way. The consensus is that with hostilities ended, those intelligence capabilities developed during the war will be lost to civilian control if a place isn't created for them, hence the cooperation between Stanton and McCulloch."

"Have they considered just letting them be lost?"

"That doesn't fit with the victors' view of what our government is *supposed* to be. Think of Greg as a double agent. I'll be holding my cards close when it comes to him, but he's useful. He provided my descriptive narrative of the nature of this beast back in Washington, and as far as Guthrie's role out here and Miller's arrival, he saved our asses. Treasury would have come out here, taken your reports, taken your investigation, and left us nothing."

Malcolm lit his pipe. "He's resigned, then?" Seth asked.

Malcolm shook out the match, then removed the pipe stem from between his teeth and contemplated it. After a moment, he said, "Did I ever tell you that Marlene and I lost two sons? Both were stillborn. Early labors. She had no problem with the two girls, just my sons. Almost lost her that second time, so we quit trying."

"You never told me."

Malcolm gave him a fleeting smile. "It's good both my girls are married, or I'd be doing my damnedest right now to match you up with one of them and cool that fever with which Mrs.

Mackey has infected you." He looked away, shrouded in the sheen of blue-gray smoke, which had enveloped the room with its sweet scent.

"In answer to your question, Greg and I are both resigned. This nation is gonna go on, son, in some form or another. I want you to be around to go on with it."

"I'd like that, too. And since it looks like I'm gonna go on with this convoluted mess, I need some information on Rebecca Mackey, and I think it resides with your predecessor."

Chapter Thirty-six

"That is one incident, Major Parker, I will never forget as long as I live." Faith Lawrence, wife of a supply officer assigned to the new army detachment in Columbus, Mississippi, smoothed her skirt and sat on a floral print settee across from the matching one she now motioned him into. The affable Mrs. Lawrence was a plump matron in a high-collared green velvet dress, and she wore her graying head of auburn hair in a bun at the nape of her neck. Her face was broad and homely. She claimed to have never seen a Marine Corps uniform before, and she appeared genuinely taken with both the novelty of it, and apparently him.

She handed him a cup of tea.

None of Ralston's records from the summer of 1863 were available. Those had been crated and returned to Washington, Malcolm had told him, and probably resided in some warehouse waiting for the archivist, if they'd been kept at all. Some records were best destroyed. Either way, they didn't need them, Malcolm continued, at least, not for the short term. Malcolm had already been aware of the arrest and subsequent "questioning" of a young Confederate widow back during that timeframe. He had not known the name of the woman involved, but he did know she'd been six months pregnant. He'd learned of the incident from a mortified Marlene, shortly after they arrived at their new post.

The cup rattled melodiously in its saucer as Mrs. Lawrence poured herself a cup of tea.

"It shamed me that those men did what they did in the name of the Union." Mrs. Lawrence's sentiments sounded close to the reiteration that Malcolm gave him of Marlene Byrnes' opinion on the matter. Marlene had apparently been quite disturbed about the incident when she heard of it two years after the fact, and it hadn't taken her long to come up with the names of the women who had been involved in retrieving the widow from her captors. It had taken Malcolm one more day to determine that one of the rescuers, Faith Lawrence, espoused to a member of the occupying force, was still in the state.

"I understand measures must be taken in time of war," the woman continued, "but the questioning of a woman in labor seems a bit too extreme for a civilized nation. Her questioners didn't represent any Union that I wish to be part of, I can tell you that." She shook a finger his direction. "But don't you dare argue with them or *you* are the traitor. They seemed to think they coined the word 'patriot.'"

"Do you know why they were questioning her?"

"No one seemed to know. They did, of course, and I would think someone senior to them. They claimed to have orders from Colonel Ralston."

"Who were they?"

"One was a lieutenant colonel in the Army, a rather young colonel with a lot of swagger, which led me to believe he was some sort of intelligence operative. The other was a civilian. My guess was he worked for Treasury, but I don't know. Maybe he was a secret agent, too, incognito. They never spoke to me after their initial attempts to quell my concerns, then intimidate me, and they didn't even bother to look my way after I solicited the help of Jessica Stevens"—she looked at him quickly—"she's Colonel Stevens' wife. He was the acting provost and he interceded with Colonel Ralston, who claimed he'd had no idea the woman was pregnant, much less in labor. As if two men alone in a room questioning a young woman of breeding is acceptable under any circumstances. If it had not been for the concern of that sergeant guarding her, she might have had her baby on the floor of that abandoned warehouse those people use for such purposes."

"And afterwards she gave you no idea what questions they'd asked her."

"She said very little, poor thing. The baby was early. She said she'd been injured the day before in an incident that had led to her arrest. I learned later there'd been a shooting over in Madison County where one of our soldiers was killed and another shot. I don't know the details on that, but she did say she hadn't felt the baby move since then, so I think she must have known in her heart he was already dead. Still the birthing had to be endured.

"She was a young widow, you know? The boy would have been their only child. I remember she begged us to let her see him, hold him, but Jess didn't think it was a good idea. I had nine children, Major Parker. Two I lost within days of their birth. I wasn't sure if we should let her see him, but my mother always said it was too hard on the grieving mother to see her baby dead."

Seth had no answer for that. He only knew there was a rock sitting in his gut that didn't belong there. "After the birth of the baby, did Ralston's men attempt to question her again?"

"I don't think so. I volunteered to keep her at my house until a determination could be made in her case, but the provost put her in one of his spare rooms. There was a guard at his house anyway. Her mother came for her a few days later, and she was released. Now you tell me what valuable intelligence had she held that required her to be subjected to such callous behavior, then just let go?"

Seth couldn't rule out that she'd been questioned while with the provost, albeit under better circumstances. "They may have determined she knew nothing."

"Hmmpf," Mrs. Lawrence groused, then asked, "do you know where she is, and if she's well?"

"I do, and she is well."

"Has she remarried?"

"She's still wearing black."

"Well, she was young and very pretty. She'll find another if she wants. Not the one she lost, perhaps, but someone."

Seth watched the smile on Faith Lawrence's face melt away. "Oh, Major!" she cried, immediately reaching over and covering his hand. "I had no idea how you felt. I do apologize."

Chapter Thirty-seven

Becky jumped at the assertive knock outside the sickroom door. It hadn't disturbed the sleeping Eli, but it had startled her and certainly Alice, who bounded from the cot they'd set up beside the bed. Betty Franklin was quick on her niece's heels. The door flew open, barely missing Alice, and Betty cried out in indignation. Becky moved to get a better view of Jubal Summers, his hand on the knob, his body rigid, and his visage stern with righteous — Becky wasn't sure what. Two steps more outside the portal stood another man, a civilian, blond with a mustache. He was dressed in a black suit, recently pressed, and behind him another man, burlier, uglier, his bowler hat still sitting on his head. He was chewing tobacco, which undoubtedly explained his stained teeth. The former graced Alice with a grim smile, while the other stared, first at Alice, then at Betty Franklin, and finally at her, and her heartbeat quickened. She knew what these men were.

Alice appeared to take stock of the situation, gave the civilian a dirty look, then settled her gaze on the Negro officer. "What's the meaning of this, Captain?" Her voice was low, but forceful, and her small frame effectively blocked entry to the room.

"Forgive the intrusion, madam," the blonde man in the dark suit said, "but I need to speak to Mr. Calhoon."

Alice made to take the door knob from Summers, but he wouldn't move his hand. "We'll talk in the hall," she said to him.

He raised his chin. Becky stepped closer, and Betty Franklin, two steps behind Alice, took her niece by the shoulders, set her aside and bodily shoved the officer away from the door. Becky figured it was more the shock than the force that made Summers let go of the knob. Betty crossed the threshold and would have pulled the door shut behind her, but Becky had already seized it, at the same time following Betty Franklin into the hall. She shut the thing with a soft rattle, separating their group outside the room and isolating Alice and Eli within.

"What's the meaning of this intrusion?" Betty Franklin was looking not at Summers, but at the first civilian. "Who are you, sir?"

Behind the unidentified men, Becky saw her mother approach from their bedroom, and to the left, in the vicinity of the dining room entry, a pensive Sergeant Zachary stood beside a curious Corporal Daws. She'd seen neither in two days. They'd accompanied this group to create an impressive illusion of force.

"I am Special Treasury Agent Walter Miller, Mrs...."

She folded her arms over her breasts. Clearly she had no intention of offering him a handshake. "Franklin. I'm Alice Calhoon's aunt. Alice Calhoon is—"

"Mr. Calhoon's wife."

He sounded reasonable, pleasant even. But that was a typical opening tactic. Becky caught her mother's eye, which had heretofore been fixed on Betty Franklin's face. Isabel raised a brow and mouthed, "uh-oh."

"What do you want, Mr. Miller?"

The knock on the door might not have disturbed Eli, but Betty Franklin's tone might yet.

"I told you—"

"Colonel Calhoon is indisposed." She turned on Summers. "And you know that. Why would you bring these men into this house and dare to bang on that door"—she whirled back to the door and jabbed the air in its direction—"like that?" Now she placed her hands on her hips and faced Summers head-on. "Your troopers have been coming in and out of that door for the past two weeks."

She must have been referring to Sergeant Zachary, who was the only one of Seth Parker's troops who had entered and exited that room almost at will.

"I know he's been seeing people. He's up to talking."

"He's sleeping, but regardless, that arrogant performance was uncalled for!"

By now a smile had formed on Isabel's face. Summers had noticed her presence, and the Miller person followed his eyes. Miller stepped back and angled his body to see her better. He nodded curtly. "Miss Hays."

"Walter, darling, I wish I could say it was a pleasure."

She knew him then, but that wasn't surprising.

Miller, his smile tight, turned back to Betty Franklin. "I had been led to believe that Mr. Calhoon was receiving visitors."

"Last week, before pneumonia set in. He's relapsed."

Summers narrowed his eyes and found Zachary. "I hadn't been told that."

"Ain't been here since day befo' yesta'day, Cap'n."

Betty Franklin had just given Eli pneumonia. It was true he'd developed a cold and they were worried, but no pneumonia yet.

"You are aware of how grievously he was wounded?" Betty asked Miller.

The man behind Miller stepped forward. "The doctor been here to see 'im?"

Betty Franklin switched her focus from Miller to the other. "Do you have a name, sir?"

He said nothing. Miller said, "Felix Roscoe. He is also in the employ of the Treasury Department."

"Well, Mr. Roscoe, the doctor saw him earlier this morning. He gave him something to help his pain and to ensure that he sleeps, which I just told you he's doing, as was his wife before you compelled Captain Summers here to pound on the door."

"We'd like to see the man for ourselves," Roscoe said.

"To confirm he's here," Miller explained.

"What?" Then Betty Franklin laughed. "Do you think we anticipated your unexpected arrival and have in the not too distant past removed a critically ill man from his sick bed to hide him from thugs"—she glared at the one named Roscoe—"whom we never for a moment expected to appear.

"Which one of you is supposed to be the leader of this group?" she asked now, almost as an afterthought. She spun on her heel and locked eyes on Jubal Summers. "You?"

"I am," Miller said.

"And what is your business with Mr. Calhoon?"

"We'd like to question him regarding the murder of Alan Guthrie, who—"

"I'm aware of the incident."

Becky cast a glance at Zachary, who gave his head a surreptitious shake.

"Then you understand our interest in speaking with Mr. Calhoon."

"You'll have to come back in a few days. And be civil when you enter this house."

She turned back to the sickroom door.

"We don't have a few days, Mrs. Franklin," Miller said, his voice now tinged with malice.

She spun like a cyclone. "You're not bothering him right now."

"Calhoon is a suspect in the murder of a loyal agent of the United States," Roscoe said sharply. "Why are you protecting him?"

Becky saw her mother's mouth open a tad, a discreet reaction to the outrage on Betty Franklin's face. Whatever Mrs. Franklin had been about to say to the horse's behind called Felix Roscoe, however, was preempted by Miller, who stepped in front of Roscoe and said calmly, "If we come back it will be today, Mrs. Franklin, and I'll have the provost. I have the authority to remove Calhoon from this house and place him under guard."

Becky, head pounding, body shaking, took a hasty step forward. Her mother moved, too, but Betty Franklin proved faster, extending her arm to halt Becky at her side.

"Becky, dear," Betty said, "in the top drawer of the dresser on Alice's side of the bed are my brother's military papers. Would you get them for me please?"

Becky hesitated.

"Go," her mother snapped, and with a quick glance at Isabel's anxious face, Becky turned to the sickroom door.

Alice was on the other side, listening, Eli's Navy Colt in her hand.

"Is that loaded?" Becky whispered.

"Yes."

Becky almost told her to put it away, but decided not to. Those men were not taking Eli out of here, not without.... "Your aunt's talking to them," she said, moving toward the bed. "I need your father's military documentation."

Becky didn't wait for Alice to retrieve it. Knowing where to look, she found it herself. She gave Alice a quick smile, glanced at the Colt in her sister-in-law's small hand, and left the room.

Betty Franklin snatched the folded paper from Becky's hand, snapped it open, and thrust it at Miller. "Mr. Calhoon's wife is the orphan of Master Sergeant Jacob Shelton, 8th Ohio, United States Army. He and his eldest son died taking Atlanta for the Union. His youngest son died less than a year later pacifying North Carolina shortly before the end of hostilities. I wonder what value the local provost"—she barked out a laugh—"who knows all that and who also knows my husband, Major Peter Franklin of the 13th Illinois, will place on that when you attempt to drag Mr. Calhoon out of here?"

The man nodded curtly. "Your brother and nephews I presume?"

"You presume correctly."

"I'm sorry for your sacrifice."

"Mine and my niece's, sir, and I'm determined she'll not be making another in the near future simply to humor the central government." She glared at Roscoe. "How dare you bring your lackey into this house and accuse me of protecting a murderer and, by implication, question my loyalty."

Miller stiffened with that, but Becky didn't perceive that Roscoe was overly bothered.

"We could hope there'll be no more sacrifice on the part of your family, but we may not be able to prevent it, Mrs. Franklin.'

"Then you'd best show up with more than the provost, Mr. Miller. And in the meantime, take your hollow threats and your paragon of patriotism"—she nodded sharply at Roscoe—"and get the hell out of this house."

Becky watched amused satisfaction settle on her mother's face, then she felt someone at her side, and looked up to see Frank Zachary beside her. "Beggin' yo folks' pardon, but if'n I might say, da colonel heah, he already be undah guard." He met Jubal Summers' eye. "Dat's what Cawprals Peters an' Daws been doin' heah all dis time." He nodded to Corporal Peters who stood away from the rest of them, in the hall near the stairs. He straightened officiously. "Ain't no need fo' evah'body to get der hackles up ovah dis."

Jubal Summers looked at Miller. "I saw Calhoon in the bed. He was sleeping."

Miller looked at the sergeant. "And he's under guard twenty-four hours?"

"Has been since he were shot. He ain't goin' nowheres, even if he could."

Miller seemed to think about that a minute, then produced a grimace along with a quick nod. "That should be sufficient, I would think. I'll confirm all this with Parker."

"You're working with Parker?" Becky asked.

"Parker's working for us," Roscoe said, and Becky felt the color drain from her face. She was thankful the hall was dim. Why this came as a shock she couldn't fathom, because she'd known it would eventually happen.

Miller expressed a curt "Good day" and started for the back door. Roscoe, eyes on Becky, lingered. "You're the half sister?" he asked.

Isabel quickly crossed the distance between them and wove her arm through Becky's. Roscoe's beady gaze shifted to her. "And the stepmother?"

"In a manner of speaking," her mother said.

Becky hadn't answered, she hadn't needed to. The man tipped the brim of his hat and left the hall. Summers started to follow, but Betty Franklin placed a palm flat in the middle of his chest.

"Where's Parker?"

Summers' eyes flashed. He was angry, and he didn't answer. To their left, Frank Zachary said, "Ain't got back from Warren County yet." Betty never dropped her eyes from Summers. "Is what he said true, Treasury is now in charge of what you and Parker were working before?"

He still didn't answer. Betty raised a brow, and at the same time, she dropped her hand. "Or maybe you don't know what you're doing?"

"I don't know that any of us know what we're doing," Isabel said, "but we are doing something. I, for one, have developed a whole new opinion of you,"—she smiled at the ruffled Mrs. Franklin—"Betty."

Betty Franklin glanced Isabel over head to foot. "Well, I'm not yet sure what to make of you, Isabel, but I do appreciate your approval of my tact."

Isabel laughed. "Or lack thereof." She narrowed her eyes on Captain Summers, who stood back watching all of them. "Unfortunately, it's not going to work for long."

"You think they'll be back?" Betty asked.

"Definitely. Despite Miller's agreeableness, he's a ruthless man. You observed the bullish arrogance of Felix Roscoe? Understand that Miller controls that man. He is oh-so-much worse. Treasury is delirious with power, and in this matter they have come with an agenda."

And Becky would bet her future hold on Muscatine that Isabel Hays knew what that agenda was.

Isabel looked toward the dining entry where Daws loitered smartly. Her gaze settled on him. "Daws, darling, let's take a ride."

The defiant Summers moved then, and Isabel jerked her gaze to him. "I could take Peters, but I assume he's still on 'guard duty'"—Summers shot Zachary a look—"or neither one. I only thought you wished to know my whereabouts at all times.

Perhaps with Treasury in charge, I no longer matter?" She smiled into his sullen face.

Summers sucked in a breath and stomped across the hall and into the dining room. "Send Daws with her," he yelled back. A moment later they heard the back door open and close. Daws looked at Zachary, who nodded. Daws smiled, then looked at Isabel. "We ridin', Miz Iz'bel?"

""We'll take the carriage and leave it at Grand Gulf. Come, daughter, I need to counsel you."

Betty placed her hand on Becky's arm. "You think she's in some kind of—"

"You may not have noticed," Isabel said, "but the timely raising of your arm prevented a bodily attack on Roscoe. A prudent reaction would have been to strike out at the smaller of the two men, but either would have been disastrous. Becky doesn't have Union *bona fides*. God forbid she be arrested for assault on a Treasury agent."

"Oh, Mother, please, I didn't intend to strike either one."

"You only intended to frighten them, darling? You should not have drawn attention to yourself with either man."

Becky turned to Frank Zachary. "Thank you for stepping in, Sergeant."

"Yo welcome, Miz Becky, and don't you worry none. Majah gonna come an' make evah'thin' all right."

How could he if he were now subordinate to them? And even then, what would Major Seth Parker consider "all right."

"If you have that much influence," Becky said, watching the reflection of her mother tie the lilac scarf that would hold her hat in place, "why can't you simply travel up to Vicksburg and have the encumbrances removed from Muscatine?"

"We're talking two different entities here." Isabel fluffed the bow and turned from the mirror. "What I need to protect Eli I can obtain indirectly through the military. What encumbers your land is Treasury and what is influencing Treasury resides in Warren County and is less enamored of me."

"Caruthers, you mean?"

"Yes."

"Do you think this Miller person is working with him?"

Isabel stepped to the daybed she had taken as her own and picked up her black leather gloves. "Miller is the Treasury agent we've been expecting from Washington. No doubt they're in cahoots. How well they're 'working' together, I don't know. Either way makes no difference to us in this matter of Eli." She caught Becky by the shoulders and kissed her cheeks. Then with the hum of satin against her wool coat, she opened the door. "After I've concluded business up north, I'm going to Rodney. I won't be back before Thursday."

"You're going to talk to Mr. Holbein?"

"I'm going to look in on The Pink Lady, and yes, I intend to talk to Toby."

"I can tell whoever asks where you are?"

"Of course, Daws being with me, I'll have no secrets."

Becky's stomach squeezed, and she laid a hand over it. Her mother disappeared out the door, pulling it shut behind her. Becky sat hard on the daybed. Back in the middle of October, she'd made one of the happiest entries in her journal that she'd made in a long time. A letter from Aunt Naomi had arrived and informed her Eli was safely home. She'd never concerned herself with the exact date of his arrival. It hadn't mattered. Nothing had, except that her brother was alive and well and home at Camellia Creek. But the mail sometimes took days. Naomi Polk had written immediately, at Eli's request, and the date on the letter would bear a closer approximation of Eli's homecoming than her journal entry. Guthrie, the dead agent, had been killed on the ninth of October. She needed to check that letter, stored away with other such missives in a desk drawer at Hickory Grove. She rose. As Eli had told Parker a couple of days ago, he hadn't known Guthrie. He hadn't been back in the area long enough. She was sure of it. A recorded date after Guthrie's death could help exonerate him.

Doubt washed over her, and she closed her eyes. It might

mean nothing to people trying to place the blame on him. But wouldn't a court require a motive?

No, it would more likely consider a motive, and if it couldn't come up with one it might summarily dismiss the need for providing such. Still the date on the letter could mean something.

And if the letter ended up compromising him, she'd burn it, which might prove an even more important reason for finding the thing.

Chapter Thirty-eight

Seth had met with Miller and Roscoe prior to his leaving for Lowndes County. He'd told them his upcoming absence dealt with a lead on the 1836 railroad charter, which might tie to the Franklin murder, and he'd meet up with them in Port Gibson in a couple of days.

That was good, Miller responded, because he and Roscoe had some leads of their own they needed to follow. Those dealt with the Guthrie murder. Miller hadn't volunteered what those leads were, and Seth hadn't asked, because he figured Miller wasn't going to tell him. But they did concern him. The two operatives, from best Seth could tell, were focused on one man, who was mighty vulnerable right now.

His trip to Columbus, Mississippi, and back, using a combination of rail and horseback, accounted for two full days. One day there and one day back to Jackson, all for a fifteen-minute chat with an albeit pleasant lady and a good cup of hot tea, the pleasure somewhat undercut by the fact he wasn't a tea drinker. His mother and sisters drank tea.

The rail between Meridian and Vicksburg was operational now, but he and Boon jumped train in Jackson for a quick trip to environs southeast of Raymond in Hinds County and an interview with Emily Mackey's old friend to verify Becky had, indeed, been at her home earlier on the day Alan Guthrie was believed to have been murdered.

Helen Morgan had, Seth thought, been pretty once, but now, despite the fact she was no longer in widow's weeds, she appeared pinched and careworn. The house where she lived had in the recent past been a fine farmhouse, large and spacious, built on the common plan of the wide central hall flanked on both sides by two large rooms replete with pocket doors which could be used to divide the rooms in two, at least that's what Seth surmised. He never got past the shaded front porch. The house had two stories and looked to have a spacious attic. The exterior hadn't seen a coat of paint in years and the interior, from what he could see down the hall, was dim and barren.

The boy, the one whose birthday Seth figured Eliza had celebrated back in October, stood between him and his mama like a sentry, until his mother had finally patted him on the shoulder and sent him back into the house, telling him everything was all right. Then Mrs. Morgan and a man she introduced as Philip Dexter, a neighbor, had joined him on the porch. Dexter, older than himself and probably a little older than the woman, might have been the reason she'd forsook her drab widow's attire for a forest green silk, years out of fashion, but well taken care of. Life went on.

She'd been polite, the man civil, when he'd explained his purpose, that being to confirm Rebecca Mackey had been present here the last ninth of October. Her son's birthday had been on the seventh, Mrs. Morgan told him. Becky had left at noon the second day following.

"Ah, Major," Poynter Cummings said from the threshold of his office. "You've returned. I was starting to wonder if the Army was gonna let you."

Seth looked at the closed door to his own spaces. None of his people lingered outside. It was dusk and past chow time. "You seen any of my troops?"

"Spain closed your office door an hour ago. Summers has been in and out all day, in company with a couple of civilians."

Cummings' knowing look told Seth that he knew. Seth walked around the counter. "You wanna talk?"

"Always, Major." Cummings stepped back inside his office, and Seth followed. "Treasury has taken this?" the editor asked and sat in his creaking swivel chair.

"They've taken Guthrie, but Army has held onto Franklin."

Cummings smiled. "Your suggestion?"

"My boss's."

"That's interesting. Your seniors aren't ready to give this up?"

"No."

Cummings waited. Seth knew he wanted him to expound, but when he didn't, Cummings asked, "Where have you been?"

Seth pondered how much to tell the man. He was officially not working the Guthrie case anymore, but of course he was, at least on the side. Tacitly, he'd just told Cummings that. "Lowndes County."

Cummings cocked his head.

"I needed to talk to a woman, the wife of an officer stationed in Vicksburg in September of 1863. They're over in Columbus now. The woman led the charge that retrieved Rebecca Mackey from an interrogation being conducted by a couple of operatives after her arrest in Madison County."

"An interrogation?"

"Yep."

"That was after her father-in-law's home was razed?"

"It was."

"Damn. I was aware of the destruction, but I didn't know she'd been questioned. Was it by Treasury?"

"All I know is that one was military, the other appeared to be civilian."

"What did they want?"

"So far no one seems to know. My senior is searching for reports on the incident, but most of his predecessor's records have been returned to Washington. The woman in Lowndes County didn't know the reason. She just didn't like its happening."

"I've heard rumors Rebecca Mackey lost a baby."

"I don't think it's a great secret, but they don't discuss it.'

"It happened then?"

"It did."

"Rebecca Mackey must know what they asked her."

"I'm sure she does, but she doesn't talk about that either, not the specifics anyway. I was kinda hopin' you knew something before I pressed her."

"Nope."

Cummings opened a drawer to his desk and pulled out a fifth of whiskey, then reached behind him to a battered credenza from where he retrieved two glass tumblers. He poured them both three fingers, and said, "Let's look at this."

Seth sucked in air with the downing of the shot. Cummings poured him another. Seth left that one sitting on the front edge of Cummings' desk and leaned back in his chair. "Let's do. In the late summer of 1863, Vicksburg has fallen. A man named Sam Caruthers is in the process of seizing Muscatine farm in Warren County under the guise of a 'loyal citizen.' The land correlates to that required for an old railroad right-of-way once chartered by the Mississippi legislature at the behest of the same 'loyal citizen' Sam Caruthers. In September, a raid is made on a farm south of Muscatine. The old master is killed, and the home is ransacked."

"It wasn't burned," Cummings said, picking up the thread, "because the daughter was inside with yellow fever and the bastards were afraid to touch her in order to get her out of the house, and they remained humane enough not to burn it down on top of her."

Seth nodded. "If Hannah hadn't been inside, they might or might not have burned the house."

"Leading one to speculate the intent was to drive the owners off and leave the property open to confiscation."

"Because that property also had land required for that old Caruthers' right-of-way. Shortly thereafter a violent raid was made on Hickory Grove plantation over in Madison County, which didn't have a damn thing to do with the right-of-way—"

"But did have one of the heirs to both the Camellia Creek and Muscatine properties."

Seth had begun to slouch, but now he sat up, stomped his brogans on Cummings' wood floor, and reached for his whiskey. "That railroad right-of-way didn't end in Claiborne County."

"And I can further add," Cummings said, "that other properties Caruthers has acquired, or tried to acquire, have not been
dealt with in such a violent manner."

"Isabel Hays says there's a distant relationship between the
Caruthers clan and the Calhoons."

Cummings shrugged. "I wouldn't know."

Seth took another sip of whiskey and resumed his slouch.
"Then in late September 1865 a Treasury operative shows up
looking for the Calhoon family." Seth frowned at Cummings.
"You seeing a connection?"

"Not yet."

"As in you don't know of one, or I haven't broached it yet?"
Seth asked.

"I don't know of one."

"The two surviving members of the family deny all knowledge
of the man's interest in them at the time of his death. As far as the
other relations the man contacted, Naomi Polk killed Laura
Blackledge, and I shot Naomi Polk."

"Pity you had to kill her."

"Isabel Hays'"—Seth shrugged as the thought struck him—
"another relation we need to consider, has already pointed that
out. Then there's the dead Jon Franklin, whom we've connected
to Isabel Hays, Naomi Polk, and Sam Caruthers."

"You didn't bring up that name you mentioned the last time
we talked."

"Martin Trueblood?"

"Yes, him."

"He ties in to the summer of '63."

"Muscatine, Camellia Creek, Hickory Grove..."

"And the arrest and questioning of Rebecca Mackey."

"Well, Major, you need to find out what they asked her."

Seth rubbed his chin. He needed a shave. "I know. What can
you tell me about the agents' activities during my absence?"

"As far as I know, they just arrived in Port Gibson today.
Came in this morning with your captain. After greeting me, they
holed up in your office for a bit."

"What did they talk about?"

Cummings smiled. "You must have told Summers I can sometimes get the gist of what's said in that office."

"I think you get more than a gist, and yes"—Seth actually regretted it in this particular instance—"I did warn Jubal to be careful what he said. At the time, he suggested we find other spaces. Instead, we decided to talk about the really secret stuff in my quarters at the hotel. So you can assume, Mr. Cummings, that what you hear is what I want you to know in order to expedite any subsequent discussions between the two of us."

"Understood, Major, and in answer to your question, the two agents wanted to talk to Calhoon. They also indicated to Captain Summers that he would be well served by adherence to their cause. Whether they implied that was to your detriment or not, I assume will be on a moment by moment basis."

"What did Jubal say?"

"He made a point of saying he was a captain in the United Sates Army. Whether that was for their benefit or mine, again I do not know.

"I guess I'll find out on a moment by moment basis. So far, things here are congenial with Treasury."

Cummings sat back. "Did they tell you why Guthrie was here?"

"They gave me a story, pretty much right in line with the one you already guessed."

"Infiltration?"

Seth wasn't comfortable working with Cummings on this. The betrayal of men working under vulnerable, even potentially deadly situations, was abhorrent, so he didn't confirm or deny. After all, nothing had been confirmed to him.

"There is, in my opinion, a problem with that theory, and that is Guthrie's wanting to talk to Rebecca Mackey."

"There was her arrest and now, we know, her questioning in '63," Cummings countered.

"Which Guthrie didn't know about. In fact, he didn't know about her until you told him. If his role was to find proof that the

Calhoons, and we'd be talking the entire family here, were involved in some sort of continued seditious activity, he should have already been aware of her and her arrest. He should have known Holland Calhoon was already dead. It's not adding up."

"It could add up for Treasury, though, if all they want is a killer for Guthrie."

Damn right it could. "Did you hear any results from their visit to Camellia Creek?

"They didn't get in to see him. Apparently he has pneumonia and an aunt by marriage who isn't easily intimidated by operatives from the Department of the Treasury."

Seth grinned. "Betty Franklin."

"Ran 'em off with their tails between their legs, to hear your sergeant tell it, albeit he did not say that in their presence."

Seth looked out the window of Poynter Cummings' office. Night was falling. "I'll need to get out first thing. How bad is he?"

"The pneumonia, you mean?"

Seth stood. "Yep."

"Zachary says he doesn't think it's pneumonia. Thinks the aunt made that up to deny them access. He also told me he smoothed Treasury's feathers by implying Calhoon has been in confinement since he was shot."

Well, Miller had just let that falsehood slip by, because he'd already told both agents he'd never had grounds for arresting Calhoon. He needed to find Miller and get this cleared up.

Poynter Cummings watched him stand. "You understand that I know Walter Miller."

"He made reference to that. What can you tell me about him?"

"He's been in and out of the area since Grant established a foothold. He's one of my inspirations in my quest for justice. Look, Parker, the morning after Calhoon was shot, you asked me if Guthrie had ever mentioned Sam Caruthers' name. I told you no."

Seth eyed him and Cummings said, "That was the truth. But has Walter Miller mentioned Caruthers to you?"

"We discussed their relationship. Reading between the lines, I assume Caruthers cooperated with him on things."

"Is that a euphemism for treachery and thievery? Those two worked very closely together. Caruthers betrayed his country, his state, his friends, and his neighbors. He ultimately betrayed his family in the worst way imaginable."

Seth opened his mouth to ask, but Cummings shook his head. "One day, when I have absolutely no doubts left about you at all, I'll tell you exactly what I mean by that. For now, rest easy that it has no relationship to what you're working at the moment, except you need to understand you're dealing with men of the lowest degree imaginable."

Chapter Thirty-nine

"**I** wasn't concerned so much with that," Walter Miller said to Seth. "The point was he was there and under guard. He is under guard now, isn't he?"

"I haven't been out there yet, but I assume so, if that's what Zachary told you and Summers was standing right there when he said it."

"Well, Summers was there, and he didn't contradict his sergeant. I think we were all relieved to have the impasse removed."

Across the table from Seth, Roscoe grunted.

"Except Felix here."

Seth had found them in the hotel dining room partaking of an early supper. "Do either of you know where Captain Summers is?"

"Out eating with his own kind," Roscoe said. "We don't break bread with the likes of him."

Miller pushed rice onto his fork. "Speak for yourself, Felix." He turned to Seth. "We haven't seen him since we got back from the Calhoon farm late morning. How was that lead on the Franklin killing?"

"Dead end."

"According to your captain, the Hays woman left shortly after our visit out there this morning. She took one of your men with her."

Well, that was just wonderful. "I've been keeping a close eye on her since I established Alan Guthrie had contact with her."

"Why?" Roscoe asked.

"I knew her to be familiar with Calhoon. I was not aware, at the time, just how close the relationship was, so I watched."

"Her and Calhoon, if I am correctly interpreting your reports."

"And intermittently Tobias Holbein, the lawyer, who I also know Guthrie contacted."

"Yes, I've talked to Holbein."

"Is that what delayed your arrival until yesterday?"

Miller set his knife and fork aside, then removed the napkin he'd tucked inside his collar. He was finished. Roscoe was long finished. Miller smiled. "I've made a number of contacts since last we saw each other, Major Parker. The sooner this is resolved, the better."

"I agree."

"I'm going to assume your man with the Hays woman will brief you as to what they did once they get back?"

"You assume correctly."

"I would appreciate knowing where she went."

"I'll let you know what I find out."

Chapter Forty

Seth had no sooner stepped from the Camellia Creek dining room into the foyer when the door to the sickroom opened. Betty Franklin rushed out and set a course straight for him, but stopped abruptly when Jubal followed him into the foyer. She glared at the man, then refocused on Seth. "I'm glad you're back," she said curtly. "I'd like to speak to you, alone, when you're done with this man." She turned on her heel and returned to Alice and Calhoon's bedroom.

He glanced at Jubal, then stepped into the study. "That's about yesterday morning, I take it?"

Jubal followed. "Yes."

"What exactly did you do?"

"Knocked on the door harder than she thought necessary."

"Did you do it, or Miller?"

"It was me."

Jubal told him this morning on the way out that Miller and Roscoe had arrived Port Gibson late afternoon day before yesterday. Before leaving for Columbus, Seth had sent Jubal a missive from Vicksburg, via the courier, to expect them, and confirmed for Jubal that the agents were assuming responsibility for the Guthrie murder. Seth and his detail were keeping Franklin's.

He didn't say anything to anyone about his visit to Helen Morgan in Raymond or about Becky's and Guthrie's activities the day Guthrie had died. Malcolm's warning echoing in his ear, he wasn't going to bring Becky up in any of this, much less in the context of Guthrie's murder, as if doing so tacitly insinuated her involvement. He was being delusional, perhaps, since Greg Dustin had already implied that possibility.

⋇

*J*ubal Summers left the study, and Betty Franklin slipped in. "You need to talk to Major Hemple in Port Gibson."

"The provost?"

"You know him? Good. You need to see the man quickly, Major. This is urgent."

"You're concerned about Calhoon's being investigated for the Guthrie murder?"

"I'm concerned he's going to be arrested and dragged out of here. He's finally on the mend. He'll die in jail."

Seth had been on his feet since the woman entered the room. Now he moved to the stove at its rear. "Mrs. Franklin, I talked to Miller last night. He's comfortable Calhoon is under guard."

"It's temporary. Isabel believes he'll be back. Now, I know Hemple. Peter is friends with him, but Peter isn't here. This is your matter," she said and thrust her finger at him, then, appearing to focus on him for the first time, she drooped. "So what he said is true, you're no longer involved in the investigation?"

"I'm involved, but no longer in charge."

She held her hands out. "So, you've been demoted?"

Sweet Jesus, she sounded like Jubal. "Treasury has assumed responsibility for a case it probably should have been working all along. I am still responsible for investigating your nephew's murder, which we believe might tie in to Guthrie's."

"I can't believe this is happening." She was looking at him, her eyes wide, seemingly appalled. "And what has gotten into your captain? The...." She caught whatever expletive she'd been about to spew out and straightened defiantly. "He banged on the door. *Banged* on it, as if we'd locked him out and he intended to knock it down. We'd just gotten Eli to sleep. He's still in a lot of pain, for heaven's sake, and no sooner does he finally fall into a deep sleep—and Alice, too, she'd been up all night—than that fool bangs on the door like he intends to storm the place. You may rest assured I was plenty upset before I got to the door, and I was dumbstruck to see your man had done it. Maybe you should tell him the Army has been relieved of the matter?"

He already had, but Betty Franklin's inadvertent implication that perhaps Jubal's enthusiasm for the case stemmed from displaced loyalty filled him with unease. He'd also let Isabel leave yesterday, with Daws, and showed little interest as to where she'd gone. "Do you know where Miss Hays went?"

Betty Franklin waved her hand. "I think she plans on intervening with someone she knows to set this Miller straight."

Seth rolled his eyes and started around her.

"Are you certain it won't help to speak to Don Hemple?" she said, following.

He didn't need Don Hemple. He didn't need Isabel, either. He needed people to quit stomping their feet in front of the damn cottonmouth.

She veered left to the sickroom, and he kept straight into the dining room and out the back door. In the kitchen, he found Zachary and Spain. Both were at the table. Both rose. "Do you have any idea where Miss Hays went off to?" he asked Zachary.

"Gran' Gu'f and a ship nawth."

"The next time we send one of our men off with her—and at the moment there's still a need for next time—ask her where the hell she's goin' before she leaves."

"Yes, suh."

Seth turned back to the house.

*B*ecky saw Seth Parker peeking in the door, and her heartbeat quickened.

Alice had gone back to sleep on the cot after breakfast, and Eli snored softly in the bed. She was careful not to change that. Parker stepped back when she came out.

"Where is your mother?" he asked when the door shut.

"Vicksburg," she answered, keeping her voice at a whisper. "She wanted to talk to someone about this situation with Eli." She raised her chin "Treasury has arrived. I assume you know?"

He nodded.

"She knows this person Miller who was here yesterday and fears he's a threat to Eli."

"But you don't know who she intended to talk to?"

"I don't, but Daws went with her. He should be able to tell you something when they get back. Oh, but she was going to Rodney before returning here. She wanted to check on The Pink Lady."

"She's going to Rodney to bring Tobias Holbein up to date."

He was right, of course, but she didn't respond to his contradiction.

He turned a step, and she asked, "Is it true you're working for them now?"

Pivoting back to her, he said, "Who told you that?"

"The other one. The one that wasn't Miller."

"What else did he say to you?"

She didn't like the dark mood reflected in his face, and she felt blood rushing to her temples.

"Did he ask you anything, Becky?"

"He asked if I were the half sister." She licked her bottom lip. "Is it true what he said?"

"Hell, yes, you're the half sister!"

She startled.

"I need to talk to you," he said. "Let's go in the study."

Chapter Forty-one

She followed without protest, but when he closed the door, she turned on him. "Is it true you're working for them now?"

"No, it's not true. Technically, I'm no longer working the Guthrie murder at all, but I am still working Franklin's." He stepped around her and walked to the desk, turned, then leaned back against it.

"Treasury has decided to get involved with Guthrie's murder. On the surface it appears almost out of the blue, but out here it correlates uncomfortably close to your brother's being shot and Jon Franklin's demise. Right now, the Franklin killing is keeping me involved, but I'm not standing in a particularly good place. To tell you the truth, Miller's agreeing to keep me around is open to conjecture."

She came farther into the room, closer to where he stood. "Having your men watch my brother might explain some of it."

"He doesn't need my men to watch your brother. He could, as he apparently threatened, come in here with the provost and take your brother. Truth is, I think he wants to keep an eye on me."

"And why would he?"

"He's armed with all my past reports to my senior."

"Ralston's relief?" she spat out.

"Yes," he hissed back at her. "Ralston's relief, who knows Guthrie was looking for you the day he was killed."

"I thank you very much for that."

"That last report was verbal and it's what you told me in my office three days ago. Miller and Roscoe, as far as we know, don't know, but they're gonna figure it out. Roscoe asked if you were the sister, so he's already looking at something, which hopefully is nothing more than a weak spot, but I've made a point of not bringing you up with them."

She thrust her chin and swallowed hard. "I apologize."

That took him so much by surprise he was almost unable to suppress a grin, but he managed.

"There's something else Ralston's relief is aware of, and he's written Ralston to try to find out the details. You could expedite things by talking to me."

"What do you mean?"

"I know you were questioned by intelligence officers following your arrest in September of 1863."

She started blinking. Watching her turn away, he cursed himself for not positioning himself between her and the door, but he was quick enough. She'd barley yanked it open when he overtook her and slammed it shut. He seized her shoulders and forced her to face him. "I need to know what they wanted."

She twisted. "Let go of me."

"Those men are dangerous, Rebecca."

"Those men were cruel and hate-filled and stupid."

"Not those three years ago. Miller and Roscoe, now."

"Let me go," she said again, spitting out the words one by one, as if each were something foul she wanted off her tongue. This time he did, and she moved away from him.

"Did they identify themselves?" he asked.

"No."

"Did you recognize them?"

She turned and glared at him.

"I need to know."

"I did not recognize them. I have no idea who they were or where they came from, and I do not want to talk about that day."

She turned her back to him, and he moved closer. "You don't have to tell me about that day. Just tell me what they wanted."

She started shaking her head, as if unsure what to do. "I don't think I want you to know," she said momentarily, her voice oddly high-pitched and laden with tears.

"Why not?" He wanted to shake her. He wanted to hold her.

"I have my own plans, Major."

"Vengeance?"

She whirled on him. "Justice."

"Southern justice," he cried. "I'm the one trying to find real justice."

She choked on a laugh. "Listen to yourself. 'True' justice, 'real' justice. You're speaking of 'legal' justice in a system bereft of such a thing. The only true justice *is* Southern justice as you put it. We talked about this three days ago, and that was before you were working with Treasury agents, who even you admit are dangerous."

"Which is why I don't want you dealing with them, dammit." He straightened. He didn't want to be cruel—as she described the men who questioned her three years ago—but he was running out of options. "I recently talked to a woman named Faith Lawrence."

She breathed in. She wouldn't meet his eyes now.

"I know you were in labor when they were questioning you.'

She blinked, still refusing to look at him. For an interminable moment he heard only her labored breathing. Then she spoke.

"My water had broken, and I was bleeding. They considered that 'so unfortunate.' All I had to do was tell them what they wanted, and I could get help for my baby."

He had braced himself when she stated she'd been bleeding. Despite the steel in her voice, her deep breaths were giving away how much this was taking out of her.

"Did their questions deal with military activity?" he asked. "Anything you might have known about troop movements?"

Her eyes did meet his then, and they filled with tears. "Good God, no. It would have almost made sense then, wouldn't it? Torturing a woman and an unborn child if the forces of unwarranted aggression had actually had lives at stake?" She squinted at him in disbelief. "How could I have known of such things? They wanted to know about a letter. A letter from Congress. They wanted to know if I'd seen it, if I had it, if I knew where my father's copy was. If it had burned with Hickory Grove.

"The day the raiders came to Hickory Grove, my baby had been moving constantly. After I was shoved and fell in the barn, I didn't feel him move again, not ever. By the time I got to Vicksburg it had been almost a full day. I was already bleeding when they sat me in a hard chair in a filthy warehouse, but I knew my baby was already dead, as was his father and my father and brother and sister. So I endured their stupid questions and listened to their sick comments regarding the fate of my unborn child and my *duty* to their perverted Union, which"—she turned and glared at him—"I will go to my grave despising. And I sat in my own blood for hours, enduring cramps, then labor pains, and said nothing beyond my screams when the contractions were so strong I couldn't stifle them, until someone, somewhere put a stop to it." Her glistening eyes remained focused on him.

"I had no idea what they were talking about. I still don't know what they were talking about. So you take my pitiful bit of information and share it with your new associates and Ralston's damn relief...." She choked on her tears.

"Becky," he said and took a step toward her, but she scurried back.

"Do with it what you will, but you leave me alone now."

She was gone. He stood for a moment, numb, staring at where she'd been only a moment before. Then he walked back to his chair and sat, sick at heart and filled with self-loathing.

But he'd profited from the ordeal he put her through. A congressional letter, which said what? Having the bastards who questioned her would help. They could fill in the what and why they'd needed the thing. Maybe Ralston could provide their names, but Seth's gut was telling him no record had ever been made of the interview. Ralston might know those details, if the interrogators told him the truth when he'd learned of the incident, assuming he really had been unaware until after the fact.

<h1 align="center">Chapter Forty-two</h1>

"She was going to Vicksburg," Seth said, watching Miller enter his Port Gibson office. "From there down to Rodney to check on her establishment."

"Business booming?" Miller said, taking the empty seat in front of Seth's office desk. Roscoe was already sitting in the other. Miller had a mug of fresh coffee in his hand. He trailed behind Roscoe because he'd stuck his head in the door of Poynter Cummings' office to say good morning. Roscoe partook of nothing, no cup of coffee, no friendly chitchat. Seth had offered him coffee, but not chitchat.

Miller settled and eyed Seth, who said, "There've been patrons every time I've been there."

Seth took a sip of his own coffee, much appreciated in the wake of a restless night. Becky's confession of the afternoon before gnawed at him, even in the cold dawn of what promised to be a beautiful late January day. Spain had the stoves going by the time he and Cummings arrived half an hour ago, and most of the chill was gone from the building's occupied spaces.

"I conducted some business there during the war," Miller told Seth.

Roscoe said nothing, simply sat quietly watching Seth, who leaned back congenially and wove his fingers together at the back of his head. "Clandestine?"

"Operations certainly, but also cotton factoring, black market—oh, transfers didn't take place, not as a rule, don't get me wrong. Agreements rather. Some interesting people patronized the place. I imagine they still do."

"You should write a book," Roscoe said.

Seth thought he might have heard sarcasm threaded between Roscoe's words, but Miller merely pondered them a moment, then nodded. "I might one day, only I'll make it about you, Felix."

Sarcasm worked both ways.

Miller turned back to Seth. "But my point is, we can't trust Isabel Hays. There are all sorts of things that make that woman successful, not just mankind's oldest profession."

"I'm aware of that, Mr. Miller."

"Who told you she was going to Vicksburg?" Roscoe asked.

Seth stiffened. It wasn't so much the question, but the way he said it, as if he were accusing Seth of something.

"She told her daughter her itinerary. I expect she'll be back today."

"You checked on Calhoon while you were out there?"

"I did, he's..."

A knock, then Spain was in the open doorway. "Majah Hemple heah, suh."

Seth rose, so did Miller once Hemple was through the door. They shook hands, Seth's attempt at an introduction cut short by Miller, who assured him he and Roscoe had made a courtesy call on the provost yesterday afternoon. Roscoe grunted a greeting, then offered a hand almost as an afterthought. He didn't rise. Ignorant and rude. By birth or by design?

"Spain," Seth hollered, "find us another chair."

The private complied, and Don Hemple sat. "I looked for you two over at the hotel earlier. Glad I've found you together." He unbuttoned his blouse and pulled a dispatch from inside. "The morning courier brought me this from the district provost." He handed it to Miller, who started to read. Hemple glanced at Roscoe, then looked at Seth. "Basically it directs that one Eli Calhoon is not to be removed from his sickbed until his condition has been appraised by a military surgeon in consultation with Calhoon's personal physician, Ephraim Lester of Port Gibson. If confinement is rendered appropriate, Colonel Calhoon, ex-CSA, is to be placed under guard at his residence." Don Hemple gave Seth a slow grin. "I don't know who the hell was involved in this, but that throwing in the civilian doctor to 'override' the army surgeon, and that's really what it means, implies a lot of influence."

"Looks like she screwed the district provost last night," Roscoe said.

Seth said nothing, but Miller sighed. "What she's attempting to do is screw us." He looked up from the paper he held. "General Wood signed it." He handed the document to Seth. "It further states that upon agreement of both physicians, any subsequent directives to move the detainee are to be coordinated through the provost marshal of Claiborne County.'

With a quick smile, Miller nodded brusquely at Hemple, who said, "I am here to serve when the time comes."

"Well," Miller said, "this, at least, makes your sergeant's attempt to mollify the situation a couple of days ago official. Not that I had any complaints with matters as they stood."

"I take it," Hemple said, "that you two gentlemen believe Calhoon killed that Treasury agent back in October?"

"He's the best candidate at the moment," Miller said.

"Why?"

When neither Miller nor Roscoe spoke, Hemple looked at Seth, who said, "I'm officially off this, Don, but there're indications that Eli Calhoon and Alan Guthrie may have known each other."

Don Hemple raised his chin. "Really? Hmm." He stood. The others did, too, even Roscoe. "Gentlemen," he said, and shook Miller's hand. He didn't look at Roscoe this time, but he did look at Seth. "I'll talk to you later.

"Oh," he said at the door, "Do let Betty Franklin know that for the moment all is well, will you, Seth? She came to visit Sally late yesterday. Sally said she was foaming at the mouth over this.'

Chapter Forty-three

Miller and Roscoe left for Hinds and Madison Counties not too long after. Miller said they wanted to talk to the sheriffs and provosts in both counties in regards to Guthrie's murder. Seth had thought those interviews would have accounted for their delay in reaching Port Gibson, or the time between Miller's leaving Washington and arriving Vicksburg, though Roscoe's recruitment probably explained that.

Most of all, Seth figured Miller would have wanted to talk to Isabel. Seth sure did, but with the directive from headquarters already in place, maybe Miller felt no compelling need to pursue the issue. Seth didn't feel such complacency, and he was particularly curious to know over whom in Vicksburg Isabel held such influence. It meant riding out to Camellia Creek and the real possibility of seeing Becky, whom he both did and did not want to face. He figured he must be feeling like a remorseful drunk who woke up in the morning to his wife's battered face. Regardless of how bad he felt about the previous afternoon, Becky had given him more information than he required and more than he had asked for, though he'd wanted to know. No matter his self-recriminations, she had shared her personal pain with him, and she'd done so willingly, just like she'd done days before in their discussion on Ralston and Trueblood.

"No, suh, we nevah did go to headqua'tahs," Daws told Seth. "We went to da house a' Judge Pendleton, outside a' Warrenton, not too fah from Vicksbu'g, but we didn't see no army where we wuz."

"You know Judge Pendleton?"

"No, suh, but all of us from dat pawt a' da county know him's house."

"The house still stands, no damage?"

"No, suh, none. He be a Unionist. I heah tell 'im always friendly to Grant an' Sherman, an' all dem gen'rals an' such durin' da wah, an' dey to 'im."

Interesting. Just he and Daws were in the office at Camellia Creek. "Tell me what you heard."

"We got to da house. Ole Mistah Pendleton come out on da poa'ch to greet 'er, real friendly, like dey know'd each otha a long time, but he tol' 'er Lila be visitin', but Miz Isabel, she laugh an' say what she had fo' 'im be worf da risk. An' he say, gib me a hint, and she say 'Sam.'

"Him's face lights up wif dat an' he say come on in. Dey lef' me sittin' in da carriage in front a' da house. In a little bit, out dey come again, still real friendly like. She smile at me an' say we goin' on back to Rodney."

"Did she talk to the lawyer?"

"Yes, suh. Went to see da lawyer early befo' we come back heah dis mawnin'."

Seth pursed his lips, then looked his corporal in the eye. "If anyone asks, you never heard her speak the name 'Sam.'"

"Who, suh?"

Seth frowned, then smiled when a big grin spread across Daws' face. "Good report, Corporal."

"*I*'ve known Lawrence Pendleton for almost forty years. He was another of Isaac's associates." Isabel's tinkling laugh was poignant with memory. "He was always friendlier to me than Isaac's other friends were. Larry likes women. The other reason for my choice in securing aid is that Larry and the district prevost have become quite close."

Seth had found Corporal Daws in the kitchen when he first arrived at Camellia Creek around eleven. When he'd exited the office with Daws fifteen minutes later, he'd found Isabel Hays drinking coffee with Cassie Franklin at the dining room table.

Chatty Cassie was dominating the conversation, which dealt with sponge-washing the scalp as opposed to the hair and some wonderful secret rinse Alice used on her hair, and she most "certainly did wash every strand, and often, too." Isabel had smiled when she saw him and requested he join them. He declined, not so much averse to the ladies' discussion, but because he really did want to speak to Isabel about Judge Pendleton. He'd apologized to Cassie, then spirited Isabel away.

"Larry established himself in Warrenton as a territorial lawyer two years before statehood," Isabel continued. "A Virginian and a true adherent of protectionism. Isaac used to get so irritated at him for that. Later, years after Isaac died, Holland told me Lawrence's proper place was with Louisiana's sugar merchants instead of Mississippi's cotton growers. But he was still likeable and well-respected for his legal abilities, if not his economic views, which I believe he limited to his social circles. In the thirties, the legislature appointed him to the bench. In the forties he sat the state supreme court. He was a powerful and respected jurist. Larry was a Whig and loyal to the Union, but he was not a Union Whig as Daws led you to believe. Sam Caruthers was a Union Whig." Isabel leaned back on the settee, the gold of her satin dress a shimmering contrast to the worn, red velvet of the couch. "Holland described Sam to me once as a Daniel Webster Whig, if that makes sense to you."

Seth nodded. His grandfather on his mother's side, the one from Fulton County, Kentucky, called the credo putting the Union before the Republic.

"Then in the early fifties Larry was accused of taking a bribe in the case of a murder for hire, allegedly paid for by the youthful and vivacious widow of the deceased. But the case was dropped, and shortly thereafter the defendants wed.

"The dead man was Silas Caruthers, a favorite uncle of Sam Caruthers. This uncle was actually two years younger than Sam. Sam had expected he, or one of his sons, would inherit Silas' property, but, alas, Amanda Strickland Caruthers had given birth to a baby boy the month before Silas' untimely death.

"His death was originally ruled a suicide, which Holland maintained it was, Amanda's baby having been sired by the co-defendant, who had been Amanda's lover long before she ever wed Silas Caruthers. Silas was a widower who'd been married twenty years without issue. Ecstatic over the birth of his believed-to-be son, he was devastated when he learned the babe was not his, and he took his own life."

"So, Sam Caruthers questioned the death?"

"Indeed he did. Of course, nothing could be proved. It was, in the mind of the presiding judge, Lawrence Pendleton, a clear case of suicide, and he dismissed the case. When Amanda turned around and wed the accused coconspirator, intending to live happily ever after with her little family off Silas Caruthers' money, Sam, according to Lawrence, decided to wreak vengeance by framing him for taking a bribe. It was well done and ruined Lawrence's career as well as his good name. Lawrence hates Sam."

"Do you believe he could have taken the bribe?"

"Anyone could take a bribe. Knowing the two men as I do, if you're asking which one is more likely to be lying, I'd tell you Sam. The truth is Lawrence didn't need money. He was a successful cotton planter in addition to being a judge, and if he were going to take anything from Amanda Strickland to dismiss the case against her and her beloved, it wouldn't have been money, but something Lawrence would have truly appreciated."

Seth cocked his head, and Isabel smiled.

"Lawrence is a pervert, Major. It's not a big secret among his associates, but I do request your discretion. His tastes are harmless, but there are some things money cannot buy, at least not from everyone. Several of my girls like what Lawrence likes, which is another reason he remains so fond of me."

"Daws mentioned the name Lila?"

"Lawrence's sister-in-law, and yes she does, to some degree."

Seth didn't say anything, so it must have been the discreet stirrings in his groin, indiscreetly reflected on his face, that propelled her on.

"She is his deceased wife's sister. Lawrence lost Patricia fifteen years ago. The sister's husband passed on six years later. Since then, they have been consoling each other with periodic games of master and mistress."

"He tells you this?"

She smiled. "During his stays at The Pink Lady, he visits my office where he recuperates between bouts, and we reminisce."

Seth drew back, widened his eyes, then asked, "What exactly did you offer Pendleton in regards to Sam Caruthers?"

"Why, I offered to help him tear Sam's little railroad all up, metaphorically speaking."

"And is that the naked truth or are you truly speaking in metaphors?"

"The naked truth is so boring, don't you think?" She leaned forward and said softly, "It's what lies unseen, behind the veil, that entices."

"Quit playing games, Isabel. This is serious."

"More often than not it is," she said, rising.

He rose, too. "Dangerous?"

"To the heart and the soul...and sometimes to life."

If Isabel did have something else on Sam Caruthers, would she have shared it with Lawrence Pendleton? He looked out the east bank of windows, down to the lake where Mattie and the two girls stumbled in the rough grass at the water's edge. The sky had dawned clear and cold. Blue skies remained, but the day had warmed some. The ride hadn't started his shoulder aching.

"Since you admit Sam Caruthers is the man you thwarted by going to Pendleton, does this confirm you believe Miller is working for Caruthers?"

"I tell you with all confidence that Walter Miller is working for himself. That may or may not put him at odds with Sam, depending on their mutual goals. And I would never presume to redirect you from your duty, Major, but I would hazard a guess that Miller's goals could be at odds with Treasury's. My purpose in meeting with Lawrence was to thwart what I believe is Sam's determination to remove Eli as an obstacle to Sam's railroad."

Well, Isabel had something on Caruthers, he was sure of that, and he didn't have enough leverage at the moment to force her to tell him what that was. "Railroad" would suffice for the time being. Her little coup, with this fellow Pendleton, had removed any residual worry they had regarding moving Calhoon from his sickbed, at least for the immediate future.

"Is Becky sitting with Calhoon?"

"Betty Franklin is in with both Eli and Alice. Becky has returned to Hickory Grove."

"What?"

Isabel's lips parted, but he snapped—"When?"—and looked out the window. "She left Mattie and the girls?"

"She left at first light, Major. She'll be back either late this afternoon or in the morning, but I would guess this evening. Betty said she was actually wearing a riding habit and went on horseback, so she planned for a quick trip."

"That area is not safe for lone male travelers, much less a woman."

"Hector's with her, and I don't need to be lectured. We are all aware of the dangers now prevailing in the state, but she didn't ask my permission. She left early this morning, before I got back. Elvie said she'd gone to retrieve a letter Naomi wrote her last fall informing her of Eli's return. She hopes it will support his case against the murder accusation. Now, I trust you're done with me?"

"Do you know anything of Sam's betrayal of family?"

She raised her chin. "Where did you hear that?"

"Poynter Cummings. My first thought was of his confiscating Muscatine from Becky and his railroad initiative at the expense of his Calhoon relations, but Cummings' accusation was spoken with a conviction belying the mere betrayal of distant cousins."

"Closer kin you mean?"

"Yes."

"Well," she said and turned to the door.

"Is that your answer?"

"Yes," she said, moving on and not looking back.

"Did you know your daughter was questioned during her incarceration in Vicksburg two and a half years ago?"

She stopped and turned back. "As to?"

"Perhaps interrogation would give you a better perspective."

The smile left her lovely face. "Interrogation?" she said slowly as if mulling the meaning over on her tongue.

"For hours."

"But why?"

"I was hoping you might tell me."

"She told you this?"

"She did. Did you really not know?"

"I knew something had happened, but I attributed that to the loss of the baby. What was she asked?"

"What Becky told me, she told me in confidence."

Seth saw Isabel's jaw tighten. "No, she never said anything to me, nor can I believe she said anything to you. Is this subterfuge a tactic suggested by your new secret-agent friends?"

"Lying and subterfuge are your tactics, Isabel."

"I've never lied to you."

"Subterfuge then, and I'd appreciate your not letting Becky know I told you this. My purpose was to determine if you knew who would have questioned her, because she claims not to know anything about what they wanted."

"Who questioned her?"

Seth shook his head. "I believe the actual names are inconsequential. The real question is who would have wanted her questioned?"

"Dammit, Parker, what did they want to know?"

"The whereabouts of a congressional letter."

He swore she paled. Then she breathed deeply through her nostrils and whirled away from him, toward the door.

"Hey, wait a—"

She spun back, index finger already raised and shaking at him. "I will promise not to divulge your indiscretion in telling me about the questioning, and in return you will respect my desire to speak no more to you on this matter."

"I need a name."

"I don't have one."

"And I'm supposed to accept that's not a bald-faced lie?"

Her smile wasn't pleasant. "Think of it as subterfuge, because I truly know nothing for sure." She was out the door and gone. For a moment he stared into the empty hall, then took his seat. He could make a wild guess as to who wanted that letter, but he couldn't know for certain without knowing why he would have wanted it and why he searched for it where he did. Besides, Sam Caruthers' access to military assets would have been limited, no matter how strong his bonds to the occupying forces. There had to have been some sort of pretense in regards to military objectives. Isabel herself had explained the reason given for the raid on Hickory Grove. Similar charges had been made regarding Camellia Creek — treason, support to the enemy. Now, Seth laughed out loud at the absurdity of it. Becky had been right not so long ago. They were at war. Such charges were nothing more than covers for rapine and plunder that were ubiquitous. "Let's go have a little fun, boys. Give these Southern traitors what they deserve." It would be impossible to prove anything in the way of a self-aggrandizing conspiracy. Besides, no one in authority cared, not then and not now. Isabel and Becky believed it was fruitless to try and find justice in a system that had betrayed them in every way imaginable.

Nevertheless, they believed the particular attacks had been purposefully orchestrated, and for a particular reason. Now he was beginning to see why. But even if Caruthers was the genius behind the crimes, someone in a position to order the so-called tactical raids for military expediency had to be involved, and he found himself pondering Becky's recriminations of Ralston and Trueblood.

And what the hell did any of this have to do with Alan Guthrie?

Chapter Forty-four

When Becky saw the mounts in front of her appropriated home on the ravaged Hickory Grove plantation, she prodded the little mare Buck had dubbed Honey into a gallop. Behind her, she heard Hector do likewise with their gelding Nate. Hector beat her to the parsonage by only a length, and she was sliding from the sidesaddle when one of Seth Parker's troopers, a saddlebag over one shoulder, stepped out on the porch.

Seconds later, she was up the steps and blocking the man's way. Hector waited at the bottom of the stairs, the bridles to both their horses in his hand.

"Where's Parker?" she said to the man. She didn't know this one's name.

"Ain't heah," the young man said, not attempting to advance.

She narrowed her eyes on him. "What's your name?"

He reached for the forage cap atop his head, then appeared to catch himself. "Private Hand, ma'am."

"What are you doing here?"

"I come wif—"

"He's with me," a voice called from within.

Immediately, Becky dropped her interest in Private Hand and stepped through the door into the dim entry. To her left, in the front parlor by her desk, stood Walter Miller. Closer to the room's entry was Roscoe, the man who had spoken to her at Camellia Creek. He watched her with arrogant contempt. Becky called down the front hall, "Polly, are you all right?"

"She's fine," Miller said.

Becky glared at Roscoe as she moved past him. Miller watched her come with an amused tilt to his lips.

"What are you doing here?" she asked.

"I'm confiscating documentation as part of a murder investigation."

She yanked open the top left-hand drawer of the writing desk. Empty, as was the one beneath it and the two on the other side. The middle drawer was open. It, too, was bare. She whirled back on Miller, who gave her one last look before turning his back and starting toward the door.

"By what right did you break into this house?"

"I told you," he said, not even bothering to look at her, "I'm investigating the murder of a Federal agent."

"And what has that to do with me?"

Miller was on the porch now. She looked over the ramshackle room once more before following him out.

"Private Hand, mount up," Miller said, before looking down his nose at Becky. "Indeed, that's a good question, madam. What does that have to do with you? Perhaps we'll find something."

Behind her, Roscoe put his hands on her shoulders and moved her roughly to one side, then stepped around her. She glared at him. "Don't you touch me again."

He touched the brim of his hat. "Then keep out of my way." There was a veiled warning in that, and her face heated. He did not move.

"Do you have a warrant?" she screamed at Miller's retreating back.

"I don't need a warrant, Mrs. Mackey."

"This state is not under martial law. You most certainly do need a warrant." She took a step forward. Again Roscoe pushed her. Shaken now, she glared at the man, and the hint of a grin shaped his lips.

Private Hand stood on the porch near her, his way partially blocked by Hector, who had dropped the bridles and climbed two steps up. Righting herself, Becky grabbed for the saddlebags draped over Hand's shoulder. A scuffle ensued, with the surprised Hand clutching the bags to him, and Roscoe grasping Becky's upper arms and shoving her hard against the railing, her outstretched hand still ahold of the bags. Pain sliced her side. Hector inserted himself between Roscoe and her, his back to Roscoe so that he protected Becky like a shield. Roscoe struck and Hector, who was not a young man, collapsed against her, then fell to the porch. Becky screamed. Roscoe raised his fist again. Sunlight glinted off brass knuckles, and Becky let go of the saddlebags and draped herself over the fallen Hector.

She wasn't sure what happened next, because she had her head bowed over Hector, but the next voice she heard was Hand's calling out, "No, no you won't."

She twisted around and looked up. Hand stood confronting the steel-eyed Roscoe, who ground out "Get out of my way, you stinking nigger."

"What the hell is going on here?" Miller barked and shoved Roscoe back before glowering down on her. "You'd best stop your troublemaking, Mrs. Mackey, or I'll place you under arrest for interference in a Federal investigation."

She rose to her knees. "I want my letters. They'll exonerate my brother and you know it."

"If they do, they do."

"I didn't see any letters, Walter, and I emptied the desk," Roscoe cooed.

Hector groaned. Becky started to lurch forward, Roscoe moved, so did Hand. Miller raised a palm and placed it square against Hand's chest. Roscoe twisted around Miller and brought himself closer to Hand.

"Whatcha gonna do, boy?" he sneered.

Hand's face hardened, and he pressed against Miller's hand. Roscoe flexed the fist that bore the brass knuckles. Miller looked at Hand. "Get mounted, now." Hand stood his ground.

Becky scrambled to her feet. "Go on, Private, before you get in trouble."

Miller dropped his arm and told Roscoe to settle down and get on his horse. "Now!" he hollered when Roscoe gloated.

Roscoe snickered, then turned away.

Hand, the saddlebags still on his shoulder, looked down on

Hector, stirring on the floor of the porch. "Do you think him'll be okay?"

Becky squatted beside Hector, her movement awkward. Her own side was hurting. "He'll be all right." At least she hoped he would.

"You should consider the consequences of the trouble you start before you react, Mrs. Mackey."

"Go to hell, Miller."

"Let's go, Hand, before we have to hurt anyone else."

"Go on, now," Becky told him quietly. "He'll be all right." Hand started away. "Private Hand?"

He looked back.

"Thank you."

He gave her a two-fingered salute, then bounded down the porch steps.

She touched a spot behind Hector's right ear. He winced, and she felt blood under her fingertips. "There's some swelling."

Hector sat up and touched the spot himself. "Fall hu't worse dan my head. Bones gettin' too old fo' hittin' da flo' dat hard."

"I'm sorry to have involved you in this."

"Heah be Polly," Hector said, and the woman Becky always left in the house when she was gone slipped out the door and kneeled beside them.

"Dat fella got a hit like a hamah."

"He used brass knuckles," Becky said, helping Hector to his feet.

Polly took his other arm, but before they could maneuver him inside, he lurched to the railing and threw up. After wiping his mouth on his coat sleeve, he said, "Seen such, ain't nevah gib no man cause to use 'em on me befo'."

And there'd been no cause today to use the things on anyone, much less an old, gray black man trying to protect a fool woman from herself.

Becky looked down the road at the dust cloud created by the retreating horses, then she and Polly guided Hector into the ransacked house.

"Dey done to'h up da mattresses, Miz Becky," Polly said.

Searching for something other than the letter so important to her? Perhaps, the same letter so important to whoever two and a half years ago? "Did they hurt you?"

"No, ma'am. Dat one white man tol' dat nigga sol'ja to kick open da do'h when I tell 'em weren't no one heah an' dey should come back. Didn't eben ask a second time, Miz Becky. Didn't say what dey wanted. Jus' tell me to open da do'h. Da white men, dey set to wo'k goin' through evah'thin'. Had da sol'ja' takin' all yo' stuff from da desk der."

They had the letter that could exonerate Eli...or be used against him. Becky sat hard in the chair. They couldn't have known of its existence. And they had her journals, four filled since the fire, with her private thoughts and fears and dwindling hopes, all for her eyes alone.

She checked the damage to the rest of the house. All the mattresses and pillows had been ripped open.

Polly, who had accompanied her, said, "We sho' gots us a big mess to clean up heah, Miz Becky."

Becky squeezed Polly's bony wrist and moved back up front. Hector was on his feet.

"Cyrus in da qua'tah?" he asked Polly, who answered yes.

"I'll go git 'im. Him'll fix up dis front do'h. You take stock a' what dey took, Miz Becky. Den we'll go tell yo' mama what dey done."

"I want you to sit down. Polly, you run get Cyrus." Becky wasn't even sure where her mother was at the moment. It was Seth Parker she had words for.

Chapter Forty-five

"**I**'ve got to talk to him man to man," Seth told Betty Franklin. She had her arms folded over her breasts, and her face was the mask of a harridan. All she needed was a rolling pin. "I know he's in there by himself."

They were in the hall, in front of the sickroom door. He'd watched Alice leave the room with Cassie not five minutes ago, and for fifteen minutes before that, Cassie and Elvie had been shunting hot water from the kitchen to the bedroom the two Franklin women used at present. He figured Alice was bathing and she'd be occupied at least a little while.

"He is resting."

"He's asleep?"

She huffed. "Not at the moment, and he won't be if you go in and bother him."

"Look, I need to talk to him in private. You're the only female in this place with whom I have a fighting chance."

"And what is that supposed to mean?"

"It means your primary concern is doing what's best for Alice. All the rest of them, Alice included, treat him like he's a newborn. He's a grown man, wounded maybe, but he's got some problems he needs to be aware of and at the same time, with a little information, I might can ward off."

"What you're going to broach with him is going to upset him."

"He's tough. He can handle it."

She raised a finger, but Seth said. 'Alice's happiness depends on him, right?"

She breathed in.

"Understand this, Mrs. Franklin, his confinement within this house is conditional. If we don't get this mess resolved, eventually an army surgeon is gonna walk through that door"—he turned and pointed in the direction of the dining room and, hence, the back door—"and declare Calhoon fit for the brig, and Dr. Lester is gonna have to agree. It's gonna happen."

Betty dropped her arms, looked down the hall to where Alice and Cassie were holed up, then nodded at the door. "I'll give you ten minutes."

Damn, it was good for her he was a nice fella.

"Feelin' better?" Seth asked, laying hold of the straight-back chair near the bed and situating it to better see Calhoon.

"Yeah," the latter responded. "Should have seen me yesterday. I was yellow."

"Still are a bit."

"I was canary yellow according to Becky, with ochre cheeks. Today I'm amber."

He was propped up on pillows, appeared to be dressed in a nightshirt, and was covered from the waist down with quilts. He needed a haircut, but someone had given him a shave recently, and he smelled of soap.

"I'm told you've fought off another fever."

"I have." His voice remained weak, but stronger than when last they spoke.

"We need to talk."

"Sit," Calhoon said, a wary curiosity in his eyes.

So, Seth sat. "Your womenfolk tell you that you're officially under arrest here at home?"

Calhoon frowned.

"They tell ya I'm no longer officially working the Guthrie case, that Treasury's taken it over?"

"Haven't mentioned that, either."

"I didn't think so, and I wouldn't have myself, but I need information, and I need you to understand why. I'm gonna talk quick 'cause Betty Franklin has me on a schedule. Guthrie was lookin' for your family. Not just you, but your father, brother, and sister—Hannah. He didn't know about Becky till he got in the area, but he found out about her. We think he was returning to Port Gibson from her house the day he was killed."

Calhoon opened his mouth to speak, but Seth anticipated him and said, "Becky didn't meet him. She'd been in the Raymond area that day, but her servant described him, that's how we know it was him. Becky made an entry in her journal.

"Now, here's where things get murky. There's a possibility the raids on both Camellia Creek and Hickory Grove during the summer of 1863 were predicated on the recovery of a congressional letter sent to your family, probably to your father."

Seth let that sink in, gauging the man's reaction. After a moment, Calhoon asked, "Does Alice know this?"

"I don't think so. She knows you're being looked at for the Guthrie murder, but doesn't know why beyond cotton thieving."

"Becky?"

"She knows more than you or me. Isabel knows plenty, too. Once I'd have said she knew everything, but now I know that's not true. There are things about that summer your sister's keeping from her mama, and there are things Isabel knows she's not sharing with anyone except maybe Tobias Holbein. The reason I came to you is to ask if, one, you know anything about that alleged congressional letter and, two, why Guthrie would have been looking, specifically, for you Calhoons."

"Do the letter and Guthrie tie together?"

"I was hopin' you could tell me."

Calhoon blew out a breath. "I wish I could. So, Treasury is trying to pin the Guthrie murder on me because they think he found me last fall, and I killed him...because of the letter?"

"Correct on your killing Guthrie, but no one has supplied a reason, and I don't know where that congressional letter fits in."

"Do you think he was involved in the raid on Camellia Creek?"

And therein would lie Calhoon's motive. "He was in the west during the fighting," Seth answered, "but his record says he served in Arkansas. There's nothing official on him ever being in Mississippi."

"What does Becky say about the raid on Camellia Creek?"

"She thinks Sam Caruthers was behind it. Isabel kinda confirms that by implying Caruthers' confiscation of Muscatine is tied to an old railroad initiative, but she's never said anything to me accusing him of involvement in the raid. But I've reviewed that right-of-way, and it requires parcels belonging to Camellia Creek."

Calhoon said nothing, and Seth asked, "Has he approached you at all regarding selling him the land he needs?"

"No, but relations are strained over Muscatine and have been for a while."

"Since the summer of 1863 I would imagine."

"Yeah," Calhoon sighed bitterly. "Since around the same time as the raid." He met Seth's eyes. "What do you think?"

His asking surprised Seth, but pleased him nonetheless, because he did have some thoughts on the matter.

"If Caruthers' initiative is legitimate, I'd think he would have already approached you regarding the land he needed for the right-of-way. At least made an effort to see if you were even amenable to selling."

"Unless he had a guilty conscience."

"Or didn't plan on having to spend the money at all."

Calhoon's visage darkened, but he didn't ask for clarification, and Seth knew that was because he didn't need any.

"Let's assume Becky is right and Caruthers was behind the raid on your farm three summers ago. Your father was dead, you were gone, and Becky was already dispossessed of Muscatine. She certainly wasn't living here at Camellia Creek. What was keeping Sam Caruthers from taking this farm as a loyal citizen?"

"It wasn't abandoned. That's how he got Muscatine. Becky had left it to help at Hickory Grove."

"*You* might claim it wasn't abandoned, but I think Caruthers and his friends in high places could have made the case it was, had they been so inclined. You need to think about that, because I have. I'm not satisfied as to why Naomi Polk wanted you dead. Let's suppose your aunt made a deal with the same man who was managing to keep Becky off Muscatine. Your surviving the war and coming home might have messed up some well-laid plans."

"You're suggesting Sam Caruthers was working with Aunt Naomi, but I gotta tell you, Parker, I know Caruthers and I knew my Aunt Naomi. Here's what I'm seein' and you're not, because you don't have the hindsight. Caruthers wouldn't waste his time working with Naomi Polk, not on any venture."

"Then why didn't he take this place away from her?"

"Are we sure he wanted it?"

"You tell me."

Calhoon didn't answer, and Seth said, "If he played a part in the raid on this farm, we must assume he wanted it for some reason, yet he made no move to run Naomi Polk off, and theoretically there should have been nothing stopping him."

Calhoon issued a soft curse. "She had something threatening him. That's just the kind of sneaky thing she would do."

"That's what your sister thinks, too, and I have to tell you, when Becky hinted at that to me, it meshed real well with my doubts about the reason for your aunt's attack on you and Alice."

"But what about Hickory Grove? You tied that incident into that congressional letter, too."

"Those two raids came close together and the one common denominator is Becky, who we should look at as a Calhoon."

Calhoon released a gentle breath. "And Guthrie was looking for the Calhoons"—he frowned—"but two years later?"

"Interesting, huh?"

"'Stretching it' might be a better way of putting it. Does Becky know about the congressional letter?"

Seth had dreaded the conversation's taking this turn. He had hoped Calhoon was aware of the congressional letter and would willingly tell him what he needed to know, but that had not proved to be the case. Now, he was about to be bombarded with questions that could potentially violate Becky's trust.

"Yes."

"So, she has concluded that Caruthers is the person looking for the congressional letter."

"Yes. She says she never saw the letter. I'd hoped you had or, at least, could make an educated guess about what it related to."

"Sorry. How did you learn about it?"

Calhoon was watching him, waiting for an answer to a reasonable question. He'd told Isabel about the interrogation, but he wasn't going to violate Becky's trust again.

"Your sister told me things in confidence," he said. "I won't betray her trust. I wanted to know what you knew of the letter and any thoughts you could share on why Guthrie would have been searching for all you Calhoons. Now, I know you don't know more, but at least you know as much as I do, and that's a good thing. Maybe something will occur to you."

Calhoon raised his chin, then nodded sagely. "So, she told you about the letter."

Seth didn't confirm it. He didn't need to. The answer was obvious.

"On a related matter," Seth said, "have you ever heard the name Martin Trueblood?"

"He's Peter Franklin's cousin."

Seth's jaw fell open. Well, wasn't that a kettle of fish to fry.

"From the look on your face, I've told *you* something."

"You sure as hell have."

"Aunt Betty and Cassie talk about him all the time. He and Peter were speculators before the war. Trueblood was stationed in Vicksburg for two years, and he talked the Franklins into coming to Mississippi."

Now Seth recalled Alice had told him about Peter Franklin's cousin the day they'd met. "He's the man who accompanied Peter Franklin to New York with Jon's body?" And he was living in Vicksburg.

"Yep. How does he fit in?"

"He validated the confiscation of Muscatine and its transfer to Sam Caruthers."

"You think he was involved in the raid on Camellia Creek?"

"Not necessarily, but I fear your sister suspects him."

"I need to talk to Becky—"

"Not yet. If you do, she'll know I'm the one who talked to you, and she might not talk to me ever again. If that proves to be the case, I'll have to leave your ass to the mercy of Treasury operatives."

"It's hard for me to believe she's confiding in you, Parker "

"She's my source for everything I just brought up with you, so believe it, and don't mess it up. It's me or Treasury. Your womenfolk think you need protection from the truth. In Becky's mind, she can't talk to you. I can and will. Be happy with that."

"Does she *trust* you?"

"Do you?" Seth snapped back, because if Calhoon didn't, could he trust the man's denials regarding both the letter and his knowing Guthrie?

Calhoon smirked. "Don't get huffy, Parker. I do tend to trust men who save my life."

But could he trust Calhoon? Well, Seth judged him for an honorable man, and in the minds of such men, Eli Calhoon did owe Seth Parker.

"In answer to your question about Becky, not completely. Worse, she claims to have her own agenda, which she implies my investigation hinders. But understand, Calhoon, this Federal investigation is happening. There is no getting around it."

"Becky's after Caruthers."

"She's calling it 'justice.' How about you think on what that congressional letter could have been about, and why Guthrie was looking for the lot of you."

"How do you fit in, if Treasury's taken the investigation?"

"I'm holding on to the Franklin murder."

"You think it's related?"

"Who the hell knows, but that doesn't prevent me from saying it is. And in regards to Guthrie's murder, keep in mind that Treasury isn't looking much beyond you as the culprit. *You* are the one they want. Your pseudo-stepmother called in some markers with a Judge Pendleton, who arranged for the district prevost to require a surgeon's authorization prior to your being removed from this house, so you're good for the moment. And Calhoon....?"

"What?"

"Stay put."

"I intend to. How is Treasury seeing Becky?"

"As far as I know, they aren't aware Guthrie was searchin' for her the day he was killed, but I figure it's only a matter of time."

Chapter Forty-six

 etty Franklin knocked on the bedroom door moments later, then entered. Alice and Cassie were about done, she told Seth. They had best finish up. Seth made one last entreaty to Calhoon that their conversation stay between them, then went off in search of Isabel, only to learn from Frank Zachary she'd absconded with Peters to Rodney.

Seth had no doubt she'd gone to Tobias Holbein about that congressional letter and Becky's being questioned. With that, he left Lawson in charge of the "prisoner," gathered up his sergeant, and returned to Port Gibson.

 rivate Hand shifted his gaze from Seth to Jubal Summers and blinked from the glare of the sun, low enough on the horizon now to blaze through the dirty glass into Seth's office.

"There's nothing she's gonna do," Jubal said.

Hand stepped forward. "Dat Roscoe shoved her. Weren't no call fo' 'im to do nuffin'. I had da bags. She couldn't a' took 'em from me. Den when her nigga tried to protect 'er, dat fella hit 'im in back da head. He weren't eben lookin' at da Trez'ry man, Cap'n. He weren't threat'nin' 'im, jus' protectin' da woman."

"Was she hurt?" Seth asked. He was pretty sure he'd kept his voice even.

"Had to been, at leas' some. He shoved 'er hard against da rail. He raised 'is fist. Had dem brass knuckles. Dat's what he hit da old man wif. An' weren't no call fo' any of it. He jus' be mean. I seen white men an' niggas bo'f like 'im. Mean. Ain't no otha way a sayin' it."

"And you're sure they didn't have a warrant?"

"Sho' I be. She eben ask'd if'n he had one an' Millah say him didn't need one."

"What did they take?"

"Evah'thin' in da desk an' we searched da whole house. Ripped open da mattresses, like dey thought she mighta hid somethin'."

"So you ransacked the place?"

"Like durin' da war. Yes, suh."

"I didn't know they were gonna do that," Jubal said.

"She say she wanted 'er letters. Say der was one she—"

A blow, it could hardly be called a knock, preceded the bursting open of the office door. A disheveled and oh-so-beautiful Rebecca Mackey, in riding habit, stood at the threshold, her breasts heaving. She looked first at him, then Jubal, and her eyes lingered a moment on Private Hand.

Seth had risen. "You're intruding, Mrs. Mackey."

"Intruding?" She seized the edge of the door, and he stepped to one side of his desk. "You've never seen intruding as I've witnessed it. Let me give you some idea of what *intruding* is."

He leaped forward and grabbed the door before she managed to slam it against the wall. Foiled, she kicked it and broke his hold. It hit the wall, but not with the force it would have had he not intervened.

"Stop it, Becky."

She turned, wide-eyed, and glared at him. "By what right did you send vandals to Hickory Grove?"

She was shaking so hard she could hardly talk.

"Ain't 'iz fault, Miz Mackey. Majah didn't—"

"Private," Seth barked, "I can defend myself against the woman."

"He is your man and you sent him out there with Miller," she choked out.

"Yes, he's my man."

Her eyes filled with tears. "You're responsible. Or is this another case where the policy makers didn't know the policy being executed by their magnificent soldiers?"

"I sent him with Miller," Jubal said.

She sneered at Jubal, then turned again on Seth. "He's yours, too."

"Men, excuse us if you would."

Hand hesitated, looked at Seth, then left. Jubal followed. Becky tried to step out of their way, but she appeared so discombobulated Seth took her arm and moved her to one side. She freed herself, and he waited until he'd seen both his men out the front door before he closed the one to his office.

"This morning, Miller told Captain Summers he needed one man to help him search a house and seize documents that might be related to the Guthrie murder."

She breathed through her nose, watching him as he spoke. "Did Miller tell him it was my house?"

"Yes."

"And why, Major Parker, weren't you consulted?"

"I wasn't here. I was at Camellia Creek hoping to talk to your mother and brother."

"That dog Roscoe hit Hector in the back of the head with brass knuckles. Hector, for Christ's sake! You've seen him. He's just a poor old man who was trying to protect me."

"Where is Hector?"

"He's at Hickory Grove. He wanted to come with me, but he was in no shape to travel, and I was in a hurry."

"So he's up and walking around?"

"Hopefully he's lying down, but he can walk around if that's what you mean. Why did they come to my house?"

"What did they take?"

"He took the letter which tells me when Eli got back in the area. He's going to destroy it and frame Eli for murder."

"That's the letter you went to retrieve?"

"Yes, he beat me there."

"Who else knew why you were going?"

"Elvie," she cried, "and she wouldn't have told anyone but Mama."

"Would you sit?"

"I don't want to sit," she spat. "I want my things back."

"What else did he take?"

"He took my journals, my letters, all the papers in the house."

"Your letters from your husband?"

Head bowed, she sank into one of the worn arm chairs in front of his desk. "I took all my letters from James with me when I moved to Hickory Grove. They were destroyed when the house burned. All the little personal items he gave me were lost." She rubbed the ring finger on her left hand. "One of the soldiers at Hickory Grove stole my wedding ring," she said with a heavy voice. "It was set with rubies and diamonds. It had been James' maternal grandmother's."

She looked up quickly. "My journals. Everything I'd written since the fall of 1863." She sucked in a ragged breath. "They were personal. I don't want those people reading them." She leapt to her feet. "I want them back. He had no right to take them. He had no warrant. What is he looking for?"

Originally, Seth's fear had been the same as hers, that somehow Miller had learned she had a letter that would exonerate her brother and the man had hastened to Madison County to get it and possibly destroy it. But why her journals and, Hand had verified this, every piece of paper in the house, even searching for something that might be hidden? Still looking for a congressional letter, perhaps?

"Private Hand said he kicked the door open."

She raised her defiant chin, but said nothing.

"What's the extent of the other damage?"

"They gutted the mattresses, pulled everything out of the drawers. The contents were strewn all over the house. Yankees find a great deal of fun in that." She stood suddenly and took an awkward step toward him. "I don't care about that. I want Aunt Naomi's letter back. I want my journals. And I want everything else I don't even know is missing."

He reached for her arms, but she folded them over her breasts and stepped back.

"I'm going to go to Mr. Holbein. The war is over. We are not under martial law. You awful people cannot do this. We are Americans, too. You all *insisted* on it, and you are not going to continue this tyranny unchallenged."

He didn't try to touch her again, but said softly, "I want you to go—"

"No! Where are those people working out of?"

As far as Seth knew, Miller had not acquired a working space in town. At the time Hand had knocked on his office door to make his report, Miller and Roscoe were at the hotel, because Hand himself had carried the loaded saddlebags up to their rented rooms.

"You can't just waltz into wherever they are and retrieve that stuff. They've taken it as part of a Federal investigation."

"They had no right!"

"That's not relevant," he said, his voice loud now. "They will arrest you, dammit. Don't you understand that? Go back to Camellia Creek right now!"

For a moment she hovered in front of him on the verge of tears, just staring. Suddenly she pivoted, and he didn't like the determination in her step. He reached out and grabbed her arm. She flinched, and he stiffened. "Are you hurt?"

"No," she answered, but she was careful in extricating herself from his hold.

"Where are you going?"

"I am going to Camellia Creek, then I'm going to Rodney to talk to Tobias Holbein, and if he can't help, I'm coming back to Camellia Creek, I'm getting my daddy's gun, and I'm going to kill Miller."

Well, he had a little time anyway.

Spain was in the outer office. "Escort Mrs. Mackey back to Camellia Creek, Private."

She started to protest, but Spain's face had lit up so, she apparently decided not to ruin it for him. His men had become quite fond of Camellia Creek, of Aunt Elvie's fried chicken and Isabel Hays' supplementary pay.

They were out the door. He closed it behind them, then

turned to his office and spied Cummings standing in the door to his own.

"You do realize Miller didn't know about that letter," the man said. "How could he have?

"And he wouldn't have had to ransack the whole house for it either."

Cummings smiled. "He's looking for something else."

"Yep, and I hope he's still looking."

Chapter Forty-seven

Seth heard the door to the front room squeak open before he'd made it back to his desk. He sat, facing the door, and locked up as Private Bo Hand was about to knock.

"Come in, Private."

He did come in, but stopped. "Might'n I close da do'h, suh?"

"You may."

"I done somethin' I shouldn't a' done, an' I weren't quite decided what to do about it." He was unbuttoning the middle two buttons of his army blouse. Now he pulled out a package of what appeared to be letters held together by a length of red ribbon tied in a bow. "She say at da house dey took da letter dat would he'p 'er brother. I can't read too good, an' sides, didn't really 'ave time to sort through 'em on da way back, so I took da whole package." He laid the stack on the desk in front of Seth. "I was gonna gib 'em to 'er, but den I thoughts dat might be too bad a thin' to do, so I thought I'd let you decide."

Seth touched the stack, then pulled it closer. After a moment, he looked up at his pensive private. "You understand, Private, that initiative is both important and dangerous. Orders must be obeyed. However, there are times when decisions must be made on the spur of the moment that dictate countermanding stated orders. The trick is knowing when the latter is the case."

Hand swallowed. "Yes, suh."

"Problem is most men tend to hide behind orders or end up misjudging the moment when countermanding is called for, or simply bungling it."

"Yes, suh, but it weren't no milit'ry action, just rightin' a' wrong."

"What you thought was a wrong."

Seth watched Hand's jaw tighten. "Yes, suh."

"Why did you steal the letters?"

He hesitated, then apparently resolved, squared his shoulders. "I tol' you what he done to dat ole nigga man. He'd a hit 'im again, but Miz Becky fell on top 'im, protectin' 'im. He'd a hit 'er, I think, if'n I hadn't moved an' Millah come.

"It ain't like I nevah seen such befo', I have. I seen a white man protectin' a nigga from a beatin' an' I seen it go da otha way. I seen white on white, dat's jus' folks' way, but no matta der's right and der's wrong. I knows, seein' what I saw, who be right and who be wrong at dat house this mawnin'. We to'h dat place up an' took 'er stuff an' da only right we had was Millah's say so. Den Millah tol' 'er dat ole man gots huht 'cause of what she done. Like folks s'posed to stand around while dey treated dat way."

"You had all the items taken?"

"Yes, suh, dey lef' me to carry da bags. I lagged behin' 'em on da ride back. Was me stuffed da papahs in da bags. I know'd where dat package was. I jus' slipped it out an' into my coat."

"Did you listen to any of their conversation on the way out or back?"

"Dey didn't talk much, no speculatin' if'n dat's what you mean. Jus' kept dem eyes on da road. Did ask me goin' if I knew da whereabouts a da house or church, but I didn't. Dey foun' it easy enuff."

Seth picked up the letters, set the package on one long end and slapped its edge on the top of the desk. He looked at Hand. "You made a good decision, Private Hand, not only morally, but in our case, tactically." He found the letter from Naomi Polk near the top of the stack, now he pulled it out and grinned at Hand. "Not only do we have the evidence, we got it without violating Miss Becky's rights ourselves. Treasury will take the blame."

Hand smiled. "You gonna gib it back to 'er?"

"Maybe, but only after I read it. Do you recall taking her journals?"

"Dey was da writin' books?"

"Four of them apparently."

"Yes, suh, but I didn' take 'em out. Jus' da letters."

"Will Miller miss the letters?"

"Yes, suh, he saw me put da letters in da bags an' she told 'im when she got der she wanted da letter.'

Seth pulled out a sheet of note paper, then penned a brief note to Becky. He folded it. "Private Lawson is at present on guard duty at Camellia Creek. I want you to relieve him. Lawson is to return to Port Gibson." He handed the missive to Hand. "Give that to Miss Becky. Don't mention taking the letters. I intend to look through them all, then decide whether or not I'll return them."

"Yes, suh."

"And stay there. I'll inform the sergeant."

"You don't want me seein' dose Trez'ry men."

"I don't want them seeing you."

The front door had no sooner closed behind Hand when Poynter Cummings appeared in Seth's doorway. Seth already had the Naomi Polk letter out of the envelope and had started reading. It was short. Cummings came in and sat in a battered chair in front of the desk. "Does the letter exonerate him?"

"No, it was dated the seventh of October, two days before Guthrie's demise."

"She would have destroyed it."

"No doubt. In fact, I can't rule out the possibility her real purpose in rushing home was for that very reason."

"But then she would have told Aunt Elvie she was going to destroy a letter incriminating Calhoon, not clearing him."

Seth handed Naomi's letter to Cummings. "Hardly incriminating, but it is something that could be used against him in proceedings that might require very little evidence to convict."

"You gonna give it back to her?"

"Yep."

"Treasury could consider that obstruction."

"Treasury *will* consider it obstruction, Cummings, but who's gonna tell 'em?"

"Not me, I'm on your side, and I'm especially on her and Calhoon's side."

Seth considered the possibility that Cummings might play both ends. Still, for the last reason the man had stated, he didn't think so. "What they define as obstruction in this case, I define as a peace offering."

"You think that will get you into her good graces?"

"It won't hurt." Seth untied the bow holding the letters together. "I'll probably return the bulk to Miller as appeasement. I wonder what sent them out to her place?"

"Do they know Guthrie was looking for her?"

"I sure never told them, but don't forget that they know why Guthrie was here, and we don't."

Chapter Forty-eight

Seth opened the door to the newspaper office next morning and braced. Spain stood at the counter, watching what was making the racket in Seth's office. Cummings was on the other side of the counter, also watching events unfold inside the room.

He closed the door to the front room with a clatter and strode forward. "What the hell is going on?" he demanded.

Spain, who'd spun with the slamming of the door, said, "He say—"

"Your office is being searched, Major," Cummings said.

Seth near about tore the counter door off its hinges getting through, and Cummings stepped back to get out of his way.

"What do you think you're doing, Roscoe?"

The man looked up at him, then yanked out another drawer to the credenza behind the desk. Most of what Seth stowed in this space were personal items and not even many of those. But there had been some work papers, now a mess on top of the desk and strewn on the floor.

Roscoe had stopped what he was doing when Seth entered. "Get out," he said, now. "I'll let you know when you can come in and clean up."

On the floor, Seth spied the rope-made boatswain's billy that he'd owned since his last year at the academy, a small item, a memento from the old retired boatswain's mate who considered Seth his finest pupil. Seth set a palm on the surface of his desk, then bent down and picked it up with his right hand.

"Did Miller send you over here for something in particular?" he asked Roscoe.

"He's wearing the knuckles," Cummings said.

"And I know how to use them." Roscoe took an ominous step closer. "You and your people are out of line here, Parker. You know what I'm looking for. If your nigger didn't give them to you, then he gave them to the woman. I almost hope you haven't got 'em because then I can—"

It was over almost before it started, probably because the dirty street fighter looking down his nose at Seth wasn't expecting it. Seth, halfway up, still supported by the desk, swung the billy hard into the side of Roscoe's left leg. He went down howling as Seth came up, raising the billy above his head then bringing it down on Roscoe's shoulder, near the neck. If what he'd been taught was valid, he'd shattered the man's collarbone and God-only-knew how many other bones in close vicinity. Roscoe didn't howl, this time, but cried out in a screech of agony. The knee, of course, was crippled. Seth should have aimed that following blow to the head. That would have ended it for good. It would have also been murder.

Seth looked down at Felix Roscoe, writhing on the floor. There was no blood, but there was a devoted enemy. Cummings was beside him. "Damn, Parker, remind me never to get on your bad side."

"Just give me time to think about it, Cummings, and you'll be okay. It's those spontaneous reactions that'll get you killed."

"I'd settle for just not getting hurt."

"Then don't overstep yourself." He reached down and tore Roscoe's right hand from his injured shoulder and pried the brass knuckles from his fingers. Roscoe was breathing hard. Seth's moving him had hurt him more. He turned to find Spain staring at him, mouth agape. "Go get Dr. Lester."

*S*eth returned to his quarters, pulled the letter from Naomi Polk out of the stash, squirreled it away in another part of his blouse, then went off in search of Walter Miller. He found him in the dining room having breakfast. Seth slapped the ribbon-bound pack of letters down on the table beside the man's plate. Miller looked up.

"You might have asked me first before sending your goon over to ransack my office." Seth yanked out the dinning room chair opposite and sat.

"You might have brought me these."

"What makes you think I didn't intend to?"

Miller shrugged and took a sip of coffee. "He was to search, not ransack."

"Bullshit, Miller, you know how the bastard operates."

"Got carried away did he?"

"He did, figuratively and literally."

Miller seemed to focus on that. "Where is he?"

"Doc's got 'im."

"You shot him?"

Seth leaned closer. "I beat the shit out of him."

Miller leaned back and grinned. "Maybe I hired the wrong man."

"For ruthlessness and intimidation, you hired the right man. I intend to have Mrs. Mackey submit a claim for the damage y'all did out there yesterday."

"Your man —"

"Was operating under your direction. Her claim will be made to Treasury."

Miller smirked. "Like so many others of late. Go ahead, have her submit it. I'll even give it a favorable endorsement. Doubt she'll ever see any compensation, though."

Seth rose and Miller looked up in mock surprise. "I thought you intended to join me for breakfast, Major?"

"I've things to do. You might want to check on your man. Doc's name is Lester. Spain can show you the way."

*B*ecky sat on the settee in front of her father's desk. Seth, arms folded across his chest, leaned back against the desk and watched her. She'd received his missive to wait on him, and she'd complied.

She looked up. She hadn't needed to read the thing, really, because the only thing that mattered was the date.

"Treasury has seen it?"

"No. You can thank Private Hand for that. He removed the letters from what they took and brought them to me before Treasury realized they were missing."

"Had you told him to do that?"

He laughed. "No. I really didn't know they were going to search your place, Becky. Hand did it all on his own initiative after you protected Hector the way you did."

"Roscoe was demeaning to everyone there, including Private Hand."

Well, Roscoe would be a bit under the weather for a while.

"And what of the other letters? Hand wouldn't have known which one I needed."

"I read them each and every one. Finding nothing of value, I returned all but that one to Miller this morning to mollify him, at least, for the moment."

She squinted at him.

"They knew the letters were missing, Becky. Soon enough they'll realize this one is still missing. You apparently mentioned it yesterday?"

She wet her lips with the tip of her tongue. She was so beautiful and so vulnerable sitting there, not sure what to do next.

"It doesn't indict him," he told her, "any more than a date two days after the ninth of October would have cleared him."

"I'm not giving it back to you."

Keeping his eyes locked on hers, he smiled, knowing he could take it from her. Knowing she knew that, too. "What do you intend to do with it?"

She looked at the stove in the back left corner of the room, which he knew was lit. She stood. "I'm going to burn it."

"Go ahead."

And she hurried to do so, as if she feared he'd change his mind. He watched her wad it up, then toss it in. She slammed the stove door shut and turned to find him watching her. "It was just a simple little thing. Two sentences, but I wanted to keep it for posterity, for grandchildren and great-grandchildren, so they could share, what was to us, a brief moment of happiness in a time otherwise filled with sadness." She started back his way. "You have no idea how much I despise the North for what they have done."

"It's not the North that made you burn that letter, Becky."

"Maybe not, but it's the North and its corrupt government that abets men such as Sam Caruthers. It's the North that has sent corrupt agents into our midst and keeps them here under the protection of the military. I'm so glad Sam Caruthers belongs to them now. He's what they deserve, because he'll turn on them first chance he gets. I can only pray his treachery results in the demise of what they're creating."

"We're all one now," he said softly, not wanting to encourage her anger. "Their demise would mean your own."

"Maybe that would be for the best, instead of allowing them to build a faux Union on the ruins of the South, desecrating our Founders' Republic."

He only allowed himself so much empathy for her sedition, so he quietly changed the subject by asking if she still intended to go to Rodney and talk to Holbein.

"Miller still has my journals, my other letters, and who knows what else."

"Does he have the journal that records the redhead coming to your home?"

"I'm still writing in that one."

"Good. Try and keep it out of his hands. Now, is there anything in the others that would imply treason?"

"Treason to the Northern government, you mean? Does a deep, unyielding hatred for Lincoln qualify?"

He held up a hand. "Anything that links you to organizations that threaten the United States today?"

"No. The journals are mostly random thoughts on my loves and losses and were for my eyes alone. That doesn't mean the likes of Miller won't read more into them."

"Anything about your brother?"

"And seditious groups?"

"Yes."

"Nothing."

"I'll try to get them back, though my standing with Miller is strained right now."

"In answer to your question regarding Mr. Holbein, I need to get home to Hickory Grove soon and clean it up, but I won't do anything unless Mama agrees to stay. I fear the possibility of the provost trying to remove Eli from this house."

"An inevitability if we don't get this cleared up."

She drew in a stuttered breath. "Thank you for giving me the letter."

"You're welcome, but you might want to say something to Private Hand.

"I intended to. Are we done?"

They were, and they entered the foyer as Cassie Franklin, still in winter outerwear, emerged from the dining room on their right and almost collided with Betty Franklin coming out of the sick-room.

"Daddy's home," the girl said and grasped her mother's hands. She gave a little bounce in apparent delight. "Cousin Martin is with him."

"And your Aunt Eustacia?"

Cassie started bouncing again. "That's the most absolutely wonderful part, Mama. She's not here." The girl giggled, then turned, apparently to include Seth in the jubilation. Becky hung back.

"I did make it to Jones' Grocery before I came," Cassie continued to her mother. "Martha has everything she needs for supper tonight."

"Cassie, where is your aunt?" Betty asked.

The younger woman graced her mother with a brittle smile. "I didn't ask. I didn't think we wanted to know."

"If only not knowing meant we'd never learn of her whereabouts."

Seth took a tentative step forward, and Betty turned her eyes to him.

"I only recently learned that your husband's cousin is Martin Trueblood, Mrs. Franklin."

"What of it?"

"He dealt with the confiscation of Confederate property during the war. It's my understanding that he was a speculator in civilian life."

"Yes. Peter, too."

"I need to talk to Mr. Trueblood."

"Is this about Jon's death?" she asked.

"Yes.

"Then come to supper," Cassie said.

Betty blinked at her daughter, as dumbfounded it seemed by the invitation as was he.

"I don't need to im —"

"Of course, do," Betty Franklin said, looking first at Cassie, then back to Seth. "Arrive around seven. You can talk to Martin then. Peter, too. We'll eat promptly at eight."

The handsome Mrs. Franklin hooked her arm through her daughter's and the two of them disappeared into the dining room, en route the kitchen, no doubt. Becky moved closer.

"I want to see him," she said.

"You should come to dinner, too."

"I was not invited."

She started away, but he touched her arm, and she tilted her head slightly over her shoulder. She did not look directly at him. "What do you plan on asking him?" she asked.

"All of it. The raids, confiscated property, the buying and selling of land...Sam Caruthers." He didn't bring up her interrogation. He knew it must be at the forefront of her mind, but she didn't broach it either. She'd tacitly done that when she said she wanted to see the man, meaning she wanted to see his face.

Chapter Forty-nine

Becky refolded the letter and stuck it back between the same pages of the old Calhoon Bible where she'd found it. The letter had been dated the 30th of August 1863. At the bottom her father had written, Luke 21:16. She read the referenced verse one more time, then slapped the Bible shut when her mother came into the room. Isabel stopped short, looked at what lay in Becky's lap, then gently closed the door and sat beside her at the foot the bed.

"What's the matter, darling?" her mother coaxed.

"I found a letter from the U. S. Congress in this Bible." She turned and found her mother's guarded face. "Dated the end of August, 1863."

When her mother said nothing, Becky asked, "Did you know it was there?"

"It was in the Bible when I found it at Naomi's house. Your father must have put it there. It was placed at the chapter and verse he annotated on the letter."

"'And ye shall be betrayed both by parents, and brethren, and kinsfolks, and friends; and some of you shall they cause to be put to death.' He believed someone close to him had betrayed him. Who, Mama?"

"The letter refers to a decades-old matter that concerned both the Calhoons and the Carutherses. Toby continued to work it at the latter's request after your grandfather said to drop it. Holland was not aware Toby continued to pursue it. After this area fell under Federal control in 1863, Sam asked Toby to draft a letter requesting the matter again be addressed. That letter in the Bible was Congress' response. Unfortunately for Sam, Congress informed all persons concerned, so Holland's learning of the matter was by accident. He confronted Toby, and they made their peace shortly after. That's all there was to it."

"That's all there was to it, Mama? My daddy was dead within days of when he must have received that letter. What did the letter concern?"

"Dear God, Rebecca, it was a property dispute, and there is no reason for you to assume it had any bearing on your father's death."

Becky glared at her mother, and for the first time that she could ever recall, her mother turned away from her scrutiny. Becky's eyes filled with tears. "No reason for me to assume it had any bearing, Mother? And what do you know of what I base my assumptions on?"

Her mother turned back, regret in her eyes.

"Aunt Naomi knew it was in there, you know? That letter was her insurance. That's why Sam Caruthers never tried to force her off Camellia Creek."

Her mother didn't question that rationale, so she must have already reached the same conclusion. But Becky's reason was because she knew that during the late summer of 1863, someone had desperately wanted that letter, and it was a foregone conclusion that person was Sam Caruthers. So, what had her mother based her conclusion on?

"When did you find this out?" Becky asked.

"This past November."

"You saw this letter?"

"No, Toby told me."

"Why?"

Her mother shrugged. "He was trying to explain Sam's obstinacy regarding Muscatine. Holland also had words with Sam. It all tied together."

Yes, Mr. Holbein had told her mother, but the reason could not have been as simple as her mother was trying to make it. Her father had had words with Sam Caruthers over Muscatine a good month before that letter was written.

"And the status of this property dispute, as you put it?"

"Overtaken by war and death. Toby doubts it will ever be addressed again."

Becky turned to the window. Outside, an ancient cypress shuddered against a clear blue sky. Dark green leaves of camellia and azalea bristled beneath it. It was a beautiful winter day, but cold and windy, best observed from inside. She placed the Bible between them on the bed, then whispered, more to herself, "It's what they wanted, now I know. What I don't know is why."

Her mother raised an arm to pull her close, but Becky stood, out of her reach.

"I want you to tell me, Rebecca, what you meant by someone wanting that letter?"

Becky furrowed her brow. "And in return, you'll clarify the hogwash you're trying to feed me now. You keep things from me, Mama, to protect me, you say. Do you ever consider that you do more harm than good?"

"I need to know what you know."

Becky shook her head. "I'd rather try to find answers on my own than deal with your well-meaning prevarication." Much to her chagrin, her voice broke, and she started around the bed. "I refuse to deal with this now. I need to find the girls. I promised Eliza a story, and Mattie needs a break."

Chapter Fifty

In Peter Franklin's brightly lit dining room, Seth weighed the speculative value of Sam Caruthers' railroad against the Calhoon-Mackey land in Warren and Claiborne Counties required to make it a reality. Then he considered its value against the price, assumed already paid. It was too high to make sense.

Cattycorner to him, one seat down at the head of the table, sat the man who had purchased a plot of Calhoon land, at above-market price Seth now knew, which included a chunk of the presumed right-of-way. At the other end of the table sat the not-so-elusive, as it turned out, Martin Trueblood, a favorite cousin and childhood friend of Peter Franklin, and the person who, if Seth had pieced this evolution together correctly, had advised Peter what land to buy.

Betty Franklin sat across from Seth. She'd placed her daughter next to him, and Cassie was in fine form. She was moderately pretty, certainly no match for her mother's beauty, but Cassie could turn a head or two and apparently had. Unfortunately she'd allowed too many of those heads, if rumor were valid, to turn hers.

Betty Franklin had brought up the subject of Walter Miller at dinner. Martin, as he'd asked Seth to call him, admitted knowing the Treasury agent. He'd had the misfortune more often than he liked of working with the man, who was quick "to confiscate from those who confiscated" in the name of the Federal government, but readily ran illegal sales of similar confiscated property, primarily cotton, for his own benefit. Miller had been involved in two operations that Martin was aware of, in which joint Army-Treasury agents had broken up illegal activities between

Vicksburg and New Orleans, and a similar one, between Natchez and New Orleans. These had taken place in the fall and early winter of 1863-1864. The thefts had continued, Martin conceded. Miller returned to Washington, and Martin had eventually gone home. Martin Trueblood readily admitted that he was back, eager to commence land speculation, and he knew where to make his investments.

Indeed he did, Seth surmised. Martin had spent two years in and out of the county clerk's office in Vicksburg, and God only knew how many trips to Jackson and other counties, ascertaining which property was available and why. Seth hadn't missed Peter Franklin's guarded glances when Mrs. Franklin's mention of Miller had led to his cousin's candid remarks about confiscated property and his desire to invest in land. How much the elder Franklin and Trueblood had discussed Jon's death, Seth didn't know, but certainly they had. As far as the land speculation went, the matter held little interest to Seth at present. He was already aware of it. What he really wanted to know was the working relationship between Martin Trueblood and Sam Caruthers during the war. Seth glanced at Betty Franklin, graciously accepting a compliment on the meal from her husband's cousin. The Franklin dinner table was not the place for further inquiries. He needed to talk to these men on his own ground.

After dessert, a darn good custard pie, which Betty Franklin pointed out Cassie had made, Seth rose to depart. Franklin and Martin were tired after their journey, and Seth had endured a trying day on his own. He thanked Betty and Cassie heartily for the meal, then turned to Franklin, who'd risen when he did. "I'd like to talk to you and Martin privately if I could."

"About Jon's death?" Martin asked.

"Yes, but tomorrow is soon enough." He turned back to Franklin. "My spaces at the newspaper office?"

"What time?"

"Ten."

"We'll be there, Major," Martin said and thrust out his hand. Seth took it, then shook Franklin's and was extricating himself from the table when Betty Franklin said, "Cassie, dear, please escort Major Parker out."

"I will," she said happily and rose.

At the front door, Cassie took his hand and, glancing behind her where there was no one, stood on tiptoe and surprised him with a kiss on the cheek. "Mama has decided she'd like to see us together, but have no fear of me, Seth Parker, I know your heart belongs to another."

The kiss had been a surprise, the revelation a shock. Not sure what to say next, he opted for deflection. "I thought you were engaged?"

She shrugged and added a sad smile. "Nathan has forgotten me. I received one letter from him before Christmas, and it lacked affectionate regard. If ever I receive a second, I fear it will say 'adieu.' No, I'm a free woman, and that concerns Mama." The girl smiled brightly and with a little curtsy added, "I know she pretends to hold you aloof, the war having been so devastating for her, but I've seen how Rebecca Mackey looks at you when you are unaware. Do not despair, sir. There is hope for you yet."

He thanked the girl for her unsolicited encouragement and went to the barn in search of Boon, wondering with each step what Cassie was telling Becky about him.

Chapter Fifty-one

"How did you learn of Sam Caruthers' plan for a railroad, Mr. Trueblood?" Seth asked, purposefully reverting to formal address with his questioning of the man. Yes, the question was leading, but Seth thought the approach would save time and give him the advantage. It was raining this morning, had started in fact before he got back to the hotel last night. His shoulder was hurting, which could account for his aggressiveness, but the pain was more nag than throb, so far.

"We didn't—"

"Pete," Trueblood said, and when Peter Franklin looked his way, Trueblood shook his head at him, then looked at Seth behind the desk. "I found out inadvertently from Caruthers himself, an accident really. In the early winter of '64 we were in the process of establishing the loyal farms, confiscation of abandoned and known Confederate sympathizers' properties and placing their farms under the management of loyal citizens. It was a way to exploit the land to compensate for the cost of the war and subsequent care of the freedmen. It also provided productive work for the freed slaves, and at the same time, their work helped accomplish the first goal."

Seth nodded patiently. He knew all that.

"Sam Caruthers was supposedly one such loyal citizen. I'd been working with him for months by that time and knew him fairly well. Personally, I would have called him just the opposite, given his support for secession and nominal loyalty to the insurrectionary government prior to the arrival of Federal troops in the area, but Mr. Caruthers knew people I did not. He basically switched sides and offered himself up as regent, shall we say, of confiscated land. One of his associates, another such loyal citizen with whom he was acquainted, happened to be in the county clerk's office on such an occasion. Caruthers and I were studying a plat map, discussing the property lines he was laying claim to, and this third individual leaned over Caruthers' shoulder, snorted, and said, I quote, 'Hell, Sam, you'll get your damn railroad yet, won't you, you son of a bitch.' Neither man smiled. I'm not sure they were actually friendly, but they did know each other."

Trueblood grinned and started rubbing his hands together. "Well, I tell you, Major, I saw profit. I knew the land Caruthers was taking. It was all in the records. And I knew the land he already had. Later, I asked a few questions of the clerk and learned that there'd been a railroad proposed by Sam Caruthers that died in the legislature back in the thirties. I managed to resist being mustered out until after the archives returned to Jackson, and I got my hands on the state records and found that proposed right-of-way." Trueblood looked at Peter Franklin. "Peter had been stationed here, too, but not long. He and I both speculated in land, and I knew for a fact, Pete liked the winters here. I pointed out the potentially profitable investment, and he decided to take the gamble."

"Did you know Jon had contacted Sam Caruthers?" Seth asked.

Trueblood frowned, but it was Peter Franklin who said, "I didn't know Caruthers' name till you told me after Jon's death."

"I kept that information from Pete, and Jon," Trueblood said. "I didn't tell Peter the name of the railroad investor until we were en route New York. That's when Pete told me you'd brought up Caruthers' name."

"That explains why Jon went behind my back," Franklin said to Seth, who nodded.

"And explains why your nephew was trying to pry the name from those who knew people. But Jon did know you were buying land for a railroad investment, right?"

"I told him last summer, but I also told him Martin didn't

want to divulge the identity of the individual spearheading the railroad."

"And now you know why," Trueblood said. "The potential you claimed you saw in that boy scared the hell out of me."

Peter Franklin closed his eyes, then opened them and focused on Seth. "As I told you before, Jonathan had little left to invest, but he appeared enthused. He wanted money of his own to put in, though all I required was his help. Once I had Cassie securely wed, Jon would have become my partner and heir to whatever we built here. That wasn't an honorable position in his opinion."

"He told you that?"

"In so many words. I think that's why he continued to pursue Alice even after she made it clear she was not interested."

"Oh, for Christ's sake, Pete," Martin Trueblood said, "She was a *married* woman. The only way for him to get his hand on Alice's money was for her to be party to her husband's murder. You and I both know Alice better than that, and we know Jon and his scheming well enough, too."

"He didn't deserve to die like he did."

"I don't know that." Trueblood leaned out of his chair, closer to the man he now confronted. "Let's think about this. For him to get away with murdering that Calhoon fella, Jon would have had to kill Alice, too. You've got to face the fact he planned to kill Alice."

"It makes no sense."

"Because he wouldn't get the money?" Seth asked in order to clarify.

Both men turned to him, and Seth wondered if they'd forgotten he was there.

"Yes, of course," Peter Franklin said. "I'll admit that I wanted Jon to marry Alice, but for more than her money. Alice was all that was left of Betty's family. We loved and still love her dearly. I knew I would never have a son. Jon bore my brother's name. Through him, at least, my father's name would continue. Perhaps it's a bit foolish, but Alice and Jon being united was ideal in my mind, if not Betty's. I knew the boy was a bit of a rake"—from his vantage point facing the two men, Seth saw Martin Trueblood roll his eyes—"but I always believed him to have character. I was sure marriage would force him to grow up."

"A 'rake', Peter?" Trueblood looked at Seth. "Shortly after his father died, Jon was accused of rape in New York. You've heard the rumors that he bought his way out of the fighting?"

He had heard them, but before Seth had stopped nodding, Trueblood was saying, "Jon lost his inheritance buying off the girl's family and keeping himself out of prison. That's why he wouldn't take a simple 'no' from Alice the day he went to her home." The man turned back to Franklin. "That's why she had to beat him off with a poker."

Franklin gave his head an emphatic shake. "I can't believe that."

"Peter," Trueblood bellowed, "Jon intended to rape Alice before he killed her."

"What about the money?" Franklin railed back.

"He didn't care about the damn money. Whatever money he needed he planned on getting elsewhere. A man with a drive like that puts all else aside, can't you understand that?"

Seth had no clear understanding of the "drive," but he had already concluded that Jon didn't visit Camellia Creek that fateful afternoon to get Alice's money. That had been lost to him when she married Calhoon.

"His plan could have been as simple as rape and murder," Seth said to the two men. "Vengeance for her spurning him. But the rape was only a prelude to murder."

"So," Franklin said, "like Martin, you believe he went out to Camellia Creek to murder Alice?"

"And Calhoon. In fact, I believe Naomi Polk intended all three of them to die, her ultimate goal to rid herself of Alice and the person who'd cast her off Camellia Creek. I believe she would have killed Jon after he'd rid her of the other two. What I would like to know is what she offered your nephew to go along with her."

Martin Trueblood snorted. "Musta really been something if it was more than Alice's fortune."

"Not necessarily," Seth said. "We've already established that Alice's money was lost to him. Anything, at that point, would be better than nothing."

"Would that Polk woman have inherited Calhoon's estate?"

"If she managed to disentangle herself from the killings of those three?" Seth shook his head. "I don't know what her plans were, but I'm told there were no provisions for her, and I would think Calhoon's half sister would have inherited the estate."

"And Betty and I would have fought it in either case," Peter Franklin said, almost as an aside. "That old woman wouldn't have lived long enough to enjoy the money even if the court ruled in her favor."

Seth wasn't sure Naomi wanted the money. She would have wanted Camellia Creek and, maybe even more, her perverse vengeance on her nephew and his bride.

"Still," Trueblood said, "she could have promised Jon a part of it. He would have been too stupid to realize he might never see it."

"He wasn't as stupid as you think, Martin."

"He's dead. Shot down like a dog on a Mississippi back road. If he'd stuck with us, we'd have all seen a nice little return on our investment and all of it made legally."

Peter Franklin bowed his head.

"Mr. Franklin," Seth said softly, "no matter what her plan, Naomi Polk didn't kill Jon. His murderer is still out there, and until we know who killed him and why, we still don't know if he—or she—is a threat to Calhoon and, therefore, to Alice. Is there nothing else you can tell me?"

Peter Franklin drew in a long breath, then looked up to the ceiling. "It seems there's to be no end to the shame and the embarrassment."

Seth kept quiet and watched the man struggle with himself. Finally, Franklin looked at him. "He told me Naomi Polk was blackmailing him."

"With what?"

"The Blackledge woman's murder.'

Seth's heartbeat picked up a notch. "And what was he paying for her silence?"

Franklin shrugged.

"Tell him," Trueblood said.

"I didn't learn about any of this until a couple of days before he was killed. He wanted me to loan him a hundred dollars, which I probably would have done if I'd had ready cash."

"You'd been loaning him money for a while," Trueblood spat out. "Money we'd consolidated for our venture here."

"That's the money you knew about," Franklin said sharply. "There were other occasions where I'd provided him money from my personal account. Anytime I took money from the common fund, it was with your blessing."

"Hmmpf."

Franklin looked back at Seth. "I didn't have funds available, and I wasn't going to dip into the kitty again. It was getting to be too much. I asked him what it was about. Always before, he resorted to the excuse of 'impressing prospective contacts'. He said wealthy and important people frequented The Pink Lady."

Trueblood guffawed. "And the most expensive whores on the Mississippi."

Franklin held up a staying hand. "I gave him the benefit of the doubt, Martin. For a little while, anyway. Even you said he could be developing important liaisons. That's why you agreed to his expenditures."

Trueblood sighed. "Yes, I did. My mistake in retrospect.'

Franklin turned back to Seth. "I asked him point blank what was going on. That's when he admitted to the blackmail. It was late, so I said we'd go to you the next day. He said little after that and retired. The next morning he came to me and asked that we delay approaching you. He feared you might actually arrest him. He was adamant that he was innocent of the woman's murder, but feared the Polk woman's lies would prove compelling since she was determined to protect her nephew, who she said was suspected of the crime. Jon told me he wanted time to prove Eli's guilt and asked if I'd give him a few days."

"So it's possible Miss Polk compelled him to do her bidding?"

"Certainly, and as for his guilt or innocence in the Blackledge murder, at the time I believed his claim of innocence." He glanced at his cousin. "Now I just don't know."

"You can rest easy on that count," Seth said. "Naomi Polk confessed to Alice that she killed Laura Blackledge, who she said presented a threat to Calhoon at a time when Miss Polk still, apparently, had some reason to protect him."

Peter Franklin leaned back in the chair. "I'm relieved Jon didn't rape and kill that woman. But that doesn't tell you any more about who killed him, does it?"

"No, but I'm still working on it." Seth turned to the other man. "Who exactly did you work for at headquarters, Mr. Trueblood?"

The question appeared to take the man back, then he said, "On paper, I worked directly for Colonel Ralston overseeing the God-awful accountability of confiscated property, the official responsibility of which Ralston farmed out to his immediate subordinate, Lieutenant Colonel Petersen. Neither man bothered me a lot. Why the Army didn't simply promote me to lieutenant colonel and relieve Petersen of that job, I do not know."

"Petersen worked special operations?"

Trueblood waved a hand. "Devil only knows the sort of mayhem he was responsible for. I know he was damn glad to have me on the job handling the other, because accounting for property had little interest for him. Acquiring it to the detriment of the enemy, now that he enjoyed, but keeping up with it after"—Trueblood shook his head—"no, sir."

"When did you first meet Sam Caruthers?"

"Hmm," Trueblood said, squinting at the ceiling. "Let's see, I think I met Caruthers shortly after I'd recovered from my bout with pneumonia. Say late July, early August of '63."

"Are you aware there was a Union raid on Camellia Creek in the late summer of 1863?"

Trueblood nodded curtly. "I am."

"Is this going to be like pulling teeth, Mr. Trueblood? What do you know of it, and most importantly, did Sam Caruthers have any role?"

He was quiet a moment, then said, "I'm the one who took the information to Petersen at Sam Caruthers' request."

"What information?"

"Sam Caruthers claimed this man Calhoon down in Claiborne County was passing operational intelligence to Confederate spies. Petersen wanted to meet with Caruthers. They met. I was not privy to that meeting, but as you are obviously aware, the Calhoon farm was subsequently neutralized."

Seth narrowed his eyes on Trueblood, and Peter Franklin said, "The man who would have become Alice's father-in-law was killed in that attack, Martin."

Trueblood held his hands out, palms up. "There was a war on, Pete. He shouldn't have been working with the enemy."

Well there was no doubt that Holland Calhoon was the "enemy," but Seth was having serious doubts about that being the reason for the attack on Camellia Creek. "From what you're telling me, Mr. Trueblood, Sam Caruthers was the man who provoked that attack."

"Yes."

"On land that just happens to include the proposed right-of-way we're trying to buy up," Peter Franklin ground out.

"The misfortunes of war," Trueblood said but there was less conviction in his tone now. "Besides, I didn't know that then."

Peter Franklin sighed.

"Mr. Trueblood," Seth said, "is there anything else you recall about that raid, and this could be important regarding Jon's murder, because despite what happened that night, Sam Caruthers did not end up with that land."

"And he subsequently expressed frustration over that, particularly when winter rolled around and we started formalizing the transfer of properties to loyal citizens. Turns out that property remained occupied despite the death of the owner and absence of the heirs. I asked him why he didn't challenge the individual squatting on the property and have the Army remove the person. I never got a good answer from Caruthers, but he seemed reluctant to take further action on the place."

The squatter, of course, had been Calhoon's aunt, Naomi Polk. Seth flexed his shoulder. "Let's return to September 1863, and a similar raid on a large plantation over in Madison County, for, as best I know, much the same reason—aid and comfort to the enemy."

Trueblood swallowed. "There were a number of such raids, Major."

"This one was at Hickory Grove plantation. Does it ring a bell?"

Martin Trueblood said nothing.

"A woman was arrested and brought in for questioning."

"I do recall that. Petersen himself questioned her along with one of his operatives, a civilian. He had a number of them. I can't remember that one's name."

"What do you recall of the incident?"

"Major Parker, what are you getting at?"

"Bear with me, sir, and answer my question. Do you know if Caruthers played a role in orchestrating that raid, too?"

Martin Trueblood filled his cheeks with air then blew out a breath. "Those two raids came within a fortnight of each other, I remember that. Supposedly there was cotton stockpiled on that farm. It was to be part of the payoff for the raid."

"Petersen was part of that?"

"As was I, dammit! We're talking the perquisites of war, here, Major."

"We're talking rapine, rape, and plunder...and theft against your own government," Seth shouted. "A Federal soldier was killed, as was a female civilian living at that farm. There was no cotton, was there?"

"No."

"The woman who was arrested—"

"I did not know there was an order to arrest anyone, much

less a woman. The only thing I was aware of was the cotton, which was supposed to be substantial.'

"Was the woman asked about the whereabouts of the goddamn cotton?"

"Major...?" Peter Franklin started, but Seth held up a finger, bidding him to be quiet.

"I don't know what she was asked."

"But you know it wasn't about the cotton, because by then you knew there was no cotton."

"Supposedly the cotton had been moved."

Seth couldn't resist a snotty smile. "When did you realize there *never* had been any cotton?"

Martin Trueblood bristled. "Look here, Parker, can I assume you're going after Sam Caruthers for some misdeed?"

That surprised Seth. "If misdeeds there are, up to and including the murder of your nephew."

"You're not planning on arresting me for anything?"

"For your 'perquisites', you mean?"

"Yes."

"How much justice do you think a Southern 'traitor' would find in a military or any Federal court for events occurring during hostilities?"

"I was thinking of crimes against the U. S. government."

"It can look out for itself," Seth said. "I'm trying to solve murders."

"Samuel Caruthers is a lying, thieving cheat. He used me on more than one occasion, all with the promise of payment that proved fruitless. So I'm going to tell you what I know.

"His initiative against the Madison County property came fast on the heels of the one on Camellia Creek. You may not be aware, but the soldiers who raided the Calhoon farm removed a lot of paperwork."

"They were looking for something?"

"Nominally military information, evidence of Calhoon's passing intelligence to the enemy. It was all provided to Petersen. The raid on the Madison farm followed within two weeks." Trueblood clenched his jaw. "Caruthers was talking to Petersen directly by this time. I have no idea of the whole truth they were concocting, but you know what kind of things Petersen was involved with, don't you?"

"Yes."

"Ralston was the senior in charge, and his was the ultimate authority for the assignment of the unit to carry out such raids. That meant my involvement. For whatever reason, Petersen did not want to run this so-called critical operational matter by Ralston. So he, on the word of Sam Caruthers, who was standing at my side as Petersen briefed me on his requirement for this latest covert operation, subtly bribed me with the cotton. And I'll freely admit that such bounties are the reason I wanted to stay in the Army, at Vicksburg, vice allowing injury and disease to send me home. I worked hard for Ralston and he appreciated it. I more than earned my bounties.

"They plundered that house, too, before burning it. The killing of the soldier gave them cause for the conflagration."

"When you say plundered," Seth said, "you mean removed paperwork?"

"That, too. It was returned to Petersen."

"The woman they arrested?"

Trueblood grimaced. "All I know is that she was detained and questioned. There was a brief stir at headquarters in that she was pregnant and subsequently gave birth to a stillborn child. It was some of the Union wives, I believe, who raised a ruckus over the questioning. Ralston put a stop to it."

"Did Ralston ask you about it?"

"He asked Petersen, and I don't know how Petersen explained it."

"What happened to Petersen?"

"He disappeared that fall in the Pearl River swamp. Went in and never came out."

God's justice or another voice silenced? "The civilian conducting the questioning with him?"

"I have no idea."

Chapter Fifty-two

Seth followed the two of them out of his office. In front of him, Peter Franklin looked to his right, and greeted, Seth assumed, Poynter Cummings. Martin Trueblood did likewise, then turned back to his left to leave. He stopped, bringing Seth up short. Franklin, in front of both of them, stood unmoving.

In the outer office, Rebecca Mackey, in ominous black, rose from the bench where she'd been sitting. She wore her coat and hat, its veil pulled back over her head, exposing her face. Her ensemble glistened with raindrops. She appeared composed and was, without question, beautiful. Seth blinked, then immediately came to his senses. He looked at her black-gloved hands, both visible and empty, thank God. She took a step toward the counter gate separating the main room from the two offices. She was studying Trueblood. The look Peter Franklin shot Seth made it clear he'd put it all together. Franklin looked at Rebecca and nodded. "Mrs. Mackey."

She nodded serenely, briefly dropping her gaze from Martin Trueblood. "Mr. Franklin." Then her eyes shifted back to the former. "Are you Martin Trueblood?" she asked.

"I am," he said, trying for polite in a wary, uncomfortable sort of way. "And to whom do I owe the pleasure?"

She offered neither hand nor name.

"Gentlemen," Seth said, "we're done here."

Peter Franklin took the hint. Martin didn't tarry, either, but gave Becky a quick nod on his way past.

Becky turned with them as they slid past her. The door clattered shut. Only now did Seth notice Spain standing quietly by his desk in the other corner of the room. "Take a break, Private."

"Yes, suh." And he was gone.

Seth glanced at Poynter Cummings taking it all in. "Don't tell me to take a break," he said.

Becky met Seth's eyes. "I came to see how dinner had gone. I didn't expect to actually see him."

"Did you recognize him?" he said.

"No, but he knows."

Seth wasn't sure Martin Trueblood had realized she was the woman Petersen questioned, but for sure he did by now, because Peter Franklin had told him.

Her gaze shifted to Cummings, then back to Seth. "Did he tell you who it was?"

"The officer who questioned you was a Lieutenant Colonel Petersen. He was directly subordinate to Ralston. He didn't know the civilian. Ralston was not aware of the assignment Petersen was working on until after the fact."

She took a step closer to the counter. "Did he tell you who was aware, who his accomplice was?"

"Yes."

She waited, he said nothing. Her eyes shifted to Cummings. "Is it because he's here that you're not telling me?"

"I'm going to take care of it, Becky."

She looked at Cummings. He said nothing either. Back to Seth, but now her eyes glistened. She raised her chin. "I don't need either of you to tell me. I've always suspected. Now, I'm not only sure it was him, but I know why he did it. But since the two of you are reticent to share with me, I'm not sharing with you."

She glided away, out the door and into the rain. Seth fought his need to hurry after her.

"Do you think she does know it was Caruthers?" Cummings asked.

"I think there's never been much in the way of doubt in her mind. What I'm curious about is whether her knowing why was the truth or just sour grapes."

"I could trade information with her. Confirm to her it was Caruthers, then you wouldn't be breaking any trust."

"What trust, Cummings? The only word I gave Trueblood was that I wasn't interested in arresting him for malfeasance.'

"A ludicrous charge to attempt, I agree."

"There's enough intrigue going on here without your conspiring with her." Seth turned back into his office. "You keep away from her or I'll break your damn shoulder."

Cummings moved to Seth's doorway. "She already knows she has a friend in me."

Seth straightened from where he had bent over his desk and shot Cummings a jaundiced look.

The man smiled. "On that note, how is Mr. Roscoe this morning?"

Seth returned to the note he was scribbling for Spain. "Dislocated the knee and fractured the kneecap, but the doc thinks he might walk normally again some day, or a close approximation thereof. He's got a shattered shoulder, too. Unfortunately it was the left one, and he's right handed."

Chapter Fifty-three

Seth came in through Camellia Creek's kitchen, sized up its occupants with one look, and wondered if it had been the most popular room in the house before the war. Certainly for the kids, but now it seemed everyone congregated here. Summertime would change that, no doubt.

"Keep your seats," he said to Hand and Peters, who started to rise when he entered. They were eating, as were Mattie and the two little girls.

"You hungry?" Aunt Elvie asked.

"No, thanks. Must be like old times with all these mouths to feed, huh, Auntie?"

Elvie turned from the stove and made a point of looking at his two men. Peters was telling Eliza some tale about his experience with a cottonmouth, and Hand had just added an aside, which made the girl laugh.

"Don't look nuthin' like my Andrew and Eli, but good to heah da talk and dem chil'ens' laugh."

"Have you seen Miss Becky?"

He had given her an hour to get back home after her impromptu visit downtown, then ridden out to Camellia Creek himself.

Elvie pursed her lips. "Not in a bit."

"Since she got back from Port Gibson?"

She nodded, and he walked out of the warm kitchen onto that covered breezeway, and indeed it was breezy. The sky was beginning to clear. It would be a cold night. February's weather was proving no more amenable than January's had been.

Cassie was in the dining room, placing clean dishes on the

buffet. "Hello," she said cheerfully, "will you be joining us for the noon meal?"

"I ate in Port Gibson before I left, but thank you. Have you seen Becky?"

Cassie stopped what she was doing and looked at him. "About fifteen minutes ago. She'd changed into a riding habit and was all bundled up. I think she might have been going after her mother."

Recalling Peters at the kitchen table, he frowned. "Isabel's not here?"

"That lawyer, the one from Rodney, arrived about two hours after I did this morning. Must have been around twelve or half past. He visited a bit with Eli, then he and Miss Hays left in his carriage. Becky got back from Port Gibson shortly after." Cassie gave him a knowing look. "I was in the kitchen when she got back. It was Miss Elvie who told her that her mother had gone off with the lawyer, so she might know what's going on."

And *Miss Elvie* might have also volunteered that information to him two minutes ago, an ominous sign. He pivoted and started back to where he'd come from.

At the kitchen table, he stopped and looked at Peters, who rose. "Do you know where Miss Hays is?"

"She an' Mr. Holbein be in wif Colonel Calhoon las' I saw."

Things were getting worse and worse.

"She say," Elvie said, taking a step toward where Peters now stood at attention, "I was to tell Petahs she had Mr. Holbein wif her an' he was not to worry."

"She lef'?" Peters cried.

Elvie nodded and Peters, eyes wide, looked at Seth. "She always comes and gits me, suh. 'Sides I shoulda seen 'em go."

"Yes, you should have seen them go, which means she snuck off." Seth glanced from Mattie to Eliza, watching him pensively. "Did your granny say anything to you?"

A big grin spread across Eliza's face. "She's not my granny, she's my grandaunt Isabel, and she told me Peters told good ghost stories, that's all."

Grandaunt vice great-aunt. Isabel, no doubt had made that

distinction. Seth glanced at the sheepish Peters then turned to the complacent Elvira Hinny, who said, "Cain't blame Petahs. She didn't want 'im comin' wif 'em. Miz Isabel waited till I call 'em to dinnah time."

"So it's fair to assume you were part of this?"

Elvira turned back to her stove. "You think whatevah you wants. Feed 'em da same time evah day. Miz Isabel knows."

"Becky went after them?"

"Yes, suh."

"Were they going back to Rodney?"

"Don't think so."

"Miss Hinny!"

She tightened her lips, then slammed a wooden spoon on the stove top. "Don't know what dem's up to, but I can tell you da direction dey all went." She stomped to the back door. "Come on," she snapped, when he didn't immediately follow. Outside the kitchen she pointed to the bridge over Lake Elizabeth. "If you turn lef' at da road instead a da way you come, da road takes you out by da qua'tah. Just pas' it, da road fo'ks. To da right be a footpaf, which be a shawtcut to Pawt Gibson. It be da way us niggas used all our lives. Mounted riders, too, but ain't wide enuff fo' a wagon. Ain't no bridges eitha. If'n you go lef', der be a good road fit fo' a wagon or a buggy. Leads to Masta' Holland's uncle's old place. Miz Becky's weddin' gif' from 'er daddy."

Muscatine.

"Miz Isabel and Mr. Toby be in a buggy, so I would reason dey done gone to Muscatine."

"How far?" he asked, already reaching for the tethered Boon's reins.

"Five mile I've heard say."

He was a good half hour behind Becky now, but figured he could overtake her, assuming her goal was not to catch up with her mother and Holbein, but to spy on them.

Seth discovered an unmanned ferry when he reached the Big Black—moored on the opposite bank. He considered swimming

Boon across, but the water was high with last night's rain and the weather was downright cold, so he drew the thing back over. It wasn't easy, given the current, and he wondered how Becky had managed alone. But she had, or she'd swum her horse over.

Not long after Boon set hoof on the north shore of the Big Black, Seth crossed the Little Bogue Desha into Warren County, and minutes later, his big gelding answered a friendly whinny. Becky's mare was off to his left, easy to spy in a winter landscape devoid of much of its greenery, but Seth figured Becky hadn't planned on hiding her. No doubt, this road saw little activity, but the mare's being here in the woods did confirm Becky's plan was to reconnoiter. He left Boon with the mare. Twenty yards beyond, the land had been cleared, and in the far distance, he saw a farmhouse in need of paint. The rear, he thought. The front faced north. He looked left, maybe fifty yards beyond, and he saw Becky leaning up against a tree, watching the house.

He snuck right up on her, his progress disguised by the rattling of the naked branches of trees at the mercy of wind gusts approaching gale force. He stopped during a lull, close enough now to reach out and touch her.

"Whatcha doin'?"

She jumped and fell back with a cry, tripping and almost toppling backward, but she caught herself without his help. Hard at her heart, she sucked in a breath. "What are you doing here?"

"I just asked you that." Then he turned to the house and raised his binoculars. "What are you trying to find out, Becky? Hmm, two carriages. Neither do I recognize, but I assume one to belong to Tobias Holbein...now the other is rather elaborate." He looked at her. She said nothing. "You're not going to learn much out here so far away from the house."

"I'm going to be seen if I get closer. Besides, Uncle Jessie has a dog, he'll start barking if I step one foot out of these woods.

"Then you just want to know who they're meeting."

"Excuse me, sir, I know who they're meeting and so do you. The house, the land, this all belongs to him, thanks to the good graces of your criminal government."

She took a step closer, eyeing the binoculars. "I'm waiting for him to leave."

He handed the eyepiece to her. She hit herself in the eye, jerked back and was about to hand them back to him, when he said, "You adjust them here." He looked her over. She was indeed in a riding habit, but was well bundled against the cold.

"Are you armed?" he asked.

She thrust the glasses back at him. From all indications, she never had gotten them to focus. "Really, Major, you think I plan on shooting him?" She laughed. "Actually that's a wonderful idea. I did, however, leave my gun behind, I was so flustered when I left the house. Perhaps you'd loan me yours?"

"Doubt you could use it any more effectively than you did these binoculars."

She appeared to ignore that, her eyes back on the house, but he couldn't believe she'd come out here alone without some sort of defensive weapon.

Distant voices. He started to raise the binoculars, but realized he didn't need them. Three people emerged from the far side of the house and came up to the carriages, Isabel Hays, Tobias Holbein, and sure enough, Sam Caruthers. "Well, at the moment, my dear, it's all a moot point"—Caruthers' voice carried in the wind—"because it doesn't appear anyone is getting anything."

"The only thing I care about is—"

The wind gusted, rattling brittle branches over and around them and making Isabel difficult to hear, but Seth did hear the word "property" and Caruthers' counter of "Federal authority." Isabel shook her head, and started gracefully toward the smaller of the two carriages with a testy, "You can take care of that."

Caruthers stabbed a finger at Holbein, who eyed him coolly. "We need to talk," Caruthers said. His voice was loud now and easy to hear. The man looked at Isabel, now in the carriage, then back at Holbein. "Alone. The usual place. Tomorrow, same time."

"I'll be in Jackson. Make it later in the week."

Well, well, Toby could hold his own with the mighty Sam Caruthers. Seth was surprised, then wondered why he should be.

"Friday then."

Still an order, but Holbein agreed. Seth looked around and saw Becky had started back toward the horses. He caught up with her. "You said you knew what's motivating Caruthers. I want you to tell me what it is."

"I know you do, just like I wanted you to tell me about your conversation with Trueblood." She took her horse's reins and started walking to the road. She kept ahead of him, and he knew she did so by design.

"You know it was Caruthers," he said after her.

"I don't need your information anymore, Major Parker."

Damn angry, stubborn woman. "All right, it was Caruthers."

At the road they mounted. One carriage was headed their way. "I wanted to know the details, how it all came about. Why the Army went along with the attack on my father's farm, my father-in-law's farm."

"Why do you need to know all that?"

"The satisfaction of having the proof of just how corrupt the entire system is that destroyed the South."

Isabel had spied them. Toby pulled the carriage up. "Well, well, my darlings," she said, "I am surprised at this alliance."

"Not nearly as surprised as I am to find you meeting with Sam Caruthers and on my farm, no less," Becky said.

"Spare me aggrieved martyrdom, sweetheart. You know my point is to get this property back for you, and your presence at this meeting would have only been detrimental."

"There's more to it than my property, Mama."

"What, darling? Justice?"

"You're the one with the answer to that." Becky glanced his way, then back to her mother. He knew she'd say no more in front of him. "So has he agreed to return Muscatine?" she asked.

"He's all bluff now, honey," Holbein said. "He's holding out more for the sake of contrariness than anything else."

The air was cold, and Seth's shoulder had started to ache. Becky looked up through the naked limbs to the clearing sky, then urged her horse onto the road in front of the carriage. Seth lingered, and Holbein said, "It was my understanding you were off the Guthrie murder."

"My presence here is due to the Franklin murder. Your lovely associate here gave my trooper the slip."

"Oh." Holbein flicked the reins and started the carriage forward. Seth fell in beside them. "And have you taken all those convoluted clues to the Franklin murder and brought them full circle back around to tie into Guthrie's?"

He glanced sideways at Holbein. "I keep tryin'."

"You frighten me sometimes, Major."

"Because I'm so deluded or because I'm so close?"

Holbein didn't respond. Becky was in sight, but well ahead, aloof...and resolved. That worried him. "So," he said to Isabel, "what did Caruthers say about the interrogation?"

Isabel turned and looked at him.

"Come on, Miss Hays, do you think I haven't put it together that as soon as you found out about Becky's being questioned two and a half years ago you ran off to Rodney to consult with your solicitor here. And do you think it has escaped me that you just met with the man who, your daughter is convinced, was behind her arrest?"

Some semblance of a smile formed on Isabel's lips. "He denies all knowledge of any questioning."

"He maintains that if Becky were interrogated that summer, it was for purposes that only the Army is aware of," Holbein added.

"Ignoring, of course, that Becky knows what she was asked," Isabel said.

"What do you think, Holbein?" Seth asked. "Was he behind it?"

"Not a doubt in my mind."

"Do you know why?"

"Because he's an idiot."

Chapter Fifty-four

ecky waited for them at the river. Seth thought she might float the raft to the other side and leave it for them to pull back, but Isabel said she'd never be so petty. If Becky were set on spite, she'd float it over, then cut it loose, leaving them no way to cross.

At Camellia Creek, Seth handed Isabel down from the buggy. She looked up at Holbein and said, "You know you're welcome here tonight, darling."

"I don't know that Becky would be particularly welcoming."

"Pshaw. That's not so, and you know it. Besides, this isn't her house."

"I'm heading to Jackson early. I'll stay in Port Gibson. Here," he said, and handed her several copies of newspapers. "Give these to Eli. I forgot to bring them in earlier."

Isabel glanced at what Seth saw was a copy of the *Chicago Tribune*. "I don't think he should see these," she said.

"There's several copies of the *Clarion* in the pile," Holbein said. "It does a good job offsetting the *Tribune*. He'll enjoy them."

Isabel nodded farewell to Seth and climbed the back porch stairs.

"You headin' back into town?" Holbein asked him.

"I want to stick my head in and see how Calhoon's doin' "

From his perch on the buggy seat, Holbein shifted to get a better bead on Seth. "Isabel said you'd asked about Sam's betrayal of kin."

"I did. The way it was posed to me, it was more sinister than the mere encroachment on the cousins' farms."

"A man's death, the abuse of a pregnant kinswoman?"

"Doesn't sound like it could get much worse, does it?"

"There's kin and there's kin, Major Parker, and I've been pondering what to tell you since Isabel said you asked. Sam has two sons. Wilson, the younger, is his by blood, but Cole, the older, is the offspring of Alma Caruthers' first husband, Alexander Terry, who was killed in a duel during the early days of Alma's pregnancy. Doubt the two even knew she was pregnant when he died. Sam wed Alma before Cole was born. Sam is the only father he ever knew.

"Alma brought Sam a great deal of property with the marriage. In '62 Sam sent both boys, ages 17 and 18, to England to sit out the war. Rumor has it that Cole didn't want to go. He wanted Sam to raise a Confederate regiment. His father had opted for secession, and Cole was devoted to both his father and the Cause. I'm told they practically shanghaied him to get him out of the country. Recently, Wilson returned to his father's house. Cole did not."

"So you believe Mr. Caruthers' forcing his son to go to England is the betrayal I spoke of."

"Hardly sinister, is it?"

"No."

Holbein shrugged. "I knew both boys, Parker. Cole was smart and honorable. He believed in the South as much as his father once claimed to. He might be disappointed in his father for forcing him off to England, angry even, but he wouldn't let that cause a permanent rift between them."

"His father's perceived treachery, then?"

"More likely, but the war is over."

"The treachery's not."

"You asked. I thought I'd give you something to consider."

"Does Caruthers mention Cole?"

"Only when asked, but Alma does. They say he's in New York, and he'll be home soon. They've been saying he'll be home soon since the war ended. Personally, I don't think he'll step foot in Sam Caruthers' house again for as long as the man lives."

"That's a pretty severe break. You know more than what you're telling me."

Holbein smiled. "I believe that's where the betrayal to which you referred lies."

Holbein looked up to the door leading from the mud porch into the dining room. The porch was empty. "She did go into the house, didn't she?"

"Yes."

"I don't know how much she's telling Becky, and I don't know how much Becky, in turn, is telling you, but Isabel plans to return to Rodney tomorrow more or less permanently. Eli is on the mend, and Miller has made an appearance at The Pink Lady. Supposedly, he's looking for evidence to implicate Eli in the Guthrie murder."

"Supposedly?"

"There's no evidence to implicate any of the Calhoons at The Pink Lady."

"Then why is she concerned?"

"I don't know that she is. I'm the one concerned, and that's why I'm telling you. Isabel is trying to beat Sam Caruthers at his own game."

$\mathcal{O}$n the mud porch, Seth almost collided with Becky coming out of the house. She'd picked up speed once they crossed the river and she'd probably beaten them back by a good fifteen minutes.

"I was hoping to see your brother," he said.

She had stepped aside to let him enter, now her eyes flashed. "Why?"

"Just want to see how he is."

She studied him. "He's in a snit, so go ahead."

He stepped into warmth and the smell of food and old wood. Cassie hurried around the corner and into the dining room. She gave him a brief hello, then was out the door, too, following in Becky's wake. Both seemed harried.

The door to the sickroom was half open. He pushed it wide. Eli Calhoon was lying on a stripped-down bed, propped up on pillows and wearing a nightshirt. He looked at Seth, who said, "I do believe this is the first time I've walked in this room and you didn't have a female hovering over you. Can I come in?"

Calhoon snorted. "If you can stand it. I haven't come up with anything. You got news for me?"

His voice sounded strong. The room smelled of soap and shit.

"Trueblood has confirmed Caruthers' role." Seth wrinkled his nose. "You have an accident?"

"Yeah. That's where my little angels have gone. Literally cleanin' up the mess. They'll be back all too soon. Do you need to close the door? They left it open to air the place out, but we could open a window."

"Naw, that's all I really needed to tell you. Wanted to check how you're doin' is all."

"Alice finally acquiesced to my desire for something other than broth. Turned out to be a little more solid than my gut was ready for, and given my condition, I couldn't get to the chamber pot. Couldn't have squatted fast enough if I had." Calhoon grimaced. "Course it was liquid and did come out the ass end, so that must say something."

"Are they done with you?" Seth asked, his hand on the back of the rocker he'd intended to turn so that it faced the bed.

"They got it all cleaned up. You know how degrading it is, Parker, to have your beautiful young wife wipe your nasty butt?"

"Never had a wife, but I've had my adult ass wiped by a woman. Bet we could never find another man to do it."

"I had to run Becky out. She was gonna stay. Said Alice couldn't get the sheet out from under me, but I'd be damned before I let my baby sister see my filthy butt, much less wash it. She left, but she went and fetched Aunt Elvie. Meantime, Cassie Franklin waltzes in all chipper wantin' to help. Good Lord in heaven, help me."

Seth sat. Calhoon was bothered and no doubt he had his womenfolk equally upset. "And how many times do you reckon ole Auntie changed your diaper?"

"Ain't no way of knowin', but she hasn't touched my naked behind since I was four."

"Oh, yes she has, and real recent."

"Yeah, well, I didn't know it, and the humiliation isn't near as bad when you're not aware of it." Calhoon motioned his hands over his body. "Look how Alice has me dressed. In a damn night shirt. Think it belonged to one of her brothers."

"Reckon all this contrariness means you're gonna survive, Calhoon."

"That's my intent. Here," he said and pulled himself forward before dropping his pale legs over the edge of the bed, "help me to the chamber pot so I can pee before they come back."

"You've been out of bed?"

"No, but it's past time."

The chair rocked back when Seth stood, then he steadied Calhoon, who took two awkward steps to the chamber pot on the other side of the nightstand.

"It's your rib?" Seth asked.

"Yeah, it and the pelvis."

"You gonna pass out?"

Calhoon started drawing up the nightshirt. Sweat had formed on his forehead. "Throw up maybe, but not pass out."

Seth looked away. "I know what you're goin' through," Seth said. "My mother and sisters were the same way with me during my recuperation."

Done, Calhoon let the nightshirt fall back to his knees. Seth turned him back toward the bed, and Calhoon asked, "Wounded, were you?"

A bit surprised by the question, Seth didn't answer.

Calhoon frowned up at him once he managed to settle onto his back. "Where?"

"Beneath my right collar bone. Damaged my lung. Bullet lodged in my right shoulder. Shoulder still gives me fits, up to and includin' now, but the most immediate threat was blood loss."

"I meant what action?"

"Warren County, Mississippi. Almost three years ago now. I was bored on the boat. Volunteered to ride with some cavalrymen trying to ferret out a battery on this side of the river."

Calhoon cocked his head. "Before Grand Gulf?"

"A week before."

Seth plopped down in the rocker and watched Calhoon's eyes narrow, then a grin moved over the man's mouth. "It was you."

Seth held Calhoon's gaze. "It was me, what?"

"The man Becky nursed. She thought for sure you died."

Seth shook his head. He absolutely could not believe this. "She hasn't said anything to you?"

"About that man being you? No. Does Isabel know?"

"How should I know? I figured she told y'all."

"Nope, and I'd bet she hasn't told Isabel either or Isabel would have said something to me."

"Well, it was me," he said. "We were ambushed just north of the Big Black."

"You were lookin' for Robert Davis's battery. That's what he said."

"He'd sunk a supply boat the week before and damaged two transports. They were having a field day. Word was there was only one battery, but he kept moving it. I'd found the cannon two nights before, in the dark. The daytime look was to confirm it was still there, then we were gonna take aim from the river. Turns out we were being watched the whole time, hadn't even gotten far enough inland to abandon our horses. I was in front. Scout got me with the first shot, and I wasn't even supposed to be there in the daylight, dammit. My horse bolted, but I managed to hold on to the pommel. The five men I was with scattered. Two received minor wounds, but I learned later they all made it back." Seth looked at Calhoon and grinned. "They went one way, and my horse took me another. I wish I could say I knew what the hell I was doin', but truth is I was tryin' to stay in the saddle and keep from drowning in my own blood at the same time. As long as I was headin' away from the action I guess I figured I was okay. Apparently, I fell out of the saddle about a hundred yards from your sister's barn. Next thing I remember I woke up in the house with her trying to stop the bleeding. Davis was there. Think he considered me more trouble than I was worth."

"At least to him." Calhoon flexed his jaw. "Curious, isn't it?"

"That she helped me or he didn't want me?"

"That she didn't tell me that fella was you." After a moment, Calhoon laughed.

"*No*"—Becky heard Eli say when Alice, tray in hand, pushed wide the door to the sickroom—"we lost it in the west."

"My personal belief"—Becky's stomach quaked at the sound of the other man's voice—"is you lost it in Richmond." Dusk was settling over Camellia Creek, and she thought surely Parker had left by now.

Alice let loose a little cry and hustled into the room. "Seth," she said, rounding the end of the bed. "Don't talk about the war. You'll upset him. He's already in a temper."

Becky watched as Seth Parker rose. "I heard," he said, "but I think he's settling down."

"And I'd like to keep it that way," Alice said.

Becky and Alice had lingered for some time in the kitchen to give Eli time to recover from his embarrassment. He'd been such a horse's behind. No one had faulted him, not even Alice, whom he'd browbeat into allowing him to eat boiled chicken at dinner-time instead of its broth. She'd not once said she'd told him so.

Eli's eyes watched Alice with tender amusement. "I'm enjoying Parker's company, honey."

"My, how times have changed, but I don't think the topic is good for your humor." She set the supper tray on the table beside Eli's bed.

"We were philosophizing over grand strategy," Parker said. He turned slightly on his heel and found Becky. She gave him a curt nod, then placed the linens she held at the foot of the bed.

"Seth," Alice started, "maybe you could help us get the clean sheets under him."

"I'll sit in the rocker," Eli said, rising to a sitting position.

"What are you doing!"

"Honey, I stood alone not twenty minutes ago and peed in that pot there. Ask Parker."

She turned wide eyes on Seth, who nodded. "He did."

"There comes a time, sweetheart," Eli said, stepping carefully to the floor, "when you've just got to let a man get well."

Alice had grabbed his right arm to help. Now Parker took the other and they maneuvered him into the rocker. "Damn seat is cold," he said. "You two forced me into this rocker before I got my skirt situated the way I wanted it."

Becky convulsed with silent laughter. Parker saw and grinned. Eli's gaze moved over them both. He said to her, "My under drawers are in the bureau."

"You're in a nightshirt so we can get to your wound, darn it, Eli," Alice snapped.

"The wound's about healed."

"No it isn't, nor have you managed to gain full control of your other bodily functions."

Oh, that made him mad. "I'm ready for—"

"No! The nightshirt is not for your convenience, Eli. It's for mine, so you're going to have to tolerate it a bit longer."

Alice was on the verge of tears; Eli saw it, too. Becky touched his shoulder, bidding him to still, but there was no need. He gave her a contrite look, while Alice, head down, no doubt to hide her tears, stomped around to the foot of the bed and picked up a clean sheet. Becky moved to the other side of the bed to help. She looked at Eli, who looked right back. "Shame on you," she mouthed, then looked at Parker, standing near Eli and taking it all in.

Eli blew out a breath, and Parker said, "It's gettin' late. I need to get back to Port Gibson." His gaze moved from her to Eli. "Good to see you're better."

"Elvie's got ham and collards in the kitchen," Alice said.

"And chicken broth," Eli said. "Lots of chicken broth."

"Eat before you go," Alice said to Seth.

"That's assuming Hand hasn't eaten it all." Parker started for the door.

"I'm sure he skipped the broth," Eli called to him. "Finish it for me, will you?"

With a violent motion, Alice shook out a sheet. "Then you'll have nothing to eat, Eli Calhoon, because it's gonna be a while before I allow anything solid to pass your lips."

Parker smiled and pulled the door shut behind him. Becky started toward the other side of Eli's bed and picked up the book that had been tossed to the floor when they'd stripped off the soiled sheets.

"His eyes go all soft when he looks at you," Eli said. She glanced up, then away, and tucked the sheet. "Why didn't you tell me he was the man you nursed back in '63?"

Her heartbeat echoed in her ears now. "Because I didn't want you to know."

"Does your mother know?"

"Not unless he's told her, too."

"It wasn't like he was tattling on you, Becky. We were comparing injuries. It was obvious he thought he was embellishing a story he assumed I already knew. Now I'm left to ponder why I didn't."

"I didn't want you to feel vulnerable to him."

"I beg your pardon?" Eli said.

Alice straightened from smoothing the sheet. She was watching the two of them now, listening.

Becky wet her lips. "Obligated for some reason, you know."

"Obligated by what?"

"His..."

"His being in love with you."

"Shut up, Eli."

Eli squirmed in the rocker. "Or your caring for him, because that, not his feelings for you, Rebecca, but yours for him is the only thing that would mitigate my regard for him."

"Well, sir, feel free to hate him as much as you ever did, because I do not care for him."

Becky saw the look Eli gave Alice, then said, too sharply, "Get up and let me help Alice get you back in this bed."

<h1 align="center">Chapter Fifty-five</h1>

"**I** hoped that you'd stay here longer," Becky said, watching her mother pack clothes in a carpetbag. "I want to get back to Hickory Grove. There's still the mess Miller made, and I need to get a crop of something in the field."

"Quit worrying about Hickory Grove and stay here. I've got to get back to Rodney. When I was there before Toby arranged the meeting with Sam, Savannah told me Walter Miller had been at The Pink Lady. His presence causes discord, particularly with one of my regulars, who has been a bit too regular for some time now."

"Who?"

"Mark Dicks. They have too much in common personality-wise, and I don't like Miller's being around. I run a high-class whorehouse, dammit, not a boarding house." Isabel looked at her. "You're concerned about Eli's being arrested?"

"He's doing much better. He got out of bed yesterday after-noon, you know?"

"He's going to heal, darling."

"Well, let's hope so, but I'd almost rather he didn't until all this is settled."

"Goodness only knows when this will be settled, but the indi-vidual who will facilitate Eli's arrest is presently increasing ten-sions at my establishment. Eli is better served by my presence in Rodney." Her mother looked at her. "And there's still you."

"You think Miller knows Guthrie was looking for me the day he was killed?"

"Yes."

"Caruthers confirmed it?"

"He did, though he really didn't point it out that way. Just took it for granted as being something everyone already knew, not to mention the recent search of your house was a dead give-away."

"Then why don't they come after me?"

"Convicting you of Guthrie's murder will not get Eli off Camellia Creek, darling. Sam wants Eli out of the way. You are not considered as big an obstacle."

"Well, I am."

Isabel placed her fists on her hips, started to speak, then dropped her arms. "It's best not to let them realize that." Her mother buckled her bag and looked around the room. "I can't say I'll miss the child's daybed, and you don't need to be at Hickory Grove right now, crop or no crop. If your darkies are gonna leave, they're going to go. How many are left?"

"Nine, and most of them are elderly. Aunt Boo has her two grandbabies. They're the only children left, ten and eleven. The Bureau has talked to her, says they'll put them in school, but she's not ready to let them go. I have managed, thanks to you, to keep everyone fed so far."

"They need to be helping."

"They still have their gardens, but it is February, Mama. I told her she should put the kids in the school. They're not old enough to do me much good, and she's well into her seventies. She may not be around to care for them much longer."

$\mathcal{T}$his morning, the courier from Vicksburg had a twelve-year veteran of the United States Army with him. Born and raised in Minnesota, Sergeant Richard Kushing was not only white, he was downright golden with flaxen hair and blue eyes and a combat veteran of the Army of the Potomac to boot. He was Frank Zachary's relief. Of all the men Seth hated to lose, Zachary was the one he least wanted to see go. Standing in front of Seth's desk, flanked on either side by Zachary and Jubal, the one anxious, the other enigmatic, Kushing appeared merely odd, an ominous next step in an evolving plan for Reconstruction. He handed Seth a dispatch that included the discharge papers not only for Zachary, but for Corporal Peters and Privates Ball, Hand, Spain, and Lawson, effective in five days. Seth looked up. "Did Colonel Byrnes indicate whether there'd be any more replacements?"

"Sir, Colonel Byrnes instructed me to inform you I was all you were gonna get, but he'd delay further discharge papers as long as he could."

The news wasn't a surprise, but Seth couldn't quell his disappointment. Despite Malcolm's philosophical resistance to what he perceived to be an overreaching Treasury Department, the Army wasn't exactly shoring up its intelligence effort, at least not for Jon Franklin's murder.

"Thank you for the report, Sergeant, and welcome to Port Gibson, Mississippi." Then the man had saluted him, uncovered and inside. All present responded to the gesture, and Seth's three subordinates left.

There was a written note from Malcolm acknowledging Seth's altercation with Felix Roscoe, along with a request he try and curb his enthusiasm for beating up his colleagues in the future — Seth could read the colonel's approval between the lines. Lastly, Malcolm had forwarded a letter from Seth's father addressed to him at headquarters in Vicksburg. He'd been expecting the note, firming up his father, brother, and grandfather's itinerary in early March. They had to go to New Orleans on a family matter and wanted Seth to accompany them. In lieu of his company, they at least wanted the opportunity to visit with him a few hours during their trip downriver.

<h1 style="text-align:center">Chapter Fifty-six</h1>

A little Negro boy summoned Seth to Camellia Creek later that week. The boy hadn't come from Camellia Creek, but from the doctor. A while back, Seth had asked Dr. Lester to let him know if and when the district provost took action on the directive to have Eli Calhoon examined by both a military surgeon and his personal physician. Miller was apparently determined to press the issue, because the military surgeon had shown up at the doc's place midmorning today.

Seth arrived with Jubal to find Miller in the Camellia Creek parlor in company with a stranger, who Miller introduced as Clem White, Roscoe's replacement. White shook Seth's hand in a forthright enough manner, but also gave him a good look over. Seth wasn't sure what to make of the scrutiny, but concluded it wasn't friendly. Roscoe had disappeared from the hotel days ago, Miller shortly after. Miller confessed he'd been to New Orleans. He needed support in his endeavors, and he had known White during the war. They worked well together.

Seth hadn't been there ten minutes, Cassie Franklin having just served them all coffee, when the door to the sickroom opened.

"Ah, Mr. Miller," the emerging army officer started, before spying Seth and introducing himself as Lieutenant Colonel Douglas French. "The man is doing exceptionally well given the grievousness of his wound, but he has a bit of a fever this morning. The wound is tender and causes Mr. Calhoon a great deal of pain, as does the broken rib and pelvis."

"Can he walk?" Miller asked.

"Not without help. Gets up to relieve himself, I understand, but even then he requires support, that's about it."

"If he can get up, he can run."

The colonel laughed. "Not hardly. Most of us regular humans lack the superhuman stamina of you clandestine operatives. Besides, I've been assured of the character of Mr. Calhoon. He wants this cleared up so he can get on with his life. That won't happen if he runs."

"And who told you that?"

"Judge Lawrence Pendleton up in Warrenton. I dined with him just last night. Provost was with us. That's why I'm here today. We decided I should get down here and get this hashed out. Dr. Lester agrees Mr. Calhoon will require at least another month to six weeks of convalescing before we'd render him fit for arrest." French smiled at Miller and thrust out his hand. "I'll be back mid to late March."

Miller looked at the proffered hand, then looked at Seth. "Byrnes is behind this."

Isabel had started it all, though Seth couldn't rule out that Malcolm was now in cahoots with the provost on that end.

The colonel dropped his hand and his friendly tone hardened. "I assure you, sir, my assessment of the patient's condition is accurate. He's not running anywhere."

"He could be given help."

"He could have been given help weeks ago and be out of the country by now, so I don't consider that a sound argument." He looked at Seth. "It's my understanding he's under military guard."

"He is."

"In the meanwhile, the month will give you time to uncover evidence to make your case."

"I have all I need to make my case, Colonel. Thank you."

"Oh, then I assume you have more than what the provost last heard, because he didn't think so."

Miller rolled his eyes and walked back into the parlor to retrieve his hat. "Let's go," he said to Clem White.

Colonel French's friendly demeanor returned with Miller's departure. He held out his hand to Seth, who took it, then turned to take Alice's. He covered hers with his other. "It was a pleasure to meet you, Mrs. Calhoon, and please accept once again my heartfelt sympathy and thanks for your sacrifice in securing our grand Union."

Alice responded in kind, of course, but Seth didn't hear what she said. He was too busy searching for Becky, who didn't appear to be here. He figured she'd been in with Alice and the doctors earlier, but now...? The colonel and Dr. Lester began some sort of animated conversation on their way out the door, and Seth looked into the sickroom. Calhoon was there alone. He frowned at Seth, then smiled at Alice as she brushed by Seth and went to her husband. "Miller is gone," she told him. "Colonel French doesn't think you'll be good for much of anything for at least another month."

"I guess that's good."

She felt his forehead. "You are a little warm. Do you feel ill?"

"Headache."

"That's the fever. Dr. Lester left you something. He's still concerned with the possibility of pneumonia." She was scurrying around now, chatting. "That nice army doctor left morphine for your pain."

"I needed that six weeks ago, not now."

"At night, maybe, when you go to sleep."

"All I do is sleep...Alice?"

"Yes?"

"Parker wants something."

Alice turned the rocker. "Come sit, Seth."

"I'm looking for your sister," he said to Calhoon.

"She went to Port Gibson," Alice said. "She wanted to look at Naomi's house."

"Why?"

"I've mentioned I don't want her living over there in Madison County alone with those two little girls," Calhoon said. "It's too far away, and it's isolated. She says she doesn't want to leave the furniture over there and it's too much to add here. Since she's not sure when she'll get Muscatine back, she's looking at Port Gibson for the interim."

Chapter Fifty-seven

Seth returned to Port Gibson the back way Elvie had told him about several days ago, the footpath, good for walking and riding, not wide enough or excavated for a wagon or carriage. Eli Calhoon told him it entered town near the north end of Farmer's Street, close to Aunt Naomi's house. She used to walk back and forth to Camellia Creek routinely. Seth figured that was the route Becky took when she left the farm, because he hadn't passed her on his way out there. More than likely it would be the path she took coming home.

The rain that had caught him on his way to Camellia Creek continued, at times quite hard. That led him to conclude she was probably still holed up at the Polk house. He needed to pry some answers out of her, but what he really wanted was to see her face.

As in the past, he entered Naomi Polk's house from the back. Becky's mare was in the carriage shed, and he put Boon in there, too, out of the weather, which was damn cold in addition to being wet. As he started up the porch steps, his pelvis warmed at the thought of Becky, and he all but forgot the throb in his shoulder.

In the parlor, he found the floor in front of the fireplace littered with ash, and the shovel in the middle of the mess. The firebox was clean, however, the ash removed down to the brick.

He heard the front door close, and a thud echoed through the spartan house, then Becky appeared at the door to the parlor, ash bin in one hand and something akin to trash in the other. She stopped short.

"Hi," he said.

"Hello, and why ever are you here?"

"I heard you were here."

"And you wanted to talk to me?" Her anxiety showed, and he figured she feared he planned to broach all those mystery-related things she'd hinted at, then vowed to keep from him, and he wondered if she regretted putting forth the challenge.

"I wanted to look at you."

"Now you've seen me, does that mean you'll go away?"

"It means we'll talk. The military doctor checked your brother earlier."

She didn't move, not even to blink.

"He and Dr. Lester agreed your brother needs to stay where he is for at least another month."

She breathed out. "Does Miller know?"

"He was there, and not too happy. Downright rude to the army doctor." Seth looked at what she was holding in her ash-covered hands. "Whatcha got there?"

"Oh," she said and looked down. "It appears to be pieces of a journal. I got caught in the rain on my way here, and I was cold. Given the weather appeared to be worsening, I thought I might stay for a bit and decided on a fire. The firebox needed to be cleaned. Anyway"—she set the bucket down, shifted part of what she held to her free hand, then extended a piece of dusty cardboard to him—"the shovel caught on this."

He took the heavy stock. It had burned to a fraction of its original size, but it was covered with cloth stamped in a diamond-shaped pattern of green and gold.

"I wanted to find more, so I poured the ash out on the front porch and sifted through it. That's when I found these."

She handed him the rest of what she'd been holding, scorched outside corners of lined paper on which handwriting was still clearly visible.

"I can make out some of the writing. It's not Aunt Naomi's."

He'd seen enough examples of Naomi Polk's handwriting over the past several weeks to agree. "You don't recognize it?"

"I think it's Laura's, but I was gonna take it home to Eli and let him look at it. Does that interest you, Major Parker, Naomi Polk burning Laura's journal?"

"Are there dates?"

"September," she said, moving closer and reaching for the clump of paper corners. The scent of lilac overwhelmed that of wood smoke. She didn't look up at him, but sorted through the various corners making up the clump. "Then, when you turn this page, there's a year given. See here." Apparently seeing how close she'd come to him, she stepped back. "Here, you see, September 3, 1865."

He wanted so badly to touch her, but sensed it would be a mistake. He had to let her make the first move, display some sort of encouragement for his advances. He considered she might never would and stepped away before he did something he would regret. "So this past fall?"

"Could this support your thoughts about Aunt Naomi and Jon Franklin and Laura and Guthrie?"

"Your Aunt Naomi was blackmailing Jon Franklin with Laura's murder. At least that's what he told his uncle."

She bit her bottom lip. "But I thought—"

"Your Aunt Naomi did kill Laura, but Jon Franklin didn't know that. He just knew he'd been intimate with her on the day she was killed, and Naomi told him she saw him leaving Laura's house."

"So that's what she used to force him to help her?"

"I think so."

She was wiping her dusty hands on her coat, more a nervous gesture than a useful one. "Did his uncle tell you that when you met with Trueblood?"

"Yes."

She raised her chin. "What else did he tell you?"

He wondered what she'd do if he asked for a kiss to tell. "I thought you were no longer interested in my information."

Her nostrils flared, and she started around him, and he did toss caution to the wind this time, and he caught her arm. For the first time ever, she didn't pull away. "Petersen and Trueblood were Ralston's subordinates. They were able to arrange the raids under the pretense of operational necessity. Both had a great deal of autonomy. Petersen was an intelligence collector. Trueblood allocated the military assets that conducted the raids. Both your father and Mr. Mackey were accused of passing information and support to the Confederacy. The attacks were easy to justify. It was Caruthers who identified those targets. Trueblood wanted the alleged cotton Caruthers claimed was stowed on the Mackey farm. He did what he did for profit. He did not know about the letter, at least he says he didn't. By then, Trueblood had introduced Caruthers to Petersen, and those two were working one on one. You were right that day in my office when you said that Trueblood and Caruthers had had a falling out. There was no cotton to be had, never had been, and Trueblood realized Caruthers had been using him. He's getting even by buying up land Caruthers needs for his railroad."

Seth liked the way she was looking at him now. He turned her so that she faced him more directly. She looked down at his hand on her arm.

"And Jon Franklin?" she asked.

"From what I've deciphered, his intent was to break away from his cousin and uncle. Caruthers said he wanted to be on the board of that railroad, but he had nothing to offer, so he was wasting his time."

She started to free her arm. "Do you think Jon Franklin could have been so foolish as to think Caruthers would just place him on the board?"

"No," he said softly, and pulled her closer. Her breath quickened. It dawned on him she'd misconstrued his "no." "I think he offered him something else."

"What?" Her eyes, steel gray, were locked on his.

"I think he was blackmailing him with something. Something his new friend Naomi Polk made him privy to."

She opened her mouth, and he kissed her quick, then immediately let her go and stepped back, out of striking distance.

She blinked in surprise, then said with a shaky voice, "And what would that have been?"

He laughed at her response, or lack of. It had been so simple.

No cries of outrage, no blows to his head, but she'd noted his chaste kiss, her eyes and voice told him so. Still, it hadn't been much of a kiss. He ran his hands through his damp hair. "I don't know, do you?"

"Knowledge of the congressional letter?"

He frowned. "And would the threat of that thing have warranted Caruthers' killing him?"

"All I know is that two and a half years ago, Caruthers was going to great lengths to get his hands on it." She looked at the journal scraps in his right hand. "Do you want me to have Eli identify the handwriting for sure?"

He looked at what he held, then at her. "Are you leaving?"

"Yes."

"It's still raining."

"I know, but I must go, now."

"I won't kiss you again," he said, and she closed her eyes. "Unless you want me to."

She reached for the journal pieces. "Do you?" she asked again.

He handed them to her. "Did you intend to tell me about finding that, or was it because I happened upon you here?"

She shrugged. "We still don't know that it will add anything."

"It adds something, Becky. Whether Naomi was trying to destroy evidence in Laura's murder or evidence in regard to the Guthrie killing, there was something in that book Naomi didn't want known."

"Then I'm glad to have been of service." She started for the poncho she'd draped over the settee, then stopped. "Thank you for telling me about your discussion with Trueblood."

"I wasn't kidding when I told you I was going to handle this." He started for the dining room where he'd left his slicker on the table. "I don't want you doing anything reckless." He pivoted when she walked into the dining area behind him. "And I'm going with you as far as Camellia Creek's quarter."

"*L*aura's."

"You're certain?"

"Oh, yes, I'm sure."

Alice handed Becky a cup of coffee, then stepped around to Eli's side. He was in bed, surrounded by quilts, but uncovered as though he'd kicked them away. He appeared to be chomping at the bit. The scent of soap hovered over that musty smell of a body being in bed overlong. Alice had given him a shave, Becky would wager, just this afternoon, and he wore a white shirt and tan trousers, the hated nightshirt discarded. A fire burned in the little stove and the room was warm and felt divine to Becky's chilled bones.

"In Aunt Naomi's fireplace," Eli mused, then looked at her. "Why were you looking—"

"I wasn't. I just wanted a fire and the fireplace needed shoveling."

Alice reached toward the partial pieces of paper Eli still held. "May I look at them?"

Handing them over, Eli said to Becky, "She fancies herself a detective."

Becky leaned closer to Alice. "Parker has seen this. Y'all apparently told him I was at the house. He knows about the dates, too, see here, September 3, 1865."

"What does he make of it?" Alice asked.

"It all ties into Aunt Naomi's killing Laura," Eli said.

"Parker told me Aunt Naomi was blackmailing Jon Franklin. She told him she saw him leave Laura's home the day she was killed."

"That's how she got him to go along," Eli said. "Laura must have made reference to Franklin or Guthrie in this journal, or at least Aunt Naomi feared she had, so she burned it."

Becky rose. "I told Parker I thought the handwriting was Laura's. Y'all need to tell him it's certain."

"*We* need to tell him?" Eli said.

"Yes, you'll see him before I will. Now that I'm sure you've got a month's reprieve from incarceration in some sort of Federal stockade, I'm going down to talk to Mr. Holbein. I want to get his assessment of Muscatine without Mama's influencing him. I'll be back in a couple of days to make sure you two are still all right. Then I'll take Mattie and the girls home."

Alice and Eli opened their mouths as one, but Becky held up a hand. "Hush, both of you. I've got to get that house packed up, and I need to check on the welfare of my remaining people, then I'll move into Aunt Naomi's house." She looked at her brother. "You'll let me rent it?"

"Shut your mouth, Rebecca. I'll give you the place for nothing"—he glanced at Alice—"but be advised we now believe in ghosts around here. Naomi Polk will probably haunt you there."

"Some of us have always believed in ghosts, brother dear, and she died here."

Chapter Fifty-eight

*B*ecky knocked, and Dinah opened the back door to The Pink Lady. Private Spain followed Becky in and placed the carpetbag on the floor. He nodded to Dinah, then looked at Becky, who thanked him, and he turned back into the cold, dark night.

All her life, this had been Becky's entrance to the bowels, or living quarters, of her mother's business establishment. From this wide rear entry, a hall led to her mother's office and the main house where clientele were greeted and entertained. From the spot where she now stood, a back staircase led upstairs to her mother's private quarters where Becky had spent her infant and toddler years, and where she later enjoyed short visits away from Camellia Creek, her primary residence after she'd reached pre-adolescence and her parents had agreed she was better off in her father's home than her mother's. During long stays, Hannah would come with her, understanding their beds resided under the roof of her mother's aunt, Marguerite Fortier, Aunt Maggie. As girls and later as young women, she and Hannah had gladly anticipated their stays in Rodney, a wealthy cotton port that had rivaled Natchez in culture and art and dress and sweet shops where they spent both Holland Calhoon's and Isabel Hays' money. The boys, Andy and Eli, had sometimes spent extended periods, too, which included, once they'd gotten older, entertainment at the opera house and family dinners in fine restaurants. Those public outings had always included Aunt Maggie and, when discretion could be managed, Isabel. Rarer trips to Natchez, New Orleans, or Memphis always included Isabel, whose face, if not her name, was not as quickly recognized. Those trips had not included Aunt Maggie. Those had been happy times, at least for the children, but Becky believed the adults had been happy, too.

Thomas, the houseboy, though an older black man closer to sixty, reached for her bag, which she'd carried from the wharf until Spain had intercepted her in the yard. "Yo mama gonna be s'prized to see you heah dis time a night."

"She'll probably rail at me, Thomas."

Her mother's cry of, "It's nearly ten!" drowned his ensuing chuckle. Becky, on the bottom footer, turned.

"Go ahead on up," Isabel said to Thomas, already halfway up the stairs. She looked at Becky. "What are you doing on the road at this hour?"

"I came by boat. I went to Grand Gulf earlier this afternoon because Eli insisted, but I missed the first packet and the five o'clock was two hours late leaving Memphis because of a fire. So here I am."

"You walked from the landing?"

"Up the path. It's not that far, Mama, and I could walk it with my eyes closed."

"Which for all intents and purposes you did. Is it still raining out?"

"Drizzling."

"Did you leave any luggage at the landing?"

"I only brought one carpetbag, and Thomas has it. Remember that I don't carry much anymore."

Her mother waved her hands, shooing her up the stairs. "I could remedy that."

"You insist on color, and I'm"—she thought about Parker's playful kiss this afternoon—"content with black."

The steps groaned in greeting. Becky couldn't remember a time they hadn't.

"I may relent with a new black crepe since you are so stubborn. James would be appalled at you."

Thomas was starting back towards them when they reached the upstairs landing. From above, someone clattered down the stairwell that led to a utilitarian third level, which housed the servants. Corporal Peters stuck his head out. "You all right, Miz Iz'bel?"

"We're fine. Miss Becky has just arrived. She's sorry she woke you."

"Aw, we ain't sleepin'."

"You should be. Goodnight." Isabel turned with Becky down the hall toward their adjacent bedrooms.

"I met Private Spain in the yard when I came in. I think I scared him as much as he did me. How many of them are here?"

"Three. The sergeant constantly rotates them in and out. Peters relieved Daws late this afternoon, and Daws went back to report."

"Report on what?"

"Why, my activities, darling."

"What have you been doing?"

Her mother laughed. "Nothing, sweetheart," she said, then caught her arm and directed her into the familiar room that had been hers over the years.

"Mother, tell me why there are so many of them here?"

"Actually I believe 'Isabel Hays duty' is how Major Parker rewards them for jobs well done. He has so many of his troopers here because he doesn't have anything better for them to do. Now, I've been told the Union surgeon has examined Eli and deemed him too weak to move for at least another month."

"Was it Miller who informed you?"

"Informed me and blames me, and I'm happy to think I did play a part."

"Is he here now?"

"He arrived late this afternoon. He's reconnoitering, I believe."

"You?"

"Toby. He has a new man working with him, Clem White from New Orleans." Her mother met her eye. "As was the case with Roscoe, they're old associates from the war days."

"I heard that Roscoe and Major Parker had an altercation," Becky said. That she'd learned from Parker's troops at Camellia

Creek. Parker had volunteered nothing about the incident, and she had not asked.

"And Roscoe is recuperating up in Warren County."

Becky cocked her head at her mother. "How do you know that?"

"Toby. The man is laid up at Sam's place."

"That's interesting, isn't it, that Sam Caruthers is taking responsibility for an incapacitated Treasury agent? I wonder if Parker knows."

"You can tell him with my blessings. Miller also said the doctors claimed Eli had a fever. He thought they were lying."

"He did have a fever this morning, but he didn't have one when I left this afternoon. He dressed after they left and for two days in a row now, his stomach has dealt well with solid food. He gets up by himself to use the chamber pot, which is a big help to Alice and Aunt Elvie. He wants out of that room, but the weather has been so cold and rainy Alice fights him about it. She looks exhausted again, and I warned Eli it was because he's being difficult."

"She could at least let him sit in the parlor," Isabel said. "Here, take off that awful hat and give it to me."

"That room is big and hard to keep warm, not like the bedroom. I think the reason he relented was because of my warning." She handed her mother her hat and started unbuttoning her coat. "Buck's been over to Grand Gulf to pick up the windows Eli ordered the end of December. When this rain stops, he's gonna start replacing the windows in the kitchen."

"Why doesn't Alice have him begin with the house?"

"Those windows, as far as I know, haven't been ordered yet." She shrugged out of her coat.

"That thing is wet. Why didn't you leave it downstairs?"

"I didn't think about it. Here, just drape it over the rocker. Mother, I've made my decision. After this visit, I'm gathering my girls and returning to Hickory Grove. I need to clean up the damage done during the search. I'm planning to pack everything up and move into Aunt Naomi's house in Port Gibson."

"And I think that's where you should be if you won't move back to Camellia Creek. Just until we get Muscatine back."

"Her house needs repairs. There's a leak in one of the bed-rooms, and the front porch is dangerous, and there are other things. I've talked to Eli about my moving in, but said nothing about what needs to be done. He says he'll give me the house, but I can't expect him to fix it on top of that. The costs are high. Everything is being imported. Our mills —"

"Are also in need of repair, and the tools and parts required for that are made in Northern factories."

"It's by design isn't it?"

"Most assuredly."

"Why would the North not want recovery? Wouldn't that be to the —"

"The South has been relegated to a colony, darling. In many ways it always has been. Now she's a vanquished nation to be fully exploited by the conqueror."

Becky looked at the back wall of her bedroom. "We're where we were when we fought the Revolution."

"We are so much worse off than when we fought, even began to fight, the Revolution. The mother country then, at least, did not despise us. In answer to your question, the manufacturers have overpriced our means for recovery to ensure we will not recover, and they are doing so with the blessing of their govern-ment if not the out-and-out direction of that government except, of course, they're all woven together. If there is any recovery, they will benefit from it directly, and they will continue this course for goodness knows how many decades. Perhaps forever. Certainly for as long as they can. We have no idea yet what all has been lost in this debacle."

Becky sank into a plush armchair. "Here," her mother said and placed the matching ottoman near her feet, "you must be exhausted."

"Are these your beliefs, Mama, or do your Yankee clients tell you this?"

"I live in a man's world, darling. For decades I've listened to them, mostly Southerners, talk among themselves in my well-appointed parlor. The opinion I just gave you is based on years of compiled knowledge."

"And Daddy's thoughts?"

"Holland knew what the price would be for defeat, but I can help you make the necessary repairs to the Port Gibson house."

Becky leaned back in the chair and closed her eyes. "There's still Eliza's property."

"And she has a fine lawyer in Jackson to protect her interests. The war is over."

Becky frowned. "The darkies and the taxes?"

"If any of them are interested, put them in the fields in return for a share of the profits. You won't need to worry about taxes for at least another year. Now...." Her mother, who'd taken the matching chair, started to rise.

"A moment, Mama, I've something to tell you."

Isabel sat back.

"When I visited Aunt Naomi's house today, I found remains of Laura Blackledge's journal in the fireplace."

Isabel's interest was subtle, but Becky knew her mother well enough to recognize it when she saw it.

"And you know it was Laura's how?"

"Eli recognized her handwriting."

"Ah."

"Parker knows about it, and he says Aunt Naomi coerced Jon Franklin to do her bidding by threatening to expose him as Laura's murderer."

"How does he know that?"

"Peter Franklin told him."

"Well, then, it's probably gospel."

"Parker also told me he suspects Jon Franklin knew something else about Caruthers. Something Parker thinks Aunt Naomi told him, and he was using it to force Caruthers into making him a partner on the railroad."

When Isabel said nothing, Becky said, "You're not surprised, are you?"

"Oh, I am. I'm surprised Parker told you all this. What are you telling him?"

"He knows about the congressional letter."

"I know he does. Have you gone so far as to show him the thing?"

"No."

"It wouldn't hurt."

Becky didn't ask her mother to explain that remark, but said, "When I 'happened' upon you and Mr. Holbein at the door to the study, you said Aunt Naomi had told Jon something that made Caruthers angry, that she'd been reckless. Was that something to do with Guthrie's murder?"

Isabel raised a brow. "I need to talk with Toby first thing in the morning. If he agrees, perhaps it's time we three return to Camellia Creek and sit down with your brother." Isabel rose. "Right now, I need to get back downstairs. Savannah and I were talking business before your impromptu arrival. You get some sleep."

Chapter Fifty-nine

"**D**aws reported she went to see Holbein Saturday mornin' after he got back to Rodney," Jubal Summers told Seth. The two of them were holed up in Seth's room at the hotel. They often met here in the morning, updating each other before venturing out to breakfast at the provost's mess hall.

"He'd been to Jackson," Seth told Jubal. "He and Caruthers met somewhere Friday. Isabel would have wanted to know what they talked about."

Seth would like to keep a closer eye on Holbein, but unless he could hire private resources, he didn't think he'd be able to fool the lawyer. Whereas Isabel welcomed the escort his troops provided—he suspected she liked the extra security—the same could not have been said of Tobias Holbein.

"If you're sure he's workin' so close with Caruthers, do you think she trusts him?" Jubal asked.

"I do think she trusts him. Whether she should or not, I don't know, but they've known each other a long time. Did the corporal have the wherewithal to watch Holbein at that point?"

"Put Lawson on it, and Lawson thinks someone else is watching Holbein. A civilian."

"Treasury," Seth said.

Jubal studied him, then nodded. "And we know Miller's been in and out of her place all week."

"Where does he go when he leaves?"

"He flagged down a packet at least twice and headed upstream. We could start tagging along."

"Our men don't have the experience to try and shadow the likes of Miller. It would further strain our working relationship and could prove dangerous for the men. Odds are he went up to Vicksburg, or more likely, he's meeting Caruthers."

"He could be complaining to Colonel Byrnes about you."

Seth wondered if Miller had complained about the altercation with Roscoe, but Malcolm had never said anything about Miller bringing it up, and Seth believed Malcolm would have let him know. That didn't rule out there being someone else at headquarters Miller was talking to.

"You suppose," Jubal said, "that Miller is in Rodney because he has an interest in the Franklin killing?"

"If he and Caruthers are working together, and if Caruthers had anything to do with Franklin's death, then I'd say there's a chance. It could explain why he acquiesced when Colonel Byrnes said I would continue to work that case."

"You think Guthrie was interested in that railroad?"

"No. There's something else."

"So you're thinkin' Treasury is workin' with Caruthers, and they killed Franklin. All the while you're doin' your damnedest to convince yourself Isabel Hays had nothing to do with Franklin's killing even though she claims she passed the man minutes before he was shot and saw nobody else. Then she left the road to lose our men she knew were followin'. She tells you she has no idea who killed the man and knows nothin' of his business when you know she does, that's why he made a habit of visitin' her whorehouse."

"Do you think she killed Franklin?" Seth asked. "We've got no weapon, her reason for deviating from her route is sound, and she never once tried to conceal her whereabouts."

"I just don't think we should rule out she played a part.'

"I'm not ruling out that she knows who did it. Shoot, I think I know who did it. I even think I know the reason. What I don't know is what Franklin used to force Caruthers' hand."

"Does she know? Because if she does and she's not telling, that's just as bad."

Seth didn't respond. After a moment, Jubal said, "She's protecting Calhoon."

And his sister. "But why does she feel she needs to?"

"She doesn't want him arrested for murder," Jubal said a little louder than necessary. "Guthrie was looking for him. You know that."

Seth looked at Jubal and wondered how much talking he'd done with Miller when Seth hadn't been around, but that was unfair. Jubal had always wanted Eli Calhoon to be the killer. Subsequent knowledge that Guthrie had actually been searching for the Calhoons when he was killed simply supported his argument, which had, up to that point, been based on little.

"Do you have any interest at all in the 'why' of it, Jubal?"

"Justice is the 'why' of it."

"Four months ago we rode in here with orders to find the killer of a man who may or may not have been involved in cotton thieving. We were drawn to Calhoon by a jealous woman hell-bent on vengeance, which theoretically handed us the faceless Southerner someone in Washington wanted blamed for the murder of the Treasury agent. But once we met him, he was no longer faceless."

"Nor was his wife, but they're both still faceless to me. If it hadn't been for your befriendin' the Calhoon woman, you'd have arrested that man in late November, and we'd be home."

"We're not looking for arbitrary justice here, Captain, that's the fodder spewed out by those justifying war and tyranny. We have a real, true mystery. There's a reason these things are happening, and arrestin' a man who fits the crime isn't solving the mystery. It's covering up a murder and—"

A hard rap on the door, then it flew open. Frank Zachary stood in the portal, a harried Private Spain in the dark hall behind him.

"Spain's got a repawt, suh," Zachary said.

Thoughts muddled, Seth rose from the table and watched a wide-eyed Spain step around the sergeant and into the bright room. "Da cawp'ral sent me, suh. Miz Iz'bel, she be dead."

Seth was aware of the skid of Jubal's chair on the floor, of the man rising, but of little else. "What happened?" Seth asked.

"Murdered real early dis mawnin'."

Seth turned to the chair behind him and grabbed his colt, then his cover. "How?"

"Shot be all I know."

"Who did—"

"Don't know, suh." The young private turned with him as Seth brushed past and into the hall. Behind him, Seth could hear Jubal Summers scrambling. "Petahs skedaddled me outa der to come tell you. Dat Trez'ry man"—Seth stopped cold and turned. Private Spain, who almost ran into him, stopped, too—"was sayin' nobody was to go anywheres."

"Miller?"

"Yes, suh, he was in da house, da Pink Lady."

"Who found Miss Isabel?"

"Miz Becky."

"Mrs. Mackey is in Rodney?"

"Got der late las' evenin'. Da cawp'ral an' me heard da shot. Ball was in da front a da house on duty. He relieved me 'bout midnight. Far as I know he was awake."

"She roomed you in the servants' quarters?"

"Yes, suh, upstairs in da attic, where we be nice and wahm."

"Had she ever quartered you inside the house before?"

"Ain't nevah pitched a tent der, suh. She say we was growin' on 'er."

Seth heard the catch in Spain's voice. Isabel had wanted his men close, for all the good it had done her.

"How soon did Miller get to the scene?"

"Got to Miz Iz'bel's bedroom right afta we did. Petahs was already tryin' to he'p Miz Becky an' Miz Savannah, but da agent man pushed 'im aside an' tol' 'im to go check da house inside an' out."

"Did Mrs. Mackey say anything?"

"No, suh, not while I was der. She looked struck dumb. Just looked at Petahs like she thought he might could do somethin', but knowin' all da while he couldn't."

"Did she say anything to Miller?"

"No, suh, not den anyways. When he come in da room, she put 'er arms around 'er mama an' hugged 'er close. Dat's when Petahs scooted me outa da room an' sent me heah. Said he didn't like da way dat Millah was takin' ovah evahthin'." Spain, his eyes glistening, looked at Seth, then his eyes darted to Frank Zachary, who'd come up to stand beside them. From the end of the hall, Sergeant Kushing was pulling on his blouse and hurrying their way. "Did we mess dis up?" Spain said. "We was s'posed to be watchin' 'er."

"No. You provided her escort and were guarding the house per my instructions to Peters. If anybody messed it up it was me."

"Majah," Zachary said, "I already sent Lawson to da liv'ry fo' da hawses."

Seth looked at the sergeant. "Office manned?"

"Can leave Lawson."

Seth nodded. "I want you to ride out to Camellia Creek and inform Mrs. Calhoon. We'll let her decide when and how to tell her husband. Proceed to Rodney from there." He nodded at his new sergeant and said, "I'll take Kushing with me."

Chapter Sixty

Alice Calhoon felt the hand on her shoulder, and she jumped, glancing quickly to her sleeping husband. Reassured by the rise and fall of his chest, she reached up and covered the old gnarled hand.

"He fell back to sleep after dressing," she whispered to Elvie. "The effort exhausts him, but he won't let me help much."

"I'm awake," he said clearly, and Alice looked at him, eyes now open. She rose to prop pillows behind his head.

"Frank Zach'ry's heah. Him wants to talk to Miz Alice."

Eli's eyes narrowed, but Alice placed a hand on his shoulder and pushed him into the pillows. He squirmed to make himself comfortable. She wasn't sure if he intended to get up or not, but she wanted him to rest a bit. He gave her a tender look, something akin to a smile on his mouth. "Do you have any idea how much your bullying annoys me? I'll have my vengeance, Alice."

"Thanks to my bullying you." She bent to kiss him, then straightened. "And I look forward to your vengeance, sweet." She turned to Elvie. "He's in the hall?"

"Yessum, right outside da do'h," Elvie said, her voice hollow. Only now did trepidation wash over Alice. If Eli sensed anything amiss, he didn't say so.

She found the sergeant in the hall, forage hat twisted in his hands. Alice felt pressure rise behind her eyes. In the dining room she heard someone setting the table. Alice took another glance at the sergeant's twisted hat and asked, "What's wrong?"

"It be Miz Hays, Miz Alice, she been murdered."

Alice reeled, and the sergeant's nervous hands became suddenly strong, and he steadied her, but not in time for her to stifle a sob. Elvie, who'd come out with her, stood with her head bowed toward the floor, and Alice knew that he'd already told her. To Alice's left, Cassie poked her head around the corner from the dining room and a look of dismay washed over her features. "What's happened?" she cried and rushed to Alice's side.

Alice shook her head and swiped at tears. She felt Cassie's arm around her shoulders, and the girl hugged her.

"Miz Hays done been kilt over in Rodney," Zachary told her.

"Oh, my God, what happened?"

"Murdered," Alice garbled out before Zachary could answer. Alice swiped her nose with her handkerchief. Calm again, she looked at Frank Zachary, worry in his brown eyes. He was such a sweet, sweet man. "Tell me what you know."

"All I know is she be shot in 'er house in Rodney."

"Do you know anything of Becky? Is she all right?"

"Miz Becky was wif 'er, in da house, I mean. She be all right far as I know."

"Where is Major Parker?"

"He be on his way to Rodney right now. I gots Private Price wif me. We headin' dat way soon as I be done heah."

"Do you know who did it?"

"I don't. Don't know if we knows. Da majah say he'd let you decide how to tell da colonel, Miz Alice."

Alice closed her eyes briefly, then licked her dry lips.

"You gots to, Missy," Aunt Elvie said at her side. "Can't keep dis from 'im."

"I fear you're right. He must be told."

"How is he?" Zachary asked.

"He's—"

Behind her the bedroom door opened and Eli, watching them all with growing interest, stepped out. "What's wrong?"

Alice's eyes filled with tears, and he held his head higher.

"Becky?"

"No, Isabel." She turned to the sergeant. "Come on in," she said, turning her husband back into the room, "you need to talk to him."

Chapter Sixty-one

A pale Savannah Sutton looked up when Seth entered Isabel's office, and he swore she was relieved to see him. The room, always tidy when he'd entered in the past, was a mess, its desk, shelves, and bureau having been rifled through, it appeared by someone in a hurry, or someone who simply didn't care.

"What are you doing here, Parker?"

Walter Miller sat at Isabel's desk. Savannah sat in a familiar balloon-back armchair in front of him. Seth had seen her in that chair on many occasions, when it had been Isabel sitting behind the desk. Savannah, Isabel's immediate subordinate, occupied the main chair in Isabel's absence, and the scene before him struck Seth as exceedingly odd. He felt a compelling need to drag Miller from behind that desk.

"I was informed my primary witness in the Franklin murder was dead."

Miller nodded. "In the wee hours of the morning. Gunshot through the heart. Appears to have been her weapon."

Seth looked at Savannah, sitting there, staring at him. She was filled with grief, he realized. Savannah had been with Isabel a long time.

"Am I interrupting anything here?" Seth asked. He was, he knew. He looked at the ransacked room. He didn't care.

Miller's eyes shifted to the lovely whore. "I think we're done. Remember, Miss Sutton, our conversation is not to be shared."

"I remember, Walter, darlin'."

Savannah moved past Seth with a wink that only he would have seen.

Seth took the chair. "Was the place robbed, too?"

"I conducted the search. I'm looking for anything that might shed some light on who killed the woman."

"Have you uncovered anything?"

"I have not."

Mark Dicks—Seth knew his familiar face—told Seth when he arrived that Miller had been holed up in this office for more than two hours, first searching the place, then finally calling Savannah in and closing the door. Before that, he'd gone through Isabel's bedroom, after he'd managed to get everyone out of it. That included Becky, who according to Dicks had secluded herself in her bedroom after Miller and Savannah managed to coax her from her mother's body.

Seth took Savannah's chair. "Might I impose on you to tell me what you do know?"

"I was in a guest room in the north wing," Miller said, "graciously supplied by Isabel herself, when I heard the shot. It was past three."

Miller had used Isabel's given name in his tale. Seth's gut burned, but he didn't let it show.

"Were you alone?"

Miller nodded. "I was. Asleep, too, as a matter of fact."

Seth wanted to ask if he'd been alone all evening, but decided, at least for the moment, it was irrelevant.

"The Mackey woman was already with her mother by the time I got there. So were Miss Sutton and your men. Isabel was dead. Her pocket derringer was on the bed beside her."

"Was there an exit wound?"

"Yes, and your man Peters was looking for the bullet earlier, but only the one shot was heard and we know the derringer had been fired. Mrs. Mackey said she heard footsteps running in the hall seconds after the shot woke her. She thinks the person was probably barefoot. She checked the hall, found her mother's door open, then found her mother. She was the first one there, then your man from downstairs, then Peters from above. No one passed anyone in the halls. At least, that's what they're all saying."

"Has the Jefferson County sheriff been notified?"

"This is a Federal matter, Parker, and you know it."

"As a courtesy."

Miller threw his hands out and barked, "Fine. If General Wood thinks such actions will help mollify this bunch of traitors and keep the peace, we'll notify him, but you'll need to send one of your boys to Fayette to do it, because I don't have the luxury of a lot of under-worked people."

Seth made a point of taking in the mess strewn over Isabel's desk and the credenza behind Miller. "What are you looking for, Miller?"

"I told you, evidence that may provide a motive for killing the woman."

"This isn't a search for evidence. You're looking for something specific."

The man sighed heavily. "Very well, Major, I am looking for something specific. Something that will implicate individuals in a conspiracy against the government."

"And what is your basis for believing Isabel Hays was involved in a conspiracy against the government?"

"I'm not at liberty to divulge that information to you. Suffice it to say that Washington was made aware of certain facts recently that implicated Miss Hays in blackmail."

Blackmail? If true, that threw a new twist into everything he was working on. "Might I ask the source of that information?"

"Privileged."

"*Miz* Becky wanted to come in a bit ago," Private Ball told Seth, "but I tol' 'er"—Ball nodded to the man at Seth's side—"Mistah Millah say nobody was to go into da room, right now."

"Where is Miss Becky?" Seth asked.

Ball indicated the door next to this one. "'Er room, suh."

They were speaking in hushed tones outside the door of Isabel Hays' second story bedroom. The door was closed, the hall, lit by a window at its west end, dim. They'd entered this wing of the house by way of what had once been the servants' stairwell off an anteroom adjacent to the dining room. Isabel, her family and personal friends, and her handful of servants who lived in the house all used it, avoiding the grander staircase leading upstairs from the foyer to the bedrooms reserved for client services. Isabel had added to this house over the years, and it really was a fine whorehouse by anyone's standards. Discreetly removed from the town proper, as the original owner, Isabel's first lover, had wanted, it had been a private refuge for him and his prized mistress.

Seth pushed the door wide. The spacious room was dark, but not so dark he couldn't see the shrouded form lying on a bed flanked by windows set in the room's single exterior wall. He drew back the heavy drapes of one window, then the other, lighting the room. He paused a moment, to gather strength, perhaps, and studied the Mississippi River a short distance away, its dark waters glinting in the sun of a beautiful February day. He turned to the bed and its covered body. A day no longer brightened by the presence of Isabel Hays, and his gut quaked. Grief. He'd gotten to know her well enough for that. He glanced at the adjacent wall, which separated him from the room next door. And empathy for Becky.

He reached for the sheet covering Isabel and folded it back to her waist. She looked older in death, pasty, but still beautiful. Her eyes were shut, her lips slightly parted. Her golden hair had been plaited for bed and fell over her left shoulder and across her breast to matt in the blood staining the white lawn gown. He rolled her to one side to confirm where the bullet had exited the body, and found the wound to the right of her left shoulder blade. Despite the blood on the gown, there was little on the sheets where she lay, and he pulled the shroud from the foot of the bed and found the coverlet soaked. That would have been where she'd fallen. "Who touched the body other than Miss Becky?" Seth asked of no one in particular.

"I did, much as you're doing now," Miller said.

"I he'ped Miz Becky git 'er up on da pillows," Ball said. "She asked me to."

Seth laid the stiff body down, then started to scan the wall across from...a palm appeared beneath his nose. In that palm lay the twisted remains of a bullet. Seth looked up and met Corporal Peters' gaze. "Dug it outa da wall dis mawnin' afta Mistah Millah heah went downstairs." Peters rolled his eyes to the ceiling. "Seems he su'ched fo' dat bullet all ovah dis room, da writin' desk, da wa'drobe, eben 'tween da mattress and undah da pillows, but couldn't fin' dis bullet. I hear he ended up searchin da whole house fo' it. Didn't take me long to fin' it though. I know'd you'd be wantin' it shawtly, so I set 'bout gettin' it befo' it turned up missin'.'"

Seth took the mangled projectile, along with a quick appraisal of the now bright room. It did appear to have been rifled through. He glanced at Miller, watching Peters, who was staring right back at him. Despite the liberty Peters took in his not-too-subtle disapproval of Miller's actions, Seth chose to say nothing. Obviously, Miller had been a bit heavy-handed with Peters. That or his corporal had learned of the incident out at Hickory Grove from Hand. Probably both. Seth tossed the meager remains of the bullet to Miller and returned his attention to Peters. "Where did you find it?"

"Ovah heah," he said, directing Seth's attention to the wall separating Isabel's room from Becky's.

"Hole weren't dis big befo' I started diggin' into it."

The damage to the rich walnut paneling was easy to see, made the more so, no doubt, by Peters' mutilation when he dug the bullet out. The thing had entered the wall just below the level of the bed a good eight feet away. Seth looked back. Miller stood on the other side of the bed, still fingering the bullet.

"The point where it entered the wall indicates the killer was standing about where you are," Seth said to Miller.

Miller tossed the bullet up, then grabbed it. His hand fisted around it. "Yes, at very close range."

Seth figured the killer to be male. "She'd just come back up. Might have surprised whoever it was in her room. In fact, he might have taken —"

Seth returned his attention to the body, to Isabel's hands. He lifted the right one and sniffed and guessed she'd been holding the gun when it fired. "She could have been killed in a struggle," he said, walking around the foot of the bed. "She was probably standing by the edge of the bed, here, and fell back across it."

Sergeant Kushing stuck his head in the doorway. "Zachary and Price are here, sir. Cap'n just rode up, too."

Seth cursed inwardly. He'd sent Jubal to draft a dispatch to Malcolm and wait on the courier. He'd also told him to make a call on Don Hemple. He hadn't told him to report to Rodney. "Sergeant, could you round up Zachary for me." He started for the door, then stopped, glanced briefly at Miller, and pivoted to find Peters. "Well done on your report, Corporal."

Chapter Sixty-two

There was no immediate response two hours later when Seth knocked on the door to Becky's room. He was about to knock again when he heard a click, and the door opened a crack. She opened it as wide as her body when she saw it was him. There was a longing in her gray eyes, and for a moment he thought she might reach for him. He wanted her to, but when she didn't, he said, "I'd like to talk to you."

She opened the door wider, then walked toward her bed. Inside, he closed the door behind him, then locked it with that same telltale click. She looked at him, questioning.

"I don't want Miller coming in here," he answered, then took in the room. The walnut panels in this room had been painted white, but despite the bright walls, the room was dark, its velvet drapes also closed. A lone lamp burned by her bed, on which she now sat down. She placed an item in the drawer of her bedside table. The room was neat.

"Do you know if Eli knows?" she asked.

"Sergeant Zachary informed him this morning." He pulled a note from his pocket. "Your brother sent you this."

She hesitated, as if she might not be able to go on, then fingered the linen paper. "This must be Alice's stationery," she said with a quavering voice, and as if the thought gave her some strength, she removed the note from the envelope.

He saw enough to know the missive was short. Below the main message, another hand had written a post script. Alice, he supposed.

Eyes brimming, she looked up. "You're going back that way?"

That took him a bit by surprise. "No time soon, but I'll send one of my men if you wish to respond."

She glanced down at the letter. "He wants us to bury her at Camellia Creek near our father, but Mama has always said she wanted to be buried here in Rodney with her people. She said Rosalind was Daddy's true love, and her being buried at Camellia Creek was inappropriate. She wanted to be with the woman who raised her."

Her voice broke, and in the golden glow of the lamp, he saw she'd closed her eyes. "Sergeant Zachary didn't indicate Eli and Alice were going to try and come here, did he?"

"Your brother was a bit too active yesterday. The news this morning added to the ill effects. He was hurting pretty bad and ended up sick to his stomach. Alice got him back to bed."

Seth found one of two matching chairs and sat. "The sergeant said he was dressed when he got there."

Becky nodded. "Yesterday, too." Becky gave him a sad smile. "Mama and I were going back to Camellia Creek soon. She said we'd break him out of that bedroom where Alice was keeping him captive, but perhaps Alice's caution is justified." Becky shot him a knowing look. "She planned on dragging Mr. Holbein along with us. I told her your theories about Aunt Naomi's coercing Franklin, then him turning around and trying to force himself onto Caruthers' railroad."

"You think she agreed with them?"

"I think she believed that's what happened. Or she was certain that's what happened and concerned you were getting so close."

Dropping her eyes, she picked up a book on her bed and placed it in the drawer. "She wanted to talk to Mr. Holbein first, but I believe she intended to tell Eli and me everything."

And wasn't that the damn way of things. "I'm sorry about your mother, Becky."

He watched her chin pucker. "Thank you," she said and closed the drawer.

"Miller searched your room?"

"While I was with Mama. I've just finished getting it back in order."

"Do you know if he took anything?"

"I don't think so. Most of my things were at Hickory Grove."

Were at Hickory Grove, meaning they'd been lost in the fire.

"Do you have any idea why he was questioning Savannah?" he asked.

"Have you talked to her?" she quickly responded, as if his question had breathed new life into her.

"Not yet, and for her sake I'm not sure I should, at least not while Miller is still around."

"He warned her not to repeat what they'd talked about, but she's in no mood to be threatened. She came straight up to me after you interrupted them. But understand this, she was always a favorite of his."

"Ah, that is interesting. And does that suggest he might have taken a reckless risk with her?"

"Yes."

"And are you gonna tell me what he asked her?"

She swiped at some dust on the corner of her nightstand. "She wanted me to. She also wanted you to know it might cause her some trouble if Miller finds out she said anything, but you already understand that."

"Yes. Now what did she tell you?"

Silence.

"If you don't tell me, I'll have to go to Savannah, which could put her in danger."

"Can we agree that he's searching for something?"

"Yes."

She leaned closer and spoke softly, "Did he tell you what?"

"I'm considering wringing your neck."

A sob echoed her sad chuckle. He wanted to pull her into his lap and hold her.

She swiped her eyes. "If I tell you what Savannah told me, you won't tell me what you know."

"You want me to go first?" he asked gently.

She nodded.

"He's looking for evidence of a conspiracy against the government to which he says your mother was privy."

"And it has to do with Eli?"

"He claimed the information was privileged. Now tell me what Savannah told you."

He could see from the way she was studying him she wasn't satisfied, but he preempted her expected question with, "If you tell me what he asked Savannah, we might can piece it together."

She made a sibilant sound, as if she didn't really trust him, then said, "He asked her if she were aware of a letter of authorization from the Treasury Department, which Mama might have had in her possession. That was after he'd checked the contents of the safe and"—she widened her arms to indicate her room— "our living areas."

"A letter from Treasury, not Congress?"

"I asked the same thing. She says he definitely said Treasury."

"What did she tell him?"

"She knew nothing of such a thing."

"Was that the truth?"

Becky held her hands out, palms up. "If you're asking if Savannah is above lying to Miller, the answer is no, but I do believe she would have confessed such knowledge to me, even given me the thing if she knew where it was."

"And your mother never spoke to you about it?"

"No, and that's the honest truth. Do you know what it is?"

"I don't know." He blew out a breath. "I'd guess it granted someone the authority to act on a matter related to the Treasury Department."

"And he thinks Mama had it?"

"He must."

"So there's a congressional letter from back in 1863 and now a Treasury letter dated who knows when?"

"Miller claims your mother was involved in blackmail."

Her eyes widened, then narrowed in apparent understanding. "I knew you hadn't told me everything."

"I needed to know specifically what he was looking for. He wouldn't tell me. He finally broke down and told Savannah what he wanted because she worked close enough with your mother that she might have been aware, plus he felt he might be able to trust her. The other persons one would assume might know are you, and more likely, Tobias Holbein."

"Then it can't have to do with Eli or me, because Mama certainly wasn't blackmailing either one of us."

Seth frowned. She was right, of course.

"He's a liar. He's not trying to expose a blackmailer," she said.

"But it's probably safe to assume he is looking for that letter of authorization. He hasn't asked you anything about it?"

"No."

"And he may not. He figured he could cajole Savannah into keeping her mouth shut, not so with you." He leaned forward, arms on thighs. "What do you need to do now as far as your mother is concerned?"

"I need to go see Aunt Maggie, tell her that"—her voice gave way to sobs. Her unexpected breakdown staggered him, then tore at his heart.

Becky rose, eyes closed, teeth clenched. "Her Izzy's dead." Words out, she managed some modicum of control and patted her pocket, then in obvious frustration reached for the drawer to her bedside table. "Oh, God...."

*H*e touched her arm, and she turned to find he held his handkerchief out to her. Her eyes were burning, and her heart was breaking. She took his offering. She'd held the useless tears in for hours now, but the thought of telling Aunt Maggie had brought it all back. "And Toby Holbein. I've got to...." She choked.

He had her arm now, and he was pulling her to him. "I sent Jubal over to tell him hours ago."

Then she was there. Warm and safe, his arms holding her tight against his wool blouse. The subtle scents of sandalwood and horse filled her senses and for a moment she allowed herself the luxury to weep. She felt his cheek atop her head. She pulled back, looked up, and found eyes filled with compassion. Heart pounding, she placed her hand on his chest and raised her chin in invitation, and he dipped his head.

His kiss was gentle, but a real kiss, as tender at the start as it was passionate with her demand. Her mind asked her what she was doing, but for just a moment more, she let need rule her. Then she drew the arms, with which she'd encircled his neck, down to his shoulders and pushed gently, breaking the kiss. His eyes, dark and clear, now filled with question, watched her. She closed hers, then placed the tips of her fingers against her lips. "I am so sorry," she said. "Please accept my apology."

"If anyone should apologize, Becky, it's me."

With a hard shake of her head, she stepped back. "I took advantage of your sympathy."

"I took advantage of your vulnerability."

"Please," she begged, "just accept my apology."

And he did.

Chapter Sixty-three

Seth escorted Becky to the home of Marguerite Fortier, nearly a mile from The Pink Lady, and left her on the front walk. She said she would make her way home, eventually. There were arrangements to be made. Despite Rodney's looking like a ghost town, there were people here, and businesses open, both inside the city limits and outside, and Becky had a mother to bury.

"How is Rebecca?"

Holbein had stood and shook Seth's hand when Seth entered the man's office. The room was dim, the shades down.

"She's managing."

Holbein only nodded.

"Jubal said you didn't say much to him."

"Walter Miller had already been here. He told me all I needed to know." Holbein drew in a breath. "To tell you the truth, I don't feel much like talking to anyone. I should go home."

Seth let that pass. "Becky says Isabel was coming to see you this morning. She'd told her mother my thoughts on Naomi Polk's coercing Jon Franklin to do her bidding by blackmailing him with Laura's murder."

"We figured Naomi used something to compel Franklin to work with her. Take a seat, Parker."

Seth sat and said, "But there's more. I believe she provided Jon something that compromised Caruthers, something with which he broached the man and promised silence in return for a place on Caruthers' railroad."

"Men can't get much stupider than Jon Franklin, to think he could waltz into a pride of lions and presume to feed off their kill."

"You don't seem surprised by my assumption."

"That Jon Franklin was attempting to force his will on Sam? I'm not. I've known for months, and so as to expedite this conversation, I'll tell you that I know this because Sam told me. Sam also told me what Jon was blackmailing him with, which I will not share with you. Miller knows, but for the purposes of your investigation you need to know nothing more than there was something. And before you ask, Sam has never confessed he killed Franklin, nor would he, and I have no proof that he did except my good sense, which isn't worth a damn thing in a court of law. You're gonna have to prove Sam killed him on your own."

"If Miller has an interest, am I safe assuming that whatever Franklin had ties to the Guthrie murder?"

"That comment, Major, has proved my brightest moment in a dark, dark day."

Meaning Holbein wanted him to make a connection between the two killings? But was it because the connection was legitimate or the opposite? Had Jon Franklin used knowledge of Sam Caruthers' having murdered Guthrie to try and force his place on Caruthers' railroad? And did Holbein's cryptic remarks mean that Holbein, too, was somehow involved in Guthrie's death?

"You could tell me, and I'd know as much as Miller," Seth said.

"Prejudicial, Parker, prejudicial."

If he were involved, it would be that.

The man swiped at his nose with a kerchief, then turned his chair, averting his face from Seth's. "I apologize," Holbein said.

"Do you have any idea who killed her?" Seth asked softly.

"Supposing I did, I wouldn't tell you. I would take care of the matter myself."

"When he came this morning, did Miller bring up the matter of her blackmailing someone with you?"

Holbein sniffed. "He ran that ploy by me, yes. I chose to ignore it, and I certainly have nothing to add to the allegation, if that's what you're asking." Holbein, composed again, faced him. "She'll be buried in Rodney? It's what she wanted."

"Tomorrow morning early. In the town cemetery."

Holbein nodded and stood. "In the family plot. If you see her, tell Rebecca I'll talk to her then, I can't face her today. Now, I'm going home. I should have left this morning when I heard. I'm not fit for work." He stuck out his hand as Seth rose. Seth figured Holbein's terminating the conversation was by design and his reason for leaving his office had as much to do with ending their meeting as it did with grief over Isabel. He took the man's proffered hand.

They buried Isabel the next morning, a cold Valentine's Day. The number of local mourners was more than Seth would have thought given the woman's profession, the suddenness of her demise and haste of her burial, not to mention the attrition of the populace. It was a graveside service, per Isabel's wishes, and the preacher was from an Episcopal church in a little Jefferson County hamlet outside Rodney. Isabel hadn't been a churchgoer, but she'd supported a number of congregations, black and white, especially since the war, in support of their small farmers hit hard by the turmoil. All Isabel's "girls" were there, tastefully outfitted in black. There were eight total, and they'd always been, in Seth's opinion, a graceful class of whores. Isabel would have made sure of that. A number of them wept profusely. They stood apart from the "respectable" people, less moved, but all solemn, and there was a large number of Negroes, which didn't surprise Seth, but did affect Jubal as had every other act of loyalty of one race to the other that he'd encountered since coming South.

Seth and his men stood aside from the rest. Becky rode to the funeral in her mother's carriage, picking up her grandaunt along the way, but chose to walk back alone. Aunt Maggie returned to The Pink Lady for a wake of sorts. The house was closed for business and would remain closed for at least a week, but the handful of townsfolk, both white and colored, had declined the invitation anyway, though a good number of people had approached Becky with condolences. That had held her back a bit, so Seth lingered and kept her in sight. He knew she saw him, though she pretended not to. Tobias Holbein had also lingered and was the last to hug her tight. They'd wept, the two of them, then departed in separate directions without appearing to say much. Seth figured words didn't matter. The grief of both was real, and they shared it as deeply as two people could.

"When do you intend to see your brother?" Seth asked Becky. He'd waited for her at the back door.

"I'll leave tomorrow," she said, removing her hat. Her face was flushed from the cold outside, her eyes red-rimmed, partly the cold, mostly the weeping. "I plan to return to Hickory Grove Monday. I'll pack up and move back to Aunt Naomi's house."

He was following her down the hall to her mother's office. She stopped short at the door, taking in the mess Miller had made of the place. Dinah moved in past her with a coffee tray. "Miz Savannah tol' me not to worry wif dis now, Miz Becky. Say she get to it afta we say our good-byes to Miz Isabel." Dinah's voice cracked with that.

Becky quickly cleared a small table. "Put it here. Is Aunt Maggie comfortable?"

Dinah chuckled softly. "You know yo' Aunt Maggie, Miz Becky. She be in der entertainin' ever' one o' dem gals an' gentlemens wif tales of yo' mama growin' up."

Dinah closed the door when she left them, and Becky sat on the leather sofa and poured Seth a cup of coffee, then one for herself.

"Mr. Holbein said he'll come over in a little bit. I want to talk to him about Mama's estate." She closed her eyes. "And other things."

"Her murder?"

"Yes, and for that reason I fear he may not come at all, but I know Mama left a will. I want to know if she made provisions for the girls."

Seth didn't say anything, but considered the comment odd, as if Becky thought her mother may have cut her wards out.

Without warning, Becky's eyes filled with tears. "What's to

happen to them now?" She waved her hands as if to take in this room, this house.

"You're referring to the girls here at The Pink Lady?"

"Of course. The women here live in pampered splendor. There are much worse places to peddle their trade, you know?"

Indeed he did.

"I've considered my options up to and including taking it over myself."

His heart crashed to his gut. "Do you know anything about running a house of prostitution?" he said, and God smite his soul, he'd spoken too harshly.

"No," she snapped back, "but I can learn. I'm not stupid."

If she stayed this course she sure as hell was, dammit. He almost rose, ready to rave, but caught himself. He had no right, and to act rashly would undermine his cause in more than one way. From everything he knew of Rebecca Calhoon Mackey, she'd been sheltered from this part of her mother's life. Holland Calhoon had demanded it, and Isabel Hays had apparently loved her daughter, and probably the man himself, enough to agree. Seth swallowed and gave real thanks now for the survival of Eli Calhoon. He would be the one to set Becky right regarding this lunatic thought, and there was also...

"What about Eliza and Pearl?"

Silence.

Encouraged, he pushed his advantage. "And what will your brother and Alice think?"

She looked away. "I know it's not practical. It's certainly not how I envisioned my life, but so much has changed in the past several years. I'm hoping she left this place to Savannah. She told me once she was thinking about doing that, that she'd made other provisions for me." She took a sip of the coffee and stood. "I need to get in with the others. You're welcome to join us. Your men are in there. She adored them, and they her"—she was rapidly blinking back tears now—"she was raised by a mulatto, Major. The Negro has always been an intimate part of her life."

"Don't let them have too much to drink."

"Sergeant Zachary is with them. He told them only a couple of rounds, then back to work."

"Not Summers?"

"He declined. He didn't make a fuss about your men going, though."

Seth did make his way to the elegant front parlor, where he drank a toast to Isabel, then watched, relieved, when his men departed without incident. Miller rose, and Seth intercepted him on the way out, requesting he brief him on the continuing investigation into Isabel's death.

Miller's newest hireling, Clem White, joined them in Isabel's office, Miller taking the desk chair, he and White the sofa. White had met up with Miller during the graveside service. Seth could only guess where the man had appeared from, but he didn't ask, figuring they might confirm his speculation during the course of Miller's briefing.

With Becky's unexpected arrival around ten-thirty the night before last, Isabel had left Savannah in charge downstairs and gone up with her daughter. She'd returned a little before eleven, and she and Savannah finished the discussion Becky's arrival had interrupted. Isabel retired at midnight. A little after two, and Savannah confirmed this was not out of the ordinary when she retired early, Isabel had returned to her secluded office. There she'd had an unremarkable discussion with Savannah regarding the clientele present: five men, not counting Seth's three, two of whom were ensconced upstairs, and Private Ball, who was out front. Ball's duty included moving in and out of the house, nominally to watch for surreptitious movements by Isabel.

An hour or more later, Isabel went back upstairs, and only moments after that, Savannah started down the corridor to The Pink Lady's front parlor. She was still in the hall when she heard the shot. Private Ball, she told Miller, had nearly knocked her down, rushing from the front of the house down that same secluded hallway. Becky and Ball were both in the room with Isabel by the time Savannah got there. Ball had hurried out to find Corporal Peters, whom he met in the upstairs hall en route the room. Savannah, devastated, couldn't remember who showed up next, but eventually everyone in the house arrived with Corporal Peters trying to maintain order, before Miller arrived and pressed Seth's troopers into guard duty. He got everyone out of the room, except Becky, who refused to leave her mother. Miller shot Seth a look and told him that was when Corporal Peters spirited Private Spain out of the house and to Port Gibson to summon their seniors.

Of the five patrons present at the time of the shooting, two, both Northern businessmen, had been in the parlor with four of Isabel's girls. The men had been relatively sober, though they were drinking and playing chess, while the women kept their glasses filled, cigars lit, and spittoons handy. Two of the women were adept at chess and had partnered, in a manner of speaking, with the adversaries, advising the men with subtle winks and headshakes as to the wisdom of their individual moves. Most evenings proceeded thusly, that much Seth already knew.

Miller had retired about nine, alone, as per his choice. The beautiful quadroon, Evelyn, was in the two-room suite she shared with the redhead, Mary Margaret, helping the latter prepare her toilette. Mary Margaret, the personal favorite of Major Mark Dicks, the same man who had been condescending about Miller's house search and subsequent questioning of Savannah, had spent the late afternoon and evening with her preferred client, the two having risen less than an hour before the shooting.

Cheri, a popular newcomer to the establishment as of last fall, had been in private quarters with a Colonel Wills, a regular who'd settled his wife and children in Baton Rouge, but frequented The Pink Lady on official trips to Vicksburg. He and Cheri had confirmed each other's presence in the wing opposite the murder scene, and Colonel Wills, with Miller's blessing had made his escape during the late morning following Isabel's death.

From what Seth was hearing, the only person who didn't have an alibi for his whereabouts other than Miller was Dicks, who said he had been in the relatively luxurious bath house, replete with indoor plumbing, which Isabel had completed the year the war started. It was separate from the main house, and Mary Margaret verified she had started the stove for him at his request and put a pot of water on to boil less than an hour before the shooting. Seth figured if the man had spent the entire afternoon and half the night with Mary Margaret, he probably was ready for a hot bath, and Ball did verify activity in the bath house well past midnight. No matter, Miller told Seth, he didn't rule Dicks out, and Dicks knew it.

Seth, for what it was worth, didn't rule out Miller either.

"I think you and I agree," Miller finished, "that she probably walked back into her room, discovered an intruder, and pulled out her gun. The intruder tried to overpower her and take the gun, and she was shot. Technically, an accident."

"Assuming the intruder wouldn't have then turned the gun on her and shot her anyway."

Miller shrugged. "I can't say that wouldn't have been the case."

Seth shifted his eyes to Clem White. "You were not on the premises, Mr. White?"

"He was not," Miller said. "I've got him watching the lawyer, Tobias Holbein. At the moment Isabel Hays was killed, Clem was in a tree about sixty yards from Holbein's front door. When Holbein came into town, Mr. White followed. I then informed Mr. White of the murder and sent him upriver to telegraph my seniors in Washington."

And who there would have cared? Seth opened his mouth to ask, but Miller preempted him with, "Privileged." Miller smiled with the ensuing silence.

Upriver to Sam Caruthers, more likely. Seth looked at the smug Clem White. He wouldn't rule him out as Isabel's killer either.

Chapter Sixty-four

Eli released Becky from his embrace, and Alice stepped up to give her a hug. "I'm so very, very sorry." It was the day following her mother's funeral, and Becky was home at Camellia Creek.

Alice fussed a bit, taking Becky's coat and hat, and shooed brother and sister into the parlor. "I'll get us some coffee. Have you eaten?"

Becky looked over her shoulder. "I'm not hungry, Alice. I can wait till supper, but Private Spain—"

"I imagine Elvie has already got his plate made. I'll make sure."

Alice disappeared, and Becky refocused on her slow-moving brother, who said, "Tell me what happened."

"Mama woke and went downstairs to sit with Savannah for a bit. It wasn't unusual. Parker thinks that when she came back up, she found someone in her room, and she drew her gun." Becky furrowed her brow. "She must have had it in the pocket of her robe, then, wouldn't you think?"

"She always had a pocket derringer on her, Becky. She never knew when she might need a weapon to protect herself or her girls, and times have gotten worse of late, not better."

"I knew she carried one. I didn't know she slept with it.'

"It would have been in the pocket of her robe."

"Anyway, he believes whoever was there tried to take it away from her, and the gun went off. We also know that Miller is looking for some sort of letter of authorization from the Treasury Department, and last evening, Mr. Holbein told me Miller's behind an investigation into Mama's banking."

"Treasury is looking at your mother's accounts?"

"Yes. Miller told Parker Mama was involved in blackmail and the matter concerns seditious activities."

Her brother didn't say anything, not then, but the look on his face conveyed both contemplation and confusion. She rose. "I need to show you something." With that she hurried from the room to retrieve the old family Bible. When she got back to the parlor, Alice was there with a coffee service. Becky sat down and showed Eli the 1863 letter from Congress. When he was done, he looked at Becky, who said, "Aunt Naomi had it, and I'd be willing to bet that's what she used to dissuade Sam Caruthers from trying to drive her off this place after Daddy was killed."

Eli flexed his jaw. "Have you shown this thing to Parker?"

"No."

He looked at her thoughtfully, then said, "And you're still thinking Caruthers wants Camellia Creek for his railroad?"

"That was Mama's prevarication. I think he wanted this letter."

Eli waved the thing in front of him. "Do you know what this letter is about?"

"Mama said it was a property dispute and Mr. Holbein was working it for Caruthers, but it concerned us, too, and Daddy was unaware. This letter inadvertently informed him. Apparently there were some hard feelings over it, but Mama says Daddy and Mr. Holbein had worked through them."

"And Caruthers?"

"I think not, and I'm guessing this letter is proof of wrongdoing on his part."

Alice took the letter from Eli.

"Does Parker think Miller killed Isabel?" Eli asked.

"He hasn't confided that to me. We trade information sometimes. Something for something. I'm never sure that he's sharing everything he knows with me, and I don't know what he's sharing with others."

"And you're not sharing everything with him." Alice said with a nod to the letter she held.

"He is aware that letter exists, but he doesn't know I have it."

"But this is not the letter you think Miller is trying to find now?" Eli asked.

"No, the one he's looking for now came from Treasury. This letter doesn't authorize anything, Eli, just tells Daddy Congress is taking no action on something, but we know not what."

Eli looked at Alice, then Becky. "And something referred to as an 'authorization' letter might indicate somebody is now taking action...on whatever it is."

"But do we even know if they refer to the same thing?" Alice asked.

No one responded, and Alice said, "I think we should show Seth this letter."

Behind them a floorboard squeaked. Private Hand emerged through the dining room, looked at the open bedroom door, then turned when Alice called to him. "We're in here, Bo."

Eli waved to him, Private Hand waved back. Thus reassured, the soldier disappeared back into the dining room, and in the span of a few heartbeats, the back door opened, then closed. Alice turned back. "He and Private Spain are playing cards in the kitchen. Their unit is being decommissioned tomorrow."

"Their permanent unit," Becky said. "Parker told me he's losing six men."

"Including Sergeant Zachary," Alice said. She looked up from the letter. "It couldn't hurt, Seth seeing this letter, could it? He knows it exists, you said."

Becky rolled her lips together. "I'm not sure we should get too trusting of him. Don't forget that Miller wants Eli arrested for killing Guthrie, and no matter what, Seth Parker is working for the other side." She turned her focus on Eli. "When they're out of options, they'll force him to follow orders. They're talking about sedition, Eli. They'll make that look worse than murder, and you know it."

"No, little sister, I don't know it, not when it comes to Parker, but I will admit that I'm not sure."

Alice shook her head. "I can't believe Seth would be part of that," Alice said.

"They can relieve him, sweetheart," Eli said.

Watching worry etch Alice's features, Becky wished she could take her comment back. She was miring Eli in a conflict he wasn't yet able to deal with. Just as important was Seth Parker himself. She didn't want him in a position where he had to make a choice between duty and them.

Between that and Alice's unquestioned trust in Parker, Becky decided not to confess to Eli that she believed the missing "authorization" letter, at least at some point, had been in her mother's possession.

Becky shot her brother a surreptitious glance. "I don't want to involve him, not yet."

Eli rubbed the back of his neck. "We could do worse than Parker," he said.

Becky rose before he could say more, then put a hand on his shoulder. "Stay seated," she said. "I'm going to rest before supper."

Alice rose beside her. "I've moved Naomi's big bed into your room and put the daybeds in the boys' old room. What with your room having windows, it's nicer for guests. I hope that's all right? It has a new mattress. Aunt Betty said the old one was awful."

Thank goodness Alice had told her about the new mattress, or she'd have made a mat on the floor. Sleeping where Naomi Polk had slept would have been too much to bear.

"That's perfect, thank you."

"We'll eat about five. Eli retires early."

Eli snorted, and Becky smiled before turning away and leaving the room. Behind her, not quite out of earshot, she heard Alice whisper "...Seth's in love with her. If lying is required, it's more likely he'd lie to protect the two of you than the opposite."

Becky closed her eyes tight. Perhaps that was her greatest fear of all. What would a woman owe a man who tainted his honor for her and those she loved?

Chapter Sixty-five

"I wish you'd stay. I'll give you forty acres..."

Dressed, Eli had risen and extended a hand when Frank Zachary entered the bedroom.

Zachary, big grin on his face, shook his head.

"Eighty."

Zachary laughed. "Naw."

"Hell, man, how many do you want? Neither one of us are gonna have hands to work it. I'll throw in Brim's mule, a horse."

"Gots me a hawse. I'm goin' west. Talked to da Freedmen's Bureau. Dey say der's talk 'a Negra army units maybe bein' fo'med to fight da Injuns. Majah got me a good recommendation, signed by Gen'ral Wood 'imse'f, to he'p me get in if'n it happens."

Eli stuck out his hand. "Thank you, Sergeant Frank Zachary, United States Army, for everything. I wish you luck and the offer always stands if things don't work out with the Army."

"Yo', sho', welcome, Colonel Eli Calhoon, Confed'rate States Army. It be a pleasure to know yo', suh, an' I thank yo' fo' da seni'ment, but I reckon I won't be comin' back to Miz'sippi, no matter what. I'll jes' keep on headin' wes'."

Alice and Becky had waited outside the door. They'd already shook hands with Hand and Spain—Becky had given Hand a quick hug, actually—waiting at the dining room portal, and wished them their best. Now Alice, a stray tear rolling down her cheek, hugged the man who she believed with all her heart had saved Eli Calhoon's life weeks earlier. Becky was the last to bid him farewell, also with a hug, his face beaming and hers, too, if a bit more damp.

Sergeant Kushing, whom Parker had sent to relieve Private

Hand of Calhoon duty, rose from his chair when Zachary emerged from the room and said, "Shoot, Frank, maybe I should cry, too."

Zachary laughed and said—"Don't let da colonel git away"—and he was gone, the two privates trailing in his wake.

$\mathcal{B}$ecky waited until Eli was alone in his and Alice's room, then closed the door and sat in the rocker next to the bed. "He reminded you of Brim. I saw it in him, too."

"And he's happy as a man can be, starting out on a new adventure."

She opened her mouth, and he said, "I think it could be the McGowan claim."

She shut that open mouth and squinted at him. "George McGowan? I know he's an ancestor, but who, exactly?"

"Our great-great-grandfather, and the Carutherses', too, on the distaff side. I fell asleep last night thinking about that congressional letter, piecing it together with everything else you and Parker have said, and it's the only thing I can come up with. At least, the only thing I can come up with that would involve Congress in a claim dealing with us."

"What was it for?"

"It's a Revolutionary War claim, and I really don't know much about it. I do know Andy used it as his inspiration for the South Carolina Dragoons killing off all the British, remember that? Conquering Mississippi for the United States?"

"That was the time he made all those tricorn hats out of Daddy's writing paper. Oh, my yes, I remember the whipping he got for that. And there was something about Hannah...?"

"She fell out of the 'headquarters' building in Jocelyn's tree and broke her arm."

"Was poor Andy blamed for that, too?" Becky asked.

"Naw, she'd been told to be careful, and she fell on her own. Nobody pushed her."

"I must have been three or four. I remember the hats and Andy's whipping."

"Well, the McGowan claim was Andy's inspiration. Daddy used to call it a moon pie in the night sky. It was supposedly dropped years ago, but Toby might have continued to work on it for the Carutherses. That could explain Daddy's anger when he received that letter. But here's the thing, little sister, that claim wasn't valuable enough, in my mind, to justify all these murders.'

"And the rumors about blackmail and sedition?"

"Blackmail and sedition can always account for dead bodies, but from what I know, Camellia Creek and Muscatine are more valuable to Sam Caruthers for his railroad right-of-way than that claim would be. We need to get with Toby and find out if that 1863 letter really is about the McGowan claim."

Chapter Sixty-six

"I've heard nothing regarding blackmail in connection with the Hays woman," Malcolm Byrnes said. "Interesting he's throwing that out here now."

"I think he's lying," Seth said. "I'm focusing on that congressional letter from '63 and now this second one, allegedly from the Treasury Department."

"And Miller wouldn't elaborate on the blackmail allegation?"

Friday, the 16th of February, near noon. He and his men had returned to Port Gibson from Rodney yesterday. He'd talked to Poynter Cummings for a bit this morning, early, and when Jubal told him Sergeant Zachary and Privates Hand and Spain had arrived from Camellia Creek, they'd all departed, in good order, from Port Gibson. The 60th was being decommissioned today and six of his men were going out with it. They'd left Kushing to spell Hand. Zachary, one of the six being mustered out, had wanted to say good-bye to the Calhoons.

It was relatively warm inside Malcolm's sunlit office. If the stove had been started earlier, its fire was long out. "The blackmail allegation is an easy explanation for her murder," Seth said.

"A subterfuge you mean?"

When Seth nodded, Malcolm added, "You are, of course, correct. Now, if her death was not an accident, we can rest assured it wasn't Miller who killed her. He wouldn't have done it before he found what he suspects she's hidden. If it was an accident, who did she walk in on, you say, searching her room?"

"Could have been Miller, under those circumstances."

"Could have. I do know David Wills, the one you said Miller allowed to leave before you had a chance to talk to him. He's been on staff in Baton Rouge since May. Family man," Malcolm added, his words rife with sarcasm. "I don't know this Dicks fella, but the name sounds familiar. There's no record of him ever being assigned to headquarters."

"Isabel told me he was here during the war."

"Yes, well, that could have meant he was with a company that simply passed through."

"She said he'd become a regular starting in October. I asked her if he was a speculator, my interest at the time still running to cotton thieving, but she said she didn't think so. Her assessment of him was he provided services for whoever could afford him."

"Security for cotton thieves perhaps?"

Seth grinned. "Maybe, but the thievery is so easy and rampant I'd think he'd have indulged on his own behalf. Isabel said he was quick to throw a punch, and her take was he would probably kill a man without blinking, but was gentlemanly in his treatment of her girls, at least in the common spaces. He came, enjoyed himself until he was broke, then disappeared and recouped, physically and fiscally, for his next visit. The pun was hers, not mine. Recuperation never took long.

"He told me he'd been out of the Army since last June. Says he finds odd jobs here and there—I took that as supporting Isabel's assessment of him—but he said he lives primarily off an inheritance. He's from Rhode Island."

"Ah ha!" Malcolm held up a finger. "I knew I'd heard that name before. Dicks, a wealthy merchant family. Daddy died in '64. There were four boys and none interested in the business. They sold the holdings and divvied up the money, so he probably was telling you the truth. I'll see what else I can find out."

Which could prove easier than imagined, since Malcolm himself hailed from a good middle-class Rhode Island family.

"And what do you know of Wills?"

"He's overly fond of the ladies. His wife comes from a well-to-do Philadelphia family, his not so much. Joined a state militia in the summer of '61 and received a commission in the regular Army in '62. Up until then, he worked at a branch of his father-in-law's loan office in Pittsburgh. To hear Wills tell it, he wasn't happy in the job, didn't like Pittsburgh, and I don't think he particularly likes his father-in-law, but the old man's got plenty to leave behind when he goes, and Wills' wife is an only child."

"What has the Army got him doing in Baton Rouge?"

"Supply. His wife and children are down here with him. Apparently she insists on following him from post to post."

Seth stifled a yawn. He was tired, not bored. "Doesn't matter, he's got an alibi. Everyone does but Miller and Dicks...and if I were to suppose Miller is lying to me, neither does his new hire Clem White."

Malcolm smirked. "Roscoe's replacement?"

"Yes."

"You know Roscoe is at the Caruthers farm."

"I didn't know that."

Malcolm studied him through a haze of blue-gray smoke, then said without prologue. "Greg Dustin wants you to come to Washington. I want you to go."

That got his blood moving. "They've turned something up?"

"Yes. When is your family due here?"

Seth quickly calculated. "Twenty-two days. How's travel?"

"Same as it's been since Vicksburg fell. We'll put you on the *Melissa Magee*. She and three sister ships rotate out of here every couple of days. They're the fast ones, official travel. She should have you in Wheeling in eight days. Take the Cumberland road to Cumberland and pick up a steamer down the Potomac. That leg should take less than a day. Nine days there, nine days back, give a day for an official boat. That gives you three days maximum to take care of business in Washington. Greg's ready for you, and I figure you'll only need a day." Malcolm pulled out his watch. "What time's the ceremony?"

"Two, then we're going to a seedy part of town. I promised to buy a few rounds."

Malcolm laid his watch on his desk. "Zachary's replacement working out?"

Seth gave his head a little shake. "He was proud to tell me he was there to replace eight men. He's on Calhoon watch at the moment, so all my old timers could be present today. He seems to be a good soldier. Don't think he's gonna make up for those eight, though. Malcolm, don't let them muster my last two men out till I get back."

"I'll do my best, and do not take a regular passenger ship out of Wheeling or you'll miss your dad for sure. I'll get you documentation. Though your uniform is probably all you'll need for that packet, we'll try to get you a first-class cabin."

Any stateroom would be fine. "When does she leave?"

"Six in the morning, can you make it?"

"Yeah, I'll brief Jubal this afternoon."

"You're gonna meet Greg's brother-in-law, Dan Fairchild, but don't forget he's Treasury. Be discreet.

"Oh, and one more thing. That question you sent up to me regarding Caruthers' oldest boy? You'll be interested to learn that what Sam Caruthers offered Colonel Petersen in return for the attacks on the Calhoon and Mackey farms was not bales of confiscated cotton, but a Confederate operative."

Seth took a moment to digest the unpalatable. "He turned in his son?"

Malcolm nodded. "I heard back from Ralston and that's what he says happened. Petersen had been operating pretty much autonomously during that time period until the raid on the Mackey farm resulted in the death of a Union soldier and wounding of another. The death of the woman, killed at the same time, got back to headquarters primarily because the wives got involved with the interrogation of the pregnant Rebecca Mackey. It was a messy situation. Petersen disappeared on a mission shortly thereafter. Ralston thinks the operative might have duped him. That or he deserted, but Ralston doesn't think the latter was the case. Petersen was reputable and dedicated. He wouldn't have abused his position for a few bales of cotton, but by the same token, he wouldn't have hesitated to raid a dozen farms or employ his questionable tactics on Southern civilians in return for a Confederate counterpart."

"And the son?"

"I'm still trying to find out what happened to him, but Ralston thinks Caruthers' terms were he not be harmed."

Seth cursed under his breath. "Just questioned and thrown into some Union hellhole."

"We're in agreement here, son, it was not a fatherly gesture, but we can't rule out the boy cooperated once his father switched sides."

No, they couldn't, but Poynter Cummings didn't seem to believe that had been the case. Tobias Holbein had implied the same thing.

"Stop back after the ceremony. I'll have documents ready for you."

Chapter Sixty-seven

<u>Washington, District of Columbia, 27 February 1866</u>

"Major Parker?"

Seth pivoted with the sound of his name. He had just alighted from the stairs, leading from his second floor room down to the lobby of the Metropolitan Hotel. It had been the Brown's Hotel when he and his family had spent two sweltering weeks in Washington during the summer of 1854.

Greg Dustin stuck out his hand. "It's good to see you again, Seth."

"And you, Colonel," he said and took the man's hand.

"I checked yesterday. I was getting a bit concerned that you hadn't made it in."

"River was high. Travel slowed a bit around St. Louis."

"Well, maybe it will make for a quicker trip home. Malcolm's telegram said you were on a tight schedule. "

"Not critical. My father and brother are accompanying my grandfather to New Orleans. They wanted to stop in Vicksburg for a quick visit.'

"Family is always important. And on that note, I trust you won't mind our breakfasting after our meeting. My brother-in-law is always in a hurry." Dustin guided Seth out the lobby door. "Dan Fairchild's his name. I mentioned him in Mississippi, if you recall, an agent with Treasury. He's rented rooms three blocks from here. We just have to wade through the mud to get there."

Fairchild's choice of his living quarters instead of the ante-room inside the Treasury building he occupied with his five-man

375

team had been for discretionary reasons, and late winter rains had made a quagmire of the unpaved streets that predominated in the nation's capital.

The man proved agreeable enough, if clipped and to the point in speech and manner, unlike the more personable Miller. Seth figured Fairchild for his mid-forties, no-nonsense, and dedicated. He'd spent the war in and out of Washington, commuting back and forth primarily to the northeast and Midwest rooting out counterfeiters and forgers. He'd been called back from Boston to work what Seth referred to as the Guthrie murder. Fairchild had laughed when, after the three of them settled around the table, Seth had referred to it as that. It was the only occasion Seth realized, in retrospect, that he heard the man laugh.

"That's not how we in Treasury view this mess," the man explained. "Guthrie's death is a clue to a bigger conspiracy of which Treasury has only recently become aware.

"I started working this after the first of the year, when the National Bank of New Orleans came back with a request to augment its gold reserves. That request immediately garnered Treasury's attention, since the last augmentation of the bank's reserves should, based on expected disbursements, have lasted it until the fourth quarter of the fiscal year. That means it should have lasted until April.

"It turns out that at the end of November the bank had cashed out an account set up in September, which honored a claim made by the heirs of one George McGowan. It was paid in gold." Dan Fairchild stopped at that point and looked at Seth. "Two hundred forty-seven thousand, seven hundred three dollars and twelve cents. The bullion was loaded onto a British flag merchant and departed New Orleans November 30. The Bank of Honduras in Belize City has confirmed receipt on the eighth of December. The money was credited to the account, again identified as the estate of George Robert McGowan. The Bank of Honduras confirms the money was moved on the ninth of December and the account closed."

"Treasury doesn't know where the money is," Dustin said.

"The Bank of Honduras is under no obligation to divulge what happened to it."

"Someone initiated those transfers, Dan," Dustin said.

Fairchild drew in what appeared to be a calming breath and returned to Seth. "The paperwork closing out the account in New Orleans is conveniently missing."

"That information," Dustin said to Seth, "was provided by your colleague Walter Miller shortly after he arrived in the west."

"According to Miller," Fairchild said, "the bank president has no explanation, nor does the senior manager who completed the transaction. The manager remembered the agent's name as being Holbein"—Seth caught Dustin's eye—"but when questioned by Miller, this Holbein denied all knowledge of having possession of any authorization regarding an individual named McGowan or his estate. Nor, he said, had he been to New Orleans in the past six months. So Miller placed him in cuffs and hauled him to New Orleans."

Dustin winked at Seth. "That accounts for part of Miller's delay in arriving at Vicksburg."

"The clerk, as well as the bank manager involved in the transaction at the Bank of New Orleans, took one look at Miller's detainee and confirmed he was not the man who had been in possession of the authorization."

"Which anyone might have guessed due to the simple fact that they found the real Holbein at his office in Rodney."

Again Fairchild focused on Dustin, this time with a withering glare. "Well, hell," the latter said, "I wouldn't have hung around if I'd just managed to get that much money out of the country." He chuckled. "I'd be with it in Honduras."

"We have to assume," Fairchild said, "that whoever was the bearer of the authorization to deal for the estate of George McGowan is the individual who now has the money or knows where it is. We have the Wells Fargo receipt for delivery of that authorization letter. It was signed for by Tobias Holbein. Since the paperwork in the bank has disappeared, I've been unable to compare the Wells Fargo signature with that of the man who moved the money. Requests to Miller to have the real Holbein provide a signature for comparison have not been filled. The Wells Fargo courier himself, who we might have asked to identify Holbein in person, transferred to San Francisco before Christmas and has since left Wells Fargo and disappeared into the High Sierras in search of gold. So far we haven't found him."

"Why," Seth asked, "given a sum that large, didn't the bank double check with Treasury?"

"The bank president was in Memphis," Fairchild said.

"Very convenient," Dustin said to no one in particular.

"Greg, I have already agreed with you that someone in the New Orleans bank participated in this theft."

"I'm merely throwing that information out there for the edification of the major, who has not been privy to what you have masterfully uncovered in a commendable period of time."

Fairchild made a point of scooting his chair closer to the scruffy table occupying a forlorn nook in the two-room flat. "Miller's not convinced the clerk or the vice president is involved. The manager who handled the transaction and the bank vice president state that the authorization the faux Mr. Holbein carried was in order and signed by a proper disbursing officer here at Treasury, with whose signature they were familiar. As far as they were concerned, the authorization was valid and remains so. They had no reason to question it. I would have checked the authorization letter for forgery had they been able to produce the letter, but as I stated earlier it seems to have disappeared.

"According to them, the letter identified Holbein as executor of the McGowan estate and authorized him to act on behalf of the McGowan heirs. Treasury has been in contact by wire with the Bank of Honduras but, unless pressed, it will not identify who deposited the money or who subsequently moved it. Common sense opines that would be the same Holbein impersonator. Our most immediate concern, of course, is where the individual moved the money. That part of the mystery is in the hands of the State Department and out of mine, at least for the present. With British bankers involved, who the devil knows what'll happen."

Greg Dustin chortled. "With British bankers involved, who the devil knows what *has* happened."

Fairchild glared at his brother-in-law. "And apparently someone over in the War Department has started a rumor this is a payoff to someone involved in Lincoln's assassination."

Seth sat forward. "Why haven't we heard that?"

"You are hearing it now, and it's bullshit. If it was a payoff for some mysterious group of conspirators, the War Department wouldn't want it out, not to mention the implication against the British. They need to shoot whatever idiot over there started that rumor, and if War hesitates, State should insist."

Dustin looked from Fairchild to Seth. "There's all sorts of theories floating around here in Washington as to why Lincoln was killed. The theories go along with rumors of high-ranking individuals destroying evidence to protect the plotters." Dustin leaned back in his chair. "And lots of Southerners are immigrating to British Honduras."

"Look," Fairchild said, keeping his eyes on Seth, "there's no doubt in my mind that this was a theft. A big theft, but nothing more. First off, no payoff is going to be down to the last damn cent. It's gonna be a nice round figure. Two-hundred thousand, two-hundred and fifty thousand."

"Not if they were trying to make it look like something other than what it was."

"Greg, are you the idiot," Dan Fairchild said, "they need to shoot over there at the War Department? The only people trying to make it look like something other than what it *is* are those with something to gain by making it something it's *not*."

"Just trying to make sure you've considered all possibilities."

Fairchild blew out a breath and returned his attention to Seth.

"Secondly, the theft was committed through proper administrative channels at the Treasury Department. The transaction is in the books. Hell, we've got the outgoing mail log showing the day the bill of exchange was turned over to Wells Fargo. Everything appears to be legitimate, and it happened right there under Treasury's nose."

"If you have the mail log, then you should know who authorized the bill."

"Oh, we've got better than that now. We've got the cancelled Treasury bill that established the account in New Orleans, with the signatures of the men who signed it. Both of them are *dead*. Died the same day that bill was logged into the mailroom."

Seth's gaze drifted to Dustin, who nodded at him knowingly.

"One was James Hurd, who worked in the bank and was killed in a dray accident while returning from lunch the day the thing went out. The other was Jacob Harding, who shot himself at his desk in the Treasury building late that same evening."

The suicide, Seth remembered, that Dustin had referred to in Mississippi a few weeks ago.

"Both of those men were authorized to approve letters of credit and sign bills of exchange with a face value as large as that one, but there should be some sort of approval by Congress for disbursal of the monies. That would have been forwarded to the Treasury Secretary, who subsequently approved payment. We've yet to turn up an authorization from the Secretary. McCulloch says there isn't one."

"From the appearance of the thing, we suspected we should be looking for a claim against the United States Government payable with interest, hence the amount being down to the penny. Armed with that, we went to the House log and found a pre-war claim—lo and behold—made on behalf of the heirs of one George McGowan, and approved by Congress shortly before the commencement of hostilities. It was held in abeyance and, pending documented evidence to the contrary, is still being held in abeyance."

"That's a lot of money for a legitimate claim," Seth said.

"Worse than the Galphin claim, but as was the case there, the principal wasn't the problem, it was the interest. In the case of the McGowan claim, the principal was only twelve thousand dollars, and that's what Congress approved. But if you take that principal and tack on eighty-eight years of interest at three and a half percent compounded annually you come up with roughly the same figure paid out to the McGowan estate last September. Like I said, everything about this was made to look legitimate."

"And the claimants?" Seth asked.

"Descend from this fella McGowan on the female side, there being no surviving McGowan males. His granddaughters' married names are Caruthers and Calhoon. Names, I understand, that are familiar to you."

Seth's heartbeat hadn't even quickened. He'd suspected when they started talking about claimants, but he'd been sure the moment Dan Fairchild spoke the words "female side."

"I know that you've validated Guthrie's searching for the Calhoons. Now, allow me to elaborate a little more. Alan Guthrie was Jacob Harding's brother-in-law. Harding was the man who allegedly signed Holbein's authorization letter and his name was familiar to Mr. Haskers and the clerk at the Bank of New Orleans. Harding, you recall, was the suicide.

"The investigative report on Harding's death indicated he had both drinking and marital problems, both of which his seniors at Treasury were unaware of, or so they claim. The night he is alleged to have taken his life, he'd demanded his wife return to her parents' home with their six children. When she argued, he hit her, more than once. The evidence was clear on the woman's face later that night when officers informed her of her husband's death.

"The police report documents Guthrie's tracking Harding to his office where he confronted him on behalf of his sister. According to Guthrie, the beatings were commonplace. He told the authorities he found Harding drunk, and the investigation supports that. Guthrie stated that he feared it had been this confrontation and his castigation that drove Harding to suicide."

"I take it we're no longer thinking Harding's death a suicide?" Seth asked.

"Or Hurd's death an accident," Fairchild answered. "What we're not sure of is their roles in the theft. Guilty or innocent? Betrayed provocateur or innocent dupes?"

"Or a double cross of dupes."

"And for that particular role," Fairchild said, "I'd guess Jacob Harding since it was his kinsman who ended up dead out there in Mississippi."

"Guthrie could have been trying to clear his brother-in-law," Dustin offered.

Fairchild looked at him. "Gregory, would you clear the name of a man who repeatedly beat your sister?"

"That would be you, my friend."

"I don't beat your sister. The only person abused in my household," Fairchild whispered under his breath, "is me, by my lovely bride and her baby brother."

Greg Dustin laughed. There, Seth caught the hint of a smile on Fairchild's lips.

"Guthrie was an operative," the man started again, the fleeting smile gone. "He'd spent some time in the west during the war. At the time of his death, he was supposed to have been on extended furlough reestablishing his sister, Harding's wife, and her children in Pennsylvania, not Mississippi."

Seth caught Dustin's eye. Fairchild noticed. Dustin shrugged, and said to Seth, "So perhaps Malcolm's and my suspicions regarding Guthrie and Treasury and covert operations were unfounded. Then again, maybe not."

Fairchild didn't appear interested in pursuing any suspicions. No doubt he'd already received, and provided, an earful from and to his brother-in-law. The point was Miller had purposely led them astray as to why Guthrie was in Mississippi last fall.

"During the war, Guthrie had run into some trouble and was removed from his assignment in Arkansas."

"He'd run afoul of an army officer with more authority than he had," Dustin clarified.

"There's no need to go into that here, because it doesn't seem to have any relevancy to his death. To make it short, Guthrie was bitter with the department over his removal, and his attitude showed in his work output. When his seniors learned of his death, they were content to let the military authority in Vicksburg resolve the issue."

"He worked in the same office as Miller?" Seth asked to confirm what Miller had told him during their initial first meeting in January.

"Miller was the senior operative, but he wasn't in a supervisory position."

"We were told Guthrie was the nephew of a big Republican donor and to get the issue resolved quickly."

"I know that now," Fairchild said, "and it sounds like the work of someone in Treasury who wanted the murder covered up."

"Probably the same person who misplaced that paperwork authorizing Treasury to pay the McGowan claim," Dustin said, and he winked at Seth.

"For all we know, that was Guthrie himself," Fairchild said to Seth after a surly glare at Dustin. "But if that is the case, we still suspect he was working with someone in Mississippi. That authorization letter went to somebody."

"And Guthrie didn't have it," Seth said, "or he wouldn't have been looking for the people he assumed would have had it."

Dan Fairchild nodded. "It or the money itself. I'm pretty certain Alan Guthrie was part of the scheme that spirited the money out of Treasury and what he told people as regards his reason for being in Mississippi was a lie to cover up his true intent. I want whoever he was working with in Mississippi."

Greg Dustin looked at Seth. "So we're back to the Calhouns."

"And there's this Caruthers fella and his progeny," Fairchild added, an observation for which Seth was grateful.

Chapter Sixty-eight

Seth made it back in seven days. All three rivers were good, as was the weather for the most part. All told, he'd been gone nineteen days, and he'd returned with a pretty clear picture of what Alan Guthrie had really been in search of last fall.

"I talked to Fairchild and Greg Dustin about it, Malcolm, but I left with both of them doubtful of my interpretation."

"Which is?"

"If Alan Guthrie was behind the ruse at Treasury that spirited the money out, why was he stumbling around in the dark when he got here?"

"So you're thinking he got wind of it and decided to force his way in?"

"Yes, and he probably learned about it from his now deceased brother-in-law. And then there's Miller. He implied Guthrie was involved in covert operations in order to cover up his own search for that authorization letter. Tell me this, Malcolm. How would it hurt, us knowing about the authorization letter?"

Malcolm flexed his jaw, and Seth pointed an index finger at him. "Miller didn't want us to know what he was looking for, but why?"

"Fairchild didn't buy it?"

"By Treasury standards, Miller's got an outstanding record. Fairchild's not ready to consider he's anything but a dedicated agent. I already know that what qualifies as a dedicated agent might well mean he's an excellent candidate for what we're talking about here."

"If he's involved with malfeasance, he's in cahoots with somebody out here, but crook or not, he has a valid reason justifying his accusation against Eli Calhoon, or the entire clan for that matter, and making it stick.

"And speaking of Calhoon," Malcolm continued, "as of right now, Summers has Daws and Price switching off guard duty out at Camellia Creek. Day after tomorrow, you're losing both men. I directed Summers to talk to the provost. Don Hemple is assuming responsibility for Calhoon in two days. Rebecca Mackey gathered up her entourage and returned with her family to Madison County four days after you left. I would think Miller would be interested in her whereabouts if there's some concern the family is about to make off with a bushel load of money.'

"Do we know where he is?"

"Summers says he and White haven't been in Port Gibson for days. My line of communications tells me he's been in both Natchez and New Orleans, so we might consider he's looking at bank employees."

"And Isabel Hays' bank accounts."

"Them, too." Malcolm looked at his watch, then rose from his desk. He grinned at Seth, who stood when he did, and nodded at the telegram he'd passed to Seth when he walked into the office forty-five minutes ago.

"If the boat's on schedule," Malcolm said, "you've got less than an hour before she docks. They could be a little concerned you're not back. I wouldn't have responded to them if I'd known you'd be back yesterday, but I was no longer sure you were gonna make it in time."

"Be happy you're not going to have to make good on your offer to put them up until I did get back. My granddaddy might have actually managed to get under your tough hide." He held up the telegram. "And I'm glad they're a day late. Gave me the opportunity to wrap up this report."

"Are you sure you don't want to take a few days' furlough?"

"I'm running out of men and time, Malcolm. I need to get to Natchez and look into Isabel's accounts. You can bet Miller has. There's not a doubt in my mind, now, that he believed she knew about that authorization and the claim."

"And her daughter?"

"We know for sure she's aware of the authorization—she's the one who told me. And she's aware of the 1863 congressional letter."

Whether Becky had added the two letters and come up with that old claim, Seth didn't know, but he couldn't rule it out, and a shiver of fear shimmied up his spine. Miller's being aware of Becky's interrogation in 1863 was a distinct possibility, as was his believing Isabel confided in her about the authorization letter, and Seth wished she hadn't left the relative safety of her brother's home.

"As soon as I've got my kinfolk back on the boat and headed downstream, I'll be on my way to Madison County to see if I can discreetly find out what she knows of the McGowan claim."

The side-wheeler *Marie Lindsey* bumped the quay, the last echo of her horn fading into the cacophony of activity that permeated a wharf already bustling before her stacks came into view upriver. Seth had been squinting at the boat for the past five minutes, shading his eyes in defense of the midday sun and its fractured, sparkling reflection rebounding off the surface of the river. The bobbing main deck was loaded with shabbily dressed passengers, white-skinned and black, mingling with men and women richly appointed. Soldiers in blue, some neatly dressed, most unkempt. Soldiers in worn and battered gray. None were familiar to him, or if they were, he scanned over them too quickly to notice. He searched for a group of three men in civilian attire, but the ship's decks were even more crowded than the quay.

"Yo."

He looked to the boiler deck and locked his eyes on his older brother, Reeves, a smile on his face and his arm moving in a wide wave over the promenade's balustrade. Seth's father, Hampton Parker, and maternal grandfather, Hugh Henry James, flanked Reeves. His grandfather, tall and still robust at seventy-nine, raised a gnarled hand in greeting. They'd found him, no easy matter, Seth figured, given that the activity they were looking down

on was about as bad as the mingling scores of people he was looking up at. Vicksburg was a busy port.

"We're coming down," Reeves shouted.

"Don't," he called back, then shook his head in company with
a series of hand motions in case they hadn't heard. "Let me get
Boon onboard," he yelled, "and I'll be up."

"They're an ignorant and backwards people, my dear, all victims of slave power that has kept them in poverty. Why, I hear
the majority of poor whites haven't the sense to close their doors
against winter simply because they make it a habit of sleeping
with them open in the summer. There's no education to speak of,
no culture, no roads other than muddy mires tying isolated ham-
lets of ignorance together. Those in power refuse to be taxed, so
there is little in the way of public convenience for all. Now that
the enlightened world has been given the opportunity to journey
into the South, it is our Christian duty to save these pathetic souls
and assure justice for the Negro. Why I—"

Hugh James pushed back in his chair, purposefully, Seth had
no doubt, grinding its legs against flooring of yellow pine. The
result was a God-awful groan. The robust old man turned in his
seat and glared at the woman, who had shut her mouth.

"Just what this devastated region needs, madam, the likes of
you following the vanguard of demons in blue you sent South. I
do imagine they'd prefer the demons. They'll have to hold their
bullets for the likes of you, the world not seeing Elspeth as she
really is."

Her face reddened. Her first challenge, if Seth were to guess.
"Do you mind, sir?" she said.

"As a matter of fact I do, but with people like you it makes no
difference. You believe yourselves God's gift to the human race."
He turned back to the table, looked at his daughter's husband
and his two grandsons, then leaned back in the dining room chair.
Apparently settled, he relaxed his tight grimace. "Let me tell you
a tale," he said, rather loudly, and with that, Seth knew the tale
was meant more for the table behind them than it was for them.

Granddaddy's telling a tale was nothing new. He told good ones, always had.

"Truth? Fiction?" Seth considered his granddaddy's reaction to the woman and grinned. "Not for mixed company?"

The woman had started talking again, this time keeping her voice lower. His grandfather snorted softly, then said, his voice congenial, if still unnecessarily loud, "Allegorical, I think you'd call this one. And as true an allegory as ever told. A tale told for a mix of victor and vanquished, the honorable and the insufferable, self-righteous hypocrites."

That "self-righteous hypocrites" part was definitely stated for the woman and her female companions at the other table. The New Englander, if her accent meant anything, was on her way to the wilds of western Mississippi to save the sinful and stupid from themselves as well as uplift the downtrodden Negro, all at the behest of God Himself—personified as the Federal government. She was the sort of individual Hugh Henry James despised.

Seth sobered.

"There once was a half sister and half brother. They had a common father, a wily, greedy old man who had no compunction about using his children for his own gain. The daughter was a beauty, only a bit older than her brother. Her father wed her to a rich old man, who, when he died, left her a wealthy widow with strong investments and a good income. A regular boon, shall we say, for the father, who then proceeded to direct and harvest his daughter's properties. She lived well, and for the self-righteous, who will say in the end she got her just deserts"—he'd raised his voice a bit and glanced at the table behind him. The woman was whispering to her companions and pretended, obviously, not to be paying attention, so Pap raised his voice a bit more at the same time turning back to find Seth's father pondering him—"we'll say the lovely young beauty became a paramour. Willingly at first, she provided a fine income for her father, and a comfortable standard of living for her brother and cow of a stepmother, who happened to be the son's true mother." This last he said loud enough to cause the table behind them to quiet completely.

"The man's hardworking son," Hugh James continued, "and I wish to be just here, also saw the fruits of his labor pilfered by the stingy old miser. This mode of existence went on for some time, the old man content living off the labor and sin of his children until in time, the children, seeing no advantage to themselves from the arrangement, discussed the matter and decided to run away from the man and begin life anew. The daughter, of course, was able to take her assets with her, the brother, his father owning the industry in which he labored, left with nothing, but by mutual agreement between the two siblings, the girl shared her profits. Let me emphasize that my purpose in making the young woman's means of income that of a harlot is to make her accountable to the self-righteous, who would never agree to her profession even though they are, in truth, pimps and whore-mothers living off it." He'd raised his voice again. There was a low murmur from another neighboring table now, due as much, Seth figured, to his grandfather's language as to the story. "The girl's purpose, of course, was to support her brother"—Hugh James' eyes twinkled—"and let's add the young man's mother here for effect—*until* he could establish himself.

"Under the agreement, the young woman required certain conditions if she were to carry on her profession, which was the source of her wealth. The young man, no longer threatened by his father's abuse of his labor and seeing a profitable future once his sister had provided him the means to establish himself, agreed to the terms."

Hugh James, obviously pleased with his tale so far, stiffened his back and placed his forearms on the table. "But, of course, once the young man had established himself, he discovered that the young woman's profession had become an embarrassment— a feeling fed by his domineering mother, the girl's stepmother. Despite the older woman's censure, her son did continue to enjoy the income. However, the girl's profession had become a source of significant strife within the home. The young man continued to support his extravagance with her largesse, while she fell more and more under the criticism of her stepmother. Confident she could live quite handsomely on her own and pursue her profession in peace, she decided to leave her unhappy home.

"Incensed by her effrontery in daring to leave the protection he provided her—not to mention the loss of wages she heretofore willingly gave to him—and determined she would not leave his house, he beat her. Then, telling his mother she must leave the room, the brother had the servants strip his sister naked, then drag her to the bedroom upstairs. There he directed them to bind her to the bed and he watched as each in turn took their pleasure from her, the sight feeding his own wicked lust. And when they were done, he sent them from the room, unbuttoned his britches and crawled on top of his sister and possessed her. Conquest complete, he kept her prisoner, selling her to his companions and to strangers. Anyone, actually, to ensure he would not lose the income she had willingly provided for so long. In return she existed with a roof over her head, food to eat, and a lifetime feeding her body to strangers."

Dry-mouthed, Seth watched as his grandfather turned to the woman, who, along with her companions, had risen from the table. The woman glared at Hugh James, who, clearly focused on her, said, "And the pimp and his whore-mongering mother wallowed in the wealth provided by a shattered whore, certain they were justified in their rapine and violence."

The woman pushed the chair in, slamming its back against the table rim.

"Enjoy your gain from the wreckage, madam," he said, "and pray there isn't a hell for those such as you."

She stuck her nose in the air and whirled with a flounce of her skirts. Briefly Seth caught the eye of one of the women with her. The companion immediately dropped her gaze and turned to follow the other women out.

On Seth's right, Reeves let out a long breath. "Well, Pap, you certainly outdid yourself with that one."

Hugh James picked up his whiskey and downed it. "Damn New England Methodists. Ain't a bit'a doubt in my mind that's what they are. You can smell their sulfurous stench for miles, as if the stink of death and destruction they fostered isn't enough. I'm glad your grandmother didn't hear what that personification of ignorance said about the South and Southerners. I'd go to my grave wed to a murderess."

"And we would have been deprived of that provocative story," Hampton Parker said. He reached for his own whiskey. "Good God, Hugh," he said under his breath, then picked up his own glass.

Hugh James rose suddenly. "I need a nap."

He was gone before Hampton could turn and find Reeves "Don't let him make more trouble."

"Afraid the woman's reaction didn't quite satisfy his needs?" Reeves said, rising.

"I doubt her jumping overboard to atone for her sins would satisfy him. But what worries me is he'll hear another opinion he's not in agreement with and start a riot."

"How bad are things at home?" Seth asked, watching Reeves step out on the promenade.

His father set his glass on the table, and Seth took Reeves' chair beside him. "Not as bad as here," the man said, "but bad, restless. Those who backed the Union have suspected since '62 Lincoln would betray us to the Radicals, and he did. Won't be long now, and we'll all be ex-Confederates. I hate your grand-father's telling me I told you so. I hate it worse knowing he was right all along."

"Kentucky can't be faulted for believing her interests were best served by staying in the Union."

"We believed the Union best *protected* our interests, son. Your grandfather used to laugh when I said that, before the war. Argued Kentucky was the only power to protect its interests and to cede such protection to the central government was a sure way to sacrifice them. He was adamant we go out the moment Lincoln called for troops to wage war on the South. He was right, and now those who opted for caution are forced to do some serious pondering."

"What exactly are you pondering?"

"Congress is not going to allow the rebel states back in on Johnson's terms. The Radicals want nothing short of the complete destruction of the South. The conservatives want to guarantee no more threat to protection and the tariff. State rights mean nothing, and the needs of the central government are paramount. That's what I'm pondering. It's been an ever-growing objective of Whiggery since its inception. The South's solution was to get out, but Davis was no novice and there is no excuse for his behaving like one. Thinking the North would leave the South alone with free-market ports and all that lost revenue was delusional. He bungled the war and signed the death warrant of the Republic, then handed it over to its executioners."

Seth contemplated his empty glass, then said softly, "Do you think they could have ever won?"

"Not the way they fought it. You'd be better talking to your grandfather about this, but it's our considered opinion that the minute Lincoln attacked, Jeff Davis should have moved north with everything he had. The South's window of opportunity was narrow. He had to work fast. Good God, Jackson could have taken D.C. without firing a shot."

"Davis didn't want Washington."

Seth's father looked at him as if he'd grown horns, and Seth grinned, because he knew what was coming.

"Davis didn't *want* war, but that's what he had. And as far as Washington was concerned, he didn't have to keep the damn, pestilence-infested place. Once the North said enough, he could have given it back."

"They'd have retreated back to Philadelphia or New York and set up camp."

"If Davis had taken the war north quickly enough, before Lincoln silenced his opposition, they might not have found a home. Back then most people up there didn't like Republicans, either, and the opposition might have flourished if either the British or French had opted in, and early strategic victories, such as taking the enemy capital, might have given the Confederacy that." Hampton Parker waved a finger under Seth's nose. "Jeff

Davis knew what he wanted and that was for the South to be left alone. Unfortunately, he wasn't willing to do what he had to do to get it. Lincoln and the bunch of ruthless bastards he surrounded himself with knew what they wanted, too, and they had no qualms about doing what they had to do to get it. For three decades men who gave credence to the likes of Lincoln have gone so with the ultimate goal to enforce their economic agenda on this nation, and for three decades factionalism over slavery, much of it created by themselves, has foiled them. The South's solution was to peacefully get out.

"In the end all Lincoln and his ilk had to do was martial their forces and cull out the weak spots. Human life was expendable and they had plenty of it to expend, hence your grandfather's so-called allegory. And the servants are just now dragging her up the stairs. The real rape and degradation hasn't even started yet."

Seth didn't look at his father. He'd known this was coming. His father and brother hadn't been silent all this time. He was aware of their dissatisfaction and second guesses, and he'd always known where his maternal grandparents' sympathies lay. Back during the fifties Hugh James' fire-eating rhetoric had been a bit of a family joke.

"I don't know what your goals are, son," his father said in a voice soft and sympathetic, "and I won't try to influence you. You're your own man and a damn fine one. I'm proud of you for doing your duty, and we'll love and support you no matter what you decide, but we're entering another struggle. If you're worried about what we're thinking, let me assure you that me and your mama won't be hurt one bit if you resign your commission and come on home."

His family had had misgivings from the start. He'd fought, in the parlance of those with whose side his family had aligned themselves, to save the Union, to protect his way of life, not to alter it, but they'd always been aware that alteration was exactly what was happening. How poignant the price of honor and duty when victory proves false.

Chapter Sixty-nine

Seth's kinsmen had wanted rooms at one of the hotels near the quay in Natchez, but those were full. They ended up with good lodgings at the Jefferson Hotel on Franklin Street. The recently refurbished Jefferson had been around since the twenties, and was a Natchez landmark, its accommodations comfortable by any standard, if not as convenient to the river. Once they'd settled in, they opted for an afternoon nap. They'd apparently made quite a night of their brief stay in Memphis. Seth took the opportunity to slip off to the Adam's County courthouse on State Street. "Spanish deeds," he remembered that old codger Ferguson at the Warren County courthouse saying, "validating British claims."

And that was what they proved to be, Spanish validations of British properties that went back to the close of the French and Indian War and had passed, from two distaff sides, to one George McGowan. The surname had belonged to the mother of Mary Ellen Price, wife to Angus Calhoon and the mother of Holland Calhoon. Her father had come to British West Florida and married into pioneers already established in the area as of the late 1760s. This had all happened darn close to a century ago.

With the clerk's help and that of an old British map, Seth deduced that the land in those ancient deeds matched up with what now made up Camellia Creek, Muscatine, and land farther north in Warren County—Caruthers' holdings if he recalled the map in the Warren County clerk's office correctly—and those old female lines no doubt explained the relationship between the two families.

A third man stepped through the door of an inner office and joined Seth and the clerk at the counter. He introduced himself as another Federal employee overseeing the workings of the county clerk in yet another Mississippi county.

"Was a pretty, young widow here this mornin' interested in these same old deeds." The man looked at the clerk. "Isn't that so, Joe?" The Federal had intervened, obviously, because the clerk failed to bring that earlier visit up.

Seth took another look at Joe.

"She wanted information on an old property claim," he said, "made against the national government. I told her we keep the deeds. It would have been a lawyer who looked at them, then drew up a claim from there."

"Do you recall a lawyer working on a case involving these particular holdings?"

"No, sir, and I've been here for twenty-odd years."

Chapter Seventy

Hugh James glanced around the muted elegance of the hotel's dining room before pulling out his chair. He didn't say anything, simply glanced across the table at Hampton Parker, who'd taken his seat without bothering to look around. Hampton looked at his father-in-law. Hampton didn't speak either.

Reeves moved around to the other side of the linen-draped table, and Seth pulled out the chair opposite his older brother. Father and grandfather flanked the younger men, and four left plenty of room at a table meant for seating as many as six. His father glanced up at the Negro waiter hovering near his shoulder. "Bourbon."

The waiter looked at the others, but his father preempted his question. "One bottle and four glasses."

Hugh James, studying the menu, said, "They're eating well."

"Never stopped," Reeves said.

"Never stopped selling their cotton," Hampton Parker said, "never did without their steak and wine and oysters. We know, Hugh. The same can be said for Kentucky and in neither case would it be the true picture. Both gave blood and sacrifice to the Confederacy."

"I'd argue both the oysters and red meat," Reeves said.

"And who did you sell your cotton to, Hugh?" Hampton asked.

"Black market, and I never asked."

The Negro placed a bottle of Kentucky whiskey near the center of the table, but a wee closer to Seth's father, and the senior Parker reached for the bottle while the waiter set a fat glass tumbler in front of each man. Hampton poured himself a shot, passed the bottle to Reeves on his left, then tipped the glass to his senior. "That's what they did."

Hugh James narrowed his eyes. The bottle was with him now, and he filled his glass to the rim, then passed the whiskey to Seth. Without spilling a drop, his grandfather raised the charged tumbler in a haughty salute to his son-in-law, then downed the entire drink. He clenched his teeth, his grimace giving way to a thin smile, and said, "Let's enjoy the damn liquor."

Hampton returned his half-empty glass to his lips and downed it. Reeves smirked at Seth and took a swig, but did not finish his. Seth filled his glass and raised it. "I'll drink to the liquor." Like his grandfather, he emptied his tumbler.

Hugh straightened and smiled at Hampton Parker. "He's his granddaddy's boy," the elder said and slapped Seth on the back.

Hampton made a point of taking in Seth's uniform and cocking an eyebrow.

"Ah, he's not to be faulted for siding with his daddy or his state. Now" — Hugh Henry looked pointedly at his son-in-law — "you'll all end up siding with me."

Hugh Henry James of Fulton County, Kentucky, returned to the menu in earnest. Seth's father said nothing, but reached for the bourbon Seth had returned to the table before steeling himself to match his grandfather's performance. Seth didn't look at the menu. Instead he looked to Reeves, who discreetly shook his head, indicating "say nothing more." For more than three years there'd been a covert estrangement between Hampton Parker and his wife's father. Mild and equanimous in manner, Hampton Parker had never allowed the rift to become more than that between himself and his less temperate father-in-law, but now, from Seth's point of view, Hugh James' bitter I-told-you-so's, combined with the acceptance on all their parts that the old man had been right regarding the central government's subsequent treatment of Kentucky, were wearing on his father. Granddaddy needed to ease up, but he had cause for bitterness, too, and the man had never once refused to break bread with his youngest grandson, despite the blue uniform, though once Seth had heard him say under his breath that at least it wasn't the one worn by the damn Army.

The waiter returned, and Seth's father looked around the table. "Steaks for all?"

All nodded, and Hugh James eyed the server. "Rare."

The Negro started to glance at the other faces.

"All of 'em," Hugh said and grinned. The waiter smiled, then took the menus Hampton Parker had gathered for him.

Reeves looked at his father. "Mama would have your hide."

"One thing I've always tried to tell you youngsters," Hugh said, shifting in his seat to look first at Seth, then Reeves, "enjoy yourself when God blesses you with distance from your women-folk." He nodded across the table. "Your daddy knows that."

Hampton Parker finished his second tumbler of whisky, and Seth turned to Reeves. "Speaking of womenfolk, how's Anne?"

"Jessie Spense managed to survive his forays with Morgan. He's home."

And was a damn hero no doubt and becoming more of one every day. "So—"

"Felicity," their father said and winked when Seth turned to him.

"Her little sister?"

"She's prettier than Anne," Hampton said.

"And more pliable, no doubt. How old is she?"

"Eighteen."

Seth pursed his lips. "And how does she regard you?"

Reeves grinned. "Seems amenable."

"Mr. Foley?"

"Considering where he cast his lot," Hampton said, "more amenable to Reeves and Felicity than Anne and Jessie Spense."

Seth poured himself another whisky and Reeves said, "That prejudice has been waning since '63, but the Foleys and us are all on the same side. Just that now the Spenses aren't the odd men out."

Hugh James snorted. "You Bluegrass bunch can be one big happy family now."

"Maybe all of Kentucky will be one goddamn happy family now," Hampton snapped.

Reeves' jaw dropped, and Seth watched Hugh James bend his long frame over the table toward Hampton. "It's too damn late!"

Seth grabbed the whiskey bottle. "Pap, have another shot, it will calm you."

Reeves choked, then coughed. "Calm him?"

Seth found the glass when his grandfather sat back, and he poured the whiskey. "I was attempting levity." Seth looked up, trying to catch his big brother's eye. Reeves, however, was no longer enthralled with the near ruckus between father and grandfather, but focused on something over Seth's shoulder. Hampton looked, too, and Seth twisted in his seat to see what had drawn their attention.

There, at a small table along the back wall and dressed in splendid, modest, yet provocative black silk and lace, sat the splendid figure of his preoccupation. His heartbeat quickened. For certain now, Rebecca Mackey was in town. Better still, it appeared she was staying at his hotel.

Her beautiful face was raised to the maître d'. They were talking, and Seth suspected the two had probably known each other for years. He turned back and now he did catch his brother's eye. Reeves, apparently misjudging the look he saw on Seth's face, said, "I'm not wed yet."

Seth pushed back his seat, and rose. "I'll be right back."

"*B*ut, no matter, my dear Miss Rebecca, we will miss her lovely presence."

Becky extended a hand to Anthony. She'd never known his last name and wondered if her mother had. The maître d' covered her hand with his free one.

"Thank you for the wine and reserving this table," she said.

"It was my pleasure, as it has always been my pleasure to serve your family over the many years." He turned away, and she was reaching for her wine when she caught sight of the golden-curled Seth Parker, resplendent in his dark uniform, coming toward her. He placed his hands on the back of the opposite chair. "May I join you a moment, Mrs. Mackey?"

Her "of course," came out mangled, and from the look he gave her, he noticed, but sit he did, then immediately leaned across the small table. "What are you doing here?"

She leaned forward, too. "I'm trying to determine the status of my mother's estate."

"By doing what?"

She considered he was being a bit impertinent and would have told him so, but she was too glad to see him. "I tried to gain access to my mother's bank account, but state law forbids it until the estate is settled." She sat back hard. "I received your missive via Eli. It said nothing. I waited weeks and weeks, and—"

"Tomorrow makes twenty-two days I've been gone, and I was told you'd left Camellia Creek and returned to Madison County. I thought you planned to move into Naomi Polk's house in Port Gibson?"

"I do, but I thought I'd make an attempt to hire laborers for Hickory Grove and contract to pay them after the crops come in, but,"—she shook her head—"it's proving difficult."

"The Freedmen's Bureau—"

"They're attempting to help, but their efforts to accommodate the freedmen are injurious to the planters. They're looking at one-month contracts now. Who wants to deal with such nonsense? Renewing contracts once a month? And even then the farmer still runs the risk of having a crop come in and no one to harvest it."

"Your people are gone?"

"Most of them now. A few of the elderly and a couple of kids are still there. When I get done here, I'm returning to Hickory Grove and packing." She bit her bottom lip. "What are you doing in Natchez?"

"I arrived today with my father, grandfather, and brother." She followed his eyes across the room and saw another handsome young man raise a hand and wave. The two older men didn't wave, but they were watching them.

"They're going on to New Orleans on family matters. I'm staying here tomorrow and working on your mother's murder, which"—he gave her a knowing look—"I'd hazard a guess, is your real reason for being here."

"Have you been in Vicksburg all this time?"

"No."

She waited, expecting him to tell her what he had been doing. Instead, he said, "Where did you get that dress?"

Her eyes widened, and she splayed her palm over the lace bodice. "It was Mama's. Do you think it immodest?"

"I think it's lovely," he said, his voice soft. "You look beautiful in black, and I much prefer this style to traditional widow's weeds."

"Mama wore it off and on for a year after Daddy was killed."

"Does she have other such mourning ensembles?"

Becky decided not to encourage the conversation further and said, "Have you found out anything?"

"Yes, and we need to talk."

"Have you been able to look at Mama's bank accounts?"

His look was one of surprise. "Is there something there I should see?"

"I don't know. You haven't looked?"

"I was planning to do that tomorrow."

"But you are authorized to look at them, are you not?"

"What has you worried, Becky?"

"Miller has me worried, of course. I tried for the past three days to track down Mr. Holbein, but he's not in Rodney. I finally came on down here, knowing full well the bank wouldn't let me see her records yet, and I was right. I am assuming Miller's looking for some significant deposit if he's claiming Mama was involved in blackmail. Am I right?"

"Yes."

"Have you seen him...did he say what he found?"

"I haven't seen or been in communication with him. I know he's been here and to New Orleans, but I don't know if he's found anything."

She braced herself. "Can I go with you to the bank tomorrow?"

A waiter moved in front of her, blocking her view of the three men Parker claimed as kin. The young darkie was lifting a crystal bowl of bread pudding to place in front of her, when Parker said, "Join us with your dessert."

"Oh," she said, "but have y'all eaten?"

"No, we're waiting for our meal, but I don't want to leave you here alone, and we need to talk."

"I don't think..."

But he was up, already directing the waiter where to deliver her dainty and, at the same time, taking a place behind her to maneuver her chair as she rose. It wouldn't be for long, after all. She was almost done, and she had yet to wrest an agreement from him about the bank tomorrow.

*S*eth hadn't introduced her using her married name. They'd have recognized it—something he hadn't considered when he insisted she join them. She was to his kinsmen, "Miss Rebecca." It had been poor form, and he felt the sting when he heard Becky say, "To mothers everywhere, no matter how awful their offspring." He looked at her, a hint of a smile on her lovely lips. She sipped her wine. She was speaking to Reeves, who now swigged his whisky. Pap and his father also acknowledged the toast. While he'd been responding to his grandfather regarding the status of Negro military forces in Mississippi, Becky had been bantering with Reeves, who was getting downright obnoxious, a flaw exposed when he had too much to drink. Thinking about that, Seth considered he might should be paying more attention to the antics of his older brother. He trusted it was Reeves, not him, who'd inspired the "awful offspring" comment.

The same young waiter who'd brought Becky dessert now placed a cup of coffee in front of her and took her empty bowl.

"Did you leave the girls at Hickory Grove?" Seth asked her.

"Yes, but Hector and Cy are there with them, and I was there only a few days ago. I plan to be home by week's end."

"Does your brother know where you are?"

Reeves looked up from his steak.

"No," Becky told him, "but he knows there could be trouble brewing for both of us and that I intended to work on this."

Seth wanted to say more—she shouldn't be in Natchez alone, without an escort—but he preferred not to admonish her in front of his kinsmen.

The men ate their steak, rare, Becky noted. Despite their protestations to go ahead and enjoy her dessert, she'd waited for them to be served. That hadn't resulted in too long a wait, and in the interim, they'd plied her with small talk and questions about who she was and where she'd come from. Since Parker had not introduced her formally by her married name, she opted to be equally discreet, though not sure why. Parker's relations were drinking heavily, and she managed to distract them by orienting the conversation around them and their trip. She now knew Seth Parker had, in addition to the menfolk here, a mother, two grandmothers, and three sisters, two older, one three years younger—her own age, actually.

Becky turned to Parker's grandfather, who, she gathered during the course of the dinner conversation, held Southern sympathies. "And what do y'all hope to accomplish in New Orleans?"

"We're going to the rescue of my wife's older sister, she's a widow and frail of body and mind"—he laughed—"well, in my opinion, she's always been frail of mind. For the past four years, she's been battling those favored by the occupying forces over the status of her husband's slaughterhouse business on the river. That bunch of thieves is tryin' to take it."

"Somebody needs to take it, Pap. She couldn't manage that business under any political environment, least of all the present one," Reeves said.

"Well, that might be true, boy, but they can sure pay her for it."

"Which is why we're going down, Miss Rebecca," Hampton Parker said, "to make sure her property is not confiscated."

"And you're combining business with pleasure, I take it, or do you intend to sway the Louisiana courts by sheer numbers?"

Reeves held up a finger. "There's a reason for that, madam."

Hugh James cleared his throat, drawing her attention to him. "Actually, the boys' grandmother, my beautiful bride of fifty-two years, has expressed a desire to keep the business in the family. It was her father's, you see." He looked at both his grandsons in turn. "Your granduncle Fred made a fine livin' off it."

"I intend to inherit Willow Wood," Reeves said, grinning at his father. "We hoped Seth would come along and take a look at it, but he says he's got work to do here." Reeves winked at her. "I do believe I see the truth of that matter."

Becky held the eye of the older Parker boy and hoped the look sufficed as a proper warning.

"I said I wasn't interested in a slaughterhouse, and I do have work to do here."

Reeves pursed his lips and raised his tumbler. He grinned at Becky, who finished her coffee. She hadn't had a chance to get Parker's agreement on her accompanying him to the bank, but she could rise early and wait on the front stoop of the bank if nothing else. It was time for her to leave them to their drinking. She placed her napkin beside her saucer.

"How did you two meet?" Hampton Parker asked her.

"She's involved in a property dispute about which I have agreed to intercede with the local authorities," Parker said.

Well, for sure he didn't want her talking, nor them knowing much—about her—or what he was working on.

Reeves smirked. "Ah, yes, the old knight in shining armor and damsel in distress, and repayment much sweeter than a journey with a bunch of familiar men." He nodded thoughtfully, made a sibilant sound, then said, "I thought it might be something like that. Now if you don't mind my asking, Miss Rebecca, what is the actual nature of your distress?"

Her cheeks heated, and she turned to Parker, who was staring at his brother with a look melding mortification with anger.

"Her property has been encumbered, and you've had too

much to drink," he said, before shooting his father what Becky judged to be a warning glance. What had Seth Parker implied to his family before he'd gotten up and come to her table?

"They've confiscated your husband's cotton, haven't they?" the grandfather said, and she turned to him.

"Cotton is not my business, Mr. James."

"Sugar?"

"I'm not a planter at all."

She felt Seth Parker lean her way.

"Then your deceased husband was a merchant?" Reeves asked. "Banker?"

She drew a breath through her nostrils. "I'm quite independent, I assure you." Now she felt Seth Parker's gentle kick beneath the table, and from the corner of her eye, she saw Parker's father wipe his mouth and place his napkin next to his empty plate. "Forgive me, Miss Rebecca, but I was certain that earlier Seth gave us to understand your husband had been a farmer."

"He was a farmer, as were his father and grandfather before him, but the status of my land is in limbo, and I do not have access to it. I have, however, through tragic circumstances, been afforded the opportunity for other ventures."

"*A*nd in return for my unrestrained gratitude, your gallant Major Parker has intervened with those mean old agents from the central government who are threatening me."

Provocative words expressed more provocatively yet. Reeves' interest was palpable; Seth could see it on his brother's face. He couldn't bring himself to look at his father and grandfather. Not one man sitting at this table had been born yesterday. She was doing this on purpose, and he was going to throttle her.

"And what is the nature of your business, *Miss* Rebecca?" Reeves asked in a sweet, assuming voice.

She smiled at him, and this time, Seth kicked her shin. Her only response was to sit a little straighter, so he bent to her ear.

"Don't you dare," he hissed between clenched teeth.

His grandfather had stopped eating now and watched them.

His father leaned back in his chair. Becky never took her eyes off Reeves.

"Why, sir," she said, "I'm the proprietress of the finest whorehouse on the river between St. Louis and New Orleans."

Hugh James' jaw dropped, and a grin stole across Reeves' face.

Seth looked at his father. Hampton's expression hadn't changed, but his eyes moved from Becky and settled on him.

Reeves caught Seth's eye. Livid, Seth turned on Becky. She was still watching Reeves, but following his brother's lead, she looked at Seth, her smile fading. Angry tears filled her eyes.

"She's a madam?" Reeves said, then guffawed. "That's better than I thought."

Becky rose, her gaze now steady on Seth. His kinsfolk stood, too, as did he once he'd regained some modicum of wit.

He tossed his napkin beside his plate. "You're not leaving." He kept his voice low. "You will explain yourself." So far they'd attracted no attention from the other diners, and he wanted to keep it that way.

"I most certainly am, and I most certainly will *not*." She turned to his relations. "Gentlemen, thank you for your gracious company. It truly was my pleasure to meet you all." Her voice hardened when she turned back to Seth, now glaring down on her. "I'll leave you to explain to your family the services you perform for the other favors you receive. Obviously, the truth didn't occur to you any more than did a proper introduction. What did you expect they'd think of me? You're just angry I played the part."

Her voice broke, and she whirled away. Diners at the table next to them looked up, but only briefly. Seth drew in a long breath. So, his attempt at subterfuge had backfired, and he tried to recall his cavalier attempt to explain their relationship, the truth of which, he admitted, he'd wanted kept hidden. What had he been thinking to bring her over here and then be secretive?

"You're her pimp?" Reeves asked, with a stupid grin on his face. Seth sneered. Hell, he hadn't been thinking at all. He'd been as drunk as his stupid-ass brother.

"Good God, Reeves, you've said enough. Shut up." Hampton Parker fell back into his chair.

His grandfather frowned at Seth. "That beautiful flower of Southern womanhood runs a whorehouse?"

"That beautiful flower of Southern womanhood is an embittered Confederate war widow, who technically *owns* a whorehouse. The Pink Lady in—"

"Rodney," his father said.

Seth squinted at his father, who shrugged. "I met an associate in Memphis. We had a drink. He told me Isabel Hays had been murdered recently. She was the owner."

Hugh James barked, "How the hell do you know that?" The older man took his seat, so did his grandsons.

Hampton Parker looked down at his plate and said, "Put your minds at ease, gentlemen. I've never been there, never met the woman, but I know men who have visited the place."

"Rebecca's her daughter."

Hugh James poured Seth another glass of brew, then filled his own. He passed the bottle to Reeves. "Well," the old man said after a moment, "you've got to separate her from that business." He shook his head then took a long swallow. "That gal ain't well-suited for it."

Seth tightened his jaw. "I think she is stubborn enough to suit herself to any kind of business she felt the need to be in. But for your peace of mind she's not in the business. She tossed that on the table for y'all to maul me. She's obviously quite angry with me."

Reeves sprawled back in his chair. His father and grandfather should be feeling the alcohol now, too. He excluded himself only because Becky's confession, in front of his family, had reamed his brain. She didn't give a damn what his kith and kin thought of her, and that hurt. He blinked at his brother.

"Did I give you cause to believe I was receiving sexual favors from her in return for my intervention on her behalf?" he asked, his voice harsh.

"Aren't you?" Reeves said flippantly, but in earnest.

"He's drunk," his father said and sat forward. "I considered it. Not necessarily because of anything you said, but more from what you didn't say, for example, her proper name. But also there's her situation. You did imply she's in distress, and you gave the impression you are aiding her in some way, and you were rather obscure —"

"Insinuating," Reeves said.

His father glanced ominously at his older son, then quickly back to Seth. "Most people, your family included — and she's very much aware of this, not to mention we're a table full of males — would assume that she's reciprocating the only way she can, in the boudoir."

"That's why *I* thought you brought her to the table," Reeves said. "And I was damn well impressed with your conquest."

"And no doubt she now considers that part of your design," his father added.

"Showing off my whore, you mean?"

"Yep," Reeves said.

"Or your lover, if you prefer," his father said, "but once, thanks to your stupid brother here, she got wind of what he was thinking, and the possibility you were party to it, the ploy embarrassed and humiliated her. Depending on how she feels about you, 'hurt' might be the word we're looking for."

He recalled her voice breaking right before she left the table. He could hope for hurt, but embarrassed and humiliated for certain. Bad as those were, they were a lot better than her not caring what his family thought of her, and bad as he felt, he felt better. "I brought her over because I wanted to keep an eye on her. She could become a victim in a matter I'm working on."

"You think she's in danger?" his father asked.

"I think she could be." He glared at Reeves. "I'm not sleeping with her. Her value to me is that she could be the key to the investigation I'm conducting."

"Oh, shit," Reeves yelped out of the blue, bringing all movement and conversation to an abrupt halt. "You're not in love with a whore, damn you."

"When I'm done with you, Miss Felicity Foley will never look at your toothless, eyeless face again."

Reeves held up a hand and snapped his fingers. "That's it! That's the missing piece my drunken brain couldn't pull out."

"What the hell are you talking about?"

"Your eyes when you look at her."

Seth narrowed said eyes. "What are my eyes telling you now, Reeves?"

His brother laughed at him. "Your eyes and her scent. Lilac." Reeves passed a glance to their father. "You know why he didn't introduce her using her married name, Dad?"

Seth bit his tongue and prayed Reeves would just pass out, but before Hampton could answer, Reeves said, "Because for some odd reason he didn't want us to know she's the one. She is *the* girl."

"Rebecca...*Becky*," his father whispered. "Becky Mackey. Dammit, son, she's the woman who saved your life?"

"Goddamn it, boy," Hugh James bellowed, causing diners to look their way. "Why didn't you just say so?"

Because he didn't want them to know, fearful they'd say something in front of her that would embarrass him.

His grandfather had sprung from his chair when he spoke and was now looking around. "We gotta find 'er. Is she —"

"Hugh, sit down," Hampton said, tightly. "I can see her from here. She's been waylaid in the lobby."

Seth jerked around to see, then breathed a sigh of relief. Acquaintances, it looked like, a man and a woman.

"Draggin' that young woman back in here in the mood she's in is not the thing to do."

Seth turned back to the table. Hugh, dumbstruck and drunk, was staring at his son-in-law. "Sit down," Hampton repeated. Reeves wiggled his grandfather's chair.

"We'll find her in the morning, Pap, before we leave. Dad's right." Reeves rubbed the back of his neck and cursed. "I'm afraid I owe her an apology I might not be up to giving at the moment."

It amazed Seth that Reeves even realized an apology was in order, much less that he was in no condition to attempt one. The table quieted after that, almost somber. Seth had not confirmed Becky was the woman he had dreamed of and spoken to during bouts of delirium accompanying a precarious recovery during the bulk of 1863 at his grandfather's Fulton County home, his doting mother and sisters ever by his side, while his father and brother took turns trekking dangerous territory straddling the Union and the Confederacy to monitor his condition and still manage their Bluegrass plantation home. No way in hell could he have kept the fact that there was someone haunting his psyche, but dammit, she didn't have to know that.

"Hmm," Reeves said after the quiet began to wear on them all. "I don't think we need to let Mama know the part about the whorehouse." He raised his glass, looked at his father, then pointed at him with his little finger and laughed. "'Specially that bullshit about 'never havin' been there.'"

Seth's gaze moved to his father. "Is she still there?"

The man looked around Seth, then nodded. "They're goin' their separate ways now."

Seth started to move.

"She's goin' to the front desk."

To get her key, no doubt, and Seth turned quickly. It was a pretty far distance, but Seth noted the general position of the box from where the clerk pulled her key. He watched her disappear from his line of sight, and he rose.

"Retirin' for the night, are you?"

Seth's gut tightened, and he turned to look at his brother, who raised a brow. Quickly, before he could decide to knock his brother's lewd ass out of the chair he lounged in, Seth said to his father, "I need to talk to her."

"Of course," the man said in tandem with Reeves' snort.

Seth ignored the latter. "I'll be back. If y'all aren't here I'll come on up to the suite."

Chapter Seventy-one

Looking at the cubbies, Seth figured Becky was in room 210 or 212, but not sure that she'd open up for him when he knocked, and not comfortable with insisting a stranger do so, he asked the clerk Rebecca Mackey's room number. The young man hesitated, took in Seth's uniform, and was about to speak when Seth said, "It's official."

"I'll get my manager."

Inwardly, he cursed the young man's departing back. Farther down the front desk, another clerk helped a customer, and to his left, a Negro doorman, impeccably dressed and graying at the temple, opened the massive door of the hotel through which a couple departed. Seth approached him and, offering him a five-dollar greenback, asked, "Which room does Isabel Hays occupy when she's in Natchez?"

The man looked at the note, looked at Seth, then said. "Dat be da ole Mr. Calhoon's chosen suite, suh."

"The best rooms in the hotel, I was told, and I should ask for it when I came to town."

The man hmmpfed, but took the note. "Two twelve. At da en' a' da hall. Cawna rooms."

"Thanks," Seth said and moved away without a backward glance.

The carpeted stairs brought him up in the middle of the hall. He took two steps to his left, then a muffled scream sent him racing.

Two-twelve, last door on the right. He grabbed the door knob to find the door open. Inside a man cursed and something toppled, and Seth shoved the door wide. The room was dark and the sconce across the hall failed to illuminate the space appreciably, but to his right, he saw the dark form of a man stop, then turn. "What's goin'—"

A hard shove from behind sent him stumbling into the room, and he nearly lost his footing. At his back, the man who had been in the room rushed past him. The door slammed shut, and in the hall, the muffled sound of feet, at least two pair, faded. He spun intending pursuit, but had no sooner found the knob when a whimper stopped him, and finding the gas wall sconce, he illuminated the room and saw Becky rising from a bed in the shadowy room beyond. She saw him and opened her mouth, but nothing came out. The lace at the shoulder of her dress had been torn from its seam. She took a few steps his way, and he started toward her as she smoothed her fingers over the tear and upwards to massage her scalp. She brought her hand away to reveal bloodstained fingertips.

Shit! His cautious first few steps toward her exploded into a fevered rush as, circling his arms around her, he lifted her up and carried her to the settee in the front room.

"They hit you in the head?"

She nodded.

He was still on his feet, and now he parted the silky strands to find where the skin had been cut. "Who were they?" he asked, retrieving washrags and towels from the washstand.

"I didn't see. I had just unlocked the door when I heard someone behind me. I started to turn, and whoever it was hit me and shoved me into the room. I tried to ward him off, but he shoved me again, so I tried to get away."

"You might have screamed."

"I did."

"It was a pathetic little cry, Rebecca."

"I don't like drawing attention to myself."

"That's the point of screaming."

She gasped at his touch. He gentled for a moment, but pushed her hand away when she tried to stop his ministrations. "Stop," he said. "Heads bleed a lot. Do you want your hair full of matted blood? Let me try to get it stopped." He applied pressure. "Do you think you ever lost consciousness?"

"Never. I think I deflected his blow when I turned at the door. Ouch!"

"Sorry. There's a cut, about an inch. Swelling, too, but the damage doesn't appear to be too bad. Of course, we can assume they didn't intend to kill you."

"You keep saying 'they.'"

"There were at least two. The second must have been standing guard for the one in the room with you. That's who shoved me on in, then they took off out of here. They probably hid in that vestibule there at the end of the hall." He removed the pressure. "Bleeding's stopped." He rinsed the rag in a bowl of water, then dumped the water into the chamber pot and started for the bell pull.

"What are you doing?"

"We should have a doctor look at your head."

"No, please, that means hotel security will get involved. The trouble would be more than it's worth, and you and I can readily guess the reason for the attack."

"Something we do need to talk about."

"Is that why you followed me up here?"

He placed the porcelain bowl on the table, then picked up two pieces of a hurricane lamp that had been knocked from a delicate Queen Anne table during the brief melee. It had fallen on carpet, neither base nor chimney had broken. His mind was clear now, completely sober. He looked at her on the settee, her pale visage softened by the glow of the gas light. God, she was beautiful, eyes large and bright, her hair in disarray. "I wanted to apologize."

"Your horrid brother is the one who should apologize."

He sat beside her. "It wasn't my brother who felt your wrath downstairs, Becky."

"You might have told them the truth. And my name! Why didn't you introduce me properly. Of course they'd assume I was your trollop."

He looked at the hands she'd folded in her lap. "I didn't introduce you by your last name because I knew they'd recognize it. I didn't want them to know you were the one who saved my life."

"Oh?" she asked with a look that indicated something between indignation and hurt.

"Like you didn't want your brother and mother to know I was the man whose life you saved."

Her chin rose higher, and she averted her gaze.

"But in my case, I didn't want them jumping to any wild assumptions. What was your reason for denying me?"

"I didn't deny you...I didn't want them to know that you might have some obligation to me or vice versa."

"You didn't want them to know you might actually like me."

"Oh, really, Parker, what sort of obtuse reasoning is that?"

"Or how about, no one would tell you anything if they knew you had developed a friendship, shall we say, for a man in a blue uniform.

"Or perhaps," she offered, "'Rebecca, let's take advantage of your friend, Parker, see what you can get out of him?'"

"Your mother asked you to do that, because your brother would probably shoot me and you both if he thought you'd resort to seduction just to ply information out of me."

"My brother married a Yankee, and he knows better than to tell me who to like. And in answer to your question, my mother did not ask me to do anything so reprehensible, and if she thought I cared for you she'd be even less inclined to do so."

"Then where did you get such a thought?"

"I thought of it all by myself."

He narrowed his eyes on her. "You thought about seducing information out of me?"

She released a much put-upon sigh.

"Why didn't you try?"

"Because I think I know more than you do, and I had to consider you might be attempting to do the same."

His heartbeat had quickened with their discourse. "I've given you information," he said softly.

"And I you, but I had Mama to think of, and I still have Eli."

"Are you protecting your brother from anything?"

"I hope not."

"I'm sorry?"

She started to rise, but he pulled her back.

"I want up."

"I need you to tell me what you meant by that."

She tilted her chin, tightened her lips and stared forward.

"Are you protecting him?" he demanded.

"Yes," she hissed, "I'm protecting him from an accusation I am sure is false, and your abject loyalty to a tyrannical government makes it impossible for me to trust you."

He blinked at her and, with every ounce of patience he could muster, forced himself calm. "You don't trust me? *You* do not trust *me*?"

He had enunciated each word carefully and hit his chest with his thumb when he said "me." Then he stood and turned and took two quick steps to one side before running his hands through his hair and coming back to stand in front of her. Becky sat glued to the couch watching him. He raised an index finger. "I have dreamed of you for the past three years. I smell lilac even when I'm taking a crap in a filthy cesspool of an outhouse. I am the last poor bastard on this planet, despite the color of my uniform, who would ever hurt you, and that includes your seditious brother." He bent and leaned into her. "The only part of you who has anything to fear from me is your heart, and you know it."

Her brilliant, glistening eyes flashed, and she stiffened her back. "The color of your uniform has less to do with my concerns than the fact you chose to wear it."

"Well I did choose to wear it, and that can't be undone. And right now the color of my uniform is the best damn friend you've got considering whatever the hell mess you're in."

He saw the subtle quiver of her throat when she swallowed, then, surprising him, she scooted away from him and sprang from the settee. He reached out and snagged her.

"No!" She slapped at his hand, but he yanked her hard to him and wrapped her in his arms. She made one soft guttural sound, and he soothed her with a gentle "hush." He felt her tense body relax, then hugged her tighter, and was pleasantly surprised when she responded in kind. The scent of lilac filled his senses, and he hardened.

"So," she said, her tremulous voice heavy, "you are comfortable with my attentions diverting you from your objectives?"

"I'm not sure what you think my objectives are at the moment, but your attentions are not diverting me from them."

Their hug relaxed, but slightly. He felt her raise her hands to her cheeks and wipe away tears he hadn't, until now, realized were there.

"I could give myself to you," she said, "for purely selfish reasons."

"I could do likewise," he said.

"I'm not as easily seduced as you."

He dipped his head and whispered against her lips, "Prove it."

Chapter Seventy-two

Seth covered her lips with his, and Becky parted hers in invitation. How long he'd wanted this! She ran her hands through his hair. He kissed her cheek, her jaw, and she raised her chin, giving him access to her neck. He picked her up, and she was light in his arms. She found, then ravaged his ear with her tongue, and a thrill heated his pelvis.

Becky sucked in a breath when he caressed a clothed nipple. "You've got too many clothes on," he said.

"As do you."

He turned her around and worked the buttons down the back of her dress, whispering that he reckoned she had on corsets and stays and bloomers and petticoats, too. All those things, she said, but turned in his arms when cold air caressed the bare skin on her shoulders, and she touched his hardness, cupped him, and he pulled the bodice from her body and reached for the laces of her stays. She moaned when he touched her, but resisted his efforts to push her onto the bed until she'd helped him undress, too. He, impatient with her efforts to force his drawers over his hips, sat on the bed and pushed them over his ankles with movements bordering on frenzied, and he pulled her onto the bed beside him and eased what proved to be adept fingers between her legs. Warmth and pressure rose and fell with each stroke of his hand, each flick of his thumb, until sensation overflowed her pelvis and coursed through her body. She pressed her nails into his shoulders to give her purchase and clung to receding waves of pleasure.

His face against her throat, he kissed her neck, then pushed himself up to look into her eyes. He entered her with one deft thrust, and thrilled with the hunger in him, she let loose a cry. He circled his arm around her neck to hold her in place and moved against her, gently at first, at variance with his initial entry, then faster, until he pressed her to him with a soft grunt and a whoop when he climaxed.

Seth woke and knew instinctively the time was near four in the morning. Beside him, Becky slept. She had spoken little after they made love, and her withdrawal worried him. He'd kept quiet, too, but he told himself that was out of respect for her. He wondered if it were him she'd been thinking of or James Mackey and whether she was sorry now to have given herself to him, their union a betrayal of her lost love.

Whatever the case, she was curled into him, his arm over her waist, her hair tickling his nose. He breathed in lilac, then rolled onto his back and a curse screamed through his sex-saturated brain. *Four in the morning!* He could hope it was earlier, but four, two, or even midnight made little difference at this point.

He threw the covers back. Beside him, he felt Becky roll over. "You're leaving me?"

"I've got to tell my father where I am." Her being awake, he felt for and found the wall sconce closest to the bed. Now able to see, he reached for his drawers, then looked over his shoulder at Becky, sleepy-eyed, her hair in lovely disarray around her face. She was beautiful, and for a moment, he considered tossing discretion to the wind and climbing back in next to her. He stood and started pulling on his clothes. "I forgot all about them."

"I'm taking your time from your family. I'm sorry."

He nearly choked on his laugh, then sat and pulled on his socks. "It's not that. They probably all passed out shortly after they got back to the room hours ago, but I've got to make some kind of revelation to them. I was expected back. When I left the dining room last night, I was on my way to apologize to you. If I don't return with some kind of excuse to head off my brother's speculation, you can well imagine what they'll think."

"The truth?"

He twisted around and looked at her to gauge her feelings. "Exactly."

"Does it matter?"

"It does to me. After I realized I'd embarrassed you at dinner, I went to some length to assure my kin that you were not a madam and I was not receiving favors from you."

"But now you are."

"No," he said roughly and stood to pull on his pants. "I'm not receiving 'favors' from you nor you from me, despite your defensive machinations with that seduction bullshit you spouted last night, and they will not be allowed to believe so."

"They will believe so."

He ran his thumb across her cheek. "How's your head?"

"There's a little ache."

He smiled at her. "And your body?"

She lay back on the pillow and stretched, then curled into a ball and faced him. "It feels wonderful."

With some effort, he focused on tying his shoes. "I can't simply show up at breakfast, you in tow."

"I don't know that I ever want to face your family again after that grand exit I made last night."

"Hush. They know you're the one who helped me."

"So you did tell them?"

"Reeves, of all the drunks at that table, guessed it. I didn't confirm or deny, but there is no doubt in their minds. And believe me, for almost three years now that ephemeral woman, who is you, has born the status of an angel in my family."

"It might have been best had they never met me. I would have always remained so."

Buttoning his blouse, he placed one knee on the bed and leaned over to kiss her. "You'll always be so. If you don't come to breakfast, they'll come here looking for you."

She said nothing, and he moved off the bed with a bravado he wasn't feeling. He found her key on the floor and held it up for her to see. "I'll lock the door behind me, and I'll let myself back in. You go back to sleep."

Chapter Seventy-three

Dawn. The room was bright, their bed of bliss-filled sin empty. He stepped farther inside Becky's suite. It had been picked up, even the bed had been smoothed, its sheets and blankets folded back neatly. He closed the door and released the breath he was holding. She stood on the private balcony, a feature unique to the rooms facing Jefferson Street, the perimeter of the hotel's rear courtyard. A white morning gown, as proper as it was provocative after the fashion her mother's girls wore a good part of their workday, adorned her body. She'd pulled the French doors almost closed, and he swung one wide, stepped up behind her, and circled an arm around her waist to pull her against him.

He sighed in relief when she melted into him. He'd feared a repulse in the light of day.

"I could have been another kidnapper," he whispered against her ear.

"I heard you when you came in," she said, and he heard the smile in her voice.

"I still could have been a kidnapper." He breathed in the scent of her hair, brushed and cascading down her back. A satin ribbon kept it out of her face, and she appeared to have cleaned up the blood.

"I know your tread," she said, caressing the arm that held her. "I can sense you." She laid the back of her head on his shoulder. Below them the first rays of sunlight caressed the tired blooms of the japonica in the garden and painted the sky blue. "I did have a thought that perhaps you wouldn't come back, that you'd gotten what you wanted and now I was out of your system."

He took her by the shoulders and turned her so she faced him.

"But then I also considered that I'm part of your investigation and you couldn't just —"

"You entered my blood three years ago and are now integral to my life cycle. You'll never be out of my system. There were nights I cursed you for a witch who'd possessed —"

"Stop," she said, and touched his cheek.

"Did you want me to have gotten you out of my system?"

"It would be simpler, don't you think?"

"There's nothing complex about this, sweetheart. Are you over me?"

She didn't say anything, then she closed her eyes tight and fell against him, her arms circling his torso and squeezing him tight. He held her in return, not sure what to make of her response — defense for herself or worry for him? Resolve or indecision?

She said, "You saw your father?"

"I did." He also saw his smart-ass brother, who rose despite Seth's precaution of closing the bedroom door in hopes he and his dad would not wake him. His grandfather slept like the dead of late.

"And your explanation for being out all night?"

"I was working."

"And Reeves accepted that?"

"I told them the truth."

She looked up at him, and he touched her cheek. "I didn't tell them the whole truth, Becky, but I did tell them you'd been ambushed in your room, and I stayed with you for fear your attackers might return."

"Did they ask whether you'd referred the incident to the authorities?"

"Dad did, but I told him in this particular case I am the authorities, and that's the truth. He knows enough not to ask further."

A grin stole across Becky's beautiful face. "And Reeves is skeptical, isn't he?"

Seth nodded, then dropped his eyes from her face and gazed at the whole of her, at the lovely lawn wrapper, her bare toes, their nails neatly trimmed, and he took her hand, pulling her toward the open French door. "Come back in. I need to check the rest of your body for injury in the light of day."

"When do you plan to move back to Port Gibson with the girls?" Seth asked Becky. He lay on the bed, his head propped on one arm, watching her.

She eyed his reflection in the dressing table mirror. His hard body was covered to the waist by bedclothes, but he was nude beneath. His sensuous mouth was quiet for the moment, his look intent, more curious than challenging. With his fair hair and green eyes, Seth Parker looked every inch a Roman god.

"I went to Jackson last week and talked to the Mackey lawyer about abandoning Hickory Grove. His primary concern is whether there will be money to pay the taxes, if no effort's made now to produce something from the land. The farm is destitute."

"You could sell part of the land."

"I know. Mama and the lawyer had already suggested that. It's an option, but truth is, I've been too occupied with Mama's death and this threat to Eli—"

"And yourself, Becky, you keep leaving yourself out of the equation, but you're in it, last night proves that. Have you spoken to your brother yet about the 1863 letter and the authorization Miller is looking for?"

"Eli knows almost as much as I do about everything."

That was a relief. Now he didn't have to expedite matters by confessing to her that he'd spoken to Calhoon about that letter.

"Another problem is Alice. She's worried for him. Despite his progress, he's a long way from full recovery."

"It'll probably take him a good year." He twisted to see the Terry clock on the table beside the bed.

"It's almost eight," she said to him. "That's why I woke you."

In the mirror, she watched him lay back on the pillows. She placed a final hairpin in her coiffure and rose from the vanity to stand over this very handsome man. He tugged the sleeve of her wrapper so that she sat beside him on the edge of the bed, and she placed her hand near his right shoulder to caress the ugly scar marring the beautiful chest she'd bathed in cool water for a day and a night and most of a second day before Union forces found him and took him away. She narrowed her eyes on the puckered skin. "It shouldn't have been so big."

"Gangrene set in before they got me to Granddaddy's house."

"But the surgeon...?"

"He was on the gunboat, part of the staff. You'd slowed the bleeding significantly, but hadn't stopped it. He said he couldn't wait for Memphis to operate or I'd end up bleeding to death."

"Did the gangrene appear before or after the surgery?"

"After. I had a bad eight months. Your brother's recovery is, compared to mine, phenomenal."

"It was probably the surgeon who gave you gangrene."

"I'm sure it wasn't you," he said, and she immediately found his eyes, certain she'd find levity, but there was none.

"What did you do after you'd recovered?"

"Blockade duty on the eastern seaboard."

"Did you go ashore again?"

"Nope. We chased a few blockade runners."

"Did you sink any?"

"Nary a one. Didn't catch any either."

She found his laughing eyes and smiled. "Your family isn't going to make a fuss, are they?"

"Possibly, but for certain if you don't join us. They are insistent on thanking you, sweetheart, and they'll be pounding on your door if you don't go up. Unless provoked, Granddad is a perfect gentleman, but he likes you, so I doubt you'll set him off. Reeves likes you, too. The provocation you observed last night was to pester me. He's like a kid sometimes, especially when he's drunk."

She opened her mouth to speak, but he said, "And I don't want to leave you on your own for any length of time."

"Meaning you don't want to leave me to my own devices, or you think someone will again try to hurt me?"

"Both. Who knew you were coming to Natchez?"

"Hector knew I was on my way to Vicksburg when he put me on the stage in Madison. Mattie might have said something to him. She's the only person who knew I was coming here."

"You should have gone back to Port Gibson and got one of my men."

"Do you have any men left?"

"A few. I lose two more tomorrow."

She blessed him with a sorrowful look, then said, "I can't order your men to escort me, anyway."

"They know—"

"And I wouldn't trust Jubal Summers to keep secrets from Miller. Do you?"

*N*o, he didn't. Becky smoothed a palm over his scar and down to his nipple, and he felt himself harden. He caught her hand. "I'm fixin' to undo the toilette you've worked so hard on."

Her gray eyes assessed him. "Have you made progress on the investigation during your absence?"

"I spent the time validating and verifying. I'm more suspicious of Miller than ever, but my doubts are not reciprocated by his seniors at Treasury."

"You've talked to Miller's seniors at Treasury?"

"My senior has a contact back there."

He had opted for discretion. Not knowing what she already knew, he wasn't ready to tell her what all he did. It had been her, after all, who'd warned about her using him.

"Have you considered doubts about Treasury itself?" When he didn't say anything, a frown creased her forehead. "Is there another woman in Vicksburg?"

He laughed out loud, relieved to change the subject. This he could handle with the truth and nothing but. "There are lots of women in Vicksburg. My absolute favorite is Marlene Byrnes, my immediate senior's wife. She feeds me dinner at her house on a routine basis. Her husband is always present. No, Rebecca, there's not another woman in Vicksburg or anywhere else. Until last night, I hadn't been with anyone since April of 1863, a slatternly barmaid who served drinks to me and several of my companions in Helena, Arkansas. I think her name was Janet, and she told me afterward that she was married. To tell the truth, I haven't been up to whoring, not physically and not emotionally." He kissed her hand. "Now, back to serious matters. Is there anything you can add to what I already know?"

She studied him for a disquieting time, then said, "I need to think. You'll give me time?"

He searched her eyes. The only reason she'd need to think on the matter was if she were keeping something from him. She endured his perusal, and he finally shoved his frustration aside and nodded. He would give her the time she sought and hope that in the end her decision would be to trust him.

"Now, stand up and turn around."

She looked at the covers concealing his body. He raised a knee in defense. "You're modest all of a sudden?"

"I'm hard," he said gruffly.

Her eyes met his, and she slipped her right hand beneath the covers.

"Becky..."

"Lay back," she cooed and leaned over him with a smile.

He smirked and fell back on the pillows, then clenched his teeth when he felt her fingers around him.

"Is it more exciting," she asked, "not knowing if you can trust me?"

He flung the covers back and pulled her on top of his naked body. She parted her lips and lowered her mouth to his, whereupon he wrapped his arms around her waist, rising to kiss her, exploring her mouth, relishing the taste of her and the scent of lilac in her hair and on her skin. Still holding her close, he broke the kiss. "As exciting for me, I would guess, as it is for you."

She placed an index finger on his lips. Quickly he moved his head and caught the offending finger between his teeth, then released it. Just as quickly he rolled her off his other side and drew his legs over the edge of the bed. "Your wicked threat has cost me my lust. Come on," he said and rose before extending her a hand. "Let's get dressed so we can go upstairs and I can attend to my toilette."

Chapter Seventy-four

"It was an attempted robbery," Seth told his grandfather who, having heard the story that led to a reconciliation between suspected lovers, had looked at Hampton Parker and suggested they postpone their arrival in New Orleans. They should stay here and help Seth catch whoever waylaid this young widow.

Seth was less interested in trying to catch whoever had attacked Becky than he was in delving into the bank records here in Natchez. That presented a greater chance of identifying the culprit than searching for an arbitrary marauder—barring his actually seeing Walter Miller or, more likely, Clem White lurking in the hallways of the Jefferson. Telling his grandpap and his brother the attack on Becky was a foiled robbery had been to head off the inevitable. His father would have figured there was more to it than that, but for the other two, the truth would be an invitation for them to stay, and Seth would accomplish nothing.

They breakfasted in his family's suite, two adjoining rooms on the third floor, but at the opposite end of the hall from where Becky roomed. Eating in had been a concession to Reeves, who didn't feel like an early morning confrontation with the outside world. His apology to Becky was almost as painful. Seth would have enjoyed it more, except that it appeared almost as painful to Becky to listen to as it was for Reeves to say it.

Seth suspected even his dad was suffering a headache this morning. Only Pap was immune to the alcohol they'd consumed last night, and that was a foregone conclusion as old as the man himself. He could drink himself into oblivion and feel no ill effects the next day.

Following Reeves' awkward apology, his kinsmen had all

thanked Becky copiously for the care she'd provided him in the spring of 1863. In return, she had graciously given them a skeletal account of Confederate soldiers recovering him in her field and bringing him to her house, followed by the time he'd cost her nursing him. She'd said that last tongue in cheek, and once during the conversation, Reeves broached Seth's continued recovery up in Kentucky, but their father had nipped it.

"We've decided on the Memphis packet at noon," Hampton Parker said to Seth an hour after they'd sat down to breakfast. The man looked around the table. "If we can make it." They'd all finished eating, except Hampton. He took a last sip of coffee. The rest of them, expressions bemused, watched him, and he them. Finally, he set his cup down. "Waiting on me, I suppose?"

"Forever, Dad."

"Eating too fast isn't healthy." He tossed his napkin onto the table and rose with the others. Seth followed Reeves into the adjoining room.

Becky turned to watch the brothers disappear, then felt Hampton Parker take her hand.

"I want to thank you again for saving my son's life."

"I believe that was done by a surgeon."

"He'd not have survived to reach that surgeon, but for you."

"You are welcome."

"His mother thanks you, too. She had instructed him to find you, you know. To see what she could do. Our church ladies have made a particularly earnest effort to help their sisters in the South."

"The women of Kentucky have been very kind, Mr. Parker. I know that for a fact. I'm really in no need of fiscal support. When I told you I was heir to my mother's estate, I was telling you the truth." At least she thought she was.

He smiled sheepishly and patted her hand. "I know, but there may be other ways, in the future, that we might be of service, and I want you to remember our offer. We can never repay what you did for us."

"I never considered payment."

"I know you didn't. Folks don't, not for deeds such as yours, but you understand what I mean."

"I do."

"It's my understanding he's here in Natchez trying to find the culprit who killed your mother."

Becky wasn't sure if this kind man were fishing for information, so she replied with a simple, "Yes."

"I know her loss ties in with other crimes, he told me that much. It must be very complicated, even dangerous, if the matter took him to Washington. I cannot imagine the involvement at that level."

She managed a weak smile. "You should heed your father-in-law, Mr. Parker. The powers that be are bent on interference at every level."

"Yes, but I fear interference might be called for in this instance." He leaned closer. "I know better regarding that story you two concocted about a robbery attempt against your person last night."

"Oh?" She wasn't exactly sure what the man implied, and she was at an even greater disadvantage in that she was still trying to digest the fact that Parker had been to Washington. She had no doubt it was in regards to the mystery shadowing her family, the 1863 congressional letter and that elusive "authorization." But her biggest question was when Seth Parker planned to share that information with her.

She turned to find Seth in the doorway of the adjacent room watching her and his father. He had carpetbags in both hands. Reeves, his hands empty, stood beside him.

"You'll be accompanying them to the wharf?" she asked.

"I'm saying my goodbyes downstairs. I'll escort you to your room first."

"We all will," Hugh James hollered, then laughed. "Make sure there are no more thieves lurking around."

$\mathcal{P}$ap and Reeves exited the lobby onto the street. Hampton Parker touched Seth's shoulder to prevent him following them.

"Commission or not, I guess your mother and I won't be lookin' for you home any time soon." He embraced Seth, who hugged him back. "Take care, son. We'll try to catch you on the return trip. Not sure yet when that will be."

Chapter Seventy-five

He dropped his bag on the floor of her hotel room. "I checked out," he said.

She smiled demurely and reached for her veiled hat.

"I fear your mode of dress will cause you second thoughts."

"I assure you, it will not be my mode of dress that will cause me to reconsider what I've done with you." She tore off the netting comprising the veil. "It's like lost virginity, Major. What we did cannot be undone."

He wanted to ask if she had regrets, but didn't want to know the answer.

"What's your favorite color?" she asked, buttoning her coat.

He almost said blue, which was the truth. Then he considered gray, which she would have seen through. He settled on green.

"It took you a while to think about it."

"I like lots of colors. Simply trying to figure what would look nicest on you. I assume that's why you asked."

"I crossed a threshold last night. It's time to move on" —even if she weren't positively sure of the direction — "blue is my color."

"And my first choice, but I was trying to be diplomatic."

"Despite the bad name you people have given it, you don't own the color blue. I offer you the Bonnie Blue Flag."

"And a perfect color, indeed."

"That's what Mrs. Mackey asked?" Seth Parker repeated. He was alone with Gerald Hilliard, president of the Old Southwest Cotton Bank. "The past six months?"

Becky had given him a general account of what transpired yesterday when she'd met with Hilliard, a trim, middle-aged man of good height and thinning hair. The man had been forbidden by federal authority to discuss Isabel's bank account with Becky and refused even to tell her if there'd been any large deposits made in the past six months, the specification set by Becky herself. Seth, however, had a general warrant signed by the district provost authorizing him access to the account information. Hilliard had graciously escorted Seth into his private office, then had a clerk fetch the appropriate documentation. He'd been equally gracious, and apologetic, to Becky for the second day in a row, and found her a comfortable area within the bank's confines to await completion of her escort's business.

"Yes," Mr. Hilliard told him, "and the estate should be settled by now. I know that young woman has her mother's debts to pay, and there is, of course, Miss Hays' business affairs, which I understand are being held in abeyance pending the state's settlement, which, in turn, is waiting for the Treasury Department's approval. Mr. Tobias Holbein, the family solicitor, told me a week ago the state action would be done, but for this murder investigation to which you referred. That has now become an unpleasant matter for this bank."

Seth frowned, and Hilliard laid a ledger in front of him. "Treasury is looking for something, simply put, which isn't in here. It's been ten days since their agents visited."

The man opened two more ledgers and laid them before Seth. "Miss Hays opened these accounts only a few years ago when the banks in Rodney closed, but she had a history of sorts with us in that her old friend, a Mr. Isaac Baker, had been a charter member of the bank and remained with Old Southwest until his death. One is her personal account, the other a business account. As you can see, there is nothing extraordinary about either, and here are her bank statements. There is no way Miss Hays could have concealed transactions involving large sums of money without my complicity, which I assume Mr. Walter Miller believes to have occurred. He has gone so far as to threaten me with an audit involving the entire bank. I told him to go ahead. I don't know what else I can do. We have not altered the accounts in this bank for any purpose and certainly not to perpetrate fraud against the U.S. Treasury." The man smiled sadly. "The purveyors of the national bank have won the day. Am I to assume the United States Navy also wishes to audit my books?"

Seth didn't know anything about audits, and little more about banking, outside his own. He was just looking for a deposit in excess of two hundred thousand dollars. "Neither the Navy nor Army, as best I know, Mr. Hilliard, and I'm confident Treasury's audit will suffice for us all if Miller does go through with it."

"The sign of a new age, sir." Hilliard sighed. "Something to look forward to from here on out?"

Discretion in regards to Seth's blue uniform, he reckoned, kept the man from saying more. The Old Southwest Cotton was a small bank with a state charter that went back to 1832. It had endured recessions, depressions, and years when cotton prices had bottomed out, and it had survived because its board had never allowed it to overextend during times when the economy boomed with high cotton prices. A sound, conservative bank during volatile economic decades and now a horrific war.

"You can see her activity was routine, year in, year out. Now, these other two accounts I intend to show you are new since last May, one in the name of her daughter Rebecca—and I shewed her this yesterday, by the way. This money is hers and not tied to the estate. The other was for Rebecca's half brother, Eli Calhoon. Miss Hays closed the Calhoon account before Christmas and transferred the money from his account to her daughter's, implying to me he no longer needed the money. Her purpose with these accounts was to protect the family properties amidst the rumors of the Confederate states being forced to pay those back taxes."

Seth leaned forward to better see the entries. There was a little over three thousand dollars in the account, but except for a twelve hundred dollar deposit in early December, representing the closure of Calhoon's account, there had been no obscenely large deposits made. In fact, the largest deposit before that transfer had been three hundred seventy-five dollars in August of 1865. At the moment, Rebecca Mackey was solvent.

"At the time of her death, it was a forgone conclusion the taxes would be deferred," Hilliard continued. "I believe Miss Hays' intent was to continue adding to the account and allowing it to grow." Hilliard cleared his throat. "When Miss Hays was in last month, she removed her name from Mrs. Mackey's account. She did not indicate why, but it's proved propitious"—the man looked him in the eye—"since Mrs. Mackey can get her hands on this money if she needs to."

Seth nodded. Isabel had begun to fear for her life and didn't want this account encumbered should she turn up dead.

"There were no large deposits made to her account," Seth said, holding the bank's heavy exterior door for Becky. "Hilliard said you specified over the last six months. Why that period?"

"That took it back to around the time Guthrie was killed."

They stepped onto the sidewalk. It was the second week of March and a beautiful, spring-like day. Natchez itself was lovely, seemingly untouched by war, though it had been touched, economically and emotionally, if not physically scarred. To the west, the river was silent, a mute requiem to a lost past.

"Do you think Miller's trying to prove she was blackmailing someone?" Becky asked. "Is that why he's looking at her accounts?"

He figured Miller was looking for a deposit in excess of two hundred thousand dollars representing the McGowan claim, but he couldn't rule out that Isabel had nothing more than knowledge of the claim and its payout, and had indeed been extorting money from those who orchestrated the crime.

"Maybe," he told Becky. He took her elbow and turned her west down Main Street.

"How big a deposit do you think we would see, if she had been blackmailing someone?"

"That would depend on who she was blackmailing and the size of the kitty. Where we need to focus our attention is what would she have had to blackmail someone with?"

Chapter Seventy-six

They lunched late at the hotel, Becky observing the quiet, well-mannered eating habits of the handsome man on whom she might be taking a reckless gamble. She was torn between broaching Seth's unacknowledged journey to Washington or keeping the information close. She opted to keep him ignorant of the fact she knew, at least for a while. There'd been a reason he kept the trip from her, but she had secrets she was keeping from him, too.

They checked out after lunch and caught the northbound Memphis packet. Its scheduled arrival in Natchez was one p.m., but it didn't arrive until three and that's the only reason they managed to catch it. The captain of the *Susannah Bright* put on extra steam to try and make up for lost time. Becky always hated when they did that, and she insisted they stay near the stern on the starboard side in anticipation of a blown boiler. Seth was told that same captain had scowled when he learned Seth had asked to be put ashore at the desolate Rodney wharf, but he'd whisked them off with nothing said and the *Susannah Bright* had steamed away with smoke billowing from her stacks. Becky never heard anything about her exploding.

Things remained all right until they walked through the back door of a much subdued Pink Lady with its shrouded windows and mirrors and black wreaths. Savannah met them halfway up the hall. Walter Miller and Clem White, she told them, were in Isabel's office.

The first thing Seth saw when he entered the office was the blown safe. It wasn't a large safe and hadn't taken much of a charge, so there'd been little damage done to the room, but what damage there was had been uncalled for. Seth knew Miller had checked the safe's contents the day of Isabel's death. Savannah had opened it for him before Seth arrived in Rodney.

Miller was sitting at Isabel's desk. "I wouldn't have resorted to damaging the safe if the lovely Miss Sutton had been more cooperative, but she claimed she couldn't open it." He gave Seth a quick politic smile. "Naturally I was intrigued."

Becky looked at Seth. "I changed the combination. We'd paid the girls. Only some contracts of Mama's were left in there. Savannah and I agreed she wouldn't have the combination for this very reason."

Miller had the alleged contracts in front of him. Clem White stood to one side of all the activity, watching. Seth asked Miller, "Did you find what you were looking for?"—thinking he might have recovered the authorization required to retrieve all that missing money.

"I didn't find anything worth having." He passed the documents to Seth. "Promissory notes mostly, and a contract for an addition to the house."

Seth handed them to Becky. "Check to make sure everything is there."

"There was never anything in there he would have been interested in," Becky said with a tired voice. She placed the documents back in the safe and pushed on its door, which fell back open.

Miller situated himself in Isabel's swivel chair and said to Seth, "What are you doing here? I was told you were on your way to New Orleans." The man glanced at Becky. "And I didn't expect you back from Natchez for a couple of days."

"How did you know she was in Natchez?"

White stepped forward. "I saw her there. Saw you, too, but I thought"—he raked his eyes over Becky—"once you'd completed your business with the lovely widow, that you had accompanied your kinsmen downstream."

Now Seth took a step in the direction of White. "Were you the one who attacked her at the hotel?"

"I believe you're the one who took advantage of a lone woman."

Miller was out of the chair and between them. "Mr. White, we've heard enough from you. The relationship between the major and his suspect is not our concern...yet."

"I wasn't aware Mrs. Mackey was a suspect in the Franklin murder."

Miller turned and nodded at White, who backed away. "She's not, but you and I both know, Parker, that the reason Colonel Byrnes insisted you stay on the Franklin case was so that Army could keep its fingers in the Guthrie thing."

"And the only reason you agreed to it was so that you could keep your fingers in the Franklin thing, which tells me they tie together and you know how."

A quick nod and again that irritating, politic smile.

Becky had moved away from the safe and now stood closer to Seth. Miller looked at her.

"It's my understanding your brother's condition improves daily, Mrs. Mackey. Despite this ruse the provost and Colonel Byrnes has perpetrated upon the Army, he should be deemed fit for questioning soon. You do understand, do you not, that there is a tie between Alan Guthrie's death and the deposit of a substantial amount of money, associated with the Southern cause, in British Honduras." He made a sibilant sound. "British Honduras is proving to be a favorite refuge for Southern expatriates and their suspect activities in regards to the United States. Your cooperation with Treasury might mitigate, to some extent, any unpleasantness required to uncover your brother's associations in that part of the world."

"You wish me to confess to killing Alan Guthrie?"

Miller laughed as if genuinely amused. "Believe it or not, Treasury does have bigger priorities than the murder of a rogue agent."

Becky said nothing and Seth was glad. Miller was baiting her, her brother the bait, and she wasn't biting.

"What were you expecting to find in that safe?" Seth asked.

"Evidence that proves Isabel Hays' involvement in conspiracy against the government. But alas, it wasn't there." He made a point of looking around Becky to the damaged safe. "It appears I've rendered your safe useless. You'll need to move those documents to the other safe."

She glared at the man, who continued, "The safe where Isabel kept her real valuables."

When Becky didn't speak, Miller looked at Seth. "You note she doesn't deny it."

"She's playing you for a fool, Parker," White said from across the room. "Do you think for a moment her mother didn't tell her what she did?"

She spun on Seth. "He's trying to find out if there's another safe."

White laughed, and Becky went rigid. Seth stepped closer and spoke softly. "You just told them there is one."

Becky opened her mouth, but Seth preempted her. "Don't say anything else. Where's the other safe?"

Wide-eyed she turned, then reached for him. "I'll tell you, but not them. Come —"

He stayed her. "It's too late, can't you see? If you show me the safe and what's in it without them, they'll accuse us of collusion."

"No one knows about that safe," she squeaked out.

"Of course they do," Miller said. "How else would I know?"

"Then why don't you know where it is?" she snapped.

"I know it exists," he said back. "I know your mother received a payment of six thousand dollars in blood money the day she was murdered, so if it's not in there"—he jerked his head toward the blown safe—"then she put it somewhere else."

Seth took Becky's hand, and she dropped her glare at Miller and blinked up at him. "Show us the safe," he said softly.

She removed her hand from his, and without a word, or a look, marched out the door and back down the hall, the three men following. In the rear entry, she hiked her skirt and started up the stairs. Once in her bedroom, she removed a picture from the wainscoting between the two windows on the back wall and slid the right stile of the central raised panel to the right. It glided no more than a quarter of an inch, just enough to release the panel's edge. On the left, she did the same, exposing a fourteen inch piano hinge. The panel swung wide on the hinge to reveal a small wall safe with a tumbler lock.

"Open it," Miller said.

"Go to—"

"Becky," Seth said, "do you know the combination?"

She didn't look at him, but began dialing. Seth heard it click.

Miller motioned to White, who seized Becky by the shoulder. Seth shoved the man, breaking his hold. White bristled. Again, Miller moved between the two, but Seth shot Miller a warning glare before gently moving Becky to one side. He opened the safe himself, reached in, and pulled out a canvas bag. Inside was a stack of newly printed greenbacks in denominations of one hundred dollars. Behind him, he heard White's hateful chuckle.

"Should be six thousand dollars, just like Walt said."

Seth turned to watch Becky sit hard on her bed. "You knew this was in there?" he asked.

"Since the afternoon after Mama was killed. I checked the safe once I was allowed back in here."

Seth heard movement and turned to see White rummaging inside the safe, from which he pulled a document. Becky jumped up from where she'd been sitting and lunged toward White. Seth stopped her. Miller held out his hand to White. "Let me see it." Miller's other hand was inside his coat, and Seth unsnapped the holster to his own gun.

Miller flicked the document open with one hand, then, his expression unreadable, he looked at White. "Is there anything else?"

"Nothing," he said and nodded at what Miller held. "Whatcha got?"

Miller handed it to him, then stepped to the bed and upended the canvas sack. Nothing else fell out.

Clem White looked from the paper Miller had handed him to Becky. "Guess this would be valuable," he said, "to the bastard of a whore." Becky pulled against Seth's hold, freeing herself as White crushed the document in his fist. He tossed the crumpled paper across the room. "Fetch, bitch."

This time, Miller made a point of getting out of the way, and Seth slammed into White and toppled him. White came up with a blackjack. He should have stayed down and gone for Seth's knee. The old boatswain at the academy had taught his cadets not only how to use such things, but also how to defend against them. Seth blocked the shorter man's blow to his shoulder with his left forearm, crashing them both against the wall, then kneed him hard in the groin, rendering White as helpless as the billy had rendered Roscoe weeks before. Holding the writhing man, Seth snarled over his shoulder to Miller, "Are you done in here?"

"Yes. Just toss him out back, I'll collect him."

Seth spun White around, placing him in a choke hold before reaching inside the man's coat and pulling the gun from his shoulder holster. Behind him, he heard Miller mumble some sort of apology to Becky—that, Seth figured, was for the "bitch" remark. Halfway down the hall with the scarcely struggling White, he heard Becky cry out something about the money. He assumed, at that point, Miller was taking it with him.

He stumbled twice getting White down the stairs, then half dragged, half hurled him out the back door and down the porch stairs. Miller stepped onto the porch behind him. "Don't ever bring that bastard near her again," Seth managed between heaving breaths.

White was coughing, trying to get to his knees. Miller observed him dispassionately. "That's the second of my assistants you've brought to his knees, Major. It's becoming a problem."

"You should upgrade the quality of your hirelings, both in character and ability."

Miller produced his quick smile, then said, "I hear you once desired to work for Treasury?" For a moment Seth thought the man might actually be offering to bring him into his confidence, to turn him, but Miller was no fool.

"I'm no longer interested in the organization." He pointed to the canvas bag Miller held. "I want a written receipt for that money."

Miller shrugged, then handed Seth the bag. "Not worth the trouble. Keep it." He started down the stairs. "Think about my offer, Major."

At the bottom of the stairs, Miller kicked a small derringer from the hand of Clem White, who'd managed to get himself, barely, to his knees. White again tumbled into the dust. "Get up,' Miller growled and picked up the gun. "You couldn't have hit him with this anyway, not at that distance."

"You Yankees used 'em for dueling," Seth called down "so you couldn't hurt each other."

Miller laughed, but White appeared to pay no attention. "You won't *see* me near her, Parker. Not next time."

Seth, body strained and heart pumping, heard the threat in the man's words. Miller grabbed the red-faced White and helped him to his feet. "Dammit, Clement, shut the hell up."

Chapter Seventy-seven

Seth closed the back door and noticed Becky watching him from the top of the stairwell. After a moment, she turned and started down the upstairs hall, out of his line of sight. Savannah, behind him with Cheri at her side, moved forward and locked the door. Cheri held out papers to him, and Savannah said, "They're what was in the safe down here. Give 'em to Becky. Creditors have been askin' about some of them. We need to make some income. Some of the girls have already left for New Orleans to see how things are there."

"You'll need to talk to her," he said. "I'll send her down."

When he got back to her bedroom, Becky was sitting on the bed smoothing out the crumpled document. She didn't look up. "It's my birth certificate."

He dropped the canvas bag on the bed, then White's gun and sat down. "Were you going to tell me about the money?"

She looked up, but not at him. "I was thinking about what to do. I asked you in Natchez to give me some time, do you recall?"

"And how much money we'd be searching for if your mother were involved in blackmail? I remember that, too."

He watched as she rose, the crumpled birth certificate again neatly folded, and reached for the canvas bag containing the money. Both she placed in the safe. She looked at White's gun, contemplated it a moment, then placed it inside, too.

"It might come in handy," he said, but she shook her head.

"I have Mama's."

"Here," he said, and handed her the papers Savannah had given him. "You might want to put those in there, too. You've got bills due according to Savannah. You need to talk to her."

She secured the safe, then closed the panel and placed the picture back over it. Finally, she turned and met his eyes. "That six thousand dollars in this safe was Miller's proof Mama'd done what he was accusing her of. I didn't want to accept it, and I'm still not sure I should." Her voice caught. "But I feared you would."

"Six thousand dollars is a lot of money, but note he wasn't very interested in taking it. All we know for sure is that Miller was aware your mother had that money squirreled away somewhere. It's not what he's looking for."

She closed her eyes tight.

"Becky, we've got to work together," he said.

Eyes opened, she said, "We *can't* work together."

His gut quaked, and he rose from the chair. "He's after something —"

"You know what it's about."

He stared at her. Something was askew, and he realized that she suspected he did, indeed, know. How could...? "Do you have it?" he countered.

She frowned, obviously confused, then enunciated stiffly, "I don't know. You tell me what it is I'm supposed to have, and *maybe* I'll tell you if I have it."

His heart, which had calmed in the wake of his altercation with White, was beating fast again. "What makes you think I know?"

"Because you didn't bother to tell me that you've been to Washington and back."

Malcolm's telegram to his family telling them he might be late returning to Vicksburg, because he'd gone to Washington.

His father hadn't brought it up to him. "My father told you?"

For a moment she said nothing, and he considered she simply wanted to keep him in doubt as to her source. Then she said, "Yes."

"I didn't tell you because I wasn't ready for you to know."

She looked away. After a moment she turned back and said, "Are you going to tell me now?"

She was angry. Worse, she was hurt. He could counter that she hadn't confided in him about the money, but that would be petty, and she had asked him for time—just this morning, though she'd known about that money in the safe for weeks, known, in fact, since Miller first accused Isabel of blackmail. But exacerbating their fight would not help the investigation, nor would it help them. Again, he found the chair and sat.

"We already knew that Miller, and Guthrie before him, were looking for an authorization letter sent to someone out here last September. That person was Tobias Holbein, the executor of a claim paid to the heirs of George McGowan."

He watched Becky close her eyes and gently shake her head, and he suspected then she was aware of the claim.

"At the same time, a corresponding bill of exchange was delivered by Wells Fargo to the U.S. Bank in New Orleans and an account was set up for the heirs, payable in specie"—he found her eyes—"that account was closed in November, the money moved to the Bank of British Honduras in Belize City. That account was closed the day after the money was deposited. The Bank of Honduras is not cooperating beyond saying the authorization belonged to Tobias Holbein and everything was in order."

"It's been paid?" she asked in a small voice.

"Months ago. You were aware of the claim?"

"Mama told me a while back that the congressional letter I'd been questioned about dealt with a property claim."

"You told your mother about your being—"

"No. Not too long ago, after I'd told you about the questioning, I found the letter in a Bible Mama had brought back from Aunt Naomi's. It's still in there."

The same Bible, he'd wager, Isabel Hays had offered to him for perusal the morning after he'd killed Naomi Polk. "So, your mother already knew about the letter?"

"Yes. She didn't know I'd been questioned about it. Didn't even realize I was aware of it, or I doubt she'd have left the thing in the Bible in our room. But I knew when I saw the thing— which said nothing more than 'the matter alluded to by Tobias

Holbein esquire of Holbein, blah, blah, blah, was still being held in abeyance and not subject for review at this time' — I knew then that it had been the reason for my questioning.

"After Daddy received that letter, he brought it up with Mr. Holbein, who in turn told Sam Caruthers the matter had been exposed. Mr. Caruthers arranged for the attack on Camellia Creek. What he wanted at that point was the letter, I think. Congress had sent the original to Mr. Holbein and a copy to each of the heirs, the Calhoon and Caruthers patriarchs.

"But I don't understand its importance. Eli says the claim wasn't worth that much. That's why he can't believe Caruthers would have been party to all this killing. Like everyone else, he thought Sam Caruthers wanted the land for the railroad."

"The principal on the claim was nice, but your brother is right, it wasn't worth the kind of carnage that's resulted from it. Not that any amount would have been. The face value on that bill of exchange deposited in New Orleans was $247,703.12. The principal plus eighty-eight years of interest at three and a half percent."

She stared at him. "My God," she said after a moment.

"Back in 1861 when Congress approved the payment of the claim, only the principal was approved. The interest was added by someone at the Treasury end. In addition to those we know who are dead out here as a direct or indirect result of this payment, two men from the Treasury Department died last fall. One death was believed to be an accident, the other, Alan Guthrie's brother-in-law, was thought to be suicide. Investigators back there now believe both were murder.

"Everything at that end was made to appear legal. Treasury had no idea anything was wrong until January, when the Bank of New Orleans requested its gold reserves be augmented."

"But Mr. Holbein should know what happened."

"Mr. Holbein was not the man who identified himself as Holbein and presented the authorization letter to the Bank of New Orleans."

"Who was?"

"Treasury doesn't know, nor does it know where the money is, other than it was deposited and then removed from the bank in Honduras. But the belief is that whoever has that authorization letter, has the money."

"And that individual is in British Honduras, don't you think?"

"Not necessarily. The letter was sent to Holbein. There is no getting around that. He told Miller he never received it, and we know he didn't close that account in New Orleans. Treasury's thinking someone at Treasury is in league with someone out here and all this might be going according to plan."

"But the money going to Honduras is a problem for Treasury, isn't it? For Ralston's relief"—her voice quivered—"sedition. A quarter million dollars could buy a good deal of trouble for the Federal government, couldn't it? That's what Miller meant with that threat to Eli."

"It's a diversion," he started, but she was shaking her head.

"Listen to me," he began again. "Someone is trying to steal that money. You need a lot more money than that to wage war."

She rose. "Is your government listening to you? If someone back there believes or just wants to believe that money is going to be used for seditious reasons, some scoundrel is gonna get very wealthy at the expense of someone else blamed for nonexistent crimes. And the argument appears valid. What 'loyal' American would dare question the soundness of the findings fabricated by the patriotic agents of the Grand Republic? And who better to blame than one of the heirs themselves?"

"And that's what I'm trying to head off."

She laughed, but the sound was choked by tears. "Oh, Seth, darling, you can't be sure that Eli doesn't have that authorization letter. For all you know, he took it off Guthrie's dead body."

He scowled. "Guthrie was looking for your brother, not the other way around."

"You can't rule out Eli had it even then...or me," she croaked. "You can't rule me out."

"I know you had no knowledge of the value of that account, Becky. You're not that good an actress."

She swiped a tear. "Thank you, for that," she said dryly, "but it doesn't change the fact that half an hour ago you considered the possibility I might be guilty."

"Yes, Rebecca, I wanted to rule out the authorization letter being in your possession. I will admit that."

"And what about Eli?" she asked.

"Do you think he has it?"

"I don't think he has it, and I don't think he knows where it is, but I don't know the truth and neither do you. And we both know that neither matters to the government."

"You're blaming the government for something individuals are doing."

"I'm blaming a government that not only aids and abets such corruption, it foments it for its own agenda, and you know it! A blatant lie that Eli has stolen that money to be used for some sort of antigovernment agenda is exactly the kind of bullshit they want to hear, because then they can counter by heaping more abuse upon the South and the real thief gets away scot-free, and the government writes off another corrupt venture as the price for victory and creation of some wonderful *new* United States."

She drew a stuttered breath, then took an awkward step his way. "I was wrong not to tell you about the money in Mama's safe, but that's my point, don't you see? I could do you wrong again."

"I don't feel wronged by you, Becky."

She shook her head. "I don't have the authorization letter, and I don't know where the money is, and depending on what it could do to the people I love, I don't know that I'd tell you if I found either one. I can't use you to help me uncover the truth under those conditions. I care too much for you to do that."

"Becky, we're not at odds in this."

"We can't risk it, not until we know."

His stomach tensed. "We can't risk what?"

"Hurting each other."

"I will never hurt you."

"You can't say that." She pointed at the picture hanging on

the wall. "You forced me to divulge the location of that safe. I am relatively certain that I can count on fewer fingers than you have on one hand the number of people who know about that thing. Now Miller knows, because *your* side wanted to know."

"I had—"

"I'm not faulting you," she said and held her hands out, palms up. "You did what you had to do, what you needed to. That's clear to me now, and I would never ask you to do otherwise. I couldn't respect you if you did. That's why I've got to break this off. I was wrong to say you forced me to divulge the location of that safe. Miller and his thug never could have. They could have beat me to death before I'd have told them, but I told you without your making a threat." She released a strangled sob. "I'm not going to stand in the way of whatever you have to do, my darling, but I'm not going to help you hurt me and mine either."

Sweet Jesus in heaven, this was getting out of control. "And what if you find something that helps both of us?"

"That would be ideal, wouldn't it? Too ideal for the present circumstances."

He stepped toward her, but she moved away. "Don't," she said. "I'm too vulnerable, and it's not fair. I've got to get to Camellia Creek. I want to see Eli, and I want to get home to my girls. I've got to talk to Savannah before I go."

She started around him, and he exercised every ounce of self-control not to grab her and pull her to him. But he couldn't have stood it if she struggled to free herself.

"Becky?"

At the door, she turned and looked back at him. "If you were to guess, who else might know about that second safe?"

Chapter Seventy-eight

Seth went with Becky to the office of Tobias Holbein. Given Becky had been trying to track him down for the past week, neither held much hope of finding him there, and they hadn't. His office was locked. Seth could imagine all kinds of reasons as to why Holbein seemed to have disappeared, up to and including his untimely demise. That made Seth all the more anxious to lay eyes on the man.

From Holbein's deserted office, Seth escorted Becky to the home of her Aunt Maggie. He didn't know where Miller or White were. More than likely, Miller had validated what he'd wanted from Becky when he'd seen the interior of that second safe at The Pink Lady. He hoped the man was content nothing more would be gained from Rebecca Mackey, at least for the moment. The threat posed by Clem White would be different, but Seth figured that, for now, Miller would keep him busy with Treasury matters and not pursuing personal vendettas.

Becky wanted Aunt Maggie to come to Camellia Creek with her, but her aunt said no. Just for a little while? Still, she said no. Savannah could check on her, then? The old woman had nodded and smiled and kissed Becky's cheek. She'd kept fresh flowers on Isabel's grave, she told her, and would continue to do so. She came out on her porch to bid them farewell. Marguerite Fortier had spent most of her life in this place, she told her grandniece, and she wasn't going to pass her remaining days in Claiborne County. The town would come back. The townsfolk were already returning. Everything would be all right.

Finally, Seth left Becky at The Pink Lady to pack and set out in search of Tobias Holbein.

❦

"Come on in, suh," Irene told Seth from just inside the front door of Holbein's home. "He be in 'is pa'lah. Jus' been mopin' these past weeks since we put Miz Iz'bel in da groun'. Dey be close frien's fo' yeahs an' yeahs."

It was dim in the open foyer, through which he slowly followed Irene, keeping some distance between them and giving her time to announce him. She stuck her head inside the open door of that same room he and Holbein had relaxed in weeks ago.

"Dat nice Majah Pa'kah be heah to see you, Mistah Toby."

"Ah, yes," Seth heard Holbein reply. His voice sounded clear and strong. "Did you let him in?"

"Ain't no need fo' you to ask me such. I ain't gonna leave a man you done shared yo' table and yo' roof wif standin' out on da poa'ch 'less you done tol' me otha'wise."

Seth heard the creak of leather. "Well, send him in, send him in."

Irene stepped aside, and Seth slipped past her. Holbein rose to extend his hand, and Seth took it. "Cold out?" Holbein asked.

"Warm, but clouds are movin' in. Think we're in for more rain."

"Storm probably. March tends to be volatile. Have a seat. Coffee?"

Seth shook his head, but he did sit. "I don't plan on taking up much of your time. I needed to ask you about something."

Holbein remained standing. "I sorta figured that's why you came."

"Can you figure what I'm gonna ask?"

"Except that it must have something to do with Isabel's death, no."

"It has to do with that allegation of blackmail Miller made against Isabel the day she died and six-thousand dollars in a safe at The Pink Lady."

Holbein narrowed his eyes. "Has he elucidated on his allegations of blackmail?"

"Not much. It's an accusation he throws out there when it's

450

convenient for him to do so, but that money was in the safe, Holbein. He knew there was another safe. Becky tells me that the second safe was a well-kept secret. Savannah wasn't even aware of it, at least she claims she wasn't. Becky doesn't think Eli Calhoon knows about it. Figured Holland Calhoon did, and, of course, Becky knew about it. The only other person she thought might possibly know was Isabel's lawyer."

Toby puffed up his cheeks, then blew out a breath. "Miller came to The Pink Lady claiming there was six thousand dollars in a safe that had been paid to Isabel by whoever she was allegedly blackmailing?"

"That's the gist, yes."

"Well," Holbein said and turned to the commode on one side of the fireplace, "this calls for more than coffee. Would you care to join me?"

Seth didn't want whiskey in his gut. In fact, he didn't want anything in his gut. His stomach had been queasy since Becky had expressed her belief they must forgo what they'd shared because duty to some greater cause on both their parts demanded it, just like generations of self-righteous fanatics, blind-eyed hypocrites, and self-serving politicians had torn a nation apart. It was all too vague and too muddled to sort out, but he'd be damned before he let Becky go, not over this bullshit. He had to solve this thing.

"No," he said. "Thank you."

Holbein downed three fingers and turned back to Seth.

"There hasn't been a bank in Rodney since the summer of '63. There's been a secure safe of some sort in that house since before it became The Pink Lady. In recent years, Isabel has graciously stowed away documents of a legal nature that I needed kept secure. She may have hinted at a second safe in the place. She never overtly discussed such a vault with me."

"Who would she have discussed it with?"

"I can think of no one," Holbein said and took his seat.

"Then how did Miller know about it?"

"Are you sure he did?"

No. It was as he figured at the time. Miller had duped a rattled Becky into confirming its existence.

"He knew about the six thousand dollars," Seth said. "He blew the safe in Isabel's office."

"And, when the money wasn't in there, he guessed there was a second safe?"

"He'd have had to be pretty sure about the money, though, to run a bluff like that."

"Which means someone told him about the money." Holbein tightened his lips. "Someone who knew that money had been passed to Isabel."

"That's how I see it."

"You tell Becky the money was mine, and that's the honest truth. I gave it to Isabel for safekeeping the day before she was killed. I hadn't even thought about it until you brought it up just now."

"Where did you get it?"

"I didn't blackmail anyone, if that's what you're thinking. I'm acting as a middleman in the premature sale of state timberland. The transaction is"—he laughed bitterly—"pending a Republican victory at the state polls."

Seth opened his mouth to speak, but Holbein stopped him with, "It has nothing to do with Isabel's death, and if you need more information on it, good luck getting a subpoena, because you'll need others for those being protected by your boys in blue, and none will be forthcoming."

"I was only going to ask how Miller knew you'd received that six thousand dollars?"

"And knew I'd secured it at Isabel's," Holbein said, almost to himself. He stared into the embers of the dying fire. The afternoon had darkened. Outside lightning split an ominous sky. "I haven't discussed that business with Miller, nor would I have had reason to. He's not involved." In the distance, thunder rolled.

"Who would have?"

"Could have been several people." Holbein looked at him, then squinted oddly. "But there was really only one."

And Holbein wasn't going to tell him who that one was, but Seth figured Holbein knew he'd already pegged the man to be Sam Caruthers.

"I know about the McGowan claim, Holbein, about the authorization sent to you, which you claim you never saw the accounts in New Orleans and Belize City, and all that missing money."

Tobias Holbein looked at him. "So does Treasury. Don't be offended, Major, when I tell you my concern for what they know far outweighs my concern for what you think you know."

*H*olbein had all but dismissed him after that, his initial genial humor replaced by a dark brooding, and Seth couldn't help but wonder what course the man had set with his silence.

It was only two miles back to town, and Seth managed to out-ride the storm, which broke over The Pink Lady not two minutes after he'd turned Boon over to Thomas. He was already in the back foyer, watching Becky descend the stairs, carpetbag in her hand, when a blowing rain started splattering against the window. Night had fallen.

"Did you see him?" she asked.

"I did. He said to tell you the money was his. He gave it to Isabel the day before she died. He wouldn't tell me how Miller knew about it except to say he wasn't the one who told him. I confronted him with the claim. He's aware of everything, including Treasury's being aware of his role. He's not concerned about me, and he's not owning up to the whereabouts of the authorization or the money, assuming he even knows."

He passed his eyes over her, dressed in winter garb to ward off the weather, then he looked through the glass in the door. It was pouring, and the damn wind gusting. "Are you sure you want to do this tonight?"

"If the packet's on time, we'll be in Grand Gulf before ten. Besides you still need to get to Vicksburg."

"That landing's not covered, and I doubt the boat will even hear our shot."

"She will, but we can wait until the rain slacks up a bit."

If it didn't let up, and if the steamboat wasn't on time, they'd be beyond soggy. He desisted from pointing that out. He feared what drove her now was not her desire to get back to Camellia Creek and talk to her brother, but to ensure nothing happened to shake her resolve regarding their relationship. Alone here tonight with him, he might sway her, or she sway herself, but in his heart, he knew her surrender would be temporary and only serve to make her feel guilty. He'd go on to Port Gibson tonight, and tomorrow he'd ride up to Vicksburg with his remaining men and usher Corporal Daws and Private Price into civilian life. Major Don Hemple, the Claiborne County provost, was assuming responsibility for guarding Eli Calhoon.

"*He*'s sound asleep," Alice answered when Seth asked after Calhoon. She kissed Becky's cheek. "Mr. Bowen and his boys were over here most of the afternoon with him, watching the barn go up. The weather's been so nice"—she frowned into the rain-swept night—"mostly. He's been out a lot the last few days, but he's still slow and tires easily. I got him to lie down after supper, and he fell right to sleep."

"I'm sorry we woke you," Becky said.

It was after midnight by the time they'd made the three-mile trek to Camellia Creek. Alice, lantern in hand, had met them on the mud porch, outside the dining room door. "Do come on in."

She stood to one side. Becky started to enter, then stopped when Seth touched her arm. Alice looked him over.

"Oh, dear," she said, taking in Seth's soiled britches and shoes. "You got stuck?"

"Once," he said, "It's hard enough navigating that road in the daylight, much less a night like this one. Look, I don't want to risk our disturbing him, so I'm not coming in. I'll just make a mess." He looked back across the breezeway, then to Alice. "Is the bridge—"

"There hasn't been enough rain for it to flood."

Seth hadn't looked forward to swimming Boon across Lake

Elizabeth. He looked at Becky, who was watching him. "I'm gonna go on to town. I'll take the carriage to the livery. In the morning, I'll head on up to Vicksburg with my troops and report. My senior might have some information for me, too. I plan to be back the day after, but depending on what I learn, or what he's learned, it may be later. I'll go with you to Hickory Grove and help you move the girls back." He looked at Alice, listening to them.

"Oh," Alice said. She stepped back inside the open door and placed the lantern on the dining room table. "I'm going to check Becky's room."

The two of them alone now, Seth studied Becky, who had turned a bit to watch Alice disappear into the house. Still bundled in black crepe, her hat yet to be removed from her head, Becky appeared soft and golden, if a wee bit eerie, in the shadows created by the single lantern light beyond. He wanted to pull her into his arms, to make everything all right between them, and when he tugged her back around to face him, he thought she might have allowed him to. Then she straightened, a subtle reminder to herself, and perhaps to him, that she was resolved. "I'm going to Hickory Grove tomorrow, Seth, as soon as I've talked to Eli."

He started to protest, and she placed her fingers against his lips. "I'll have Buck take me into Port Gibson. I'll go by stage. Hector and Cyrus are still at Hickory Grove, that much I'm sure of. I'm as safe there as I am here with an injured brother who sleeps twelve hours a day. Besides, I think Miller knows now that I don't have what he's looking for." She sighed. "Darn, I should probably remain here and protect Eli."

"Warn your brother and Alice. I'll talk to the provost before I leave for Vicksburg in the morning. Your brother should be safe enough, though. Miller's holding out for his arrest, then he can question him at will."

He turned to go, and she cautioned him, "Be careful. Either of those men will shoot you in the back without blinking an eye."

That was probably true. He nodded, turned away, then

almost slipped and fell when she spun him back around. She kissed his cheek, then for the briefest of moments, her arms were around his shoulders. He squeezed her tight, and she pressed her face against his throat, then abruptly pushed away before disappearing inside the house.

Chapter Seventy-nine

Seth fidgeted. "Given all that, has Colonel Dustin passed you anything additional about that stolen money being used for a pro-Southern movement in Central America?"

"You think Miller's comments were a ploy, using her brother to influence Rebecca Mackey?"

"Yes." Seth sat in the upholstered chair in front of Malcolm's desk. He'd just finished updating his senior on the events of the past three days, sans the consummation of his relationship with Becky and her self-imposed rift from him. "And he has her worried. She'll never cooperate with Miller, but she's more wary than ever about cooperating with me."

Malcolm puffed on his pipe, then removed it from between his lips. "If you recall, during our initial conversation with Miller, I led the conversation that way, not necessarily because of happenings in Central or South America, but a belief Treasury was trying to covertly consolidate intelligence assets here in the west. Miller picked up on my concerns. Could be nothing more than he's feeding us the seditionist threat to deflect us from the truth. The man is a far cry from stupid."

"Fairchild says this is nothing more than theft."

Malcolm pointed the pipe stem Seth's way. "Yes, but keep in mind that Fairchild's not an operative. He's an expert in forgery and counterfeiting, and it's my experience that experts sometimes can't see beyond their own expertise. Wipe that grin off your face, Major. I recognize my prejudicial shortcomings, at least."

Malcolm admitted he had prejudices. Whether he knew which ones were actual shortcomings was a different matter. "That's why I wondered if you'd heard from Dustin. Anything more about that rumor the money was payment for the Lincoln assassination?"

Malcolm grinned around his pipe stem. "Nothing more, but it is interesting, isn't it? All that money, rumors of seditionist offensives, assassinations, and murder."

"If I didn't have the feeling that most of the trouble is purposefully created I'd be more excited. It's like creating Mary Shelley's monster from dead body parts. Why do it? Sleep with a beautiful woman and make a baby."

"Because creating life the way God intended doesn't make one God. It's about power and control, both of which are brutal and gruesome." Malcolm sat forward. "After you've got your boys mustered out, I'm going to try and get you in to see General Wood. He's got your letter."

"He's holding it?"

"He intends to approve it with regret."

Why the hell Seth rated more than a standard approval of his resignation letter, he couldn't fathom. "It's not like I've had a lot of success with this present assignment, Malcolm."

"Not so. You might be surprised to know the general has followed this case with interest. You plan to reapply to Treasury?"

"I'm working all the Treasury I ever plan to work, right now."

"Are you sure you don't want to stay with the Navy?"

"Spent too much of the war laid up in bed in Kentucky. My best days were spent as a junior officer on an *Army* staff. Afraid I've lost too much ground to make up for."

Pipe in hand, Malcolm leaned back in his swivel chair. "You made two impressive night forays into enemy territory before you let yourself get talked into that damn daytime excursion."

"I didn't get talked into it, I volunteered."

Malcolm leaned back and smiled wistfully. "Well, something critical might be said of your judgment, but you were young. Depending on the outcome of this case, the general could help make up for some of that lost ground."

"Malcolm, you and I both suspect that if I'm even allowed to uncover the truth in this case, I won't be welcomed in the present and maybe future administrations, depending on how far into the future the Republicans have things wrapped up. I don't want to be part of this government. You said so once yourself, there's too much of Kentucky in me. What has happened and will continue to happen spits in the face of everything I was raised to believe in."

"Your granddaddy getting to you?"

"It's Dad now. He's been aligning with Pap since '63. He never did vote for Lincoln, you know. Despised the man and despises his sanctified memory and the Republicans more with each passing day."

Seth looked up and watched Malcolm bring his pipe to his lips. After a moment the man blew out a puff of smoke. "I don't know that I'm gonna like the country that emerges from this nightmare, either. God knows I never particularly liked Whigs or Republicans myself, and let's face it, they're in charge now, and worse, the Radicals are on the ascent." Again the pipe, again a puff. "Of course, I don't like the Democrats either." He stirred with that and asked, "Have they talked you into going back to Kentucky?"

"Made hints."

"But you're not going back."

"My plans are to stay here."

"And farm a little patch right here in Warren County, I'd wager." Suddenly, Malcolm was animated, pipe stem in the air. "That brings up another thing. A fella south of here pulled Mark Dicks' body out of the Big Black early this morning. He hadn't been in there long. The Claiborne County sheriff found his discharge papers inside his coat pocket and turned the matter over to the provost. That's why I'm aware of it. Would appreciate it if you'd do the identification."

"What happened to him?"

"Had a couple of holes in his head. Small one right behind the left ear, a very large one at the opposite temple."

"He was executed." Seth had stated the obvious out loud, but more to himself than Malcolm.

"When's the last time you saw him?"

"Talked to him the afternoon following Isabel Hays' burial, close to a month, now." He met Malcolm's gaze. "That's damn interesting. He was one of the two men who had no alibi the night Isabel was killed."

"And I'd told you he was heir to a nice nest egg back in Rhode Island, if I recall."

"You did."

"I was mistaken. There had been a lucrative business, but the Dicks boys' daddy had a history of dissipation. He was a chronic gambler and a happy drunk. Problem apparently worsened after his wife died about ten years ago. He'd squandered most of the company's money. The boys probably did get a little, but odds are your Major Dicks was on somebody's payroll."

Chapter Eighty

Pearl was sick with a bad cold. Hector had come from Hickory Grove and told Becky that Mattie was worried. The baby kept crying and pawing at her left ear. Her fever ran high. Mattie had sent for the doctor, but he hadn't come as of yesterday afternoon, and Mattie wished Becky would come home. Buck was hitching up the buggy to take Becky to town to catch the stage when Hector got there.

Becky had eaten an early breakfast with Alice. Eli had risen earlier still, eaten, then gone to monitor progress on his barn. A young corporal had accompanied him out the door. A white soldier, regular Army. More and more of them were appearing. This particular one worked for the provost marshal assigned to Port Gibson, Alice told her. All Seth Parker's Negro troops were out of the Army officially that day, except for Captain Summers. He had a little longer before he, too, would join civilian ranks.

Oh, she had almost forgotten that they had received a letter from Sergeant Zachary. He was well and still heading west.

Eventually Eli had wandered back in, his guard following. Everything there appeared cordial. Aunt Elvie kept the man fed, him and whoever would relieve him later today, but the very thought of Eli under guard, no matter how amenable, filled Becky with dread. The timing of Eli's arrival home in tandem with Guthrie's death and the disappearance of all that money predicated on an authorization letter she knew her mother had once had in her possession didn't bode well for Eli, and after he settled into bed for a rest, she snuck in behind him and told him she crossed paths with Seth Parker in Natchez, and she told him how much that claim he wished to discount was really worth.

She did, in fact, tell him everything pertinent about her foray to Natchez. She did not include telling him of her reckless relationship with Seth Parker, which might or might not prove painfully pertinent, but she certainly didn't consider it any of Eli's business at this point. She did tell him they'd shared information and what that information was. She didn't tell him about the attack on her person, but rather couched Parker's accompanying her back to Rodney, then Camellia Creek last night, in terms of the major's fear that he suspected someone looking for the money might believe she had it and could do her harm. Most importantly, she told him about Miller in Rodney, the second safe and the money inside, and finally she broached her biggest concern of all. "Do you remember when I told you not long ago that they'd make sedition look worse than murder?" Eli nodded that he did. "Well, Miller came right out and told me Treasury had bigger concerns than Guthrie's murder. He claims the money secreted out of the Treasury Department has gone to support continued Southern sedition from a base in British Honduras and that you're part of the cabal. Though he hasn't come right out and said it as such, it follows that he's claiming you killed Guthrie because Guthrie was on to the conspiracy."

Chapter Eighty-one

It was a poignant moment, Seth's losing the last of his colored enlisted and, for all intents and purposes, putting an end to his troop, if not an end to the assignment. Not yet, anyway.

Given the nature of what he was working on, Seth wasn't sure why he got the men in the first place and wondered if Malcolm had thought through their purpose when he'd acquired them to augment the detail. Certainly Seth had needed help, and Malcolm had expressed concern that available white troops might prove more threat than boon, but Seth had received nothing but support from the provosts with whom he'd dealt these past two months, and if blind eyes were being turned to illicit trade, it was happening on their watch. In retrospect, Seth suspected Malcolm had wanted to keep the Guthrie investigation separate from routine army matters. That would have had to do with his senior's early, and at the time unvoiced, suspicions regarding covert operations on the part of Treasury. No matter, his Negro troops had proven dedicated, loyal, and trustworthy, and they had, as it turned out, proved exceedingly valuable. He was proud to have led them.

Shortly after he'd bought Corporal Daws and Private Price one last round and offered a last handshake, he'd returned to Malcolm's office. Malcolm got him in with General Wood about four. The general had touched upon Seth's resignation letter, expressed his disappointment—that was standard—and told him he'd endorse it within the week. The final disposition, Seth knew, lay with the United States Navy.

Approval up the chain would take time. He hoped he would finish this case as a major in the Marine Corps. If not, he'd have to finish it as a private citizen. He had no intention of leaving Mississippi for any length of time.

"There are rope burns on his wrists. He was bound. This was an out-and-out execution, Malcolm."

Malcolm nodded at Seth, who was twisting Mark Dicks' stiff hands to better view the wounds.

"He was beat up pretty good, too," Malcolm said. "The doctor assures me most of that happened before he went in the water. Doesn't think he was in there more than a couple hours, if that long. He'd been weighted, but not good enough. That or his body caught on something before it reached the bottom."

"Where was he found?"

"You'll find that interesting, too. North bank of the Big Black in Claiborne County, about a mile downstream from a ferry linking a road between Warren and Claiborne Counties. You done?"

Seth nodded that he was, and Malcolm motioned him out of the back room of the livery. "I looked at it on the map," Malcolm said when they were on the street. "It appears to be the same road that links the Calhoon and Mackey farms."

"I had a feeling you were gonna say that," Seth said. "That is curious, isn't it?"

"I thought you'd think so."

Isabel told him Dicks had started spending a lot of time at her establishment in the early fall. That would have been around the time of Guthrie's appearance and subsequent demise. Or did it coincide with the authorization letter and the establishment of the McGowan account at the Bank of New Orleans...or the return home of Eli Calhoon? Any or all, the timing was right. At first light, he'd rouse Jubal and Sergeant Kushing and they'd mosey roughly sixteen miles down to the Big Black.

Eliza, her flushed face beaming, rushed down the steps to greet Becky with a hug that almost knocked Becky over.

"You're in time for supper," she said, squeezing Becky tighter. "Polly just finished it."

"And I feared I'd missed it." She eyed the buggy she knew belonged to Dr. Mitchell Pritchard of neighboring Madisonville. "How is our Pearl? I see the doctor has come."

"Finally," the girl said. "He was over at Mrs. Ramsey's house. Jake was sick all night long."

"Oh, dear. That doesn't sound good, but he must be better now if the doctor left him, don't you think?"

"Yes," she said.

"You look a bit peaked yourself. Is your ear hurting, too?"

"My throat hurts a little. Mattie says I'm getting a cold."

Becky, her hand at Eliza's back, had reached the porch when the front door opened and the doctor stepped out, Mattie at his heels. He looked down at Eliza. "We were just coming to fetch you, young lady."

"I saw Aunt Becky coming."

"Oh, you did, did you? Well, I guess that's a good enough reason for running off. You go on with Miss Mattie now and let me talk to your Aunt Becky."

Eliza took Mattie's hand. At the same time Mattie's stricken gaze found Becky's eyes. Becky's blood chilled.

"I'm glad you're back," the doctor said softly when the two were gone.

Becky started to tremble. "What's wrong with her? I came as soon as I got word."

"It's not Pearl," he said, taking her by the elbow and motioning her to a weathered rocker. He sat in the one next to it. "Pearl has an ear infection. I gave Mattie drops for the pain and a little home remedy for the fever. She's sleeping now."

Becky held her relief as Dr. Pritchard's head sank, and Becky stared down at the weathered hand now reaching for her own. "I've been at the Ramseys' all night," he said. "Little Jake died a couple of hours ago."

"No," she said, her voice ringing inside her head.

"Diphtheria. We think it was from well water over at the abandoned Blount place. The kids drank from it on Sunday."

The doctor's face blurred. "Which kids?"

"Jake and Eliza. Janet, the Ramseys' oldest girl was with them. It was warm. The younger ones were running a lot, she said, and got thirsty. She drew the water herself and gave it to them. She didn't drink."

Becky stared at him.

"Mrs. Mackey, I asked Eliza when I got here. Her throat is sore, and she has a fever."

Chapter Eighty-two

The morning was cool and weeping, sodden with lingering mist and heavy dew. Shortly before reaching the Big Black, Seth and his two remaining men left the road for the farm of Steve Henshaw, the man who'd found Dicks' body. Once they found him, Henshaw asked Seth if the Army was thinkin' a Southerner did it. When Seth told him he believed the death tied to other murders possibly committed by nefarious Northerners, the man had grinned, as if he thought Seth were toying with him, which he was a bit. Then Henshaw showed them where he'd found the body.

The farmer didn't take them by way of the road, but followed a cow path winding through his property and ending on the trampled and muddy bank of the river itself. "He was here," the man said, then pointed to his mutt of a dog, sitting on his haunches, tail wagging and tongue lolling. "Ringo's barkin' brung me."

Sergeant Kushing patted the beast on his head.

"He's a good dog, Ringo is."

After answering a few more pertinent questions, Mr. Henshaw and Ringo left to do more important tasks, and Seth and his men searched several yards up and down the river bank. They didn't find anything, but Seth hadn't figured they would. Dicks had been tossed into the water upstream; he'd washed ashore here at a bend in the river.

After an hour's search, the three had mounted and headed east along the riverbank.

The ferry landing, the one he'd used to cross the river the afternoon Becky had followed Isabel to Muscatine, was a good winding mile, closer as the crow flies, from where the body had come ashore. If Dicks had been killed and thrown in the river on the night they thought, that would have been the same night he and Rebecca had returned to Camellia Creek from Rodney. The weather had been stormy, and there'd been a lot of rain.

They checked the area around the landing, then the ferry itself, before crossing the river and checking the south bank. Nothing, as Seth had expected. Finally, confident they'd made a good effort, he and his two men recrossed the Big Black and continued up the road to Muscatine.

"Yo," Jubal Summers called above the yelping dog scurrying between the legs of their mounts.

An old black man shuffled out onto the porch of a cabin in need of whitewash, but its roof line was straight and its walls square. It appeared to have two rooms, and Seth figured it for the overseer's cabin.

"Are you Uncle Jessie?" Seth asked him.

The old man settled the dog. To one side of Seth, Kushing's horse snorted and tossed his head.

"Yes, suh," the old man said.

Behind the man, the young Negress Seth had spoken to last fall stepped up to the threshold. Becky had called her Lettie.

"We need to talk to you about anyone you might have seen here a couple of nights ago."

"Yes, suh." The old man came farther onto the porch, and Seth dismounted. Jubal and Kushing followed. The sergeant took the horses' reins.

"Come on down here, Miss Lettie," Seth called to the girl, who smiled. "We'll need to ask you, too." He refocused on Jessie. "The house is locked, but we need to check it. Can you get us in?"

"Yes, suh, I can. Do Mr. Caruthers know you heah?"

"He does not."

Lettie moved to her father's side.

"We found a body on the riverbank a couple of miles downstream. That was yesterday morning. We want to check to see if the man was possibly killed here."

They were both silent.

"Ain't nobody accusing you, old man," Jubal said. "We just want to know if you recall anyone here two nights ago."

"Da night a' da sto'm?" Jessie said.

"Yes," Seth answered.

"Didn't see nor heah nuffin'," the old man said. "But thundah' clappin' mighty loud all night long. Mighta missed somethin' or might not a heard it over da racket."

Jubal's eyes narrowed. "Heard what?"

"Why, any ruckus you be askin' about. You say der was a killin', right?" He looked at Seth, who nodded.

"Da dead man be shot?"

Seth nodded again, and Jessie continued, looking at Jubal. "Gunshot, dat's what I be talkin' about. What you think?"

"He could have been lynched," Jubal said.

"Coulda been," the old man snapped, "but I didn't heah dat neitha."

"Did you see anyone here?" Seth asked.

"No, suh, but black as pitch out heah in da night."

"Lights in the house?" Jubal asked.

"No, suh, but me an' da gurl, we go to bed right afta da sun goes down. Ain't lookin' fo' no lights, an' da house is a good bit away."

"Bahn is closah," Lettie said. She was looking at Seth.

He met her eyes, then looked at Uncle Jessie. "Can you let me in the house so I don't have to break the door down?"

"Yes, suh," the old man said and started ambling up the path in the direction of the house.

Seth turned to Kushing behind him. He nodded further down the same path they were on. The barn was visible from where they stood. "You check the barn. The captain and I will meet you there when we're done in the house."

The girl had more or less told him to go to the barn, but he wanted to see the house. Jessie let them in through the front door. The place was empty, and their boots and brogans echoed through the rooms. Seth mentioned the cleanliness of the place to Jessie.

"Lettie, she keep it clean. Hopin' our people come back soon."

Jubal turned to the old man. Uncle Jessie was dark of skin, his gray hair cropped close to his head. He wasn't a tall man and had a bit of a paunch, the baggage of age. His clothes were worn but clean, and his brogans scuffed, their soles ragged.

"Your people?" Jubal asked.

"Our white folks, da Calhoons. Masta James Mackey, he be kilt in da wah, but we keep hopin' Miz Becky'll come on home. Only reason we still heah."

"Mr. Caruthers is employing you?" Seth asked.

"Yes, suh. He give me my pay, but ain't da same."

Jubal snorted and Seth meandered into the room, where, as best he could recollect, Becky had placed him the day he'd been shot. Today the space was barren and dim. There were no curtains on the windows, but the house was shaded by water oaks and pecan. Despite the breeze outside, the day was warm. No windows were open, and the house smelled musty.

Four large rooms and a central hall. He walked out the back door. The kitchen was there, attached to the porch via a breezeway, much as the one at Camellia Creek. The place had a nice layout and could easily be added to. He was stepping back into the hall, when he heard the pounding of boots on the front porch. The door flew open, and Kushing called, "Major?"

"Yo," Seth said, and stepped into the sergeant's line of sight.

"You can stop searchin'. I've found what we're lookin' for in the barn."

*B*lood and gore and nasty, buzzing flies. Not to mention the stench. Unless Uncle Jessie simply hadn't had occasion to enter the near-empty barn over the last two days, there was no way he could have missed the carnage. Seth figured he had expected the mess and had purposefully avoided entering the building. That, or the old man had entered the place, then pretended he hadn't. Seth had little doubt the girl knew what they would find inside.

Strewn in one corner were four short lengths of hemp rope. They were, Seth figured, the remains of one length that had been cut from Dicks' wrists after he was dead. Against the back wall of the structure was a ladder-back kitchen chair speckled with blood. Seth surmised the killer or killers had tied Dicks to it. That same person or persons had probably asked him a few questions he may or may not have answered. Some degree of satisfaction achieved, the killer had then placed a gun to Dicks' head and blown his brains against the wall. The bullet was there, too, lodged in a rough plank of yellow pine.

Despite what Uncle Jessie had told them, he and Lettie had heard the ruckus that night. Lettie had subtly told Seth so. Maybe she remembered him from last fall, otherwise he had no idea why she should trust him. Maybe she just hoped this would cause a problem for Caruthers, and he wondered if she'd actually seen the man here that night. That he'd sort out later, or get Becky to sort it out, which would be easier.

Bullet in his fist and a wee bit queasy, Seth pivoted on his heel and started for the door of the structure. A damn fine barn, he noted, but for the stench. He stepped out and sucked in fresh air. Jubal and Kushing had beaten him out. "Well, gentlemen," Seth said, "we need to keep moseying up this road. I'm told it will bring us, eventually, to the home of Sam Caruthers—"

"To da ole home place," Jessie interrupted him. The old Negro had been waiting outside. "Ain't no house der now. Ain't been one der fo' thirty yeahs, but you'll know da site when you get der. Da jonquils 'bout done bloomin' now, but dey still green all 'round where dat house used to be.

"Long befo' dat ole house fell in, Sam Caruthers' daddy built a big house mo' to da east. But da road, it keep goin' an' hit da Pawt Gibson road to Vicksbu'g. Dis ole way crosses it, so stay on it. You'll come to da new place eventu'ly, jus' latah dan you be thinkin'."

"How much later?" Seth asked. He knew the road of which Jessie spoke. It was simply a matter of how long it would take to reach the Port Gibson-Vicksburg Road from here.

"Late afta'noon, I reckon, less you lathah dem hawses good and eben den won't be much fasta. But dis road still be da quickest way from where you standin' now."

Seth thought of Becky isolated at Hickory Grove, but this couldn't be helped. He had to find Sam Caruthers and try to ascertain how much the man knew about the murder that took place in the Mackey barn two nights ago.

<h1 style="text-align:center">Chapter Eighty-three</h1>

Seth and his men found the old home site eight or nine miles up the ancient trail, now a relatively improved post road, and they crossed the Port Gibson-Vicksburg Road roughly two miles northeast of that. From there Seth knew where to find Caruthers' place, which they reached around four that afternoon. Samuel Caruthers was at home, his wife told Seth. She was as courteous as ever, but the warmth of her earlier hospitality had been replaced by a subtle coolness. Either blue uniforms were no longer as welcome, blue uniforms covering black skin weren't particularly favored in the parlor, or, most likely, the family had taken a personal aversion to Seth.

Regardless of the reason, Mrs. Caruthers had led him and his captain to her parlor, offered them a cold drink of water and left them to wait twenty minutes on her husband. The patriarch and his younger son were equally reticent, but polite. Both readily shook hands with him and Jubal, then Sam Caruthers beckoned everyone to sit before asking the reason for their visit.

"The body of a former Union officer was found washed up on the bank of the Big Black yesterday morning," Seth began without preamble. "He was a regular at The Pink Lady in Rodney. You are aware Isabel Hays was murdered there a few weeks ago?"

Indeed he was. So sorry to have heard it. A short questioning ensued as to who Seth thought killed her and why, to which he was noncommittal, and what the hell did any of this have to do with the Caruthers family?

"Mark Dicks was one of two men who couldn't account for his whereabouts the night Miss Hays was shot. His turning up murdered, and our knowing the lay of the land in the vicinity of where his body was found, I did some snooping. We're pretty certain he was murdered in the Mackey barn."

Caruthers pondered that a moment, then said, "And you assume, that because I have possession of the property, I had something to do with the killing?"

"Actually, it was knowing you had possession of that property that caused me to look there."

Wilson leaned forward. "You're saying you already suspected Dad in this man's murder?"

Seth looked at Wilson, then back at Sam Caruthers. "Did you know Mark Dicks, Mr. Caruthers?"

The man studied him, then said, "What are you fishing for, Major?"

"I suspect Mark Dicks was working for someone who had him secreted at The Pink Lady."

"And for what purpose would this particular someone have stowed the man within the confines of that establishment?"

"I suspect he was there to report on Isabel Hays."

"Or her employees," the younger Caruthers said, and a smile moved across his face. "That could prove entertaining, Dad, but under those circumstances wouldn't that someone's money be better served by simply going—"

"Or her extended family or her clientele," Seth said in a voice devoid of nonsense.

Wilson's smirk disappeared. To his credit, Sam Caruthers didn't ask who Seth meant by that, but the fact he didn't ask said more than if he had.

Seth leaned forward and addressed the man behind the desk. "I don't believe Mark Dicks was there to report on sexual activity, though allegations of blackmail have been bandied about. That crime, however, has been attributed to Miss Hays herself, and I do not believe Mark Dicks was working for Miss Hays. I think Miss Hays knew something or had something that someone else wanted. I think Mark Dicks was working for that individual. I think Mark Dicks was working for you."

"I have nothing more to say to you, sir."

Seth rose abruptly, and Jubal did likewise.

"The farm is isolated and for all intents abandoned," Wilson Caruthers said. "Anyone could have used it. Did you happen to talk to the servants there?"

"I did. They neither saw nor heard anything. It was stormy that night. Killer left a mess though."

"Well," Jubal said when they'd retrieved their horses from Sergeant Kushing and mounted, "if he had anything to do with it, he knows you're onto him."

"Which was my intent, and I do think he had something to do with it. The man's dying the way he did and where he did is not coincidental. If Caruthers didn't do the killing, he knows who did and why."

Chapter Eighty-four

"How do you do? My name is Ursula Spate." The woman, a stranger to Becky, glanced at a thin man next to her on the porch. "This is my husband, the Reverend Josiah Spate." She extended a hand. "And you are?"

"Rebecca Mackey," Becky said, and took the woman's limp hand. She offered her hand to the man, who took it with a firm shake. The man's black coat and white tie would have identified him as a minister, even had the woman not introduced him as such.

The Mrs. Reverend Spate was dressed in a black frock with a touch of white lace at the collar, and it occurred to Becky they'd come to offer solace. The wreath was on the door, plain for anyone to see, but she made no move to ask them in. When she opened her mouth to ask how she might be of service, the man said, "It was our understanding that this is the pastor's home."

Becky braced. "It was. The last minister was Daniel Beazley. He and his wife left here three years ago."

"He went into Confederate service, I understand," the reverend said.

"He did. His wife went to her parents' home in Alabama. I haven't heard from her since the war ended. Are you searching for them? Daniel, I believe, was unhurt in the conflict."

"No, no, madam. I am here in Mississippi working with the Freedmen's Bureau. I've just recently learned of the availability of this church."

"Availability?"

"That it was here, abandoned," Mrs. Spate said, with a smug tilt of her chin, "and might be made available for religious and educational services to the freedmen." The woman placed her hand over her heart and stepped forward, nodding her head woefully, as if sorry for what she was about to say. "We do not wish to disturb you, my dear, but might we ask what you are doing inhabiting this property?"

Since it was common knowledge to everyone around here that she and what was left of the Mackey family had been living here since the late summer of 1863, Becky doubted the veracity of that statement. "Do you have any authorization for asking?"

The woman's eyes widened, and she didn't respond. Her husband said, "It seems the proper authorities had been unaware of the existence of this church..."

Heart quickening, Becky stepped full onto the porch and pulled the door shut behind her, forcing the reverend back a step. The house faced east and the hour neared noon, but the warm sun still managed to kiss the hem of Becky's black dress. The Spates moved closer together.

"I imagine," Becky began, "the proper authorities to whom you refer assumed these two structures had been destroyed along with everything else on this farm, and was therefore not made available to the confiscation schemes of the past two years. You are Northern Methodists, are you not?"

The woman startled. "We represent the one true Methodist Episcopal Church, if that's what you mean, Mrs. Mackey."

"It is my understanding," Becky said, "that those properties seized by the government at the behest of your church over the past two years are being returned to their rightful owners."

"That is correct," the man said, "but given this church stands idle with no claim made to it by anyone, and there being such great need for sound structures, we hoped to put it to good use."

Out of the corner of her eye, Becky saw Mattie come around the side of the house. She was carrying Pearl, who pushed at her breast, a silent demand to be let down.

"We were unaware there was a squatter on this property."

"But you most certainly were aware there was an inhabitant on this property, sir!" Becky said.

The reverend bridled. "These properties belong to the Diocese of the Methodist church, and given the lack of interest of the Methodist Church, South, we intend to lay claim to them."

"This house and the church belong to the estate of Thomas Langdon Mackey. They and the land they are built on were donated to the Methodist Episcopal Church by his father in 1832 and rechartered in 1844 under the Methodist Episcopal Church, South, the Mackey family holding a life estate in the lands, buildings, and outbuildings as well as any other improvements on the property with the written obligation that said property will revert to the Mackey estate should the church ever cease its ministry through dissolution, war, pestilence, or any other act of God."

He made a point of turning and looking at the church across the road. "That church stands idle."

These two people had come out here with more in mind than inspecting the property. They hoped to intimidate her into moving off it. Silently, Pearl waddled up the stairs at the end of the porch, using her hand to steady herself. Mattie hovered close behind. The baby was coming to her, Becky knew. Poor little thing was lost without Eliza. Finding footing on the porch proper, she made a funny squeal and began running, arms out, to Becky.

"And idle it will remain until the Southern Methodist Church sends a minister to assume responsibility for the congregation of this district," she said, bending down to catch the child up in her arms.

"Liah?" the baby asked, her eyes wide.

Becky looked at Mattie, who shook her head. The Negress would have taken the child, but Becky didn't offer her up and instead turned to the couple.

The woman stepped forward. "I'd always heard mulattos are beautiful." The woman looked from Pearl to Becky. "Particularly desirable to Southern men, as I understand it. Mr. Mackey's offspring perhaps?"

"Ursula!" the man said, and from the look on his face, he truly was offended by his wife's comment.

"I doubt you understand much of anything, you loathsome

creature." The porch groaned when Becky stepped toward the woman. She had to hold on to Pearl, because if she dared turn the baby over to Mattie she'd slap this Mrs. Spate.

The woman fell back when Becky took yet another step toward her. "And your ignorance proves how much you do not belong here. Truth is, mulattos are appealing to most men, not just Southern ones, and this baby is the offspring of my niece's nanny, who was raped by a Federal soldier, whom the likes of you in your self-righteous bigotry felt compelled to send down here to show us the wickedness of our ways, and in so doing proved how right we really were about the lot of you insufferable people in the North."

"The Northern Methodist Church has the sympathies of the central government, madam," the man, said, "and we intend to pursue this issue. It's a sin to leave a fine building like that empty when there's so much need."

"And a home such as this inhabited by traitors when so many loyal are in want," the woman added.

Becky pivoted toward them, then sidestepped to expose the wreath they darn well should have already seen. "This house is in mourning. I'll deal with whatever forces of evil you send this way whenever they should arrive. For right now, get off my porch and off Mackey land."

Josiah Spate eyed Mattie before turning to the stairs. "There are others who might be amenable to God's true word."

Mattie moved closer to Becky. "We gots our own church. Don't need da likes of you folks heah." With that, she took Pearl from Becky and went into the house.

Chapter Eighty-five

Seth sent Jubal and Kushing back to Port Gibson, then returned to Vicksburg to report. Malcolm put him up for the night, and in his office the following morning, Malcolm told him that he wouldn't be able to get Seth in to see the general until early afternoon. Seth had finally spent ten minutes briefing Wood at a little after one.

Another lead came to Seth now, that being Judge Lawrence Pendleton, the man Isabel went to see after Walter Miller had first come to Camellia Creek intending to arrest Eli Calhoon. Isabel had given Seth her side of the story, and it worked well for her purposes, he reckoned. Still, knowing the judge's side of what she told him might prove valuable.

According to the provost's office, Pendleton's home sat about a mile off the Vicksburg-Warrenton road, the turnoff being two miles north of Warrenton. "Easy to find," Seth was told, and, indeed, it took him little effort to find the small but stately plantation home, two stories with four pillars spanning the wide front porch. Water oaks, white oaks, and red surrounded the property, shaded comfort for Mississippi's hot summers. The grounds were manicured, though had yet to receive their spring cleanup.

On the north end of the porch, a young man sat in a rocker. He acknowledged Seth with a nod, but instead of rising to meet him, looked away to the woods north of the house. Odd, and curiosity getting the best of him, Seth started toward the seated man instead of to the front door.

A pleasant breeze traveled the length of the west-facing porch and the man turned again when he heard Seth approaching, then rose awkwardly, and Seth realized he was injured.

"Don't get up," Seth said, too late. The man was on his feet, so he stuck out his hand. "Seth Parker," he said. The other man took his hand. "Cole Terry," he responded. "Is it me you're here to see, Major?

"Judge Pendleton."

"I figured. He's my uncle, and he's inside."

It was a dismissal of sorts, though not spoken in an unfriendly manner. Seth figured the fellow simply wanted to sit back down, and given the way he favored his right leg, Seth wondered... No, both feet wore black brogans.

Cole Terry was tawny-haired and green-eyed and would stand a good six foot when fully straight. He was young and handsome, though Seth guessed he was recovering from bad health or his injury, because he was thin of face and the dark frock coat hung loose on his frame. On his lapel he wore a simple unit pin captioned C.S.A.

"Terry?" Seth asked.

The man cocked a brow. "It was my father's name."

Seth smiled at the crafty deflection, and he figured Cole Terry understood that he knew. This man was the boy Sam Caruthers had raised from birth to be his own, then had betrayed. "Good meetin' you, Mr. Terry."

A Negress opened the door when Seth knocked. Some ways down the dim central hall, a tall man, elderly but still spry, stepped out of a room and listened as Seth told the servant his business.

"Bring him to my office, Nell," the man called after a moment. "I'll see the Major."

Yes he would, come hell or high water, but Seth was happy to allow the pretense of choice in the matter. The man was a judge, after all, and his cooperation made things easier.

Now, a glass of cool water on the table beside the wing chair Lawrence Pendleton had directed him to, Seth watched the judge sit forward in the matching chair next to him.

"On the day you're referring to, Isabel came to me and requested my intervention with the district provost marshal in

Vicksburg. It seemed this Treasury agent Miller"—he waved a hand in the air—"was back in the area and, in league with Sam Caruthers, was trying to have Eli Calhoon arrested for the murder of that agent over in Hinds County last fall."

"She actually said Miller was working with Caruthers?"

Pendleton guffawed. "She did, not that she needed to tell me that. Those two were in cahoots during the war. Sam Caruthers has his greedy claws latched on to her daughter's property here in Warren County. Miller probably played a role in drawing up the paperwork." He looked at Seth and shrugged. "But I don't know that for certain. Maybe Isabel did, she never said. I was damned surprised when Miller pulled up stakes and headed back to Washington in the spring of '64, what with so much more left to plunder."

"He might have been relieved for his behavior."

"If so, why is he back here, now? More likely he's being rewarded for his misdeeds. Listen, Major, nobody back there cared what men of Miller's ilk were doing in the South. They don't now, either. The worse, the better."

"I would have thought you—"

"The nation I believed in is gone, Major, on both sides of the Mason-Dixon Line. Let's get back to Isabel and Sam, shall we?"

Seth nodded. "You interceded with the provost?"

"Yes, but that only worked because the Army in Vicksburg teamed up against Miller. The provost was able to insert a requirement for medical approval prior to Eli Calhoon's removal from his home. It's temporary if Treasury chooses to pursue it."

And Seth figured Miller would.

"What I want you to tell me, sir, is what Isabel Hays offered you in return for your intercession with the provost."

"Isabel wouldn't have had to offer me anything, God bless her," he said softly and looked away. "All she'd have had to do is ask." He turned back to Seth. "In this particular matter, she had something detrimental to Sam, and Sam and I are old enemies. If there is anything I can do to thwart Sam Caruthers' endeavors, I am happy to oblige."

"In what endeavor did the two of you thwart him?"

The judge studied him a long moment. "She said he needed Calhoon's Claiborne County property for a railroad right-of-way. Sam always had this big, self-aggrandizing dream of a railroad providing Natchez access to the east." The man rolled his eyes. "To accomplish that, he planned a north-south route to Vicksburg where his line would pick up the Mississippi Southern. It was a doltish plan designed for purely mercenary reasons. Rail through Vicksburg is not what Natchez envisioned then or now. What Natchez needed, Albert Blackledge provided back in the fifties, and that's what needs to be rebuilt. Nevertheless, Sam plans to try again, and if the Republicans do manage to get control of the Mississippi legislature, he could sell that white elephant to them."

"That's all, the railroad?"

Not taking his eyes off Seth, Lawrence Pendleton leaned his head back against the chair. "Do you think Sam Caruthers had something to do with Isabel's murder?"

"I do."

The judge frowned, then pointed a finger at Seth. "She was often enigmatic in what she said." He dropped his finger, tightened his lips, then looked at the ceiling. "Let's see, how did she put it? I said something to the effect that it was always a pleasure to deprive Sam of anything he's lusted after for as long as he'd wanted that damn railroad." Pendleton settled his gaze back on Seth and shook his finger again. "She laughed at that and said, 'Oh, I'm thinking he's waited longer for things more valuable than that damn railroad, Larry.' Then she gave me a right passionate kiss on the lips and added, 'and your protecting Eli will deprive him of that, too.'"

"You didn't ask what that was?"

"Nope. I was satisfied with the kiss, and she wouldn't have told me anyhow."

Chapter Eighty-six

The planks of Camellia Creek's mud porch groaned with Seth's weight. Through lace curtains covering a repaired window, he watched a shadow flit around the dining room, and his stomach quivered with hope Becky had been to Hickory Grove and was back to stay. He knocked, and after a moment, the door flew open and Alice smiled up at him. "You're just in time for supper."

Gosh, she looked good. Glowing. That was the word he'd heard used to describe a pregnant woman, but there'd been times over the past several months Seth doubted this young woman would carry her baby to term, much less glow in the interim.

"You're radiant," he said, and she laughed. He swept the cover from his head and stepped inside. Dusk was falling, but days were longer. "You're eating late."

"We are." She closed the door and stepped around him. "Eli's been out with the builders all afternoon. He's just now washed up." She stuck her head into the foyer and called his name, then came back to the sideboard. "He's putting on a clean shirt. I need to get the lanterns lit."

"He's not retiring with the sun?"

"Not tonight." She leaned closer. "He carries a cane with him, and by afternoon, he's using it, but he's doing good."

She knelt down in front of the cabinet and pulled out another plate. That made three settings, and he forced back his disappointment.

"Becky's at Hickory Grove?"

"She left the morning after she got here," Eli said from the doorway, "but we're expecting her within the next week. She's made the decision to move into Aunt Naomi's house." Calhoon stepped into the dining room, then extended a hand. He didn't have the cane Alice had mentioned, but he was moving awkwardly. Given the bullet had fractured the pelvic bone, Seth was amazed he was getting around as well as he was.

Seth took his hand. "They told me you were out and about. Nothing like seeing to believe it."

"Not even real tired today." The man circled his arm around Alice's waist and pulled her against him. "Little mama here might be though."

"I feel wonderful," she said and freed herself to continue supper preparations. "Sweetheart, could you light the lanterns, I can scarcely see what I'm doing."

She removed the spare tablecloth covering the dishes on the table, leftovers from dinnertime. A platter of fried chicken sat on the sideboard along with a bowl of rice and hot gravy.

"You still under guard?"

Calhoon took Seth's hat. "Oh, yeah. He's in the kitchen. Elvie's feeding him. Not nearly as personable as your troops though. Them I had something in common with. These new fellas are all Northerners."

Seth leaned against the door jamb and watched Calhoon make his way to the hat tree. "Did anyone go with Becky?" he asked.

"She told us your concerns," Alice said, "and in answer to your question, Hector came for her. Pearl had an ear infection." She stepped back and looked at her table. "We're ready to eat."

Seth turned to the mud porch. "Let me wash up."

*S*upper proved pleasant in addition to tasting good. These two were happy, Seth realized. Calhoon's recovery had been precarious, but it looked like he'd made it, although even now the matters that had brought Seth into their midst shadowed them. Between gentle smiles at his young wife and concentration on his food, Calhoon gave Seth several surreptitious glances. He had questions and so did Alice.

Alice rose, then commanded both men to keep their seats when they would have stood. "I'll take these dishes to the kitchen. Elvie graciously allowed me to make a pound cake, so we have dessert. Do you both want coffee?" Her eyes twinkled when she looked at her husband. "Might keep you up."

"I want some," Calhoon said, and Alice looked at Seth.

He didn't have any reason to stay up. "Might help keep me in the saddle till I get into town."

"Stay the night here," Calhoon said when Alice had left. "It'll give us a chance to talk. Alice is aware of what Becky told me, and she's worried about Miller's accusations of conspiracy."

"And you're not?"

Calhoon shot him a sardonic smile and twisted in his chair to snag a bottle of bourbon from the sideboard behind him. He managed the whiskey, but ended up having to get out of his seat to reach the tumblers. "What does he have to implicate me?"

"How much did Becky tell you before she left?"

"She told me that old McGowan claim paid out nearly a quarter of a million dollars, that all these killings are apparently the result of people trying to get their hands on it, and there's some bullshit story being spread around by Miller and the Treasury Department that I killed Guthrie because he was aware of some conspiracy I'm part of to bring down the empire Lincoln forged."

Seth snorted. "Those are your words, right?"

"Yes, but that's the gist of what she said. Is it accurate?"

"Pretty much. She wasn't aware of the rumor that the money is a payoff to Lincoln's assassins."

Calhoon stared at him a moment, then said, "I didn't think it could get more bizarre than that huge payout for the claim."

Seth handed the glass back to him. "Things do appear a bit odd. How about another drink?"

Calhoon accommodated, then hid his dirty glass in the sideboard. The bottle he pushed in front of Seth. "I'm not supposed to be adding alcohol to my wounded liver."

"The doctor's probably right about that."

"That's Alice, not the doctor. Look, until Becky described it after Isabel's death, I had heard nothing about that claim since I was a kid, and I haven't seen Toby since before Isabel's death.

Becky told me he has admitted working the thing at Sam's insistence, but it was you who told her it had actually been paid. She hasn't been able to find Toby since. She says you have."

"Yeah. Holbein admitted to me that he worked the claim years ago, admits your father told him to drop it, but is otherwise noncommittal regarding the McGowan account or the letter authorizing him to settle the estate. He doesn't deny knowledge, he says *nothing* when pressed. But according to the mail log at Treasury, the letter was mailed to him. The bill of exchange was delivered to the Bank of New Orleans by Wells Fargo. The two documents went out the same day to two different recipients. Everything was routine and done through proper channels. No one even suspected anything was wrong until two months later when New Orleans came up short on its gold reserves. That set the church bells ringing. Treasury agents took Holbein to New Orleans where bank personnel confirmed he was not the man who'd presented the authorization."

"And the gold went to British Honduras?"

"The Bank of Honduras in Belize City. Someone opened an account in the name of George McGowan, presumably using that same authorization letter. The money was deposited, then the money was removed and the account closed the next day. The money's disappeared, and the Bank of Honduras is not cooperating with our people. The matter has been turned over to the State Department, but Treasury agents in Washington believe whoever has the authorization letter has the money. The question is how did that person get his hands on an authorization meant for Tobias Holbein?"

"Why the devil isn't anyone looking at Sam Caruthers? He's the one who had Toby working the claim."

"Exactly, and Miller and Sam Caruthers became fast friends during the war. But let's be reasonable. Miller wouldn't be looking to arrest his partner in crime, not when he could use that ploy to eliminate a potential threat to the scheme and competing heir to the claim, that being you."

"So you think they've been working together all along?"

"Somebody had to work this on the Washington end. Miller went back there in '64, then returned when things started coming apart out here. Someone out here has fouled things up. But I don't think they know who, and I'm not sure they've ruled out one another."

"You think Toby's part of it?" There was doubt in Calhoon's question, but there was little doubt in Seth's mind. Holbein had to know what was happening. Hell, he'd even admitted such.

Alice bustled back in with a cake on a plate and a pot of coffee. Both men stood. She told them to sit, then immediately told Eli to scoot out of the way so she could get to the dishes. The first thing she found was the dirty glass, sniffed it, then looked at her sheepish husband. She stood and placed the glass in front of him. "Do not put dirty dishes away in the cupboard, Eli."

That's all that was said. Moments later a slice of buttered pound cake was melting on Seth's tongue.

"It's good, darlin'," Calhoon said to his wife. "Still warm."

"The coffee?" she asked.

"The cake, sweetheart. The coffee's hot as it should be. Everything is perfect."

Seth echoed the compliment.

"Thank you," she said and sat down. "You two can continue your conversation."

Seth looked at Calhoon, who nodded.

"Holbein's the answer," Seth said, "but I can't get anything out of him. I don't know what he's telling Miller, but if Miller's in cahoots with Caruthers and Caruthers is in cahoots with Holbein, it follows that Holbein is in cahoots with Miller. But I've got one last itch that I can't scratch. Holbein has given me the impression it's less about refusing to help me than it is about his wanting to handle matters himself."

Calhoon appeared to mull that over. "I don't know what Toby is thinking. Becky believes Isabel knew what was going on and she and Toby were in agreement. I've got to be honest with you, I can't believe Tobias Holbein would ever double deal my daddy, and I know Isabel never would, so something isn't adding up."

"Do you think you could get the truth out of Holbein?"

Seth watched Calhoon's gaze travel to Alice. "Might can," Calhoon said.

Alice sat pensively, watching the two of them. It occurred to Seth this conversation disturbed her, and he realized, as Calhoon apparently already had, there was no way she'd let Eli Calhoon take off on a journey to Rodney to speak to Tobias Holbein, not anytime soon, not without a fight.

Seth cleared his throat and made a face at Calhoon.

"I've got no secrets from her, Parker," Calhoon said.

"But he can't travel yet," she said, suddenly animated.

"And he's officially under guard," Seth added to calm her. "I'd have to get approval from the provost." He frowned. "Your guard still eating, or has he taken up residence in the kitchen?"

"He's playing poker with Buck. He knows there's an officer in here with Eli."

"Good." Seth rested his eyes on Calhoon. "You've got big problems in that no one knows where you were the day Guthrie was killed, all that missing money, and a government thriving on rumors of Southern threats to the powers that be. Those same accusations could also be randomly tossed at Becky, should those powers so decide. We need to find out what happened to the money."

He turned to Alice. "And you've got to understand, if your husband is as innocent as I hope he is, I need him involved."

"And you've few men left. Will you get white officers now to help you?"

"If any were offered me at this point, I'd be highly suspicious of them. There are too many unknowns at the Washington level, and I'd be wary of who recommended them and why.

"I've still got Jubal and a sergeant. I'm no longer saddled with watching your husband and Isabel. My focus on who I need to be watching has narrowed mightily of late, and to tell you the truth, I don't want to be second-guessed by any new players I can't trust. As soon as I get Becky back here, I can concentrate efforts on Tobias Holbein and Sam Caruthers."

"Becky's concern," Calhoon said, "is that you still don't know it wasn't me who killed Guthrie."

"I know what Becky's scared of, but no matter how much I believe in your innocence, I don't count for much. You are deep in the woods with this. On top of it all, there's real danger, not just regarding your possible arrest for murder and charges of treason, but to life itself. One of The Pink Lady's regular clients was found murdered day before yesterday. He was there the night Isabel was killed and was one of two men who couldn't account for his whereabouts when she was shot. He was murdered in the Mackey barn."

"Dammit," Calhoon said. "I wish she were here."

Alice covered Calhoon's clenched fist with her small hand. Given that reaction, Seth decided not to broach the physical assault on Becky in Natchez. He didn't know if Becky had told her brother, but since Calhoon didn't bring it up at this apropos juncture, Seth opted to keep quiet about it.

"I'm going to Jackson tomorrow morning and talk to the Hinds County sheriff. When Miller and I first talked, he had a question regarding Guthrie's clothing. I didn't give much thought to it at the time because the question appeared to relate to Guthrie's murder being a robbery. At least, that's what I thought Miller was relating it to. Now I'm thinking that wasn't the case.

"From there, I'm going to Hickory Grove. I need directions. It's my understanding Guthrie had trouble finding the place. Depending on how much packing Becky's got done, look for us back in a couple of days."

Chapter Eighty-seven

Seth, with Jubal and Sergeant Kushing, left the Natchez Trace a good mile and a half south of the road Eli Calhoon told him led to the abandoned Methodist Church and its pastor's house where Becky now lived. He wanted to see the plantation house proper, its barn, and outbuildings, or what was left of them, to better assess what had happened here more than two and a half years ago.

He saw the Corinthian columns from the road, four to a side and spread roughly fifteen feet apart to accommodate wide walls. The devastation proved to be about what he'd expected. Those magnificent, classic Greek-revival columns, much like those gracing his grandfather's home in Fulton County, Kentucky, were all that still stood.

Rubbish filled the space enclosed by the blackened columns, the home's remains flattened by more than two and a half years of rainy springs, summers, falls and winters. Ash, silt and filth nourished the vibrant scrub now dominating the ground where once a magnificent home had stood. A warm breeze rattled the brittle limbs of the trees closest to the ruined house. From a distance, these had appeared dead, but on closer inspection green shoots and buds sprouted from the crags this spring, life forced from a seemingly dormant host. No longer trimmed and lovely as he could imagine them, but chaotic and ugly, symbolic testimony to the brutalized South.

He rode around the entire perimeter, then stopped at the charred remains of another large building.

"Kitchen," Robert Kushing said and nodded to blighted earth a good seventy yards away. "Should be the barn yonder."

The barn, where Emily Mackey had shot an Indiana soldier raping her daughter's nanny and in turn was shot herself; where the pregnant Becky, who'd accompanied her sister-in-law in the imprudent rescue attempt, had been hurt. He shuddered to think what else might have happened that she had never spoken of. She'd been arrested and forced to watch as the house was plundered, then burned.

A hint of nausea invaded his gut, and he tapped Boon with his heels and rode that way over a grass-choked road. His two men followed.

There was nothing much to see, just charred remains, these, too, returning to the soil. He didn't speak, nor did Jubal and Kushing, who probably weren't sure what tack to take on this place, not knowing his. God, it was quiet here, the sun pounding down on them in what promised to be a hot day. Off to his right, a narrow road disappeared into an island of woods surrounded by fallow fields, where the craggy stems of cotton waited, after more than two years, to be cleared. It had appeared, at least, to have been harvested. The quarter would be at the end of that road, he figured, secluded in the woods. An isolated little village built on a spring-fed creek where its inhabitants had known a degree of autonomy and self-reliance. He knew some darkies remained on this place. They were one of the factors that brought Becky back from Camellia Creek. Them and a stubborn determination that neither Northern interlopers, nor treacherous Southern opportunists, should dare consider this place abandoned. Seth ground his teeth. That darn corn she kept talking about should be sowed within the month, but the fields were yet to be cleared, much less plowed. No sign that anything was being done to revive a once thriving farm, and he wondered how much actual help Becky had left.

He followed the road around the barn, Boon's hoofs, like those of the other two horses, nearly silent on the dusty earth. Within fifty yards, he came to a broader dirt road, which, when he glanced back, he saw led to the front of the house, as Eli Calhoon said it would. Roughly a mile in front of him, the road would come to the church and the pastor's cottage, which according to Calhoon was the original Mackey homesite. The first house had been built in the late twenties by James Mackey's aging grandfather, a Scots-Irish émigré from North Carolina. It served the family until wealth enabled the building of the larger home. The original house and two acres of land had been donated to the Methodist Church in the late thirties or early forties, Calhoon wasn't sure of the date, to serve this part of the county. The Mackeys had constructed this back road, now rough and in need of grading, to accommodate the family on Sunday mornings. Rough it might be, but it was also beautifully tree-lined, and now shaded with the bright green leaves of spring.

The population had dwindled when the Yankees came and burned Hickory Grove. The pastor had sent his family to the then safer environs of Alabama, and he had entered Confederate service. Becky, after her short incarceration at Vicksburg, had returned to this devastated place and assumed residence in the abandoned preacher's house. She kept with her the orphaned Eliza Mackey, the sole heir to this ravaged property, the last of the Mackey blood, and according to Becky's brother, a compelling responsibility.

*B*ecky had managed to keep her eyes dry all morning. She blotted the ink on her correspondence. In the central hall, off to her left, she heard the shuffle of Mattie's feet, then the familiar creak of that central floorboard. The woman stopped in the middle of the hall, first looking at the front door before turning to Becky at the desk in the parlor. That's when Becky heard the horses and glanced through the lace curtains to catch sight of the riders. Men in blue, coming from the south, and her gut clenched. They disappeared around the corner of the house, out of sight. Slowly she rose, then caught the Negress' wary eye.

"God, Mattie, I can't deal with another man in blue today."

Mattie stepped toward the door, behind the wall, and disappeared from view. A moment later she reappeared and said, "It be Majah Pahkah, Miz Becky."

Her heart skipped. "He's not alone."

"Dat nigga sol'jah Summers be wif 'im an' another sol'jah. Him's white."

Becky braced her arms against the desk for support. Mattie stepped inside the room. "Majah ain't gonna do you harm, baby, not on pu'pose." She sobbed suddenly. "Might be him can he'p."

Becky shook her head and started for the entry. "If they weren't here, there'd be no need for help."

Through the glass, she saw Seth climbing the steps, heard his brogans clomp on the wood. Booted feet followed. She swung the door wide. Mattie caught it and followed her onto the porch.

*S*eth noticed the wreath the moment his foot touched the first step. Anxiety overtook his anticipation at seeing Becky, and his heartbeat quickened.

He was on the porch when the door opened, and he swept the cover from his head. Becky stepped out, chin high, eyes bright and defiant...and red-rimmed. He wanted to greet her with a kiss, but under the best of circumstances, that would not have been appropriate. She said nothing, so he said, "Becky."

"Close the door, Mattie," Becky said without looking at the woman, then folded her arms over her breasts. "What can I do for you, Major Parker?"

He tensed, confused. They had not parted with hostility. He glanced at the wreath. Behind him, his men were still. Jubal had made it as far as the porch, he knew. He suspected Kushing lingered on the steps. Seth looked at Jubal. "Give me a moment."

Jubal glanced at Becky, then made a point of looking at the wreath before motioning Kushing off the stairs and following him back to the horses. Seth turned to Becky.

"I'm back in disfavor?" he said softly.

Tears filled her eyes. "For something another bastard in blue has done." She covered her face with her hands. "I'm sorry. That's not fair to you."

"Becky, what's happened here?"

She turned to Mattie who stepped to her and caught her in

her arms, and the old black woman sobbed, squeezing Becky to her, then laid her cheek on top of Becky's head.

Dear God in heaven. He stepped toward them. "Here, let's go —"

But Becky pushed out of Mattie's arms and held up her left hand to stay him. "No." She straightened, sucked in a stuttered breath, then faced him. "Eliza's dead."

Despite having seen the wreath, despite his brief attempt to brace himself, to prepare for what she would tell him, disbelief churned his gut. It was more than the child's death that moved him. It was the empathy and love he felt for this beautiful young woman. He watched her wipe her eyes.

"How?" he asked.

"Diphtheria. She died day before yesterday, during the night. And this morning, they..."

She broke down completely then, and he sidestepped, determined to get the door open, to shuffle them all inside, but Mattie cried, "An' dey done come and took our Pearl. Dey took dat baby from us dis mawnin'. Say she be an o'phan an Miz Becky ain't got 'er bes' int'rest in min'."

Seth had stopped. "Who took her?"

"Mattie, I don't think there's —"

"*Who* took her, Becky?"

Becky blinked at him, and he swore he saw hope in her eyes. "Major Chase from the Freedmen's Bureau. He came with a Major Thatcher, the —"

"Provost marshal. I know him. I know Chase, too." He turned slightly. Jubal had returned to the bottom of the porch steps. Robert Kushing held back. "I wonder why they would take an orphan out of a home —"

"Dat nasty ole preacher's wife was behin' dat. I know it sure as I'm standin' 'ere. 'Er an' Missy had words yesta'day 'bout dis house, so she an' 'er hateful ole huzban' went back an' gots da Bureau to come an' take our baby Pearl."

Seth looked down at Becky, a pained expression on her face. "Can you talk?"

She nodded.

"What preacher's wife?"

"They're Northern Methodists. They've been coming down here since before the war ended and taking Southern churches."

"You don't need to say more. I'm aware of what they're doing, but that policy has changed."

Becky was nodding. "Yes, but they thought they could work around that since this one is empty and the Methodist Church, South, has shown no interest in it. I think they planned to occupy it, or get the Army to confiscate it for them. Unfortunately for them, I was here in the pastor's cottage, and they need to drive me off, but by the terms of the Mackeys' agreement with the Southern Methodist Church in Montgomery, this property reverts to the Mackey estate should the church abandon it.

"As of yesterday those two weren't even aware of the original agreement. All the Mackey records were destroyed when the house burned, but I found the church's original copies in the pastor's office yesterday afternoon. No one's come about the church. They were all bluff there. Then this morning"—her voice gave and Mattie picked up.

"Dey come for Pearl after breakfas' dis mawnin'."

"She was crying. She was so scared, and she doesn't understand where Eliza is."

"Oh, lawd, 'av muh'cie," Mattie cried and covered her mouth. Becky took one step toward the older woman, then Seth saw Becky's eyes move past him, down the steps to where Jubal Summers had approached. He looked as the black man turned away and returned to his horse, his back to them all. Becky bypassed Mattie on the porch and went down the stairs to him. He didn't turn to look at her as she moved up beside him, just tilted his head slightly as she spoke to him. To Seth's surprise, he let her take his hand. He nodded after a moment, her talking to him all the while, and Seth watched Jubal Summers raise his free hand to his eyes. Becky let him go, then squeezed his arm and started back to the porch. Seth felt Becky would have hugged him in shared grief had Jubal been more amenable, but Seth knew the man wasn't. But that child now mouldering in the ground had pierced the disdain the man held for white Southerners, or for the white race in general. A pinprick, which would quickly heal. But right now, at this moment, pierced him it had.

Chapter Eighty-eight

An abandoned plantation house two miles west of Canton was now the home for Madison County's orphaned freedmen, Seth learned when he arrived at Major Edgar Chase's office on the outskirts of the county seat. Chase, with whom Seth was acquainted, said he had removed the child from the custody of Mrs. James Mackey earlier that day at the insistence of the Reverend Josiah Spate, who informed him the child was an orphan being kept at the plantation for dubious intent and that disease was present within the house.

"Diphtheria," Seth said.

"I know." Chase moved around to the front of his desk. "That seemed a valid enough argument to me at the time. What dubious intent the good reverend felt Mrs. Mackey intended for the child I've yet to ascertain, but certainly her removal from possible contagion seemed valid enough. I've subsequently learned from the local physician the child had not been exposed to the contagion that killed an older child at the residence two days ago." Chase turned and picked up his pipe. "The army doctor examined her, and she's with the other children."

"I want that baby back, Ed."

Chase straightened. "I considered that might be your intent when you asked about her, but the Spates came with the provost marshal. You've got me between a rock and a hard place here."

"Tell me how to get to the orphanage."

Behind him, Seth heard Jubal Summers move, the better, he figured, to observe Chase's response to Seth's demand.

Edgar Chase sighed, then stepped away from his desk. "I'll take you myself. My wife is there. She's a teacher. So is Eleanor

Thatcher, the provost's harridan." The man grabbed his cover from a peg on the wall. "You know her, I believe."

"She only stops crying when she's worn herself out," Amy Chase said to her husband. She looked at Seth, then Jubal, who was straining to see down the central hall, from where they could hear a child wailing. "She's beginning to wear on us all. Some of the little darkie girls have tried to console her, but they've about given up, and she will not eat."

A woman, whom Seth recognized as Eleanor Thatcher, joined them from what was once a parlor. Now it appeared to be an office, with at least three desks, a large one in the middle of the room and two along the back wall.

"You know that child?" the woman snapped.

"I do," Seth said.

She squinted at him. "You're here because you want to take her back to wherever it is she came from?"

"The only home she's ever known."

The woman smiled suddenly and held out a hand. "I thought you looked familiar. It's good to see you again, Major...Seth, isn't it?"

"And you, Mrs. That—"

"I told you to call me Eleanor the day you joined us for dinner. Please continue to do so. As I told you at the time, I have the dubious distinction"—she smiled at him, then nodded at Edgar Chase—"by separate contract with the Freedmen's Bureau, of managing the care for these poor, displaced children."

"That child is not displaced. She has a good home and people who love her and whom she loves in return. I want her back."

"And may I ask what involves you in this particular matter?"

"It's a personal interest."

"Ah." She stuck her head into the former parlor, now an office and called, "Lilly, child, go fetch my husband would you, dear?"

A Negro girl of perhaps thirteen slipped from the room, said, "Yes'm," then glanced quickly at the rest of them and ran out the front door. Eleanor Thatcher perused the taciturn Edgar Chase and said, "I fear we may need added authority in this matter." Ignoring Seth, she started down the hall, toward the room that held the wailing baby. "Come along, Major, and let's try and ascertain what is going on here."

Pearl stood crying in the middle of the room, tears and snot and sweat covering her little face. Her body was tense, her breathing hitched. Two Negro girls, between the ages of eight and ten, Seth reckoned, were trying to comfort her, to no avail.

"She's most difficult," Mrs. Thatcher said.

"She's absolutely miserable is what she is," Amy Chase added.

Behind him, Seth heard Edgar Chase blow out a breath. "I couldn't take too much of this," he said.

"Which is why," Eleanor Thatcher said, as Jubal pushed his way inside the door of the room and squatted, "God made women patient."

Seth wasn't convinced women held mastery over patience.

"Pearly," Jubal called, then called again.

The crying baby, flanked by her sitters, turned and saw him. Still wailing, arms open wide, she came to him, fell against his chest, and wrapped her arms around his neck. Jubal scooped her up and stood. The crying stopped. "Hush," he said to her. "You hush now, everything is gonna be all right."

Seth wasn't sure of that and wished Thatcher would get here so they could get this resolved.

Pearl pushed back and looked at Jubal, licked at the phlegm running from her nose, put her tiny hands on each side of his jaw and forced his face to hers. "Liah?" she said. She blinked, her eyes bright with hope. "Liii'ah?"

"What's she saying?" Amy Chase asked.

"She's asking me where Eliza is," Jubal said. Seth noted the clutch in his voice, though he wasn't sure the others did.

"Eliza?" Eleanor Thatcher asked. She looked at Seth when Jubal didn't answer.

"Eliza's the six-year-old who died two days ago at Hickory Grove. This child's mother was Eliza's nursemaid. She's dead. Eliza more or less adopted the baby."

"Which the likes of Ursula Spates," Mrs. Thatcher spat out, "would construe as making the baby poor little Eliza's slave."

Seth had heard the front door open. Now heavy footfalls followed, approaching from down the hall. Bill Thatcher stuck his head in and his wife spun to face him. "For the love of sweet Jesus, William, what were you thinking? A family buries one child and you take the remaining one away by force!"

The man blinked.

"Where is the order you signed to remove this baby from her home?"

He frowned and looked at Edgar Chase. "It's on my desk."

"Well, it needs to be in the stove."

Poor Bill Thatcher squinted at her, then turned an accusing eye on Chase. "I got my validation from the Freedmen's Bureau. Edgar agreed this child needed to be removed from that house for her own good."

Eleanor Thatcher's lips tightened, then she held up an index finger and waved it between her husband and Edgar Chase. "I knew this wasn't right. Knew by the way that baby was dressed she wasn't a displaced mongrel. Do you remember, Amy, I made note of her pinafore earlier."

Amy nodded. "I thought so, too. I told you so."

"I want that order rescinded."

"I beg your pardon?" her husband said. She was embarrassing him, Seth realized, not that she seemed to care.

"I think that is in order, Bill," Chase said.

"Well, hell," William Thatcher bellowed at his wife and threw his arms wide to take in Edgar Chase. "Talk to him. He wrote the damn thing."

Eleanor Thatcher took that still pointing index finger and thrust it against her husband's chest, forcing him back a step. "Don't you talk to me like that in front of others."

Chase caught Seth's attention and rolled his eyes as Eleanor Thatcher skirted around her husband, then past the teenaged Negress, Lilly, who'd followed the provost into the room. "And now I'm going to have a few choice words with Ursula Spates."

In the dim hall now, she turned to look at all of them, still standing in the bright room. Seth didn't know what the others were thinking, but he figured remaining still until she'd disappeared was the most prudent course. "She's hosting tea," the woman forced out between clenched teeth. "*Tea* with other spouses of the occupying forces who wish to ingratiate themselves to the almighty Methodist Episcopal Church"—she preened haughtily — "in order, I assume to advance their husbands' careers."

William Thatcher's eyes widened, and he rushed after her. No doubt he had something left unsaid he wished to convey to his agitated wife, or maybe he was simply thinking of his wife's proposed indiscretion and the impact on his own career.

The young Negress Lilly watched them disappear, then skimmed her gaze over Seth and Jubal. "Dat Miz Thatcher, 'er be somethin', I tell you. 'Er huzban' tell me all da time dat she be meaner dan a badger. Say she don't take no guff from nobody." The girl shook her head and her smile widened. "'Er be a congregation'ist from Mass'chusetts. Um hmm. An' 'er don't like Miz Spate one bit. Calls 'er one a dem rabit Meth'dists. Dat mean she be like a mad dog." The girl laughed and skipped toward the door. "Sho wish I could be der to see 'er light inta dat mean ole Spate woman. Sho do. Oh, da howlin' an' slobberin' Miz Thatcha gonna whup outa 'er."

"Oh, dear," Amy Chase said to no one in particular, "Eleanor has been looking for a reason to berate Ursula Spate since the woman got here." By all indications a calm and capable woman, Amy folded her hands in front of her and looked askance at her husband. "All that aside," she said, "I do believe rescinding the writ is in order."

Chase looked at Seth, then little Pearl, calm now in Jubal's arms. He handed his wife his handkerchief, said, "Wipe her nose if you would, dear," then rested his gaze on Seth. "Take the child home, Seth. I'll take care of the rescinding order."

Chapter Eighty-nine

Seth saw the women waiting on the porch, then watched them rise from their rockers as he and his men drew closer. Becky moved to the stairs and placed a hand on the railing. Seth knew the moment the two realized they had the baby, because Mattie, who had stayed behind Becky, threw her hands in the air and started down the porch steps.

Jubal still held Pearl. Seth had left her with him because she knew and seemed comfortable with him. She hadn't made a peep since they'd climbed in the saddle and started back to Hickory Grove.

"Oh, thank da sweet lawd." Mattie, in tears, held up her hands to take Pearl, who reached down to her with hungry arms. Jubal readily handed her over. Mattie came up beside Seth, yet to dismount, thanking him over and over.

He looked to Becky, just now coming down the stairs, a smile on her face and her eyes brimming. He dismounted. "Thank you," she said, and for a moment her smile lingered.

"They were pretty happy to give her up."

Kushing took Seth's bridle, then turned to Jubal. "Here, Cap'n, I'll water 'em."

Mattie brought the baby to Becky. Pearl reached for her, and Becky squeezed the baby to her breast. She closed her eyes, and when she couldn't control the tears, turned and started up the porch stairs, the baby clinging to her neck. Then Pearl pushed away, and catching Becky's face in her hands, much as she had Jubal's at the orphanage, said, "Liii'ah?"

He could only see the back of Becky's head shake with a symbolic negative, and the girl repeated the question. Becky kissed the baby's cheek quick, then handed her to Mattie, who began to cry again. God, this was a forlorn place.

Seth turned on his heel to Jubal, but Mattie checked whatever he would have said. "Polly's got some dinnah left ovah in da cookhouse, suh, if'n you and yo' men want to eat."

"Gather up Kushing," Seth told Jubal, "and y'all eat. I need to talk to Mrs. Mackey."

She'd waited for him on the porch, just outside the front door, which she held open, then slipped inside with his approach.

He closed the door and followed her into the parlor, mercifully cool this hot afternoon. The room was on the east side of the house and dim this time of day.

"What happened?" she asked.

"Suffice it to say the powers that be are satisfied that here with you is where Pearl needs to be." He swallowed. "The culprits were the Spates, Becky, no one else intended harm."

She didn't respond with any invective directed at ignorant people with good intentions. He thought she might. Certainly he could relate, but she didn't, in fact, respond at all. The fight had left her.

"Have you sent word to Camellia Creek yet about Eliza," he asked, "because as of last night they didn't know."

Becky shook her head and tried to speak, then sank onto a brown velvet settee. She waved a hand toward a writing desk, its surface well appointed with pen and inkwell, a lovely astral lamp, and stationery.

"I'd started a letter. Perhaps you would take it if you're going back soon?"

He drew in a breath. As far as he was concerned she would break the news in person when he delivered her to Camellia Creek, but he only nodded. Now was not the time for a row.

She turned on the couch and looked at him more fully. "You can sit."

Hat in hand he sat beside her on the settee, close, but not too close.

"How was Eli?"

He leaned forward on his thighs, absently twirling his cover over and over in front of him. "Good, so's Alice. They actually seem happy." He straightened, then placed the kepi on his other side. "I realized early on that they cared for each other, but they weren't happy. Everything about their relationship was strained, but that peculiar tenseness that lay between them is gone now."

Becky looked at the table in front of the settee. It sat on an oval rug and was draped with a doily. He looked around the room with its polished furnishings, lace curtains, and sparse whatnots and pretties.

"You must have cleaned up since Miller's visit. I don't see a lot of damage."

"Mattie and Polly had things in good order before I got back. The only permanent damage Miller did was to the door, and he ripped open the bed mattresses. For the most part he simply made a mess."

"Your brother told me the Union soldiers didn't visit here that day back in '63."

"The trees hid it from the big house. I think they would have found it eventually, but Emily's actions diverted them. The lieutenant in charge appeared shocked by everything that happened. His men raping a Negress, the shooting of a woman. Emily killed one of his men. Shot him in the groin with his pants down." She grimaced. "She had a shotgun. Shot wounded a second man. The sergeant shot her. No doubt that officer knew he'd lost control of the situation. Given the offense, he torched everything and left."

"With you."

"And as many of our personal belongings they could carry."

"Becky, did anything else —"

"He wasn't a rapist," she said quickly. "He was disgusted to realize some of his men were. He took me to Vicksburg for questioning. You know that part of the story." She drew in a deep breath, and he watched as she unclenched her fists. She began again. "I'd been knocked down in the barn. There was a struggle with me trying to get to Emily. Captured, I guess would be how they regarded thwarting my efforts. I don't know if I could have

505

saved her if I'd been allowed to stay. Certainly Mattie knew more about doctoring than I did, so I doubt it.

"It was a rough ride back to Vicksburg. I went into a long, slow labor, but I knew my baby was dead. Not long before the men came to question me, one of the guards, a middle-aged corporal, asked me if I was in labor. I've always suspected he's who got word to Mrs. Lawrence, who intervened and eventually put an end to the questioning. I was moved to more comfortable quarters where my son was born dead. The women wouldn't let me see him. They were trying to be kind, of course, but I'll never..." Again, she balled her hands in her lap, crushing the lace handkerchief between white-knuckled fingers.

Forgive, he thought. Not the women, specifically, who'd provided her help and sympathy, which Becky would have never needed if they and their brutal men had not come South to begin with.

"What's to become of this place now?" he asked.

"Daddy Mackey left the farm to his oldest and second sons first, then to his grandchildren, male first, then female. In the end there was only Eliza. After her, the land reverts to a cousin in east Tennessee. Emily, then I, have been in contact with him since Daddy Mackey's death. He has living sons. I've a letter ready to send to him, and I've finished the one to the Mackey solicitor in Jackson. I'll post it tomorrow."

"There was no provision for you?"

"None. Why should there have been? Had Daddy Mackey known how quickly things would change, I think he would have made arrangements for both me and Emily."

"What kind of person is this cousin, do you know?"

She shrugged. "A good man with a fine family as far as I know. He's a merchant. I think he might have been a Unionist. Has a small farm. He incurred some losses with the war, one son I think, but there were others who survived. I'm sure they'll want this place if they can cover the taxes." She turned slightly to look out a window. "It doesn't matter to me now. I want to go home, but I hate to leave...."

"Eliza's with her mother and her grandfather."

"And a grandmother she never knew and great-grandparents and...." Becky placed a hand on her forehead. "There's only a handful of darkies left here now. They won't work, except for Hector and Cyrus. I asked Mr. Jake Mackey, that's the cousin, to consider giving the two of them forty acres each. I believe Daddy Mackey would have approved, but he never even thought about such things when he wrote his last will. Never considered what has happened could have happened."

"When you say home, do you mean Rodney?"

She blinked at him. "Camellia Creek."

And that meant there'd be no row on that point. But they still needed a plan of action, and he preferred making one on a full stomach. He needed to see to his men, he told her, then he'd be back.

*F*rom the window of the detached kitchen, Seth watched the skirt of Becky's mourning dress billow in the evening breeze. She held little Pearl and stood with Mattie inside the wrought-iron fence of the Mackey section of the churchyard, saying good night to little Eliza Mackey. Mattie was obviously weeping, and after a moment he saw Becky circle the black woman's shoulders with her free arm and pull her closer. Little Pearl appeared to say nothing, simply looked down at what the two weeping women looked at, unable to comprehend what had happened.

He'd eaten after his men. Behind him now, he heard Kushing ask Jubal if he'd like to play cards—he had a deck—but Jubal declined. He wasn't a card player, he said, and he didn't drink. Seth figured Kushing thought Summers pretentious, but Seth sensed more. The man was grieving and, no doubt, didn't relish doing much of anything with anyone, not that he ever had. Jubal had walked out after that, stating he was riding out to see the slave quarter.

Seth sensed the amenable, towheaded sergeant move up beside him. Kushing hailed from Minnesota, he'd told Seth when he reported in. Now he was a twelve-year lifer, regular Army.

"The little girl was the woman's niece, sir?"

"Yes."

"How old was she?"

"Six."

"Darn shame. My mama had only one little girl. Four boys and one girl. Lost the girl when she was three. Typhoid, the doctor said. Mama never was the same."

"How long since you've been home?"

"Six years. Went home to bury Papa before the war. Mama had passed on when I was twelve. I was the youngest 'cept for the girl. My oldest brother has the farm. He has three kids, two boys and a girl. My other two brothers moved into town. They're partners in a feed store. Only one of them is married. No kids yet. The unmarried one fought with a local unit formed up that way. Made it home okay. How about you?"

"Never married."

"Never figured to be taking orders from a marine officer."

"And I never figured to be giving orders to army sergeants, but I've been doin' it a lot lately."

*M*attie said Becky was in her bedroom and pointed the way. Seth had been hesitant to disturb her, thinking she might be sleeping, but they needed to talk. He was going to insist she return with him to Camellia Creek tomorrow. He knew, of course, they were in agreement on her going to Camellia Creek. It was the tomorrow part that caused him to worry.

He'd sent Jubal and Kushing back to Port Gibson an hour ago. They wouldn't get back until well after dark. He didn't confirm anything to Jubal, and he didn't give him or Kushing anything to do. His investigation centered mostly on Holbein and Caruthers and Miller now.

He knocked gently on the door at the end of the hall.

"You can come in," she said, and he wondered if she really did recognize his tread.

Becky stood silhouetted against the north-facing window, dusk's gloom filtering through the leaded glass. She had a towel in her hand. A wash bowl sat on the stand at her side. Her eyes were puffy, but dry, and he realized she'd just washed her face. "I'd feared you'd left," she said.

"No." He moved into the room. "Mark Dicks is dead," he said and watched as she studied him. "Murdered. His body washed ashore in Claiborne County on the north bank of the Big Black. We found the place where he was killed."

He paused, and after a moment she asked, "Where?" The way she posed the question, he knew she suspected.

"Your barn at Muscatine."

"Do you know who—"

"I suspect Miller or Caruthers, but I haven't put it together yet. You didn't tell your brother you were attacked in Natchez, did you?"

She came closer. "I hope you didn't either."

"No. He didn't bring it up, so I didn't, but he needs to know. I've sent Jubal and Sergeant Kushing back to Port Gibson. I told them I'd be back tomorrow. I'm taking you and Mattie and the baby to Camellia Creek. I don't want to fight about this." He turned and reached for the door.

"Where are you going?"

He turned slightly on his heel so he could see her. "I meant to give you privacy. I'll be in the house."

She stepped closer and touched his hand. "Stay with me."

He watched tears fill her eyes.

"I'm sorry," she said, her voice breaking. "I want us back to where we were in Natchez, to where I was going to buy a blue dress to wear for you. I've lost my country, my land, my family, my little niece who I was responsible for." She drew in a deep breath. "The only good thing I've lost is my heart, and I'm no longer proud enough or strong enough to deny it. I need you, and I'm tired of worrying about the risks involved."

He started to take a step, but she held up a palm. "There's something else I've got to tell you first, then you can decide if you still want me."

He stilled with that to wait her out.

"I've struggled with this since Mama died, but I've got to tell you, whether it damns me or not. Back in January, I eavesdropped on Mama and Toby Holbein. At the time I didn't know what they were referring to, but I know now it was the authorization letter. Mama had it, or had had it, and did something with it."

He opened his mouth—

"It was Mr. Holbein's and she'd gotten hold of it somehow. He admonished her for being more reckless than Aunt Naomi, but he didn't seem to be angry."

Becky waved her hand when he started to speak. "No, I have no idea what's become of it. She didn't give it me. I don't think she gave it to Eli, and trust me when I tell you that's the only reason I haven't told you until now."

"You feared she might have given it to him?"

She nodded. "At some point, yes. And don't tell me you never considered the possibility that it was Eli that walked into the Bank of New Orleans last November with that authorization, because in my wildest nightmares I've considered the possibility myself. But I don't really believe it. I truly believe Mama tried to keep Eli as ignorant as she kept me. She wouldn't have wanted him drawn into this. She would have wanted to protect him. He's Holland Calhoon's last remaining son."

She stepped back. "Now you know everything I know."

He reached her with one quick step and crushed her to him. After a moment he pulled back and found her lips in a kiss gentler than his hold.

"We're already past where we were in Natchez," he said when he ended the kiss. "We crossed that threshold, and there's no going back. You said so yourself. I'll stay with you tonight, but I won't make love to you. Neither one of us is suffering from that need, not with grief burrowing into our very souls. You need to be held, and it's enough for me to do the holding."

He walked her to the bed, where he laid down and pulled her against him. Her squirming soothed to stillness and a soft sigh assured him he'd eased her grief. She did not weep. In the space of minutes daylight was gone, the room dark, and head upon the pillow, he closed his eyes and breathed in the scent of lilac, and slept.

He woke at first light, the room as heavy with night's waning shadows as his head was dulled with sleep. Becky lay beside him. They'd never pulled down the covers. Despite the warmth of the day before and the expectation of a warm one to follow, it was March, and the morning was chilly.

She turned in his arms and laid her cheek against his chest. Outside, the first haze of light caressed the dark leaves of the japonica near the house's wraparound porch and bleached the sky from black to gray. He nudged her, and when she looked up, he kissed her, and she returned his kiss.

"This mattress is uncomfortable," he said.

"This mattress is missing half its stuffing."

His hand brushed over the gentle bulge of her belly, and he thought of the baby she had lost. He would give her another. He took her hand.

"Marry me," he said.

<h1 style="text-align:center">Chapter Ninety</h1>

Seth turned her so she again spooned against him. "Today."

It was a statement, not a question, just shy of a command.

"I will marry you, but not today."

"Why not?"

Despite his earlier effort, she rolled back, forcing him up, and he hovered over her, waiting.

"We're going back to Camellia Creek today," she said. "I can't fathom telling Eli and Alice that we've wed and, 'oh, by the way, Eliza died three days ago.'" She shook her head, more a wobble really. Her eyes had filled with tears at her words. She curled away from him. "I just can't do that."

"It bothers me, too. We'll keep the nuptials secret, at least from family."

She rolled back and frowned at him.

"Bodies are startin' to fall from the trees, darn it. I can protect you better when you're my wife."

"Only against the powers in charge. That's not what killed my mother, and it's not what killed Mark Dicks."

"Or Jon Franklin or Alan Guthrie, but I'm not so sure that some degree of association with the powers in charge won't prove useful." He punched his pillow and stacked it against the headboard, then leaned back as she sat up. "I wasn't part of the rebellion, honey. That gives me some protection. I know lots of good people who are not part of whatever it is that we're up against. They're in positions to help me and will. And there's Muscatine."

"Muscatine," she echoed. "And all this time I thought it was me you cared about."

He smiled and smoothed his index finger along her crepe-clad arm. "Investigating Dicks' murder gave me an opportunity to get a good look at the place. We can be happy there, Becky, if that's what you want."

"What about Kentucky?"

"Already divvied up, and I'm not included, though they would probably try to fit me in somewhere if they had to. There's still the slaughterhouse in New Orleans, but I am sure I don't want that."

She played with a brass button on his blouse. "We'll have Pearl?"

"Yes, Pearl is ours. And Mattie and Hector and Cyrus—"

"And Polly and Jessie and Lettie."

"Any of your people, if they want to stay."

Chapter Ninety-one

Calhoon took Pearl from Mattie's arms and passed the baby to Alice, who'd followed him down Camellia Creek's front steps. Hector climbed from the wagon seat, while Seth dismounted and swung Becky from where she'd been perched since late morning. It was now near dark, and Seth was thankful for the longer days.

On the other side of the wagon, he heard Calhoon ask Mattie where Eliza was. This was followed by Mattie's muffled sob, and Calhoon's anguished curse. Instantly, he appeared around the back of the wagon, followed by Alice, still holding Pearl.

"What has happened?" he asked, in a voice filled with compassion and his tender gaze on his sister. Seth knew this was hard for her. The family had to be told, and grief would be faced and shared, accepted dutifully, not hidden away. The hurt filled him at the same time it hit Calhoon, and Alice, pale and bright-eyed, brought her free hand to her mouth. She said nothing, but he saw her shudder with silent sobs, and Pearl circled her arms around her neck and laid her head on the woman's shoulder as if now she understood.

"Diphtheria," Becky managed, then she was in Calhoon's arms, sobbing against her brother's shoulder.

"Three days ago," Seth said.

Calhoon looked at him, then gently pushed Becky to arm's length. "You should have let us know," he said. "You've dealt with everything yourself?"

"We had to bury her quickly. Seth's been with me since yesterday."

Seth moved up behind her and placed his hands on her shoulders. "I'll talk to your brother. You go on with Alice."

Calhoon was watching him, but Becky didn't see. She had started toward Alice, who now let loose a little sob and took Becky into her arms at the same time Pearl went to Becky.

"Come inside the house," Alice said, her voice heavy. They joined a weeping Mattie at the back of the wagon, and Becky took the old Negress' hand and tugged her along with them.

"Dear God," Calhoon said with a shake of his head. "Will this never end?" Then he swallowed and stuck out his hand. Seth took it. "How is she doing?" Calhoon asked.

Seth drew in a long breath. "Better," he said and looked for Hector. He found him already unloading trunks. "She'll be all right now that she's here."

*W*ithin the hour, Seth found Becky in the bedroom that he'd slept in night before last. Alice had told him that in happier times, Becky shared this room with her older sister Hannah. He knew she had more recently shared it with her mother. It would be theirs, he supposed, but he could hardly move in until they'd told Calhoon and Alice they'd wed — just this morning, in fact, by the justice of the peace in Madison. Seth had filed the license in Canton while Becky and Mattie packed trunks.

She turned with the click of the door closing. "Did you eat?"

"Yes," he said, and sat on the bed. "You need to get something, too."

"I will."

"I talked to your brother about sending Buck and Hector back over to Hickory Grove this week and moving the furniture out of the parson's house like you wanted. He said he would."

"Really, it belongs to the Mackey cousin —"

"Not the church?"

She pulled a book from a bottom drawer, then reached up to place it atop the dresser. "More than any one entity, I suppose, the Southern Church, but if not," she said, arranging the clothing inside the drawer, "certainly the cousin in Tennessee. As I understand it, Daddy Mackey furnished the place. That's why Theresa left everything when she returned to Alabama."

Becky stood. "You might consider me selfish, my darling, but should they come back, and I fear they might, I do not want those Northerners to get a thing in that place. We can keep the stuff here. I'll write the cousin and tell him."

"I don't think you're selfish. You wrote to Montgomery?"

"Yes, but I don't know what they can do. The Methodists in the North are waging a holy war against the South and the government is complicit."

"It's for the cousin to sort out, I reckon."

She picked up the book she'd found in the dresser drawer and absently thumbed through it before placing it beside a coal oil lamp. "Did you tell Eli?" she asked.

"About us, you mean?"

"Yes."

"I wanted to, but we said we'd keep it secret."

Finally a smile, and it was a sweet one, too. "And you don't think Eli would lie for you?"

"Two months ago, Eli and Alice made a habit of keeping secrets from each other. I'm pretty sure those days are behind them. If I tell Calhoon, he'll tell Alice. Did you tell Alice?"

She shook her head and started back toward him. "Did anyone see you come in here?"

"No."

"I guess we're going to have to tell them."

"If we want to share this bed, for sure." He pulled her onto his lap and kissed her behind the ear, and with a gentle sigh, she laid her head on his shoulder. "But we don't need to tell them today," he said, "because I won't be here tonight."

She sat up straight. "But it's our wedding night."

She'd said the words without conviction, and he kissed her quick. "We had our wedding night in Natchez. I need to get to Port Gibson. Your brother's not out of danger of arrest, and the same could be said of you. And so you know, your brother is now aware of the attack in Natchez." He situated her more comfortably on his lap. "We'll tell them about our nuptials in a day or two, when the news of Eliza's death won't be so raw."

Chapter Ninety-two

"What are you still doing here?" Seth asked.

Poynter Cummings was leaning back in his chair looking at the door, anticipating, Seth assumed, him peeking his head in.

"Waiting for you as a matter of fact."

Seth figured the time to be a little after seven in the evening, their shared spaces quiet, the glow of the lantern welcoming. The lamp was lit in his office, too. "Why?" he asked.

"To make sure you get all the facts. I'm not certain that you will."

Cummings' gaze followed Seth as he moved to the chair in front of Cummings' desk. Seth sat and the editor said, "Miller was here this afternoon late. He told Summers to let you know he'd seen the provost and intended to push the issue of Calhoon's arrest. Your boy Summers suggested that if Calhoon were still not made available, Miller might suggest Rebecca Mackey be substituted, because he suspected you'd grown overly fond of Mrs. Mackey and, given the option, you might be a bit quicker to act against Calhoon."

"Jubal told Miller that?"

"Yes, Parker, he did. That man is neither your friend nor loyal follower, not that he's a friend to anyone white, including Miller. The man has ambitions and it's not to make rank. Surely you've noticed?"

Seth's gut was churning. "I'm well aware of the dislike, but not the treachery."

"Yeah, well, you should be more attentive to betrayal, because things get worse. They talked a little too long, and Miller was still here when a Negro corporal from headquarters arrived with an urgent dispatch for you. The corporal insisted on giving it to you himself, but Summers pulled rank and intimidated the man into giving it to him. Said you were due back this evening and he'd pass it on. I don't need to tell you, I'm sure, that Miller wanted to see the missive also. A loud discussion ensued. I closed my own door so as not to draw attention to myself, but as you know, I can hear what transpires in that room. Summers seemed to be in the dark, but Miller apparently understood whatever was in that message, and Summers was plenty sore at Miller for not telling him what it was about." Cummings pursed his lips. "Got kinda ugly actually. Miller used some rather crude expletives in regards to the Negro race, but in his defense, Summers started it, then ended with a harangue about a Negro state in which no whites were allowed. Miller slammed the door on his way out. My impression was he was in a rush, the catalyst being that missive meant for you."

Seth rose from his chair and started for his office next door.

"Not in there," Cummings called after him, and Seth heard Cummings' chair creak as he rose.

"I searched earlier," Cummings said, appearing in the doorway to Seth's office as Seth reached for a drawer pull.

"I searched them all. Summers took it with him."

Seth slammed the drawer shut. Back to the hotel, then. He started to the door, and Cummings stepped out of his way. Seth asked, "Did you glean anything from their discussion about the actual content of the message?"

"Clem White's dead."

Seth spun around and stared at Cummings. "No details?"

"I don't have any."

Seth grabbed his kepi from the peg by the outer room's main door and turned. "Poynter," he said.

The man raised an eyebrow.

"Thanks for waiting."

*S*eth rapped on the door to Jubal's hotel room. It opened after a moment and Jubal Summers, his blouse and shoes off, looked him up and down. Irritated at the scrutiny, Seth bowled inside the room, surprising Jubal and forcing him back. "I understand you've assumed responsibility for my personal correspondence from headquarters," Seth said curtly.

Jubal blinked, then he lifted his blouse off a ladder-back chair and reached into an inside pocket. He handed Seth the opened envelope, which had been addressed specifically to Major Seth Parker. Seth, near rigid with anger, glared at his second in command, then pulled out the short missive from Malcolm.

"Missing details," it read, "but Tobias Holbein shot and killed Clem White late this afternoon at home of Judge Lawrence Pendleton. Pendleton told the provost it was a clear case of breaking and entering. Caruthers' oldest son was also in the house. Provost is keeping the matter confidential, per my request."

And there was a reason Malcolm wanted the incident kept quiet. He hadn't wanted Miller to learn of it. That meant Caruthers probably was unaware also. Now Jubal Summers had shown Miller the missive. Seth swallowed, and gathering every ounce of patience he could muster, he looked Jubal in the eye. "You opened my personal correspondence, and you shared this information with Miller."

"You weren't here. You were busy on personal matters, Major, sir."

Seth drew to full height, livid at the contempt in Jubal's voice. His captain continued, "Miller was in the office when the courier arrived. He's supposed to be working the case—"

"What case, Captain? You had no idea what was in that missive. It was personal to me. And as far as the shooting was concerned, do you know what the word 'confidential' means?"

Seth noted the workings of the man's jaw. "Where's Miller?" he asked.

"I believe he went to the livery."

"That's enlightening. You gave him everything I know. Did you get anything in return, because I can assure you he's the reason for 'confidential' being in this note? Answer me, dammit!"

"He seemed bothered, but wouldn't tell me anything."

"How long ago did he leave my office?"

Jubal said nothing and Seth bellowed, "How long?"

"About an hour."

"Any idea where he went?"

"He didn't say."

Sam Caruthers or Lawrence Pendleton.

"Rouse the sergeant. You two get up to Pendleton's—"

"It's night and I don't know—"

"You think you can find your way to Grand Gulf, mister?" Seth shouted at the man, now visibly strained. "Have the ship put you off at the Hennessy Bayou landing. There's a trail. About a mile up the bayou, that trail junctions the Vicksburg-Warrenton Road, and you're almost there. Pendleton's house is brick, four columns across the front. Ascertain, first, that Miller did not go there. Unless you run into some unforeseen trouble, continue to headquarters and report to Colonel Byrnes, who should be at his private quarters by now, what you found at Pendleton's place. I'll get Don Hemple to send a telegram to the colonel and let him know Miller's aware White is dead."

"Where are you going?"

He hesitated telling the man, but it was a reasonable question from his subordinate. "To the Caruthers' place. I'll put that in the telegram, too. By the time you get to Vicksburg, I hope to be on my way there myself. Miller has an hour on us, so get moving."

Jubal's lips curled into a sneer. "You actually think the Army is after Miller?"

"I think the Army has doubts about what Miller is up to and is trying to find answers. Your tipping him off has jeopardized that."

"You are the one who doesn't know what is happening here! Headquarters is filled with Southern sympathizers, all of them determined to retain the old order."

"Miller's words, Jubal? Pray tell why the hell would that be? They're trying to maintain order all right, but not the *old* order. Right now they've got their hands full maintaining any order at all, and Miller is a criminal feeding on chaos."

"I don't need Miller's words, I can think for myself, and I'm thinking chaos is what's needed right now, if we're ever to set things right."

"A cleansing, Jubal? As if there hasn't been enough of that over the past five years." No matter, Seth was done with Captain Summers. He'd just have to hope Miller's desperation was taking him to Caruthers, not Tobias Holbein in Warrenton. Truth was he had no idea what Jubal Summers had unleashed by sharing with Miller the fact that Clem White had been shot at Pendleton's home.

"You are relieved, Captain Summers. You are to report to Colonel Byrnes in the morning. Your unit wanted you back anyway. Now, I'm happy to oblige."

Jubal laughed in apparent disbelief. "You can't—"

"The hell I can't. You're confined to quarters tonight. You be out of here at first light. Direct to Vicksburg, do you understand? Or I swear I'll have your ass court-martialed for disobedience of a direct order."

Seth stepped into the hall and bellowed Kushing's name. A door opened two rooms down.

"Sir?"

"You've got guard duty tonight, Sergeant. Captain Summers is confined to quarters until daybreak at which time you are to escort him to headquarters in Vicksburg. If he refuses to return to headquarters, you are not to interfere with him, but confirm his intentions not to do so, then report first to the county provost, then to me, if you can find me. I'll brief the provost."

"Yes, sir."

Jubal stood in the open door. He heard every word. The ploy was to ensure Jubal did indeed return to Vicksburg. Hell, Don Hemple might even lend him a man if Jubal made trouble. He didn't think Jubal would try to team up with Miller, they were at odds now, but he couldn't trust that for certain.

The dutiful sergeant stepped back inside his room to retrieve his blouse and boots, both of which he pulled on in the hallway. Seth shut Jubal's door, then made a quick stop in his own room before leaving the hotel. He could only guess that Clem White's attempt to break into the Pendleton house had something to do with Tobias Holbein's presence there. Seth had little doubt that Holbein knew where all that money was, but the first thing he wanted to check was the people at Camellia Creek, and removing the issue of Calhoon's guard would give him some flexibility regarding his new brother-in-law. He had more to arrange with Don Hemple than a telegram to Malcolm.

Chapter Ninety-three

"What are you doing?" Seth asked Calhoon, who'd reentered the parlor, cavalry boots in hand.

"I'm going with you," he said, and sat down on the settee next to Alice, who simply stared at her husband. "I figured you anticipated that, and that's why you got rid of my guard."

"I got rid of your guard because I didn't want him subject to a bullying Treasury agent who might show up here attempting to talk to you, and the guard not knowing any better."

Alice still wasn't saying anything. Calhoon looked at her, then returned his attention to his boot.

On Alice's other side, Becky rose slowly from the settee. First boot on, Calhoon again glanced at his wife. "I've got to go with him, honey. I can tell you're dead set against it, but I know that trail to Muscatine like the back of my hand, and he's gonna need help."

"And what about beyond Muscatine?" Becky said.

"Moon's three-quarters full and will be up for a few more hours, at least." Calhoon looked over Alice's head, to the new parlor windows. "Clear night, too. Shouldn't be any trouble seeing the road."

"You're not as familiar with the road beyond Muscatine." Becky, wide-eyed, looked to Seth. "Wait till morning."

"He could be there and back here by morning," Seth said. He turned to Calhoon. "But I don't like leaving them here alone."

"Trying to dissuade me, Parker? Humoring my wife and little sister? You said yourself you're not sure where Miller went or if he's even up to anything. Besides, our womenfolk won't be alone. Buck and Hector will be on guard." Calhoon stood and pushed his second heel into his cavalry boot, then straightened. "There's no way I can let you go off into Caruthers' territory alone, not in good conscience. I think you're right about Miller and Caruthers working together on this, but you yourself said Toby is the key. I'm still not sure we wouldn't be better off going to Pendleton's and finding out what that shooting was about this afternoon. If Toby knows something about the money..." Calhoon looked at Becky. "We *don't* know anything about that money, do we?"

Becky rolled her eyes, and Seth cursed himself for leaving Kushing with Jubal. He needed him. "Are you sure you can ride for any length of time with that wound in your belly?"

"The rib and the pelvis are the problems, not the belly, but if I prove more trouble than I'm worth, I'll stop and let you go on alone."

$\mathcal{I}$t was going on nine when they left. Calhoon had taken a quiet Alice in his arms. They embraced, then kissed. Seth had watched a moment, then turned to find Becky near his side. He pulled her to him. She was in her nightgown and robe—the household had all been about to retire when he'd rode back in nearly an hour ago. The kiss he gave Becky, and she'd returned, had been a passionate one full of promise and hope and worry, pregnant with fear it might be their last. When they moved apart, he turned to find Calhoon and Alice watching them. Seth said nothing. He stepped back, then reached for the kepi he'd set on the dining room table when he arrived. "Let's go," he said to Calhoon, and then he was out the back door.

They moved out fast, Seth following Calhoon, who did know the trail well, though with the bright moon and a clear night, Seth didn't think he'd have had any trouble following it. They made the Big Black in under three-quarters of an hour, the water shimmering beneath the waxing moon that still hung well above the western tree line. The river was up with the spring freshets and the ferry was on the other side, but they opted to pull it back rather than swim the horses across this narrow expanse of river. A swim might have proved dangerous in the dark.

"What exactly are your intentions regarding my sister?" Calhoon finally asked when they'd secured the raft on the other side. Seth almost laughed. He knew damn good and well the man had been wanting to ask him that for the past hour. His curiosity had finally worn him down. Seth put his foot in the stirrup and pulled himself into Boon's saddle. "Well, Eli, I tell ya, I've been in love with your sister since the spring of 1863."

Eli, back in the saddle himself, pulled up alongside him, and Seth made out his face in the silver glow of the moon. There were beads of sweat on the other man's forehead, and Seth swore his walking had been marked with a hunker in addition to the limp.

"Well, *Seth*," Eli said, "I think she kinda likes you, too, but what are your intentions?"

Seth looked away, squinted at the dark, tree-shrouded road ahead, then back to Eli. "We wed this morning in Madison. I wanted it done quickly, wanted her protected by my uniform. We didn't tell you and Alice because—"

"Of Eliza."

"It wasn't a fit time for a wedding, but I didn't want to wait."

"I hope you didn't try to convince her with that 'protection in a blue uniform' argument."

"Not in those exact words, no, but like you said, she kinda likes me."

"Hmm." Then Eli stuck out his hand. "Congratulations."

"Thanks," Seth said, and shook his new brother-in-law's hand.

Eli nodded toward the road. "Well, hell, shall we mosey on up the road to your encumbered farm?"

*I*t wasn't too long a mosey from that point, half an hour at a canter. The main house was dark, as it should have been. A good hundred yards beyond loomed the shadow of that fine barn where Robert Kushing had found Mark Dicks' murder site. Just to the west sat the cabin that years ago belonged to Uncle Seamus' overseer, Eli told him, the place where Jessie and his daughter Lettie now lived.

The dog started barking before they'd made it as far as the deserted main house, and shortly after a light had gone on in the more distant cabin. After a moment, a man's voice hollered "Who's der?" into the night. That disturbed both him and Eli, made clear by the latter's soft curse, because the times demanded discretion, not bellowing at unseen threats in the dark.

"It's Eli, Uncle Jess."

"Ohhyee," the man cried back. "Git yo'se'f on ovah heah, boy. Thought we was nevah gonna lay eyes on you ag'in."

"Here," Seth said, "give me the reins, and I'll water the horses. I'm glad we roused 'im. You need a break."

Seth headed to the barn. Behind him he heard the glad shouts of the old man and the happy squeal of the girl, asking Eli when Miz Becky was comin' home.

*I*n the warm glow of the lamp inside the cabin, Eli looked Jessie and Lettie over. They were dressed.

"What are y'all doin' up? It's gotta be after eleven."

Jessie closed the door and motioned Eli into a chair. "Lettie jus' got in from da kitchen. We gittin' all kinds a visits dis night."

"Who?"

"Trez'ry man. You comin' from Camellia Creek?"

Eli's belly had been hurting him, and he'd hoped to relax a bit in Bo Collins' old rocking chair. "Yes. He was headin' north?"

"No, suh. He be headin' south. He headed nawth way befo' suppa time, but he didn't want no suppa den. 'Stead, he stops back by jus' a bit ago. Dawg already rousted me an' da girl from bed, so he asks 'er if'n der be food lef', an' she fix't 'im a plate."

"We should've passed him."

"Sho' should've if you be headin' nawth."

Eli rose. "He must have heard us coming and hid off the trail."

Looking a bit nervous now, Uncle Jessie rose, too. "Dat Millah fella come by early yesta'day afta'noon wif da younger Caruthers boy. Dey was on der way to Pawt Gibson. Den dis afta'noon, like I say'd, back comes Millah, den back he come goin' da otha way jus' a little bit ago."

Eli had his pistol, but his rifle was on Johnny. "Uncle," he said, and nodded to the rifle Jessie had stood by the fireplace when they came in, "that ole Dickert rifle of Uncle Seamus still shoot?"

"Sho do. Good, too. Gots me a fox tryin' to get in da coop night befo' las'."

"It's ready to go?" Eli said, moving toward it.

Jessie picked it up and handed it to him. "Been ready since da spring a' '63."

*S*eth pushed Boon at the shoulder. He stood between the two horses, them vying for the narrow trough outside the barn. The darn stupid beasts had nigh squashed him. Boon lumbered to one side, swishing his tail, and Eli's Johnny stepped closer, nudging Seth into Boon. Seth had just raised a hand to Johnny, when he heard a click so soft as to be barely perceptible.

He squatted as he spun, but his equilibrium shattered when a rifle shot rent the night. A second gunshot echoed the first in tandem with a flash of fire, downward, not twenty feet from him. Seth curled his body, hands over head, as both horses wheeled away, and Johnny knocked him over in his haste to overtake Boon. On the ground, Seth heard the beating of their hooves above the beating of his own heart, and somewhere in the distance, the sound of the blasts still ringing in his ears, Seth heard Eli Calhoon's voice calling, "It's me, Seth, it's me."

The shots, the shouts, and the dark, not to mention nearly being trampled, left Seth short of breath and generally confused. He rose on weak knees, his wrist aching. In his right hand, he held his Colt, but couldn't remember drawing it. "What the devil?" he asked himself, watching Eli's shadow kneel beside a dark form on the ground.

"Dead," Eli said and looked Seth's way. "Son of a bitch was about to shoot you in the back."

Seth moved closer as Jessie, lantern in hand, bounded up behind Eli. Eli reached over and retrieved the dead man's pistol, still in the would-be assassin's grasp. The scene was well-lit now.

The girl Lettie burst into the circle and grasped her daddy's arm. Eli rose, then bent and flipped the dead man on his back.

"Walter Miller," Seth said, and Eli looked up at him.

"Yep, well, it looks like you finally caught me red-handed killing a Treasury agent."

Seth blinked at him, then at Eli's weapon.

"You all right?" Eli had resumed a serious tone.

"'Bout the only thing I can say for myself is this time I didn't shit my pants." He looked at Eli. "How did you know?"

"Uncle Jessie said he'd just come through, headed south. We should have passed him. It was a foregone conclusion he'd heard us comin', doubled back, and was out here plannin' to bushwhack you."

Seth stepped forward and took the rifle from Eli, then laughed. "I was saved by a Kentucky rifle?"

Eli nodded at the rifle. "Best weapon ever made as far as I'm concerned. Andrew and I learned to shoot using that antique."

Seth looked up the small rise from where Eli had taken his shot in the dark and said, "Looks like you learned pretty damn good, too. Eighty yards?"

"Nah, I stumbled halfway down. Probably no more than sixty or seventy."

In the light of a near full moon, no less. "How did you know for sure you weren't aimin' at me?"

"Us Johnny Rebs can make out a face in the dark at a thousand yards."

"Yeah, and fight ten men to your one."

"Correct. Unfortunately we were required to fight twenty."

Seth frowned at him, and Eli said, "All right, maybe not all us Rebs can make out a face in the dark at a thousand yards, but when we're shootin' at shadows, we can tell the difference in one belonging to a man who's six foot seven and one that's five nine."

"I'm only six foot three and Miller was close to six foot."

"What can I say? The chances were fifty-fifty I'd get it right."

Seth snorted, then stuck out his hand. "All bullshit aside, it was a darn good shot. Thank you."

"This make us even now?"

"We're keepin' score?"

"Not from here on out, I reckon." Eli looked from him to the dead man, then back to Uncle Jessie and young Lettie before settling on Seth. "I was hopin' we'd be about done with this game, but Uncle Jessie has pointed out to me that we still have a problem."

Chapter Ninety-four

Turned out to be more than a problem. It was a dilemma. With Miller's attempt to murder Seth, there were no lingering doubts in Seth's mind as to Miller's role in the theft of the money from Treasury. Sam Caruthers' role was also substantiated. Holbein's role remained obscure. Eli swore the man would never have betrayed his father, and Seth didn't believe Holbein had ever been at odds with Isabel.

So, where to now? Find Caruthers, Holbein at Pendleton's, or return to Camellia Creek and confirm their assumption that Wilson Caruthers would make no move until he'd heard from Miller. They had to assume that Miller and Wilson had come to Port Gibson yesterday with some specific plan in mind. Learning White had been killed over in Warrenton had required a change in plan, sending Miller back up to Sam. Plan revised, Miller had started back south to team up with Wilson. Theoretically, with Miller dead, Seth and Eli should have all the time in the world, but assumptions often prove hazardous.

Seth left a note for Malcolm and a couple of one-dollar greenbacks with Jessie, asking him to deliver the message along with Miller's body as soon as there was good light. Eli assured him Jessie was reliable. In the missive, he explained the circumstances of Walter Miller's demise. The man had been shot in the back, after all. He also told him there was now enough evidence to bring Sam Caruthers into headquarters for questioning. He'd wait to hear on that—Malcolm might yet tell him to go over and interrogate Sam Caruthers at his farm rather than have army personnel bring the man in.

Chapter Ninety-five

Becky opened her eyes with the rattle of the door. Lantern light crept eerily across her quilt. Though she'd tried, she had not been able to sleep.

"Are you awake?" Alice asked.

Becky sat up. "Has something happened?"

"Nothing," Alice assured her, and Becky relaxed. "I can't sleep. Even if our concerns all prove for naught, Eli shouldn't be out. He's not sat a horse since the beginning of January, and he's not recovered, Becky."

"I know." Becky rose and bade Alice place the lantern on the table beside the bed, then sit. In the wake of a warm day, the room, closed off from perceived threats outside, had become oppressive. Now, Alice's companionship, along with the warm glow of the lamp, comforted Becky enough that she opened one of the floor to ceiling windows. A cool breeze washed over her. "I'm frightened sick," she told Alice.

"I couldn't help but notice, nor did it escape your brother's attention that your relationship with Seth Parker has changed."

"I've decided to be happy again." The breeze proved a wee bit cooler than Becky expected, and she pulled on her wrapper before sitting by Alice on the bed. "What time is it?" she asked.

"Nearly two. We shouldn't expect them back tonight, do you think?"

"No, I think Seth plans to go to Vicksburg and find out what he can about that shooting in Warrenton."

The door creaked. Becky's heart skipped, and she looked up into a darkly shadowed face she was certain belonged to one of the Caruthers boys. Beside her, Alice gasped.

531

"And how much does Eli know about it, Rebecca?" the man said. He shut the door behind him.

"Wilson?"

"It's been a few years, but I'd know you anywhere, too. You favor your mother."

Becky rose slowly. Alice would have, too, but Wilson drew a handgun from inside his frock coat. "Stay where you are"—he cocked his head—"Mrs. Alice Calhoon, I believe?"

Becky, throat dry and heart palpitating, said, "You don't need that thing, put it away." She stepped in front of Alice, who immediately pushed at her to get her out of the way.

Wilson shouted for them to be still, then motioned to Becky with the barrel of his gun. "Step away from her so I can see what she's doing."

Becky did not move. "What do you want?"

"I'd hoped to speak to your brother...or mine. Has Cole been here?"

Becky frowned. "It was my understanding Cole was in New York."

"Cole has been back in the area since last fall, and I believe both you and your brother are aware of that. Y'all knew it before Daddy did."

"Why would we know before...did your brother not return from England with you?"

"You might not be aware of that, but my brother preceded my return to Mississippi by almost three years. Against our father's wishes, I should add, which has resulted in a bit of an estrangement within the family."

"I am sorry to hear that."

He laughed. "Don't be. Just give me the details of what y'all have planned."

"What we've...planned?"

He grabbed Becky roughly by the arm and shoved her to one side of Alice. "Quit being coy. Where is Eli?"

Becky rubbed her arm. "He's gone to talk to your father."

"Hah!"

Becky glanced at Alice, wide-eyed, watching the intruder. She was scared. So was Becky.

"Does he know what Holbein received?"

"I beg your pardon?"

"Holbein received something by courier a couple of days ago, Rebecca," he enunciated slowly. "What was it, and who sent it?"

"Is that what the man shot in Warrenton was trying to find out?" Alice asked.

A frown furrowed Wilson's forehead, and he contemplated Alice, before returning his gaze to Becky.

"You damn well know it's as much ours as it is the Calhoons'. My dad worked that thing long after Holland washed his hands of it. The claim was legitimate. It would have been stupid to give it up."

Becky licked her bottom lip. "Defrauding the other claimants isn't legitimate."

The man's face darkened. "What did Holbein do with that money?"

"I've never discussed the claim with him. I didn't even realize what all this was about until recently."

"I can almost believe that. Holland's little bastard wouldn't have been privy to it. Guthrie dug up your name by accident, but he always knew about Eli. Oh," he said, shaking his head with feigned sorrow, "but your mother.... That idiot Guthrie went to her searching for Eli, and that's where the real damage was done. He'd clued the beautiful, pragmatic, and deviously smart Isabel Hays to the fact that something was amiss. After Guthrie was killed, Cole filled in the gaps for her, you do realize."

"Is that why you killed her?"

"Her death was an accident. She came upon Mark Dicks searching her room. He tried to take the gun away from her, and it went off."

Becky blinked back tears and stiffened her spine. "But you'd have had to kill her then anyway, because she knew what you were up to."

"She already knew, and we knew she knew. Oh, she didn't

know we had Dicks working there. True, that advantage would have been lost to us, but we wouldn't have killed her for knowing about him. We couldn't kill her. Dad's figured for a while now that she knew what happened to the money."

At the foot of the bed, Alice stirred, and Wilson Caruthers, the gun unsteady in his hand, turned on her. "Do you want to live to give birth to that baby, Mrs. Calhoon? Because I can assure you I don't give a damn one way or the other."

Becky, blood rushing to her head now, reached out a hand. Wilson's failing composure could make him more dangerous still. "Don't move, Alice."

"Yes, don't," Wilson mimicked and turned the gun on Becky. "Where is the money?"

"I have no idea." She wondered if he were here alone, but quickly surmised that he must be. A cohort would have made an appearance by now.

Wilson emitted a sound somewhere between a laugh and a snarl. "You are wearing heavily on my patience, cousin. We know Holbein and your mother...and my damn brother were all working to get that money, but Daddy is the one who had the guts and the brains to get it out of Treasury. I'll be damned before I let you people rob him."

Becky resisted the urge to look at Alice.

"Why in the world," Becky asked, "would Cole be working with us?"

He snorted. "Oh, Rebecca, haven't you heard? Cole and Eli are lieutenants in an organization dedicated to the continuance of the South's struggle against the Union."

Alice rose. "That's not—"

"Alice," Becky cried, "sit down. It's a tale he and his friends have concocted to hide the truth."

Despite Becky's interruption, and much to her dismay, Wilson pointed the gun at Alice anyway, the same place he directed his wrath. "My brother," he snarled, "doesn't want our Daddy to have the money."

"Because your father is a traitor to the South and to the

Republic," Becky spat, hoping he'd turn the wavering barrel from Alice, but it was only his gaze that shifted targets.

"I don't want to get nasty, Rebecca, but I'm going to give you one more chance to fess up about that money, then I'm going to shoot your brother's pregnant bride."

Becky glanced at Alice, whose pale countenance was riveted on the man.

A floorboard groaned behind her. Wilson's eyes shifted a scant instant before his hand holding the gun jerked toward the sound.

"Git down, Miz Becky!"

*T*he moon sank lower as Seth and Eli headed south, no longer providing the light it had when they'd ridden north. During the trip back, the two men had fed off each other's anxiety, pushing their mounts as hard as feasible along the dark road to Camellia Creek, and Seth suspected Eli was in pain.

Now, lights in the house despite the late hour, they'd consoled one another with the expressed belief that the women had been unable to sleep from worrying over them. Still, Seth wasn't going to feel at ease until he held Becky in his arms.

In the quiet darkness of Camellia Creek's nearly completed barn, pleasant with the scent of new wood, a gingerly moving Eli Calhoon lit a lantern. Immediately, Seth growled for him to put it out.

"Get the doors," he said to Eli, now struggling in the commanded darkness. But he did get them shut.

Seth struck a match, then squatted beside a man lying on the ground. Eli limped up beside him, squatted, then relit the lamp. "Hector."

Seth felt the man's head, then pulled his hand back, sticky with blood.

Eli laid his ear on Hector's chest. "He's got a heartbeat," he said, rising awkwardly and retrieving his rifle from his gear. Seth rose, too, and wiped his hand on his pants.

"You go around front," he said to Eli, "I'll take the back." Eli nodded and started to the front of the barn. Seth was following him out when a shotgun blast shattered the quiet night.

Covering her head with her arms, Becky dropped to the floor, as did Alice, and a blast ripped the room apart, throwing Wilson Caruthers backwards against Hannah's upholstered chair, and sending both crashing to the floor. Ears ringing and body shaking, Becky started to rise. She looked first at Alice, also rising, then around to see Buck step through the man-high window, reloading his shotgun as he came.

He snapped the barrel in place and pulled Becky, who'd been in his line of fire, to her feet, then pushed Alice behind him and cautiously approached the prone Wilson. Buck kicked the chair off him and rolled the body over with his booted foot. "Good."

Alice had moved beside her, and Becky pulled her close as Buck turned to them. "It's all right. He dead."

Now Becky was aware of Pearl's wails from above, and she extricated herself from Alice to go into the hallway and shout up the stairs.

With Mattie's confirmation that she and Pearl were all right, Becky turned to Buck and hugged him without a word.

"Foun' Hector on da flo' a' da bahn when I come to spell 'im. Knew somethin' be bad wrong."

"He's hurt?"

"Yes'm."

Becky picked up speed as she started down the hall to the back door.

Seth saw the back door open, then Becky running across the porch and down the steps as if the devil were at her heels. He braced to see who followed her. Alice, then Buck, and he relaxed. He called to Buck, who held a shotgun, before catching Becky in the yard and pulling her into his arms.

"Eli," he yelled, "we're in the back."

Chapter Ninety-six

Midmorning. Seth had gotten maybe a couple of hours sleep. Becky, he was certain, hadn't slept at all, waiting by Hector's side until Buck had fetched poor Ephraim Lester from town once again. They'd been careful in moving Hector, but the doc said he wished they'd left him prone on the floor of the barn. Head injuries were such precarious things. Nevertheless, Hector had come around about nine that morning, head splitting and throwing up, but he knew his name, knew where he was, and he knew every face they brought in front of him. The doctor pronounced him on the mend, told him to stay in bed, and ordered him to keep his head still. After sharing breakfast with Seth — Eli was sleeping and Alice had snuck in with him — the doctor pronounced Wilson Caruthers good and dead. Seth had kissed Becky, told her the cat was out of the bag — she seemed too exhausted to comprehend what he'd said — then he and Dr. Lester had loaded Wilson Caruthers' shrouded body in the buckboard and, along with Buck, they'd set out for the Claiborne County sheriff's office.

After discussing the killing with the sheriff, he'd informed the provost of events. There was a telegram from Malcolm waiting for him on Don Hemple's desk, Hemple having been unable to find anyone but Poynter Cummings at the newspaper office. The missive — "S. Caruthers dead. Details lacking. Will advise when informed" — had been sent during the wee hours this morning, prior to Malcolm's receiving anything from Seth. Seth had looked at Don Hemple, who shrugged, then the two of them had gained access to Wilson Caruthers' hotel room, but they found nothing prejudicial to the man or his father.

Back at Camellia Creek by noon, he and Eli listened to Becky relate Wilson's comments regarding, most interestingly, his older brother, Cole Terry Caruthers.

Seth had just finished a late lunch with Eli and was on his second cup of coffee when Sergeant Kushing found him. The sergeant had accompanied Jubal Summers to Vicksburg as ordered, and he had in hand a longer missive from Malcolm responding to the one Seth had sent him that morning by Uncle Jessie.

Sam Caruthers was dead, that he knew. What he hadn't known was the man had been dead since ten o'clock the night before. That's when Mrs. Caruthers had been awakened by a pistol shot. She found her husband in his office. The coroner had identified the bullet as coming from a .22 caliber gun, doubtlessly a derringer. It had entered Caruthers' head right between the eyes. The man had died instantly.

Eli stood beside Seth, reading Malcolm's missive along with him. Seth looked at Eli, and Eli at him. Eli said "Toby" at the same time Seth said "Holbein."

Chapter Ninety-seven

"Come in, gentlemen," Tobias Holbein said. "I figured you'd beat me back here before breakfast, Parker, and you, Eli, are a most unexpected pleasure. Miss Alice finally let you out of the house?"

"I broke out last night," Eli answered. "I figure I've set my convalescence back about six weeks."

Holbein laughed, then looked at the servant who'd escorted them to this now familiar parlor in Tobias Holbein's modest farmhouse. "Thank you, Irene. Please close the door and ensure we're not disturbed." Holbein eyed Eli, who took a chair in a familiar manner, then slid his gaze to Seth. "You do have Miller?"

"He's dead," Eli answered. "I shot him last night while he was taking aim on Becky's new groom."

Tobias Holbein grinned broadly at Seth, who'd yet to take a seat. "Congratulations, Major. You are, I presume, the lucky groom?" Holbein rose and started for the commode near the cold fireplace. "This calls for a celebratory drink."

It was a lovely late afternoon, quite warm, but Holbein's parlor was comfortably cool. Seth took the matching wing chair next to Eli while Toby poured three tumblers of whisky. "Has Wilson Caruthers turned up anywhere? I am a bit worried about him."

"He's dead, too," Seth said. "One of Eli's servants killed him after he broke into Camellia Creek in the wee hours of this morning and threatened Alice and Becky with a handgun."

Holbein looked away. "Pity that. He was so young and it was Sam who...well, it doesn't matter now. It will be hard on Alma, but with his father gone, Cole will move home." Holbein looked at Eli. "No repercussions for the freedman?"

"It was Buck, and no, a clear case of self-defense."

"I met Cole when I visited Lawrence Pendleton a few days ago," Seth said to Holbein. "He introduced himself to me as Cole Terry. Seems he's dropped his stepfather's name. I know he was an operative, and I'm assuming he had a role in all this. I'd sure like some clarification."

"His role was small, but critical. Cole spent all of 1864 and half of '65 in solitary confinement in a Union prison in upstate New York."

"So much for sitting out the war in England," Eli said.

"Cole came back in '62," Seth said. "He joined Confederate service in Virginia, then returned to Mississippi as an operative. He was captured in the early fall of 1863."

Eli frowned, and Holbein said, "His father sacrificed him for special favors. Sam argued he would make it up to him after the war was over, that Cole would find it all worth it. And, of course, Cole was not to be hurt. Never mind his leg being broken during his capture, not to mention Sam didn't receive any word on his condition for the next year and a half. He didn't know whether he was dead or alive. Cole was an army prisoner."

"And in return, Sam got...?"

"Petersen's aid in trying to recover that 1863 congressional letter sent to your father," Seth told Eli. "Petersen arranged with Martin Trueblood for the military raids on Camellia Creek and Hickory Grove."

"Peter Franklin's cousin was part of this?"

"Not directly," Seth answered. "Trueblood introduced Sam to Petersen. That's the liaison Sam really wanted. In return for the introduction, Sam allegedly identified farms for raids that would produce large quantities of baled cotton awaiting sale on the black market. Petersen validated the operational necessity. He, of course, wasn't after cotton, but a Confederate operative. Petersen got his operative. Sam didn't recover the letter because they bungled the raid at Camellia Creek, and Naomi Polk found it—something Sam Caruthers didn't realize until after the raid on Hickory Grove."

Eli looked from Seth to Holbein. "Sam thought Becky had the letter?"

"By that time, she was the only known heir in the vicinity," Holbein said. "The fact they took extreme measures against what was basically a houseful of innocent women was unimportant. The use of such tactics against Camellia Creek was no more justified. But then I would argue Lincoln's war was uncalled for in its entirety.

"Burning Hickory Grove increased the chances the letter would be destroyed. Emily Mackey made that suggestion—and that's pure speculation on my part—an easy one to carry out. I would be willing to bet that had Hannah not been sick, Camellia Creek would have met the same fate and for the same reason."

Eli, his face dark, said nothing.

"Yeah," Seth said, "it takes a lot of finesse to run a sloppy war. Anyway, Trueblood didn't get his cotton because there was none. It was simply a ploy on Caruthers' part to seduce the man into teaming him up with Petersen. Trueblood considered himself used, and his subsequent buying of land along Caruthers' proposed right-of-way was his way of getting even and his due. He knew nothing of the claim. Peter Franklin knew nothing about the raids or the interrogation of Becky. He was nowhere around. He came to Mississippi at his cousin's request after the war to speculate in land."

Eli leaned back in his chair. "As long as I can manage to steer clear of Trueblood, I should be okay. Having to keep away from Peter Franklin might have proved a problem."

"And it all proved for naught. Sam didn't get the letter and lost a son to boot. Cole is a dedicated Southerner," Holbein said, "more so now than ever. He thought the man who raised him was, too. Sam was already dealing cotton on the Mississippi with Northern agents by the time Cole got home. That was months before Vicksburg fell. Sam knew some pretty unsavory people and had made some prejudicial alliances, which Cole believed his father cultivated for information. Cole in turn passed that information to his seniors. The intelligence was good early on. He began to doubt his father's dedication to the Cause, however, after Grant crossed the river. He probably should have developed doubts before that, but what son would? On two separate occasions the information he passed to his Confederate handlers proved faulty and men died. Cole underwent some strenuous questioning from his own side at that point. At the same time, his seniors told him things about his father's activities that he hadn't known. After that, he took to searching his father's office rather than use the information Sam passed to him openly. He also took to eavesdropping outside open windows. Tables had turned by late summer and the United States Army realized it had a problem, which, in turn, it traced back to Sam.

"For the purposes of our mystery, Cole met Miller at his father's house, and as an adjunct to Cole's snooping, he became aware of the claim and the letter I had sent to Congress that summer asking the claim be reviewed. Cole was equally aware of his father's chagrin when Congress responded to all claimants instead of only me, exposing my work on the claim. Holland believed himself duped and was angry." Holbein gave Eli a stern look. "I made my peace with your father. Like him, I never believed that claim would be paid. I continued to work it for the Carutherses because they asked me to, and I'd have made certain the Calhoons got their part if it ever amounted to anything.

"But truth be told, Sam's chagrin was justified. He needed that letter back because by that time he did intend to cut out not only the Calhoons, but also me of my ten percent. Between the time I sent my letter and Congress responded, Sam had forged a new alliance with a devil who had a hand inside Treasury's vault, or would as soon as he managed his transfer back to Washington. In return, Walter Miller wanted the Calhoon share of the principal and interest. I was not aware of what they were up to until this past September when I received a letter resolving the claim and authorizing me to act on behalf of the McGowan estate.

"To say I was surprised would be an understatement, and that final sum was laughable to the point that I simply did not believe any of it. We'd decided after that uproar with the Galphin claim not to sue for the interest, and here I had in my hand a letter that said this claim had been paid *with* interest.

"I almost went up there to let Sam know what I'd received, then thought better of it. The receipt of that letter left a niggling suspicion in the back of my mind, and I wondered if he was behind it somehow. I decided to wait and see what happened. I sealed up the letter and asked Isabel to put it in her safe. Then a couple of weeks later, Guthrie shows up looking for the thing.

"I told him I didn't have it. He was adamant that I did, but I insisted he produce proof that I had such a letter. He couldn't, which made me suspicious of him, because I certainly had received the thing, and if he were legitimate he should have been able to produce evidence against me. Failing with me, he started searching for the Calhoons and the Carutherses. Certainly he had seen something implicating the lot of us.

"He got wind of Isabel, either through Naomi, Laura, or that newspaper man in Port Gibson, Cummings. That was Isabel's first inkling something was amiss. In the meantime, Guthrie visited Sam, who wasn't home at the time. Alma talked to him. It was she who told Guthrie where he could find Cole.

"Shortly after I'd had the pleasure of meeting Guthrie, Sam approached me. He'd been advised by Miller that the letter authorizing action for the McGowan estate had been mailed to me, not to Sam. Miller had apparently directed the authorization letter be sent to Sam. He never did explain how he messed that up, don't even know if he knew, but their having been found out, Sam confessed that back in '63, he'd partnered with Miller to spirit that money out of Treasury. The authorization now having gone astray, they were compelled to bring me back into the plot."

Holbein smiled, then took a sip of his whiskey. "I must commend myself on my machinations. I told Sam I hadn't received the authorization and asked if Miller could prove it had actually gone out. I had them between a rock and a hard place. Sam had no way of knowing if the letter had gone out as Miller claimed, and Miller couldn't be sure I hadn't received the thing and now Sam and I were conspiring against him or if I were acting alone.

"Unbeknownst to me at the time, Guthrie found Cole, who knew what Guthrie was talking about, but he feigned complete ignorance. Guthrie's subsequent murder piqued Cole's interest, and he approached Cummings in Port Gibson, who had been editorializing mercilessly in his paper about the murder. Then, Eli not being home, Cole went to Isabel whom he'd liked since he was a little kid. She took what Cole told her and put it together with Guthrie's threats and innuendo, then took it upon herself to violate my trust and see what I'd squirreled away in her safe." Holbein looked at Eli. "Then you came home."

Seth rubbed his chin. "I'd like to know about the claim itself."

"It is the Robert McGowan claim," Toby said. "It's not a big secret. It's been presented off and on before disinterested and hostile Congresses since it was first drafted in 1807. And no, it was not I who drew it up, but my mentor, who briefed me on it twenty-one years later in 1828. I was still a young man then and an even younger lawyer.

"It was a good claim, as justified, in my opinion, as Galphin's, if not more so. The principal was twelve thousand dollars, and when it was submitted thirty years after the incident, the interest on the claim was already large, but still would have been manageable if the United States Government had paid it at the time, but it didn't. Decades later, the Galphin claim over in Georgia left a bad taste in Holland's mouth. He'd have been content with the principal, but he drew the line at the excess of all that interest. But the Caruthers clan did not want to withdraw the suit, so I didn't withdraw it. During the years of a Whig congress I didn't pursue it, nor were our Democratic representatives eager to present it, so for years after the Galphin fiasco, I let it lie." Holbein looked at Seth and grinned. "But that didn't answer your real question, did it? You want to know what it was for, don't you?"

"I am curious."

"Are you aware of the James Willing Raid?"

"Generally."

"Then suffice it to say that, in 1777, the Continental Congress financed a river-borne offensive against British West Florida led by a Pennsylvanian who had previously resided in the Natchez area. James Willing and his pirates came down the Mississippi, plundering every British plantation they came upon. Just south of the Big Black stood the home of a wealthy British planter who had emigrated here in 1766. His young wife died within the first two years, and he remarried a wealthy French widow by the name of Claudette Benet. She didn't live long, and by 1770 we find him married to Claudine Maignon, another widow of substantial means. Between his British grant and his wives' holdings, George Robert McGowan had acquired substantial property.

"The Benet woman died leaving McGowan no issue, but she did leave a two-year-old daughter by her first husband. The Maignon woman gave him two sons and another daughter, Sarah Michelle. Both boys died before they reached adulthood, but at the time of James Willing's raid there were four of them, McGowan and his wife, his young stepdaughter, Cecilia, and a three-year-old boy. McGowan himself was not present when James Willing's pirates landed—and this is critical to the validity of the McGowan claim—he was in New Orleans, passing information to Oliver Pollack regarding a shipment of naval stores from the Natchez district meant for the Royal Navy. Spanish ships, sailing covertly under the American flag and manned by, nominally, American crews were able, based on McGowan's information, to intercept that shipment and divert it in support of the American cause.

"The Natchez district was for the most part Tory in its sympathies, but the Maignons were French Huguenot and Robert McGowan, much smitten with his beautiful wife and himself Scots-Irish, identified, discreetly, with the American cause. Willing plundered the plantation, burned the man's barn and inadvertently, or so he claimed, set fire to the McGowan house, which burned to the ground."

"McGowan's family?" Seth asked.

"Unharmed, but for being left homeless."

"And the two daughters...?" It was all too obvious where this was headed.

"Cecilia Benet McGowan—he legally adopted her—wed a Pepper when she was sixteen. Her only surviving child, a daughter, wed a neighbor, David Caruthers, somewhere around the turn of the century. Caruthers was a young Revolutionary soldier from North Carolina. He and his bride settled on his soldier's grant southeast of Vicksburg. His property bordered on that of his father-in-law."

Eli shifted in his seat and said, "Meanwhile, back at the old homestead, my grandmother, Mary Ellen Price, the only surviving child of James Price and Sarah Michele McGowan, wed a South Carolina émigré, Angus Calhoon."

"Your grandfather," Seth stated. "So there's really no common blood between you and Caruthers."

"There is not," Eli said, "but there are the common holdings from the female line descending from Robert McGowan. Daddy regarded the Carutherses' claim through the Benets as speculative, since the land had already fallen under the McGowan's by the time of the raid and all evidence indicates the house Willing burned was built on land originally belonging to the Maignons."

"Nevertheless," Toby said, "McGowan had legally adopted the Benet girl. Their rights were valid, and the Carutherses were always the primary pursuers of the claim."

Seth turned to Eli and asked, "Was there ill will between the two families?"

"No," Holbein answered. "Angus would have had no qualms dividing the money. The original claim of 1807 was drawn up by David Caruthers himself, who was a lawyer. For years after his marriage to the Pepper girl, he doesn't seem to have been aware that the potential claim was there, but when he learned of it, he pounced. Wars, depressions, which party was in power, all mitigated against settlement, and after the Galphin claim was paid out over in Georgia, embarrassing the Taylor administration, the McGowan claim appeared hopeless, but Sam held the reins of the Caruthers clan by that point, and greedy Sam did not falter.

"During the congressional elections of 1858 it all finally came together—a friendly representative with pull inside the Thirty-sixth Congress. The claim, for the principal, slipped through the House on the eighth of January 1861."

Eli stirred. "You gotta be kiddin'."

"Believe me, I speak not in jest about either the approval or the date."

"And the significance is...?" Seth asked.

"That was the day before Mississippi signed its Ordinance of Secession," Holbein answered. "Needless to say, Treasury held the payout in abeyance."

"But you went back and asked Congress to reconsider the claim."

"At Sam's request and against my advice. I'm not sure what Southern Whigs are thinking half the time, but they do not appear to understand that Northern Whigs, much less Republicans, do not think as they do. Sam Caruthers had been consorting with the Federals since well before Grant landed on this side of the river. In the summer of '63, with Vicksburg in Union hands, and given his self-proclaimed faithfulness to the Union, he was certain he'd receive a payout of the claim.

"Given the tack he ultimately took, he doubtless regretted not having listened to me. That 1863 letter became a problem beyond announcing to Holland he'd pursued the claim without his knowledge. Even worse, Naomi Polk ultimately ended up with the letter, and she was an unpredictable threat. For Miller's plot to work, discretion was paramount. What Sam and Miller planned to walk away with, they didn't want to share with anyone. Indeed, it was dangerous to do so, because the more people who knew what they were about to do, the more likely they'd ultimately be caught.

"Attrition helped him some. First Andrew was killed, then Holland and Hannah. Sam was pretty much convinced Eli had managed to get himself killed off, and was not at all happy to see him come home." Holbein looked at Seth. "But with a little help from the vengeful Laura, you focused on Eli as Alan Guthrie's killer."

"She never actually told me Eli had met Guthrie," Seth said.

Holbein shook his head. "I think she was being careful. My guess is that at the time she approached you with that possibility, she wanted to cause trouble for Eli, not see him hanged. She was holding her hand close, so to speak, but Naomi saw her working with the Federals as potentially exposing the claim. She knew making Federal authorities aware of the actions on the claim at this point would most likely result in its forfeiture. Sam didn't want to lose the money, and Naomi didn't want to lose her advantage over Sam.

"Naomi had known, ever since Sam tried to force her off Camellia Creek after Holland's death, that he might try to shut her up for good, so she took Holland's official letter and a detailed history of the conspiracy perpetrated by Sam and hid the information away with the warning he'd be exposed should anything happen to her."

"We have the letter sent to Daddy, but there was nothing with it," Eli said.

"Mark Dicks found her testimony sewn into a chair in her bedroom after she failed to meet Wilson at the hotel the evening she was killed," Holbein said. "Earlier in the week—apparently right after Eli had run her off Camellia Creek for good—Naomi contacted Sam with her convoluted plot to kill both Eli and Jon Franklin. She'd already fueled Sam's ire when she told Jon Franklin that it was Sam who was building the railroad for which Jon's uncle and cousin were buying up land. Trueblood had declined to divulge Caruthers' name to either Franklin.

"She compounded her offense by telling Jon about the claim, which he subsequently used to try and blackmail himself into a partnership on Sam's railroad."

"What insane reason did she have for telling a fool like Jon Franklin that?" Eli asked.

"You hit the nail on the head with 'insane,'" Seth said. "I think it was the consolation prize for his willingly giving up all chance of getting Alice's fortune—by agreeing to kill her and you along with her."

"I would concur with that," Holbein said. "Doesn't make

sense otherwise, and it was both stupid and reckless on her part. On the same night Naomi planned to eliminate both you and Alice, Sam meant to force her to divulge where she'd hidden the evidence against him. Then Mark Dicks was to kill her. By the time Dicks met Wilson at the Port Gibson Hotel, they knew Naomi's plot to kill Eli, Alice, and Jon had failed, because it was Dicks, on his way to Port Gibson to team up with Wilson, who came upon Jon on the Rodney-Port Gibson Road. He took the initiative and killed him. You, Parker, beat him to Naomi."

"Wilson told Becky that Dicks shot Isabel trying to take her gun away from her," Eli said.

"Yes, an accident. That's how Sam explained it to me, too. Sam has explained a lot to me recently."

"What made him suspicious of Isabel?" Seth asked.

"He'd always been suspicious of her. Do you recall the day we met him at Muscatine?"

"Yes."

"She confronted him about the raid on Camellia Creek, insinuating she knew it was about more than the railroad. He took note. I think he might have realized at that point she and I were working together."

"Did you believe him a threat to you?"

"Most certainly. He and Miller both, and becoming more of one every day."

"Did he tell you who killed Guthrie?" Seth asked.

"Mark Dicks pulled the trigger, but it was Sam who made the decision. Sam had informed Miller that this agent Guthrie was in the area and asking questions about him and the Calhoons. Miller responded that Guthrie had no authority to be there and was after the money. Sam, of course, didn't want Guthrie asking anything that might clue one of Holland's heirs to the existence of the claim. He took Miller's response as his license and dispatched Mark Dicks to Port Gibson to remove Guthrie. On his way to town, Dicks stopped at Muscatine and Jessie informed him that a Treasury agent had been there just that morning asking about Becky. Dicks went on to Port Gibson, confirmed Guthrie was not there, then started up the Natchez Trace in search of his prey."

Holbein lifted his glass and sipped, then placed it on the table beside him, leaned back, and laced his hands over his belly. "I must say, Mark Dicks could be an expedient fellow. He'd never seen Alan Guthrie, but when he met a lone, southbound rider that day, he casually asked if he were Alan Guthrie. Guthrie asked why he wanted to know. Dicks told him he worked for Sam Caruthers and Mr. Caruthers understood Mr. Guthrie would like to talk to him. Guthrie told Dicks he'd found his man, at which time Dicks whipped out his pistol and killed him."

"Who killed Dicks?" Seth asked.

"Miller's man White. Miller considered Isabel's death suspect. He called it sloppy work, made all the more so since Dicks claimed to have netted nothing in return for it. The bottom line was Miller didn't believe Dicks, and I further believe Miller had doubts about Sam. White's subsequent questioning of Dicks, unknown to Sam, by the way, uncovered Treasury's file copy of the authorization letter sent to me, *and* the Treasury Secretary's original authorization to pay the claim. Signed by Salmon P. Chase, no less." Holbein winked at Seth's frown. "A fine forgery, I assure you. Sam concluded Dicks found both back in October when he searched Guthrie's hotel room in Port Gibson. That or he'd taken it off Guthrie's body the day he shot him."

"I'd wager off his body," Seth said. "I double checked with the Hinds County sheriff a couple of days ago. He told me the bottom hem of Guthrie's coat lining was open. He didn't think much of it during his investigation because the coat was well worn, but on reflection, he agrees it might well have been torn open." Seth gave them both a knowing look. "Seems Miller asked him about the condition of the coat a few weeks ago."

"So Miller had doubts about Dicks early on, because Sam told him from the start who killed Guthrie."

"But if Guthrie had proof supporting his accusations against you," Seth said, "why didn't he show it to you?"

Toby nodded. "I didn't think he had any proof because he didn't confront me with anything. Now I think his reticence in showing me that letter may serve as posthumous testimony to his having killed his brother-in-law last September. Guthrie thought he could intimidate me into confessing the whereabouts of the money without using the letter. I believe he was holding off, but it wouldn't have mattered had he shoved it under my nose. I knew by that time he was a thief and very probably a murderer. I'd have laughed in his face and told him to go ahead to the authorities, knowing, of course, that he couldn't."

"He couldn't have used that copy to access the account in New Orleans?" Eli asked.

"No," Holbein answered. "What White found on Dicks was clearly a copy and annotated as such. To move the money, Guthrie would have needed the original. We don't know what Dicks would have eventually done with the letter. Probably used it to blackmail Sam. Anyway, Miller used that as evidence of Dicks' perfidy to mollify Sam for having killed his man."

"Who killed Sam, Mr. Holbein?"

Holbein's eyes widened in mock surprise, and he leaned over the arm of his chair, bringing himself closer to Seth. "Why I assume Walter Miller did. Isn't that what you were thinking?"

When Seth learned that Sam Caruthers had been shot around ten on the evening he and Eli were racing to get to him, that had indeed been his first thought—Miller had killed him and was rushing back to Port Gibson when he crossed paths with him and Eli.

"Did Miller have a motive for killing Caruthers? And with a .22? A .22, Holbein! Did Miller even own such a weapon?"

The Humpty-Dumpty lawyer smacked his lips. "Doesn't sound like his sort of weapon does it?" He smiled wistfully. "It was, however, Isabel's weapon of choice."

"Do you own one?"

"I do," he said, and rose, making his way to his desk from which he withdrew a mahogany box. From it, he took a round-butted pistol. "Fired it just yesterday, at a squirrel in Larry's yard. Missed. I always do. Not good for distance, you know.'

"Squirrel hunting with a derringer, Toby?"

Holbein smirked at Eli, at the same time handing the gun to Seth. "It's not loaded. I cleaned it this morning."

Seth handed the gun back to him, and Holbein returned it to its place in the mahogany box.

"When did you learn Sam Caruthers was dead?"

"Lawrence roused me from bed at one this morning. I was at his home in Warrenton last night."

"And earlier that afternoon," Seth added. "We know you shot Clem White there."

"Yes, breaking and entering. He didn't identify himself."

"He was after something you took there."

Holbein looked at Seth, who added, "Wilson let it be known to Becky and Alice that he was curious as to what you'd received by special courier."

Holbein shrugged. "I didn't take time to ask what the man wanted. A proper warrant and identification might have saved his life."

Seth doubted it. The man had showed up in broad daylight, after all. "What did the provost say about that shooting?"

"The provost and Larry are quite chummy, shall we say, which is why Isabel went to Larry to gain that medical restriction in the face of Eli's potential arrest." Holbein leaned back in his chair. "We're all one big happy family that goes back a long, long ways." He took another sip of whiskey and smiled at Seth. "Need I say more? Anyway, I was still there last night when Alma sent word to her son that Sam was dead."

"And all that about the railroad was just a deception?" Seth mused.

"Not a deception. Sam's always dreamed of that railroad. It simply wasn't relevant to this matter."

Eli was lounging comfortably in his chair, listening. Seth imagined he was tired, despite his sleeping earlier. He could be hurting some, too. They'd come by boat from Grand Gulf, which was easier on him than the horseback ride would have been. Now he stirred. "Toby," Eli asked, "where the hell is all that money?"

Chapter Ninety-eight

Tobias Holbein rose from his chair and again made his way to his desk. "Two days ago I received a letter by, it just so happens, special courier"—he winked at the two of them—"confirming my purchase of forty percent interest in an emerald mine from a British-based consortium headquartered in Rio. The purchase was made on behalf of my clients, Angus Elijah Calhoon, Rebecca Calhoon Mackey, and Cole Terry Caruthers, who are now part owners of the property in partnership with the British-Brazilia Mining Consortium." While he'd been talking, Holbein retrieved a sheaf of papers and meandered back to his chair. "The transfer of stock was completed by the Bank of Honduras."

Eli frowned. "The money has been invested in a Brazilian mining company?"

"An emerald mine."

"Who closed that account in New Orleans?" Seth asked.

"One William Rothenham, an old, old friend of Isabel's. He's been in and out of New Orleans since before the war ended and on occasion came up as far as Natchez. He and Isabel would meet there and *reminisce*. Officially, he's with the British embassy in Rio as part of the economic and trade delegation. In reality, he's the representative of the Bank of England in Central and South America, and he and Isabel have swindled the government of the United States out of nearly a quarter million dollars in shimmering California gold, and reinvested it, for all intents and purposes, in the Bank of England. And I will deny, under oath, ever telling you any of this."

Seth glanced at Eli, who sat looking at Tobias Holbein with a smirk on his mouth. "But I have a witness," Seth said to Holbein.

Eli looked at him. "I haven't heard a word since 'special courier.'"

"It'll be made up for out of the South's hide," Seth said softly.

"The South's hide has always been expendable as far as the North is concerned. Minor as it is, this is a victory for a handful of Southerners."

Seth turned back to Holbein. "And you're taking no credit?"

"The deed was done, no pun intended, before Isabel made me aware of it. For a fraction in time, she did consider I might have actually betrayed Holland."

"And what about your ten percent?"

"Seems I made a twenty-four thousand dollar investment in a Honduran sugar refinery. It was a bit of a surprise, but I understand the industry is doing well there, and Willie has passed assurances it cannot be traced."

Seth sucked in a breath. "I've got to tell you two, I'm a little uneasy about that mine."

"Just don't say anything, Major. The United States will not recover that money, not even if it is ever able to trace it, and the only thing you're guilty of is a conscious effort not to strain international relations. But poetic justice aside, it was a valid claim." Holbein cleared his throat. "It won't bring Holland and Isabel back, but there is some satisfaction in Sam's knowing.... Well, never mind that."

"Sam's knowing before he died what Isabel had perpetrated. Is that what you'd been about to say?"

Holbein didn't answer him, but Seth knew the only way Sam Caruthers could have known that was if Holbein told him right before he put a bullet between his eyes. He could see Holbein doing that. Miller hadn't killed Sam. Miller was already on his way back to meet with Wilson. Together they were going to try and force Eli to divulge the whereabouts, if nothing else, of the authorization letter, and hence learn the fate of all that money. Seth flexed his jaw and shifted his gaze from Holbein to Eli. Eli gave him a knowing look and said, "I don't care."

Seth didn't care either. There was justice and then there was justice. "I assume that special courier letter is what Clem White was after at the Pendleton house," Seth said.

"Good chance. He'd been spying on me off and on for weeks." Holbein held up another document, which he handed to Seth. "That was the other matter Isabel raised with Larry Pendleton that day she went up to talk to him. He'd been holding it for me."

A short writ, signed by General Wood's adjutant, returning the lands belonging to James and Rebecca Mackey to the widow. "I think my sweetheart will be a lot happier with this," Seth said, passing the writ to Eli, "than with the emerald mine."

Eli read the thing, then handed it back to Seth. "I imagine you are right. The point is, are you?"

Sudden relief washed over Seth, and his ensuing laughter sounded downright giddy to his ears. "Oh, yeah, I've already submitted my resignation. Becky and I will be at Muscatine."

"I've done a little checking on that particular mine you two and Cole Terry are invested in," Holbein said.

As one, Eli and Seth turned to him.

"It's lucrative, not that I would have expected ole Willie to have done less by Isabel. Apparently, the consortium had been hoping for an expansion, just needed an infusion of cash. Would either one of you care to wager that Willie owns a substantial interest in that mine?"

Chapter Ninety-nine

From the parlor, Becky heard Seth whistling. This evening the tune was the *Bonnie Blue Flag*. Some evenings it was *Dixie*. He did it for her, and it made her smile. She rarely spoke of the war or the Federal government anymore. That she did for him. He himself was concerned with the course Reconstruction was taking. She knew that because she listened to him and Eli talk when they were together. They rarely ever argued except about what type of opposition the one or other thought should be employed, but they agreed opposition to the unfolding tyranny was in order.

She walked out on the porch and watched him come, long and tall, a slouch hat on his head. He raised it in greeting, then wiped his forehead with the sleeve of his cotton shirt. He was tan and robust and happy, and with him by her side, she forgot the world outside Muscatine and let him make her happy.

The sun had disappeared behind the tree line to their west, but there was still good light. A cool breeze picked up, and inside the house, she could hear Mattie getting Pearl down for the night. Seth should have time to go in and say goodnight. The baby had become attached to him, a fact that seemed to surprise him as much as it did Becky. But he had responded to Pearl's sudden hugs and raised arms in kind.

He climbed up two steps, so that he stood over her, then drew her to him for a kiss that, despite its sweet start by a tired man to a tired woman, quickly became passionate, and she pushed him away with a laugh.

"Polly's got supper on the table," she said.

He sat on the top step and pulled her down beside him. "I'm hot, let me rest a minute and cool off."

"If I keep still too long, I might not get moving again. Did you finish getting the corn in?"

"Yep. I hope we're not too late. Jessie thinks we'll be okay. What did you get done?"

"Lettie and I finished the pea patch."

"Painters done?"

"With the parlor. I was putting things in place when I heard you coming." She leaned against him despite the heat, and he circled an arm around her shoulders. "I'm dirty," he said.

"I don't care." She turned her face up for another kiss. "Wash up, then go say goodnight to Pearl before she falls asleep." She started to rise, but he caught her for one more kiss.

"I love you, Rebecca Parker."

"And I love you, my darling Seth."

Historical Note

The primary setting of *Honor's Banner* is Claiborne County, Mississippi. For a brief history of the county and Port Gibson, the county seat, I refer the reader to the "Historical Note" found at the end of this novel's prequel, *Camellia Creek*.

Honor's Banner takes place during the first three months of 1866, a period marking the close of Presidential Reconstruction (May-December 1865), during which Mississippi wrote a new constitution, held elections, and reestablished law and order under the auspices of a civil government elected by her taxpayers. It also foreshadows Congressional Reconstruction and the growing power struggle between President Andrew Johnson and his Republican Congress for control of Reconstruction policy. The struggle culminated with the fall elections of 1866 when the Northern populace gave the Radical Republicans full control of Congress and ensured the demise of the war-ravaged Republic our founders had created in 1787 when they framed the Constitution.

In handing Reconstruction to the Radicals, the Northern populace lent credence to Radical determination to reconstruct the Southern states into the image of those making up the "progressive" North, thereby making the South fit to join a Union they claimed it never left. In that, at least, they failed. The Old South had been summarily and senselessly butchered, but what rose from its ashes was not what the conqueror envisioned, but rather a scarred image of what the South managed to salvage of itself from the carnage. But that is the stuff for other tales.

During that winter of 1866, the two houses of Congress debated what would become the 14th Amendment to the United

States Constitution. For the past century and a half this amendment has been used and abused by lawyers and the government to alter the founder's republic beyond recognition. What it did was ensure the final victory of Henry Clay's American System. The Fourteenth Amendment subjects the states to the scrutiny and arbitration of a Federal government no longer limited in supremacy, succinctly put, to national defense, international relations and trade, and interstate matters. Governing the people, which had been the responsibility of sovereign state governments, now fell to the whims of a central government exercising powers it was never meant to have. The Fourteenth Amendment is anathema to the compromise agreed to by the advocates of strong central government and those supporting the rights of independent states, and it is as unconstitutional today as it was the day it was declared ratified 150 years ago, not only in concept, but in its passage. From its earliest inception, ratification of the Fourteenth Amendment by the Southern states was tied to their reentry to the Union.

Congress passed the proposed Fourteenth Amendment in the summer of 1866 and sent it to the duly elected and recognized state legislatures across the South. Like the Thirteenth the year before, the Fourteenth Amendment was sent for ratification to states that had not been represented in Congress at the time of its passage, an egregious violation of Article V of the United States Constitution. Mississippi's Democratic legislature refused to pass it. Such intransigence in the face of Radical demands meant continued deprivation of representation in Congress and no voice in matters of national importance — including those which directly affected the state.

At the time of my story, the political map of Mississippi comprised a long-dominant Democratic Party willing to sacrifice representation in a criminal Congress in order to keep control of the state; conservative old-line Whigs/Republicans and more pragmatic Democrats willing to work with Congress to bring the state back into the Union and gain representation along with the delusional hope of fiscal benefits that might result from such representation; and the Radical Republicans determined to wrest control of the state from the Democrats and ensure control of the Republican Party and the Radical agenda within the state forever—and that's not hyperbole.

In the minds and voices of Radical Republicans, Southerners were unfit to govern the South and should be driven from Dixie and/or subordinated to "loyal" Americans from the North. They maintained that stance even when dealing with Republican Scalawags who cooperated with them. *All* Southerners needed to be "trained" in governance and maintained in subordinate positions while they learned to be good "Americans." The more arrogant of this group believed that the Constitution was no longer fit to govern a nation whose star, with the destruction of the "state-rights" South, was on the ascent.

A key factor was the Negro vote. The majority of taxpayers, members of the Democratic Party, tried to nullify it, while the conservatives and Radicals vied for it. The price for the more pragmatic conservatives was isolation from white Democrats.

At the moment Seth Parker lays Naomi Polk in her grave at the end of *Camellia Creek*, the Radicals in Congress have yet to consolidate their power. Indeed, that will not happen until after the fall 1866 elections. As of the opening chapter in *Honor's Banner*, President Johnson has recognized the civil government of B. G. Humphreys in Mississippi, as well as the state's 1865 constitution, notable for its failings only because it was not a "progressive" constitution as were those governing the Northern states. Civil government and the courts are functioning, and progress is being made toward the monumental repair of the state's infrastructure, devastated by war. These meager positives are evolving despite a flailing economy, the result of an unreliable labor force of vagrant freedmen, which the Federal government supports from the sale of abandoned property that their owners can no longer sustain due to lack of income—a vicious cycle brought on by a combination of self-righteous ignorance, arrogance, and design.

In a few words, *Honor's Banner* is set during an anxious time, which anticipates the coming battle to save the state from a cabal of men who are determined to destroy all opposition to Federal imperium, their vanguard being the petty tyrants determined to profit from prevailing conditions. These petty tyrants, both the interlopers and those homegrown, provide the fodder for my story.

My antagonist, Sam Caruthers, is an unprincipled scalawag, a traitor to two nations. I developed the man from my study of Mississippi's Scalawag governor and senator, James Alcorn, who, I wish to emphasize, was not the criminal Sam Caruthers was. Caruthers is a fictional villain, the bad guy, lacking in character, honor, or principles. Though I have problems with a number of things Alcorn did and with the alliances he made, I do not consider the man unprincipled or without honor or character. He was a Whig, therefore a life-long opponent to the Democratic Party, but he was also a Southerner. He believed the only way to rid ourselves of the Yankee contagion infesting our homeland was through representation in Congress. He believed that representation could only be realized through cooperation with the Republicans. Capitulation to Radical demands, he said, would be rectified at some future date. I liken this tactic to that of giving up a beachhead. Once the enemy has it secured, odds are you aren't going to throw him off—best not ever let him get a foothold. I've written a series of blog posts on James Alcorn (http://loblolly-log@blogspot.com) for anyone interested in further study of the man and this period.

My inspiration for the fictional Robert McGowan claim, at the heart of the mystery driving *Honor's Banner*, is the Galphin claim referenced in the story. The Galphin claim was a real Revolutionary War claim made infamous because President Zachary Taylor's Secretary of the Treasury paid to the lawyer on record fifty percent of sixty years of interest at six percent on a principal of $43,500. That amounted to $191,000 in interest, a total payout of roughly $235,000 (or $4.1 million in today's money). Ninety-five thousand dollars, or $1.66 million in today's money, went to the lawyer, who just happened to be President Taylor's Secretary of War, George Crawford of Georgia.

All these men were Whigs—including the President (at least he ran on the Whig ticket. He was really an unaffiliated soldier, the "hero of Buena Vista"). You can imagine the reaction of the Democratic Party, which excoriated the payment as a raid on the U. S. Treasury with the complicity of the President's cabinet (the Attorney General, Reverdy Johnson, also played a role).

I would like to expound here on what is known to history as the "Galphin Affair." George Galphin was a Scots-Irish émigré from County Antrim, who came to Charleston, S. C., as a young man and became a successful Indian trader as well as Indian commissioner, well respected by both the British Crown and the Creeks and Cherokee with whom he traded...and to whom he extended a great deal of credit.

By 1775 the natives were over their heads in debt with no way to pay their creditor(s). The creditors pointed this out to the Crown (which leaves little doubt the credit had been extended on behalf of the Crown to keep the natives happy—and in Britain's debt). Of course, that didn't pay the creditors' creditors, and Mother England stepped in, concluding a treaty with the Creeks and Cherokee in May 1775 that ceded 2.5 million acres of land in parts of South Carolina/Georgia to the Crown. The Crown was to sell the land and pay off the creditors. The Crown agreed to pay Galphin £9,791 sterling (and some change). However, the Revolution broke out before Mother England sold the land, and the good guys (including Galphin) won the war, leaving Britain dispossessed. Georgia took possession of the land, part of which had been earmarked to pay off Galphin's claim, and parceled it out to her soldiers as their reward for victorious service. Galphin had not received his reimbursement from the Crown, and now hadn't a prayer of doing so.

George Galphin was an American patriot. He is credited, by virtue of his relationship with the Creeks and Cherokee, to have foiled British attempts to enlist those tribes in a war upon the vulnerable white population then inhabiting those portions of South Carolina and Georgia where he operated. In his defense, he did not make a claim against Georgia or the United States, but his heirs on the distaff, or female, side did. The same year George Galphin died, 1780, the state of Georgia passed an act binding her to pay claims made by those who had been loyal to the United States during the Revolution, principal plus six percent interest per annum. I'm reading between missing lines here, but it appears the Galphins made no claim at that time, the patriarch passing on as he did. Perhaps he didn't wish the claim pursued. We do not know. Then in 1790, the general government (known affectionately today as the Federal government) passed the Assumption Act, which set up an account rewarding the contributions made by the various states during the Revolution, then paid the states accordingly. The Galphin claim had not been brought before the Georgia legislature as of that time and did not make the cutoff for the Assumption Act.

In 1793, thirteen years after George Galphin's death, a son-in-law submitted the claim to the Georgia legislature, under the 1780 act, in which Georgia said it would honor claims to those loyal to the United States. For each year up until 1826 (when the heirs may have temporarily given up), the Georgia legislature sent the claim to committee, which declared what a good, valid claim it was by the 1780 standard...but, alas, there was no money to pay for it, short of heavy taxation of the citizenry. Of course, with interest accumulating, that situation grew worse with each passing year.

Then, in 1832, Virginia's courts caught up with Virginia and determined that back pay, with interest, was due three officers who had been promised recompense way back during the Revolutionary War. It amounted to a lot of money, and Virginia could not pay it. Virginia went back to Congress and requested it pay the debt under the 1790 Assumption Act, and Congress did. At this point Georgia's legislature decided the state should make a similar request regarding the Galphin claim. When Congress received Georgia's request in 1836, it asked President Jackson to query Georgia Governor William Schley as to the validity of the claim virtually unknown, I'm guessing, outside of Georgia. The governor came back to the president with the details, and Andrew Jackson subsequently told his Congress the claim was good. The only matter left to decide would be who paid it — Georgia or the United States. (The Whigs loved to point this out subsequent to the furor that erupted after the payout. Jackson, of course, was a Democrat.)

Governor Crawford, in the interim, pressed Georgia's senators and congressmen Berrien, Stevens, and Toombs to get the United States to pay it, and on 14 August 1848, twelve years after President Jackson told Congress the claim was valid, Congress directed the Secretary of the Treasury to pay the amount that the secretary found due. James K. Polk, another Democrat, was president at the time.

Well, the agreement was principal plus six percent interest per annum. Polk's Treasury Secretary, Robert J. Walker, when paying the principal, stated, "...the facts being of a peculiar character the claim for interest remains an open question." In other words, what he found "due," he wasn't comfortable with. He further said he would abide by the guidance of the Attorney General if he had doubts about what he was doing. Apparently he did nothing regarding the interest — it was August of Polk's last year, and it appears he passed the buck to the incoming Taylor administration.

Taylor took office in 1849 and made George Crawford his Secretary of War. Zachary Taylor was not aware of Crawford's interest — pun intended — in the case, nor were his Treasury Secretary, William Meredith, and Attorney General, Reverdy Johnson. But John Berrien, Georgia's senior senator, who had pressed the claim before Congress for years, at Crawford's request, certainly was aware of what Crawford had to gain. Berrien, a fellow Whig, had also been around the Senate long enough to know what it would look like when it all came out in the open. It was Berrien who pressed Meredith to broach the interest issue with Attorney General Johnson.

So, Meredith went to Johnson. Johnson, in turn, reviewed the 1780 Georgia legislature's promise to her veterans/patriots, the U.S. Congress' 1790 Assumption Act, and the 1848 approval by Congress which rather indecisively directed Secretary Walker to pay what he saw as due. What that previous, Democratic, Congress had done was left the decision on the interest payment to the discretion of the Treasury Secretary. Attorney General Johnson, when actually asked, told Meredith the matter did not fall within the Treasury Secretary's discretion. The interest was due and should be paid. So Meredith paid it and did severe damage to the Taylor administration. My source for sorting all this out, by the way, was Georgia Senator Alexander Stephens' congressional testimony given a couple of years after the debacle occurred.

As regards my fictional Robert McGowan claim, there were no imprudent promises made to Mississippi's Revolutionary War heroes on the part of her legislature, nor submissions for a portion of the expenditures made under the 1790 Assumption Act. The state did not exist at the time of the Revolution, and most of Mississippi's Revolutionary War heroes moved in *after* the fighting, many onto land granted as rewards to soldiers from the east. But Revolutionary War actions did take place in what is now Mississippi, the best known events centering on James Willing and his 1778 foray down the Mississippi River into British West Florida.

I here briefly outline the Willing Raid. For a more detailed history of the event and the strategy that precipitated it, I refer the reader to: *The American Revolution in the Old Southwest: The James Willing Raid* beneath the "History Lovers" button at my website: loblollywritershouse.com. (http://www.lobollywritershouse.com/llwhhistoryjameswillingraid.html).

The Willing raid was the truncated strategy of an original plan developed early in the conflict by Major General Charles Lee, Commanding Officer of the Southern District and the Virginia Committee of Safety, to send a force down the Ohio and Mississippi Rivers and capture British West Florida, thereby gaining control of the Mississippi River for the Americans as well as the ports at Pensacola and Mobile.

The Continental Congress' Commerce Committee approved the plan, the feasibility of which had been tested in the fall of 1776 when Captain George Gibson, with eighteen men and a boy, descended the Ohio-Mississippi Rivers from Fort Pitt to New Orleans. There Gibson met with Oliver Pollock, a Scots-Irish merchant, who had arrived in New Orleans in 1768 on the heels of Alejandro O'Reilly, the enforcer who had established order over rebellious Frenchmen hostile to the prospect of life under the Spanish crown. France had ceded New Orleans to her Bourbon cousins in Madrid, vice having it fall into British hands at the close of the French and Indian War (1754-1763). Paris had not bothered to ask the opinion of French Louisianans in making that decision.

Pollock served O'Reilly's commercial needs and those of the Spanish governors who followed. History credits Pollock, a sincere American patriot, with financing the American Revolution in the west, and I offer, as a historical tidbit, his development of a symbol for the Spanish peso consisting of an elaborate "p" inside an "S." He gave us our dollar sign, folks.

Under Pollock's heedful eye, Gibson treated successfully with the Spanish Governor of Louisiana, Luis de Unzaga y Amezaga. This liaison led to the delivery of 9,000 pounds of "British" gunpowder to Fort Pitt in April 1777, just in time to prevent the fort's capitulation to the British, and it established a line of communication between Colonel George Morgan, the American agent for Indian Affairs and Deputy Commissary General for Purchases in the Western District, and Spanish Louisiana—discreetly eager to help the Americans thwart the British, though not eager enough to risk war between Spain and Great Britain.

Morgan, familiar with British West Florida, proposed an invasion force of 1,000 men to overwhelm the 300 British troops stationed there for defense. Initially, he had the support of the Continental Congress. Henry Laurens of South Carolina, fearful of spreading American assets too thin (it's one thing to take the area, another to hold it), walked Congress back from a full-scale invasion. At this point, the Continental Congress' "Commerce Committee" proposed a scaled-down version of the plan.

Robert Morris, the wealthy Philadelphia merchant known as the financier of the Revolution, had an equally successful partner in Thomas Willing, also of Philadelphia. Thomas was James Willing's older brother. Morris sat on the Commerce Committee as did Henry Laurens, who apparently didn't have a problem with a "scaled-down" version of the plan. Morris had business interests in New Orleans and a good friend in Oliver Pollock.

And now the plot thickens.

Between 1771 and 1777, James Willing had, ostensibly, tried to make a go of a business supplying flour to the British Army in British West Florida. When that failed, he bought a plantation between Natchez and Baton Rouge. That failed, too, the result, apparently, of waning initiative and love of a good time. He enjoyed visiting his Tory neighbors, eating their food, drinking their liquor, and promoting the American cause. When he had, through dissipation and insult, managed to isolate his influential neighbors, he returned home to York, Pennsylvania—the British occupied Philadelphia at the time—a bitter (more likely, a broke) young man. It was James' familiarity with the Tories along British West Florida's east bank of the Mississippi that prompted Thomas and his partner, Robert Morris, to recommend James to the Commerce Committee for a Colonial Navy captaincy and give him command of the abbreviated foray into British West Florida.

By the time the expedition of twenty-nine men reached Walnut Hills (Vicksburg), Willing's group had plundered a number of British fur-trading posts and grown in number to 100 men. One would like to think these recruits were converts to the American cause, but I doubt it—evidence indicates they simply heard the siren's call to rapine and plunder. Many of the men who joined Willing owed money to the British merchants they plundered along the way. The looting, razing, slaughter of livestock, and theft of slaves (650 in all) grew worse as Willing continued south into the area where the folks who had shared their food and bread with him resided. Such was the fate of the fictional George McGowan's farm in my story. In Pensacola, the Governor of British West Florida, Peter Chester, had expected an invasion ever since Colonel Gibson visited New Orleans in 1776. After a year and a half waiting for an invasion that never came, he had grown complacent and could not react quickly enough to protect British residents along the river.

Willing made it to New Orleans, set up base, and continued forays north against British citizens, many of whom he initially promised not to plunder. Bernardo de Gálvez, the new Spanish governor, in an effort to portray at least the image of neutrality, offered refuge to those British who had lost their homes. Willing's rowdy men created havoc in the city, and he himself promoted conflict in the streets with the "refugees" his pirates had created. Pollock and Gálvez, it appears, were at best able to exercise only marginal control over the group. The British holed up in New Orleans, however, conveyed the duplicitous situation to Governor Chester in Pensacola.

Worst of all, a major part of Willing's mission had been to secure supplies for the Colonial Army back east, and while Pollock was busting a gut to get the goods headed north before the now angry bulldog arrived back on scene and put things to right—by British standards, I mean—Willing and his pirates were using up the profits from the plunder and challenging Pollock over division of the spoils. Pollock, trying to load a merchant ship with arms for the return to the east, and yet to be reimbursed by the Continental Congress, was losing money. Clearly, in the eyes of Pollock and Gálvez, it was time to get Willing out of New Orleans. I wonder sometimes if Pollock remained friends with Morris after all this, but I imagine that for men like them, dealing with the likes of Willing and his crew was simply the ho-hum price of doing business.

In August, Lieutenant Robert George, the nephew of George Rogers Clark, snuck out of New Orleans under the nose of British warships and eventually got Pollock's arms to his uncle in the Illinois territory. In November, Pollock and Gálvez managed to spirit James Willing and ten of his men out of New Orleans on a private sloop, which the British overtook at sea. Except for a brief escape from imprisonment on Long Island, for which offense he was placed in irons, Willing spent the rest of the war in a British prison. He was exchanged on 3 September 1781.

Except for a brief disruption of British trade between West Florida and the West Indies, primarily in lumber and slaves, and $75,000 in plunder, the Willing Raid did little to enhance the American cause in the region and much to hurt it. Willing's primary mission had been to open up the Mississippi River to American commerce. Now, with British warships on the prowl, Americans not only couldn't move under their own flag, they couldn't move under the Spanish flag either. How much of that failure can be attributed to the abuses of Willing and how much to the strategy, I don't know.

American objectives aside, the heretofore limited ambitions of a reticent Spain expanded. Within the year, British Manchac, Baton Rouge, and Natchez fell to Gálvez. Mobile fell in 1780 and Pensacola in 1781. By 1783, Spain and her young, former ally were squaring off for control of the Old Southwest, and I imagine Madrid was wishing it had the British back.

This brief Spanish interlude into the region's history explains the Warren County clerk's comment to Seth Parker regarding "Spanish deeds validating British claims."

I based the method Walter Miller used to spirit that money out of Treasury in 1865 on the actual steps taken in the Galphin claim, to wit: Congress approved the claim and sent it to Treasury. Treasury paid it. In my story, Congress had approved the claim in 1861, but had not authorized Treasury to pay it.

I had a bit more trouble trying to come up with a scenario explaining the actual mechanics involved within Treasury's bank itself. In my story, I have Walter Miller, intimately familiar with local and regional forgers, create a forged letter from Salmon Chase, dated to Chase's last day at the Treasury Department in the summer of 1864. Miller gave the forgery to the dissipated Jacob Harding in accounting, whom he coerced into authorizing a letter of credit to disbursing for the amount of the claim plus the interest (which Chase's forged letter authorized, Congress' valid approval did not). The innocent head of disbursing, Jim Hurd, not comfortable with the face value of the bill of exchange, had second thoughts and decided to delay sending the letter and bill of exchange to the Bank of New Orleans until he talked to the treasurer himself, an intent he made known to Jacob Harding. Frightened by that prospect, Harding informed Miller of Hurd's intentions, and Miller arranged Hurd's "accident." Now involved not only in financial malfeasance, but also in the murder of Hurd, Harding got his vengeance on Walter Miller and his cohorts in Mississippi by sending the letter authorizing access to the McGowan account in New Orleans to the lawyer on record for the old claim, the heretofore clueless Tobias Holbein. Miller had directed Harding to send the authorization to Samuel Caruthers. This sleight of hand on Harding's part demolished Miller and Caruthers' entire scheme.

Alan Guthrie knew all this because his brother-in-law told him before Guthrie killed him the night of 1 September 1865. Initially, Walter Miller did not know what had gone wrong, but he was smart enough to put two and two together in early October, when Sam Caruthers informed him Alan Guthrie was in Mississippi asking questions. Following Sam Caruthers' reckless elimination of Guthrie, Miller, in his near-autonomous capacity of senior agent in his office, created the subterfuge with the Republican donor uncle, pending the discovery of the missing gold from the bank in New Orleans and his finagling an assignment to Mississippi to ostensibly work Guthrie's murder case.

I accomplished the delay between the movement of the money and the discovery it was missing with the simple legitimacy of the transactions themselves. Treasury did not realize the money had been stolen until the Bank of New Orleans came back with a request to augment its gold reserves. This did not occur until the very end of December, when New Orleans could not meet a certain (and irrelevant for the purposes of this tale) payment. Since Treasury, based on known expenditures, had already provided the bank with enough gold to meet its projected requirements until the end of the fiscal year, Treasury's first question was "why?" Even then, it took time for the accountants and clerks to figure out why New Orleans had come up *way* short.

As far as the actions of personnel at the bank in New Orleans, I attribute that successful ruse to the machinations of William Rothenham. Yes, his name is an oblique feint at the legendary intrigues of the Bank of England/Rothschilds over the centuries to which I neither give nor deny credence. Mine is a story of fiction. I wish merely to make it believable. A character with such a connection, in my opinion, helps my story work.

Willie's intimate acquaintances within the banking industry and his assumed familiarity with the operations of the New Orleans Federal Bank enabled him to slip the money out from under the noses of bank personnel. He followed up with a carefully placed bribe and retrieved the requisite documentation in order to prevent tracing the transaction. On the surface, everything appeared legal, and given the familiar signatures on the bill of exchange from Treasury there was no reason for suspicion on the part of honest bank personnel.

Regarding the Parker family's thoughts on the deteriorating situation in Kentucky, let me first note, for those readers who may be unaware, Kentucky is a Southern state, which suffered divided loyalty during the war. Many Kentuckians who opposed secession and managed to keep the state in the Union did not do so out of a blind belief in the Union, but more pragmatically to protect their way of life. In the minds of those people, the state's economic interests, including slavery, were safer under the protection of the Constitution.

Likewise, an imposing number of Kentuckians believed the interests of Kentucky were best served by joining her Southern sisters and leaving the Union. Enough such secessionists existed to create a separate Confederate government within the state.

Thus one of the thirteen stars on the Confederate Battle Flag belongs to Kentucky. The other border state is Missouri. A missing star belongs to Maryland, the state whose fate, I have no doubt, Kentucky would have shared had she opted to leave the Union, that being military occupation and martial law early in the conflict.

By 1863 and the signing of the Emancipation Proclamation, Kentucky's vacillating population knew it had been betrayed by the central government, and by the time of my story, the majority of Kentuckians were aligning themselves to fight the egregious overreach and tyranny now being displayed by a Congress drunk on blood and power. Kentucky, not being a disloyal/defeated state, was better situated to fight back legally, but despite representation at the national level, she was still outnumbered in Congress and had a battle at home to repel the forces of evil trying to gain control of her legislature. Like everywhere else across the South, the battle would prove bloody.

The incidents which prompted Hugh James' allegory during the river journey south from Vicksburg to Natchez and Josiah Spate and his wife Ursula's aborted attempt to remove Rebecca Mackey from her home and seize the property that by agreement belonged to the Methodist Episcopal Church, South and/or the Mackey estate, I conjured from the activities of the Methodist Episcopal Church, North's activities prior to the war, during the war, and during Reconstruction.

The Methodist Episcopal Church, South, separated from the northern branch of the Methodist Episcopal Church in 1844, in a schism over slavery. At the time of the split, assets were divided up amicably. It was not until the next general conference of the Methodist Episcopal Church that animosity appeared, and that animosity manifested itself in the Northern church. In time, the Northern church's hate grew to envelop not only the Southern church, but the entire South.

The beliefs expressed by these people in their own journals —
The Central Christian Advocate, Ladies Repository, Methodist, Methodist

Advocate, *Methodist Review*, *Missionary Advocate*, *Western Christian Advocate*, and *Zion's Herald*—to cite only a few; minutes of their annual conferences; and the official publications of the Methodist Episcopal Church bring to light a self-righteous, hate-filled, insufferable people incestuously tied to the central government, which supported their ultimately failed effort to scour the South of the Southerner. I am not speaking of the imposition of their brand of religion on the South, Methodism is Methodism. I am talking about social and political mores they incorporated as part of their religion. These people believed that the Republicans (especially the Radicals) were intimately tied to God's will for the nation, that Methodism was loyalty, and that the North's victory over the South was the signal for the initiation of a great moral regeneration of the nation.

At the time of my story, physical subjugation of the South was complete, and the Methodist church was sending "missionaries" south to remove the institutional debris and reorganize Southern society, restore civil order, and ensure dependence on moral and religious influences. The central government was heavily sprinkled with fanatics in powerful positions. The Methodist Episcopal Church was painfully political. It was the religious wing of the Republican Administrations of that day and was, I quote, "the God-appointed church to redeem and possess the South." In the eyes of these people, the South was a malignancy affecting the nation, and the only hope was that the Methodist Episcopal Church would impregnate the South with Northern ideas and civilization.

I could go on in this vein, but suffice it to say the endless stream of words from these peoples' mouths, which they proudly put in print, were so belittling and hateful it is hard not to think of those who spoke them as caricatures. Indeed, to portray these people in fiction makes them look like cardboard villains. Sadly, they were real, and they truly believed they were God's gift to the nation and the South's only salvation.

In support of my fictional confrontation between the Spates and Rebecca Mackey at Hickory Grove in March 1866, I submit that in November 1863, the War Department issued an order applicable to the Southwestern states of the Confederacy authorizing Northern Methodists to occupy "all houses of worship belonging to the Methodist Episcopal Church, South in which a 'loyal' minister, appointed by a 'loyal' bishop of said church, does not officiate." *The War Department, y'all!* This refers to territory that by the summer of 1863 had fallen under Union control and included a significant part of Mississippi. Aided by the United States Army, these people occupied the property of the Southern Methodists. At the time of his death, Lincoln had begun returning these properties to the Methodist Episcopal Church, South. This reversal of policy continued under Andrew Johnson. The Methodist Episcopal Church was not in bed with Johnson, though it had been with Lincoln to some extent. Rather, the Methodist Episcopal Church was in bed with *Congress*. This change in policy proved a problem for the Church in that there was a dearth of locations where their adherents could worship. The existence of an empty church in which the Southern Church had indicated no interest would have been quite a temptation for the likes of the Spates in early 1866. Given the nature of such people and the focus of the powers that held sway at the time, the scenario I presented is a plausible one.

Northern Methodists worked intimately with the Freedmen's Bureau in support of freed slaves and later had roles in the puppet Reconstruction civil governments established in the occupied states. Their primary adherents, ultimately, proved to be freed black folk, and to their rare credit, the Northern Methodists did play an important role in establishing early educational facilities for the illiterate black man.

For a good overview on the Northern Methodists during this period, I refer the reader to Ralph E. Morrow's *Northern Methodism and Reconstruction* (1950).

I have been unable to find a definitive history of intelligence assets in the western theater during the war. We have the works of Lafayette Baker and Allan Pinkerton, who worked primarily in the eastern theatre and in the North, but I have found nothing inclusive consolidating operations in the west. I'm speaking of covert operations, spies, double agents and black market activities. I have no doubt they occurred—there was a major war on, after all, and both sides participated. I can understand the lack of material from the Southern side. Any man who might have liked to put his memoirs out there for literary consumption could end up incriminating himself, which would not be good in the wake of defeat, but there weren't any swaggering secret agents in Treasury or the Army that appear to have jotted down their recollections of glory, and their activities would have more likely inspired awe rather than trial by a military tribunal, though in the interest of *true* justice, the opposite would have been the case.

My speculation regarding the usurpation of military intelligence assets into Treasury's Secret Service and the Army's reaction to it (at least by those in the Army whose bailiwick would have been intelligence gathering and analysis) is just that, speculation. My sources for what little definitive information I have are the first chapter of *The Secret Service* by Philip H. Melanson, Ph.D., and a series of blog posts by the American Numismatic Society's *Bank Note Reporter*, Fred L. Reed III. Reed's work on government operatives' forays against counterfeiters during and after the war provides a good view of the character of the men making up Treasury's Secret Service at that time.

Contrary to popular belief, Abraham Lincoln did not, on the day he was killed, authorize the official establishment of a secret service under the Department of the Treasury. A more likely scenario would be that Treasury Secretary Hugh McCulloch caught Lincoln's arm following that last afternoon cabinet meeting and said, "I wanted to talk to you about this secret service thing," and Lincoln responding, "hmm—sounds like a good idea. Handle it." That night, of course, Lincoln was shot by John Wilkes Booth, and Treasury took Lincoln's alleged words for action.

While still Secretary of the Treasury, Salmon P. Chase convinced War Secretary Edwin Stanton to assign Colonel Lafayette Baker, head of the War Department's Army intelligence assets that composed the National Detective Police, to help Treasury. Though his assets were employed in support of Treasury, Baker remained directly subordinate to Stanton. By the summer of 1865, Baker, due to his "extracurricular" activities, had fallen out of favor with Stanton. So it was that on 5 July 1865, after an exuberant Fourth of July celebration, Secretary of the Treasury Hugh McCulloch appointed William P. Wood chief of Treasury's Secret Service Bureau. Wood's new position fell directly under the Solicitor of the Treasury, Treasury's head lawyer, Edward Jordan, an old Ohio Whig turned Republican who had been given the position by Chase back in 1861. Note that though Hugh McCulloch made Wood's assignment to Treasury, it was Edwin Stanton in War who handpicked Wood for the job.

Back in 1862, Stanton had tapped this same old friend for Commandant of the Old Capitol Prison in Washington, D.C. It seems Wood had served Stanton well in a patent dispute between equipment giants Massey and McCormick. I won't go into the details of the case here, but I will say that the suspicion of fraud perpetrated by the Stanton and Wood contingent in favor of McCormick haunts the case to this day. I mention this to give the reader an idea of the relationship between these two men. Before the war ended, Wood had become Superintendent of Prisons in the District of Columbia, and he was reported to have been very effective in gleaning information from prisoners ranging from Confederate soldiers, vocal northern Democrats known as Copperheads, spies, blockade runners, draft opponents...anyone and everyone who might possibly be opposed to the Union cause (translate that as "opposed to the Federal government").

Wood, as it turns out, was another swashbuckling, legend-in-his-own-mind Baker-type individual who participated in guerrilla warfare during the Mexican War and reputedly accompanied William Walker on his ill-fated attempt to establish the Republic of Nicaragua as an English-speaking colony (1855-1860). While chief interrogator for the Union and commandant of prisons, Wood expanded his law-enforcement repertoire to include anticounterfeiting. When Wood assumed his position in

Treasury on 5 July 1865, his primary mission was, in the words of either McCulloch or possibly Jordan, "...to restore faith in the nation's money." Jordan, as Treasury's head lawyer, then told him, and we are sure *he* spoke these words, "Our policies and rules can take shape as your work progresses." Yeah, faith in Monopoly money was paramount. Faith in the laws of the Republic, however, didn't matter—just make up legislation as required.

Imagine how happy the South must have been to be back in the warm, safe fold with men such as these.

I will cease with the sarcasm and characterization of Wood and the men he would subsequently hire to support his "anti-counterfeiting" efforts. Counterfeiting has no relevancy to *Honor's Banner*, and the reputed heyday of Treasury's success against terrorism in the unreconstructed South resides in the future, and will make its way into another historical note down the road. What I want to point out is the shifting of Army intelligence assets under Baker to Treasury under McCulloch/Jordan/Wood, all with the obvious blessing of Edwin Stanton, Secretary of War. As far as Army's high command was concerned, U. S. Grant, very much aware that his future was tied to the Republican Party, would have gone along. The regular Army's thoughts on the matter, as heard through the mouth of Malcolm Byrnes in the text of my novel, are my thoughts on what I believe his take would have been. As a retired intelligence officer, albeit Navy, I believe the regulars would have resented it, fought it as best as they could, but in the end, yielded to political expediency.

Regardless, covert operations during the war and the dark days of Reconstruction that followed are great stuff for fiction, and I intend to put my imagination to work in future novels.

I hope you enjoyed *Honor's Banner* and that this historical note has dispelled any lingering doubts you may have harbored regarding the plausibility of the story.

If you enjoyed *Honor's Banner* don't miss Charlsie Russell's award-winning first novel

The Devil's Bastard

Natchez on the river, 1793. The Spanish Fleet controls the Mississippi, and the Dons rule their rowdy British and American subjects with a patient hand. The location is strategic, the land fertile, and within two decades, cotton will be king. Into this web of international intrigue, the rich and powerful Elizabeth Boswell welcomes her orphaned grandniece Angelique Veilleux and introduces the impoverished beauty to a world of privilege. But power has enemies and wealth demands a price. Rumors state that Elizabeth's success stems from dalliance with a lustful demon that still prowls her family farm of De Leau outside Natchez.

At the center of this ominous legend is Elizabeth's grandson, the handsome and dangerous Mathias Douglas, who saves Angelique from degradation and death near the end of her journey to Natchez. Mathias is the son of the doomed Julianna,

Elizabeth's only daughter. Mathias's father, locals whisper, is Elizabeth's demon.

Despite the dark legend, Angelique cannot quell her feelings for Mathias, for whom she would make any sacrifice. An outcast, Mathias is cruelly tested by Angelique's affection. Determined not to dishonor her, he callously puts her aside. But Elizabeth has other plans and offers him the family farm at De Leau to marry the girl. Soon Angelique finds herself desperately in love with the man who has conquered her body and possessed her soul.

But something in the swamps surrounding De Leau stalks her, and nightmares invade her dreams. What she perceives as Mathias' indifference to the threat leaves Angelique isolated and afraid. She begins to doubt her grandaunt's motives for sending her to De Leau, as well as Mathias' role in Elizabeth's plan. Resolving her doubts means uncovering the secret of Mathias' sire.

From Mathias and Angelique's first meeting to Elizabeth Boswell's revelation at story's end, *The Devil's Bastard* is a splendid read. First and foremost a sensual romance, it is also a well-researched historical with a haunting mystery.

Don't miss Charlsie Russell's second award-winning novel

Wolf Dawson

Ten years after the Confederate Army reported him killed in action, dirt-poor Jeff Dawson returns to Natchez, Mississippi, a wealthy man and purchases White Oak Glen, the once opulent home of the now impoverished Seatons, the aristocratic family that years ago shattered his own.

Burdened with her drunken brother, Tucker, and besieged by greedy relatives, Juliet Seaton struggles to hold on to what remains of her farm. Now she finds her family faced with a new menace in the form of a marauding wolf that slaughters valuable stock and assails the mind of her alcoholic brother. Tucker Seaton warns his sister that the man occupying White Oak Glen is a ghost, who in the form of that vicious wolf seeks to destroy what is left of the Seatons.

An infant when events occurred setting her family against the Dawsons, Juliet appears pitted against a neighbor hell-bent on avenging his sister, who died in childbirth after being violated by a Seaton male. Jeff's grandfather was part Creek Indian.

Local legend states he terrorized unfriendly neighbors with tales of his ability to shape-shift into a deadly wolf. Unidentified persons lynched the colorful old man following the savage killing, apparently by a wolf, of the Seaton who raped Jeff Dawson's sister.

But Juliet finds the handsome Jeff a living, breathing man, hot-blooded, to boot. His seductive touch weakens her resolve and blinds her to the danger he poses. Jeff, however, is no longer compelled to destroy the Seatons, if he ever was; they have destroyed themselves and left the vulnerable Juliet to his mercy—mercy he's quite willing to give, though he's not ready to let the feisty beauty know that.

Into this explosive mix of fear and distrust comes a sadistic killer, and what this fiend kills is not Seaton livestock.

With the countryside ablaze with suspicion directed toward Jeff, he and Juliet overcome mutual distrust and strip away a lost generation's hatred as quickly as the clothes covering their bodies. Old lies give way to new truths, lust to love, and together, the lovers set out to uncover not only a killer, but the identity of the spectral beast haunting the countryside.

Don't miss Charlsie Russell's third award-winning novel

Epico Bayou

In the fall of 1897, a grand old gentleman of Handsboro, Mississippi dies a very wealthy man, and much to the chagrin of Lionel Augustus's siblings, he leaves the bulk of his estate to his estranged bastard son, Clay Boudreaux, and his beloved step-daughter, Olivia Lee. There is but one stipulation to Lionel's will, the two must wed.

For reasons of their own, the two young people agree to marry, sight unseen, but only days after her marriage by proxy to Deputy Sheriff Clay Boudreaux of Galveston County, Texas, Olivia learns her husband has died in a house fire and her extended family intends to contest the terms of the will. Exacerbating her situation, a mysterious stranger, claiming to be the dead Clay, but who her family warns is Clay's older brother Troy, invades Olivia's opulent home and accuses her of hiring Troy to kill Clay . . . and yet another henchman to eliminate Clay's killer.

Olivia and the handsome stranger, whoever he might be, both have sound reasons for confusing their roles in the plot to murder

Clay Boudreaux, reasons dealing with duty, justice, and survival. Neither is sure of the role the other plays in the Machiavellian plan of Lionel's siblings, nor is it clear if Lionel's brother and sister are the only subversives working to sabotage the terms of Lionel's will. So clear is the present danger, it overshadows the dark secret driving Lionel's bizarre stipulation that Clay and Olivia wed.

Set on the Mississippi Gulf Coast at the close of the nineteenth century, Charlsie Russell's third novel is both a romantic charade and a compelling mystery, pitting the wit and will of one wary lover against the honor and sheer determination of the other, even while the sinister machinations of dangerous foes force them into a grudging alliance.

Though the tangled mystery sets this novel apart from her edgy Gothics, *The Devil's Bastard* and *Wolf Dawson*, Ms. Russell's *Epico Bayou* still features those tried and true elements of suspense, sensual romance, and historical setting that characterize her work. Pure escape. Don't miss this journey!

And if you like what you've read so far, look for

River's Bend

Rafe Stone came back to Mississippi seeking justice and the house irrevocably linked to everything that makes him who he is. But the magnificent structure that began life as a one-room, French-Dominion log cabin and grew into an antebellum showcase south of Natchez has fallen into disrepair and into the hands of a savvy Mississippi City businessman by the name of Josephus Collander. The astute Collander has no use for the tax-draining piece of real estate; moreover, he needs to unburden himself of a recently acquired orphaned niece who, through no fault of her own, is wreaking havoc within his household. The house is not for sale, Collander tells the disappointed Rafe...but he can have it for nothing, if he'll accept it as Delilah Graff's dowry.

Rafe's desperation, coupled with Delilah's beauty, makes the decision, albeit a reckless one, easy. But what secret in the siren's past would cause a seemingly kind and responsible kinsman to barter her to a stranger?

Tragedy, followed by a difficult childhood, has left Delilah jaundiced toward life, bitter toward men, and eager for the independence she is sure is coming. Instead, the financial support her beneficent Uncle Joe promised is suddenly forfeit, and he has called in his markers, compelling her to wed a man she does not know. Worse yet, her uncle doesn't appear to know much about the handsome Rafe Stone either. Adding to her discomfort, this Mr. Stone takes her to Natchez, a city where her name is synonymous with disgrace. There he moves her into a house rumored, over the course of its nearly two hundred years, to have hosted treason, robbery, adultery, and murder. A house still reputed to harbor the specter of a vicious killer.

And who is Rafe Stone, the man to whom she has sworn her troth and under whose roof she sleeps at night? A man who claims to be a stranger to Mississippi, yet knows more about the ominously majestic River's Bend, and its past, than he should? What is his link to the dark legends haunting River's Bend and to the ghost walking its rambling halls? Is he the personification of her nightmare or an unbidden dream come true?

Mystery, suspense, romance, and history, dear reader. Enjoy this look back to the time when the memory of the Old South blossomed into legend.

And if you haven't already read it, make sure to go back and read
the prequel to *Honor's Banner*,

Camellia Creek

In September 1865, Lieutenant Colonel, Confederate States
Army, Eli Calhoon, returns to his war-ravaged plantation, Camellia
Creek, outside Port Gibson in Claiborne County, Mississippi, resolved to begin again. But Mississippi, like the rest of the South,
lies prostrate in the wake of a devastating conflict that wasted its
population and destroyed what had been, only four years earlier,
the third strongest economy in the world. More troubling, the
South's recovery is now overseen by a victorious enemy determined that the Southern economy, as well as the South's influence within the Union, will never be revived. For Southerners,
getting a spring crop in the field is as far out of reach as is the
payment of five years' back taxes Congress demands from the
states in Rebellion to pay for the war it waged against them.

Orphaned Alice Shelton, late of Ohio by way of Chicago, has

come to Mississippi with her aunt and uncle, Betty and Peter Franklin. Peter is a speculator in search of investment. A veteran of the war, he knows opportunity exists in the defeated South. His preference for a home for his wife, daughter, and niece is the lovely Camellia Creek. In company with the Franklins are Peter's widowed sister-in-law Eustacia and her son, Jonathan, who Peter believes is the perfect match for Alice, heiress to a fortune.

Alice's widowed father, Jacob Shelton, and his two sons were killed in action during the war, fighting for the Union. The losses have left Alice in despair so deep her aunt fears Alice might take her own life.

Seth Parker, Major, United States Marine Corps, has come to Mississippi on orders at the request of a friend and military senior to investigate the murder of a U.S. Treasury agent, which possibly ties in to cotton thefts rampant among the white army officers stationed in Mississippi. The powers that be prefer he find a Southerner to blame, but the senior officer is not so sure. To investigate the death, Seth is given a troop of nine men, all Negro members of Mississippi's Native Guard, for the most part former slaves recruited into the Union Army during the war.

Desperate times call for desperate measures, and in a lawless South, desperate measures are gambles that sometimes pay off. When an indiscretion not of her own making lands the lovely Alice into the hands of a determined Eli Calhoon, he blackmails her into marriage and brings her to Camellia Creek, where she is haunted by Jocelyn LeBlanc, an ill-fated beauty who died under mysterious circumstances decades earlier. In addition to Jocelyn's ghostly presence, war's aftermath, murder, and jealous greed vex Alice, threatening her newfound desire to live, a desire ignited by the very man who could be plotting to snuff it out.

About the Author

Charlsie Russell is a retired United States Navy commander turned author. She loves history, and she loves the South. She focuses her writing on historical suspense set in her home state of Mississippi.

After seven years of rejection, she woke up one morning and determined she did not have enough years left on this planet to sit back and hope a New York publisher would one day take a risk on her novels. Thus resolved, she expanded her horizons into the publishing realm with the creation of Loblolly Writer's House.

In addition to writing and publishing, Ms. Russell is a mother, grandmother, and homemaker.

To learn more about Charlsie Russell and Loblolly Writer's House, visit www.loblollywritershouse.com or visit her blog at http://loblollylog.blogspot.com.

Follow her on Twitter, @CharlsieRussell, and on Google+ as Charlsie Russell.

Loblolly Writer's House

Order Blank

Tear this sheet out and mail order to: **Loblolly Writer's House**
P.O. Box 7438
Gulfport, MS 39506-7438

Item	Price*	Qty	Total
The Devil's Bastard	$16.00	_______	_______
Wolf Dawson	$16.00	_______	_______
Epico Bayou	$16.00	_______	_______
River's Bend	$16.00	_______	_______
Camellia Creek	$16.00	_______	_______
Shipping free:	0.00		

Total payment: _______

Would you like a signed copy?
Tell me how:_________________________________

____

Send to:

____

____

____

* Price includes 7% Mississippi sales tax
For Bookseller rates visit: www.loblollywritershouse.com